# Books by J. B. PRIESTLEY

## FICTION

| | |
|---|---|
| Adam in Moonshine | Bright Day |
| Benighted | Jenny Villiers |
| The Good Companions | Festival at Farbridge |
| Angel Pavement | The Other Place: short stories |
| Faraway | The Magicians |
| Wonder Hero | Low Notes on a High Level |
| Laburnum Grove | Saturn Over the Water |
| They Walk in the City | The Thirty-First of June |
| The Doomsday Men | The Shapes of Sleep |
| Let the People Sing | Sir Michael and Sir George |
| Blackout in Gretley | Lost Empires |
| Daylight on Saturday | It's An Old Country |
| Three Men in New Suits | The Image Men |

## PLAYS

| | |
|---|---|
| The Roundabout | Private Rooms |
| Duet in Floodlight | Treasure on Pelican |
| Spring Tide | Try It Again |
| Mystery at Greenfingers | Mother's Day |
| The Long Mirror | A Glass of Bitter |
| The Rose and Crown | Mr. Kettle and Mrs. Moon |
| The High Toby | Bright Shadow |

Dragon's Mouth (with Jacquetta Hawkes)

## COLLECTED PLAYS

| Volume I | Volume II | Volume III |
|---|---|---|
| Dangerous Corner | Laburnum Grove | Cornelius |
| Eden End | Bees on the Boat Deck | People at Sea |
| Time and the Conways | When We Are Married | They Came to a City |
| I Have Been Here Before | Good Night Children | Desert Highway |
| Johnson over Jordan | The Golden Fleece | An Inspector Calls |
| Music at Night | How Are They at Home? | Home Is Tomorrow |
| The Linden Tree | Ever Since Paradise | Summer Day's Dream |

## ESSAYS AND AUTOBIOGRAPHY

| | |
|---|---|
| Talking | Delight |
| Open House | All About Ourselves and Other |
| Apes and Angels | Essays (chosen by Eric Gillett) |
| Midnight on the Desert | Thoughts in the Wilderness |
| Rain upon Godshill | Margin Released |
| The Secret Dream | The Moments and Other Pieces |

Essays of Five Decades

## CRITICISM AND MISCELLANEOUS

| | |
|---|---|
| Brief Diversions | British Women Go To War |
| The English Comic Characters | Russian Journey |
| Meredith (E.M.L.) | Theatre Outlook |
| Peacock (E.M.L.) | The Olympians (opera libretto) |
| The English Novel | Journey Down a Rainbow (with |
| English Humour | Jacquetta Hawkes) |
| The Balconinny | Topside |
| English Journey | The Art of the Dramatist |
| Postscripts | Literature and Western Man |
| Out of the People | Man and Time |

# The IMAGE MEN

# The IMAGE MEN

*J. B. Priestley*

AN ATLANTIC MONTHLY PRESS BOOK

Little, Brown and Company   *Boston • Toronto*

Published originally in England in two volumes entitled *Out of Town* and
*London End*. With the author's permission this American edition in one
volume has been slightly abridged.

ATLANTIC—LITTLE, BROWN BOOKS
ARE PUBLISHED BY
LITTLE, BROWN AND COMPANY
IN ASSOCIATION WITH
THE ATLANTIC MONTHLY PRESS

PRINTED IN THE UNITED STATES OF AMERICA

# DRAMATIS PERSONAE

| | |
|---|---|
| *Alfred* and *Florrie* | Servants at the *Institute of Social Imagistics* |
| *Frank Angle* | Chief Whip of the Government |
| *Alan Axwick* | Opposition Member of Parliament |
| *Harvey Bacon* | A radio interviewer |
| *Stan K. Belber* | Area Representative of the Kansas City and West Coast Agency |
| *Roger Belworth* | Leader of the House of Commons |
| *Ben* | An assistant to the Prime Minister |
| *Simon Birtle* and his wife, *Gladys* | A newspaper magnate |
| *Lon Bracton* | A film comedian |
| *Dr. Edith Brede-Smith* | Instructor in the English Department of the University of Brockshire |
| *Professor Denis Brigham* and his wife, *Gladys* | Head of the English Department of the University of Brockshire |
| *Alfred Brimber* and his wife | A boss at Meldy Glebe's film studio |
| *Bob Brodick* | General Secretary of the Prime Minister's party |
| *Rod Bruton* | An editor in a publishing company |
| *Budgy* | Lon Bracton's girl friend |
| *Professor Donald Cally* and his wife | Head of the Sociology Department of the University of Brockshire |
| *Charry* | Managing Director of a publishing company |
| *Eric Chetsweth* | Primrose East's useless young man |
| *Clarice* | Assistant to Radley |
| *Sir Emery Clavering* and his wife, *Lady Clavering* | House guests at the Sturtletons' |

| | |
|---|---|
| *Cliff* | An official of the Prime Minister's party |
| *Jeff Convoy* | Brockshire Representative, National Confederation of Students |
| *Commander Crast, M.P.* | Security Chief, Ministry of Defence |
| *Ilbert Cumberland* | A shop-owning tycoon |
| *Paul Cumberland* and his wife, *Sonia* | Son and daughter-in-law of Ilbert; in the hotel business |
| *Dave* | An official of the Prime Minister's party |
| *Mrs. Dobb* | Secretary to Vice-Chancellor Lapford |
| *Dorothea* | Meldy Glebe's maid |
| *Mrs. Elfreda Drake* | Assistant Director and General Secretary of the *Institute of Social Imagistics* |
| *Primrose East* | An ex-model; a student of sociology at the University of Brockshire and a member of the *Institute of Social Imagistics* |
| *Beryl Edgar* | Typist-receptionist at the *Institute of Social Imagistics* |
| *Jocelyn Farris* | Chef at the Rose and Heifer |
| *Mrs. Fletcher* | Mr. Meston's daughter |
| *Sir Henry Flinch-Epworth* and his wife, *Lady Mildred* | Leader of the Opposition party |
| *Foster* | Jimmy Kilburn's man |
| *Albert Friddle* | A student of sociology at the University of Brockshire |
| *George* | One of Simon Birtle's editors |
| *Meldy Glebe* | A film actress; a client of Wilf Orange's |
| *Major Gerald Grandison* | Owner of Audley Enquiries, a private-detective agency |
| *Greenleaf* | Executive head of Fitch, Berg and Greenleaf, advertising agents |
| *Ben Hacker* | A television interviewer |
| *Mrs. Hartz* | Secretary to Professor Saltana in London |
| *Dr. Hazel Honeyfield* | Instructor in the Sociology Department of the University of Brockshire |

| | |
|---|---|
| Professor Hugo Hummel | Head of the Psychology Department of the University of Brockshire |
| Marion Ilbert | Mrs. Mere's cousin; Dr. Tuby's landlady in London |
| Paul Ilbert | Her husband; a civil servant |
| Ernest Itterby and his wife, Ethel | Prime Minister |
| Merleen Jacobs | A young cabaret star |
| Jadson | The Prime Minister's press man |
| Jeff and Betty | Night-club owners and performers |
| Ted Jenks | Writer-in-residence at the University of Brockshire; author of Stuff It, Chum |
| Jimmy Kilburn | A Cockney millionaire |
| John James (Jayjay) Lapford and his wife, Isabel | Vice-Chancellor of the University of Brockshire |
| Leslie | Lon Bracton's bodyguard; an ex-boxer |
| Lingston | Advertising Manager of Bevs Ltd. |
| Dan Luckett | Owner of an American restaurant chain |
| Frank Maclaskie | An American businessman; an old acquaintance of Elfreda's |
| Maria | The Lapfords' maid |
| O. V. Mere | Editor of a new Redbrick monthly magazine |
| Eden Mere | His wife; later a member of the Institute of Social Imagistics |
| Mr. Meston | A 'cello player |
| Mike Mickley | A student of sociology at the University of Brockshire |
| Mrs. Mumby | A radio producer |
| Charlie Murch | An American friend of Frank Maclaskie's |
| Murch | A television interviewer |
| Mrs. Stephanie Murten | Major Grandison's secretary |
| Sir Leopold Namp | An industrialist; a member of the Academic Advisory Board of the University of Brockshire |
| Jacques Nazaire | A public relations man |
| Daphne Nugent-Fortesque | Alan Axwick's fiancée |

| | |
|---|---|
| *Sir Rupert Nugent-Fortesque* | Chairman of the Opposition party |
| *Sally Nulty* | Sir Henry Flinch-Epworth's daughter |
| *Wilf Orange* | Agent for Lon Bracton and Meldy Glebe |
| *Sir Herbert Ossett* | Head of Pennine Fabrics |
| *Sam Peachtree* and his wife, *Betty* | An American adman |
| *Malcolm Petherton* | Head of the Philosophy Department of the University of Brockshire |
| *Petronella, Duchess of Brockshire* | Wife of the Chancellor of the University of Brockshire |
| *Rupert Pickrup* | Opposition Member of Parliament |
| *Elizabeth Plucknett* | Public Relations Officer of the University of Brockshire |
| *Povey* | M.C. of *During the Week,* a television programme |
| *Mrs. Prake* | An authority on housing; a guest on Professor Cally's television programme |
| *Archie Prest* and his wife, *Sara* | An English adman |
| *Radley* | A television producer |
| *Brigadier Rampside* | A public relations man, in the Ministry of Defence |
| *Phil Rawbin* | A photographer-artist |
| *Reg* | An official of the Opposition party |
| *Mrs. Ella (Kate) Ringmore* | An executive of Prospect, Peterson and Modley, advertising agents |
| *Betty Riser* | A columnist employed by Simon Birtle |
| *Clarence Rittenden* | Registrar of the University of Brockshire |
| *Professor Cosmo Saltana* | Director of the *Institute of Social Imagistics* |
| *Dr. Sittle* | Medical Officer of Health; a guest on Professor Cally's television programme |
| *Ezra J. Smithy* | Dan Luckett's assistant |
| *Dr. Stample* | Librarian and Public Orator of the University of Brockshire |
| *Ken Stapleford* and his wife, *Ruth* | Minister of Possible Developments |
| *Professor Anton Stervas* and his wife | Head of the Economics Department of the University of Brockshire |

| | |
|---|---|
| *Orland M. Stockton* | An American lawyer |
| *The Earl of Sturtleton* and his wife, *Lady Harriet* | A political figure, and his restless wife |
| *Vi Tarriton* (or *Farriton*) | Charlie Murch's girl friend |
| *Tasco* | Meldy Glebe's director |
| *Sir James Tenks* | President of the Board of Trade |
| *Rolf Tenzie* | A public relations man |
| *Dr. Lois Terry* | Instructor in the English Department of the University of Brockshire |
| *Lady Thaxley* and her daughter, *Lucy* | Owner of Tarwoods Manor |
| *Dr. Owen Tuby* | Deputy Director of the *Institute of Social Imagistics* |
| *Turner* | A reporter for the *Brockshire Gazette and Advertiser* |
| *Geoff Wirrington* | Deputy Opposition Leader and Shadow Home Secretary |
| *Mrs. Nan Wolker* | Advertising Manager of Pennine Fabrics |
| *Barry Wragley* | An American, currently at Oxford |

# Volume I: Out of Town

## PART ONE

# 1

It was the end of a wet Monday afternoon in autumn. Professor Cosmo Saltana and Dr. Owen Tuby were sitting in the Small Lounge of Robinson's Hotel, Bayswater, London W.2. Robinson's is one of the city's few remaining good old-fashioned hotels, known to several generations of visitors for its quaint inconveniences and quiet discomfort. The Small Lounge, decorated in various despairing shades of brown, is one of its saddest rooms, but guests may have afternoon tea served in there, close to its sullen little fire, never quite out but never quite in. But Professor Saltana and Dr. Tuby were not talking over the remains of afternoon tea, which they had not ordered because neither of them felt he could reasonably afford what it would cost. They were in fact discussing how they could best meet their hotel bills, for though they had separate rooms, they were close friends and had decided earlier to pool their resources.

"As soon as my cousin's back in London," Dr. Tuby was saying, "he ought to be good for at least fifty pounds."

"Are you sure?" Professor Saltana asked him.

The bright hope faded and Dr. Tuby shook his head now in no more than the dim yellowish lighting of the Small Lounge. "No, I'm not. To tell you the truth, Cosmo, I'm not sure of anything. I was a fool not to stay out East. At least I could live cheaply out there while looking around for something to do. Nothing's turning up in London. And now here we are, old man, paying through our noses to sit in the sodden ruins of an Empire."

"Quite so," said Professor Saltana. "I ought to have gone to Africa. Join the beginning, not the end. Not a bad-looking woman, that," he added, after a pause.

"No, she's not. We exchanged half a smile this morning. I was going into breakfast as she was coming out. But now she's too worried to notice me. Something in those papers she's staring at. Important official-looking stuff, probably legal muck. It always has women worried."

They stared across at the woman, the only other person in the room. She was probably about forty, a plumpish blonde type, thickening perhaps but still looking quite trim — and obviously prosperous — in a dark red suit.

Robinson's only pageboy, a kind of changeling, came into the Small

Lounge, crying plaintively, as if for a lost mother: "Miss-us Dray-ick, Miss-us Dray-ick!"

"Yes, I'm Mrs. Drake," she told him.

"Wanted on the telephone."

And out they went, Mrs. Drake leaving the papers on the sofa. "She's a Mrs. Drake," Dr. Tuby announced.

"I gathered that," said Professor Saltana dryly. He was a dry sort of man.

"Can't help feeling curious," said Dr. Tuby, getting up. "I'll take a peep."

"You're a cad."

"I know. Always have been. Watch the door." There was no sensible reason why he should tiptoe across, but he did. He bent over without touching the papers, took a quick look, then hurried back. As he sat down he met his companion's enquiring look with a slow smile.

"Well — what?"

"Don't tell me you're a cad too, Professor Saltana?"

"Of course I am. Anything interesting?"

"Could be. American setup. The Judson Drake Sociological Foundation. Hadn't time to take in anything else. What do you think, Cosmo?"

"Might be something. Might not."

"You may remember," said Dr. Tuby, smiling again, "that I was urging you this morning to forget philosophy and try sociology. If I'm ready at a pinch to prefer it to Eng. Lit., a subject in great demand but poorly subsidized, then you ought to be prepared to drop your old moral sciences, to which nobody's prepared to give a penny. Just consider — "

"No speech, Owen, please. Save it for Mrs. Drake."

"You think then — " He stopped there because he heard the door open. Mrs. Drake returned to her sofa slowly, sat down, and began fumbling her papers rather blindly. A moment or two later, she began rummaging through her handbag, obviously in search of a handkerchief. When the two men heard a choking sound coming from her, and saw that she might be about to hurry away, they exchanged a quick look and a nod, then moved across together.

"Mrs. Drake," Dr. Tuby began, "please forgive this intrusion. I am Dr. Tuby and my friend and colleague here is Professor Saltana. We couldn't help noticing that you are in some distress, and we are wondering if there is any way in which we could be of assistance to you. After all, we are fellow-guests. I must explain, though," he continued, giving her time to collect herself and stop dabbing, "that I am not a medical man. Mine is an academic doctorate, and I am in fact a sociologist."

"We are both sociologists, Mrs. Drake," said Professor Saltana. "And if there is anything we can do — "

"You're very kind," said Mrs. Drake between sniffs, "and really it's quite extraordinary — I mean, it just shows — and it's not the first time it's happened to me either — I mean, just when I've really needed some help, it's come along — out of the blue, you might say. Oh dear — I must look a sight. I know I feel one. I can't explain anything properly, looking like this. You'll have to excuse me for a few minutes." She got up. "I'll leave these things here and come straight back. Don't go, please. You *can* help me, I'm sure." She was now moving away and called over her shoulder: "I don't know if you gentlemen would like a drink. But I know I would, and they'll serve it in here. Large whisky-and-sodas? I'll tell the waiter."

"Highly emotional, possibly," said Professor Saltana as soon as she had gone, "but not entirely a foolish woman."

"Certainly not. Intuitive of course rather than intellectual. The idea of the whisky-and-sodas — large too — was intuition almost raised to the power of genius. By the way, she sounded English to me, not American."

"English, but has lived in America."

"We don't take another and better look at her papers, I think, Cosmo?"

"Wouldn't dream of it now that she's our hostess, Owen."

"Exactly what I feel. Point of honour. And now, Professor Saltana, is it in order to welcome you to our faculty or department?"

"Sociology?"

"Sociology. And, remember, Cosmo, *you* said it. I didn't. *We're both sociologists, Mrs. Drake,* you told her. No prompting from me, don't forget. You're in with me now up to the neck. But in *what,* God knows."

"We shall see," said Professor Saltana in his own dark brooding fashion. And Dr. Tuby was silent and thoughtful too, until Mrs. Drake returned, sleek and smiling now, and followed by the waiter carrying three handsome whiskies and three bottles of soda water.

## 2

"Well, I feel much better already," said Mrs. Drake, after she had signed for the whiskies and taken one herself. "Thanks to you two. I'm still in trouble — you don't get out of *that* just by doing your face, though it helps — but if I can just *explain* to somebody who'll understand, it won't seem anything like as bad. Oh dear — where do I start? I'm Mrs. Judson Drake, originally Elfreda Hoskins. English, of course — born and brought up in Highgate. About fifteen years ago I went to New York as a secretary. I moved around, the way you do over there, and ended up as secretary to Judson Drake, who was the big man in a little town called Sweetsprings, in Oregon. He was years older than me, nearly sixty, and of course everybody out there thought I'd worked that divorce

and then married him just because he was rich. And it's not true. I don't
say I was as crazy about him as he was about me, but I really was fond of
him. He was kind of sad and simple outside business, as if he never knew
where he was or what he wanted. But in business — lumber and other
things — he was a real tiger. Well, we were married nearly five years
and I made him happy — at least as far as he could be happy, being so
puzzled about everything except business. He passed away just over a
year ago."

By this time she had of course been able to take a good look at both
of them. They were so sharply contrasted that there was something
vaguely comical about them, taken as a pair — like Laurel and Hardy,
she thought. But of course neither of them actually looked like Laurel or
Hardy. The Professor was tallish and thin, with a long sunken-cheeked
face, black hair white in streaks and deep-set eyes that might be a curious
dark green: an odd and perhaps rather frightening man, somewhere
between fifty and sixty, she guessed. He was clean and neat but rather
shabby, which was of course all right for a professor to be.

"My name, Mrs. Drake, is Cosmo Saltana. My paternal grandfather
was Spanish, but I am English by birth and upbringing and am a graduate of London University. For many years I taught philosophy in various
universities in Central and South America; I speak fluent Spanish. I have
had to make many moves, partly no doubt because I was restless but
chiefly because in that part of the world there is so much political in-
stability. One year you may be dining with important ministers; the next
year you find yourself hounded by the secret police and about to be sum-
marily arrested. The young men are your students in March and a revolutionary committee or guerilla fighters in June. This makes academic
life very difficult. Moreover, I decided some time ago to move from
philosophy to sociology." He hesitated a moment. "One last point. If it is
possible to save any money on Latin-American academic salaries, paid in
unstable currencies, then I have never learnt the trick of it. So now — I
prefer to be entirely frank with you, Mrs. Drake — I am a poor man.
I ought not to be staying in this hotel. I can no longer afford it."

"Isn't that wonderful?" cried Mrs. Drake, glowing with admiration.
"I mean — coming straight out with it like that. I haven't heard a man
say he was poor for years and years. All Judson's friends were rich. He
didn't like poor people. He said they hadn't tried hard enough. Well now,
what about you — Dr. — Dr. — oh, isn't this silly of me?"

"Dr. Tuby. Owen Tuby. Part-English, part-Welsh. Honours degree
at Cambridge, doctorate later in India. Taught English language and
literature for many years — in India, Malaya, Hong Kong. But became
increasingly interested in sociology — "

As he explained why, very eloquently, Mrs. Drake stared at him in
delighted amazement. He wasn't much to look at; not at all impressive
like Professor Saltana. He was rather short and quite chubby, almost a

little fat man. He was going bald and had a large pink baby-face. His spectacles, rimless and round, magnified his eyes, big anyhow and a lightish brown, so that they seemed enormous, adding to the general baby effect. But there was nothing childish about his voice, one of the best Mrs. Drake could ever remember hearing. It was not too deep, not too light, wonderfully clear, resonant, musical, just honey in sound. He seemed a nice man but one to beware of, until you knew where you were with him, because with a voice like this he could talk a woman into anything.

"And as you must realize, Mrs. Drake," he concluded, "I am fond of talking, either in public or in private. Otherwise, my accomplishments are very modest though not without social value. I can draw lightning caricatures and play the piano a little."

"With feeling," said Professor Saltana, "but with appalling inaccuracy."

"Quite true — unfortunately," said Dr. Tuby. "I must add that Professor Saltana has a passion for the clarinet, which he plays with both feeling *and* accuracy, quite beautifully." And he bestowed upon Mrs. Drake, like a benediction, an entrancing smile.

Before anything could be said, six people, a family party, marched into the room, as if under orders to take it over at once. "This'll do, I think," said the leader, all aggression and hostility, exchanging glares with Mrs. Drake. She finished her whisky and then got up.

"I think we've had enough of this place, don't you?" she said, giving the remaining five of the invaders a collective glare, and led the way out. She did this without another word, clearly unwilling to offer the Enemy the tiniest scrap of information.

They halted in the corridor outside.

"I've had such a worrying scratchy sort of day — you've no idea — that I'd like to go up and have a long leisurely soak in the bath. You must dine with me. Will you? Oh — that's wonderful. I'll ask for a quiet table and some really good food — if they have any. Quarter to eight, shall we say? And while I'm resting and recovering, you two could be working out what you'd like to do in sociology if you were given the chance. Couldn't you?" And her look was as appealing as her voice.

"Certainly," said Professor Saltana.

"Our heads are bursting with plans," Dr. Tuby told her.

"Quarter to eight, then. I must fly." And off she flew, leaving them to cross the entrance hall in the direction of the bar.

"I see this as an all-or-nothing situation, Cosmo. A tide in the affairs of men and so forth. This insistence upon ready money in the bar — to a man who's been signing chits for twenty years — is appalling, but unless we're ready to venture a pound or two on whisky, then we're not fit to deal with this situation, not the men for Mrs. Drake and the Judson Drake Sociological Foundation."

## 3

The dining room at Robinson's, like almost everything there, is irregular
in shape, and at the far end there is a table in a nook, a close fit for four
but admirable for three. This was the table that Mrs. Drake had secured
for them.

"Now then," she began, after the waiter had brought the smoked
salmon, "I'll tell you all about it. Why I'm here. Why I was feeling so
upset. You see, my husband left over two million dollars, after taxes.
Some of it went to his first wife and her son — his son too, of course —
Walt, who also has a big share of Judson's various businesses. Walt's a
stinker, like his mother. Then of course some of it came to me. The rest,
a million dollars or so, was divided equally between two Judson Drake
Sociological Foundations, one for America, up there in Oregon, and one
for England, chiefly to please me. Which of course it did." She dis-
tributed a wide and pearly smile between them, but the next moment
looked sad. "Poor Judson!"

It is not easy to look deeply sympathetic while eating smoked
salmon.

Feeling that his best was probably not quite good enough, Dr. Tuby
risked a question. "Your husband took a great interest in sociology,
did he?"

"Only the very last year, when he suddenly found out about it —
something on the television, it was. Really educational, he thought, and
at the same time good for business, not like so much of this educational
stuff, if you don't mind my saying so, Professor Saltana, Dr. Tuby. And
I do hope," she added rather wistfully, "that if you can do something for
me, it'll be something that's both educational *and* good for business —
just for Judson's sake."

"It will be," said Professor Saltana. "*It is.* But our turn will come
later. Tell us about the English Foundation, please, Mrs. Drake."

"Well, as you can imagine," said Mrs. Drake, "Walt Drake and his
mother and their lawyers were dead against this English Foundation and
me coming over to set it up. The fuss isn't over yet — trust them — and
if they can catch me out and have it all upset — they will. That's why
I had to bring over Professor Lentenban. I didn't want him, though of
course I knew I couldn't set it up all on my own, but they agreed to him.
And if you want my opinion, knowing what I do now, I think it was
rigged from the start."

"There was something wrong with Professor Lentenban?" Dr. Tuby
tried to look thoughtful, scholarly, in a sociological way. "I seem to know
the name. Don't you, Saltana?"

"I associate him — rather vaguely — with one or two interesting little social experiments — not entirely successful, though." And the Professor frowned, tightened his lips, gave his head two slow turns to left and right, as if he had had doubts about this Lentenban for years.

"And I'll bet they weren't entirely successful," cried Mrs. Drake. "Gin and pills — that's Professor Lentenban. I must admit his wife warned me. But they'd been fighting — and that's when a woman will say anything about a man. After two days on the boat — he wouldn't fly — I thought him very peculiar. Never left his cabin all day and then wanted to sit up and talk all night. Giggling a lot too. Then I saw what it was. Pills by the handful — all colours. A proper 'pillhead,' as they call 'em over there. By the time we landed at Southampton I wasn't getting any sense out of him. Giggle, giggle, giggle. Had to handle him like a baby. Called a doctor for him here — only two days ago, Saturday — and off he went into a nursing home. Went to see him yesterday, then this morning. Giggling away and didn't even recognize me. Then they rang me up — you remember, that pageboy coming for me — to say I needn't call again for a couple of weeks because they've put him under sedation. That's when I was so upset. Not sorry for *him* — he'd asked for it — but for myself. Here I was, all on my own, not knowing where to start, with Walt Drake and his mother and their lawyers all just waiting to pounce on me. Ah — this looks nice."

A saddle of lamb had been wheeled up to them — this was a different Robinson's tonight — and the wine waiter was watching Professor Saltana anxiously as he tasted the claret. It was some minutes — and fine luxurious minutes too — before any more private talk was possible. Then the two men looked expectantly at Mrs. Drake.

"So when you two came across and spoke to me — and did it so nicely too — I was feeling quite helpless and miserable, not knowing where to turn."

"If you depend upon us, Mrs. Drake," said Dr. Tuby, "we promise not to giggle."

"Gin, no doubt," Professor Saltana added, "but none of those pills."

She laughed but then looked serious and asked if *they* were serious.

Professor Saltana nodded twice, looked hard at her, and held up a long finger. Then, after a moment's silence, he said, "*Social Imagistics.*"

She stared back at him. "Social what?"

"Imag-istics. Concerned with public images."

"The selection, creation, projection," cried Dr. Tuby, "of suitable and helpful images. You must know, Mrs. Drake, how immensely important the image is now in politics, advertising, business. Of course you do. Well, Professor Saltana and I are preparing a course — two courses in fact, one elementary, the other more advanced — on what we propose to call *Social Imagistics.*"

"Oh — but that's wonderful. Poor Judson would just have loved that. *Social Imagistics.* Yes, yes, yes. Even if he'd knocked off his gin and pills, Lentenban would never have thought of anything as good as that. My — aren't you clever, both of you? But where do I come in?"

"You come in with the Judson Drake Sociological Foundation," said the Professor.

"If you prefer to stay away, you stay away," Dr. Tuby told her. "But if you decide to work with us — as I hope you will — then the *Institute of Social Imagistics* would be headed as follows: Director — Cosmo Saltana. Deputy Director — Owen Tuby. Assistant Director and General Secretary — Elfreda Drake — "

"Oh — I'd love it. And that would settle Walt and that lot." As she received no immediate reply, she looked rather anxiously from one to the other of them. "Wouldn't it?"

"Probably it would — in certain circumstances," said Saltana slowly, thoughtfully. "But we shall have to create the circumstances." He stopped there because the waiters were back again.

Indeed, it was not until coffee and brandy were in front of them, and the two men, after being urged by their hostess, were smoking the best cigars Robinson's could offer, that Saltana explained what he had meant. "To create the circumstances, we must attach the Foundation — and ourselves — to a university. This would, I hope, silence your American critics. It would also be much more economical than setting up an independent institute, which if we'd sufficient money I'd have preferred."

"But there's plenty of money." Mrs. Drake was astonished. And he'd called himself a poor man!

After awarding her one of his smiles, Dr. Tuby took over. "Plenty of money if we could spend it almost at once, Mrs. Drake. But I've been working it out — over the cheese. The half-million or so dollars would have to be invested. So let's say it produced an income of about eight thousand pounds a year. An independent institute would earn nothing at first and couldn't expect other grants, not until it became well known. Meanwhile it would need suitable premises in London that would have to be furnished, staffed, widely advertised — "

"Of course I know that," cried Mrs. Drake. "But there's always my money — "

"And what are your Americans going to say?" said Saltana. "That the English Foundation isn't soundly based. That it has no official academic backing. That — "

"No, you win. We'll have to go to a university. And if you two know how to do that, well and good, because I haven't the foggiest notion. I wouldn't know where to start."

"In a sense, neither do we," Dr. Tuby admitted, smiling, "having been abroad so long. But if you're prepared to leave it to us, we'll spend tomorrow obtaining the best possible advice. Which of all these new universities would be the most suitable for our purpose. Which vice-chancellor is the most likely man for our *Social Imagistics* department. Once we know that, we go into action. Mrs. Drake, why don't you look around the shops tomorrow — you've been wanting to do that, haven't you? — "

"Of course I have — "

"If we've any luck tomorrow, then on Wednesday the three of us call on the vice-chancellor we've chosen." Saltana sounded brisk and businesslike. Certainly an iron head there.

But Dr. Tuby was ready now to respond more generously to the whisky he had drunk before dinner, the claret during dinner, the brandy after dinner. "We choose, we move, we strike," he announced. Then, holding Mrs. Drake's entranced gaze, he intoned:

> *Yet was there surely then no vulgar power*
> *Working with us, — nothing less, in truth,*
> *Than that most noble attribute of man,*
> *That wish for something loftier, more adorned,*
> *Than is the common aspect, daily garb,*
> *Of human life. . . .*

"I don't know what that was all about," Mrs. Drake declared, "but I could listen to you for hours, Dr. Tuby."

"Be careful — or you may have to," said the Professor, dryly but not sourly. "Now is there anything else you'd like to discuss, my dear Mrs. Drake?"

"There's this — but there's not going to be any argument about it. From tomorrow morning on, I'll take care of all your expenses. It's the least I can do, seeing you'll both be working for me and the Foundation. You agree? Good! Now tell me again — what is it you want to do? Social what?"

"*Social Imagistics.*"

"That's it — *Social Imagistics,*" she cried enthusiastically, no iron head herself. "My God! Poor old Judson would have loved that. Do you think that if I went to a spiritualist medium I could pass it on to him?"

"I doubt it," Saltana told her gravely. "You'd only find yourself in a dark basement trying to talk to a Red Indian."

# 4

Saltana and Tuby had spent nearly half the morning telephoning from Robinson's, being passed on from the Ministry of Education to University Grants to *The Times Educational Supplement* to this one and that one, so that it was nearly twelve o'clock when they reached the man they really wanted, O. V. Mere, editor of the new Redbrick monthly. He was on the top floor of a large building just off Fleet Street, a warren of editorial offices filled with ironmongery, jazz, nursing, hotel-keeping, bringing up babies, fashions for men, wrestling, the shoe trade, linguistics, and lingerie. O. V. Mere's office was at the end of a white-tiled corridor that suggested a severely hygienic prison. But the office itself was quite different; filled with cigarette smoke, review copies waiting to be sold, pamphlets waiting to be read, letters waiting to be answered; a cosy higgledy-piggledy. And no sooner had they set eyes on O. V. Mere than Saltana and Tuby exchanged triumphant glances. This was their man. They had dealt in their time with dozens of him.

He was a slack, untidy, chain-smoking, ash-and-dandruff sort of man. Above his smouldering cigarette he seemed to peer out of some desert of cynicism where the ruins and bones of innumerable schemes for higher education might be found. He had one of those uninflected voices that are like hard stares. He never really smiled but sometimes the cigarette in the corner of his mouth would wobble a little.

"Well," he said, after they had introduced themselves, "I know all about the new universities. Wouldn't be here if I didn't. What can I tell you?"

Saltana gave him a brief account of the Judson Drake Sociological Foundation, and then mentioned *Social Imagistics.*

"Social what? Imagistics, did you say?" said Mere, without removing the cigarette that smouldered away. "Who came up with that one?"

"We did," Tuby told him smartly. "Professor Saltana and I. We've just invented it."

The cigarette wobbled. "To do what?" He gave Tuby a look.

Tuby returned the look. "The selection, creation, projection of suitable and helpful public images."

The cigarette wobbled again. "You might have something too. But why a university?"

Saltana took over. "Our association with the Judson Drake Foundation," he said smoothly, "demands a beginning on a sound academic basis."

"I see," said Mere. Then silence. He looked at them; they looked at him. All three of them might have gone into that desert together, to stare at the ruins and bones.

Saltana came out of it first. "If you gave us some advice we were able to follow successfully, Mr. Mere, I would ask the Foundation to offer you at least a token fee — say, twenty-five guineas."

Mere nodded his acceptance. "Once you were established I might come and do an article on you myself. Now let me think." His eyes, always half-closed, were now completely shut. Then, after about half a minute, he opened them almost wide. "Brockshire," he announced.

"Brockshire?" This was Saltana.

"Oh — Brockshire!" Tuby sounded surprised — and indeed he was, remembering as he did a county of sheep and stone walls and pretty villages. "A university there! Good God — they must be coming up like toadstools."

Then Saltana thought he must be going out of his mind because he distinctly heard Mere say, "It's really a moved-out cat."

"We're not with you, Mr. Mere," Tuby told him. "What's a cat got to do with it?"

"Ah — you heard it too, Owen." Saltana sounded much relieved.

Mere wobbled his cigarette at them and then spoke very slowly, as if addressing an infant class. "*Cat* is our term for a college of advanced technology. If you take, roughly, the area between Gloucester, where the technical college was originally, and the county town of Brockshire, Tarbury, there's been a rapid industrial development — agricultural machinery, light engineering, fertilizer plants, all that kind of thing. So the money's been coming in. The University of Brockshire's only half-built yet, but most of the staff's been engaged and already there are five or six hundred students. I'm told they're aiming at two to three thousand. I haven't been there lately, I must admit." And Mere returned to the desert.

"And where do you go when you do go there?" Saltana asked with a touch of irritation.

"Tarbury. It's only about a couple of miles away. Not a bad old-fashioned market town. Big square, decent old hotel, that sort of thing. You might enjoy it. I hate the bloody place."

"Well, why do you suggest *we* go to Brockshire?" This was Saltana again, not yet free of his irritation.

"Chiefly because of the Vice-Chancellor there. The V.C. is all-important. You agree? Of course. And this is why I suggest Brockshire. The Vice-Chancellor there is John James Lapford, always known as Jayjay. He was Director of Education for Brockshire for many years. I know Jayjay very well. Worked under him once. We don't like each other — and his wife's almost Lady Macbeth in my book — but that's beside the point. He'll listen to me. He knows I know what's cooking. And he wants to know what's cooking. He's had no real university experience since he came down from Cambridge. And he's had to work like hell from scratch, bunging in social studies and humanities on top of the advanced technology he took over. Moreover, he'd give almost anything to look right out in front. He can take any amount of publicity, always could. Fundamentally he's a timid sod, lying awake wondering if he's done the right thing, but even so he'll risk making a fool of himself rather than chance being left behind and out of it. Then there's another thing. You're in a hurry, aren't you?"

"We're in a hell of a hurry," said Saltana.

"Then Jayjay's your man. He can be rushed. Doing from scratch a hurry-up job, he's got more room to move in quickly than the vice-chancellors of the genuine new universities have. He's not as clamped in as they are by academic advisory boards and senates. I don't say he could hand you a department, but he might be rushed into letting you work inside an existing one, if it was on the cheap — "

"It needn't cost him a dam' penny," Saltana declared emphatically.

"Well then, say the word — and I'll ring up Jayjay this afternoon and tell him I'm giving him the first crack at — what's it? — oh yes — *Social Imagistics.*" Mere gave them his look again, and the cigarette wobbled.

"Then I say the word," cried Tuby enthusiastically. "And you do too, don't you, Cosmo?"

"I suppose so." Saltana was still resenting that stare. "What's it like down there — Brockshire?"

"Very beautiful," Tuby put in hastily.

"In summer, for a few weeks," Mere said. "Any other time it's raining or freezing. And you're trying to instruct a lot of young clots on a building site. Look — I generally go out for a drink or two at this time. No objection to a pub, have you?"

"Not unless it's closed," said Saltana. "Let's go."

In the lift going down, Mere told them that this particular pub was a Fleet Street favourite and that he nearly always found his brother-in-law there, collecting material for paragraphs out of which, believe it or not, he made a dam' good living.

The bar was packed with men fortifying themselves with gin and whisky to keep alive the spirit of *Areopagitica* and already almost mewing like a Milton eagle, with here and there some of their feminine colleagues, not Miltonic and screaming like seagulls. It took Mere some minutes and two rounds of gin-and-tonics to find his brother-in-law, Fred Somebody-or-other, free to listen to him. Fred, a surprising figure, was a short, wide, red-faced man, dressed unsuitably in tweeds and looking like a mad farmer. Holding himself aloof from this Fred talk, Saltana became involved with a red-haired woman, an up-to-date embittered version of Queen Elizabeth the First, who insisted on telling him how the column for teenagers she ran was driving her out of her mind. It was Tuby, more eloquent every moment, who gave depth, richness, sparkle, to Mere's account of them and *Social Imagistics* to Fred, who still looked as if he might be ready to sell them a score of ewes. Then Fred vanished, and then Mere vanished, after promising to ring up Jayjay about teatime, and then Tuby bumped into a Reuters man he'd known in Singapore and soon found himself pressed to one end of the bar by a number of jolly good fellows, and washing down stale sausage rolls with whisky presumably paid for by total strangers. He could just catch an occasional glimpse of Cosmo Saltana, taller than his new companions, and could tell by his flashing eye and haggard look that he was arguing ferociously about something — and not, Tuby hoped to God, about *Social Imagistics* or who ought to pay for the drinks, which neither of them could afford.

It was nearly two o'clock, with the room thinning out, when a scarlet Dr. Tuby and a deathly pale Professor Saltana, looking like an old-fashioned Hamlet, were able to meet and decide to leave. "A very useful morning, I think, Cosmo," Tuby said very carefully, knowing he would have trouble with *useful,* as they left.

"Possibly, Owen, possibly." Saltana was gloomy. "But I took a dislike to that fellow Mere. Also, I've had too much to drink and nothing to eat." He turned up the collar of his peculiar huge overcoat, which always looked as if it had been made for him by some tropical tailor who had never seen an overcoat. "Raining again, too."

5

John James Lapford, Vice-Chancellor of the University of Brockshire, was staring out of the biggest window of his room on the eighth floor of the Admin. and Refectory Building. He often did this, sometimes feeling elated, at other times feeling rather depressed. This was one of these other times. It was raining again — Brockshire has a high rainfall — and there seemed to be far too much standing water down there among the temporary huts, the half-made roads, the idle machines probably sinking into the mud. If any men were working anywhere — and most of his university still didn't exist outside the architect's model on the table behind him — there was no sign of them; and the contractors were already over six months behind their schedule.

Hoping to lighten his spirits, he looked across at the three other buildings already up, two of them, Science and Engineering, actually in use. But he could see only the upper floors of these two, rising above the low grey bulk of the Library, for which his architect had contrived a genuine Cotswold look. The Library was still unfinished inside, where Dr. Stample, the University Librarian and Public Orator, was still short of shelving and various furnishings, and not a single row of books had yet been installed. And this was a worry, no spirit-lightener, because Jayjay had already arranged for the Duchess of Brockshire, wife of his Chancellor, to come and open the Library towards the end of this very term. Even so, Jayjay was warmed by what he saw. Unlike those new vice-chancellors who had been compelled to build within or close to city limits, he had not had to fight for space, with the further result that he and his architect, himself a Cotswold man, had not had to run up a lot of grimly functional semi-skyscrapers. Even Science and Engineering were broad rather than high, almost cosily Cotswold.

The Vice-Chancellor was a tall bulky man, oddly built for an intellectual because his head seemed disproportionately small for his body, as if Nature, round about 1910, had had a whimsical notion to start developing some humans along the lines of the old dinosaurs. However, there was nothing reptilian about his face — his permanently surprised eyebrows, his restless pale eyes, his anachronistic semi-cavalry moustache. When agitated, especially at an important committee meeting (he owed almost everything to his committee-handling), he had a trick of keeping his heavy body quite still while moving his head quickly from side to side, like a sea lion looking for fish tossed from any direction. It was during these moments too that his voice, to his disgust, often rose to a squeak.

He went across to a side table where there were several exceptionally small wine glasses and a decanter of pale dry sherry. Wishing he could risk something stronger — after all, it was that kind of day — he had just taken his first sip when he heard a knock. He looked up to find himself confronted by an extraordinary figure, which some time machine might have brought from Henry the Eighth's Hampton Court. "Oh — I say — look here," he began, only narrowly missing his squeak.

"Good morning, Vice-Chancellor." The visitor, removing his enormous purple velvet cap, turned himself into Dr. Stample, Librarian and Public Orator. "Here it is. What do you think, Vice-Chancellor? About right for a Public Orator — on ceremonial occasions only, of course — eh?"

"Rich — quite impressive — certainly, Stample." He looked harder at the robe, purple and pink and heavy with gilt. "But you won't enjoy four or five hours of it on a hot July day."

"I don't mind, Vice-Chancellor. And I can hardly remember a really hot July day. Shall I accept it, then? On approval at the moment." Stample began getting out of the robe.

Jayjay was about to say *Yes* when, as often happened, he suddenly remembered something and somebody. "I think I'd like my wife to take a look at it first. Strong views about this kind of thing. And she'll have to sit there in front, staring at it while we perform. So why not leave it here — *and* the hat — Stample, that's a good chap?" He watched the robe being carefully folded for a moment or two, then went on: "By the way — and I mention it because you might help us here — we were wondering last night if we couldn't somehow develop the *traditional* side of the university — y'know, a few quaint but appealing forms and ceremonies. Kind of thing third-year men explain to the freshmen. No reason why Oxford and Cambridge should have it all. Give it a thought, will you?" he concluded hastily.

Somebody else had arrived, to keep an appointment with him, and it was already quarter to one and he was due back home, where some people were lunching with them, at one-fifteen. "Come in, Professor Cally. Thank you, Dr. Stample."

Professor Donald Cally, head of the Department of Sociology, was the physical opposite of his Vice-Chancellor. He had a slight body but an unusually large head that seemed to have more than its share of bone. His forehead, various ridges, chin looked as if they ought to be polished, not merely washed, every morning. He was in his middle forties, and a very solemn man who didn't even pretend to have a sense of humour, would not have known what to do with one. He had a loud voice that he never made any attempt to modify, and generally spoke as if he were addressing a class of mentally defective children. Isabel Lapford detested him, and never stopped telling her husband that his appointment had been a mistake. But in fact it was his voice and manner that had secured him the chair of sociology at Brockshire. He had been only an Assistant Lecturer at Edinburgh when, with some other sociologists, he had taken part in a television series. When the others had hissed or mumbled in an academic fashion, he had been so loud and clear, so well-equipped to talk to idiots, that he had been the one outstanding personality of the series, with a photograph in the *Radio Times*. This was the kind of man Jayjay wanted at Brockshire, especially for sociology, and he offered him the professorship at once — undoubtedly a catch. Even so, after a few minutes of Cally, he did find himself not altogether out of sympathy with Isabel's idea of the man.

"Do sit down, Professor Cally. I'm having a glass of sherry. Can I tempt you?" And if he wanted a refusal, he couldn't have put it better. Cally must have been resisting temptations ever since the age of twelve.

"Vice-Chancellor," Cally began sternly, "you mentioned over the phone a Professor Saltana and a Dr. Tuby. So far I can't find them anywhere. No sociological publications listed under their names. No attendance at major conferences. If you can give me time, I could make further enquiries — "

"No, no, leave it. After all, as I must have told you, I'm seeing them — and this Mrs. Drake — this afternoon. About four o'clock. But not here. I've decided to see them at home."

"You have?" Cally sounded almost accusing.

"Yes. This Mrs. Drake being with them. And my wife thought perhaps a cup of tea — eh? By the way, do you see the *Post?*" He went across to his desk, still talking, "Paragraph about these people, this morning. Paper's here somewhere. I marked the paragraph. Take a look at it."

Cally didn't read it aloud but neither did he keep it to himself. In a peculiarly irritating fashion, he brought out, loud and clear, the significant bits, rather as if he thought Jayjay couldn't read at all. "Professor Saltana Director Judson Drake Sociological Foundation . . . Dr. Tuby Deputy Director . . . trying to decide which university . . . *Social Imagistics* . . ." It was like having newspaper placards and headlines shouted at you.

"They'll explain their *Social Imagistics,* no doubt," Cally said as he returned the newspaper.

"Of course — naturally." Jayjay was still feeling irritable.

"Very irregular though, isn't it?"

"What?"

"Just ringing up, then coming straight down here."

"The way I like to work myself, Professor Cally. Contemporary trend and pace. I'm working here to create a *modern* university. Essential part of the New Britain. After all, that's why *you're* here, Donald." The *Donald* was new, but he felt he might have been rather too sharp with him.

"I understand that, Jayjay."

A little too quick with that *Jayjay*, Lapford told himself. "I must go in a minute. People coming to lunch."

Cally nodded. "Will you be wanting me to attend this tea party for them?"

"No, no, no — not necessary at all."

Cally, who had all the bone for it, looked stubborn. "But of course it's understood, Vice-Chancellor, that if they do come to work here, they'll have to do it in my Department."

"Yes, yes — I ought to be familiar with academic etiquette by this time. Only one thing I need to know. Have you any space for them?"

"It's a tight squeeze as it is. But if you think it's all that important, I might manage half a hut."

"Not much to offer them, is it? Foundation comes along — American money behind it — then the best we can do is half a hut. They've probably already got half a skyscraper over there. How important it might be, of course, I don't know yet. But I have an idea — one of my hunches, if you like, Donald — that it easily might be. Look — I must run. Would you mind telling them downstairs to redirect Professor Saltana to my house?"

# 6

At the very time, that Wednesday, when Vice-Chancellor Jayjay Lapford was driving home to lunch, Mrs. Drake and Saltana and Tuby were finishing theirs on the 12:05 from Paddington to Moreton-in-Marsh. After being out of England so long, Mrs. Drake had not felt equal to hiring a car and then driving them to Tarbury. And she disliked maps, timetables, travel arrangements, and so did Saltana, but fortunately Owen Tuby loved them — Hyderabad to Calcutta, Kuala Lumpur to Bangkok, anything — and had spent a happy half-hour at the porter's desk at Robinson's devising the neatest way to get them to the University of Brockshire.

They had had large pink gins before lunch, a bottle of stone-cold

Beaune during lunch — not a good meal but better than it used to be, they all agreed — and were now having what Saltana called *a touch of brandy* with their coffee.

"It's a funny thing about you two," cried Mrs. Drake, who was excited and gay and looking splendid in her fur coat and new dark blue tweed suit. "I've noticed it already. Shall I tell you what it is?"

"I insist," said Saltana, smiling at her.

Tuby, who was staring out of the window, at nothing but the rain, kept silent. He was nearer the window; Mrs. Drake was sitting opposite them.

"You see, that's just what I mean," she continued. "When one of you's up, the other's down. Now last night at dinner, Professor Saltana, you seemed quite grumpy — I don't mean you were rude or anything — but, y'know, you were a bit down. And there was no holding Dr. Tuby — I haven't laughed so much for years. And now you're all cheerful — and look at him!"

They both looked, and that brought his face slowly round. "*Empty pastures blind with rain,*" he whispered, as if talking to himself, not to them.

"Say that again, Dr. Tuby." It was almost a command.

He smiled out of an infinite melancholy. "*Empty pastures blind with rain.*"

"My God — you could have me crying in a minute. Laughing, crying — I don't know how you do it. Does he have that effect on you, Professor Saltana?"

"Not at all. What about your empty pastures, Owen?"

"I'm trying to remember who wrote that line. Rossetti perhaps. Years since I read him. What I *am* remembering, without particularly wanting to, is my youth — the vanished golden roads, the lost years — "

"You're off again." Mrs. Drake shook her head at him. "Now — stop it."

"Certainly," said Tuby mildly. "As a matter of fact, I was miserable when I was young. I was born to be a rather overweight middle-aged man. And Cosmo there hasn't reached his peak yet. He was intended from the first to be an intolerant fierce old man."

"Now that reminds me — you saying *Cosmo* like that," said Mrs. Drake. "I think we've overdone these 'professors' and 'doctors' and 'mississes.' Why can't we be Cosmo — Owen — Elfreda?" She looked from one to the other. "You don't object to calling me Elfreda, do you?"

"I already call you Elfreda in my mind," Saltana told her, giving her a grave little bow — in his occasional Spanish style.

"So do I. I said to myself as soon as I saw you this morning, 'This dark blue is wonderful for Elfreda,' I said to myself."

"And you agree, Cosmo?"

"I do, Elfreda. But — " and now he looked immensely grave — "I must make a point here. When we meet this Vice-Chancellor, we must be Mrs. Drake — or perhaps Mrs. Judson Drake — "

"That's what they always called me in Oregon — "

"And Dr. Tuby and Professor Saltana. We approach this fellow on stilts — "

"We'll have to leave that to you, Cosmo. Won't we, Owen?"

"No, no, I can do a small stilt act, Elfreda."

"And I shall take a high line, right from the first," said Saltana. "It's possible, of course, that Mere's opinion of this fellow Lapford is wrong. I disliked Mere myself, as Owen knows."

"Ten to one he's not wrong, though, about his Jayjay," Tuby declared with some emphasis. "But the high line, certainly. You're doing Brockshire a favour. The Judson Drake Foundation is almost slumming. Yes, a hard high line, Cosmo, from you. If a little softening needs to be done anywhere, then leave that to me. Agreed?"

"Agreed."

"Now you two just listen to me for a minute," said Elfreda. "You know I like you both. Wouldn't be here if I didn't. But now and again — just now, for instance — you talk to each other in a way that makes me feel uneasy. You sound so *cynical*. And Judson wouldn't have liked it, I know — not outside business. He thought universities and social sciences and professors and everything were wonderful. Well then — " But there she had to stop, in order to pay the bill, and then they returned in silence to the first-class compartment they had to themselves.

Tuby settled down into his seat as luxuriously contented as a cat. "Cosmo will answer you in a minute, Elfreda. Meanwhile, I'll tell you a secret. You've said I've been down this morning, but the truth is — I've been enjoying the kind of self-indulgent melancholy only possible in extremely comfortable conditions. And the secret? Well, believe it or not, this is the only time in my life that I've travelled in England in a first-class compartment."

"Me too, me too," cried Elfreda. "I was only a shorthand-typist — not even a real secretary — before I went to America, and — don't forget — this is the first time I've been back. Now what about you, Cosmo?"

"Only once," he told her bravely. "And then only for about twenty minutes. I was told to pay the extra fare or clear out. I cleared out. Which brings me, Elfreda, to your complaint — "

"No, not really a *complaint*. I only said that sometimes you make me feel uneasy — when you suddenly seem quite cynical — "

Saltana held up his hand. "Please allow me to explain, Elfreda. Owen Tuby and I, as you know, are quite different characters. But we are alike in this — that up to now we have each played a role as honourable as it is ancient — that of the poor wandering scholar — "

"It goes back not hundreds and hundreds but thousands of years," cried Tuby, alight. But then his face darkened. "And now the old trails are being covered with concrete. The universities look like factories, are controlled by five-year productivity plans, cut down staff to buy computers. Instead of the wandering scholar — "

"That's enough, Owen. You can deliver that speech some other time. And you'll enjoy it, Elfreda. It's one of his best. But now you must listen to me." He paused but refused to allow her to look away. "As I told you, I am a poor man. I am also fifty-five years of age. I may be rich in experience — as indeed I am — but who cares? If I make you feel uneasy by sounding cynical, I am sorry. But I am being honest with you, Elfreda. I *am* cynical. So allow us, please, a little cynicism, a little cool planning, some deliberate performing perhaps, a bit of bluffing and hocus-pocus at times — eh?"

"All right, so long as you don't expect much help from me. You're a wicked pair, you are — and I'm just an innocent woman."

"Elfreda," said Tuby softly, "you underrate both yourself and your whole sex." His eyes were already closed and he dozed for a while, but then — the complete traveller — he awoke to look immediately at his watch and to announce that in a few minutes they would arrive at Moreton-in-Marsh. They had brought suitcases, and Tuby said that if Saltana would be responsible for them, he himself would arrange for their further transport to the university. "And I shan't accept any kind of car. We must arrive in style, and there's a lot of car snobbery about nowadays. What we need is something quite large and either very new or very old."

He explained this to the taxi-driver in the drizzle outside. "Haven't you anything else? Something you use for weddings and funerals? We'll be taking you to the other side of Tarbury."

The driver was a young man with a lot of hair and no cap and a wide grin. "What you want is our old Daimler. But I'm warning you — she's slowed up a lot lately — fluid flywheel's not behaving. She'll take best part of an hour to Tarbury."

"Doesn't matter. We're in no hurry. Pop off and bring her along. Oh — and will you be driving her? Well then, I wonder if you'd mind borrowing a chauffeur's cap and wearing a dark overcoat or something?"

"Funeral-style, like? Right you are. But it'll cost you three or four pounds — Tarbury and back."

Tuby, trying to look like a wealthy eccentric, lifted a limp hand and waved him on his way, then joined the other two in the waiting room. "We'll have to wait a few minutes. The car out there wasn't good enough. We're going to Brockshire funeral-style — but it'll help, I think."

"When you said *funeral-style,* I thought you were joking." This was from Elfreda, half an hour later, as the ancient landaulette moved majestically through the dim Cotswolds landscape. "But like hell you were. I hope we've plenty of time. And what does it smell of? I'm trying to think. A damp attic?"

"It's reminding me of an old colleague of mine," said Saltana, "a Professor Orzoni. He was always damp too. Roughly the same smell."

"It's her hoot that I don't like." They were separated from the driver by a stout pane of glass, but Tuby lowered his voice. "He might have warned me about the hoot while he was warning about the fluid flywheel — whatever that is — misbehaving. It's one of the saddest sounds I've ever heard. Lament for a lost world, perhaps. I see myself meeting this Vice-Chancellor with a tear-streaked face. Perhaps the driver doesn't notice it — just a hoot to him. However, he does look like some kind of beatnik chauffeur now, though it's long odds against his getting out and opening the door for us."

"He wouldn't sit with that glass there if we were in Oregon. He'd be turning round telling us about his wife and kids. Wouldn't do here though, anyhow. My God — I'd forgotten how narrow and twisty the roads are."

They went rumbling and sadly hooting on and on until at last Tuby, peering out of the window, said, "This must be Tarbury. People are staring. Some derision from the young. The hoot will soon be heartbreaking. Like one of your adagios, Cosmo. By the way, have you brought your clarinet?"

"I have. I may need it — entirely for my own sake. When words fail me, in triumph or despair, I play my clarinet."

"You do indeed, Cosmo." Tuby was still observing what he could see of the world outside. "Tarbury — yes. Pleasant old town, this part of it. Market place now. Hotel — The Bell — solid, old-fashioned, comfortable, no doubt. Can you see, Elfreda? We may have to spend the night there, don't forget. Ah — he's pulling up. He's asking the best way to the university. Only two or three miles away, Mere said. We should be there in a quarter of an hour."

Finally they arrived at what looked at first like a derelict mining camp. "I realize now what Mere meant," Tuby muttered, "when he talked about young clots on a building site." The old Daimler lurched and groaned, backed out of dead ends, turned, stopped, turned again, and brought them at last to a real building, quite large too. Back in his courier service, Tuby nipped out at once, only to be told that the Vice-Chancellor was expecting them at his house. They couldn't miss it; on the left, about a mile nearer Tarbury.

Elfreda didn't mind, perhaps because she was feeling so nervous, but Saltana responded to the news with a kind of cold fury. "The line I'll take with this fellow," he announced, "will now be even higher and harder."

"But won't it be much nicer at his house?" said Elfreda, wondering for the ten-thousandth time why men got angry about nothing.

Saltana didn't reply in words but made a noise rather like an old steam train starting. The Daimler was now back in the derelict mining camp and was trying hard to get out of it. Six students waved and cheered.

"I've been giving this change of venue a little thought," Tuby began. "And I think it tells us something important about Vice-Chancellor Jayjay Lapford. He's a man who's afraid of his wife."

"Now how do you make that out?" This was Elfreda, of course. Saltana was still busy being angry.

"When I rang him just after six last night, he was still in his room at the university, where he arranged to meet us this afternoon. But then, I think, he went home and told his wife. She said at once that it all seemed very strange to her and that she wanted to be there when he met these people. Remember, Elfreda — because I think we mentioned it to you — that Mere told us something about her, namely, that she has money and is socially ambitious. She didn't want to meet us at the university — that would look odd — so she told Lapford to switch the meeting to their house, where we'll be examined over the teacups. And he agreed. Why? Not because it was more convenient for him. It couldn't have been. No, simply because he's afraid of his wife. It follows, therefore, that we'll have her to deal with as well as him. Cosmo?"

"You might be right. But I'll leave her to you two."

They had turned into a longish straight drive and were lumbering up to a big Queen Anne sort of house. Tuby pulled at the glass panel and told the driver to hoot a little and then, when he had stopped outside the house, offer a brief impersonation of a chauffeur not in the wedding-and-funeral but important-calling business. They were late, and the afternoon was darkening fast in the drizzle. A curtain moved in a lighted room upstairs: probably Mrs. Lapford taking a peep. They got out and before a bell could be rung the front door was opened. Not Mrs. Lapford, naturally; a grim foreign woman in black, like a housekeeper in one of the old-fashioned mystery plays: and she showed them into a square hall where Vice-Chancellor Lapford himself met them, and proved to be as tall as Saltana but smaller in the head and bulkier in the middle; and he took them into a large, off-white drawing room with a lot of modern art glaring and scratching at them, and said they must be ready for a cup of tea and that his wife would be down in a moment.

# 7

Even after she had heard those people arriving, Isabel Lapford lingered for another moment or two in front of her mirror. She decided all over again that while she wasn't pretty, or of course beautiful (except perhaps at certain infrequent times when she couldn't see herself but *felt* beautiful), she could call herself handsome — looking forty perhaps, but not forty-five — and, above all, *interesting.* Because she was an interesting person to herself, she was certain she looked interesting, though uninteresting people, especially if they were common as well, might never notice or understand. She was wearing her beige twin-set and her pearls, all very boring of course but *safe,* as the wife of the Vice-Chancellor, however interesting, ought to appear to be on this kind of occasion.

She hurried downstairs and reached the drawing room just when Maria had taken in the tea things. Jayjay as usual went bumbling and mumbling through the introductions; fortunately she remembered the names from his account of the telephone call yesterday evening. Mrs. Drake, the American widow, who was just about to take off a pastel mutation mink that must have cost thousands and thousands, looked smart but was too determinedly blonde and by any decent English standard looked rather common, like a woman in one of those very noisy American musicals. Professor Saltana was tall, thin, actorish, with peculiar eyes, apparently dark green like the shabby suit he was wearing. Dr. Tuby was chubby and a light-brown-and-pink sort of man — pink face and tie, light-brown hair and eyes — suit, also shabby: definitely English, unlike Professor Saltana, and probably common, not at all interesting. On the whole, a disappointing trio.

While she was pouring out and making the customary polite remarks, Jayjay, not at ease and well below his usual form, was blundering rather than entering into talk with Professor Saltana.

"Donald Cally, from Edinburgh, is head of our Sociological Department here. Absolutely first-class chap. Member of the team that did a survey of social ritual among urban lower-middle-class groups and then appeared on television. Cally was a notable success. I snapped him up at once for Brockshire."

Professor Saltana ate a scone and said nothing.

There was some danger now that Jayjay's head might begin its sea-lion act. "You've heard of him, I imagine? No? Well, I must confess I was talking to him this morning and he said he knew nothing about your work in his field."

"I'm not surprised," said Professor Saltana coldly. "You might ask him if he knows what Baez and Lorkheim are doing in Brazil, what Montra and Saditowsky have done in Argentina, and what Bargholtz and his young men are doing in Montevideo." He swallowed some tea while still staring hard. "You must know, Vice-Chancellor, even if Professor Cally doesn't, that Edinburgh, Brockshire, and the B.B.C. don't enjoy any monopoly of the social sciences."

Jayjay laughed uneasily. "I'm sure Cally isn't suffering from any such delusion."

But that wasn't good enough for Isabel, who felt that the man had been downright bloody rude. "What do you call your thing?" she asked him frostily.

"What thing?" Professor Saltana stared at her now.

"You mean *Social Imagistics,* don't you, my dear?" Jayjay put in hastily.

"I suppose I do, darling. But what *are* they?" She raised her eyebrows at her husband and then at the Professor.

To her surprise it was the Drake woman who replied, quite boldly too. "It has to do with the selection, creation, projection of suitable public images." And pride was in her voice and eye.

"Well, well, well! Thank you, Mrs. Drake." But now she looked at Professor Saltana. "But I'm not sure I believe in this image thing." And that ought to take him down a peg or two, she felt.

But it didn't, obviously. "I can't reply to that — if you wish me to answer you, Mrs. Lapford — until I know what you mean. Are you saying this image thing, as you call it, doesn't exist? Or that it exists, but that you disapprove of it?"

My God — it was suddenly like being back at St. Anne's, taking a tutorial with old Miss Dalby. But that was twenty-five years ago, and she wasn't having any now. "Of course I know it exists, Professor Saltana. What I'm really saying is that I don't know why it should exist and I'm suspicious of it."

"I see." And that was that. Damned cheek!

But for once Jayjay came to her rescue. "It's not entirely unimportant, that line of objection, is it? And I'd be interested to know what you'd reply to it, Professor Saltana."

"No doubt," said Saltana dryly. "Though Mrs. Lapford might prefer my colleague, Dr. Tuby, who can be more eloquent on this subject — or indeed almost any other — than I can be."

Isabel glanced across at the chubby man, whose appearance didn't suggest eloquence. The eyes magnified by his spectacles seemed to twinkle at her. Almost impudently. She gave the sombre dry Professor Saltana a challenging look. "No, let us hear you."

"Certainly. We are compelled to accept public images. First, because modern life is increasingly complex. We have to take more into account, especially in public life, than we can cope with, unless we are experts. Secondly, we are all strongly influenced by the mass media, which cannot do otherwise than simplify and so are inevitably concerned with images. You may dislike all this, Mrs. Lapford, just as I dislike seeing more and more motorcars and sometimes wish the internal-combustion engine had never been invented. But the cars are with us — and so are the images. We ignore them both at our peril."

"Thank you." She could be dry too. "What about another cup of tea? No? Mrs. Drake? Dr. Tuby?"

"If I may — thank you," said Tuby, twinkling at her again. "Delicious tea. And perhaps a little of that orange cake. I haven't seen an orange cake for years and years." And he gave her a rich warm smile.

"I quite agree with you of course, Professor Saltana," Jayjay was now saying. "By the way, have you always been in sociology?"

"No, I taught philosophy for many years. As a neo-Hegelian — hopelessly out of fashion, I need hardly say. So I went over to sociology. Intellectual slumming — until, with Dr. Tuby's help, I conceived the idea of *Social Imagistics.*"

"All very exciting," Jayjay told him. "But Dr. Tuby very naturally felt he couldn't say very much over the telephone yesterday evening — so what exactly is your plan?"

"The Judson Drake Foundation can do one of two things, Vice-Chancellor," said Saltana coldly, almost harshly, and staring hard. "It can set up, preferably in London, an independent *Institute of Social Imagistics.* It has the necessary funds — "

"Ample, I'd say," cried Mrs. Drake. "Ample."

"No, Mrs. Drake," he told her in a rather warmer tone. "Not ample — but certainly adequate." He stared at Jayjay again. "Or — it can begin its work in association with the sociological department of a university. It consulted Mr. Mere — "

"Oh — of course it was Oswald Mere who put you on to us? He was my assistant at one time — "

"And you didn't like him — obviously. Neither do I. But he was strongly recommended to me as an authority in this particular field. So we decided to approach you first. But of course if you're not interested — "

"Oh — but I am, I am. I'll say at once — it's our kind of thing. Of course I don't know what Professor Cally's attitude would be — "

"One moment, Vice-Chancellor. How old is this Professor Cally and what was his academic status before he came here?"

Jayjay hesitated, and his head began to do its turning trick.

Isabel *thought* she disliked this Saltana man, but she *knew* how much she detested Cally. So she rushed in with — "He's about forty-five and he was an Assistant Lecturer before he came here."

"Indeed. Thank you, Mrs. Lapford. And thank you for giving us tea." Saltana seemed to rise slowly out of his chair to some immense frozen height. "Mrs. Drake, Dr. Tuby, we appear to be wasting time we can't afford to waste — "

"No, no, no — *please!*" Jayjay was now a sea lion desperate for a fish. "I've given you the wrong idea. Only a question of academic etiquette — "

"I am ten years his senior, Vice-Chancellor, and I have been a full professor for twenty years. Mrs. Drake — Dr. Tuby — "

Jayjay was now putting a hand on his arm. "Look here — why don't we go across to my study — and go into the whole thing? Isabel, you'll excuse us, won't you? Come this way."

"Very well." Saltana flashed a look at Tuby. "I think Mrs. Drake should join us, if you don't mind. And if Mrs. Lapford wouldn't object to entertaining Dr. Tuby? He will tell her anything she wants to know."

"A great pleasure," said Dr. Tuby, who was standing up too and now gave her a little bow. He waited until the other three had gone, and then somehow, just by the way he settled into his chair, created at once an atmosphere of cosiness and intimacy. "I wonder if you'd allow me to smoke a pipe, Mrs. Lapford? All right? How very kind of you!"

"My husband sometimes smokes a pipe," she told him, not really intending to say any more on this subject but somehow finding herself unable to stop. "But when he does, it never seems quite real. He's appearing to do it rather than really doing it. I've often noticed actors smoking pipes like that on the stage."

"So have I." He was now filling a black little pipe, but he stopped for a moment to give her a look that had more than polite interest in it. "They puff too hard and flourish their pipes too much. Clever of you to notice that."

"I'm not sure if I ought to be pleased or annoyed. You hadn't come to the conclusion that I was a stupid woman, had you?"

"Certainly not." He had his pipe going now and twinkled at her through the smoke. "One glance told me you weren't, even though I'd been told you were something of a snob." But he said it with a smile.

"I *am* something of a snob. But I haven't time now to explain why. You must tell *me* something. Is your friend Professor Saltana always as bad-tempered as this?"

"Certainly not. It's quite unusual. But now and again his Spanish grandfather takes charge of him. This happened today when we arrived at the university and were told we had to come on here. Saltana didn't like that — felt he was being messed about. I didn't object myself. I was as curious about you as you were about us."

For a moment Isabel didn't know whether to be angry or to laugh. Then she laughed. "I can see I shall have to be very careful with you, Dr. Tuby — that is, of course, if it's decided that you stay here. And now you can tell me, as we're being so frank with each other, why you made Brockshire your first choice? You did, didn't you?"

"We did. And for the reason that Professor Saltana gave you. We consulted this man Mere and he suggested Brockshire. It's as simple as that, Mrs. Lapford."

"Not quite so simple from our point of view, Dr. Tuby. Indeed, rather worrying. Oswald Mere's an old acquaintance of ours. We don't like him. He doesn't like us. And he's a vindictive fellow. So — "

"He might be *wishing* us on you. That's what you mean, isn't it? And I think, with all due respect, you're quite wrong. He didn't pretend to like you and your husband. For that matter, he didn't pretend to like *us*. We appealed to him as an expert. He answered us as an expert. You know, Mrs. Lapford, there's a neutral area in the masculine mind that women are apt to overlook. In that area we neither declare war nor celebrate a peace treaty."

He stopped to relight his pipe, and Isabel was content to wait for him to continue. She had completely revised her first estimate of him; chubby and light-brown-and-pink, perhaps a little common, he remained; but he was far from being uninteresting; he was very quick and perceptive and had a quite unusual charm of voice and manner, unlike almost everybody else — that loud-voiced lout Cally, for instance — on the staff of Brockshire University. But then she had to remind herself that he and the other two might be gone in the next half-hour. And what a bore that would be!

"We wanted a new university, not too bogged down. And a vice-chancellor — and this was more important — who wasn't afraid of something new but ready to welcome it. If Mere gave us the right advice, he would earn a fee. And clearly he wouldn't if he was giving his malice an airing. He knew at once that Cosmo Saltana was no fool. And I'm not entirely stupid myself. Neither for that matter — though you may query this — is Elfreda Drake. By the way, I wish you'd try on that fur coat of hers — "

"Good gracious — certainly not! I couldn't do that. My dear man, what an idea! What on earth put that into your head?"

"You must forgive me, Mrs. Lapford. I've been out East for years and years and I'm quite out of touch with good manners. And it's such a magnificent affair, that coat, not the kind of thing I'm used to seeing, and — between ourselves — I couldn't help thinking earlier that perhaps Elfreda Drake — bless her! — is a little too short and plump to set it off perfectly."

"Well, as a matter of fact, she is."

"Quite so. Then, just now, I couldn't help wondering how it would look on somebody taller, straight, slender, handsome and distinguished in appearance and manner — like you."

She laughed. "You wicked man. I believe you are, you know. Well, just to please you — but for God's sake keep your eyes and ears open for that door — "

"Never fear." As she slipped round the tea table, he took the coat off the chair for her. It was all quite ridiculous, but even so she couldn't help feeling rather gay and excited as she stood before him, sketching the posture of a model, in this superb coat.

"Perfect! Just as I imagined. Thank you so much." And as she was now in a hurry to get out of it, he helped her and then carefully folded the coat and returned it to the back of the same chair. And Isabel had only just settled on the sofa when Maria came to clear the tea things.

"Wouldn't you like a drink now, Dr. Tuby?"

"Thank you, yes — so long as it isn't a pale dry sherry."

She laughed. "And how did you guess that that was just what it was going to be?"

"It nearly always is, I've found, in high academic circles — "

"Well, we have some whisky too. Unless you've taken it into the study, Maria. No? Then bring it, please — and some glasses and soda water." She looked enquiringly at him as the woman went out. "No whisky yet in the study. Does Professor Saltana drink whisky?"

"He does indeed. And if anything had been settled, he might have asked for some. There might of course be some difficulty about our accommodation here — "

"And salaries too. I happen to know that Jayjay — my husband — is close to the limit of his present budget — "

"No, no — salaries don't come into it. The Foundation will be responsible for our salaries — "

"Oh — well!" And she was surprised to find how relieved she felt. Then she laughed. "I can tell you what your accommodation would be. Professor Cally told my husband just before lunch, and then after lunch, when our guests had gone, my husband told me. Half a hut." And she laughed again.

"Half a hut? And one of those huts? The Judson Drake Foundation in half one of those huts?"

"But Dr. Tuby, you must have seen for yourself how we are situated." She stopped because Maria came in with the whisky tray. "I'll have it here, please, Maria. Dr. Tuby, I'd better give you some whisky at once — after that shock you've had."

"Thank you. It will help, certainly. And you are joining me, I hope — um?"

It was really far too early to be drinking whisky — a weak nightcap was all that she usually allowed herself — but in this atmosphere that Dr. Tuby appeared to be able to create at will, it seemed unfriendly not to join him.

"I propose to be entirely frank with you, Mrs. Lapford," he began solemnly, after she had taken her first sip and he had had a good gulp.

"People who begin like that are generally anything but frank." But she smiled at him. "After all, why should you be?"

"I'll tell you why. One of two things must happen now. We go or we stay. If we go, I shan't care what I've told you. If we stay, then I believe that you and I will soon be friends, and then I'll be glad to have been open and candid with you."

Thank God this man wasn't trying to sell her anything! But perhaps he was. She resisted a curious feeling of helplessness that was stealing over her. "Very well. Tell me your secret — if it *is* one."

"Please regard it as a confidence." His voice fell to a whisper. "Without boring you with any details, I must explain that Mrs. Drake anticipates a certain amount of trouble from the Americans. You see, there are two Judson Drake Foundations — one operating over there, the other here. This is one reason why Professor Saltana, as Director, and I, as Deputy Director, decided that the British Foundation must be associated with a university. Mrs. Drake would then be in a position to reply to any hostile criticism — "

"And all the more hostile because she's a woman — " Isabel was a keen feminist.

"Of course. Now then, I ask you — *half a hut!* And when the American Foundation has probably moved already into two or three sound-proof floors of a skyscraper!"

"Oh — damn!" It came out before she could stop it. She suddenly saw these three shrugging and going, leaving behind a muddy wilderness of Cally and his like. "Even if you two men didn't mind — "

"And we would, you know, especially Saltana — "

"It wouldn't be fair to poor Mrs. Drake. I can just imagine what those Americans would say. But what can we do? Please think of something, Dr. Tuby." She knew she was now looking and sounding like a fellow-conspirator, but she didn't care. She regarded him anxiously as he emptied his glass in a fine careless fashion — the result of being out East so long, perhaps.

"I don't know, of course, how the Vice-Chancellor and Saltana are getting along. Perhaps quite nicely, the question of accommodation for the Institute not having been reached yet. So let's see if you and I can answer it for them. I can see just one way out." He leant forward and put his glass close to the decanter, waited a moment, then continued in a hurried whisper. "Quite apart from the Foundation, Mrs. Drake is a fairly wealthy woman and not afraid of spending money. Now if there were a furnished house of some size in the neighbourhood that she could rent for the time being — a place where the three of us could live comfortably while also using it as headquarters of the Institute — "

"Wait — wait!" Isabel heard herself almost shrieking. It was absurd, not like her at all. Then she went on hurriedly but in a more sensible tone: "I don't suppose you know how much Mrs. Drake might be willing to pay — no, of course not, I'm being stupid. But there *is* such a house — quite big and very well furnished — about halfway between here and Tarbury. It stands well back from the road, so you probably didn't notice it. Tarwoods Manor, it's called — God knows why. It belongs to a Lady Thaxley, an elderly widow, who lives there with an unmarried daughter. And they were dining here only the other night, and she was telling me how they longed to go off to Bermuda or somewhere for the winter — only they couldn't afford it. I believe she'd let it like a shot, though Mrs. Drake would have to bargain with her — she's a grasping old thing — "

"Mrs. Drake is as innocent as an egg about some things," said Tuby gravely, "but I fancy she's an excellent businesswoman. But of course you must talk to her yourself, Mrs. Lapford — "

The door burst open and Saltana, an outraged grandee white with fury, came striding in, followed uneasily by Mrs. Drake and the Vice-Chancellor.

"*Half a hut!* That's what the University of Brockshire offers us, Owen — *half a hut!*"

"Yes, I know, Cosmo — but — "

"The *Institute of Social Imagistics* — the Judson Drake British Foundation — offered half a hut on a building site! You and I sit up night after night making great plans for our Institute — training the pick of the promising youngsters — soon reaching out to industry, commerce, advertising, the political parties — "

"Yes, Cosmo, but just listen — " And now Tuby had raised his voice, but Saltana thundered on.

"Prominent industrialists, tycoons of commerce and advertising, leaders and chairmen and general secretaries of political parties — can we write to them from half a hut — can we ask them to visit us in half a hut — can we — "

"*Shut up!*" And Dr. Tuby bellowed it with astonishing force and ferocity. He really was an extraordinary little man, Isabel thought. She almost loved him.

"Why, Owen?" And Saltana was surprised, not angry.

"Because Mrs. Lapford and I have already by-passed that half-hut. Yes, Vice-Chancellor?"

Jayjay, whose head had been turning and wobbling ever since he entered, swallowed hard (an invisible fish, perhaps) and then replied apologetically, "I was about to say that if you proposed to entertain distinguished visitors, no doubt some temporary arrangements could be made — "

"Mrs. Drake, Professor Saltana," Isabel cut in sharply, "can I give you a drink?"

"You can, madam," said Saltana.

"Oh — whisky?" Jayjay's tone and glance at her were reproachful. "I had thought of suggesting a glass of sherry — "

"Whisky will do, Vice-Chancellor," said Dr. Tuby. And now he took charge of the situation, as Isabel had been hoping he would. "It will save time and temper if we divide now. Mrs. Lapford, will you please explain your idea of the furnished house to Mrs. Drake and your husband?"

"And leave Professor Saltana to you, Dr. Tuby? Of course. Excellent!" Isabel gave him a special quick look. "But who moves away and who stays here, near the whisky?"

"We do," he told her firmly.

"Certainly," said Professor Saltana.

She began laughing and found it hard to stop. "Do you mind, Mrs. Drake? It's quite an exciting plan. Come on, Jayjay darling, you're with us." But no sooner were they on the move than she had to halt and turn because Dr. Tuby was calling to her. "Yes! What did you say, Dr. Tuby?"

"I only said 'My dear Mrs. Lapford.' To claim your attention for a moment. To ask you to remember that the difference between pale dry sherry and whisky is profoundly symbolical."

"Certainly," said Professor Saltana.


*8*


"Of course the whole place will look its worst now," said Mrs. Lapford as soon as they were out of her car. It was now after six and still drizzling; the Vice-Chancellor had an engagement he couldn't get out of; the ancient Daimler was conveying Saltana and Tuby to The Bell at Tarbury; and Mrs. Lapford, enthusiastically bustled into action by Elfreda, had telephoned Lady Thaxley, so now here they were at Tarwoods Manor. "It will all look quite different on a bright morning," Mrs. Lapford continued, as they hurried to shelter in the enormous doorway. As they reached it, she added just for emphasis: "A bright morning makes all the difference, doesn't it?"

"It does," said Elfreda. "But when can we expect one — next May?" Actually she was still feeling nervous, now that the men had gone and she was on her own with Mrs. Lapford, even though Mrs. Lapford seemed nothing like so cold and stiff as she had been before Owen Tuby talked to her — trust him! And now there was this old Lady Thaxley to be faced, and her unmarried daughter, and this whacking great Tarwoods Manor. It was all exciting, though. Even Mrs. Lapford, though she pretended to be calm and easy, was excited underneath, Elfreda knew.

Would a butler answer the door? Or weren't there any butlers answering doors now? Elfreda just couldn't see herself coping with a butler. But then it was all right because she found herself being introduced to the unmarried daughter.

"My dear, you don't mind being rushed like this, do you?" Mrs. Lapford was saying, back in her high-society manner. "It's too bad, I know, but you see, Mrs. Drake, who's come all the way from the Far West, does want to decide quickly — if your mother's interested in the idea — "

"Oh — Mummie is — and so am I. We're both desperately keen to join up with the Grove-Pearsons in Bermuda — heavenly!" Miss Thaxley, who was tall, thin, pale, seemed to be a kind of worn-out schoolgirl of forty. Whether she said *heavenly* or *beastly,* her voice never changed. "Do keep your lovely coat on, Mrs. Drake. I know how you Americans like to be warm, and even I find this house beastly cold at the moment — something has gone wrong with the central heating."

"Not permanently, I hope," said Elfreda.

"Oh — I'm sure not — really. The truth is, we have a man who

comes in — and he's got 'flu or something. Mummie's in the little breakfast room — trying to keep warm — so we'll go along there, if you don't
mind." She led the way across the huge dim hall. "And how is the university, Mrs. Lapford?" As if it were an invalid aunt.

Lady Thaxley was quite unlike her daughter. She was broad and
square both in face and figure; she had an untidy fringe of cropped grey
hair, and what with that and her leathery square face she looked like an
American football coach. She was rather deaf, so she shouted and you
had to shout back at her: it was a real shouting match while she was
around. Another wearing thing was that all the lighting on the ground
floor was very dim; there seemed to be hundreds of switches — which
the daughter, Lucy, worked hard at — but nothing happened with most
of them and the lights that did come on must have had bulbs of uncommonly low wattage. So the drawing room seemed to be colossal, easily the
largest room Elfreda had ever seen in a private house.

"It's very big, isn't it?" she shouted.

"Big? Of course it is," Lady Thaxley shouted back. "Some people say
it's the largest in the county. Never use it, of course, now. Three or four
years since I saw it without the covers."

"Perfect, though, for your main lecture room," Mrs. Lapford whispered to Elfreda. She kept up this whispering while they looked at the
other rooms on the ground floor, and Lady Thaxley was obviously suspicious and shouted "What? What?" several times.

The kitchen was on the same scale as the drawing room. Elfreda had
seen nothing like it since a pantomime of *Cinderella* she had been taken
to as a child. Impossible to imagine anybody boiling a couple of eggs here
for Lady Thaxley and Lucy: it asked you to start roasting an ox. Elfreda
couldn't help laughing.

"Amusing, I dare say," Lady Thaxley shouted. "Fine old kitchen
though. Not in use now, of course. Little gas range in the pantry. No use
to you either, Mrs. — er — Drake — is it? Told Mrs. Lapford at once
couldn't tolerate students living here. Out of the question. A few quiet gals
perhaps, but none of those horrible-looking young men breaking everything. Quite out of the question." She glared round at all three of them.

"Oh — Mummie — really — honestly!" cried Lucy.

"Lady Thaxley, don't you remember?" Mrs. Lapford shouted quite
bravely. "I did explain that Mrs. Drake wanted a house for her Institute.
It won't be a students' hostel."

Elfreda tried hard not to laugh again, but the sight and sound of
them glaring and shouting in this gigantic pantomime kitchen, waiting
for the comic brokers' men, was too much for her.

"We'll just look at a few rooms," said Lucy, moving them out. "There
must be about thirty altogether, including the staff rooms on the top
floor. Actually we no longer use the biggest bedrooms. Mummie's room,
which you can't have, is much smaller than they are — and mine's quite

tiny." They were now at the foot of the main stairway, a tremendous affair that divided at a half-landing. "You'll find you've lots and lots of space up here, Mrs. Drake. But at the moment it's all beastly cold — and rather damp, I'm afraid."

And she was quite right; it was. It was also very depressing, and Elfreda, for all her enthusiasm about renting a big house, had to fight hard against an impulse to clear out and forget about Tarwoods Manor. However, she was a sensible woman and had had plenty of business experience both before and after marrying Judson Drake, and after about a quarter of an hour of dim corridors, shuttered rooms, mildew and moth-balls and starving mice, she led the way back to the staircase. "Haven't time for any more, Miss Thaxley. And I'd rather talk to you than to your mother — easier on the voice. Now then — supposing I wanted the place — what are you asking?" She had always been a direct, almost brutal bargainer. She stopped at the half-landing and looked the agitated Lucy straight in the eye.

"Well — actually — Mummie says fifty guineas a week — "

"Too much."

"Oh dear! She thinks it's awfully cheap for a furnished house as big as this — "

"Its size is against it. And I have to heat it and light it properly. Cost me hundreds of pounds, just to move in and make it work. But if I take it, you and your mother can go away knowing you won't be coming back to a wet ruin. As it is — and you must know this — the place won't be worth anything in two or three years' time." Then she hastily changed her tone. "Oh — no, don't be like that."

For Miss Lucy Thaxley, forty if a day, was standing there crying — not sobbing, not making a sound, but just letting the tears run down her long pale face. "I'm sorry," she gasped finally. "And I know what you're saying is true, Mrs. Drake. I tried to tell Mummie. And I must get away — I must, I *must*. You can't imagine what it'll be like — just the two of us here — all winter. It's *hell*."

"I'll bet," said Elfreda, deciding to pull her out of this by giving her something to think about. "Now listen, Miss Thaxley. I don't even know if I want the house yet. That depends on what happens tomorrow morning at the university. But *if* I do, this is what I'm prepared to offer, take it or leave it. Are you listening?"

"Yes, I am, Mrs. Drake — really I am. Do go on."

"Right. I take it for six months, beginning this week, at a hundred and fifty pounds a month. And I'll pay you three months in advance — four hundred and fifty pounds down — "

"Oh — that could make all the difference. I mean, it would pay our fares, wouldn't it? Oh — please — please — talk to Mummie — "

"No. Mrs. Lapford hasn't time. And I've had enough. *You* talk to her. Then you can ring me — at The Bell — either tonight or early in the morning. And don't start raising the ante. No bargaining. It's take it or leave it. And remember — that's *if* we decide we're staying here at Brockshire."

## 9

It was after nine next morning, Thursday, when Owen Tuby hurried into the dining room, which was full of men staring very sternly at newspapers while they chewed away at sausage and bacon. When you see English businessmen at breakfast in a hotel, Tuby reflected, it is hard to believe they are not conquering the world. He then thought he would feel better if he were wearing another and newer suit, perhaps a tweed, not the thick and hairy kind but something more in the gentlemanly Brockshire style. He joined Cosmo Saltana, who wasn't attending to a newspaper but to a kipper, which he was pushing about rather than dissecting.

The breakfast menu the waitress handed him looked wonderful at a first glance, as if time had run back, but then on closer observation proved to be stiff with frugal alternatives. So, by ordering a kipper, Saltana had deprived himself of everything else except toast and marmalade.

"Oh — well — I think — bacon and eggs," Tuby declared, giving the order a richness and sweep.

"Egg and bacon," said the waitress, cutting it down and impoverishing it at once.

"The truth is," Tuby began, though without any encouragement from Saltana, "the English hotel breakfast is now a melancholy ghost. Out of England, rolls and coffee will do — or, further out, perhaps a slice of papaya and two pieces of toast — quite enough, really. But here you're haunted by gigantic breakfasts that vanished years and years ago — by kippers and haddock as a mere starter, by huge plates of ham and bacon, kidneys, fat pork sausages, eggs *any style* — "

"That's enough," said Saltana. "You've made your point, Owen. I take it Elfreda's not coming down."

"No, breakfast in bed. I heard her asking for it last night after dinner. Why most women prefer eating either in bed or under a tree is still a mystery to me. No rain this morning, by the way; not even any drizzle; almost a fine day. Auspicious perhaps — um?"

"It depends on us, not on the weather. Elfreda sent a note along to my room this morning, really only saying what she said last night — we must try to rush things through as soon as possible today, so that she knows where she is."

"The house and everything? Very reasonable." Tuby's breakfast arrived and he began to deal with it. "Do you still feel happy about Elfreda's control of all finance, Cosmo?"

"Certainly. It's her responsibility. Moreover, she knows far more about handling money than we do, Owen."

"She could hardly know less than I do. Tired sort of egg, this. Been hanging about too long — lost interest." He buttered some toast hastily. "Now let's see if I've got it right. You start at three thousand pounds, I at twenty-five hundred — isn't that so? — and there might be enough left to pay a graduate dogsbody and a typist. Right? Good! I wasn't sure because I drank rather too much before dinner when we were arguing with those two imbeciles. Professor of History too, wasn't he, the bald one? What about the other, the one with all the hair?"

"Senior Lecturer in Economics, no less. Lapford must have been scraping the bottom of the academic barrel. Started late, of course. And universities going up like cinemas in the 1920's." Saltana helped himself to marmalade and brooded for several moments. "I need hardly tell you, Owen, I don't propose to stand any dam' nonsense this morning from Lapford's Professor Cally — the television hero — "

"Mrs. Lapford obviously dislikes him. Did I tell you? And Lapford's afraid of her, I think. But afraid of Cally too."

"The Vice-Chancellor," Saltana declared sardonically, "is not what we sociologists occasionally like to call an *inner-directed* type. But he's not an unpleasant fellow. We might have done much worse. And he must have sense enough to realize that with us he has everything to gain, nothing to lose. No salaries to pay, and now not even a roof and space to provide. Mind you, Owen, he must agree that any money we make outside the university belongs to us, not a penny to him."

"Of course. And this includes any fees paid to the Director and Deputy Director of the Judson Drake Foundation and the *Institute of Social Imagistics*." And Tuby made a lip-smacking sound to which his breakfast could hardly make any claim. "By the way, suppose this fellow Cally or somebody suggests some lectures, seminars, and so forth — eh?"

"Why not?" Saltana was lighting a cheroot. "It'll help to clear our ideas — or give us some. I could take the seminars, you deliver the lectures. Wouldn't worry you, I imagine, Owen."

"Barring real science — and by that I don't mean the social sciences — I'm prepared to lecture on anything. But we ought to pick up a few books on sociology, if only to learn the jargon. The University Library, I suggest." He offered his friend and colleague a wide grin.

"Yes, Owen, but don't show 'em that grin this morning. Solemn as owls, remember."

"Easier for you than for me, old man. But I'll try hard. We meet Cally at eleven there, don't we? Plenty of time even if we take a bus. It's fine too. We might wander round the town and exchange a few thoughts."

It was just after eleven when they found their way into Cally's room or office, which seemed to be about a third of a hut. However, the walls were covered with books, plans, charts, God knows what; there was a longish table at one end; and about half a dozen chairs of the shiny wooden sort. Cally was alone, and seemed to have been marking papers. He got up and came forward to greet them, but without a smile. There didn't appear to be room on his face, so tight with bone, for any smile arrangements. But he was about to say something when Saltana got in first.

"Professor Cally? I'm Professor Saltana, Director of the Judson Drake Foundation, and this is my colleague and the Deputy Director, Dr. Tuby." They shook hands.

"I've coffee laid on," said Cally. "I'll just give them a shout." He didn't give anybody a shout, but disappeared through a door in the wall, which Tuby hadn't noticed. Drifting idly towards this door Tuby saw that it had some sort of timetable or syllabus pinned on it. *Thursday 10:00 A.M.*, he read, *Professor Cally — Organization and Analysis of Field Data for Group Studies.* "Well, well, well!" he called to Saltana, who was getting out of his vast peculiar overcoat.

"What have you found there?" Saltana was now out of his overcoat and was trying to decide where to put it.

Tuby hurried across, the door in the wall being still partly open, and said in Saltana's ear, "At ten this morning Cally was talking about — and I quote — the Organization and Analysis of Field Data for Group Studies."

"Good God!"

"And I think, Cosmo old man," he continued hastily, "you and I dropped that kind of thing some time ago — "

"Certainly. Concentrating on *Social Imagistics.*"

They had just time to exchange a look before Cally returned, followed by a girl carrying a coffee pot and by two young men with cups and saucers. "Put everything down there," Cally shouted, pointing. "Then I'll introduce you. Professor Saltana, Dr. Tuby, while we're taking coffee, I thought you'd like to meet some of my fellow-workers in the Department. Dr. Hazel Honeyfield. Albert Friddle. Mike Mickley."

Tuby didn't waste much time taking in Friddle and Mickley. Friddle, clean and neat, had a long sharp nose and prominent teeth — a rodent type. Mickley wore a thick dark blue jersey and dirty corduroy trousers, had long hair and needed a shave, and ought to have been playing an electric guitar somewhere. But Dr. Hazel Honeyfield was something else, and Tuby attached himself at the first decent opportunity. She was a rather small, delicious brunette, about thirty, midnight and cream when in repose, sparkling and dimpling as soon as she talked or listened, no matter how idiotic the subject. A lecherous man (and so was Cosmo Saltana, only *he* wouldn't admit it), Tuby gazed at her with admiring cupidity. He even tried to drink the coffee she had given him, which was horrible.

"Oh — Dr. Tuby — I do hope you and Professor Saltana decide to work here." No doubt she was merely being polite, but the lustrous eyes,

the perfect little nose, the dimples, the red lips, only about six inches
from his, seemed to be crying out for a midnight assignation. My God —
what a wench!

"So do I," he told her, smiling. "Though I don't know why you
should feel that, Dr. Honeyfield."

"Your *Social Imagistics*. It sounds so exciting." She hesitated, then
came an inch or two nearer, as if she were about to kiss him. "Tell me
something, please, Dr. Tuby?"

"Anything — anything."

She looked as if she were going to ask him if he loved her, but what
she said was, "Do you worry about status?"

"Whose status?"

"Oh — your own status, of course, Dr. Tuby." She laughed merrily
— probably no sense of humour — then looked solemn. "Do you worry
about it?"

"Not at all. My friend Saltana does to some extent, but I don't. Not
a damn. Why?"

"I'm planning a Status Enquiry for Tarbury. Really only a students'
pilot project. Later, when Professor Cally can give me leave, I'm hoping to
conduct a real investigation in depth — chiefly status of course — for
Cheltenham."

"Splendid, splendid!" He put one hand on her arm — not bare,
worse luck, covered by the crimson wool of her jersey or whatever it was
— and managed to get rid of the coffee cup his other hand was holding,
and then by a gentle pressure contrived to move her further down the
room, away from Saltana, Cally, and the two young men, saying at the
same time in a low voice, "I wish you'd tell me a little — in confidence,
of course — about those two young men. Might be extremely useful to
me, Dr. Honeyfield."

She responded at once to this appeal, as he had known she would,
and moved with him further down the room. If it had had some cosy
corner, some intimate recess, they would have been in it, but it wasn't
that kind of room, just as Cally hadn't the kind of face that belonged to
that kind of room.

"The rat-faced chap now," Tuby whispered, to bring her nearer,
"what about him?"

"Albert Friddle?" She was so close they might have been watching a
moonrise in Venice. "He's from Manchester — working for his Ph.D.
He's quite intelligent, very conscientious and hard-working. Only — well,
he's very political — committed to the New Left and all that — and very,
*very* argumentative. Whatever you say to him, in two minutes you're involved in an argument about the trade unions or Africa or South-East
Asia — "

"I know them. *In* South-East Asia too. As a matter of fact," he added, looking down the room, "I think he's arguing at this moment with my friend Saltana. Listen!"

"You must realize, Mr. Friddle," Saltana was saying, "discussing Latin America with you I'm at a serious disadvantage. Whereas you've never set eyes on it, I've lived there for the last twenty years."

"That never worries the Friddles. Stop listening, Dr. Honeyfield, please. What about the other chap — Mike Something — with the impudent face and the beatnik getup?"

"Mike Mickley? He's doing a post-graduate course with us. It's all rather disgraceful — he won't do any serious work — and Professor Cally and I feel that his whole attitude is too negative. And apart from that — " she looked and sounded embarrassed — "I've had a lot of trouble with him — you know — "

"I don't, but I can imagine it. Instead of regarding you as an instructor, a colleague, a fellow-worker, he insists on approaching you as a *woman* — " Dr. Tuby shook his head.

"But that's it — exactly, Dr. Tuby. How clever of you! But I'm sure you *are* clever — probably really brilliant. Will you be giving any lectures?"

"I might, y'know. Professor Saltana and I were discussing it this morning. But of course we haven't decided yet about bringing our Institute here. This might be the right place for *Social Imagistics,* then again it might not." A touch of severity would do no harm here.

"Oh — but you must — *please!*" Lips parted, eyes enormous, and a small hand — dimpled too — arrived on his arm like a warm heavy petal. He covered it with his other hand and exerted a tender pressure.

"Dr. Honeyfield," he told her tenderly, "Saltana and I can no longer look for data in the field. We must concentrate on *Social Imagistics.* But we're still dependent upon work like yours — the Status Enquiry, for instance. And I assure you, Dr. Honeyfield — "

"Oh, *do* call me Hazel. Everybody does."

"I do assure you, Hazel, it will be a bitter disappointment to me if I'm not here to share the results — to reap and enjoy the harvest — of your Status Enquiry."

He was now holding her hand away from his arm and squeezed it a little and then felt it respond. But before anything else could happen, the outside door was flung open, and in came the Vice-Chancellor, like an elongated turtle, his head looking smaller than ever because he was wearing an overcoat nearly as large as Saltana's.

" 'Morning, everybody! Too late for coffee, I imagine. Professor Saltana — Donald — oh — and there you are, Dr. Tuby! Now — perhaps just the four of us — eh?"

The delectable Hazel took the hint and melted away. Mike Mickley gave a knowing grin all round, hunched his shoulders, and went out slowly. Friddle looked as if he didn't want to go at all, and Saltana looked

as if he were ready to carry him out. By the time Friddle had gone, Jayjay
had taken his Donald to one side, and Tuby and Saltana met in the middle of the room.

"Next time, Owen, if there should be one," Saltana muttered rather
sourly, "you take Friddle and I take little sweetie-pie."

"I left the East because it's filling up with Friddles. Pity we can't
rope in little Hazel," he went on softly, "but Cally would never part with
her. And for academic reasons, not yours, Cosmo. What about that Mickley lad?"

"Cleaned up and out of fancy dress, he might be useful, Owen. He's
no fool, though Cally obviously thinks he is. If they offer him to us, I'll
take him. Rather have him with us than against us."

"Well now — why don't we sit down?" And Jayjay sat down, making quite a performance of it, now very much in the chair in all senses.
Tuby lit his pipe when he had sat down, so Jayjay followed his example,
but in a showy, unreal, actorish way, as his wife had said he did. Saltana
lit a cheroot, rather in his Spanish-conspirator manner. Cally looked bony
and wary.

"Now then," Jayjay began as Chairman, waving his head a little.
"The chief difficulty — accommodation — can be overcome by our accepting Mrs. Drake's generous offer to make herself entirely responsible
— by taking over Tarwoods Manor — "

"Which means, Mr. Chairman," said Saltana, speaking with impressive gravity and weight, "that the university can have our Institute
and the Judson Drake Foundation working in association with it at no
cost whatever. No salaries or expenses to be paid. No building to be
equipped. Nothing."

"We appreciate that, don't we, Professor Cally?"

Cally nodded several times. Then he looked disagreeable. "Even so,
Vice-Chancellor, speaking as the head of your Department of Sociology,
I have to ask this question. Is this Institute in my Department or not? If
it isn't, then I've no more to say — "

"Good!" said Saltana, who had to slip it in very quickly. "Now, Mr.
Chairman — "

"Just let me finish," Cally shouted. His ordinary tone was a shout —
or would be for anybody else — so that when he wanted to shout, as he
did now, he was deafening. "But if this Institute *is* to be in my Department — "

Here he paused, which gave Jayjay a chance to say very quickly,
"And that's the idea, of course — "

"Then there are certain things I must say," shouted Cally. He
wasn't trying to shout now, just speaking emphatically, but it came out
as shouting.

"Why?" asked Saltana in a flash.

All three began talking at once, and Tuby, who was sitting rather apart from them, stopped listening. For years he had cultivated this art of not listening, of thinking about something else at noisy meetings. Now he put himself and Dr. Hazel Honeyfield in one of the large ground-floor bedrooms at the Oriental Hotel in Georgetown, Penang, and while she still went on and on about Status he began undressing her. He did this slowly, with discretion, with taste, and was just unfastening her brassière when he heard his name being called. All three were looking at him.

"I'm so sorry," he told them. "What is it?"

"I was just saying, Dr. Tuby," said Saltana with marked emphasis, "that you'd have no objection to giving a few lectures."

"Certainly not. Preferably public lectures. I like an audience."

"Excellent — excellent!" cried Jayjay, keeping his head still for a moment. "Just what we need."

"But on sociological subjects, I take it," Cally shouted sternly.

Tuby smiled at him. "Why not? It's a wide field, isn't it?"

"Certainly," said Saltana.

"I'd be the last to deny that." Cally looked from Saltana to Tuby and then at his Vice-Chancellor, whose head was on the move again. "But this image approach — where's your breadth of enquiry there, your wide range of interest, your social depth? I don't see it."

"You don't see it? Good God!" Saltana stared at Cally for a moment, turned to Lapford and raised his eyebrows, then flashed one of their signalling looks at Tuby. "Owen, tell him the kind of thing we're doing. Just briefly, of course."

Nice quick work, no doubt, but all the same a dirty trick, signal or no signal. "Be glad to — if you're really interested, Professor Cally," said Tuby slowly. "But let me get this pipe going again." He was an old hand at this delaying action: all slow and easy, rustic-philosopher style, he tapped his pipe very gently, gazed into its bowl, then very carefully re-lighted it, wondering what the devil to say. But by the time he had puffed a little in Cally's direction — amused, faintly condescending puffs they were — he had something that would have to do.

"Well, let's take one of our more elementary lines of development of the Public Image. And you'll notice I'm ignoring the complicating factors of Sex, Age, Class, Income. I'm just offering you the bare bones."

"I'm sure," said Saltana, risking a glance at the Vice-Chancellor, "that's what Professor Cally would like — just the bare bones."

A faint snickering escaped through Jayjay's moustache, to which he hastily raised a hand.

"Ignoring not only all the complicating factors of Sex, Age, Class, Income, but also all group functional and dysfunctional aspects," Tuby continued, "and without any consideration of Pattern Maintenance, Adaptation, Goal Attainment, and Integration — "

"Certainly," said Saltana approvingly.

"Simplifying everything — and it's what you'd prefer, isn't it, Vice-

Chancellor? — along this one particular elementary line, we're doing this
kind of thing. We take, for example, the *Deliberate Blur* or *Softened Edge*
where the public image has been found to be too sharply drawn. Very important in the commercial and advertising fields when preliminary work
has been rushed and not satisfactory. But we make a distinction between
the *Deliberate Blur* and the *Softened Edge* — you should hear Professor
Saltana on that — brilliant! Another special study of his is what we call
the *Sudden Explosion* — an immediate staggering magnification of the
particular image — only for big campaigns of course. One of my own
specialties, useful occasionally in the commercial field but of far greater
importance in political life, is the *Reverse Image*. Let us say you have projected your party leader as a modest fellow, a family man, a decent quiet
·chap really. But there are crises. At home and abroad, the scene is darkening — *Light thickens and the crow wings home to the rooky wood.*
Your only chance now is the *Reverse Image*. You project the huge, bold,
defiant born leader of men. I can offer you a crude example — primitive
stuff because *Social Imagistics* was unknown twenty-five years ago. For
thirty years Churchill had been regarded as our most irresponsible leading
politician, a brilliant flibbertigibbet. Then, after crude but effective *Reverse Image* work, we accepted him as the one man we could depend
upon — Will o' the Wisp to the Rock of Gibraltar in one move — "

"Fascinating — fascinating — eh, Donald?"

"I'm not saying it isn't, Jayjay," Cally began cautiously.

"Well, that's the kind of thing," Tuby cut in sharply. "And while the
Institute must preserve a certain independence — we have to work along
our own lines, naturally — the Director and I don't oppose a reasonable
amount of integration with the university. He's ready to take a seminar or
two with some really bright students. I'll give a few lectures. But we'd like
one or two people from your Department to do some work with us. For
example, what about Dr. Honeyfield?"

"Quite impossible," said Cally stiffly. "She has a complete plan of important work for the whole academic year. You could take Albert Friddle?"

"Certainly not," said Saltana coldly. "We're running an institute, not
a half-baked debating society. We haven't met all your people, I suppose — eh?"

"No, there are one or two — "

"I'll tell you what I'll do." And Saltana contrived to sound immensely generous. "I'll take Who's it — post-graduate fellow — wan-
dering-folk-minstrel type — off your hands."

"Mike Mickley, you mean, don't you?"

"Now there's an offer! Better accept it, Donald."

"I *am* doing, Vice-Chancellor," said Cally grimly. He looked at Saltana. "You take him. But I must warn you. He's nothing but trouble."

"I've had hundreds of 'em. Sons of dictators, some of 'em. And Dr.
Tuby's not without experience — eh, Owen?"

"Me? I've had mad Indian princes, Malayan anarchists, Chinese revolutionaries."

"Vice-Chancellor, you'll have to excuse me," Cally shouted, getting up. "I'm due elsewhere. Now there's just one thing. This house you mentioned may not be ready for some time, I fancy. Meanwhile, do you want to make use of this half of a hut — ?"

Tuby saw Saltana's face darkening, so he made haste to reply. "We'll talk to Mrs. Drake and let you know later, Professor Cally. Until then — as they say on television — goodbye!"

"All went very well, I thought," said Lapford as he left with Saltana and Tuby. But he kept them standing just outside the door with him. The day was still fine in a mild and melancholy fashion. Men and machines were at work. The University of Brockshire was going up. Its Vice-Chancellor gave it an approving nod — or series of nods, all round. "You handled Donald Cally very cleverly, if I may say so. I think we can take it, can't we, that everything's more or less settled? You agree? Good! I leave it to you to tell Mrs. Drake to go ahead with the Thaxley house. I'll telephone my wife — she's rather keen on this house business. Oh — yes — I think we ought to prepare a statement to be sent to the Press. Can't neglect the papers. What are you two doing this afternoon?"

"After a fairly light lunch," said Saltana, speaking with great deliberation, "I propose to retire to my room, take up my clarinet, and practise the third movement of the Brahms Clarinet Quintet in B minor, opus 115."

"You're joking — "

"Certainly not," said Saltana severely. "I've been waiting for years to have a shot at that glorious quintet. You must have a string quartet here surely, Vice-Chancellor?"

"I don't think so — not yet. But there might be one in the offing, so to speak. I'll ask my wife. She's musical and I'm afraid I'm not. What about you, Dr. Tuby, this afternoon?"

"I'm free — if there's anything you want me to do?"

"Oh — splendid! Come up to my room for a cup of tea — any time after four. I'll have Miss Plucknett there — Busy Liz, we call her. She's attached to the mass media section of our English Lit. Department, but she's mostly working as our Public Relations Officer. Lot of Fleet Street experience. She'll amuse you, I think, Tuby. And between us we can hammer out something to keep the Press happy. And now I must run along. 'Bye!"

They remained to watch him — not running of course but flapping along, in a kind of walrus fashion, at a fair speed. "I saw you with Dr. Honeypot, Owen, while I was coping with those imbeciles. Two, anyhow — the Mickley youth said nothing and just grinned, but I caught a look in his eye. That's why I claimed him. But there you were with Dr. Honeypot — and this afternoon it's their — what did he call her? —

Busy Liz. Have a care, Owen, have a care. There's work to be done."

"God save us! Listen who's talking!" Tuby's manner was deliberately vulgar. "Without a word of warning, you dump Cally and his sus-
picions and questions straight into my lap. I had to improvise like a
bloody madman — "

"You were most impressive, Owen — "

"Now look, Cosmo. You're the Director. You're the *Social Imagistics*
big chief. So — as soon as you've finished with your clarinet this afternoon, you don't take a nap or wait for the bar to open, you sit down and
do some work for a couple of hours. Otherwise, the next time you toss
the ball to me, I throw it straight back at you. If there's work to be
done, Cosmo, you do some of it. Come on, let's walk back to Tarbury."

## 10

At last there came a longer interval of silence, and Elfreda, waiting outside Cosmo Saltana's door, felt she could now risk interrupting him. And
indeed, after she had knocked and had obeyed a shout to go in, she found
him putting away his clarinet.

"I listened outside for a few minutes, Cosmo, and it sounded beautiful — really beautiful — "

"That's Brahms, not Cosmo Saltana who's still botching it. Sit down,
Elfreda. I can see you're quivering and almost on the boil with excitement. Smoke a cheroot with me."

"Oh, I couldn't — thanks all the same — I'd be sick." She sat
down and then he did too and lit a cheroot. "I don't know how you take
it all so calmly. Or are you different inside?"

"Do you mean different from you or different from what I appear to
be outside? No, you don't want to bother with that. Quite right. What's
your news then, Elfreda?"

"Well — " and then she stopped to draw a long deep breath, which
she knew she was going to need — "I've taken the house and a man's
gone to do an inventory and Isabel Lapford and I are planning like mad
and I'm going to buy a car, not a big one, a neat little British car you
can park anywhere, and in a minute I'm rushing off to meet the Lapfords for tea in his room and a Miss Plucknett who does the publicity
will be there and so I think will Owen Tuby but I don't know about
you — "

He shook his head. "Between now and dinner I must do some work.
*Social Imagistics* of course. There's a great deal to be done, and somebody must stay away from tea parties. Not that I'm criticizing Owen
Tuby. He's doing what he can to help. But somebody has to think things
through. And as Director of the Institute, I accept that responsibility."

Elfreda gave him a respectful look and several nods. There was no doubt Cosmo Saltana could be very impressive when he wanted to be. It was quite right that he should be the Director and Owen Tuby only the Deputy Director. She could see him standing up for *Social Imagistics* or anything else. He would make mincemeat out of Walt Drake or any of that lot. "I wanted to see you quickly," she told him earnestly, "because I feel I ought to send a cable now to the Americans — to Walt Drake, Judson's son, you remember — I think of him first of all — telling them what's happened. Don't you think I ought?"

"Certainly. They were uneasy and suspicious, I seem to remember," he said loftily.

"I'll say they were. And they know now that Professor Lentenban's out. I could write, of course — "

"No, no, Elfreda. Cable. They're the kind of people, I imagine, who need cables."

"Yes, they are. But what do you think I ought to say? That's why I'm bothering you."

"Quite right, my dear Elfreda. Now — let me see." He looked around for some paper.

"You don't need to write anything," she told him. "I've a notebook here and I can still take dictation — if you don't rush it."

"I suggest your cable runs as follows: *Judson Drake Foundation now associated with Institute of Social Imagistics Department of Sociology University of Brockshire. Stop. Director Institute Professor Saltana Deputy Director Dr. Tuby. Stop. Letter will follow meanwhile all enquiries to me care Brockshire University* — " He broke off. "Do you want to say anything about Lentenban and his pills and giggles? No? Then that's it, I think. All the necessary information is there."

"And it's going to look very impressive, if you ask me. Cosmo, I don't know what I'd have done if I hadn't met you and Owen Tuby."

"I'm glad we did meet, Elfreda," he told her gravely. "But please don't underestimate yourself and your ability. It's a common fault of women in our new societies really dominated by the masculine principle. Behind their show of brisk efficiency, their almost arrogant aggressive façade, the women are too anxious, too humble. In older societies, where the feminine principle is still largely respected, the women pretend to be humble, passive, yielding, but are in fact proudly self-confident — princesses, then queens, and finally, when they dominate the whole family scene, despotic empresses."

Elfreda was late arriving at the tea-meeting in the Vice-Chancellor's room. She felt at once that so far things couldn't have been going very well up there. Isabel Lapford seemed genuinely glad to see her — they were equally anxious to dive straight into plans for Tarwoods Manor — but otherwise was erect and quivering a little, back in her thin, handsome, aristocratic style. The Vice-Chancellor himself appeared to be vaguely disturbed; his head was moving a lot. And Owen Tuby was not his usual twinkling and smiling self at all, and was smoking his pipe not in any companionable fashion but as if he were really sitting by himself somewhere a long way off. What had gone wrong? Did Owen as well as Mrs. Lapford dislike Miss Plucknett?

Elfreda had met dozens of Plucknetts all the way from New York to Portland, Oregon. There was nearly always one of her on every local paper. This particular one — the university's Busy Liz — was a shortish square woman about forty who had a sharply pointed nose, a helmet of black hair, probably dyed a bit, one of those wide rubbery mouths that can talk forever, fancy crimson spectacles that never did anybody any good, and a pea-soup-coloured suit that was dead wrong for her. As soon as they were introduced, she told Elfreda that she was crazy — but just crazy — about America — and wasn't it the most? She gave the impression that she'd spent most of her life over there, whereas in fact, as Isabel Lapford told Elfreda afterwards, she had spent three weeks there on one of those new cheap trips.

"Now then," cried Miss Plucknett, "surprise, surprise, surprise!"

"Just a moment, Liz," said Jayjay. "I must explain to Mrs. Drake what's been happening."

"Before you do," said Elfreda, who always liked to get her own news in quickly, "I must tell Dr. Tuby I've just sent a cable to America — to Walt Drake."

"What did you say?" Tuby sounded uneasy.

"Oh — don't worry — I didn't write it. I got Cosmo Saltana to dictate it to me. Just this." And she repeated the cable very carefully.

"Good." And he gave her not only an approving nod but also a smile — not one of his big melting ones but still — a smile.

"That really gives us a basis for our press statement," said Jayjay. "But of course we can enlarge it a little. We haven't done the statement because Miss Plucknett asked us to wait until you were here, because she has a big surprise for us. And apparently it could play a part in our press release — "

"We hope," said his wife icily.

"All right, all right, I've been a nuisance," cried Miss Plucknett. "I know it, I know it. I often am — it's part of my job, as I see it. But this is the difference between getting a little paragraph buried away somewhere and getting a column and probably a photograph." She jumped up and clapped her hands, in one of the most revolting little-girl-acts Elfreda had seen for some time. "Surprise, surprise, surprise! Really, truly — and big — *big!*" She looked round and then waited a moment. "You'll never guess who I have in this very building, just down there in the Refectory, probably having a raw egg beaten in milk — you'll never never guess."

"Either General de Gaulle — or an anticlimax," Tuby muttered.

She ignored him and now divided her appeal between Isabel Lapford and Elfreda, who thought she must have large breasts and a loose bra because around there she was wobbling with excitement.

"Well, you'd never guess, so I'll tell you. Primrose East," she announced triumphantly.

This was such a flop that Elfreda suddenly felt sorry for her. "Primrose East? I think I've seen that name somewhere, but don't forget I've only just come from America."

"I seem to know the name too," said Jayjay, probably out of kindness. "Don't you, Isabel my dear?"

"Certainly I do. She's a model — and quite well known — "

"Well known?" Miss Plucknett was almost screaming. "Primrose has been one of the top models for the last two years. She must have been earning at least three hundred a week — "

"I dare say. But what's she doing here? I can't believe our Refectory is famous for its raw eggs beaten in milk — "

"Oh — for God's sake!" Miss Plucknett in her despair turned to Jayjay. "Now look — this could be the biggest thing we've had so far. And I was lucky. I admit that — I was lucky. Though I take some credit for nipping in like lightning. It happens that a man I know works for Simon Birtle. I don't suppose you know about him either, Mrs. Drake, but he happens to control a national daily, a Sunday, three provincial dailies, and four or five magazines. It also happens that Simon Birtle is interested in Primrose East — no sex in it, I'm told, just a fatherly interest. She spends week-ends with them in the country — they like having a famous top face around — that sort of thing. And it seems that Primrose is tired of being a model, just somebody to be photographed. Now she wants to be educated. She wants culture. She's persuaded Simon Birtle to send her to a university. And as soon as this man I know told me this, I dived in head first. Why shouldn't Primrose East come to the newest of the new universities — Brockshire? And that's what I've been up to, Jayjay. Went to Town yesterday and brought her down today. Now I shouldn't have to draw a diagram for you. We have this Drake Foundation and Social Image Institute story — a nice little story, no doubt, but with no wide appeal. But Primrose East going to Brockshire, with Simon Birtle telling his boys and girls to feature it, that can't miss. So what do we do? We tie it all up in one lovely big package. Primrose has come here to work at the new Image Institute. My God — she's an image if there ever was one — and here she is in Brockshire sitting at the feet of the new image experts — Professor Thing and Dr. Tuby. And it's not just one story — it's a dozen. I could milk it for months. I'm crazy about it. Aren't you? Jayjay?"

"I can see its possibilities — yes. Mrs. Drake?"

"Well, I can too, of course," Elfreda said. "But it depends on what Professor Saltana and Dr. Tuby feel. Owen?"

"I don't know, Elfreda. I really don't know." Tuby looked as dubious as he sounded. "I haven't even seen the girl."

"I'll have her up in a minute," Miss Plucknett said impatiently. "I was about to say I can't keep her waiting down there much longer. She might march out in a huff. Though of course she doesn't know anything yet about this Institute thing. But what's worrying you, Dr. Tuby? I mean, apart from the fact that you obviously don't like me."

"I don't think I dislike you personally, Miss Plucknett." And he actually gave her one of his smiles. "It's just that I'm prejudiced against English people who try to talk like Americans. And remember, please, that Professor Saltana is Director of the Institute, and I'm not sure what he's going to feel about it. But if you're feeling anxious about Miss East, why not bring her up here? Isn't that the sensible thing to do, Vice-Chancellor?"

Jayjay said it was. Miss Plucknett hurried out. Jayjay now turned to his wife. "What do *you* think, my dear?"

Even before Mrs. Lapford spoke, Elfreda knew exactly what she had been thinking. "I'm entirely against it, of course," she began coldly. "I've never liked this *Busy Lizzery,* as you know, but money had to be raised and good public relations could help. But now we're going much too far. After all, this *is* a university — not a film or a musical we're promoting. The kind of publicity we shall get from Simon Birtle and his rags will be vulgar and stupid and will do us far more harm than good. Surely you can see that, can't you, Dr. Tuby?"

He took out his pipe, looked at it, and nodded slowly. "I can see that it might, Mrs. Lapford. And an Institute that is chiefly concerned with the choice and projection of images obviously can't afford to begin by creating a wrong image of itself. Mrs. Drake and Professor Saltana and I will have to consider this little problem very carefully."

"Of course, of course," Jayjay said rather eagerly. "And I feel I ought to accept your final decision — for or against — "

"Oh — Jayjay!" cried his wife, not looking at him, closing her eyes.

Elfreda up to this moment had not asked herself what the Lapfords felt about each other. Now she was certain — it came in a flash — that Isabel was entirely out of love with her husband, didn't even feel the affection she herself had had for poor Judson. If Jayjay was afraid of his wife, as Owen Tuby had argued so cleverly before he had even seen them, then what she felt for him in return was a kind of weary contempt. It was all in that *Oh — Jayjay!* But Tuby was talking now.

"And surely there's some confusion here," he was saying. "We don't have to think in terms of Miss Plucknett's immediate news story, no matter how often she claps her hands. You can admit this girl as a student without bringing our Institute into it. And indeed she may want to take English, French, physics, chemical engineering, God knows what. Then, if you want them, your Busy Liz can still get her news stories, interviews, photographs, whatever her job demands."

"Quite so, quite so," Jayjay said hurriedly. "I hadn't overlooked that point, of course. And the girl may have already had a subject — or subjects — in mind. I'll have to ask her, naturally — "

He stopped there because Busy Liz was now bringing in Primrose East, who at least knew how to make an effective entrance. Elfreda felt at once that she must have been one of the British models who had been photographed in New York and Los Angeles and had been seen on television. She was wearing a severe black dress, showing a lot of long slender leg, no hat, of course, but plenty of straight ash-blonde hair, and managed somehow to look both arrogant and forlorn: a pale princess who had been thrown into the water somewhere, rescued at the last minute, then hurriedly dried, dressed, combed, and powdered to pay this visit. She had of course the kind of figure perfect for showing clothes; but once again Elfreda wondered why any man would ever want anything to do with it, except, out of pity, to find some blankets, hot milk and nourishing food for it. While they were being introduced, Elfreda glanced across at Owen Tuby, to see how he was taking her, but caught neither love nor lechery in his face, just amusement. Busy Liz Plucknett of course couldn't keep still — as if she'd just brought Primrose East over the side in a landing net — and looked like screaming *Surprise, surprise, surprise!* all over again.

"Is it true, Miss East," Jayjay began as soon as they had settled down, "that you're tired of being a model — no matter how rich and famous?"

"Well — yes — actually — it is." Her words came out as if a female ventriloquist were really doing it, perhaps from the next room.

"And you don't think you might find life as a student rather dull? Not that *we* think it's dull here. We're all finding it quite exciting." He might have gone on, but he happened to catch his wife's eye on him.

"But you do understand, Miss East," said Mrs. Lapford in that careful manner which nearly always means that a snub or an insult is on its way, "that at a university one is *continuing* one's education, not *beginning* it?"

Miss Plucknett glared, muttered, "Oh — for God's sake!" and stamped out of the circle. Primrose East ignored her and simply went on staring at Isabel. She had large pale-blue eyes, dead right for this kind of stare. Then in the same sleepy-little-girl–ventriloquist's-doll's voice there came her reply.

"I think — it's you — who doesn't understand — Mrs. Lapford. Is that right — Lapford? I'm twenty-three — nearly twenty-four— actually. And I left — a university — to do modelling — "

"Oh dear! Then I must apologize, Miss East. We weren't told that." And she gave Plucknett an angry look.

"Quite so, quite so," Jayjay put in hastily. "Very interesting. Now you simply want to catch up. Where were you?"

"Leeds."

"And why did you prefer to do modelling?"

"Leeds."

Elfreda and Tuby laughed, and, after a little hesitation, Busy Liz laughed harder than they did. Primrose East stared round at them, without the tiniest hint of a smile. She was either a deep one or quite daft.

"I was — going to say — I'd hardly any money — at all. Four of us — in one little back bedroom. Bloody murder," she added, without any change of tone.

"It must have been. And what were your special subjects up there, Miss East?"

"Only one — I cared about — actually. Sociology."

"Indeed! That's very, very interesting. Don't you agree, Dr. Tuby?"

But Dr. Tuby was busy laughing. This annoyed Miss Plucknett. "What's so funny about a sensible girl wanting to do sociology, Dr. Tuby?"

"It would take too long to explain, Miss Plucknett. And don't look at me like that, Miss East. With that pure pale-blue gaze of yours, it's like having to face an early morning that's one huge reproach — "

"Aren't you working rather too hard at it, Dr. Tuby?" Mrs. Lapford enquired, all sting and with no real honey.

"Then — to business," said Tuby briskly. "Vice-Chancellor, may I suggest that Miss Plucknett takes Miss East back to the Refectory, perhaps for another egg-and-milk, while we have some further discussion here?"

"It would save time, I think," Elfreda told them all, and then exchanged a let's-get-on-with-that-house look with Isabel Lapford.

Jayjay had now pushed himself out of his chair, up and up. "If you wouldn't mind, Miss East. And we oughtn't to be too long, Liz. I know you want to send something out as soon as possible. But Mrs. Drake is right — we'll save time this way."

"I still don't see it," Miss Plucknett grumbled, "but you're the boss — I hope. Let's go, Primrose dear."

Primrose moved towards the door as if somewhere behind it a hundred buyers and fashion writers were waiting for her. Plucknett's back grumbled all the way. The others waited in silence until they had gone.

"I took your point, of course, Dr. Tuby," said Jayjay. "There couldn't be any frank discussion while they were still with us. Now — go ahead. Oh — do you want to say something, Isabel?"

"Just this. While the girl's different from what I expected, my opinion remains the same. A lot of stuff about her coming here, first cooked up by Liz Plucknett and then served by Simon Birtle, would do us far more harm than good. Now then, Dr. Tuby? Or would you rather Mrs. Drake tells us first what she thinks?"

"Yes, I would. Elfreda?"

"I'm out of my depth. I just want to do what's best for the Institute, and I'll go along with Dr. Tuby and Professor Saltana, whatever they decide. I'll only say this. I was dead against that girl at first — didn't like the look of her, didn't like the sound of her, don't like models anyhow, just a lot of snooty, spoilt clothes-horses — but then I changed my mind. She's an oddball — but no fool, and in the end I rather liked her. What about you, Owen?"

"You said it *for* me, Elfreda. I mean, so far as the girl herself's concerned. If I were you, Vice-Chancellor, I'd let her come here and do sociology. And if that includes her working with us at the Institute, that's all right with me, though of course Saltana must decide that. What I don't want, what I absolutely refuse to have, is what Miss Plucknett calls her lovely big package — her Institute story tied to her Primrose-East-goes-to-college story, like a white mouse tied to a rocket. Or am I working too hard at it again, Mrs. Lapford?"

"Shut up," she said hastily. "No, I mean, go on. Don't stop to pay me back." And she pulled a little face at him. A give-away, that, Elfreda decided. After all, these two had only had one real session together, yet already she could step out of character to pull a face at the artful little devil.

"I'm not blaming Miss Plucknett," the artful little devil continued blandly. "Though she's going to blame me. She's only doing her job. But Mrs. Drake, Saltana, and I have a job to do too. And we can't teach people to choose and then project the right images if we start ourselves with the wrong image. So Miss Plucknett must tell her Primrose East story quite separately, not mentioning the Institute at all. That can come later, if necessary. Meanwhile, she puts out on our behalf — and yours too, of course, Vice-Chancellor — a sober little account of our joining you here, which you and I can draft in the next ten minutes. Do you agree?"

"I do," Mrs. Lapford put in promptly.

"Of course, of course," Jayjay said, looking relieved. "And we do that before we have them back, don't you think?"

"Certainly. And to save time, why don't you have your secretary in while I telephone Saltana from her room? Don't move. I'll tell her." And Owen Tuby, who could be very energetic when he wanted to be, as Elfreda had noticed before, was on his way to the next room without waiting to hear what the Vice-Chancellor said.

"I'm still not sure if we ought to have this Primrose East here at all," Isabel Lapford said, looking at her husband.

"Why not, my dear? If a girl wants to stop standing about in ridiculous postures, prefers to resume her education, get a degree, and then do something useful, we ought to be on her side." Jayjay sounded almost rebellious — for him. "Don't you agree, Mrs. Drake?"

"Yes, I do." But she gave her Tarwoods Manor ally an apologetic glance. "What's your objection, Mrs. Lapford?"

"I don't like the idea of the silly publicity. That's one thing. The other is — well, after the kind of life she's led as a successful model — and I'm not thinking about sex now — she probably won't be able to settle down as a student and may have a bad effect on the other students, both the girls and the men — no, come in, Mrs. Dobb. Mrs. Drake, I don't think you've met the Vice-Chancellor's secretary — our invaluable Mrs. Dobb."

Elfreda had met dozens of invaluable Mrs. Dobbs too, and might have turned into one herself if Judson Drake hadn't been so miserable at home, though this Mrs. Dobb was thinnish, watery, and so invaluable she obviously never stopped being over-anxious — always a great mistake. Feeling a bit queenly and gracious, Elfreda dictated — at Jayjay's request — what she had said in her cable, to Mrs. Dobb, who was all humble attention and deference. Jayjay made a few notes and then, when Owen Tuby returned, smiling, he sent Mrs. Dobb back to type the cable plus his notes.

"What did Cosmo say?" Elfreda asked Tuby.

"He agreed. Which doesn't mean that he was agreeable. He was in one of his darker moods."

"Has he any other?" This was Mrs. Lapford, doing her mock-sweet act. Though no bitch and not quite a cat, Elfreda told herself, Isabel Lapford seemed much nicer when there were no men around.

Tuby gave her a slow sweet smile. "My friend will soon surprise you. Meanwhile, my dear Mrs. Lapford, until you know him better — " And then, still smiling, he intoned, but almost in a whisper:

> For I remember stopping by the way
> To watch a Potter thumbing his wet Clay:
> And with its all-obliterated Tongue
> It murmured — "Gently, Brother, gently, pray!"

He paused a moment, artfully, then went on in a brisk tone: "But it's a good thing he stayed in his room to work. Miss Plucknett wouldn't have found him a helpful cooperative colleague. *I'm* not looking forward to meeting her again, I must confess. Vice-Chancellor, you'll do this modest little press release much better than I could. It's really much more important I should go with these ladies and take a first look at — what is it — ?"

"Tarwoods Manor," Mrs. Lapford said quickly. "And I think that's a very good idea. Isn't it, Mrs. Drake?"

Elfreda said it was, and Jayjay hastily agreed with her. "I really must ask Liz to bring the East girl up again, and it might be better if I see them alone, to tell them what we've decided."

"Much better, darling," his wife told him. "Unless Liz starts screaming — and then you weaken — "

"Really, my dear!" His head began to move. "We've arrived at a sensible decision, and Liz must accept it. Off you go. And thank you, Mrs. Drake, Dr. Tuby — you've been most helpful."

In the lift going down, Owen Tuby said, "It's not quite drink time but it soon will be. Are these manorial people, mother and daughter, likely to offer us some refreshment?"

Mrs. Lapford laughed. "Oh — yes, my dear Dr. Tuby. You're in for a wonderful time. Except of course that old Lady Thaxley is deaf and against everything, and her poor daughter is terrified, and I don't suppose there's been a drop of whisky, which is what you're after, in the house for the last year or two."

"Don't laugh too soon," Elfreda said. "There might be some somewhere — the old lady might like a nip now and again — and if there is — you'll see — this man'll talk her into offering him some. You don't know him."

"I'm beginning to. And you're quite right. I laughed too soon." And then Elfreda saw that she looked quite thoughtful.

# *11*

As Tuby had rightly concluded, Cosmo Saltana was in one of his darker moods. He was by temperament and training a sharply critical man, and now for once he was himself the subject-object and victim of this power of criticism. To begin with, his attempt at the Brahms third movement had disappointed him. He was suffering, of course, from loss of practice, living in these damned hotels, not having a real room of his own, but even allowing for all that, he'd been shockingly bad. Then what followed, after Elfreda had come and gone, had been even worse. All very well airily announcing he was going to do some work on *Social Imagistics,* but what in fact had he done? The pitiful entries in his notebook supplied the answer. Owen Tuby had done far better, wildly improvising in Cally's office. The purely inventive side of the thing would have to be left to Owen. He would have to admit defeat and inferiority there. His was the better mind — as Owen himself readily admitted — but not for this vague purpose. "No apologies, old man," he'd said when Tuby rang him from the Vice-Chancellor's office. "You're not interrupting very much. My trouble is — that when I try to think about *Social Imagistics* I start thinking about something more important."

But dissatisfaction — the worst kind, with oneself — remained, to torment him. He tried to defy it by reading a little Cervantes, whom he loved above all other writers and carried with him everywhere in a Spanish pocket edition. (Shakespeare, as he kept telling Owen Tuby, might be broader, bigger, gaudier, but didn't live long enough — and was perhaps too prosperous — to reach depth after depth of irony.) Then, abandoning the mind to attend to the body, he took a leisurely hot bath, smoking a cheroot in it, dressed as carefully as he could with his woefully limited wardrobe, and went down to the bar, still in a baddish mood. He took his notebook with him, partly in the hope that a whisky or two might release a few ideas, but also because if he stared at it in a corner he might discourage any approaches by people like that bald Professor of History and that mop-haired Senior Lecturer in Economics.

There seemed to be about a dozen people in the bar. History and Economics were there, but he gave them an absent-minded frowning nod, ordered, and received his whisky, then took it to a little table near the opposite end of the bar. He drank about half his whisky, lit a cheroot, then stared hard at his notebook, wondering how long Owen Tuby would be. But he couldn't help overhearing the idiotic chatter of four youngsters, three lads and a girl, who were standing at the bar counter. Keeping up his pretence of being deep at work, he threw an impatient glance or two in their direction. This brought the girl into view as she was more or less facing him, and indeed might have been staring at him. He could hardly see her face, but she had long straight fair hair and seemed to have a very fancy fur coat, like Elfreda's, slung carelessly over her black dress as if it were a cape. She didn't appear to be saying much; the lads, showing off, were doing most of the talking. Then, just as he was finishing his whisky, there was some whispering among them. One of the young men detached himself from the group.

"Excuse this," the young man began softly, "but she's wondering if you have anything to do with the university."

"Who is?"

"*She* is. Primrose East. You recognized her, didn't you?"

"No — why should I?"

"Oh — I thought everybody did. But the point is, she wants to know — "

"Yes, you told me that. So she sent you here, and now I'm sending you back. If she wants to know who I am, she can come and ask me herself." And Saltana picked up his notebook and began frowning at it, just as if the youth were no longer there. And then of course he wasn't, but a few moments later neither was his glass. The girl had come across and taken it to the barman, all without a word. Saltana stopped frowning, closed his notebook, and stood up, staring in astonishment at her as she waited at the bar and then came back with the glass, now holding what looked like a double double. The girl didn't put the glass down but held it, regarding him anxiously.

"It *was* whisky — wasn't it? The man — said it was. And no soda — no water — that's right — isn't it?" She had a faraway voice, without any expression in it, like somebody under hypnosis.

"Thank you, yes. I like a little ice — ah, there's some in — good! And now if you still want to know who I am, I'll tell you. I'm Professor Saltana — Director of the *Institute of Social Imagistics*." They were still standing, facing each other across the little table, no doubt looking idiotic.

"I hoped — you were. And just — for once — I was right." It would be wrong to say that her face lit up, because it wasn't that kind of face, but if it had been then it would have done, Saltana concluded. "Look — there's a better table — in that corner. Please — please — will you sit there — with me?"

"Why?"

"So that we can talk — by ourselves — nobody listening. Please, Professor Saltana!"

"I don't know that I want to talk — but on the other hand I don't want to listen to those young imbeciles — so go ahead." He followed her to a table in a corner to the right of the entrance. She was still carrying his whisky. She arranged it so that they didn't sit facing each other, but side-by-side and very close together, bang in the corner, as if they were about to hold hands under the table, which was something Saltana had no intention of doing. Now she pushed the whisky towards him.

"Thank you. But don't *you* want something to drink?"

She said she didn't and that she never drank anything except milk with an egg in it and a very occasional glass of champagne. Then she explained about being Primrose East the famous model, an image really, and how she had decided to graduate in sociology at Brockshire University and had already talked to the Vice-Chancellor and had met Dr. Tuby. Saltana drank his whisky and grunted from time to time to show that he was still listening. She wasn't easy to listen to for long because of her faraway, under-hypnosis voice, which would have made a good substitute for a sleeping pill.

Then she put a hand on his wrist, a hand so delicate and cold it might have belonged to a frog. "Professor Saltana — please, please — you'll let me come and work in your Institute — won't you?"

"I don't know. We'll have to see. It'll be two or three weeks before we're ready to start. Mrs. Drake has taken a house for us. They offered me half a hut, and I told them not to be ridiculous."

"Would you — tell me — not to be ridiculous?"

"I can easily imagine it."

"Oh — how marvellous! I hoped — you'd be like that. I'm so tired — of men — who aren't."

"Nonsense, girl! You talk as if you'd been the Queen of Sheba."

"I have — only no Solomon. Tell me something — please — Professor Saltana — " She hesitated.

"Well, go on."

"Do you — find me — sexually attractive?"

"Not in the least."

"Perhaps — you don't like — women."

"Certainly I do. But you're not my idea of a woman. You're too young and too thin. I like plumpish women with round arms and great white thighs and firm large breasts."

"I'm so glad — I hoped you'd say that — perhaps I could — find one — for you — "

"Well meant, no doubt. But you're coming here as a student, not a procuress, young woman."

"Oh — Professor Saltana — I love you."

"Rubbish!"

"It isn't — honestly. Do you know Simon Birtle?"

"No. Never heard of him."

"How marvellous! He owns newspapers — and magazines — and things — "

"Well, the few men I've met who owned newspapers, magazines and things, I heartily disliked. Megalomaniacs!"

"Oh — yes. Simon is. If I asked him — to come here — would you meet him?"

"I don't know. Sometimes I feel like meeting people, at other times I don't. I'm a second-rate intellectual, a fifth-rate clarinet player, with the temperament of a prima ballerina."

"I think you're wonderful — just to be able to say that — like that. You're easily — my favourite man. Now tell me — please, please — about *Social Imagistics*."

"All right, briefly. But sit over there so we can talk properly and not look as if we're canoodling."

"What a lovely word!" she said as they changed places. "So much better — than *necking* and *smooching*. We canoodle. You canoodle. They canoodle. From now on — I shall canoodle."

"You can't. You're the wrong shape. Now then — *Social Imagistics*. We live in a world increasingly dominated by the image. There are so many of us now. Our urban industrial societies are so highly organized, so complicated. And we depend more and more upon mass media, which in their turn are compelled by their very nature to deal in images. Therefore — " But he stopped. Owen Tuby had arrived.

"Cosmo. And Miss East," Tuby cried, smiling and twinkling. "May I join you?"

"None of that," Saltana growled. "You know dam' well I've been waiting for you."

"Oh — Dr. Tuby — " and the girl was standing now — "please, please — may I bring you some whisky — you like whisky — do you?"

"I do indeed. With soda — and not too much soda, please."

"And some more — for you — Professor Saltana." And she took his glass before he had time to reply.

"How did you two get acquainted?" Tuby asked as they watched her move elegantly towards the bar counter, now thick with people.

Saltana told him. "And either the girl's a bit cracked or she has a strong masochistic streak in her. I've been bloody rude to her and she's loved it. Tired of being flattered and spoilt, I suppose. Would she be any use to us or just a nuisance, Owen?"

"A nuisance at first, perhaps, but very useful when we begin to branch out. By the way, Elfreda's gone up to change. And I'd go up to change, if I'd anything to change into — after going round Tarwoods Manor. Looked like a location for a horror film to me, but the women — Isabel Lapford was there too — see all kinds of possibilities that I missed. As a nest-builder and home-maker, I'm a dead loss. And so, I imagine, Cosmo, are you. We're both living-out-of-a-suitcase types. What are we going to do until that place is ready for us? Stay on here and work in half a hut?"

"Never! We must talk to Elfreda at dinner. But here comes our wait-ress-de-luxe. I'll say one thing for her — she knows how to get served quickly."

"She could probably earn about fifty guineas just being photo-graphed carrying these whiskies. Ah — how very kind of you, my dear!"

"My pleasure, Dr. Tuby." She put down the drinks and then went drooping in and around the chair Tuby held for her. "I know — you're a charmer — a real sweet-talker — as a coloured girl I know always says. I knew it — at once — when I met you — with the Vice-Chancellor. But I warn you — it doesn't work with me. I love Professor Saltana. I've already — told him so. And he says — I'm too young — and the wrong shape. Do you think, Dr. Tuby — he might change his mind?"

"Certainly not," Saltana said promptly.

"He never changes his mind, Miss East." And Tuby smiled at her. "Unlike me. I'm always changing my mind. Sometimes I wonder if I really have one. Whenever I look for it, I never find anything very much."

"Because your mind is then doing the looking," Saltana told him. "This was what was wrong with Hume's famous argument. If there is nothing that is continuous and more or less permanent, then how would we know — "

"I don't want to break into the class," cried an angry voice. "But I must tell you people you're the end — the stinking end."

Saltana stared at her. "Anybody know this woman?"

"I must introduce you," Tuby said. "Professor Saltana — Miss Liz Plucknett, in charge of public relations and publicity for the university."

"And do go away," Primrose East told her.

"I'm not angry with you, Primrose dear. I wasn't meaning you at all. It's these two I'm furious with — my God, I am! They've gone and bitched everything. I'm blazing, blazing, blazing mad."

"You look it, Miss Plucknett," said Saltana coldly. "So why not go away and be furious elsewhere, instead of standing over us like an infuriated cockatoo?"

"Parrakeet, I was thinking, Cosmo," Tuby remarked thoughtfully. "But you may be right — cockatoo — "

"Shut up — and don't be so bloody insulting. I've got a surprise for you two — a very nasty surprise. I'm not sending out anything — not a word — about your Institute. Jayjay thinks I am, but I'm not. If you won't play it my way — tying it up with Primrose for a big story — then I won't play it your way. All that's going out from me about you two is a dead silence. Come on, Primrose dear — let's get together on your story. You don't have to bother with these conceited clowns."

"Don't be silly," Primrose said. "Just go away. I'm begging them — to let me — work with them. And we're all — getting along — beautifully. Or were — till you came."

"Now don't be difficult, dear. I simply have to put out a story about you coming to Brockshire University — "

"Then you must say — I'm hoping to work under Professor Saltana — and Dr. Tuby — on *Social Imagistics* — "

"I've just told you. There isn't going to be a word about these two."

Primrose might still sound faraway, but she could be firm. "Then just forget — all three of us — "

A face with a slight squint now appeared above Miss Plucknett's shoulder. "Miss Primrose East, isn't it? Thought so. Now, Miss East, there's a buzz going round — "

"Don't say a word to him," Plucknett screamed. "He's a reporter on the local rag — "

"Hold it, hold it," cried the young man. "I'm not keeping this story for the *Brockshire Gazette and Advertiser* — no bloody fear! I've got ambition, I have. I know when I've got it made. This goes straight through either to the A.P. or Birtle's editor-in-chief. Now then, Miss East — "

"Stop, stop, stop, stop!" And Busy Liz, now in a frenzy, really was busy. She had twisted herself round and was actually shaking the reporter, who began protesting loudly. Everybody in the bar had turned to look at them.

"Oh — Professor Saltana" — this was Primrose — "please, please — do something."

"Certainly," said Saltana. And he immediately got up, strode forward, and pulled the two apart, glaring from one to the other. "Miss Plucknett, stop making a fool of yourself or *you'll* be in the news."

"Let go of my arm, you're hurting me."

"Very well. But clear out. Now, young man, what's your name?"

"Turner. And I wish you'd let go of *my* arm."

"Stop wriggling, then. Now, Turner, come back about half-past nine and we'll have something for you. Hang about, make a nuisance of yourself, and you'll get nothing. And I might possibly break your neck." Saltana had released him now, but still held him there by the sheer weight and force of his authority. "Nine-thirty? Right?"

"Yes, sir." And Turner hurried off.

"Oh — Professor Saltana — " Primrose began as he sat down. And she leant across the table and kissed him.

"Stop that, girl!"

"It's no use — I just love you — "

"Too young. Wrong shape."

"I know — but I'll just go on and on — loving you — and I promise not to be a nuisance — "

"I heard all that shindy." This was Elfreda Drake, ready for dinner. "No, I'm not sitting down. I want to eat, not lush it up in here."

"Can't I — come and eat — with you — please, please — Mrs. Drake?"

"Why? So you can go on trying to seduce Professor Saltana? Are you staying here?"

"I'm not staying anywhere." Primrose's voice was now forlornly far-away. "I didn't make — any arrangements. I've nearly forgotten — how to. Agents — and people — did it. But once — I'm a student again — I'll be all right. But you can't go — and leave me here. And that horrible Plucknett woman — may come back. Please, please — dear Mrs. Drake — "

"Oh — all right. Come with me and I'll get you fixed up." Elfreda smiled at the girl but then looked sternly at the other two. "You men go and wash and brush up. You've been here long enough. We'll meet in the dining room. Come on, Primrose."

The men had *Gentlemen* to themselves and so were able to talk freely, with that return to an earlier innocence which the male so often discovers among urinals and washbowls.

"Cosmo, what are we going to do with that young woman?" Tuby asked over his washbowl. He was a quiet neat washer. "Y'know, she might be very useful later on."

"Certainly. But there's a more important question to answer, Owen." Several moments passed before he said what it was; Cosmo Saltana was one of those men who put far too much energy into their washing — splashing, spluttering, groaning, like midnight Macbeths. "Yes, Owen old man." He was now trying to make the best of about a square foot of clean towel that the machine allowed him. "The real question is — what the hell are we going to do with *ourselves?*"

"What do you mean?" Tuby had replaced his spectacles and was now arranging rather than brushing his thinning-out fine hair. "We're all set here, aren't we?"

Saltana joined him at the long looking-glass and began wasting more energy brushing his hair, which was still fairly thick. "Not until that house is ready. I'm not going splashing around, looking for some corner of a damned hut."

"Ah — yes. You're right, of course. Bad for our prestige — our *status,* as Hazel Honeypot would say — to be seen just hanging about for several weeks."

"Exactly. We ought to go away until Elfreda thinks the house is right for us — and the Institute. We'll put it to her at dinner — or after dinner — "

Saltana broke off there because Bald History and Mop-head Economics came in, and not before time too, because one of them drank gin-and-tonics and the other must be awash with bottled light ale. Having been avoided earlier by Saltana, they were unfriendly.

"I'll just say one thing," said Bald History, looking and sounding nasty. "If you're so concerned about images, you might ask yourself what this girl, Primrose East, will do for the image of this university."

"Ball it up, if you ask me," said Mop-head. "Just *my* opinion, of course."

"You could take that up with your Miss Plucknett, who brought her here," Tuby told them. "You must have overheard her denouncing us because we refused to be associated with Primrose East's publicity. Though now I rather like Primrose."

Saltana eyed them severely. "The girl is ready to drop hundreds of pounds a week to finish her studies at Brockshire. Though not, I gather, to read history or economics. Owen, I've half a mind now to give that young reporter, Turner, the whole story. If only to prove to these two they're talking a long way out of their fields. Leave images to us. You empty your bladders."

"I suppose," Tuby said as they went out, "we've still time for a quick one — "

"No, Owen, we'll go straight in even if Elfreda and the girl keep us waiting. Didn't they give you anything at Tarwoods Manor?"

"When I was a small boy, staying with my grandmother, she used to dose me with something called *Skullcap.* It would have been dead right for Tarwoods Manor."

Unlike the bar, the dining room had no shaded lights and cosy corners. It was a very high room, lit ruthlessly from the top, so that everybody there looked rather ill. There were three middle-aged waitresses, who all looked as if they were really head nurses rushed from the nearest hospital, and a youngish Welsh head waiter called Evan, who tried to look and behave like an Italian head waiter in a bad film. Now he showed them to the table they usually had, and of course Elfreda and Primrose

East weren't there. They examined without much interest the dinner menu, which had even more alternatives than the breakfast menu.

"Soon they'll be telling us it's knife *or* fork," said Tuby.

"With spoon a shilling extra." Saltana glanced again at the menu, then looked up. "If Elfreda isn't dead against our going, Owen, where do you suggest we go?"

"I don't know. I've been wondering. London would be best, but it would be too damnably expensive. And Paris or Rome would be worse."

"We should of course go somewhere to broaden and deepen our sociological studies, Dr. Tuby."

"That is my own view, Professor Saltana."

"What about Dublin?"

"A brilliantly scholarly suggestion, Professor. Dublin it must be — at least for a start." He got up and raised a hand. "The ladies are here."

A good deal of the talk during dinner came — in slow motion — from Primrose East, answering questions put to her mostly by Elfreda. It appeared that as a top model Primrose had done a lot of travelling but all in a curious and most frustrating manner. She had never been given time to see anything except the particular background necessary for the photographs. She had adopted the same old poses, though of course in the newest clothes, against Indian temples, African huts, Australian racecourses, Mayan ruins in Yucatan, the Thames Embankment, highland lochs, night clubs in Montmartre, gambling dens in Newcastle. And one reason why she had had enough of it was that the most fashionable and expensive photographers were getting wilder and wilder in their idiotic ideas, and had already been suggesting to her agent that she should stand on an elephant in Jaipur and sit among walruses somewhere in the Arctic Circle. And Saltana and Tuby were entranced by her dreamlike account of these extravagant imbecilities. But it all took time, and the dining room was almost empty when their coffee came and close behind it the young reporter, Turner, and a photographer.

"The picture's not on," Primrose said in what was almost a businesslike tone. "Can't pose yet. Still under contract. You'll have to wait a few weeks. Sorry!"

"I'll wait just outside the door — this dining-room door, not the hotel — and then risk a candid shot. So just forget me, Miss East."

"Pull a chair up, Turner," Saltana told him. "Then I'll give you a statement about the Institute."

"Okay — but I must have an interview with Miss East — "

"That's up to her. You can do it at another table when you've got my statement. Ready?" Saltana waited a moment or two, then dictated what was only a slightly more ample version of the cable he had given Elfreda that afternoon. "And that's all from me," he concluded. "You can now sit at that table over there and talk to Miss East."

"Do I tell him — I'm crazy about you?" Primrose asked as she got up.

"No, you don't. Keep it dignified — academic — you're a student now, not a model. And I want you to go over there because Dr. Tuby and I have to discuss some private matters with Mrs. Drake."

"And I've something important to say to you two as well," Elfreda said as soon as the other two had left them. "But you can start."

"Thank you, Elfreda. Owen?"

"Oh — I'm going to be softened up, am I?" she said, looking at Tuby.

"Elfreda my dear," Tuby began, not smiling but using a lot of charm. "Cosmo and I are devoted to you, as you must know by this time. But we both feel strongly that until Tarwoods Manor is more or less ready for the Institute, we oughtn't to hang about here. It's not good for us, for the Institute, for the Judson Drake Foundation. If we could help you by staying here, of course we'd stay."

"Like a shot," said Saltana. "Even if it meant some decline in status. But we'd hinder, not help you."

Elfreda looked sad. "I hate the thought of being here on my own, but I'm afraid you're right. With Mrs. Lapford's help — and both of us screaming at everybody all day — I hope to have that place fit to live and work in by the beginning of November. Where do you two want to go?"

"Well," Saltana began, rather loftily, "there's a man doing some interesting new research at Trinity College, Dublin — so we thought, for a start, Dublin."

"For some interesting new research?" Elfreda laughed. "I can remember when I was a little girl my mother used to say *I believe you, but thousands wouldn't.* Well, there's one thing. You can't leave until Monday morning. The Lapfords are giving a buffet supper on Sunday. Not entirely for us, of course, but, Isabel says, so that we can meet some of the university people. And you're not getting out of that. I promised."

"We'll be there," Saltana told her. "I'll go out of a sense of duty. Owen — because he's mad about drink and women. Hello — they're trying to turn the lights out on us." He glanced across the darkening room to Primrose and the reporter.

"Now there's this other thing, the most important," Elfreda said, looking hard at them. "I want you two to realize that with this Plucknett business we've made an *enemy* here. No, no — don't start any pooh-poohing. The look she gave me, in the doorway, after you'd let her go! She's not going to forgive any of us. She'll be bursting with spite from now on. I know the type — "

"Elfreda, you're making too much out of a silly woman," said Tuby.

Saltana nodded. "Certainly."

"You're very clever, both of you, but you can be too self-confident. She's public relations here and Jayjay believes in her, even if his wife doesn't. And she's now an enemy — right inside." Elfreda hesitated a moment. "So what? I know, that's what you're saying to yourselves. But you're forgetting something. Walt Drake — and those Americans."

"You don't think, my dear Elfreda, you're also making too much — " But Tuby found himself checked.

"Just listen a minute. I've lived with Americans for years and years. You two haven't. Now up to a point, they're rather innocent. Up to a point, they're very kind and generous, far more so than we are. But they're also, a lot of 'em, bloody unscrupulous and ruthless."

"Who are?" This was Primrose, joining them after the reporter had gone hurrying off.

"Not you, dear. Not us." They were all up now, moving forward under the sad last light of two high bulbs. The severest of the three waitresses was coming to clear the coffee things. Tuby happened to be in front, and as she approached, he stopped and held up a finger:

> For I must talk of murders, rapes, and massacres,
> Acts of black night, abominable deeds—

All in such a strange and sinister tone, half-chant, half-whisper, that Primrose gave a little scream.

"Well," said the waitress, "you go and do it somewhere else. Dining room's closed."

# 12

Major Grandison put down the receiver, touched a bell that would let his secretary know she could show the man in, and then took another look at the card she had brought in earlier. It read: *Stan K. Belber, Area Rep. Kansas City and West Coast Agency, You Ask Us — We Tell You.* Then he stood up, ready to receive Stan K. Belber. He was as handsome and as determinedly English as his office, which had dark panelling, sporting prints, and some excellent replicas of old furniture. Major Grandison, who was in his early fifties and wore a beautiful dark blue suit and a regimental tie, looked himself a kind of replica, perhaps of Douglas Haig. He had a square ruddy face, a grey cavalry moustache, and those clear eyes that look as if they are demanding the truth, from somebody if not from their owner.

He shook hands with Stan K. Belber, who had a long nose, muddy eyes, a brown suit that Major Grandison would have rejected on sight, and needed a shave. "I'm sorry I had to keep you waiting, Mr. Belber. I was tied up on the phone with something rather urgent that brought me here this morning. As a rule I'm not here on Saturdays at all. Do sit down."

"Nice place, Major. Class. That's why I'm here. Knew your Audley Enquiries had class. You've heard of us of course — Kanco for short. Third or fourth biggest detective agency in America right now. Most of our work comes from the Coast these days, I need hardly tell you, Major."

"No, no — know all about you, Mr. Belber. Actually we've worked with you a good many times. With the agency, not with you yourself of course."

"We've got a screwy case this time. A college comes into it — for Chrissake!"

Major Grandison, perhaps to hide his disappointment, produced a short barking laugh. "A college, eh? Well, it'll make a change. Where is it?"

Belber looked through some cables, letters, notes he had brought out of an inside pocket. "Brock-shyer," he announced finally. "And they don't call it a college, it's a university. University of Brock-shyer. Know it, Major? Could it be a phoney?"

"Oh — no. Not possible."

"Well, can you see me there, asking some funny questions?"

"I wouldn't advise it, Mr. Belber. Not a background you could merge into. And you might easily run into trouble."

"I know it. That's why I'm here, Major. Now — could you take a quick look into this case yourself, Major?"

"A quick look — yes. I can't be away from this office for long. It's really my show nowadays. But I have several bright young men and a couple of clever girls, each one of whom could take over, if necessary. They'd be cheaper, of course — say a hundred dollars a day. My own personal services would cost you two hundred a day, plus reasonable expenses, but by going myself I could probably save you a good deal of time and money."

"Sure you could, Major. When could you start?"

"Not today. But I might run down there tomorrow. I like to get some air on Sunday. Now — what's it all about?"

"As I said, it's a screwy case," Belber began. "And don't think I'm not emptying the bag for you. I'm giving you all I've got so far, Major. Case comes from our office at Portland, Oregon, working for some attorney. Now let me get it right, what there is of it." He stopped to read a cable. "A woman called Mrs. Judson Drake is over here setting up the British end of something called the Judson Drake Sociological Foundation. She's cabled these lawyers in Portland to say she's using the Foundation to help run — hold it — these goddam names!" He waited a moment. "To help run something called the *Institute of Social — Image — Image — Imag-istics* — I guess that's right. *At the University of Brock-*

shyer. Director of this Institute is Professor Saltana. Deputy Director —
Dr. Tuby. So where's the case? Why come to us? Before I ask you to give
a guess, I'll tell you that the Oregon attorney's client is a guy called Walt
Drake, son of the late Judson Drake by an earlier marriage. So —
where's the case?"

"Guessing wildly, of course, I'd say they're thinking in Oregon that
Mrs. Drake is either too innocent — and so, easily imposed upon — or
not to be trusted, and that they'd like to know more than they do about
Saltana and Tuby."

"That's just what they go on to say — but all of course in that cautious lawyers' language. They smell something — or they *hope* they do."

Major Grandison smiled and then fingered his moustache. "And
they'd be happier if we reported back that there's something dam' fishy
about this whole business, and that Saltana and Tuby ought to be in-
vestigated."

"Major, it's a pleasure to work with you. And you and Audley Enquiries can do it where I wouldn't know where to start. It's your case. I
don't know the strength of it yet — moneywise — they're writing me —
but it'll certainly stand that quick look of yours."

"Well, Mr. Belber, if I thought it was hopeless I wouldn't waste my
time and their money. It's certainly worth an opinion based on a preliminary enquiry. If a university weren't involved — if these fellows had
persuaded Mrs. Drake to set up an independent institute to be run by
them — I'd be more optimistic. But it's only fair to warn you — and I
mean you, not your clients — that the chances of an English university's
being imposed upon by a pair of dubious adventurers are very slight.
We're rather more careful over here than you are."

"I'll buy that, Major. But let's remember that money's tighter on this
side — and in my experience a British artful guy can beat them all for
sheer goddam artfulness."

Major Grandison laughed. "I wouldn't know about that, Mr. Belber.
But it cuts both ways. I'm a fairly artful guy myself. Well — " and he got
up and held out a hand — "we're both busy men. I'll go down there tomorrow, ask some discreet questions, and keep my eyes and ears open.
You'll have a report in a few days' time."

"Major, I'll say it again — it's been a pleasure."

After Major Grandison had seen Belber to the outer door, he asked
his secretary to follow him into his room.

Stephanie was always worth watching. She was somewhere in her
early thirties; rather short but not dumpy, very trim, always looking well
dressed without being showy, always quick and efficient in every movement. She had innocent light-brown hair and much less innocent dark
eyes; and she was one of those youngish women, not uncommon now in
London, who are presumably English and yet have about them a faint
foreign air, not to be traced to any particular nationality, just a general

foreignness, perhaps because their parents were exiles or because they have lived at close quarters with foreign lovers. Stephanie was officially a Mrs. Murten, but nobody at Audley Enquiries, not even the other two secretaries, knew anything about Mr. Murten. One reason why Major Grandison liked her was that she was naturally close-mouthed, rarely venturing any confidences; and she would in fact have made an excellent detective agent. But Grandison, a selfish man, preferred to keep her as his own secretary, though there were times — and he hoped this was going to be one of them — when he took her away with him not just to get her into bed — though of course there was that too.

"I'm taking over a case for that man Belber," he began, as soon as she had sat down and tasted her drink. "It means motoring down to Brockshire tomorrow and staying a day or so. I'd like you to come with me, Stephanie."

She nodded. "Business or pleasure?"

"Both, I hope. We'll have to nose around and make some enquiries at the University of Brockshire. I think you could be very helpful. I have an idea that the nearest town of any size is Tarbury, so you might look it up and see if there's a decent hotel there. If there is, book rooms for tomorrow night."

"Two singles this time?"

"Better, I think, Stephanie. But of course if they're adjoining — better still. We're not going as Audley Enquiries, of course — I'll be a director of something — but we'll use our own names and you'll be my secretary. I want to play this fairly straight."

"Doing what?"

"Making enquiries, my dear. Which reminds me. You have your notebook here? Well — after you've booked the rooms — and I'm assuming now the hotel's in Tarbury — ask the girl at the other end, not forcing it, if she knows anything about these people — take 'em down — a Mrs. Judson Drake, a Professor Saltana, a Dr. Tuby."

"I'm not sure I know how to spell Saltana. But at least I can say it. Now I'll make sure there *is* a decent hotel at this place — Tarbury. And if there is, I carry straight on — as directed."

"Good girl." There was some work waiting for him on his desk and he spent the next quarter-of-an-hour attending to it. Then Stephanie was back.

"The Bell, Tarbury," she announced. "Not many people on Sunday nights, so they've given us two rooms sharing a bathroom, which always seems to me the neatest trick of all. Your three — Drake, Saltana, Tuby — are actually staying there — "

"What luck! Couldn't be better."

"For Sunday, it couldn't. But you'll have to work fast. Mrs. Drake's staying on. Saltana and Tuby are leaving on Monday morning. The reception girl doesn't know where they're going. She loves them all — terribly nice and all that — but that may be just reception-desk marzipan. So we're all set for Tarbury. Country clothes, of course, but do I take a long dress? We might be invited to something."

"It's always possible. Let's say — a quiet long dress."

"I'm leaving a note to Miss Gross asking her to take over from me and telling her where we'll be on Monday morning. What time do you want to start?"

"I'll pick you up outside your place at half-past eleven and we'll lunch on the way. A dam' good lunch too, if we can find one. The Kansas City and West Coast Agency can afford to do us proud. I'll look up one of the food guides."

Stephanie permitted herself a little smile. "I have an idea — a hunch, if you like — that I'm going to enjoy this trip. Though I haven't a clue what it's all about."

"Belber hadn't much for me. He'd only had a cable. Well, be ready at half-past eleven tomorrow and on the look-out for a handsome middle-aged man in a Bentley."

Major Grandison watched her go and then idly mixed himself another drink. No, he wouldn't be a director of anything at Tarbury; directorships can be checked. Perhaps a retired soldier, now a gentleman farmer. But would a farmer, however gentlemanly, be accompanied by an expensive-looking secretary? Well, he could decide on a good cover with Stephanie, perhaps over lunch. She could be a niece deciding rather belatedly — perhaps after a disastrous marriage — to read sociology at Brockshire University. He grinned as he raised his glass. Saltana, Tuby — here we come!

## 13

Cosmo Saltana was shaving when, early on Sunday evening, Owen Tuby came to see what he was doing. "Sorry," he mumbled through the lather, "but I've been playing my clarinet. No hurry though, is there?"

"Not for the Lapfords' party — no," said Tuby, sitting down. "We've another hour or so. Elfreda won't be down before eight. But I like to prepare for a party."

Saltana, who was now shaving his upper lip, and with an old-fashioned cut-throat too, made a sound that might mean anything. Tuby chose to interpret it as a demand to explain himself.

"I like to lay a foundation of a few strong drinks. Ten to one the Lapfords will be offering their guests a choice of cheap sherry, beer, or some horrible mixture of Yugoslav wine and lemonade. Now, as you know, Cosmo, I'm not a drinking man."

"I don't know." Saltana had finished with his upper lip.

"Oh — come, come! A drinking man is one who'll go on pouring it out and then down even when he's alone. I never do that. I'm essentially a sociable drinker. But I admit I like a few strong drinks before a party, chiefly because everybody looks and sounds better when I arrive in a faint alcoholic haze. In a country where prohibition was rigidly enforced, I doubt if I'd ever go to a party. I had some difficulty there in India."

"It doesn't always work with me." Saltana was now wiping his face. "Sometimes it goes the other way. After the drinks, everybody looks uglier and sounds sillier — and I walk out of the damned party. And the trouble is, I never know in advance which way it'll go."

Tuby filled and then lit his pipe. "Another thing is — I promised to meet a man and a girl in the bar. I went down at teatime and as neither you nor Elfreda turned up, I drifted into conversation with these two. A Major Grandison and his niece, very good-looking girl." He didn't expect any reply from Saltana, who was busy cleaning up and preparing to dress, and so went rambling on. "He's very much the pucca retired regular soldier — farming now, I believe — and as a rule I dislike the type — and I've met a lot of 'em in the East. But this fellow's different. Rather naïve, perhaps, but honest, open, and not too stiff. And he freely admits he's a fish out of water here. He's come with his niece — Stephanie Something, just getting over an unhappy marriage — to explore the possibility of her enrolling as a student here. And what do you think she wants to read?"

"Sociology," Saltana replied promptly.

"Now how did you guess that?"

"By your tone of voice, my dear Watson. You'd never have used that tone if she'd wanted to read modern languages or chemistry." Saltana was now brushing his hair with unnecessary vigour. "And we have to meet them in the bar, have we?"

"I said we would. You don't mind, do you, Cosmo? We shan't be landed with all the drinks. They're both extremely well dressed, and he drove down here in a socking great Bentley."

"How do you know? Did you see it?"

"No, but he happened to mention it."

"A bad sign. A car status-symbol type, as we sociologists say. Well, I'll join you on one condition, Owen. For once, I get the girl, you the man. You prattle away about Singapore and Bangalore with Major Roger de Coverley, while I look deep into the eyes of Stephanie Something, pretending to advise her on sociology. Switch over, do the dirty on me, Owen, and I walk out on you. *D'accord?*"

"Of course. And anyhow, I'll enjoy talking to Major Grandison. And if you're ready, let's go."

The bar was almost empty and Saltana had no difficulty recognizing Major Grandison and his niece at once. They were sitting at a table with drinks in front of them, a handsome well-dressed man of about fifty or so and the niece, a sleek smooth number, perhaps thirty, dark-eyed but with rather fair hair, who looked as if she had recovered from her unhappy marriage some time ago. Major Grandison jumped up, with a welcoming smile, and after introductions insisted upon bringing them their whisky himself. Saltana seated himself very close to Stephanie — introduced as Mrs. Murten — looked deep into her eyes as he had promised to do, and began talking at once in a rather low and intimate tone. "Not a pleasant day for motoring, I imagine, Mrs. Murten. Had you far to come?"

"Not too far. From London. I live there — in Hampstead — and Uncle Gerald called for me."

"He lives there too, does he?"

It was only a fraction of a moment's hesitation, but Saltana noticed it, together with a tiny flicker in her eyes. "Oh — no. He's farming now that he's retired from the Army. He drove up from Kent." She gave him a dazzling smile. "You know Kent, I suppose, Professor Saltana?"

"Hardly at all. I've been out of England for years, Mrs. Murten. In various parts of Latin America."

"Oh — do they have sociology in Latin America?"

"Why not? The social sciences aren't a monopoly of the English-speaking countries."

"Of course not. I'm being stupid. I *am* rather rusty and stupid, I'm afraid, after my marriage and everything, y'know. But I do hope I'll be able to come here, even though I am rather old to begin now, and perhaps take sociology under you and Dr. Tuby. Uncle Gerald thinks I have a chance. Do you?"

"I don't know. I'm too new here. Won't you have another drink?"

"Thank you, I'd love one. A very dry martini. But Uncle Gerald will get it." She dropped to a whisper. "He *adores* buying people drinks. Something to do with the Army, not farming." She looked across the table, raising her voice. "Uncle Gerald — I'm dying for another martini — "

"No, no, no, I'll do this," Saltana told them both. There was no waiter in the bar and now he took their two glasses to the counter. "You know how I like my whisky," he said to the barman. "And also I want a large and very dry martini. Vodka perhaps instead of gin." He turned to look back at the table, while he was waiting. Tuby and his new friend, the Major, were deep in talk, but Stephanie remained aloof from them and appeared to be staring thoughtfully in his direction. People were beginning to line up along the bar counter. Among them he noticed young Mickley, gave him a nod, and received a grin. The barman produced the two drinks and asked for eighteen-and-six. Saltana handed him a pound note and said he didn't want any change, but added that the drinks were a hell of a price. The barman winked, jerked a thumb at the martini, as if to indicate that that was where the money had gone, but not in vain, and then went to attend young Mickley and other new arrivals.

"Did you always do sociology, Professor Saltana?" Stephanie asked, after she had thanked him for her martini and had tried it.

"No. I used to teach philosophy."

"Why did you change?"

"I wanted more money."

She seemed rather taken aback by this candour. "I wouldn't have thought somebody like you — a scholar, a university professor — would care about money."

"I don't much. But *he* does — I mean the barman. And the manageress of this hotel. And the people who own it. And the tobacconists who sell me my cheroots. They don't say, 'Here comes dear Professor Saltana — a scholar, a teacher — we'll knock off sixty percent for him.' When they stop caring about money, I'll care even less."

"But you can't expect to make much — at a university like this — can you?"

"Too early to say yet." He drank some whisky; she took more than a sip of her martini. "Now, Mrs. Murten — or can I call you Stephanie? Good! Now, Stephanie, I've done what people rarely do in this kind of talk, and at the same time I've paid you a fine compliment — *I've told you the exact truth.*" He looked hard at her. "Now suppose you pay me the same compliment."

"No, that's for a man, not a girl. You can't expect *us* to tell you the exact truth. You can't, can you?" Her eyes flirted with his. "But I might try — if you ask me nicely, Professor Saltana."

He nodded, waited a moment, then asked sharply, "Do you work for a living?"

"Oh — indeed, yes. I have to. I refused to ask for alimony."

"What do you do?" Again he was sharp.

"I'm a secretary. With a West End firm that imports French and Italian silks."

"You look very smart. You must have a good job."

"Oh — I have. I've done quite well."

"And like your work?"

"Love it."

Then he pounced. "Then why do you want to leave it to become a student here?"

She tried indignation, as they so often do. "Well really — Professor Saltana! You don't have to bully me, do you? I'm not under cross-examination, am I?"

He was as slow and easy now as he had been sharp and hard before. "I'm sorry, Stephanie," he told her smilingly. "But I have to ask a few questions. Suppose Dr. Tuby and I do our best to override regulations to have you accepted as one of our sociological students here — and then you find you're hard up or you suddenly long to return to those French and Italian silks — eh?"

But now — not to Saltana's surprise because he had noticed the glances they exchanged across the table — Uncle Gerald came to her rescue. "Stephanie, my dear, Dr. Tuby tells me that he and Professor Saltana are leaving shortly — to attend a buffet supper party at the Vice-Chancellor's house. It would be a wonderful opportunity to meet him socially, wouldn't it? And Dr. Tuby has kindly offered to ring up, to ask if he could take us along."

"Oh — that would be marvellous — "

"I'll do it now," said Tuby rising.

Saltana also got up. "You do that while I leave a message at the desk about the morning. Will you excuse me — Stephanie — Major?"

"No objection, have you, Cosmo?" Tuby muttered as they left the bar.

"Certainly not. Go ahead, Owen."

"I've rather taken a fancy to him — amusing chap and he's been to a lot of places I know — and you must admit," he continued, raising his voice now that they were out of the bar, "she's very attractive."

"Very," Saltana said dryly. "She's also a hell of a liar."

"Really? Are you sure?"

"Dead certain. But you go ahead." He turned aside at the reception desk. The girl, who was bored and liked Saltana, sprang up to attend to him. "Tell me, my dear," he began softly, "did you happen to be on duty when Major Grandison asked for a room or rooms here?"

"Yes, I was, Professor Saltana. Yesterday morning. London call. For two singles. I thought it was a secretary ringing up — but now I think it must have been his niece — sounds like the same voice. And I told her that you and Mrs. Drake and Dr. Tuby were staying here."

"You did? But how did you come to do that, my dear?"

"Why, she happened to ask — after she'd booked the rooms, two adjoining singles — if I knew anything about you. That was all right, wasn't it?"

"Certainly. You know, my dear, I shall miss you after tomorrow morning. By the way, have you a London telephone directory — the one for the letter M?" Then, without leaving the desk, he looked for and found *Murten, Stephanie* at an address in Hampstead.

Tuby, all smiles, was leaving the call box as Saltana approached. "Well, that's all set," Tuby said. "Isabel Lapford will be glad to see Grandison and his niece if we'll take them along."

"You toddle along with the good news, Owen. And order a drink for me. I'll join you in a minute or two."

Saltana put the call through to Stephanie's number. It was a long shot, but girls often shared flats and there might be a girl only too eager to answer the phone. And there was. No, he was told, Stephanie had gone off with her boss.

"You mean the importer of French silk?"

"No, I don't," the girl told him. "You've got the wrong Stephanie or the wrong Murten. This one I'm talking about is with Audley Enquiries — you know — private-eye stuff — "

"Oh — I'm so sorry — my mistake." A long shot but bang in the bull's eye. Saltana moved briskly in the direction of the bar, humming the fourth movement of Mozart's Clarinet Quintet — and ran into Stephanie, who halted him.

"Do *you* think I could wear a long dress for this party? Won't be a bit much, will it?"

"My dear Stephanie," he said gravely, "you're a very attractive young woman, as you must know. And I think it's your duty to put on anything that will make you even more attractive — lighting up the whole scene."

"Many thanks, Professor. And now I'll tell *you* something. I'm beginning to feel I'm completely out of my depth with you. You're just not the kind of man I know how to handle. Well, I must fly."

Saltana continued with the Mozart — *pom pom pum pum da-di-dee-di pum pum* — and found Owen Tuby and Major Grandison sitting at the same table, with a third whisky waiting for him.

"Any ideas on transport for this party?" Major Grandison asked.

"Certainly," said Saltana. "And quite clear-cut. Tuby, who's more energetic than I am, goes up to tell Mrs. Drake what is happening. Then she takes me to the party. When Stephanie's ready, you take her and Tuby in your car. He has to go with you because it was he who spoke to Mrs. Lapford about you. And there's no reason why Mrs. Drake and I should wait for Stephanie. So I go in her car. I defy you to improve on that plan. Owen, off you go to explain to Elfreda."

After Tuby had left them, Major Grandison gave Saltana a charming smile. "You seem to have impressed my niece — Stephanie. At least, that's what she told me."

"I hope she also told you that she's working for an importer of French and Italian silks. If she didn't, there might be some confusion."

The Major opened wide his clear blue eyes. "I'm afraid I don't quite follow you there, my dear fellow."

Saltana ignored that but returned the stare. "If I did impress her, then it's because I told her the exact truth. I propose to do the same to you, Major."

"Do — by all means. Though we still seem to be rather at cross-purposes." He swallowed some more whisky.

"I taught philosophy for many years in Latin America," Saltana began in a casual manner. "But of course there was no money in it. And I'm into my fifties, in a world where money seems to be all-important. We've all been turned into consumers."

"I'm with you there, Professor. So you felt there was money in sociology — um?"

"Possibly. Possibly not. We'll see."

Grandison was now looking thoughtful. "Where does Mrs. Drake come into this?"

"Ah — let me tell you about her, Major. I have an idea you haven't had time to be properly briefed. Elfreda Drake is a very pleasant woman, simple in some ways, shrewd in others. I'm very fond of her. When Tuby and I met her, by accident, she was in some distress. She'd come over here, to establish a sociological foundation, with an American Professor of Sociology with the improbable name of Lentenban. He was mixing gin and pills all day, and she had to get him into a mental home. Then she didn't know what to do until we agreed to join forces with her and — at our suggestion — came down here."

"Interesting, of course. But I don't quite understand why you're telling me all this, my dear fellow." His retired-officer–gentleman-farmer bewilderment was almost perfect.

"Then why ask me about Mrs. Drake? Come, Major, while your manner's excellent, you're not being very clever, nearly as bad as Stephanie. Audley Enquiries ought to be able to do much better." As Grandison opened his mouth to protest, Saltana went on: "No, no, don't let's waste time. I know the pair of you are from a detective agency. And I'll bet five to one you're being employed by an American agency, farming out the job. Owen Tuby, who can be very artful but also very naïve — it's the Welsh in him — thinks he's made a new friend. And I won't spoil his evening."

"You mean that?" And Grandison regarded him curiously.

"Certainly. Now just a word or two about me. I'm a fairly tough character, Major Grandison."

"I believe you. And so would Stephanie."

"I've taught philosophy in some funny places. I've also known a number of American agents, government and private. Some of 'em will try anything."

"I'll go along with that too, Professor. I've worked with 'em."

"Well, you can report every word I've said to you and your secretary — or whatever she is. It's all been the exact truth. Give it to your American colleagues, then tell them you've done with the case. And advise them to keep away. Tuby and I are leaving here in the morning. We've nowhere to work for the next three weeks, not until Mrs. Drake has a house ready for our Institute. That means she'll be on her own. And I'll admit she's afraid of what the Americans might try. She knows how unscrupulous their private detectives can be. Now I'm warning you — and them. If I have to be ruthless, then I'll be bloody ruthless."

Major Grandison nodded, as himself now. "I take your point. But just one thing. This *Social* — what is it? — of yours — "

"*Social Imagistics?*"

"That's it. Let me make a quick note of it while you explain what it's all about."

Saltana began explaining at once, but after a couple of minutes Tuby ushered in Elfreda, whose mink coat was wide open to display a dress of shouting scarlet. Saltana could see that Major Grandison, with the manly charm turned on to the maximum, was genuinely impressed.

Her car had already been brought round to the front of the hotel — Elfreda understood this kind of thing; after all, she had been the wife of a millionaire — so that a minute or two later they were moving off.

"Sorry I had to drag you away, Elfreda," Saltana said as soon as they were out of the square and driving was easier. "But I've had a few neat whiskies and it's time I ate something. If there's anything at the Lapford's fit to eat."

"Well, there is — though it might not last long. Isabel Lapford has been helping me with the house, so I've spent most of the day helping her with the party. I'm not a bad hand with buffet food." She concentrated on her driving for some moments. "Now that Major Grandison! I'd almost forgotten about that sort of man — the real old-fashioned English officer and gentleman. Doesn't exist in America, of course."

"No, not with that packaging and label — "

"What does that mean?"

"I'm sorry to disillusion you, Elfreda," he continued dryly, "but Major Grandison is an enquiry agent — or private detective. His agency is called Audley Enquiries. And it's us he's after. I made certain of that. I doubt if he's working directly for your Drake people and their lawyers. I'd say that as soon as they got your cable, they took it to a big American agency. This agency in turn asked Grandison to look into the case."

"My God — Cosmo — are you sure? How can you be?"

"Owen Tuby had some talk with them at teatime, took a fancy to them, swallowed anything they chose to tell him. That made them overconfident and careless, especially the girl. Now when I was left alone with Grandison, I was careful not to tell him any lies. He's welcome to check any statement I made. And if he should question you, do exactly what I did — tell him the truth as you see it. Nothing fancy — the plain truth. And it's my opinion that when he comes to write his report — and I'd say he's very thorough and conscientious — he'll tell the Americans he can't find anything wrong with your Foundation and the Institute — "

"I'm glad to hear it. But that doesn't mean they won't try. And — my God — I've just remembered — I'll be here on my own for the next three weeks — "

"I told Grandison that — "

"You *didn't!* Wait a minute, I'll let this idiot get past. Oh — a woman too! I never would have thought it. Now then, Cosmo — you're beginning to frighten the hell out of me — "

"Take it easy, Elfreda. I was fairly fierce with Grandison, telling him that if anybody decided to be ruthless, then I'd be ruthless too. And he believed me. Now it's possible they may not drop the case, even though

Grandison advises them to drop it, but the decision will rest with your Drakes out there in Oregon, and with reports going through several hands, this is going to take time. So don't worry, my dear Elfreda. I'll take the full responsibility. And as I told Grandison, I'm a fairly tough character."

"I wouldn't deny that. What about Owen Tuby?"

"He hasn't found them out, and I don't propose to spoil his evening."

"You're spoiling mine."

"I hope not. And you had to know. I can tell Owen any time tomorrow. Now if Grandison starts talking to you — and I'll be surprised if he doesn't — try to behave as if you accept him and the girl at their face value. And, I repeat, simply give him truthful answers to his questions. He's no fool and he's used to people lying to him. Incidentally, when he asked me about you, I told him frankly I'm very fond of you."

"And was that the truth?"

"It was, my dear Elfreda. And now, take it easy — and enjoy the party. Like our friend Owen, I hate the dam' things myself, but it may be a chance to meet some of our colleagues."

"You'll be nice to them, won't you, Cosmo?"

"Can't promise that, Elfreda. All depends on what I think about them."

"Oh dear! I think I ought to tell you that while Isabel Lapford almost adores Owen Tuby, she doesn't like *you* very much."

"Don't break my heart. Talking of adoration, what the devil's become of Primrose East?"

"She went to stay with the Birtles — you know, the newspaper and magazine man." She slowed down. Several cars were waiting to turn into the Lapford's drive. "Lots of people already. Goody, goody! I know it's silly at my age — but I still feel excited — almost lit up — going to a party."

# 14

Not five minutes after Elfreda Drake and Saltana had gone, Stephanie entered the bar, now wearing a long dress, brown with splashes of light and darker yellow. "You look magnificent," Tuby told her, "and all the professors' wives are going to hate you."

"It doesn't follow," Stephanie said. "Men have some wrong ideas about that. Now look — I hurried like mad, so now I refuse to be rushed off without having a drink. One for the road, please, chaps."

"No, Dr. Tuby, I'll do it. I've learnt the art of getting served quickly." And Major Grandison marched towards the bar counter.

"I wish I'd learnt that art," Tuby said. "That — and getting taxis. Cosmo Saltana's good at all that, almost in your uncle's class."

"He's a frightening man — "

"Who? Saltana? Not really."

"But the way he looks at you — "

"He's had to spend years dominating Latin American students. It must have been his masterfulness that fascinated Primrose East — "

"Primrose East — the model? Where does she come in?"

"She was here, the other day. She wants to graduate here, under us at the Institute. She kept following him around, saying 'Professor Saltana, I love you.' " Tuby was an excellent mimic, and Stephanie began to laugh. "And he kept replying, 'You're too young and the wrong shape.' "

"Well," Stephanie said, still laughing, "I'm not too young — and I don't believe I'm the wrong shape. Not that I'd tell Professor Saltana I loved him. Because I don't. Though I can understand how a girl might. There's a great shortage of dominating and rather frightening men, especially if they're intelligent as well. Nearly all the girls I know agree about that."

"No use to me. I can't do anything about my appearance and it's too late to change my manner. I tried growing a beard once but only looked like a bad German painter, probably living in Rome, about 1875. Ah — thank you, Major Grandison. It's a very large whisky, isn't it? After I've dealt with this, I'll begin to feel a trifle plastered. Not a bad preparation for a party, though."

"That's what I always think," said Stephanie. "But then I nearly always begin to feel a bit sick — and rather depressed. What happens to you, Dr. Tuby?"

"Faces are larger and clearer, voices are louder, and life seems to offer far more possibilities — mostly an illusion of course. I've done a lot of drinking with my friend Cosmo Saltana and he appears to stay just the same, though he may feel a little different inside."

"I meant to ask you this," Major Grandison said casually. "How did you come to team up with him."

"We met towards the end of the war — in the Army Bureau of Current Affairs. Then I went East, he went West. But we ran into each other again, at a Unesco educational conference in Honolulu. Then we kept in touch. And here we are. We make a good team just because we *are* so different. I sprout a lot of little ideas while he holds on to and steadily develops a big idea. I'm more eloquent and persuasive, but he's more forceful and commanding."

"I can imagine that." The Major still sounded casual, as if merely making conversation. "A fairly tough character, you'd say — eh?"

"Well, I would," Stephanie put in hastily.

"And you'd be right," Tuby told her. "Unlike me and you perhaps and certainly most people, Saltana has something inside him that *doesn't give a damn.* If he's with you, he's with you. But if he feels you're against him and he has to be against you, then he'd go on and on and pull the place down to get at you. He's one of those rare men who really aren't afraid of anybody. He can think and he likes using his mind, but in a sense he's a spoilt man of action, who might easily have been a ruthless revolutionary commander. From what he's told me, he nearly became one on several occasions." He looked at Stephanie and then at her Uncle Gerald. "It's not likely that either of you will be having much to do with Cosmo Saltana. Even so, please take this tip. Don't try any covering up, any lying, because he'll see through it all in a flash — and then you'd be sorry."

"I'll bet," said Stephanie, giving her uncle a quick look.

The Major nodded and then finished his whisky. "I think we ought to be toddling along now to this party, my dear fellow."

In the Bentley, Tuby sat in front to direct Grandison and felt careless and opulent and very much in a party mood. And it was some time since he'd been to one. Thanks largely to Major Grandison and Stephanie, now he'd laid just about the right foundation on which to build a triumphant social evening.

"What sort of chap is this Vice-Chancellor?" The Major asked when they were out of the town.

"Oh — large, rather empty sort of chap. Quite amiable, but determined to be right there with the trend."

"Aren't we all?"

"I may be just now," Tuby said. "But if I were given a university to play with — and I knew I couldn't be kicked out for a few years — then to hell with the trend! Everybody calls him Jayjay, incidentally."

"What about his wife?" This came from Stephanie at the back.

"She's not as well liked as he is. A snob and snooty, they say. But I prefer her to him. We're almost friends. I'll introduce you to her as soon as we arrive, then you're on your own. Remember — I'm new myself, hardly know anybody. Look out for Elfreda Drake. She'll know where the good food is because she helped with it. Otherwise you can be given some horrible muck at these academic parties."

"I suppose you'll be engaged in some learned talk with the professors, won't you?" said Stephanie, out of her darkness.

"Not if I can help it," Tuby told her firmly. "Food and drink and the leering and lustful pursuit of attractive women — that's my programme at a party. Twenty to one it's the Major's too."

"You can safely offer fifty to one, my dear fellow." He overtook several cars, probably poor little academic jobs. "Let me know in good time where I turn in, will you?"

A number of cars were parked just off the road, but Grandison-plus-Bentley ignored that humble nonsense and swept into and up the drive, parking or no parking. A university porter took care of them, recognizing grandeur when he met it. The night was rather misty and not cold; the Lapfords' door was wide open; and from it came the sound, the hard desperate clatter, of English-speaking people trying to enjoy themselves. Nicely loaded as he was, Tuby wasn't repelled or intimidated by it. Mixed feelings stirred in him, but they ranged only from a cheerful social impudence to a vague amorousness. Clearly, the Lapfords knew how to throw a party. Drawing room, dining room, study, all had their doors wide open and were brightly lit. There seemed to be people in all of them, though they were thickest in the dining room, no doubt already wolfing away. It was there, near the door, he found Isabel Lapford, bright-eyed and handsome in charcoal grey with some touches of crimson, and he promptly introduced Stephanie and Grandison. Elfreda, noticeable in her scarlet, was in view, eating something and listening to an oldish hairy gremlin. Tuby almost pushed Stephanie and Grandison in her direction, and then immediately lured Mrs. Lapford away — he was a master of this art — saying, "I've something I want to tell you."

This brought them out into the hall, as it was intended to do. "And I've something to *give* you," she said, smiling. "Unless of course you're going to say something unpleasant."

"On the contrary. I wanted to tell you at once that the new dress is a triumph and you look ravishing, Isabel. I insist upon the Isabel tonight."

"Of course. And I must have greeted at least fifty people tonight, and you're the first person who's made that sort of encouraging remark. The men don't notice, and most of the women sulk at one. Now — wait here and you'll get your reward." She darted through a side door. Two people came up, as if he were a statue and they were about to stand and stare at him. He pretended they weren't there, as he didn't like the look of them, and they moved slowly towards the drawing room. One was an unshaven young man wearing a torn corduroy jacket and a dirty shirt, and the other was a very wide woman with thick spectacles, like a menace in disguise in a spy film. Isabel Lapford returned, carrying a large plate crowded with delicacies and an enormous whisky-and-soda.

"Specially for you," she cried gaily. "Elfreda chose the things to eat, and I've just mixed the drink. Don't tell anybody it's whisky. We've only enough — "

"I know, I know, I know, my dear Isabel. And I'm most grateful. Bless you!" He took the plate and giant glass from her, then looked for somewhere to put one of them. She showed him a chair in a corner above the side door and facing the drawing room and the study. There was a little table there, too.

"I'll leave you to gorge and guzzle," she told him. "I must circulate. But I'll come back soon to introduce you to some people."

"Don't be too long. Oh — where's Saltana?"

"He's in the study, glaring and growling at Malcolm Petherton, our head of Philosophy. He's Oxford and one of the linguistics lot — "

"Oh — I know. What do you think you mean when you think you mean anything. Cosmo'll hate him. There may be bloodshed — if your linguistics man *has* any blood. No, don't go for a minute. Tell me who were the odd pair who came and stared at me." And he described the dirty young man and the wide woman.

"Odd pair is right," Isabel Lapford said. "Both in the English Department. She's Dr. Edith Brede-Smith — Anglo-Saxon and Middle English — a great authority on *Beowulf*. Also on her brother, who's a Consul-General somewhere. You take your choice, either *Beowulf* or the Consul-General, though late at night she's been known to let rip with *Piers Plowman*. He's called Ted Jenks — and in my opinion he's one of Jayjay's mistakes. He's been given a year here as a creative writer — you know."

"I do know. What's he written?"

"One novel, which I couldn't finish, all rough and tumble — *Stuff It, Chum*. And one of those stark revealing plays — it was done without scenery one Sunday night at the Royal Court — about an incestuous window-cleaner, which is going to be done here this winter, God knows why. He's very arrogant and, I think, quite stupid. He keeps that very dirty shirt specially for parties. By the way, if you should want to see Jayjay, he's holding forth in the drawing room. Now I really must do my duty. See you later."

Sitting in his corner, just off the track of people moving between the dining room and the drawing room or the study, Tuby began eating some excellent ham mousse and was careful to take only a sip or two of his enormous whisky-and-soda, feeling that if he lowered that and then started moving around, he might be more than half-plastered and say and do anything. Then after several people had crossed the hall, not noticing or bothering about him, a youngish woman, early thirties perhaps, looking lost and rather sad, went slowly to the drawing room and then came out again, obviously not knowing what to do with herself, looked at him, hesitated, then drifted nearer.

"Hello!" And he smiled at her, hoping she would look less lost and sad. She was badly dressed, thinnish, with mousy and rather untidy hair, and would be generally considered quite plain, though Tuby, more perceptive than most men, decided it was because she had no excitement inside, no strong current of feeling, to light her up. She had the sort of eyes — large and of a light-hazel shade — that could suddenly darken with fear, out of feeling so vulnerable, or equally suddenly blaze with wonder and delight. And it was his business, Tuby felt, to put a torch to them.

"Hello!" It was a listless reply, but she drifted nearer still. Then, as she noticed his heaped plate and giant glass, she behaved exactly as he hoped she would. He guessed she was one of those people, shy and vulnerable, who keep silent too long but are then capable of blurting out something that would shock more robust extrovert types.

"My goodness!" she cried. "Where did you get all that food from? All I got was a little sausage roll and a boring sandwich. And I'm hungry. And then just beer. And that's not beer you seem to have a pint of. I don't call this fair do's." It was only half-humorous. There was indignation in her eyes.

"I'll explain in a moment," he told her. "But don't I first find you a chair? Is there one? Yes, over there. No, I'll get it." There was a light painted chair against the wall between the drawing room and the study, probably thought to be too fragile for party work, and he went across and brought it back, placing it on the other side of the little table.

"Sit there," he commanded. "You can either take over the fork or eat with your fingers. The drink is whisky-and-soda. I use this side of the glass, you the other. And if you think this is all too informal and you're disgusted, then you can apologize for making remarks about my supper and then buzz off. Which is it to be?" But he smiled as he said it.

"I'm staying." And she sat down. "But I won't take your fork. Fingers somehow. And a little of your whisky first, thank you." She only took a sip. "Now explain how you do it."

"I'm a newcomer, so I'm given special treatment. And I've made friends with Mrs. Lapford."

"More than. I've ever done. I'm Lois Terry and I'm in the English Department. I have a Ph.D. actually but I prefer Miss Terry — or Lois."

"Then you're Lois. My name's Owen Tuby. I was given an honorary doctorate out East, so I go round as Dr. Tuby."

"So you're the Dr. Tuby that all the rumours have been about — paragraphs in the newspapers — Primrose East and all that — *Social Imagistics.* Somehow you don't look it. I've seen the other man, your colleague, Professor Saltana, and he *does* look it — but you don't."

"What do you teach, Lois?"

"Sixteenth and seventeenth centuries. I did my thesis on Jacobean tragedy — "

"What — all those daggers, poisons, rapes and incest, skeletons and madmen! It's like looking for scraps of poetry in a bombed graveyard. Who's the head of your English Department?"

"Professor Brigham — Denis Brigham. He's here somewhere. He and I get along all right though we don't really agree about anything. He's one of that Cambridge lot and keeps telling his students what they needn't read, which suits them, of course — "

"O-ho, he's one of those, is he? Then I'm dead against him. I just saw another two of your colleagues — the *Beowulf* expert, who looks like an East German agent disguised — and Ted Jenks, the creative writer — what is it? — *Shove It, Pal* — "

"No. *Stuff It, Chum.*" And Lois, who ten minutes earlier had looked completely incapable of such a thing, now began giggling. Tuby regarded her with approval and passed the giant glass. There wasn't much left on the plate now. He took a couple of biscuits and a piece of cheese. "That slice of apple flan is for you, Lois. It was meant for you from the beginning. I'll bet you live alone and eat sketchy little Sunday lunches, don't you?"

"Yes, I do. Unless somebody's coming and I cook a proper meal. If you'll come to lunch next Sunday, Dr. Tuby, I'll give you roast beef and Yorkshire pudding, apple pie and cream — "

"Sorry, my dear, but I'm off in the morning." It wasn't fair; together with those revealing great eyes, she had a face that was short of a skin; her disappointment couldn't be hidden. "Only for three weeks, though. Saltana and I can't start until Mrs. Drake has this house, Tarwoods Manor, all ready for the Institute. Saltana sternly refuses to do anything in huts — "

"I've never seen anything else yet — "

"Then you must finish the whisky — "

"Oh — I couldn't. I'm feeling rather silly and giggly already — "

"Then I will." And he did, and though far from feeling silly and giggly he knew that from now on faces would be larger and clearer, voices louder, and life would appear to offer some astounding possibilities. Then, as he lowered Gargantua's glass, he found he was looking at Isabel Lapford, who was raising her eyebrows at Lois.

"Oh — hello — Miss Terry — no, Dr. Terry — isn't it?"

"No, not Doctor, please, Mrs. Lapford — just Miss — or Lois — or anything." She was scrambling up, a deep pink, painfully embarrassed.

"I promised to come back to Dr. Tuby," Isabel continued smoothly, "after he'd eaten something and had a drink, so that he could meet at least a few people he ought to know."

"Yes, of course — that would be a good thing, I'm sure," Lois said rather wildly. "But I ought to tell you I've eaten half his supper and drunk nearly half his whisky. But he asked me to. He took pity on me. He's sweet, isn't he?" She gave a nod to Isabel and a smile to Tuby, and off she went.

"Well — well — well!" Isabel cried. "I don't know whether to be cross with you or not. That was my special treat for *you* — not for Lois Terry — "

"She looked so lost and sad, poor girl. But I liked her, though she's not my idea of a Lois."

"Nor mine. And I wish somebody'd tell her how to dress and do her hair. I don't know her well — she's an odd young woman — but Jayjay believes she's rather brilliant."

Tuby went a little closer and put a hand on her arm. "Isabel," he began in little more than a whisper, "it's possible I've been too long away, but she seems to me — and I'm ready to bet on it — exactly the kind of girl who's had one of those long tormenting messy affairs with a married man, one with several children and a haunting conscience, years of hasty notes, waiting at the telephone, uneasy nights, after falsifying the register, in the back bedrooms of country pubs, catching sight on the wall, while undressing in the cold and damp, of *Thou, God, Seest Me*. And then — "

"No, don't. Not that it's ever happened to me — "

"You're not the type, Isabel. These girls move inevitably towards suffering, grief, desolation, a lonely boiled egg on a tray — "

"Stop it. You're not really sorry for them, Owen. You're just showing off and enjoying yourself." She was pretending, with an exaggerated frown, to be severe with him, but perhaps it wasn't all pretense. "Like poor Lois Terry we all think you're sweet — at first. But now I believe I know you. And you're a wicked little man, probably quite hard-hearted really. I don't like your friend Saltana, but I may be all wrong. Probably he's the better man."

"But of course he is, my dear. I'd be the first to admit that. The trouble with me at this exact moment is that I've had just enough whisky — mostly with Grandison at the hotel — to make me feel sad. Now a touch more, especially if you'd join me, Isabel — "

"There you go. Well — perhaps later. Now you must be good — and circulate with me. You haven't had a word yet with Jayjay, who — and this is strictly between ourselves — is rather worried about something. No, I'm not going to tell you. After all, nothing may happen. Now — come along." And she led the way to the drawing room.

The Vice-Chancellor's head was waving above a group in the middle of the room. Several people were trying to talk one another down, and among them Tuby noticed Donald Cally, shouting away, the relentless Albert Friddle, and Ted Jenks, the creative writer. A tough experienced hostess, Isabel pushed her way straight through to the waving head.

"Here's Dr. Tuby, darling, longing to have a word with you."

"Ah, Dr. Tuby — welcome aboard! I hope somebody's been looking after you."

"Extraordinarily well, Vice-Chancellor." He said that just to see if he could say it — and he could, with lots of bogus enthusiasm too. "A party wonderfully devised, contrived, executed, if I may say so." The loud arguers were still at it but had moved away a little, releasing Jayjay, no doubt to his relief.

"And where's Professor Saltana?"

"When last heard of, he was in the study arguing with your philosophy man — "

"Oh — Professor Petherton. Oxford. Very sound, very keen. Somewhat of a catch for Brockshire, I feel. What are they discussing, do you know?"

"It's probably linguistics versus neo-Hegelianism. And as I neither know nor care about either, I'm leaving them alone, Vice-Chancellor. You've heard we're leaving you for a few weeks?"

"Mrs. Drake told me. Sensible move, I think, until Mrs. Drake and my wife have got Tarwoods Manor in order for you. Yes, Liz?"

For now Busy Liz Plucknett, completely ignoring Tuby, had newly arrived at Jayjay's elbow, apparently with urgent and perhaps rather desperate news from somewhere. Tuby rejoined Isabel, who was keeping a worried eye on her husband and Plucknett while pretending to listen to two fat Central Europeans to whom she hurriedly introduced Tuby — Professor Anton Stervas of Economics and his wife.

"You wish to know what I think of such parties," Mrs. Stervas whispered. "All the food is *tarrible*. You come to my parties, Dr. Tuby, and averythink there will be deleecious. You promise?"

"I promise." It was then he noticed, in a corner, the genuinely deleecious Hazel Honeyfield hemmed in by the oldish hairy gremlin he had previously seen talking to Elfreda. He muttered something to Mrs. Stervas about having a message to deliver to Dr. Honeyfield and made for her corner.

"Sorry to break in," he began blandly, "but I have a rather urgent message for Dr. Honeyfield." She was wearing a happy arrangement of cherry red and dark blue, and she seemed to have more curls, dimples, curves, than ever.

"Oh — yes, Dr. Tuby," she cried eagerly. "This is Professor Hugo Hummel, head of Psychology."

"I have already heard and read of you, Dr. Tuby," said Hummel, who seemed to be another Central European. "And I wish to speak with you, from a psychological standpoint, about your *Institute of Social Imagistics* — "

"I look forward to that, Professor Hummel. But as Dr. Honeyfield is a colleague — and as there's something important I want to tell her — if you don't mind — "

"Of course. It is understandable. Later, perhaps, Dr. Honeyfield, then — " And that took him off.

"I thought you ought to be rescued, my dear," Tuby said, gently moving her further into the corner. "And I've two messages. First, you're looking tantalizingly, madly delicious tonight. Secondly, I've been longing to tell you how bitterly disappointed I was when Cally refused to let us claim you for our Institute. We asked for you at once, and he offered us Friddle — for God's sake!"

She smiled and dimpled at him. "Could you be a bit tight, Dr. Tuby, dear?"

"I could — yes, a bit. Do you mind?"

"Not at all. I wish I was. But you must have been drinking hard before you came here. Don't tell me that sherry or beer or cup — "

"Ah — that's just what I said there would be here. And I guessed the cup would be a mixture of Yugoslav wine and lemonade — ugh! Actually," and now he dropped to a whisper, "there *is* whisky on the premises, as I discovered when I paid my first visit here. Probably kept in a safe somewhere. There is something about me — an innocence, a helplessness, a direct appeal to the maternal instinct — that persuades Isabel Lapford to bring out, stealthily, secretly, the whisky."

"You could talk her into it. I can just imagine. But you know very well I couldn't."

"She doesn't dislike you — surely? Hazel, nobody could dislike you. I refuse to believe it."

"You know very well it's different between women. No, we don't dislike each other. But I couldn't talk her into anything, and she couldn't talk me. We don't *listen* in the same way as we do to a man like you. Oh — you're holding my hand again, are you?"

"Yes. Do you mind?"

"Not if nobody can see. And you're very clever about that. I've been reading Kuhn's *Study of Society* — and considering his point about the choice of coffee, tea, or milk in a restaurant being part of a hierarchy, and about the behaviour selections of having cream or sugar and tilting the cup, and I think I'll have a special restaurant-and-teashop section in my Status Enquiry — "

But Tuby was laughing, not being able to help it.

"Stop it!" She was furious, and, just as if they had known each other for years, she shook him. "You'd never laugh if I were a man," she went on angrily. "Just because I'm a woman and you think I'm rather pretty, then it's all absurd and you can laugh — "

"No, no, no, Hazel my dear, I'm not laughing at *you*."

"Of course you are. And let go of my hands."

"Not until you promise to stop knocking me about. Why should I laugh at you? I take pretty, intelligent women very seriously — and you're deliciously pretty and of course extremely intelligent — "

"Then what *were* you laughing at? There must have been *something* — "

"Can you keep a secret?" This was in a whisper, and now he was holding her lightly just above the waist. "Probably not, but I'll have to risk it. I was laughing — now, take it easy — at *sociology*."

"He doesn't mean it, Dr. Honeyfield." The voice, grave and deep, came over his shoulder and belonged to Cosmo Saltana. "And I suspect he's half-plastered, though on what, God knows." Tuby gave ground and then Saltana was able to introduce Elfreda and Stephanie to Hazel Honeyfield.

"And I must say, Owen," Saltana said, scowling at him, "you seem to be able to do yourself damned well on this sort of occasion. I've had nothing worth drinking and about an hour disputing in the other room with a dim imbecile — one Professor Petherton. Poor Grandison — though it serves him right — is still there, trying in vain to escape from a Professor Gutstern, a physicist, and an enormous and implacable colleague of yours, Dr. Honeyfield, a certain Dr. Dorothy Pawson."

"Oh dear — yes!" cried Hazel Honeyfield. She looked at the other two women, then all three giggled a bit. At this point, Isabel Lapford, probably feeling curious, hurried across and joined them.

"Now, Cosmo my boy," said Tuby as he made room for Isabel in their little circle, "we've really made a corner in the party's supply of beautiful women."

Cosmo, not a man to miss an opportunity, was now talking quietly to Hazel Honeyfield, with Stephanie, perhaps hoping to be frightened again by those eyes, listening in. Though not excluding Elfreda, with whom he exchanged a quick look, Tuby concentrated again on Isabel Lapford. "You know, Isabel, this is the sudden dead time of a party, when most of the people who are just routine party-attenders have gone but the choice spirits haven't yet rallied, the party within the party hasn't yet come alive, and when even a very good hostess like you, my dear, begins to feel weary, jaded, lost in a boring maze. I'll miss you — but why don't you sneak away for a quarter of an hour and sit somewhere alone over a strong drink?"

Her fine eyes awarded him a flash of thanks. Then she was brisk and decisive. "I can't do that, Owen, but I'll do the next best thing. Elfreda, I'll bring you and the others a drink shortly. Meanwhile — and this is important — while I'm out of the room will you please keep close to Jayjay? And Owen, you can come and help me."

He followed her out, across the hall, through the side door, then along a corridor into some sort of small pantry. He hesitated about closing the door, but she did it for him. Still silent, she poured out two whiskies, a small one for herself, a larger one for him. She looked at him, gave him a small twisted smile, raised her glass almost as if this were going to be a toast, then drank.

He did this too, looking hard at her, then put down his glass, leant forward and held her lightly by the upper arms, and kissed her, full on the lips but gently.

She did nothing and said nothing for a moment or two, but then, after he had released her: "That was rather stupid. I ought to be furious. But it's a party. You're not tight but you aren't sober. You're obviously feeling amorous — getting every attractive woman into a corner and offering her extravagant compliments — "

"Only one. My colleague — Dr. Honeyfield — "

"Don't be silly. She's really no more your colleague than I am. And she has no sense of humour and comes straight off a chocolate box. But I did bring you in here — though I didn't do it to be kissed." She took another sip.

"I'd like to explain that kiss. You see — "

"Not now, some other time. This is important, as I said to Elfreda Drake. You can listen while you help me with the drinks. A large whisky for Saltana — you must know how he likes it — and a smaller one with soda for Jayjay. You do them. I'll do gin-and-tonics — one for Elfreda and two for those girls — I suppose we can't leave them out."

"But what about the other people still in there?" Tuby asked. "Won't it look odd?"

"Oh — damn — yes, of course. I've stopped thinking. You carry on and I'll tell Maria, or one of the girl students who are helping, to go round with a tray of whatever we have left. Shan't be a minute. Then I *must* explain."

He poured out the whiskies for Saltana and Jayjay, then hurriedly added a little more to hers and his, taking a quick pull of his neat and then adding a little soda. There were no faces enlarging themselves, no sounds growing louder, but possibilities were increasing and being enriched: he was now far from feeling sober.

As soon as she returned, she began at once: "We could be in trouble tonight, Owen. Students. They're holding an indignation meeting. A few of the more dashing or rebellious types bring out a rather messy rag they call *The Brocken*. It's run into censorship trouble. The Registrar, Clarence Rittenden — I don't think you've met him, have you? — he works tremendously hard but in a rather neurotic way so that he tends to overdo everything — well, he's along there at the meeting, and at any moment may come and report to Jayjay. Which explains why poor Jayjay isn't quite *with* this party."

"I see. But why worry, my dear Isabel? Bless your heart, I've been entangled with hundreds of students' protest meetings and demonstrations. All more excitable than your lot. Indians, Malays, Chinese — screaming their heads off! Years and years of it. I'm an old hand now. And I tell you — not to worry."

"All very well. But if you're an old hand, Jayjay isn't. And he's still trying to raise more money. He's good at that — he's really pretty good at the whole business of running a new university — don't underrate him just because he's not as artfully cajoling as you are or as bold and determined as your friend Saltana. He's easily the best possible man they could have found for Brockshire. But he won't be good, in fact he'll be at his worst, if this situation suddenly turns nasty."

Tuby nodded thoughtfully. "I can imagine that, Isabel. He'll be too deeply divided, split between trying to maintain his still-new authority and his progressive the-young-must-be-right attitude. Like being a New Left general. Oh — I can see that, my dear." He gave her a quick hug. "But I still think you're taking it all too seriously." He drank some whisky.

"Yes, but that's not all. And we'll have to hurry this up. Pass me that tray for these drinks. You see, there's Liz Plucknett. You saw her in there."

"I did but pretended not to. Same with her. We don't like each other, Plucknett and I. But she works for your husband. P.R.O. Plucknett."

"She's disgusted with him, feels he let her down. She hates you and Saltana, and she and I have always disliked each other. If there *is* any trouble tonight, she'll make the most of it, feeding it to Fleet Street. She may even have a photographer hanging around. If it finishes her here, she won't care. She's already threatened to leave. Now do you understand why I'm worried? With Jayjay as he is — with Liz Plucknett ready to do the dirty on us — "

"And a neurotic Registrar and that bunch of assorted professors along there — and creative Ted Jenks barging in — "

"Be quiet. I know. So — " and she gripped his arm hard — "do you think you and Saltana could help us, if necessary? It might be all the better because you're newcomers."

"Of course, my dear Isabel. Command us. If it's persuasion, then I'm your man. If they have to be overawed, it's Saltana. Good God — you should hear some of *his* reminiscences. He's had students with bombs and machine guns — fascists, communists, anarchists — the lot. I'll have a quick quiet word with him when I give him his whisky — "

The drawing room seemed to have attracted people from the study, for now it was well filled and the party was going into its second and livelier phase. Isabel took Elfreda's and Jayjay's drinks from the tray and joined them. Tuby, after some dodging about, got back into the corner.

"By special arrangement with the management, gin-and-tonics for you two girls."

"Oh — thank you, Dr. Tuby," cried Hazel, dimpling and sparkling away, "I'm dying for one."

"Me too," said Stephanie. "And you've got some lipstick at the corner of your mouth, Dr. Tuby, dear. Part of the special arrangement?" And the pretty creatures made big eyes at each other, and giggled happily.

"Whisky for you, Cosmo."

"And about time too," Saltana growled, taking it.

Tuby took his own glass, put the tray against the wall, drank in time with Saltana, then muttered, "And I promised to have a quick word with you." Still keeping to a mutter, he hurriedly explained why Isabel Lapford was feeling anxious. "And I told her," he concluded, "that if necessary we'd take charge — perhaps in our capacity as newcomers."

"Certainly," said Saltana. "Most certainly." Then, after drinking again, he dropped to a whisper. "A rather tantalizing situation here, my lecherous friend. Stephanie shows signs of being fascinated, but is probably pledged for the night to her employer, that dissolute humbug, Grandison — "

"But he's her uncle — "

"Nonsense! But we can go into that later. As for Hazel Honeypot, of course I don't know what her domestic situation is — has she a place of her own, do you know? — and then again, though she might grant one certain favours in an absent-minded fashion, one might have to listen to all that damned sociological rubbish half the night. By the way," he continued, about to drink again, "is there more where this came from?"

"I don't know, Cosmo. I emptied the bottle and didn't see another one. But of course — "

"Ay, so you're here," Cally shouted. "Professor Saltana, Dr. Tuby — my wife."

"And I've been hearing so much about you from Donald," said Mrs. Cally, shaking hands as if they'd just been brought in from a sinking ship. She was not as unattractive as her husband, that shouting monument of bone, but she was so brisk, scrubbed, red-cheeked, blazingly blue-eyed, so like a Scots nurse, that Tuby felt that at any moment she would slip a thermometer into his mouth.

"You're liking it here in Brockshire, are you, Dr. Tuby?" she enquired anxiously, as if secretly wondering if his bowels were open.

"I don't know, Mrs. Cally. Haven't had time to decide. And we're off again in the morning."

"You are? I don't think Donald knows that." Her eyes were now clouded with suspicion. Donald's authority was being challenged.

Tuby dismissed this topic. He moved a little closer to Mrs. Cally. "What do you hear about this trouble with the students? Any news?"

"You mean about their daft wee magazine — *The Brocken?* Donald says they're having a protest meeting tonight. It'll be over now, I'm thinking. Just a storm in a teacup, I'd say. They want to go on printing their silly dirty jokes — "

"But there is, wouldn't you say, a question of principle involved, Mrs. Cally?" This came from a thinnish, haggard-looking chap, who turned out to be the Professor Denis Brigham, head of Eng. Lit., whom Lois Terry had mentioned. And indeed Lois herself had arrived too, still looking mousy, untidy, plain, yet somehow full of a strange promise, like a landscape on a dull day. It was typical of her, Tuby thought, that while she still looked undernourished and forlorn and vulnerable, suddenly catching his eye she winked at him. At the same time Tuby felt his glass being gently but effectively snitched away. She had worked it so that they had a little space to themselves here.

"Whisky again. I don't know how you do it," she said, almost severely. "Well — " And she took a sip and handed it back to him.

"Like so many shy, ultra-sensitive, terribly vulnerable persons, you obviously have at times the cheek of the devil."

She ignored this. "I've had my eye on you, Dr. Tuby. All you do at this party is to wheedle whisky out of Mrs. Lapford and then leave her to talk to pretty girls, probably suggesting they take you home."

"Quite wrong. The subject's never been mentioned. And I've plenty of possible transport."

"I'm not thinking of that kind of transport. Incidentally, if you can bear a very small, very old, very uncomfortable car, you're welcome to share mine. After all, I took half your supper. And if, like me, you're bored now," she continued bravely, her eyes too bright, too much colour in her thin cheeks, "well, I've half a house to myself in Tarbury and if you're not too sleepy I could make you some coffee or tea and we could talk — and I mean, just talk — "

"What kind of tea?" Tuby felt he had to say something.

"Lapsang Souchong that I can't afford. And I know how not to spoil it. You probably think this is more of the cheek of the devil."

"No, I don't. Very kind of you, Lois. So hang on, please, until we know — hello — do you hear that?"

She did and so did everybody else. The party sound died down to a whisper as the noise outside increased and came nearer and then seemed to invade the house. Tuby had been half expecting this demonstration, and anyhow had known many others ten times the size that this must be. Yet he noted how the immediate effect was still the same — a flicker of fear that would soon flare up into panic or go roaring into anger. It was absurd, he reflected. If you listened to what was being shouted out there, it was just so much silliness from excited lads and girls bent on being silly. But if you simply heard the noise, without really listening, it was charged with menace, releasing in the dark of the mind all manner of ancient alarms and apprehensions: it was the inflamed mob, the revolution, the end of civilization. Then he must have laughed aloud.

"I don't find it funny ha-ha," said Lois, who was now standing so close to him that he could feel her quivering. "Though I'm glad you do. I know it's nonsense. But all the same it frightens me. Not the actual students, of course, but the crowd thing — the noisy mindlessness — as if they might be all different now — "

"I know. That's what I was thinking, before I laughed. Now what's happening?" There was some confusion around the drawing-room doorway.

"That's the Registrar, Clarence Rittenden, talking to Jayjay. All day and every day he's as nervous as a kitten. Now he's trying to terrify Jayjay."

"And he might be succeeding," said Tuby, who could see the Vice-Chancellor's head waving away. The people near the doorway drew back. Three students, two youths and a born-to-demonstrate girl, had arrived, and they were joined at once by Ted Jenks, who began talking loudly before they had opened their mouths. Tuby couldn't catch all he said — there was now quite a buzz of speculation in the room — and soon found himself wondering about the Ted Jenks accent. Tuby was deeply interested in accents, and this was one he had never noticed before this time in England but that now he seemed to hear everywhere. He had heard it coming belting out of the transistor sets the youngsters carried. It was the accent of the pop singers, both male and female, who when they wanted to cry *My love I give to you* turned it into *Mah lerv Ah geeve tew yew*. And to his ear, which was sharp, this was an accent without any historical or regional background, not belonging to any England he remembered; as if it had just been manufactured along with the pop records and transistor sets. And now Ted Jenks's voice was raised high in this peculiar accent — he might soon be singing his protest to a guitar accompaniment — and Jayjay, waving and flustered, was trying ineffectively to interrupt and remonstrate. The three students and Rittenden, almost the soprano of the group, were joining in; the students outside seemed to be raising some defiant and possibly obscene chorus; there were shouts and cries now from some of his fellow guests; and then he saw Cosmo Saltana and Elfreda, led by a pale and rather wild-eyed Isabel Lapford, pushing their way towards him.

"You'll have to excuse me, Lois," he told her with a smile of apology, releasing the arm into which she had been unknowingly digging her fingernails. "I think I may have to keep a promise."

## 15

Just before the students arrived, Elfreda had caught sight of Grandison, coming in at last from some other room and looking round for Stephanie. And she had decided there and then that she wasn't going to allow them to slip away, race back to the hotel, hurry upstairs to bed (and she knew what that meant), without having it out with them. It was all very well Cosmo Saltana dismissing Major Grandison so confidently, after he'd told her about him, the artful English-officer-and-Gent devil, on their way here. Cosmo was that kind of man; while he was talking to you he could make you share his confidence; and she'd meant it at the time when she'd said she wouldn't worry but would enjoy the party. But in fact she hadn't really enjoyed the party — a lot of it had been boring — and the worry that had been a nibbling little mouse was now a giant gnawing rat. So her only hope of starting tomorrow with any peace of mind, she'd decided, was to have it out with this artful Grandison here before the party was over.

Well, then these silly students came — all about some equally silly
magazine — making a noise outside, sending in this deputation of three,
and encouraging this young writer, Ted Something with the dirty shirt,
to start a loud idiotic speech. None of this bothered her. It interfered
with her Grandison plan, that was all. At least it did until she noticed
that her new friend Isabel Lapford, of all people, was now in a state, and
not just because these students were spoiling her party. After some urgent hissing in her ear and arm-clutching, Isabel pushed her way through
towards Cosmo Saltana, still in a corner with that pretty Dr. Honeyfield
and Stephanie, but with Major Grandison there too now.

"Tuby told me, Mrs. Lapford," Saltana muttered as soon as he saw
her. "So if you really want us to take over — "

"Oh — I do, I do — please — "

"Then let's get Tuby. Lead on." And he threw over his shoulder:
"Sorry to break it up, ladies. See you later, I hope."

And Tuby was ready for them when they found him, at the other
side of the room, with the pale and rather plain girl with the huge lamps
of eyes.

"Right, Cosmo." Tuby was smiling. "How do we work it? One of
us outside, the other here — eh?"

"Only way. I'll take charge of 'em here if you can calm 'em down
outside. Might be a bit rougher for you — "

"But you'll do it better here."

"Certainly. And you'll be better with an audience. Come on. You
ladies stay here. I'll have to do some pushing and shoving. You can easily
slip out, Owen. Right, then."

The next moment, to her surprise, Elfreda found herself deserted
entirely. Feeling a fool standing there alone, she edged her way round
the people crowding nearer the Vice-Chancellor and the deputation, and
returned to join Grandison and the two girls, now a little way out of their
corner.

They could just see Saltana muttering something into the ear of the
Vice-Chancellor, who was standing. A moment or two later they could
hear Saltana talking to the deputation and its friend, Ted. "As you probably know," he began, "I'm a newcomer here — "

"Yes, we know," Ted interrupted. "So you're not in this. So why
don't you keep out of it?"

"Why didn't *you* keep out of it?" Saltana thundered. "I mean this
party. If you're a guest, why don't you behave like one? If you've stopped
being a guest, why don't you clear out? And if you don't want to be a
guest of the university, why don't you go away and do some work?"

"I've just as much right — "

"The Vice-Chancellor invited you to Brockshire," Saltana continued, easily topping Ted, "and now you're helping to ruin a dam' good
party he's giving. Now shut up — I want to talk to these three." His tone

changed. "You're students. I know about students. I've had thousands of them. And I know you didn't come here to ruin a dam' good party, just when it's warming up — "

"No, we didn't," said one of the students. "But we had a meeting — "

"You had a meeting and you have a grievance. Why not? But instead of standing about here, spoiling other people's pleasure, why don't we adjourn to the study with the Vice-Chancellor — and the Registrar, if you want him — and sit down and talk it over? I tell you, wars have started and then gone on and on, just because people wouldn't sit down and talk it over. And if you're wondering about the fellows and girls outside, then you needn't, because my colleague and friend, Dr. Tuby, is now addressing them. So off we go to the study, to exchange a little sense, and no doubt Mrs. Lapford will forgive us and provide a few drinks and sandwiches. Come on, now. Vice-Chancellor, you lead the way, if you please."

And of course it worked, as Elfreda had known it would for the last minute or two. As they went out, she turned and smiled triumphantly at the other three.

"All right, you needn't tell me," cried Stephanie. "What a man! Fascinated me from the first minute."

"And saw through you, my dear, in the next half-minute," Major Grandison told her, rather sourly.

"I must go and hear what Dr. Tuby's saying to them outside," Elfreda said.

"And so must I," pretty Dr. Honeyfield declared warmly. "Let's go. He's the one who fascinates *me*." They were now on the move together. They pushed their way into a small group at the front door. "Listen. There he goes!"

"We're not really different, you know," Tuby was saying in his clear but enchantingly warm voice. "We're only a little further on, where all of you will be soon. And further on to where, God only knows. But we're not really different — "

"Yes, you are, Doc," cried a voice from somewhere out there. "You're getting Primrose East." This brought an enthusiastic roar.

"I doubt it," Tuby told them, coming in at the exact moment. "I doubt it, gentlemen. It'll be one of you in the end, I believe. But it won't be *any* of us — we'll hardly see her before she's gone — if you're going to let a grievance spoil a party. Anybody's grievance, anybody's party. I'm a great grievance man myself. My God — I've carted grievances all the way from Madras to Hong Kong. But gentlemen — and I'm not talking to the girls now; they understand this — gentlemen, I say, it's a terrible thing for a man my age to come back to England after years and years away — and then what? Why, to find the first good party I've drunk my way through suddenly threatened with ruin — and just at the time when

I'm beginning to wonder who'll be taking me home — and all because of something that ought or ought not to be printed in a magazine. Now, I feed on print. I like magazines. But not tonight, gentlemen, not tonight. I know, you feel your liberty's at stake. I don't blame you. But here and now — tonight, not tomorrow — what I feel is at stake is *my* liberty to enjoy this party — and the liberty of the Vice-Chancellor and Mrs. Lapford to entertain their guests — and the liberty of those guests to be happy here. Yes, there's a deputation in the house. I saw them come in. And you're wondering what's happening to them. Well, if I know anything about my colleague and friend, Professor Cosmo Saltana, he'll have them sitting round a table now, talking it out, not just making noises. And these negotiations could take some time. And I don't know about you, but I find the night's turning cold — "

Which reminded Elfreda that *she* was feeling cold, and she moved back into the hall. Grandison and Stephanie were standing there, probably waiting to go.

"They won't be long out there now," she told them. "Dr. Tuby'll have 'em moving off in a minute. But before *you* go, Major Grandison, I have to talk to you. It won't take long. And you needn't leave us, Stephanie. I know you're his secretary — at Audley Enquiries — "

"Just a moment, Mrs. Drake," said the Major. "This is rather important. Did you yourself discover who we were or did Saltana tell you?"

"He told me. I'd never have known."

"That's not bad then — eh, Stephanie? Let's have our little talk, of course, Mrs. Drake. But not here, I think."

He was right, because the people round the front door were now coming away from it, and they were followed in by the pale girl and Owen Tuby, his duty done, looking cold and tired. He escaped from some people who obviously wanted to congratulate him, then came up and took Elfreda to one side.

"I'm going in a minute, Elfreda. Lois — Miss Terry — is taking me to her place, not far from the hotel, to drink some China tea." He was speaking very quietly. "Just tea and talk. Nothing else. In half an hour she'll be telling me all about some long sad frustrating affair — "

"I'll bet," Elfreda whispered. "You be nice to her — poor girl. But then of course you will be, Owen. And don't forget I'm taking you to the station in the morning — "

Before he could reply, Isabel Lapford turned up from nowhere, at ease now.

"Well, you certainly kept your promise, Owen," Isabel told him. "You were wonderful, both of you. But you especially." She looked at him and laughed. "And now I suppose I'll have to pour some more whisky into you."

He smiled at her rather sleepily, but even before he spoke Elfreda knew there was something going wrong. "No, Mrs. Lapford. Not now.

Perhaps not ever. But thank you for the party. Goodnight. Goodnight, Elfreda — see you in the morning." And off he went.

Isabel stared at Elfreda, stricken. "Why, why? What have I done? What have I said?"

"We can work it out tomorrow, my dear," said Elfreda soothingly, though she knew exactly where Isabel had gone wrong and was surprised that a woman of her sort could be so dense. Apparently Isabel Lapford knew a lot about education but not much about men, so thick one minute, so sensitive and touchy the next minute. But now Isabel was being thanked by departing guests, so Elfreda rejoined the Major and Stephanie.

There was a party-fizzling-out feeling that was getting Elfreda down. She wished she was hurrying away from this house, in which she'd spent most of the day and half the night, with a man she liked. She wished Saltana and Tuby weren't going away or that she was going with them. She wished she wasn't in her forties and putting a bit too much weight on. If she'd been by herself she might have cried a little, to wash this self-pity away. But here she was, and Grandison was waiting for her to begin.

"All right, we talk." The only thing was to try to be tough. "I was Judson Drake's second wife. His first wife's still alive and she has a grown-up son, Walt Drake. They don't like me and I don't like them. They and their lawyers tried to stop me setting up a British Judson Drake Foundation. They said I didn't know about such things, which was true; I didn't, though I'm not the fool they take me for. Now I'll guess what's been happening. Walt Drake or his lawyers went to a Coast detective agency, to find out what I was up to and if possible to do the dirty on me. That agency got on to you — to dig around a bit here. I don't know what you've dug, but I'll tell you this. Cosmo Saltana said he'd given you the exact truth and advised me to do the same."

"Quite," said the Major. "And I imagine that you have, Mrs. Drake. And if you have, then why worry?"

"Did I say I was worrying?"

"No, but you are, you know."

"And I wish you weren't," Stephanie added. "I'm not pretending now. I like all three of you."

"Why, so do I, my dear." The Major flicked his moustache with his left thumb, but then gave Elfreda a quick shrewd look. "So why worry, Mrs. Drake?"

She looked hard at him. "What's the name of this American agency, Major Grandison?"

"Oh — no, no," he protested. "I'm sorry, but I simply couldn't tell you that. It's never done, you know, it really isn't. But does it matter?"

"Yes, it does. Before we married, I was Judson Drake's secretary, and I had to deal with several American detective agencies. I don't like 'em. I don't trust 'em. They can be unscrupulous, they can be ruthless. You must know that, Major Grandison."

He offered her a quick shrug. Stephanie looked as if she wanted to say something, but then checked herself.

"All right, if you won't talk, then I'll have to keep on talking." She didn't pretend to be annoyed. "I'm not soft and silly — don't think that. But Saltana and Tuby are going away for three weeks. I can't possibly go, I'm too busy. And I don't like the idea of an American agency trying to dig for dirt round here. Not when I'm on my own — and very busy. Of course I'm worried. And — for God's sake — just show me a little consideration. After all, you came here under false pretences, telling a lot of dam' lies, and when we found you out we could easily have made monkeys out of you both — but we didn't, did we? Even got you in here, didn't we?"

"You did indeed." A little more moustache work. "Though I don't regard this evening as a high spot in my social career. At this very moment I'd give a pound or two for a stiff whisky-and-soda."

"All right, that's that." And Elfreda turned away, her eyes smarting with the tiny tears of anger, but both of them together gently pulled her round.

"We're friends, Mrs. Drake," said Stephanie. "We really are."

"Quite right, Stephanie my dear. Now you must listen to me, Mrs. Drake. I can't tell you who's employing me. It simply isn't done in my business. But there is something I can tell you. Two things, in fact. My report will be entirely favourable. I shall state quite definitely that the Judson Drake Foundation over here isn't throwing its money away. It's done well to associate itself with this *Institute of Social Imagistics* and Professor Saltana and Dr. Tuby, who are in my opinion unusually capable and intelligent men. And privately — to you, Mrs. Drake — I'll add that I think they're going to be wasted on this place and you may have some difficulty keeping 'em here."

"Now don't start me worrying about something else, Major Grandison. But thank you for that report. However," Elfreda continued dryly, "you must know very well they don't want a favourable report. And they're capable of ignoring it."

"That's up to them. I've done with the case as soon as I send in this report. But now we come to the second thing, my dear Mrs. Drake. And this really *is* doing you a favour. I'll hold up my report as long as I possibly can. After all, I wasn't told it was urgent. And by the time it's got out to the Pacific Coast, and the agency there has reported to its clients, and the clients have discussed the report and come to a decision to call off the enquiry and not waste any more money — or — to start again and be tougher about it, then your three weeks will have gone and you can leave it to Professor Saltana — "

"Leave *what* to me?" For the man himself had quietly joined them.

"I can explain later, Cosmo. But I must tell you, before they go, that these two are all right. They're behaving like friends."

"I'm no friend," cried Stephanie. "I *want* the man."

"Not on our expense sheet," said Grandison. "Come, girl, we must go. I need a drink." He looked at the other two. "Probably see you both in the morning. Hope so."

"*He* needs a drink," Saltana muttered as he watched them go. "What about me? Talked myself into a desert with those young clowns. What about Owen?"

Elfreda told him what had happened to Owen Tuby and was just about to describe the strange little scene between Tuby and Isabel Lapford when the lady herself appeared. She was carrying two glasses.

"This is for you, Elfreda," she began. "Gin-and-tonic. And you'd like this whisky, wouldn't you, Professor Saltana?"

"Certainly. Many thanks."

"You see, Elfreda, I'm not making any mistake this time." She looked at Saltana. "You probably won't believe this — but your friend Dr. Tuby actually refused a drink and then went off in a huff with Lois Terry of the English Department. Can you believe it?" She sounded and even looked edgy and brittle, Elfreda thought, like somebody about to crack at any moment.

"I can, Mrs. Lapford," he told her carelessly, as if dismissing the topic. "However, he seems to have talked a hundred demonstrating students out of your garden. Not as easy as it looks. By the way, what's become of my new friend — sweet little Dr. Honeypot?"

"I'm jealous," Elfreda announced. She was a little, too, but felt better as soon as she'd proclaimed it.

"Oh — I think she left with Donald Cally and his wife. Tell me, Professor Saltana," Isabel went on — and asking for trouble, Elfreda felt at once — "do you and Dr. Tuby really chase women all the time — or is it pretense?"

"That's one of those questions that can't be answered properly because they never should have been asked." Saltana stared hard at her. "No, no, I don't mean because it's ill-mannered. But it's based on the assumption that Owen Tuby and I can be lumped together. In point of fact — and certainly as far as women are concerned — we're so different that any question like yours doesn't make sense. Ah — Vice-Chancellor — all clear?"

His head quite steady now, Jayjay had come up, holding what looked like a large whisky. "All clear — and no harm done, except that it did rather spoil our party. I think Clarence Rittenden was largely to blame, my dear — "

"Of course," his wife said sharply. "And that arrogant lout, Ted Jenks. He was a mistake from the first — "

"It still doesn't follow, my dear. If you invite a creative writer — "

"Creative writer, my foot! We must have half a dozen people on the staff who can write better than he can — "

"It's not quite the same thing — "

But Saltana crashed in. "Mrs. Drake and I are about to leave. So may I put a question to you two?" He looked at her, then at him. He dropped into a confidential tone. "Do you ever stay up late and get quietly plastered together?"

"No, we don't," she snapped. Jayjay said nothing, probably not knowing how to take the question.

"You ought to try it some time," Saltana told them gravely. "Perhaps tonight. Well, Elfreda, I think we ought to go." And she agreed, thankfully.

A few minutes later, she and Saltana were outside, looking for her car. They didn't say anything — Elfreda had often noticed that after a gabby party the night, waiting there, huge and dark, told her to shut up — and it was not until they were in the car that they began talking. "I don't think those two liked being told they ought to sit up and get plastered."

"It might work, though. Lapford's not a bad fellow — bit empty, bit weak, too anxious to be out in front yet still doing the right thing — and now he's obviously being cut down by her contempt for him. And she doesn't know it all. In some ways he's better than she is. To my mind — and I don't expect you or Owen Tuby to agree — she's one of these clever-silly women who are just a dam' nuisance. What did she say to Owen that annoyed him?"

Elfreda, busy now edging the car on to the road, explained briefly the *pouring whisky* remark.

"Exactly what I mean," Saltana said with a certain relish. "If she'd thought for a week how to infuriate him she couldn't have done better. Clever-silly. I'll keep on talking, Elfreda, so that you can concentrate on the road. The woman's half in love with him, thinks she's already gone too far, so tries to cut him down too. Now he's off — and she won't know where she is."

"You needn't tell *me*. I know about women, Professor. For the next two or three weeks, she'll never ask me a direct question about him but somehow his name will keep turning up in our conversation. Not that all women are like that. But her type is. Her nasty question about women-chasing was trying to get at him, not at you."

"Certainly. And you're wondering now exactly what I meant when I told her that Owen Tuby and I are quite different. I'll tell you." But he waited until they were safely past some great roar and dazzle. "Well, you could call me a waiter-and-pouncer. I don't do anything until I'm ready to pounce, which isn't often, I may say. Tuby's the opposite. He can't resist charming the women, softening them up almost at once, as if immediately bent on seduction. But this is deceptive. You might call him a semi-seducer. That girl who's taken him home is in no danger of being conjured into bed. She can talk and he'll talk, stroking her as if she's really a speaking cat."

"Most of us like it — up to a point, but after that we have to be persons and get on with something real — sharing a life. Has he ever been married?"

"Not really. He lived with an Indian girl for some time and was about to marry her — but she died. Then there was a Chinese girl, but after a few months, quite amicably, they broke it up. And don't let him know I told you."

"I won't. And I remember what you said about yourself. Fear of Latin-American in-laws and family parties. Disreputable affairs instead, I'll bet. Here — I'd better attend to my driving." But when at last they turned into the lighted streets, with few other cars, she began again. "I'd like to keep you up a few minutes, Cosmo, after I've parked the car. There won't be any time in the morning for serious talk. And I think this *is* serious. It comes out of something Major Grandison said to me. And we're not going up to one of our rooms. It's not the sort of talk you want round a bed. Find a corner for us in that lounge place — "

"Certainly. But don't be bossy, Elfreda. You're not in America now — "

"I was just about to say *please* when you interrupted me. And here we are. You nip out. The place looks all locked up. Warn the night porter there's somebody else coming in — "

"Good God — woman! What's the matter with you? Why don't you tell me how to ring the bell?"

"Sorry — I must be nervous."

When she went in, after parking the car round the corner, the hotel seemed deserted, almost dark, and melancholy in a late-Sunday-night fashion. But there were dimmish lights at each end of the lounge, which was a long narrow room that always reminded Elfreda of some sort of sitting place on a ship. At one end two men were sitting close together, muttering and mumbling, as if they were plotting the end of the world. At the other end Saltana was waiting, half-lost in the smoke of his cheroot, and as she trotted along to him she suddenly thought how horrible it would be if he suddenly turned into somebody else. Then she wished again they weren't leaving, or that she were going with them. No — blast it! — she was becoming too dependent on these two men. And by this time Saltana, telling her the room was almost too warm, was helping her out of her fur coat.

"I talked to Major Grandison, Cosmo," she began. "I told him the truth, just as you asked me to do." Then, making use of a good memory, she gave him everything that Grandison had said. "And I'm sure he meant it."

"Very decent if he did. And I'll tell him so if I see him in the morning. Perhaps I was rather too rough and tough with him earlier, in the bar. But something's on your mind, Elfreda. What is it?"

She waited because the end-of-the-world men, both rather fat, now slowly pushed themselves up and then went lumbering out. "It was when he said that you and Owen Tuby would be wasted on this place, and that I might have some difficulty keeping you here. It gave me a shock. Here was I — getting this dam' great house ready — "

He stopped her. "No, no, no! Your mind's jumping around too much, my dear."

"But you're going off for three weeks, and I suddenly realized I don't know what your plans are — if you have any. Have you?"

"Certainly. One — definite but short-range. To dig in here, to establish a base. You know all about that, we've discussed it. Second — not definite, it can't be yet, and long-range — "

"What to do? And for God's sake — don't say you can't tell me. Just remember, I'm really out of my depth all the time. Now — please, Cosmo!"

He put a heavy hand on her arm, giving one of his rare smiles. It was really better than Tuby's when it did come; Tuby had too many and had no dark sardonic face to light up. "Easy now, my dear. We could never have made the first move without you. Besides, we're devoted to you, fondly devoted, Elfreda. And no plan of ours will exclude you, unless you want it to. That I can promise." He nodded solemnly, leant back, took a pull at his cheroot, then used a brisker and almost impersonal tone. "Now — *you* imagine we're going to Dublin — and perhaps a few other places — to drink whisky and enjoy some lively talk, don't you?"

"Knowing you two, that's just what I *do* imagine — "

"And you're quite right," he said coolly. "But we're going to do some work too. We really are. All set."

"What sort of work?" She half-believed him, half-didn't. That's why the pair of them were both maddening and fascinating. Impossible to see clean through them as she always had with poor Judson.

Saltana held up his cheroot as if it were now a miniature torch and a symbol of progress. "Planning exactly what the Institute does in that house of yours. Lectures, seminars, research projects, the lot. Digging in, academically. But at the same time planning to obtain the maximum respectable publicity — press, television, radio. And we can do it — and when I say *we* now, I'm including you."

"Me? I wouldn't know where to start." Protesting, she had raised her voice.

Saltana raised his. "You will — after a few weeks' helping us to run the Institute. Don't underrate yourself, my dear Elfreda. You learn quickly. And you impress people. Tuby and I were agreeing about that, only this morning."

"We were." And there was Tuby, ambling toward them. His overcoat was wide open but its collar was still turned up at the back; his hat was tilted towards one side; he was smoking a pipe; his spectacles were further down his nose than they usually were; and he suggested something between an enlarged cherub and a dissolute priest. He removed his hat with a flourish and bowed to Elfreda. "Perfectly true, my dear. We decided we'd never find anybody better to complete the team."

"Owen, you've been drinking," Elfreda said severely.

"Two cups of China tea, that's all, I assure you."

"Probably an aphrodisiac in your case, my boy," said Saltana. "So she had to throw him out."

"True in one sense, not in another. The poor girl began her sad story — as I knew she would — but not having told it for some time or to such a sympathetic listener, she began to weep and said she ought to go to bed and finish her crying there. I agreed very readily. But I think you were discussing something important — plans, perhaps?"

"Yes, all this work you're going to do in Ireland." And Elfreda found herself adding a sceptical sniff.

"Quite right. We are, y'know, Elfreda. May I?" No other seat being available in that corner, Tuby was now perching himself on the arm of Elfreda's very large armchair, leaving her sitting between him and Saltana, feeling rather ridiculous.

"We'll be planning the work of the *Institute of Social Imagistics*," Saltana announced, "under the auspices of the British Judson Drake Sociological Foundation and now attached to the University of Brockshire." He rolled it all out with mock pomp, but Elfreda knew he was at least half-serious.

"All the work of a few days," cried Tuby. "An astonishing achievement, you must admit, Elfreda — "

"Probably unmatched in academic life," said Saltana, now ready to be delighted with himself.

"Stop that, both of you," she told them sharply. "Talking like that can change the luck."

Taking an arm each, they lifted her out of her chair and then walked her very slowly, arm in arm, towards the door. Not knowing whether to be cross or to giggle, she decided against both, and turned businesslike. "Now don't forget you're off early in the morning. You've packed, of course?"

"Certainly not," said Saltana.

"A man who packs the day before shouldn't go to Dublin," said Tuby. "Unless, of course, it's all different now."

"It will be," Saltana concluded in his deepest and most melancholy tone. "Nearly everything is."

# PART TWO

## 1

It was a Tuesday afternoon in early November, a murky and sodden afternoon too, when Owen Tuby returned to Tarbury and took a taxi from the station to Tarwoods Manor, which from now on he hoped to be able to call the Institute. He didn't even know if Elfreda would be there. They had told her not to expect them back until Friday, but then they had changed their plans. Tuby felt quite strange in the taxi. After all, he had spent only a few days in Brockshire and now had been away from it for nearly three weeks. He felt the same about Elfreda, for though he was ready to be fond of her she no longer seemed quite real, more like somebody he'd read about in a novel. He'd noticed this about himself before. Even a week-end in any place would make it seem real, solid, inevitable, whereas the place he'd come from and might be going back to would become remote, dreamlike, almost Tasmania or Patagonia.

After dismissing the taxi, he decided against marching straight into the house. He didn't live there yet. So he put down his two bags and rang the bell. It was answered by a thick middle-aged man with a large moustache and a darkly suspicious look — a kind of generalized Mediterranean type. "What do you want?"

"I'm Dr. Tuby. Is Mrs. Drake here?"

"Yais. But she say you come Friday." More suspicion.

"Well, I've come today instead. And these are my bags — so — would you mind — ?"

The hall was much better lit and warmer than it had been before, but it looked much the same. The man had brought in the bags, but still had that suspicious and sulky look which Mediterranean types all too often put on. "I go tell," he muttered in his moustache, which belonged to some obscure brigandry among the olive trees, and left Tuby standing there, feeling disappointed and rather melancholy. He had seen himself making a triumphant return to Brockshire, forgetting that the old Irony and Anticlimax Department is always at work. He stared about him, but not really taking in anything very much. Moments passed like leaden giants.

Then Elfreda came hurrying downstairs and it was all different. She was wearing a brown jersey and a shortish tweed skirt and looked slimmer and younger than his memory of her. And all excited and genuinely pleased too. "Owen Tuby," she cried, returning to her American manner. "And am I glad to see you — wowie!" And her arms went round him and she kissed him heartily.

After Tuby had washed up, he found Elfreda already in her room, from which most of old Lady Thaxley's possessions had been removed. At one end, away from the door, was the office stuff — a desk, typewriter, telephone, filing cabinets — but nearer the door and a small wood fire, just to look at because the house was centrally heated, was everything that suggested a cheerful and comfortable sitting room.

"I like this," he told Elfreda, making no comment on any details because he never really noticed them, only the general effect and atmosphere. "Congratulations!"

"Wait till you see what we've done to the rest of it. This was easy. The drawing room and the dining room were murder. Oh — thank you — Florrie. Dr. Tuby, this is Florrie, who's doing our cooking."

She was one of those thick and wide Northcountrywomen who always look flushed with anger as if they have just been insulted. "How do, Doctor? But Friday Ah was told, not Tuesday. Oh — don't apologize — we can manage, we can manage — but Alfred's a bit put out." She was setting out the tea things on the table.

"I'm sorry," Tuby told her, smiling. "But there were urgent business reasons. Please tell Alfred it couldn't be helped."

"Trouble with Alfred he's not got used to housework yet. Making beds, dusting, an' so forth. He's a loovely waiter — soon as Mrs. Drake gives a big dinner party, he'll be in his element — you'll see, Doctor — but he thinks housework is beneath him. That's right, isn't it, Mrs. Drake? He's proud, Alfred is. That big moustache is half the trouble. Goes against the grain taking it round making beds and dusting. An' Ah can quite understand. But as Ah keep telling him — he has to keep moustache — moustache won't keep him nor me neether. Another for dinner then — eh, Mrs. Drake? Well, Ah can stretch it."

"I like Florrie," Tuby said as Elfreda began pouring out the tea, "though I'm not sure about Alfred. Where did you find them?"

"They were helping to run a small hotel this side of Gloucester and didn't like it. I've been lucky — you ask Isabel Lapford. Florrie's a good cook, and Alfred might be worse. I suppose they're married but God knows when, where, or how. You can tell where Florrie comes from, but Alfred — and that's not his real name — is a mystery man. I can never make out which end of the Mediterranean he comes from. Could be anywhere between Cyprus and Gibraltar. You mention any place down there, he's been. But never mind about him. We've a lot to talk about, Owen. Give me your news and then I'll give you mine."

"Well — " but he had just taken a large bite of buttered toast and had to wait — "it's like this. We went to Dublin and it rained. We went down to Cork and it rained. We went across to Galway and it rained. And we had a lot of talk and whisky — "

"You needn't tell me that. I know you two. At least, now you're back I do. But I'll tell you, Owen, there were times when I was slogging away, getting this house ready, and I suddenly felt I didn't know what I was doing. You and Cosmo Saltana stopped being real, as if I'd dreamt you — and the Institute and *Social Imagistics* and everything that happened three weeks ago — do you know what I mean?"

"I know exactly. Felt it myself just half an hour ago. But when we were away, Cosmo and I kept each other going. And believe it or not, we've been *working*. We've really got down to it. We know what we want to do and how to do it."

She regarded him curiously. "You know, Owen, I believe you. Somehow you're different."

"If you think I am, wait until you meet Cosmo Saltana. Iron — but red-hot. A man of destiny. He's sent me ahead to get things going here while he does what he thinks ought to be done, for a few days, in London." He drank some tea. "Now then — to business. He wants a quick survey, for *Social Imagistics,* of the West End. Clothes, restaurants, amusements, what's *in,* what's *out* — the lot. If you'd like to go, if only for a change, that's fine — he can use you. But if you feel you'd be more useful here, enrolling students, telling 'em what we've planned, then of course you stay — "

"I could do with a change — but I'll have to think about that."

"Now what about that model — Primrose East? Has she changed her mind?"

"Certainly not. She's here — in this house — living here. She insisted. There was so much fuss about her coming, and I had a room for her, so I said she could. Been here nearly a week and made herself very useful, I must say. So has Mike Mickley. He's living here too.'"

"With Primrose East?"

"Go on — you're as bad as Mrs. Cally. That's what he'd like of course, but she's not having any. She still says she loves Cosmo Saltana — you remember? I didn't move in till they did too, and believe me, Owen, I've been glad of their company *and* their help. They're upstairs now, moving some of the furniture and knick-knacks around. We'll go up and see them shortly, after I've shown you round downstairs."

"We must talk first, Elfreda. Now, what's your news? Any threat from the Americans?"

"I've heard nothing from Walt Drake or his lawyers. That could be good or bad. But Mike Mickley told me the day before yesterday — yes, Sunday it was — that he'd heard some American had been nosing around asking questions. And as soon as he told me that, I wished to God you two were back."

"Well, we are. Tough businesslike types too. No-nonsense men. Keen, hard, steely-eyed. Now what's the general picture? How do we stand with the University of Brockshire?"

Her smile vanished. She hesitated before replying. "Well, there was all this fuss and publicity about Primrose coming here, and some of the students did one of their parades — all on her side. Busy Liz Plucknett did nothing — she's against us; I told you she would be — it was that local reporter and the London people Primrose knows. The Institute's well known before it's ever done anything — "

"Fuss and notoriety have created a backwash, have they?"

"I'm afraid they have, Owen. Some of it's just jealousy. Cally's making a lot of trouble because a lot of students want to enrol here. And he says he can't allow it until he's approved the courses here — "

"He's quite right, of course. We'll attend to him."

"His wife and that Mrs. Brigham — English Professor's wife — go on as if we were going to run a cat house here — if you know what I mean. And Mike says some of the other professors — like Milfield, the bald History man, and Professor Petherton, Philosophy, the one Saltana was arguing with, you remember? — have been getting at the Lapfords. So Jayjay's beginning to look sideways at me. As for Isabel, she helped me no end at first here but lately she's cooled off, hasn't been near for a week. That's your fault, Owen. And you know it. She didn't like the Primrose East fuss, of course — she was against it from the first — but it's really *you*. When at last she got it into her head, after skirting round the subject for days and days, that her silly remark about pouring whisky into you had really annoyed you, then of course she didn't blame herself for making such a silly remark, she blamed you for being so rude to her. And I've been longing ever since to ask you why you said — what was it? — *Not now. Perhaps not ever.* And the way you said it, not angry, just smiling and sleepy, really made it worse. But why *did* you say that to her?"

"I said it because I meant it, Elfreda."

"Yes — but why, why? I mean, you're such a good-natured man, such a sweet man. And you'd been getting on so well with her — to say the least. So why? It was only the kind of silly remark any woman might make."

"No, it wasn't," Tuby said mildly. "*You'd* never have made it. And certainly not in that tone of voice. That — the way it was said — angered me. I hadn't heard that particular tone, which belongs to a peculiarly English class insolence, for a long time. Look — Elfreda — we'd had a free-and-easy little passage between us, then as a friend she'd asked me to help her husband out of a situation he mightn't be able to cope with. But when it's over and she's trying to thank me, she suddenly feels she has to recover her dignity, to be grand for both herself and her husband, so down it comes from on high." And, with diabolical mimicry, he quoted her *And now I suppose I'll have to pour some more whisky into you*. "She asked for what she got. One final point. And this is for you too, my dear. Cosmo Saltana and I aren't a pair of alcoholics. These demands of ours for whisky are half a joke. And a protest against the pale, thin, dry entertaining that people like the Lapfords, not really convivial or even genuinely hospitable, try to fob you off with. We haven't to have whisky. We didn't take a drop for two whole days in Cork," he added solemnly. "A man there had some superb claret. By the way, have you laid in any good Scotch, Elfreda? I'm a little tired of Irish."

She shook her head at him, laughing. "You're a one, you are, Owen. You could talk Isabel Lapford round in two minutes."

"I don't propose to, not unless she makes a genuine apology for using that insufferable tone to me."

"Enough of that," said Elfreda. "Do you want to know about your other girl friends?"

"Certainly."

"Well, that pretty little Hazel Honeyfield has called here three times to ask me when you were coming back. She pretends it's all sociology."

"Ah — you've missed the point there, my dear. It *is* all sociology. Any sex would be on the side. But I must see Hazel soon. She could be very useful to us from now on. It's a dam' nuisance Cally won't let her join us. What about Lois What's-her-name? — Terry?"

"The one with the big wounded eyes? She's worried about you, Owen. Oh — yes, she told me, over coffee in the Refectory. She feels she ruined the end of that party for you by taking you home and then going into a weeping fit. If you ever agreed to go home with her again, God knows what she'd offer you — her *all*, I'd say."

Now back in his chair, Tuby frowned across the table at her. "On this level, men and women are always at cross-purposes. Where you're sentimental, we're cynical. Where we're sentimental, you're cynical. I can't imagine myself entering into a casual relationship with that particular young woman. It would exist in the wrong atmosphere."

Alfred came in with a tray. "Room is ready, Doctor." But he still looked and spoke as if he suspected that Tuby was a fraud. If Elfreda hadn't been there, Tuby would have felt like one, so strong, so dark, so overpowering was this suspicion, apparently arising from long experience of conspiracies and secret passwords and customs officials and police inspectors with even larger moustaches.

"Thank you, Alfred," said Elfreda. Then, to Tuby, "Before you go up, come and see what I've done with that drawing room. You remember what a horrible place it was?"

Tuby did, and now hardly recognized it. The near end, newly furnished with a lot of collapsible little chairs, screens, and a dais, could be used at once for Saltana's seminars or Tuby's lectures. It all looked so new, bright, functional, that it was impossible to imagine that old Lady Thaxley had ever set foot in the place. In all sincerity, Tuby congratulated Elfreda most warmly as they went down the enormous room towards the screens.

"It's still a drawing room on this side, you see," Elfreda said as they passed the screens. "If it's just us and a few friends, we keep it like this. If we want to give a party or a concert or something, then we take the screens away and open it all out. Quite comfortable, you see. And I've even had this old grand piano tuned. The tuner said it wasn't bad for its age. Try it. I seem to remember you said you could play the piano."

"After a fashion. Something between — and rather below — a pianist in a Northcountry pub and one in a second-rate cocktail bar. However, let's discover how it sounds."

He began playing various odds and ends he remembered; his technique was deplorable but, after playing for hours at rather drunken parties out East, he had a good memory for all kinds of popular old-fashioned stuff; and he had a dashing manner that deceived everybody — except people like Saltana who knew and cared about music.

Elfreda was not one of those people. "But you're marvellous, Owen. We must have some musical parties."

"So long as I'm not performing. I couldn't even turn over properly."

"Well, well, well!" A cheeky voice coming from a cheeky face— Mike Mickley. (And Tuby decided then and there to take some of the cheek out of him.) He was wearing a ragged sweater, paint-spattered pants, and old tennis shoes. "And don't look at me like that, Dr. Tuby. I've been working like hell upstairs. Ask Elfreda."

"Mrs. Drake told me." Tuby was still sitting on the piano stool.

"How are you on boogie-woogie and rock 'n' roll?"

"I'm not. I can just manage the simpler tunes of the Twenties and early Thirties," he continued, getting up and closing the piano, "and play with feeling waltz themes from Central European operettas dating from 1908. Oh — hello, Primrose!"

"Darling Dr. Tuby!" She was drifting towards him, and was wearing a kind of mob cap, a pink overall, and a lot of black stocking. She was obviously delighted to seem him but her voice, as faint and faraway as ever, couldn't cope with enthusiastic recognition. "What — a nice surprise! But where — is my lovely — Professor Saltana?"

"Still in London."

"Well then — I'll have to kiss you — instead." Which she did. And Tuby was just able to catch sight of young Mickley glowering at them. Cheek going already.

"Now if you'll all sit down," said Tuby, settling on the piano stool again but still facing them, "I'll explain what we want you to do — and why."

"Is it an order — from Professor Saltana?" Primrose asked. "Is he going — to tell me — what to do? Yes? Heavenly!" She draped yards of stocking over the arm of a big chair.

"He wants you two — and Elfreda if she feels like it — to report to him by lunchtime tomorrow. Robinson's Hotel."

"Who's paying for this?" Mickley demanded.

"The Institute is. I'm leaving the details of your assignment to Professor Saltana. But your Institute work starts tomorrow in London. In Department-of-Sociology terms, you'll be gathering data in the field. You can tell Professor Cally that, if he should ask you." Checking a grin before it really widened, he regarded them severely again. "*Social Imagistics* demands an immense amount of up-to-date information — for example, about where and how people live, about clothes and shops, restaurants and amusements — and while I'm looking after things here, our Director — "

He hesitated a moment, which gave Primrose just time to cry in faint ecstasy, "Oh — I adore that."

"I say our Director wants to make a start in the West End tomorrow. A lot of his questions you'll be able to answer immediately — especially you, Primrose; this is where you're going to be very useful to us — but even so, you may have to go out into the field, as we sociologists say, and of course if necessary question your friends. Elfreda, unless you'd absolutely hate it, my dear, I think you'd better go too. Cosmo will need somebody badly — just to get down the information — it's coming in from other people too — and then start arranging it. Will you go? Good! I'll be all right here until the end of the week on my own, though I ought to borrow a secretary from somebody. By the way, Mickley, do you possess a suit?"

"Just one. Bought it for a wedding."

"Wear it. But take one of your beat outfits with you — for the dark edges of the field."

"I shall — drive up — tonight," Primrose told them, a drowning maiden suddenly being rescued. "I can stay — with the Birtles. No, Mike — I'm not taking you. I can't — drive at night — and fight off passes. Did you say — Robinson's Hotel?"

Tuby said he did, and told her where to find it. "But don't go there looking for Professor Saltana until about eleven tomorrow morning at the earliest."

"I haven't a car at the moment," Mickley said. "But if Elfreda'll take hers, I'll do the driving. Okay, Elfreda? Fine!"

Primrose having taken off for London, only the three of them sat down to dinner, looking rather lost, like the survivors of some catastrophe, at the end of the immense dining table. Elfreda said she had finally decided against moving it out, or indeed making changes in the dining room itself. "After all, we might want to give dinner parties."

"Just for Alfred's sake," said Mike Mickley, now looking spruce in his suit. Alfred himself was looking even sprucer, having changed from a dingy houseman's coat into a white jacket with a black bow tie, and was serving everything as if it cost fifteen pounds and had been flown from Strasburg and Paris. Under the spell of his tiptoeing and bending and finger-flicking, Tuby found ordinary conversation almost impossible and felt he ought to be asking Elfreda and Mickley if they had been to the opera.

At the end of dinner Alfred left them with a few apples that he almost transformed, by sheer magnificence of manner, into giant pears, huge black grapes, and a pineapple. Elfreda announced she had things to do, obviously prepared to spend one of those curious letter-pad–sewing-basket–bathroom-work female evenings that would drive the impatient male mad with boredom. Mickley said there was a debate at the Union, with two minor politicians in attendance, that he wouldn't mind catching; Tuby said he'd go along too; and Elfreda offered them her car.

"I didn't know you had a Union here," Tuby said as they went out to the car.

"No building yet. Amenities still to come. But there are these occasional debates in the big Refectory room. Oxbridge style, though — the whole bloody traditional works. But you were at Cambridge, weren't you? So perhaps you like this Union Debate bit — eh?"

"Certainly not. I spoke a few times myself just to try myself out at public speaking. The fact is, I enjoy hearing myself speak in public but hate listening to other people. So no debates. And I wouldn't have thought the lads and girls here would want this bogus Parliamentary caper."

"Some of them do. And Jayjay and Rittenden and Stample have been mad keen, trying to paint Redbrick black. They'll be ordering plastic ivy soon. Here's the garage. It's not locked."

They were moving down the drive when Mickley next spoke. "I don't know if Elfreda told you, Dr. Tuby, but now you three have split this place as if you'd taken a hatchet to it. Poor old Jayjay's under pressure. And he was already a divided man. He likes to be well out in front and yet safely behind. You and Saltana really have him bloody rattled. After all this publicity, he'd feel a fool if he asked you to leave. But then there are people telling him he'll soon feel a fool if he allows you to stay. Cally's one of them — " He stopped talking until they were safely on the main road. He seemed to be a careful driver, like several dashing types Tuby had known, the opposite of those timid conforming little men who turn into demons behind the wheel of a car.

"I gather that Cally's against us now," said Tuby. "I don't blame him. We're supposed to be in his Department and he has students wanting to enrol with us — "

"I'll say he has!" Mickley was very emphatic.

"And as yet he hasn't a notion what we're going to do. No, I don't blame Cally. I'll talk to him in the morning. Tell him I need a secretary, too."

"My God — you're cool — you and Prof. Saltana. And nobody can say you aren't. Tell me, why did he say I could join you?"

"I don't know. You ask him tomorrow. And don't be too cheeky. He's not as easy-going as I am."

"I wish you'd tell me what we're up to." And it came out too casually.

"Certainly, my boy. We're about to run the *Institute of Social Imagistics* — under the auspices of the Judson Drake Foundation."

"Now — look — "

"*You* look — there's a dam' great bus coming round the corner — "

Once the car was parked inside the university grounds, they decided to split up. Mickley remembered that he would have to tell a girl, probably working in the Library, that he was going to London. And Tuby said he could do without the car, either begging a lift from somebody or, if the worst happened, being ready to walk back to what he now firmly called the Institute. When he went up to the big Refectory he found it well filled, with the debate already in progress on a platform at the far end. There were microphones up there and two loudspeakers high on the walls. Some students, who recognized him and grinned a welcome, offered him a seat, but he preferred to keep standing at the back, not knowing how much of this stuff he would be able to take.

Not very much, he soon told himself. The amplification was rough and cruel. It was like looking at imbeciles twenty feet tall. On and on the old solemn idiocies came booming or squeaking from those boxes on the walls. *Do I understand that the Honourable Proposer . . . May I suggest to you, Mr. President, sir . . . Our Honourable if not Gallant Friend, the Opposer of this motion . . .* on and on. What they were debating he neither knew nor cared, but so long as he stood there, wishing he could light a pipe, he couldn't avoid hearing the broken-backed rhetoric, the epigrams that fell flat, the endless appeals to *Mr. President, sir.* Suddenly he found himself lost in an immense yawn, closing his eyes as his hand went up to his mouth. When he opened his eyes he saw that a young woman was standing quite close, making a face at him.

"Hello!" said Lois Terry.

"Oh — hello — Lois!"

"Are you going?"

"Yes."

"So am I." Then, with the door closed behind them, she stopped and looked at him. "If I promise — solemnly promise — not to start weeping again, will you come and drink tea with me?"

"Certainly, Lois. A pleasure."

"Just talk. No sex activities. No pouncing."

"I'm not a pouncer, my dear. I talk you into it. But I'm not tonight.

*You* don't weep. *I'm* brisk and impersonal, though not quite *Mr. President, sir.*"

"Good! Let's hurry before anybody nails us. You'll find the car as uncomfortable as ever — perhaps a bit worse."

It was, too. They seemed to explode and bump their way to Tarbury so that continuous talk was impossible. But once he had admired her sitting room again — it was untidy but light and elegant, enjoying its own spring of yellows and delicate greens — and she had made the tea and he was enjoying a pipe of an Irish cut plug, the talk flowed easily, as if they were old friends. Unlike so many university women, she was a good listener and didn't want to prove how bright she was all the time. She sat on the floor, at the other side of the gasfire, her elbows on a pouffe, her head in her hands, looking up at him with those enormous eyes that lightened and darkened with the play of his talk as he described, at her insistence, his Irish journey.

"And now that's enough about Cosmo Saltana and me," he said finally. "Tell me what's been happening here. And I'm not being polite. I really want to know. Don't forget, I'm one of you now."

She waited a moment, frowning a little, her eyes clouding. "You know — when you say that," she began slowly, "somehow I just can't believe you. I *know* you aren't one of us. Saltana neither. I feel you're just passing through. If you'd never come back I wouldn't have been surprised, though I'd have been disappointed. I felt it that night at the Lapfords' party — you weren't the kind of men who settle in a place like this. You were just pretending to start teaching here. You wouldn't dream of working with somebody like Donald Cally — or Dorothy Pawson or that idiotic Albert Friddle. I leave out Hazel Honeyfield because I know what would be going on there. I noticed the way you looked at her that night. And that's why we women will be so easily fascinated. We know you're not one of us. You're both strange men passing through, coming from somewhere unknown, on your way to somewhere unknown. That's why we like you — and the men don't. They're envious. They know you don't care a damn."

"But I do, my dear Lois. Didn't I ask you what's been happening? I want your news."

"Well, let me think. There's great excitement in Eng. Lit. because Denis Brigham has persuaded his old Cambridge master, now retired, Professor Steril, to come and give a public lecture. It's called *Notes Towards a Reconsideration of T. S. Eliot.* The Brighams are giving a party for him afterwards, but you won't be invited. He's one of the profs who've protested to Jayjay about this Primrose East publicity — "

"Nothing to do with me," Tuby protested. "I wasn't even here — "

"They blame you, though. They know she's there in your Institute. And Gladys Brigham and some of the other sour wives are going round talking about orgies — "

"I've never been in on an orgy. I was promised several in advance out East, but they'd always cleaned the place up just before I got there."

"Don't you think you'd laugh? I always feel I would — and then spoil it for everybody."

"You'd have to be plastered, I imagine."

"Then I'd be sick. I always am. Now — what else? Oh — Duncan Mack, our Drama Director, has begun rehearsing Ted Jenks's play — "

"The one about the incestuous window-cleaner?"

"That's the one. He asked me to be in — I act a bit — but I turned him down. You haven't met Duncan Mack, have you? I think he was away when you were here before. He's one of the silliest men here — perhaps *the* silliest, because he's silly *and* theatrical. But who told you what the play was about? I didn't."

Tuby thought for a moment. "It was Isabel Lapford."

"When you were wheedling all that food and booze out of her — other things too, probably. Well, there's a rumour going around — and your Mrs. Drake said something about it — that you were rude to her later that night and that now she's against you. Which means that poor old Jayjay will be, sooner or later. He can stand up to the profs but not to his wife as well. Does this worry you?"

"Not much, no."

"I thought not. You behave as one side of me always *wants* to behave — and did behave, you remember, when I didn't even know you but asked you about all that food and drink you had. Instant influence, that was. I'm not like that at all as a rule — a kind of mouse. And your friend Saltana would always make me feel like one, whereas I can be downright impudent with you. I suppose you know that Mrs. Drake adores you both?"

"We're very fond of her — Elfreda. She and young Mickley join Saltana in London tomorrow. Primrose East rushed off tonight. It's work — not fun and games. Indeed, you can tell Mrs. Brigham and her friends from me that there aren't any fun and games. All work — on behalf of *Social Imagistics*." And by the time he had enlarged on this topic, facing a certain quizzical scepticism in those telltale eyes of hers, he felt he ought to go. He was ready to walk home but she insisted upon taking him in her car, now protesting more noisily and jerkily than ever. So they exchanged only a few words along the way. But when they stopped outside the front door and he began to get out before saying goodnight, she got out too and came round to him.

"I've loved it tonight," she began, coming closer. "No weeping this time, you see. Or ever again, I fancy. Let's have another session of tea and talk very soon — please. And thank you."

And she put her arms round his neck and gave him a kiss that might not have been impassioned but was a good deal more than a peck. It was then that somebody, unseen and unheard though not two yards away, exploded a flash bulb in their faces.

## 2

"Professor Saltana, you haven't changed — the least little bit," Primrose East said fondly. They were in Robinson's Small Lounge where everything had begun.

"Neither have you," Saltana told her gruffly. "Still too young, still the wrong shape."

"You wait. I've put on — nearly five pounds. I'm eating — like mad. I still love you."

"Certainly not. Now — to work — "

"Please — *please* — just one thing first. I'm staying — with the Birtles — *you* know. And they wonder — if you and Elfreda — could dine with them — tomorrow night. Could you?"

"I could. I can't answer for Elfreda. Anyhow, you'll be meeting her here at five o'clock. Now listen, girl. We *Social Imagistics* people need to have a great store of facts at our disposal. You know the West End. What you have in your head already, don't bother about. You can dictate it all later. You're here to check what you're uncertain about. Move around and ask questions, make use of your friends if necessary and tell 'em it's sociology. You've the rest of today, all tomorrow and Friday. Fill notebooks. Pile up the information."

"With — what's *in?*"

"Yes, if it's not likely to be *out* by next week. Use your own judgment. I believe you're a shrewd girl, Primrose, behind all that vague drowned-nymph flapdoodle — "

"No, darling — please! Not flapdoodle. Part of an image buildup."

"I'm sorry, my dear. You're perfectly right and I ought to have known. It's exactly what we're after. Now off you go — and look in about five. I'm depending on you, Primrose. And don't sit languishing there, making big eyes at me. Get to work, girl."

After murmuring that she was utterly and quite maddeningly devoted to him, Primrose drifted out, looking extremely expensive and very beautiful in her own way and much further *in* than anybody Robinson's — not an *in* place — had seen for a long time. Saltana rang up the Redbrick expert, O. V. Mere, to confirm they were meeting here at Robinson's at 12:45 for a drink or two in the bar and then lunch. He and Tuby had agreed that Mere, who had now had his fee, should be brought into the picture again, as early as possible too, which was why Saltana, who didn't like the fellow, was nobly offering him lunch. Then, for the third time, Saltana rang a secretarial agency, and the woman there, behaving as if he were demanding a prima ballerina, promised he should have an experienced temporary for the late afternoon that day and possibly for several hours the next day. His final telephone call was to Audley Enquiries and Mrs. Stephanie Murten, who was delighted to hear that he was back from his holiday, had a dinner engagement that night that she would cut short if he really wanted to see her as soon as possible, and would receive him at her Hampstead address at about quarter-past ten if that wasn't too late for him. And it wasn't, he assured her. Then he went out to search Bayswater for a stationer's, to buy typing paper, carbons, and several more notebooks.

When O. V. Mere arrived in the bar at Robinson's, he looked scruffier than ever, as if he had spent all Monday and Tuesday covering himself with cigarette ash and dandruff. Saltana greeted him politely, almost warmly, host to guest, but couldn't help regarding him with some distaste. He himself was wearing a new suit, acquired, like Tuby's, in Dublin.

After they had ordered and tasted their drinks, Mere said casually, speaking as usual out of the corner of his mouth not busy with his cigarette, "Noticed you giving me a look when you first saw me, Saltana. Asking yourself why the hell I have to come to a respectable hotel for lunch looking like this. After all, I can't do too badly. So why don't I improve my appearance? Now, you're going into the image racket. So why this image?"

"You want a serious reply, Mere?"

The cigarette wobbled, proving that Mere was amused. "A little test question really, Saltana. Just to see if you're any good."

"On the subject of the O. V. Mere image — eh?" Saltana stared at him in silence for a few moments. "Well, it's all quite deliberate, of course. Two reasons for this particular image. First, you're always dealing with people who have old-fashioned ideas about journalists — cynically careless about appearances, knowing their own power and influence they take no pains to impress the outsider, and so forth. Secondly, having to seek information from second- and third-rate academics, who feel they're underpaid, you look as if you're even worse off than they are, so they don't mind doing you a favour. It's good thinking, Mere, but perhaps rather out of date. You might seriously consider building up and then projecting a *Reverse Image,* but this is a mere snap judgment. You might want to consult us properly later on. But let's go and eat."

This was a mistake — as Saltana realized not long afterwards in the crowded dining room. Mere was one of those men who don't eat, who just keep on smoking and drinking and should not to be taken into dining rooms but handed a sandwich in the bar. Having turned a decent helping of Irish stew into an ashtray, he leant forward, knowing his plotter's voice would never be heard if he didn't, and said, "I gather you may be running into trouble at Brockshire."

Saltana nodded. "Tuby's just gone down there and he called me this morning. Didn't think it serious, but he hasn't got around yet. There's something else that might really be serious — rough stuff — but I don't think you mean that. You're talking about Lapford and the Primrose East publicity — eh? Incidentally, Tuby and I weren't even in this country when that ballyhoo started."

"You're being blamed, though, Saltana."

"So — we're being blamed." He didn't offer a shrug because he was busy cutting close to the bone of a chop, but his tone was a kind of shrug. "Who tells you these things, Mere? Got a spy down there?"

"Let's say — a correspondent. And I'm not going to tell you who it is."

"You refused me before I asked. You said you might do a piece on Brockshire, Mere. Why not come down and see for yourself what's happening?"

"Can do. Next week, perhaps. Think you've had all the publicity you need?"

Saltana stared at him. "Come off it. I haven't seen much of this muck, but it's not what we want. Wrong image."

"That's my opinion."

"We'll do the image-changing, Mere. That's our department. But I seem to remember your saying something before about television or radio or both. And for anything there, I'd be grateful."

"Enough to split the fees?" Mere enquired softly.

"For a first chance — yes. And perhaps a commission afterwards. Though I must warn you, we don't care about being television or radio *personalities* — as they call 'em, God help us! We're looking for something quite different."

Mere's cigarette wobbled. "You surprise me, Professor." One eye, already drooping, closed in a slow wink. "I thought you were just a pair of scholars, returning from a long exile."

"Now I really will surprise you, my friend. Because that's just what we are — at heart and where we really live. But never mind about that. What can you get us on the air? And I mean as soon as possible — not next April."

"There are two things I can line up quite soon. I happen to know the producers. One's a radio interview — people-in-the-news kind of thing — about a quarter of an hour or so — just right for Tuby, I'd say. The other's more important — an appearance on a television programme, you may have seen it, *Every Other Day* — very popular, big audience, and all the other producers try to catch it. And that's for you, I'd say. Ever done any television?"

"No. Tuby has — out East. But if you can fix this, Mere, I'll risk making a first appearance. I've watched it here — and I have an idea or two how it ought to be done."

"Don't be too confident. I've been on several times — discussion programmes about education — and it's trickier than it looks, Saltana."

"I wonder. Well, we'll see. You talk to your men, and Tuby and I will try not to let you down. We might even be good. Owen Tuby will, I know."

After O. V. Mere had gone, and Elfreda had arrived from Brockshire with young Mickley, Saltana found a large armchair in the corner of the entrance hall, settled into it with his notebooks, and stared at them for a few minutes before dozing off. He was sharply brought back to consciousness by a woman with a thin beaky face above a black mackintosh that seemed to conceal an incongruous short stout body — a Mrs. Hartz from the secretarial agency. "I've brought a portable in case you haven't a machine," she announced. "Where do we go?"

"Well — up to my bedroom, I suppose."

"Oh — no, you don't."

"I don't what?"

"Even if the agency allowed it, I wouldn't. Oh — no!" Her voice rang with a savage glee. She might have been a policewoman in a totalitarian state.

"I must say, Mrs. Hartz," he observed mildly, "the idea of dalliance — at this hour, here and with you — hadn't entered my mind."

"That proves nothing," she retorted. "I'd trouble last week with a man at least eighty — in a sitting room, too."

Saltana could have done some retorting. Instead, he passed her a notebook and asked her if she could read his writing. After staring darkly at it, as if it might offer her unimaginable obscenities, she announced reluctantly that she might be able to make out what was there. "But I can't start copying here, can I?"

"There's a colleague of mine, a Mrs. Judson Drake, upstairs. I don't know her room number but you can get it from Reception. Explain how we're situated," he ended wearily. He always felt rather weary at this time of day. He added another notebook to the one she already had, then watched her waddling away. He lit a cheroot but soon let it go out. This entrance hall wasn't quiet but it was very warm, and soon it faded like a dream, which was probably what it really was.

This time it was Primrose East, perching on the arm of his chair and tracing his nose with a delicate cold forefinger.

"Don't do that, girl," he growled, shaking his head.

"I've been — madly busy — and you've been here — asleep. Though I must say — you looked sweet. Now — what do we do — darling? Go up — to your room?"

"Certainly not." He felt he might as well do a Mrs. Hartz while he was at it. "Even if the hotel allowed it, I wouldn't. Oh — no! Elfreda's here — they'll give you her room number. Report to her."

"Is that — an order, Professor Saltana?"

"It's an order, Miss East."

"I obey — instantly." She got up. "But later — when I'm off duty — could I come to the bar — and buy you — a lovely large whisky? And tell you about dining with the Birtles tomorrow night?"

It was about half-past ten when Stephanie admitted him into the Hampstead flat she shared with some other girl, the one Saltana had spoken to on the telephone that Sunday night. It was a large room with a wide divan against one wall and a number of big unframed canvases on the other walls, pictures that were mostly white backgrounds with a number of very thin brown or black objects set in front of them. Saltana gave them a glance and then gazed with admiration at Stephanie herself. She was wearing some sort of yellow-and-maroon striped housecoat, very little make-up, and with her hair smoothly drawn backward and her demure dark glance, she looked at once innocent and wicked, a delectable combination.

"The art you see is contributed by my room-mate, who's away tonight. Her boy-friend-in-chief — her magic man — is a painter, and he keeps bringing his stuff here. He's one of these Lancashire geniuses we seem to have far too many of now. I can't bear him. But his work's worth looking at."

"I prefer to look at you, my dear Stephanie." And he told her how she looked.

"I don't have to believe a word you say," she told him, pretending not to be pleased. "I know why you're here — just to ask me what's happening about that enquiry."

"That was in my mind when I telephoned you," said Saltana, a cunning old hand, "but as soon as I saw you, it went clean out of my mind." He took her face gently between his hands and kissed her, without passion at first, just to make her feel at ease with him; and then of course the kisses changed, the housecoat was unzipped, lights were mostly turned off, and the divan was pressed into service.

Some time later, as she purred and nuzzled against him, she said, "I suppose you think it's like this every time I go away with Gerald Grandison."

"I haven't given it a thought, my dear. I've been too busy enjoying myself — and enjoying you enjoying yourself — which is, you must admit, as it should be. I'd forgotten Major Grandison's existence. One thing at a time."

"I don't think that works with us. A woman can't help thinking of several things at a time. Comparing — among them. Gerald Grandison likes to imagine himself a dashing sensualist — having the pretty little secretary, y'know, old boy — whereas in fact he's not at all satisfactory — and I hate to think of all the nights I've spent lying awake in hotel bedrooms. But now with you — you wicked old professor, you — I'm half-asleep now. And it's rather a shame because I'm quite fond of poor old Gerald."

"Well, don't blame him, my dear. It's largely a question of polarity, and that depends again on essential psychological types. That's why this 'good in bed' talk is such damned nonsense. Making love isn't playing billiards."

"I wouldn't know about that, my darling," she murmured. "But don't you want to ask me anything about the enquiry and that American agency?"

"Yes, I do. And I'll tell you why, Stephanie. Owen Tuby, who's already down in Brockshire, phoned me this morning. Now, late last night, when a girl took him home to our Institute building and they were embracing at the front door, a flash bulb went off in their faces. And he thinks — and so do I — that means your American agency have ignored Grandison's favourable report on us, and have now moved in themselves."

"Well, you're right, they have. And I'd have told you even if you hadn't put it to me. Gerald's bloody annoyed about it, but of course he can't do a thing. It's all out of our hands now. A man called Belber is in charge of the enquiry, but he's not working on it himself. He's sent some young American down there — to do the dirty on you — but we don't know his name or even what he looks like. So you'd better behave yourself around that university or you'll be seeing flash bulbs. When you feel like misbehaving, Professor Saltana, you ring up a Mrs. Stephanie Murten, who seems to be the right psychological type with first-class polarity laid on. Kiss me."

A little later, Saltana said, "By the way, who and where is Mr. Murten?"

"He's a stinker. And at present he's running a glass factory in Czechoslovakia, where he's very welcome to stay, as far as I'm concerned. Polarity — nil. And not even any manners. Now it's my turn to ask a question. No — several questions. Do you take that Mrs. Drake to bed?"

"No. Never even thought of it. Though we like each other."

"Short on polarity, I hope. Next — how long are you staying in London and what are you doing the next few days?"

"Until Sunday, probably. And tomorrow night I'm dining with a man called Simon Birtle — some sort of newspaper and magazine tycoon — "

"My God — I'll say he is! Where does he come in?"

Saltana explained about Primrose East while she returned to her housecoat and he began to dress. "I'll telephone you the day after tomorrow, my dear," he said as she brought him a drink.

"I'm a fool if I take the call, but of course I will. Then it'll be more polarity and before I know where I am I'll find myself falling in love with you, when I know dam' well that's not what you want and it's all wrong. We idiot women bounce round town looking so smart and gay when half the time we're all churned up inside, waiting for letters, waiting for telephone calls, waiting for love — real love, trusting love, secure love — "

He put down his drink, took her gently in his arms, and she cried a little. "Say something," she said finally. "Just something — anything worth remembering — "

"It's true I hoped to get some information out of you, Stephanie my dear. But I wouldn't have come here so late if you hadn't attracted me from the first, and I wouldn't have made love to you at all, however ravishing you were looking, if I hadn't been genuinely fond of you as a person. And that's saying something, because I'm not easy to please. I'm a rather cantankerous old devil — battered, almost broke, and years too old for you, my dear Stephanie — "

"Don't be silly — no, you're not being silly, I take that back. Now don't forget to ring me — when is it? — Friday morning. I don't care if we meet and just talk. You can still be nicely polarized if you're only talking, can't you?"

"Certainly," said Saltana, and not long afterwards kissed her goodnight. In the taxi, he reflected again how different the sexes were in their relation to appearance and reality. A woman's persona — as for example Stephanie's suggestion of exotic sophistication, of experience enamelled and varnished — disappeared with her clothes, leaving her naked not only in body but also in an essential femininity. But men, appearing comparatively so much alike, removed their dull garments and then might reveal themselves as ardent and tender lovers, stammering and ineffectual idiots, bullies and brutes — and even monsters. This meant that women in these early sexual encounters were offered more excitement — but what a gamble, what a risk!

He arrived about eight o'clock, the following evening, to dine with the Birtles, who had a large house in Mayfair, close to Park Lane, complete with a butler. Primrose took charge of him in the long stately drawing room, where half a dozen people were drinking cocktails. Birtle himself wasn't there, and Saltana soon realized to his annoyance, for he was hungry, that this was going to be one of those dinner parties, not uncommon in Latin America, at which you arrive at eight and are lucky if you are sitting down to eat by nine-thirty. Primrose presented him impressively to Mrs. Birtle, plump, soft-voiced, motherly, rather like a farmer's wife in a children's story about barnyard animals. She told him at once she was so glad that Primrose was happy working for him.

"If you're glad, then so am I, Mrs. Birtle. But you realize she's hardly begun yet." He accepted a large martini and then took almost a handful of nuts, to nourish himself through the long wait.

"She's *so* enthusiastic about you, Professor Saltana," she continued, smiling. "She seems to have what we used to call a *crush* on you. We tease her about it."

"She'll soon get over it, when being ordered about's no longer a delicious novelty."

"Oh — I'm so relieved to hear you say that. We couldn't help wondering — naturally. And we were hoping you didn't take her seriously. I know there's been a lot of stupid gossip about my husband's interest in Primrose, but it's all quite simple really. You see, we had a daughter, Diana, who was about her age, and we lost her — in a terrible motor accident. And when we began to see photographs of Primrose everywhere, we thought she looked so like our poor dear Diana — sometimes it was really quite striking — I often felt dreadfully upset — you can imagine how a mother would feel, Professor Saltana. So in the end you might say we almost adopted her. Oh dear — more people. You must excuse me — "

"I thought, darling," said Primrose, arriving with what appeared to be a goblet, "you ought to have— a lovely large whisky — here — "

"Thank you, my dear, though I've already had two socking great martinis. Still — as you've brought it — thank you."

Primrose gave his arm a delicate little squeeze and gazed at him fondly. She was faraway again. "Darling — you'll be sitting next to Gladys — that's Mrs. Birtle — at dinner — so you could just hint — at images and things — couldn't you?"

"Not if you bring me any more whisky, girl. Take it easy until we've been given something substantial to eat."

Primrose took Saltana back to Mrs. Birtle, who appeared to be in the coils of a woman who might have been hurriedly sketched by Toulouse Lautrec.

"Betty Riser," Primrose hissed. "Bitchiest columnist in London."

"Never heard of her," Saltana muttered.

"Oh God — I adore you," Primrose replied, turning her hiss into a whisper. "Betty, this is Professor Saltana, my Director — at the *Institute of Social Imagistics* — at Brockshire."

"I know, Primrose dear," said Betty Riser. "I saw a teeny-weeny story about it somewhere. When do you expect to make my column, Professor?"

"Any time now."

"Oh, you do, do you?"

"Yes. Where does it appear?"

"Don't you know, Professor?" Mrs. Birtle began, trying to be helpful.

"Of course he does," cried Betty Riser angrily. "He's just being bloody rude, that's all."

"I'm not, you know. I don't read many newspapers. And when I intend to be rude, I'm much ruder than that. I'm really downright offensive. I'm quite capable of telling people I've just met that they're being bloody rude." He looked hard at her — wondering why she thought so much green round her eyes improved her appearance — but he hadn't raised his voice and had kept a mild, even tone. He'd known for years that unpleasant things said in a pleasant voice leave most people feeling baffled. It is to the angry tone that they respond with even more anger.

Betty Riser gave a glance at Mrs. Birtle, who was looking bewildered, then one at Primrose, who was contriving to appear demurely unconcerned. She hesitated a moment. "I think this image thing of yours could be rather a racket. Couldn't it?"

"Certainly."

"Oh — you admit it, do you?"

"I admit it *could* be a racket, I didn't say it *was* one, Miss Riser."

"That's not good enough for my column. Make it one thing or the other — and I'll quote you, Professor."

"Better try this — have you a good memory, Miss Riser?"

"I'm famous — or notorious — for it — "

"Then try this. *I told Professor Saltana that I thought his Social Imagistics could be rather a racket. He replied that it could be but that in fact it wasn't, as a good many people might soon discover for themselves.* Any use to you, Miss Riser?"

"Might be — yes. But tell me — for background — what have you been doing mostly for — oh — say, the last twenty years?"

"Mostly teaching philosophy in various Latin American universities."

"Why — for God's sake?"

"Why not? Sunshine. Odd amusing people. I enjoy speaking Spanish."

"But you came back — why?"

"Time for a change. And I had a few ideas that might work here and not there. And if all that's any use to you, Miss Riser, then print it. If it isn't, then don't. Just as you please."

"And you can add — that I adore him," said Primrose.

"Now, Primrose dear," Mrs. Birtle began. "Oh — Simon's here — at last."

Simon Birtle was a shortish plump man in his later fifties. He had a round face with rather small features and a browny-yellow complexion so that he suggested a worried and somewhat bad-tempered mandarin. He didn't drink, his wife explained hastily to Saltana before introducing them, so that they would go into dinner immediately. Which they did, and Saltana found himself sitting on Mrs. Birtle's right, at the end of a long and narrow dining table, opulently appointed. As there were about a dozen people there, Saltana seemed well out of earshot of his host, much to his relief, for there were things he wanted to say to Mrs. Birtle without being overheard. And fortunately she seemed anxious to talk to him, as if Primrose had persuaded her he was some new kind of wise man.

"I hope you won't mind me talking about my husband, Professor Saltana."

"Certainly not, Mrs. Birtle." He was attending to some excellent smoked trout. In doing this he happened to catch the eye of his other neighbour, Miss Primrose East, who gave him a lightning wink and then deliberately turned away, thus leaving him free to exchange confidences with Mrs. Birtle.

"I've been married to Simon Birtle nearly thirty years, and nobody knows him better than I do. And it worries and grieves me — the way people misunderstand him. Take the people who come here, people who work for him. I can see they're not really enjoying themselves, though he wants them to. You see, Professor Saltana, they're afraid of him. And that's all wrong. I ought to know, and I say he's a kind man and a generous man. I know for a fact he pays them more than they'd get anywhere else — half as much again, he says."

Saltana drank some Chablis, then nodded at his hostess. "That's one reason why they're afraid of him, Mrs. Birtle. He pays them too much."

"Now I can't have that," she began, rather indignantly.

"Please let me explain. People live up to their incomes these days. They can't help it. Now suppose your husband pays a man seven thousand a year when his market value is round about four thousand. He and his wife and family are geared to seven thousand. Therefore he's terrified of losing his job and equally terrified of his employer. His relations with them would be easier and pleasanter if he paid them less."

The butler gave Mrs. Birtle some sort of mineral water and then asked Saltana if he would take claret. Saltana said he would but proceeded to finish his Chablis, which was good. For non-drinkers the Birtles — or perhaps their butler — were admirably attentive to the needs of their guests. After two large martinis, Primrose's goblet of whisky, and now these wines, Saltana felt he would have to keep an eye on himself. He had an idea that already he was speaking with that precision which belongs to foreigners and the educated English who are not quite sober.

Mrs. Birtle had been giving his observations some thought. "I see what you mean, Professor, though I'm sure Simon does it all out of kindness and generosity. He doesn't *want* people to be afraid of him. It worries him nearly as much as it worries me. He's often mentioned it."

Saltana swallowed some roast beef, then tried the claret. "Mrs. Birtle, I'm concerned in my work with the choice and projection of suitable images — "

"That's what Primrose tells us — though I must say I don't really understand it — and I'm not sure she does — "

"She soon will. She's hardly begun yet. But the truth is, if you don't mind my saying so, Mr. Birtle has chosen — and is still busy projecting — quite the wrong image. I'm not blaming him. He might be said to have inherited the image with his career. It's the Napoleonic image of the newspaper proprietor. Harmsworth began it and probably took the title of Northcliffe so that he could use the Napoleonic initial — N. This tradition has been closely followed, and your husband is one of the latest victims of it. This image demands a dictatorial style, an overbearing manner, policies really based on sudden whims, wild alternations of parsimony and generosity, of camaraderie and savage tyranny, roars and insults on Monday and cheek-pinchings on Tuesday — the whole Napoleonic outfit. It's no longer a good image, from any point of view, and your husband should not only change it but completely reverse it." He hastily finished his wine and then added artfully, before she was ready to speak: "And this is where you come in, Mrs. Birtle."

We are always ready to come in, and motherly Mrs. Birtle was no exception. "I don't see what I have to do with it, Professor Saltana. I'm just a nobody as far as Simon's work is concerned. Still, if you say so, I'm curious to know just where I come in. So please tell me."

"Certainly." But he waited until one of the two parlour maids had cleared his plate and the butler had refilled his glass. "Women who are good wives have an instinctive and often quite brilliant ability to correct or balance their husbands' chosen images. This faculty is so remarkable that if I were consulted by a happily married man about his image — and I hope to be working in this field shortly — I wouldn't bother about his wife's image, knowing that she would attend to it herself, consciously or unconsciously. Now the image you project at the moment is perfectly adjusted to correct your husband's. You are quiet, soft-voiced, kindly, concerned, motherly — "

"Well, thank you very much, Professor. If that's what I am, that's just what I want to be — just that and nothing else." She smiled at him and he did his best — and not too boozy a best, he hoped — to return her smile in a gravely professional manner.

"But when you say *just that,* you make my point for me, my dear Mrs. Birtle. It suggests you don't really think it's enough, that something in you, important to you, escapes the image, that you might not always want to be so quiet, that sometimes you might like to raise your voice, turn off your sympathy, suddenly stop feeling maternal. So that if your husband changed his image, almost reversed it, then your own image, balancing his, might be closer to what you really feel about yourself, a great gain."

She offered him one of those deprecating laughs that are always false. "Professor Saltana, you're a clever man. And it's all much too clever for me."

He looked hard at her. "Are you sure, Mrs. Birtle?" he enquired softly.

She returned his look for a moment or two without speaking. Then she said, "No, I'm not," and gave him a tiny sketch of a smile before turning to her other neighbour.

When Mrs. Birtle had taken the women away, the men moved up to be near their host, who seemed to be in his camaraderie mood, ready — like royalty — to laugh heartily. His four editors, if that is what they were, gave a performance of enjoying themselves like actors on the first night of an under-rehearsed play. Saltana lit the magnificent Havana he'd been offered and settled down behind it to listen and not to talk. But after a good deal of facetious Fleet Street stuff, he was compelled to say something.

"George," said Birtle, using his cigar as a pointer, "why don't you ask Professor Saltana to do a piece for you on his new Institute — images and all that?"

"Glad to, Chief." George, a worried anteater, turned to Saltana. "Fifteen hundred words — perhaps a bit more if it's really up our street."

"What's your street?"

"*The New Woman* — now over two million. Marvellous chance — publicity-wise!"

Saltana shook his head. "Sorry! Not right for us. At least — not yet."

Birtle stared at him, frowning. "I don't see why you should say that, Saltana. You're new around here. We understand this kind of thing."

"I know you do. But you don't understand *my* kind of thing, which is as new around here as I am." Saltana felt he was being rather too sharp. "Sorry again! And thanks for suggesting it."

Much later, in the drawing room, after Saltana had talked to various people and was two-thirds of the way down another goblet that Primrose had brought him, and when indeed he was thinking of leaving, Birtle got him into a corner. "My wife's just had a quick word with me, Saltana. Were you serious or just making conversation?"

"Both. But she wanted to talk about you. So she did, and then I did."

"Something about me having the wrong image, wasn't it?"

"It was. If she has a good memory — and I'll bet she has — then ask her to repeat what I told her. But if she hasn't, then forget it."

"But I want to know. Damn it, man — you were talking about *me*."

"If my hostess chooses a topic, I don't like to dismiss it — "

"You're hedging. Now — look here — is it true you think I'm putting out the wrong image of myself? Give me a plain answer."

"Certainly. That's what I said. That's what I believe. But that's as far as I'm going, at present. We're only just beginning at the Institute. If you like, I'll let you know when I'm ready to be consulted professionally — "

"You're not serious — "

"Certainly I am."

Birtle stared at him, and Saltana noticed for the first time Birtle's eyes — rather small, reddish-brown, almost hot out of an oven. "This may be all very well for young Primrose or even my wife — and lots of other women, for all I know — but I don't think I'm ready to take you seriously, Saltana."

"It's you who should. It's not necessary for them. But if you're happy about the effect you have upon other people, the particular image you project, then of course forget everything I've said. No, no — that's all, now. Except I must thank you for an excellent dinner and an entertaining evening. And now I must thank Mrs. Birtle. Goodnight!"

After going down to the other end of the room, Saltana had to wait for a few moments while one of the editors explained to Mrs. Birtle that he must now rush back to his office. Then, as soon as they were alone, Mrs. Birtle said anxiously, "I saw you talking to him, Professor Saltana. What did he say to you?"

"I imagine he'll tell you, Mrs. Birtle. He's not ready to take me seriously yet. But I've told him I wasn't ready for him yet — that is, if he wanted to consult me professionally."

"He wasn't — well, angry with you — was he?"

"Not quite. I didn't give him time. But I much preferred our talk, Mrs. Birtle. And I do thank you for having me here tonight — "

"You must come again, Professor Saltana."

"I'd enjoy that, but I may not be in London again for some time. I must go down to Brockshire, probably on Sunday."

"Me too." This was Primrose, now at his elbow.

It was she who led him out, and when they were in the hall, but before he'd been given his hat and overcoat, she gave him a little kiss on the cheek and, with her lips still close to his ear, she said, "If you're in the mood — we could nip up to my room — without anybody knowing — "

"My dear Primrose, the more you talk like that, the older you make me feel, so that the gap between us widens."

"Well, at least — and your hat and coat are here — let me run you — back to terrible old Robinson's. Please — *please!* My car's just outside."

She talked, presumably about the evening, all the way to the hotel, but he couldn't hear what she was saying, and anyhow he was beginning to feel very sleepy.


## 3


After he had spoken on the telephone to Cosmo Saltana, on Wednesday morning, and a cold rainy morning too, Tuby wasn't sure what he ought to do next. He tried smoking a pipe over *The Times,* which was offering a sound balanced view of things that were obviously unsound and at least half-barmy; but his conscience troubled him, so he sought out Alfred.

"Alfred, I'm going along to the university and I shan't come back to lunch. So please tell Florrie. But I'll be in for dinner — just a chop and a bit of cheese or something, tell her."

Even though it made less work for him, Alfred didn't think much of this style of living. "Tomorrow, Doctor — or next day — perhaps you give big nize dinner for friends maybe," he said hopefully.

"I doubt it, Alfred. But perhaps for one friend — some lady." After all, there was Lois Terry, there was Hazel Honeyfield. "We'll see."

"Is telephone. I answer." And Alfred hurried away.

Following him slowly, Tuby was just in time to be handed the receiver. "Is student. He speak for you."

"Dr. Tuby here. You want to speak to me?"

"Yeah. Jeff Convoy. National Confederation of Students. Brockshire representative." He spoke in a low mysterious tone and was not easy to hear. "Must talk to you soon as possible, Dr. Tuby. How about a coffee in the Junior Refectory at eleven sharp this morning? Urgent. Got a car?"

"No car. I'd walk but it seems to be raining hard — "

"Bus stops outside your gate at 10:25. Gives you plenty of time to get to Junior Refectory by eleven. Dark blue cardigan and yellow scarf. Can't miss me. Jeff Convoy. Very urgent you get the picture, Dr. Tuby. Can't explain over the phone. 'Bye!"

Even his telephone manner suggested a conspiratorial type, and as soon as they shared a table and some uncommonly bad coffee, in an otherwise empty corner of the big Refectory, Tuby realized that Jeff Convoy was nothing if not a conspirator, one who had probably stood up in his playpen and asked for his box of bricks in a whispered aside. He was a thin serpentine youth with narrow eyes and a lop-sided face. He smoked a cigarette as if every puff was a signal agreed upon by a secret society.

"Want you to understand this, Dr. Tuby. We're with you. Ten to one the N.U.S. will be too. But the N.C.S. is definitely with you. Strong resolution — no bloody beating about the bush — passed at a meeting last night. If what happens is what I think'll happen, we take direct action on your behalf." He glanced around and then stared hard at two waitresses, ten yards away, as if they might be pointing a special mike. "So keep in touch. They'll have to move soon. Then give me the word — and — *bingo!*"

He waited, obviously expecting an enthusiastic response, and Tuby felt genuinely sorry to disappoint him. "I'm glad you're with us, Jeff. That's fine. But I must also tell you I don't really know what you're talking about."

Jeff looked around, leant forward and let his cigarette fall into his coffee cup, and then went into that emphatic mutter peculiar to conspiratorial types. "There's a definite movement to get you out. The latest is they're going to bring in the Academic Advisory Board, who'll tell 'em what they want to hear — that your Institute and this Drake Foundation don't meet the requirements — blah — blah — blah! Now I've got two of our fellows working on this. For instance, was the Academic Advisory Board asked to approve Cally's appointment? Or Brigham's — or Milfield's? If not, why is it suddenly starting to operate now?" And he looked as if he were suffering from an acute neuralgia, but this, Tuby realized, was his special cunning look. "Let them try that one and we'll show it up for what it is — bullshit. We're solidly behind you. The minute they say you have to go, we'll say you're staying. If they don't want you, we do. And we're entitled to have a say in the way this place is run. We fought that battle — and won it — term before last, on not having exams decide everything. Jayjay had to climb down. Well, some of us have been looking for another issue to demonstrate student solidarity — and we think you're it."

"Well, thank you, Jeff — though I'm not sure we want to be *it*. Anyhow, the Director of the Institute, Professor Saltana, won't be back here until the end of the week. In the meantime, Jeff, there's something important you and your fellows could do for us. Do you happen to have noticed an American around here?" And he asked this very quietly, almost out of the corner of his mouth.

"Ah — you're on to that, are you? Well, as it happens I haven't seen him myself, but one or two of our chaps have. Fattish type — but young — crewcut and big specs. Asking questions. Says he's writing a British Redbrick piece for an American mag. Carries a camera. Why? Are you on to anything there, Dr. Tuby?"

As this was obviously meat-and-drink to Jeff, Tuby felt that the least he could do was to spread a generous feast. He went straight into the complete conspiratorial manner — first, a look round, then eyes narrowed, a leaning forward, the emphatic mutter — hard to do for a novice but not impossible. "Jeff, if he's the man I think he is, he exploded a flash bulb almost in my face, late last night. And Professor Saltana and I — though Saltana's now looking into it in London — believe it's about ten to one this fellow's an enquiry agent — an American private eye — who's here to get something on Mrs. Drake and the Institute. The Americans are dead against Mrs. Drake running this Foundation."

"Christ — so that's it, is it?" Jeff was so happy he nearly raised his voice. "An American agent — eh? Think he's working with the Establishment here?"

"Not yet, I imagine. But he soon might be, once he knows how things are here."

"At the drop of a hat, I'd say. Now how do you suggest we play this?"

"Very, *very* quietly." Tuby put on what he hoped was a cunning look. "No public protests. No complaining to Jayjay. No making an issue out of it. In fact, Jeff, I suggest you don't repeat a single word of what I've told you. Can you keep a secret?"

"Can I? It's the only thing I *can* keep. All I'll say — just to two or three of our chaps — no girls; he's probably screwing several of them already — is that I've discovered that this American's some kind of agent and we don't want him nosing around here with his camera and he could have a few little accidents — " and he repeated this very slowly — "just — a — few — little — accidents. And thanks for telling me."

Tuby took his time leaving the Refectory, then trudged through the rain and mud across to the two huts allotted to the social sciences, well aware that at the end of one of them he would find Cally's office. But he didn't find Cally himself. There was a thin girl, wearing a dingy sweater, typing away and giving the impression that this wasn't the life she'd planned for herself.

"Good morning! Do you happen to know where Professor Cally is?"

The girl stopped typing for a moment but didn't look at him. "No I don't."

It couldn't be easy, Tuby reflected, to make typing sound bad-tempered, but this girl could do it — perhaps her one accomplishment. He went to the door that had Cally's notices pinned on it, the door behind which Cally kept his assistants and the coffee, and he listened for a moment or two. Somebody was lecturing in there. Hazel Honeyfield? No such luck, he concluded.

He tried the girl again, going near her to be heard above the clatter. "Who's lecturing in there — do you know?"

"Dr. Pawson."

"Thank you!" Determined now not to acknowledge utter defeat, he pulled out a chair, sat down and stared hard at her. Finally she had to meet it and stop her typing.

"What is it this time?" she demanded crossly.

Tuby offered her one of his best smiles, a winner for at least thirty years. "I do apologize for interrupting your work," he began, in the tone, another winner, that went with the smile. "I'm Dr. Tuby — *Institute of Social Imagistics.* Just two more questions I'd like to ask. First, we're in urgent need of secretarial help over there, otherwise we can't give Professor Cally copies of our proposed courses. Do you know if the university has allotted a secretary to us?"

"No, I don't. But I'd say — you haven't a hope. What else?"

"This second question's rather more personal. Why do you appear to be so bad-tempered? I'm simply curious. I'm not trying to be offensive."

"Oh — very well, if you must have it. In the first place, I don't think I ought to be here, copying this sociology stuff, when I've work of my own to catch up with. In the second place, it's raining and I've a cold coming on. And in the third and last place — anyhow, I'm fed up to the bloody teeth."

"I get the impression there are lots of youngish people like you — fed up to their bloody teeth. What's the explanation?"

"The climate's getting worse — damper and drearier all the time — and there are too many of us, all getting in each other's way or queueing up for some sort of muck. My old grandfather lives with us at home — not here, near Bristol — and to hear him talk about what it was like when he was my age — he's over eighty now — you'd think the sun was always shining then, and there were never too many people, and you could eat your head off for about ninepence. Oh — yes, he's piling it on, and forgetting the bad days, but he can't be lying all the time, can he? And what the hell am I going to be telling the kids when *I'm* eighty?"

"You can tell them you had names then and not just numbers, and that sometimes you could do more or less what you liked. Where do I find Mr. Rittenden, the Registrar?"

"He's moved into a temporary office in the Library Building — ground floor. And you needn't apologize again for interrupting me. Did me good. 'Byebye!"

The last time Tuby had seen Rittenden, that Sunday night at the Lapfords' when the students were demonstrating, he had seemed nervous indeed, almost shaking with anxiety; but even now in his office, with no students within sight or hearing, he was far from appearing calm and collected. He suggested an agitated ecclesiastic. Clearly he didn't want to see Tuby, but, on the other hand, didn't feel equal to *not* seeing him. He achieved a miserable kind of compromise by fussing with papers on his desk and picking up pens and pencils and putting them down again — a hard-pressed administrator.

"Now, Mr. Rittenden, what's happening?" Tuby enquired, quite pleasantly.

"You're referring, I take it, to your Institute and the Judson Drake Foundation, Dr. Tuby, and their relation — um-um-um — to the University of Brockshire — "

"Yes, of course. When Professor Saltana and I went away, three weeks ago, everything appeared to be settled, so that Mrs. Drake, accepting a suggestion by Mrs. Lapford, agreed to rent a furnished house here. And indeed we went away so that she could put the house in order for our Institute. Now I've just come back and already I'm hearing some astonishing rumours."

"Well, it's really a question — um-um-um — of the Academic Advisory Board. I admit we've been a little lax there — chiefly owing to the fact that we weren't creating a new university, like York, Sussex, Warwick, and the rest, but were giving a long-established college of advanced technology the newly acquired — um-um-um — status of a university. But the fact remains that our Academic Advisory Board can demand to be consulted. And this is what has happened — um-um-um — in your particular case, Dr. Tuby. The result, I'm afraid, of some unfortunate publicity. Not your doing, I hasten to add, but equally not ours. Indeed, Miss Plucknett, who's in charge of our public relations, was one of the first to complain to the Vice-Chancellor — "

"I'll bet she was — "

"And then unfortunately we had a strong protest directly from a member of our Academic Advisory Board — Sir Leopold Namp."

"Who's he?"

In his reply Rittenden seemed to borrow, by an astral process, some of the amplitude and grandeur of Sir Leopold; he appeared to be larger and weightier; his voice deepened; and he regarded Tuby with something like contempt. "Sir Leopold is one of the most prominent industrialists in this part of the world. He was a generous patron of the old college, and he's been equally — if not even more — generous — um-um-um — to the university." Somewhere about that *um-um-um* Rittenden was switched off from Sir Leopold and began to look frightened again.

"And who else is on your Board?" Tuby asked idly.

"Two other industrialists in addition to Sir Leopold. The present Chief Education Officer of Brockshire — Jayjay's successor. An H.M.I. And somebody nominated by Oxford. I admit they haven't met for some time — um-um-um — but now Sir Leopold — for one, I know — is insisting upon a meeting as early as possible — in view, of course, of these recent developments."

"And what will they do then — shoot us?"

Stung by the despairing envy of the fearful for the bold and careless, Rittenden managed to look and sound disapproving. "Frankly, Dr. Tuby, I don't think that if I were in your place — um-um-um — I'd take this matter so lightly."

"I'm a frivolous character, Mr. Rittenden. Oh — hello, Dr. Stample!" He had met the University Librarian at the Lapfords' Sunday night party.

"Back again, Dr. Tuby — eh? No, don't go. I'm sure you'll be interested in this." Stample was almost bursting with excitement and importance. "Registrar, it's all arranged. I can be ready by the first Monday in December. And the noble lady has definitely agreed to perform the opening the next day — the first Tuesday in December. All arranged. Isn't that jolly good?"

"It's jolly good indeed, Stample. Jolly, *jolly* good!" Rittenden was genuinely enthusiastic. There was nothing here, so far, to frighten him.

Stample turned to Tuby. "Sorry, old man! Must be wondering what all the excitement's about. Well, what it amounts to *is* — on the first Tuesday in December the Library will be officially opened by the Duchess of Brockshire."

"The Duchess of Brockshire," Tuby repeated slowly.

"That's the noble lady. Her husband, the Duke, is our Chancellor."

"Is there a *Who's Who* here? Oh — there, behind you, isn't it, Mr. Rittenden? Mind if I consult it for a moment?" And Tuby, as he grasped and then opened the fat volume, began asking himself if he hadn't had too much Brockshire and so got on to the wrong track and would soon find it was some other duke she had married. Only one line mattered and then his finger found it: *m. 1947 Petronella, y.d. Rev. Herold Corby.*

And as he restored the volume to its shelf he found it impossible not to laugh.

The other two were so curious that they hadn't exchanged a word. Stample got in first. "Found something amusing there, Dr. Tuby?"

But he had stopped laughing. "Damn! I never noticed where she lived — "

"Are you talking about the Duchess of Brockshire?" cried Stample.

"Yes. She's an old friend. Knew her very well before she was married, and if she's coming here I ought to write to her."

Purposeful and rapid for once, Rittenden wrote in a notebook, tore off the page, and handed it over. "Address and telephone number," he announced. "Their place is only about thirty miles away."

"One of our five-bob stately homes," Stample said cheerfully. "I don't know if you're through here, Dr. Tuby — "

"I am — yes. So I'll leave you." He looked from one to the other of them. "I can find a drink and lunch of sorts up in the Senior Refectory, can I? Good!"

It was still rather early and there weren't many people up there, just one group standing at the bar and another and larger group already lunching together and talking hard. He didn't recognize anybody but he got the impression that he'd been recognized — with perhaps some whispering and nudging. But this might be the morbid product — and he'd known it before — of a sense of alienation. As he took a whisky to a small table near a window, still dark with rain, he thought how this particular atmosphere, even if it was only imagined, could soon begin to cut him down, shrivel and defeat him. He needed sympathy in which to expand and become more himself, unlike Cosmo Saltana who could thrive, grow, harden, and gain force just by facing hostility. He ate some ham croquettes, mashed potatoes, and cabbage that might have been prepared by a frogman fifty fathoms down, and some kind of steamed pudding he'd been warning himself against for years. Then, when he lit a pipe over coffee, he began to consider and sort out, in all their ripeness, his memories of Petronella Corby, now Duchess of Brockshire and pledged to open their Library on the first Tuesday in December. Should he telephone or write to her? But after all this publicity they complained about, she ought to know by this time he was here. And if she did, then why no enquiry, no message? Surely to God she hadn't turned into a *real duchess* (whatever that meant, because after all he'd never met one), a stuffed performer of ceremonies, an armour-plated opener of libraries, a choky-voiced we-have-met-heah-today type — not Petronella! But he couldn't escape the feeling it could have happened. Too much rain, too many people!

However, once he was outside, the rain had almost stopped and there were vague suggestions that a sun might be shining somewhere. He took the bus into Tarbury, to buy a paperback or two and perhaps a rich mixture as a change from the Irish cut plug he'd been smoking. But the Irony Department was ahead of him there, Wednesday being the half-day when Tarbury closed its shops. The afternoon was fine now and had indeed a rather sinister glitter after the rain, so he walked back to the house — no, the Institute — busy not so much with his thoughts as with his chances, not good, of avoiding being splashed by passing cars. The Institute seemed even larger and emptier than it had done when he left it. He felt like a man who had promised to look after a sick white elephant.

Up in his room, he took out his notes for lectures to students at the Institute, but he felt at once he could do no more work on them because — and it came in a flash — there never would be any students. This was entirely an irrational conclusion — after all, Saltana didn't even know yet what was happening — but Tuby often acted upon these intuitive flashes. He pretended to think, though he knew very well his mind didn't work that way, being essentially intuitive and so either leaping forward or not moving at all; and then after a time he didn't even pretend to think but simply enjoyed the extraordinary sunset, one of those that occasionally arrive in an English November like good news from another planet. It was as if a painter of genius was at work outside the window with pale gold, deep touches of the palest purest blue, and masses of a dark maroon turning to indigo. He was still watching it fade out when Florrie came with a trolley of tea and buttered toast. He hadn't set eyes on either her or Alfred; how they knew he was in and ready for tea, he couldn't imagine; but why question another miracle after the sunset?

"Nay, yer want light on in here, Dr. Tuby — Ah say, yer want light on, don't yer?" she cried, an instant challenge to the miraculous.

A minute or two later, he pointed to the small television set and said, "Florrie, how do I work this thing?"

"Ah can tell yer that 'cos it's just like one Mrs. Drake got for Alfred and me." Then, after showing him the various switches and adjustments, she went on: "But yer'll get nowt now but kids' programmes. An' yer don't want them, do yer? Ah say, yer don't want them."

He hastily replied that he didn't but might want to look at something later.

"Alfred's mad on Westerns. Can't keep him off 'em. *Bang-bang-bang!* All alike — *bang-bang-bang!*"

After tea, he went into the big room and played the piano for half an hour or so. When he stopped he found Alfred was there, nodding and smiling in admiration. "Is very good, very nize," Alfred told him. "Is deener olright half-past seven for you, Doctor? Me an' Florrie go to see feelm in Tarbury. Is okay?"

Back in Elfreda's room, he stared at the telephone and wondered if he ought to ring up Saltana, to tell him all he'd learnt during the morn-

ing, then decided he didn't know enough yet. Next he wondered if he
ought to ring up *somebody*, almost anybody would do, but couldn't bring
himself to choose a number. All this time, of course, the telephone itself,
which if he'd been busy would have been clamouring for his attention,
remained obstinately silent. Apparently nobody wanted to have a word
with him. Let Tuby moulder and rot in his idiot mansion, they were telling one another. This challenged his manhood. He went upstairs and
worked on some image notes until dinner; then, after chop, cheese, and
whisky, stayed below, worked for another hour, switched on the TV
news, and then tried a play about a rather nice girl, an imbecile of a
young man, and various relatives of theirs who seemed to have been collected from old farces. Before the play ended he fell asleep, and when he
woke up he was being talked to straight from the shoulder by one of
those no-nonsense-old-chap parsons. He switched the thing off and went
to bed.

He spent most of Thursday morning not ringing anybody up, which
can take time if you bring a confused mind to it. After that, as the rain
seemed to be holding off, he walked into Tarbury, bought a few things,
resisted the temptation of lunching in The Bell, and contented himself
with a drink and a couple of sandwiches at a pub down a side street. He
went out by bus to the university, determined to put a few questions to
Jayjay before talking to Saltana but was told by Mrs. Dobb, the secretary,
that the Vice-Chancellor was still away. So he peevishly picked his way
across to Cally's office, that miserable third of a miserable hut. It was
empty. Not even that complaining typist this time. The room next door,
where Dr. Pawson had been lecturing the previous morning, was empty
too. Sociology had vanished from the University of Brockshire. Tuby took
from Cally's shelves a large volume entitled *Functional Analysis of
Groups,* then sat down on a damnably uncomfortable chair to smoke his
pipe at it and to wait until somebody came. It was after four and he had
just had to switch on the lights when Cally came bustling in, carrying
books, files, God knows what.

"Oh — it's you, Dr. Tuby," Cally shouted. And Tuby remembered
just in time that Cally always shouted, so that he needn't reply at the top
of his voice.

"Yes, Professor Cally," he said quite softly. "How *are* you?"

"I'm well, I'm well." Cally was now doing a fussy disposing act with
his books, files, whatnot. He was trying to hide his embarrassment,
Tuby felt.

"And what have you been up to while we've been away?" Tuby enquired softly, in a kind of Head-of-Secret-Police role.

"Oh — carrying on, just carrying on." Cally was faking his disposing now, putting a book in one place and then trying another. "There's
plenty to do when you have an understaffed department, Dr. Tuby, with
field work into the bargain."

"While we were away, Saltana and I spent a lot of time working out possible courses — lectures and seminars — for students who wanted to come to the Institute. We were, of course, proposing to discuss them with you. But now I'm wondering if we were wasting our time."

It was no use; Cally had to abandon disposal and face his visitor, who was still smiling sleepily at him. And in order to do this, Cally had to be angry. "You're wanting a straight answer to a straight question, are you, Dr. Tuby?" It was a super-shout — had to be, of course. "Well, I know a lot more than I did when you were here before. I know that you and Saltana have high academic qualifications in your own fields, but that you've none whatever — absolutely none whatever — in the field of the social sciences. And when I found that out, of course I had to report it to the Vice-Chancellor. And at the very same time — and this had nothing whatever to do with me, Dr. Tuby — the Vice-Chancellor received a complaint from the Academic Advisory Board, which had been giving him a free hand to make his own appointments but now felt a line had to be drawn — yes, a line had to be drawn. Have you spoken to the Vice-Chancellor yet?"

"No, he's away. I'm waiting to talk to him before I phone Saltana in London to tell him what's happening. Probably I needn't tell you that Saltana's very different from me, Cally. I'm soft and easy, almost a poached egg, whereas Saltana's a hard and aggressive type, a good friend but a ruthless and terrible enemy. He's told me stories," Tuby continued with relish, "that have made my blood run cold. I shall keep away when he talks to you and Jayjay — that is, if he finds he has to. I'm quite different. I'll merely offer a mild protest. Before too many lines are drawn about appointments, I must ask you to remember, Cally, that Saltana and I have never been appointed to anything here, that we don't cost the university a penny, that we're giving you something, you aren't giving us anything."

"We would be," Cally shouted — and manfully, Tuby felt, respecting him for it. "Oh — yes. We'd be giving you students, lads and lasses who come here to learn, to be duly qualified, to work for a degree. And if I sent them over to your *Institute of Social Imagistics,* whatever that may be, I'd be failing in my plain duty as head of this Department. What are your qualifications for teaching them — in this subject, I mean, of course? As far as I can discover — they're nil."

"Are you sure, Cally? I'm thinking now in terms of knowledge and ability, not about certificates and other pieces of paper."

"They come here for certificates and other pieces of paper, man — "

"A good point, Cally. But I'll tell you what I'm ready to do," Tuby continued, smiling. "We commandeer the biggest room in the place, one evening, and invite an audience. You lecture for half an hour on any aspect of sociology you prefer. I lecture for the next half-hour on the very same subject. Then the audience can decide who'd be cheating the students out of their time."

"A university can't be run on those lines, as you know very well, Dr. Tuby. I refer you to the Vice-Chancellor. I've done my part." Cally looked at his watch and, as if by magic, Dr. Hazel Honeyfield, in a red coat and all rosy and smiling, came tripping in. "Hazel, I must be away now. You've not forgotten we're expecting you this evening? Seven-fifteen, as near as you can make it." And then he was gone.

"My dear Hazel," cried Tuby, going to take her hands in his, "I've been thinking about you all the time I've been away. And you're even more delicious than I remembered." He gave her a little kiss.

"Oh — Dr. Tuby — "

"Owen — Owen, Hazel — "

"Owen — is it true they're going to turn you out?"

"Turn us out? How can they turn us out when we're not in? We're occupying a house rented by Mrs. Drake on behalf of the Judson Drake Foundation. This university doesn't give us a sausage. Forget it, my dear. What are you doing these days?"

"A rather sweet little enquiry at Tarbury, into pot plants as status symbols. Have you begun anything?"

"I'm just looking into things here — peering into the murk — but Saltana and Mrs. Drake, Primrose East and young Mickley, are working out in the field, gathering data in the West End — "

"Oh — lucky them! So you're all alone in that huge house."

"I am — except for a rum but efficient married couple. Now obviously you're going to the Callys' tonight — "

"Yes — and I'm taking a dreadful cousin who's staying with me at the moment. She's a harpist, believe it or not, who's just fled from the arms and bed-sitting-room of a viola player, and if she wasn't with me I'd ask you to dinner tomorrow night, Owen dear — "

"Give her something to do — she could wash her hair and then dry it practising the harp — and dine with me tomorrow night. The food's excellent, I'll find something fit to drink, and you can tell me about sociology, which I'm now accused of being entirely ignorant of, while I sit wondering and staring and occasionally breaking in to praise your eyes, your nose, your lips, your hair, and every dimple — "

She kissed him quickly. "All right, you wicked man. About quarter to eight then, tomorrow night. I've a seminar now. Sorry I can't run you home in my little car — "

"Oh — I'll walk, I'll walk — happy, thinking about tomorrow night."

And he did walk, but passed most of the time wondering if he ought to ring up Saltana now or wait until he'd talked to Jayjay. He was still undecided when he went up to his room, taking the two paperbacks he'd bought in Tarbury, and hadn't finally made up his mind when he took one of the paperbacks down to Elfreda's sitting-room-office to have a drink there before dinner. Then, on a sudden impulse, he rang the Lapfords' house, asked Maria if the Vice-Chancellor had returned, and was being told he hadn't when Isabel cut in, obviously from an extension, asking him who he was.

"This is Dr. Tuby, Mrs. Lapford." He spoke as if they'd never met. "I'm anxious to talk to the Vice-Chancellor as soon as possible, so that I can ring up Mrs. Drake and Professor Saltana in London — to try to explain to them what appears to be happening here."

"I'm not expecting him until lunchtime tomorrow. I could arrange for you to see him in the afternoon, if you think it's so important. How is Miss Primrose East?"

"I don't know, Mrs. Lapford. She's in London too. They're all doing some work there — sociological work too, you may be surprised to learn. So I'm here alone, trying to understand — " But then he cut himself off, a trick he had learnt years ago. After a few minutes, the telephone rang and he ignored it, feeling sure the call wasn't coming from London.

It must have been a couple of hours later, probably just after nine, when he heard a car coming to a sudden and perhaps bad-tempered stop outside. The ring of the bell sounded impatient and bad-tempered too. As Alfred was much further away from the front door, probably lost in a Western too, Tuby went to the door himself, admitting Isabel Lapford. Anger — and she was full of it — suited her, giving her a high colour and eyes that almost glittered. A handsome woman, undoubtedly.

"I didn't want to come here," she said as he showed her into Elfreda's room. "I realize it's all rather stupid. But if we're still on speaking terms, Dr. Tuby, there are things I want to say to you before you talk to my husband tomorrow." She looked him up and down with haughty defiance.

"Let me take your coat." His tone couldn't have been milder. "It's very warm in here, you'll find, Mrs. Lapford." His manner made hers look ridiculous, and of course she knew it. He felt she could have slapped him. As it was, she allowed him to take her heavy coat as if he wasn't really there or some machine was doing it. "*Do* sit down," he added, indicating an armchair. "Make yourself comfortable."

It is not easy to sit in an armchair while preserving an icy disdain, but she did her best, carefully avoiding his twinkling glance. "First, I must tell you that when I was helping Mrs. Drake to put this house in order for you, she took me into her confidence. She was very much afraid — poor woman — that the Americans wouldn't allow her to set up the Judson Drake Foundation here herself. And you and your friend Saltana might have thought of that when, as we know now, you passed yourselves off as sociologists. An unscrupulous mean trick, in my opinion."

Tuby pointed to the telephone. "She's staying at Robinson's Hotel. I can give you the number. Then you can tell her yourself."

"I'm talking to you now, Dr. Tuby," she replied angrily. "You and Saltana are no more sociologists than I am."

"You might be one, at that. Saltana's a philosophical sociologist. I'm a literary sociologist. Cally's a television sociologist — "

"Oh — don't be stupid. You know what I mean."

"I know what you think you mean. But the fact remains, you're sitting at this moment — rather out of temper — in the *Institute of Social Imagistics* — "

The telephone was ringing. "Excuse me."

"Which is just a lot of impudent nonsense."

He held up a hand, regarding her gravely. "You're quite wrong. But never mind about that — "

"You know very well that you and that wretched Oswald Mere rushed my husband, who's too impulsive sometimes, into accepting you here — "

"Jeff Convoy here," said the low mysterious voice. "Can you talk? Anybody with you?"

"Yes, there is," Tuby told him. "So keep it short, please."

"Can do. Brief progress report. That American you mentioned had an accident to his camera, this morning. Too bad! Now he's just had another. Accidentally pushed into that pond just outside the Eng. Lit. huts." Jeff added a conspiratorial chuckle or two. "And there's a rumour going round you people are going to be pushed out. Well, say the word and we move — direct action — "

"Thanks," said Tuby hastily. "I'll bear it in mind. Must ring off now." As he returned to his chair, he gave Isabel Lapford an enquiring look. "You were saying?"

"You've placed the Vice-Chancellor in an extremely difficult position. He's desperately worried — and so am I, for his sake. For once the Academic Advisory Board — "

Tuby stopped her. "I know about it. Sir Leopold Thing and the rest. Terrible!" He gave her a slow smile. "Have a drink. Whisky?"

"All right, I will. As I've done one stupid thing," she went on rapidly, not quite sure how they stood now, "I might as well do another. But I understood that as I'd insulted you no more whisky was to be offered or accepted. Why this change?"

Tuby was busy with the drinks. "Perhaps because you look even handsomer when you're angry," he threw at her. Then, smiling, he handed her the glass.

"Thank you. But why should one rather silly remark — "

"It was worse than silly. And it had nothing to do with whisky. You'd appealed to me as a friend to cope with a situation you were afraid your husband couldn't cope with. But then, when it was over, your pride rushed in. You had to be on top somehow. So I had to be turned from a friend into the shabby boozy little man who had to have your whisky *poured* into him — "

"Oh — shut up, for God's sake!" She had forced herself into being angry again. He sipped his drink and didn't even look at her, though he guessed she had taken a drink too, rather larger than his. When she did speak, the anger had gone; she spoke quietly, rather wearily. "You're right, of course. You're clever, and I no longer expect men to be so perceptive. The kind we get here are just thick and wooden. But it was for Jayjay, I'm sure, not just for myself. I'm still devoted to him — in a way. And I was annoyed with you because you could do what he couldn't do."

"So what?" he said carelessly. "He can do things I can't do."

"Of course. But perhaps not as far as a woman is concerned. Anyhow, I apologize. And it's a long time since I apologized to a man. I *am* proud, I confess it." She waited a moment, then, as if impulsively: "I wish you wouldn't talk to Jayjay tomorrow. After all, the Board doesn't meet until next week, and nothing's settled yet. You don't have to see him, do you?"

"No, I can leave him alone. But I must warn you, Isabel. Saltana'll be back on Sunday and when he knows what's happening, he'll soon be talking to Jayjay." He let that sink in, and then, using the same measured tone and looking hard at her: "I'll add another warning, my dear. One I didn't give Cally and Rittenden — they're not worth bothering about. When Saltana and I first came here, we were half-playing, not taking anything very seriously. Now we're working. We're on to something and we're not letting it go. We're lining up our own kind of publicity — not that Primrose East muck — "

"Well, that'll be a pleasant change — "

"Never mind the repartee," he told her sharply. "Try to understand what I'm saying. If we can all be polite and then work out a decent compromise, no harm'll be done. But if you encourage your husband to talk to Saltana as you did to me when you first came in here — *Social Imagistics* so much impudent nonsense, that kind of thing — then, I'm warning you, Isabel, we'll work faster and hit harder than you people can. And don't forget, you can't turn us away. The Institute stays here until we're ready to move — "

"Except that it won't be an institute — "

"It'll be any dam' thing we want it to be." He was very sharp, very hard.

She got up. "I don't see how I can stay after that. I thought we were going to be friends again. After all, I *did* apologize. And I'm sorry I did now." She looked defiant, but was doing too much blinking.

He went nearer. "Come, come, my dear. I was only giving you a little warning. For Jayjay's sake — and even more, for yours. You're a proud woman. You're ambitious. You're landed with a technical college

half-made into a university, with some fairly dim-witted types all round
you — "

"Oh — shut up! As if I didn't know!" She was blinking furiously.
He took hold of both her hands. "Oh — I never finished my drink." He
released one hand and she reached down for the glass and emptied it.
"Clarence Rittenden told me on the telephone yesterday that the Duchess
of Brockshire's an old friend of yours. But he's such a fool — and I know
you'll say anything — so I didn't believe it. She isn't, is she?"

"We were very good friends once, years ago. She was a young repertory actress then — about my social level. I may write to her, to tell her
I'm here, if she'd like a bit of slumming."

"She won't have much time. After the opening ceremony and tea,
we're giving a smallish cocktail party for her, then after dinner she's going to the opening night of our play — "

"Not Ted Jenks's incestuous window-cleaner play?" cried Tuby, delighted. "If Petronella's still anything like the girl I used to know, she'll
fall out of her seat — laughing."

Isabel ignored that. "Then a party after the play."

"If she hasn't changed too much, I'll lure her here — "

"You will *not*." And more than half-enraged by his impudence and
this possible threat to her carefully planned Duchess day, she shook him.
He responded by grasping her firmly and kissing her. For a moment or
two her lips trembled and opened, but then, with an obvious effort of
will, she pushed herself away. "My God — you *are* the limit! For sheer
damned cheek, you can't be beaten. And if anybody had told me an hour
ago, I'd be wrestling with you — allowing you even for a second to kiss
me — I'd never, never — "

"That's enough, my dear Isabel. You sound just like an outraged
maddened schoolgirl — 1930's vintage — I'm the *limit* — "

"Shut up. And give me my coat. I'd have to go now, even if you
were behaving yourself, which of course you aren't doing — as I might
have known." When they were on their way to the front door, she began
with a light contemptuous laugh and then said, "How many of these
rather silly young women who kept enquiring about you have you *lured*
here so far, Dr. Tuby? No, don't tell me. It's all too stupid." But when
he was about to open the door for her, she stopped him. "Now I'm serious. Will you keep your promise to leave Jayjay alone tomorrow?"

He opened the door and she stepped outside. "Yes, I will. So you
haven't entirely wasted your evening, my dear Isabel."

"I never thought I had." She kissed him quickly, put a hand on his
cheek, then hurried towards her car. As he watched it go, he thought
what a pity it was that although he'd enjoyed a number of women, meeting them on level terms of desire, mischief, and affection, he'd never
played — and never would play — the old elaborate game of seduction.
There, going down the drive, carrying a load of mixed feelings, telling

herself how devoted she was to her husband and how the wife of a Vice-Chancellor ought to behave, was a woman now ready for every move in the game, a super-seducee. But what he regretted, he thought as he went indoors, was the lost superb strategist and tactician in himself. Otherwise, he was better off with sociological sex and delicious Dr. Honeypot.

On a sudden impulse — and damn the expense! — he rang up Saltana the next morning, Friday, before either of them had had breakfast. "Cosmo, they're trying to turn us out here," he began, and then explained what was happening. "Jayjay's been away and I haven't seen him," he said in conclusion. "Now I think I'll leave him to you, Cosmo."

"Certainly, Owen. Leave it all to me now. O. V. Mere's coming down next week, and I can use him. We'll all be back on Sunday in time for a late lunch. Tell the cook. Oh — and if you're doing nothing much, you might enquire about the possibility of getting together a string quartet — for the Brahms Clarinet Quintet. Longing to try it. Thanks for ringing, Owen!"

After breakfast Tuby went into a cosy huddle with Alfred and Florrie about the dinner he should provide that evening for Dr. Hazel Honeyfield. Not too light, not too heavy, he insisted; and they hadn't to be told why, knowing dam' well why he was making such a fuss. Their final choice was a rather delicate chicken dish, one of Florrie's specialities, preceded by a small quiche lorraine and followed by a sweet soufflé. Tuby told them he would be responsible for the wine. Then he rang up Isabel Lapford.

"I've spoken to Saltana. He was calm and cheerful. He's anxious to try the Brahms Clarinet Quintet — he plays the clarinet quite well for an amateur — and he wants me to start enquiring about a possible string quartet. I wouldn't know where to begin, but I have a vague idea Jayjay said you were interested in music, my dear."

"I am. And it's time we had some here. There's a boy in Chemistry who plays the violin and a girl in Languages. There's a rumour we have a viola player somewhere, and I'll try to find out for you. But we don't seem to have a 'cellist, not in the university, but I've been told there's an old man in Tarbury — he's a retired civil servant, I believe — who used to be quite a good 'cellist. His name's Meston but I'm afraid I haven't his address and he isn't in the phone book. I think he lives with a married daughter, and it's definitely somewhere in Tarbury. You'll have to enquire yourself about him, but I can attend to the other three."

"Well, I have to go into Tarbury — to buy some decent wine — "

"Why — are you entertaining?"

"A sociological friend, my dear — "

"Oh — that one! Straight off a chocolate box, as I told you before. I don't admire your taste." And she rang off, probably in a female fury.

Though he couldn't afford them, he bought a bottle of Traminer and one of Chateauneuf du Pape that might have been '59, as the label declared, and then again might not. Then — cleverly, he thought — he enquired about Meston at the post office, and ten minutes later was ringing the bell at his address. A rather handsome woman in a faded housecoat stared suspiciously at the wine parcel he was carrying and announced at once she'd no intention of buying anything. He told her, smiling, he wasn't a salesman but a sociologist, Dr. Tuby, looking for somebody to play the 'cello — Mr. Meston perhaps — um? Her response was immediate and extremely interesting: "Oh — I read about you in the paper. Something to do with that girl who's a famous model. Come in. Dad's in the back room. He'll be pleased to be asked, though he doesn't bother with his 'cello much now." She led the way into the back room. "Dad, this is Dr. Tuby who wants to ask you about 'cello playing."

Meston was an ancient gnome type, who seemed to be wearing a lot of cardigans, and stared indignantly over his spectacles, and was a bit deaf and liked to be grumpy. He flung down the paper he'd been reading as if he never wanted to see one again. "Lot of rubbish. More and more rubbish. Not worth printing. And television's as bad. On and on and on about nothing. 'Cello? Nobody wants to listen to music here. It's a backwater. That's all — a backwater. Used to play a lot one time. We had a Board of Trade quartet — three of us, anyhow. Other chap, second fiddle, came from the G.P.O. Brahms's Clarinet Quintet? Tall order, I'd say. Heard it, of course — beautiful work — but never played it. Tricky as hell, I'll bet. Always tricky — Brahms. Give me Haydn. Try some of the old Haydns like a shot. You what? I see — your friend's the clarinet player. Have to give me a score and a week or two with it. Even then I'll make a fool of myself. But I'd rather make a fool of myself than just sit here. Wouldn't you — eh? Want to hear me try something over for you? Eh? No time. Busy man, I suppose. Used to be a busy man myself. Old nuisance now. And you want to be off, I can see that. Tell your friend to let me have a score of the Brahms if you can't find anybody better. I'll have a try, silly as I look. And come again. Enjoy a talk."

"Dad's a bit tetchy these days," his daughter said as she went with Tuby to the door, "though not with the children. He's good with them. And I couldn't help hearing what you were saying. He's a lovely 'cello player. You wouldn't think it, but he is. I hope he can play for you. It'll take him right out of himself. And after all, that's what we all need, isn't it?"

"Sometimes, not always," Tuby told her, smiling. "Often I enjoy just being right *in* myself. Exploring myself. Hello — where's my parcel? Oh — you have it. Thank you so much. Oh — by the way — are you on the telephone?"

"Oh — yes. My husband has to be," she replied proudly. (What about telephone-status for Hazel?) "And of course you might want to ring up Dad. It's 39842. You could write it on your bag — 39842." They exchanged smiles on the doorstep. "Fletcher's my married name, and of course you know Dad's. Thank you for coming to see him. Come again, Dr. Tuby. Can I say this?" she asked shyly. "I think you're ever such a nice man."

Not a bad morning's work, he concluded as he went to the bus stop — he was ever such a nice man; he'd found a possible 'cellist for Saltana; and Mrs. Fletcher's opening remarks proved that the Primrose East publicity, however deplorable, had had some effect. He must remember to tell Saltana that.

Hazel arrived at twenty-five to eight, wearing a rather short bright green dress, with a darker collar, black stockings, and more make-up than usual. Alfred ushered her in and then waited upon her later in a somewhat confused impressive manner, being divided between the roles of the majordomo of a great establishment and the waiter in a rather shady restaurant, assigned to one of the private rooms. Tuby was glad to discover there was no pecking and wine-leaving nonsense about Hazel. She ate and drank level with him, relished the food, which was excellent, and enjoyed and praised the two wines he had bought. "But you don't live like this all the time, do you, darling?" she enquired innocently, eyes sparkling, dimples at play, a smiling and talking peach.

"No, my dear, not quite. But not too badly. How about you?"

"A boring little mess, most of the time. I *can* cook but it's such a bother just for oneself. And my cousin — the harpist, y'know — doesn't drink and doesn't care what she eats. Still, if I lived like this all the time, I'd soon be too fat. Perhaps I am now. What do you think?"

"I think you're perfect, my dear Hazel. I drink to you."

They were now waiting for the soufflé. Hazel had already dismissed the telephone (the pride of Mrs. Fletcher) as a possible subject for a status-symbol enquiry, doing it very nicely too, and had then gone on, during the second course, to ask him what he felt about clique symbols and various projections and affirmations of group spirit and solidarity; and now, to his relief, they were having a break, probably only brief, from sociological topics. So after he drank to her, she drank to him. "And I already feel a bit tight," she told him, with dimples hard at it, "but in the pleasantest way, not like one feels at parties with their horrible punches and stuff. I love my work but I hate being at this kind of soggy half-baked university. I don't think I'll stay. But I expect you'll be gone long before I will, darling. I just don't *see* you here — except, of course, at this minute — lovely! I was at the Callys' last night — remember? — and he started on you and Professor Saltana and that nice Mrs. Drake, with about a dozen people listening, and I turned on him and was *furious* with him. Oh — and so was that rather odd girl from English, who says you go and drink China tea with her. Do you?"

"Lois Terry? Yes. Just twice. Tea and talk."

"Nothing else?"

"Nothing. I like her but she doesn't have the immediate and disastrous effect on me that you do, Hazel."

"Why disastrous?"

But Alfred made a triumphant entrance with the soufflé. "Sorry you wait but now is olright — exacta *moment*. You see."

They ate in silence and dreamy contentment. There was a light, not very strong, at the other side of the room, near the door, and then nothing but the four tall candles, in their silver holders, that illuminated and flattered their end of the long dining table. And Hazel by candlelight was even more delicious than the soufflé. Some instinct, some intuitive sense of a scene, not always working in her, mercifully kept her silent. Certain thoughts were passing through Tuby's mind, but he sensibly decided to keep them to himself. Yet they involved her because they were concerned with lust, that dog with a very bad name. But there was more than one kind of lust, Tuby reflected rather dreamily, and the failure to recognize this and all the furious indictments of the lustful chiefly came from men who anyhow feared and disliked women, and probably knew how savagely and cruelly they themselves would behave under the spell of their senses. They couldn't understand — though most women could — that lust needn't necessarily turn another person into an instrument, a thing, but could exist, be mixed with, an amused and perhaps tender affection, not to be confused with all-demanding love with its insistence upon a life together. Or you could put it another way, Tuby told himself while still keeping silent but looking and smiling at Hazel, that the old idea of love and lust glaring at each other over a barbed-wire entanglement was nonsense. But he also reminded himself that Burns, an authority in this field, might have been right when he declared in effect that too much lust, never arriving at love, finally hardened the heart. What was passing through Hazel's mind, as she sat there answering his glances and smiles, he couldn't imagine. Perhaps — God save us! — thoughts concerned with what was status-enhancing and group-affirming.

Dinner ended, he led her by the hand back to Elfreda's room, where they had their coffee and then switched on the television news. An important decision by the Government was to be reached in twenty-four hours, but until that time — nothing. So nearly all the news was about this nothing. Special planes had been chartered so that reporters could land in distant places and talk about this nothing. Men spoke about it from Paris and Washington. There were expensive and complicated nothing interviews. Never had more been done for nothing. "You don't want this nonsense, do you?" he asked Hazel. "Of course not. I'll turn it off."

She was anxious to talk now, apparently about status-personality.

He apologized for interrupting her. "I want to know what you think about all that, my dear. But I must show you," he continued hastily, "my bed-sitting-room upstairs. I wish you'd seen this place before we took it over and Elfreda Drake got to work on it. I wouldn't have thought it possible to come back and find myself so comfortably installed. Come and take a look at my little place. But carry on about status-personality." Which she did, all the way upstairs.

Once safely there, he took her in his arms and gave her several lingering kisses. Her mouth had responded happily to every demand of his, but as soon as it was free of these demands she wanted to know what he thought of group-institution feedback. As he unfastened her dress and unhooked her bra, revealing breasts at once exquisite and nobly ample, he insisted that she should tell him first, and at length, what her opinion was of group-institution feedback, which she did while absent-mindedly, it appeared, helping him over the trickier stages of further disrobing. During this time he remembered quite sharply how, after meeting her during his first visit to Cally's office, he had imagined himself undressing her while he was pretending to listen to the discussion among Saltana, Jayjay, and Cally; and he wondered again whether a scene clearly shaped in the imagination might not influence future events, pouring themselves into a channel already made for them. But now, with the delicious melting creature there naked before him, events moved faster and further than they had done in his imagination, and sociological jargon gave way to vague protests, meant to be brushed aside like the thinnest veils, and little squeals and delighted moans. Yet afterwards, after many cries of "Darling, darling!" and then some murmuring and nibbling at his ear lobe, she had gently withdrawn the bare arm round his neck and had sat up, and had then said quite seriously, "But darling, you haven't told me what you think about group-institution feedback, have you?"

And he kissed her lovely warm cheek. "No, Dr. Honeyfield, my sweet poppet, I haven't. So I'll tell you now. I think it's wonderful."

## 4

Elfreda and Saltana were back in Tarbury, behind Primrose and Mike Mickley of course, by about half-past one, after three hours or so of one of those November Sunday mornings in England that seem so quiet, soggy, and sad; and just before two o'clock all five of them were sitting down to Florrie's roast beef and Yorkshire pudding. It might have been her fancy, but it did seem to Elfreda that Mike looked more hopeful and Primrose friendlier. As for Owen Tuby, he seemed rather quiet but still twinkled away at everybody. He pleased her too by praising Florrie and Alfred, who had, it appeared, cooked and served a superb dinner for him on Friday night.

Saltana gave him a look. "Not for you alone, my boy. Don't tell me that."

"Well no," Tuby said smoothly. "I happened to be anxious to discuss some aspects of sociology — group-institution feedback, and that kind of thing — with a colleague here, Dr. Honeyfield."

"That sounds a bit dim and dreary," said Primrose, who then, a moment later, had to turn to Elfreda. "What's the matter with Professor Saltana and Mickley?"

"Men'll laugh at anything, dear," Elfreda told her.

"My God, Doc," cried Mickley, "you're cool — you really are. Isn't he, Prof?"

"He's spent years in the mysterious and inscrutable East, not in Birmingham and Hammersmith. But enough of that," Saltana continued, frowning at the two youngsters. "Orders now, you two. After lunch Mrs. Drake, Dr. Tuby, and I must hold an emergency meeting of the senior officers of the *Institute of Social Imagistics*. Miss East, Mr. Mickley, your attendance is not required. But your services are. Please unload the files from the two cars and arrange them in some sensible and pleasing order in Mrs. Drake's office."

"Okay, Prof," said Mickley. "Can do. But is this meeting of yours really no concern of ours?"

"Just what I was going to ask," said Primrose.

"You can't attend it. But if it arrives at any decision in which you may be involved, you will be informed as early as possible."

"Cosmo, why are you talking like this?" Tuby asked plaintively.

"That's it," cried Primrose. "Why are you, darling?"

"Several reasons. First, I'm trying to stop you calling me *darling*," Saltana told her severely. "Secondly, this will be a serious meeting and I want to create in you a serious attitude of mind towards it. This particularly applies to Dr. Tuby, who must try to distinguish between sociology and sex. Thirdly, I was talking like that just for the hell of it. So — we hold our meeting in one of our rooms upstairs, and then, perhaps after tea, I shall retire and practise the adagio of the Mozart Clarinet Concerto in A major."

"Prof, there's an embryo jazz group taking shape over there," said Mickley earnestly. "They could use a clarinet — "

"Certainly not, my boy. Unthinkable. Yes, Owen?"

"There's a possible string quartet here," Tuby began, and then explained what Isabel Lapford had told him and how he had visited old Meston, the 'cellist from the Board of Trade. So of course Elfreda had to know how he came to be talking to Isabel Lapford — about violinists or anything else — when they were not supposed to be on speaking terms, and then *that* had to be explained, while lunch was coming to an end, and Saltana was brooding over string quartet possibilities, and Primrose and Mike Mickley were exchanging those bright satirical glances which the young reserve for one another while their elders are talking as if they were really human beings.

Tuby had more explaining to do when the three of them settled down in Saltana's room upstairs. It was chiefly for Elfreda's sake, as Saltana had already heard most of his news over the telephone. "I haven't seen Jayjay at all yet. I promised his wife not to see him as soon as he came back, then I decided I might as well leave him to Cosmo."

"Quite right," said Saltana. "I'll deal with him when it should be necessary. Go on, Owen."

"I doubt if he'll be able to stand up for us even if he really wanted to. He's already up against pressure from inside his university, from the professors — and their wives — who don't want us. Lowering the tone — and so forth. In a few days, when his Academic Advisory Board meets, it's almost certain he'll be up against pressure from the outside, from Sir Leopold Namp and the rest of them. Do you see Jayjay defying them all, inside and outside? I don't."

"Neither do I," Saltana growled.

"Well, what would that mean?" Elfreda was beginning to feel alarmed. It was all very well for the men, who, as she had noticed before in similar situations, were quite ready to enjoy feeling aggressive; but she simply felt threatened and vulnerable.

"I'd say it's about ten to one," said Tuby carelessly, "that by next Sunday Jayjay will have told us that very reluctantly he's come to the conclusion that our Institute and your Foundation, Elfreda, can't be any part of the University of Brockshire. In short, we're *out*."

"Oh — dear! But he can't turn us out of this house. I rented it. He didn't — "

"No, no, no, my dear Elfreda," cried Tuby. "They can't turn us out in that sense. But it would mean no students could take courses here. Somebody like Primrose, if she wants a degree, can't stay on here. Mike Mickley would be told he'd have to leave us or lose his post-graduate grant — "

"And the Drakes and their lawyers would claim the Foundation hasn't been properly set up over here. Oh — my God!" She turned instinctively to Saltana. "What are we going to do, Cosmo?"

"I'll tell you what we're *not* going to do, Elfreda. We're not going to sit about waiting for unpleasant things to happen to us. We'll make the moves." He was now Field-Marshal Saltana, Elfreda thought — not without a touch of bitterness — ready to have a hell of a good time, planning this, doing that, while she crept away into a corner to cry. "First thing, Owen, we test the strength of this Board before it meets. This probably means Sir Leopold Thing — Namp. Now it's Sunday and he'll be spending the week-end at some country mansion of his, not too far from here. Owen, go downstairs, get his number, ring him up, and tell him I want to see him on a matter of some urgency. Early this evening, if possible."

"Ay, ay, Cap'n!" And Tuby went at once.

Elfreda regarded this Field-Marshal Saltana with some doubt. "Why did you send Owen Tuby to do it, instead of doing it yourself?"

"Because I'm the Director and he's the Deputy, and it sounds better if the Deputy asks for the interview on behalf of the Director. Owen understands that. In fact it was he who first pointed this out to me — when one of us had to ring up Lapford from London, you remember. Don't imagine for a moment," he added severely, "that I'm in the habit of making my friend run errands for me. This is part of the game we have to play."

"Well, don't overplay it, that's all," Elfreda told him, with what she hoped was equal severity. "And, if you can, just stop for a minute or two being Director and War Lord Saltana. I'm a mature woman, not a spoilt girl like Primrose who wants somebody to be sharp with her. By the way, didn't you think she was nicer to poor Mike at lunch?"

"No, I didn't."

"You mean, you thought she wasn't?"

"Certainly not. I didn't observe what was happening between them. Elfreda my dear, there are some things, from a correct clarinet technique to the fate of logical positivism, in which I take the keenest possible interest. But the courtship of Primrose East and Mike Mickley is never going to be one of them. Tell me about it — I'll listen with pleasure — but don't ask me for my own observations because there'll never be any. Though I must add that what happens to that courtship may depend on the events of the next few days. Indeed, on what happens when we talk to this Sir Leopold — "

"*We?* Oh — you mean you and Owen Tuby — "

"No, I don't. Owen would make one too many. Elfreda, if the man doesn't live too far away and you feel up to it, I want you to drive me there and then see him with me. I wouldn't insist on this if it wasn't extremely important. One of the youngsters can do the driving if necessary, but you must be there when I talk to this man. You're involved financially and emotionally, my dear, so I want you to understand what we may have to do and exactly why we'll have to do it. No orders now. I'm asking you as a friend."

This was an appeal she couldn't resist. But while agreeing to go with him, naturally she felt her curiosity ought to be satisfied. "What is it we may have to do, Cosmo?"

"I'm not mystery-mongering, Elfreda. But I think it would be wrong to tell you that before you hear what this man has to say. Otherwise, you won't go with an open mind. You must judge for yourself how Tuby and I may be situated."

She gave her impatience another outlet. "Oh — well, we're talking like this when the man may be hundreds of miles away — "

But he wasn't. Tuby returned to say that Sir Leopold was only about twenty miles away, relaxing (his own term for it) at his country place, and that although he considered this proposed interview highly irregular, he would be available between six and seven.

"Good! Thanks, Owen! What does he sound like?"

"Large, pompous, and delighted with himself. You'll have to watch your temper, Cosmo. Really, I ought to be doing it."

"No, it's my job. I can be a smoothie if necessary. I'm taking Elfreda because she has to see for herself what we may be up against. But perhaps she oughtn't to drive."

"I'd rather not, in the dark," Elfreda told them. "And perhaps if we took both Primrose and Mike, and they have to wait in the car — "

"Dangerous," Saltana cut in to observe, "because either they'll start necking, if only to pass the time, or they won't. This means that on the way back we'll have either a dreamy driver or an angry one. Both equally dangerous. But just to please you, my dear Elfreda, I'll risk it. Owen, we ought to have some music after supper tonight. The world is too much with us. Why don't you ring up Mrs. Lapford and ask her to find us a fiddler or two — and a pianist — "

"But Owen himself plays *beautifully* — "

Saltana regarded her with compassion. "For half an hour in a dim cocktail lounge, possibly. But *music* demands some foundation of accuracy — "

"He's quite right, Elfreda. Of course, Isabel Lapford may play herself. Anyhow, I'll get on to her. Any objection if she wants to come herself — assuming she can stop being a Vice-Chancellor's wife for a couple of hours? Elfreda?"

She shook her head. "I like her. Though *you* might find it awkward, Cosmo."

"Not if she can supply some music, my dear. And we won't have a word about anything else. Go to it, Owen my boy, pouring honey into the telephone. Elfreda, please see if the youngsters will pilot us to Sir Leopold the Magnificent. I must do some unpacking — music included."

They left at twenty to six, with Primrose driving her own car and Mike sitting beside her because he alone knew the local roads, not easy to negotiate on a dark and wettish night. Sitting in the back, pressed close to Cosmo Saltana because there wasn't much room there, Elfreda found herself enjoying this cosy setup even though she felt rather worried about this talk with Sir Leopold. He didn't sound the sort of man Saltana would like, and she couldn't see Saltana as a smooth and easy performer. And she told him so, warning him not to lose his temper.

"Elfreda, here's a solemn promise," he replied. "You'll be there. And I hereby assure you, Mrs. Drake, that I won't make a single angry remark *until you do*. Until then I'll be as mild as milk. If you like, I'll bet on it."

"No need to do that. So long as you promise. And I don't suppose I'll open my mouth." Which turned out later to be one of those things better left unsaid.

Sir Leopold's house was about the size of the Institute but much grander inside, with more lights, more people about. A foreign houseman, an Alfred clean-shaven and tidied up, kept them waiting in the hall and then conducted them into a library, a beautiful octagonal room full of polished and shining leather and dark wood and shelves of calf-bound books. It rather frightened Elfreda, who sat near the edge of a chair while Saltana moved around and peered at the bookshelves. She heard Sir Leopold just outside the door, telling somebody not to be a dam' fool: it was like a star entrance in an old-fashioned play. He looked just as he had sounded — a bulky and bristling man in his fifties, crimson to purple in the face, a high-blood-pressure type. He was surprised to see Elfreda — though the houseman must have told him something, so perhaps he'd kept his face looking surprised — but was quite good-mannered with her. She knew at once, however, that he didn't like the look of Saltana, that Saltana didn't like the look of him, and that there'd be trouble.

"As I told your chap over the phone," Sir Leopold began as soon as the three of them were sitting down, "this is highly irregular and the other people on the Board might object to it. But I'm used to taking short cuts. Often they save valuable time. Want to speak your piece first, Professor Saltana? Or do I speak mine?"

"You first, Sir Leopold." And Saltana was milder than milk.

"Very well. Always took a great interest in the college — my father helped to found it — we've taken on a lot of its students — and I'm equally interested now that it's the University of Brockshire. Proud of it, you might say. Now there's no doubt the Vice-Chancellor acted hastily when he agreed to bring you people into his Department of Sociology — very important department, in my opinion. And you can take it from me that when the Board meets on Thursday, we shall ask him to reverse that decision. When you see him, I think he'll tell you he made a mistake. The fact that the Board is meeting at all really tells him what our conclusion will be. And of course I've already had some talk with him."

"And what did you tell him when you did talk to him?" Just a shade sharper, but still mild. It looked as if Saltana might keep his promise.

"I deplored the kind of publicity your arrival at Brockshire had encouraged. I also told him I was astonished to learn that he had invited you to join his staff without enquiring if you were properly qualified to teach sociology. And he knows now you are not. To put it bluntly — and as you asked for this interview, I feel I'm entitled to speak plainly — you bluffed him, you and your associate Dr. — er — "

"Tuby — Dr. Tuby," Elfreda heard herself saying. "And I do wish you wouldn't talk as if they were pretending to be a pair of surgeons or something. All these qualifications!"

"Mrs. Drake, I'm an industrialist, and if a man came to me claiming to be an experienced electrical engineer — "

"We're not talking about electrical engineers," cried Elfreda. "They might blow up the works — "

"Allow me, Elfreda," said Saltana, still quite smooth and calm, though she herself had already almost lost her temper. "Let me take the points you make. The publicity you complain about had nothing to do with Dr. Tuby and me. We weren't even in this country. Next, then. Dr. Tuby and I never offered ourselves as teachers of sociology. We asked to set up our *Institute of Social Imagistics,* financed entirely by the Judson Drake Foundation, in association with Brockshire and without costing it a penny. Broadly speaking, it's a sociological project — "

"*Very* broadly speaking, I'd say," Sir Leopold interrupted him to say, with a sneering air of triumph that maddened Elfreda. "And quite unsuitable for any university."

"You don't know anything about it," she told him warmly. "It's concerned with the choice and projection of suitable images. A very important subject now. And Professor Saltana and Dr. Tuby are two of the cleverest men I've ever known, worth a hundred of that daft American Professor of Sociology I was sent over with. Or your Professor Cally, for that matter. And how do you know what they're doing is unsuitable for a university?"

"I'm not here to answer your questions, Mrs. Drake. If Professor Saltana has anything more to say — and doesn't take too long saying it — I'll listen to him. But I think the least *you* can do is to keep quiet."

At this, Elfreda was about to explode, but Saltana checked her. "Sir Leopold, I'll be quite brief. You needn't listen long. In fact, all you have to do is to give me a direct *Yes* or *No* to a few plain questions." And to Elfreda's surprise — and disappointment — Saltana spoke quite calmly and very quietly. "You believe our *Institute of Social Imagistics* should not be associated with the university or be approved by it in any way?"

"Yes, I do. I think I've made that plain."

"And you've already convinced Vice-Chancellor Lapford he made a mistake, and your Board on Thursday will officially confirm that?"

"Yes, yes, yes!" Sir Leopold was obviously impatient. "And I don't think we need waste any more time — "

"Just one more question." And Saltana now spoke very softly indeed. "Now you've already mentioned publicity. In view of this publicity, won't your decision immediately place Mrs. Drake, Dr. Tuby, and me in an obviously humiliating situation?"

"It might — I don't know." Sir Leopold waved it all away. Elfreda could have slapped him.

"And you don't care?"

"Frankly — no. It was your own doing. You took that risk." He got up, done with them.

Saltana got up, and then, to Elfreda's astonishment, looked hard at

Sir Leopold and then offered him a small slow smile. "That's all. Elfreda my dear, let's go."

As soon as they were outside the front door, to which Sir Leopold had made no effort to conduct them, Elfreda clutched Saltana by the arm fiercely, almost ready to shake him, and cried, "Cosmo Saltana, I simply don't understand you. There was I, making you promise not to lose your temper, and then when I lost mine because he was so damned high-and-mighty and rude and insulting, instead of telling him what you thought about him, really blasting him, all you did was to ask him quiet little questions — just taking it all — "

"And leaving him pleased with himself, eh? Come on, it's damp out here, let's get into the car." She had released him, and now he put her arm through his, to go down the steps.

"Yes, of course, leaving him pleased with himself. And why — why?"

"I'll tell you why, my dear. He's the sort of man who can work fast if he has to. I didn't want him to forestall me. And that's what he just might have done, if I'd told him what I longed to tell him — that now I propose to make a monkey out of him — *and* Lapford."

"But how — how?"

"Tell you tomorrow. We can't do anything tonight." They were now at the car, and he opened the door for her. Primrose and Mike Mickley seemed to be busy arguing. "All right," Saltana told them masterfully. "Drop that and let's go. What's the time? Twenty to seven? Well, don't kill anybody, girl, but take us back as fast as you can. We'll have a little party tonight. But a musical party," he added sternly.

Elfreda settled back, snuggling against him a little, and began thinking about parties. But then Mike turned round and asked what had happened at Sir Leopold's.

"Nothing," Saltana told him sharply. "What we have to do now is to get back home safely and in good time. Keep your eyes and minds on the road, you two. Elfreda, meditate and snuggle."

Tuby met them in the hall, beaming and rather excited. "The musical party's on," he cried. "Eight o'clock. Isabel Lapford's a pianist and she's coming and rounding up one or two fiddling students. His daughter's bringing old Meston and his 'cello. And I've invited one non-playing guest — "

"We know her," said Saltana. "Dr. Hazel Honeypot."

"Wrong, Cosmo. It's a girl from Eng. Lit. called Lois Terry, who needs cheering up. Elfreda, you'll have to get a move on. The drink situation isn't bad, but I don't know about food — and I feel we ought to lay on some sort of buffet supper. What's your news, Cosmo?"

"A hell of a packet. Let's go upstairs and I'll give it to you."

It was ten to eight when Elfreda hurried upstairs to change, bursting in on Saltana and Tuby to tell them to stop plotting and go below to receive their guests. "That'll allow me a little more time. And Florrie's got everything in hand. But no eating until about nine or so. Drinks, of course, any time."

"Good work, Elfreda! Down we go, Owen my boy!" And Saltana picked up his clarinet and an armful of music.

It was already a wonderful little party, Elfreda felt, when she went down, looking her best, and joined it. They were all in the big drawing room, not far from the piano; drinks had been served; the music was just beginning. Isabel Lapford, not looking haughty and aloof at all, but eager and happy, had brought a fat girl student and a thin boy student; there was this old 'cello player, with his rather handsome, shy, married daughter; and Tuby's friend, Miss Terry, the plain girl with the huge eyes, was sitting there not missing anything, her eyes like great soft lamps, no longer plain now, not a bit of it. And of course her own four — bless 'em — now floating high above institutes and foundations and grants and degrees and quarrels and arguments.

Except now and again when a lovely little tune emerged, Elfreda didn't understand or much enjoy this kind of music, and anyhow she had to keep quietly dodging in and out to see how Florrie and Alfred were making out in the kitchen and the dining room. Actually it was half-past nine before supper was ready, and even then she had almost to drag them away from the piano and their other instruments, promising them they could start again as soon as they felt they'd had enough to eat. What delighted her wasn't the music itself but the sort of common feeling or atmosphere it created, making this a different kind of party, stripping the hard social skin off people, turning them into their real selves, eager and warm and alive, more like happy children. Why in the name of God couldn't they always be like this?

Well, they went on playing, in various mixtures of people and instruments, until after midnight, and Elfreda could have done with less music and more talk, and anyhow she was beginning to feel tired and there would still be some clearing up to be done, now that she'd told Florrie and Alfred to go to bed; and yet it stayed a wonderful little party, right to the very end, with a special kind of innocence and happiness in it, not quite belonging to this world — at least the way we'd made it. But when all the thanks and kissing and hand-shakings were over and they'd gone and Owen Tuby was helping her to clear the dining room, it was different, straight back into this world.

"Owen, they were all saying we must do it again — especially Isabel Lapford — "

"Of course. Quite right."

"Yes, except that it won't happen — can't happen. You won't see Isabel Lapford at that piano again — "

Tuby, who'd mixed a fair amount of whisky with the music, stared at her. "Elfreda, what's the matter with you?"

"Nothing, nothing — except we may declare war tomorrow on the University of Brockshire."

"Christ! I'd clean forgotten."

5

Not long after breakfast on Monday morning, they were talking up in Saltana's room. They had left Elfreda below in her office, where she was re-arranging the files with the help of the two youngsters. They needed this time to themselves before going into action, because for once Cosmo Saltana and Owen Tuby weren't in complete agreement.

"Why go soft on them?" Saltana demanded.

"For that matter, why be so tough? Why not a joint statement saying we're separating by mutual consent? Then nobody's feelings are hurt."

"I wish to God now you'd come with us to see this Sir Leopold. Why — Elfreda was a dam' sight angrier than I was, and shouted at him. No mutual consent and sparing of feelings for Sir Leopold, my boy. We weren't good enough for his tinpot university, and he was ready to tell the world as much."

"No doubt. But, after all, Jayjay's running this place — "

"Since when? And a man who allows himself to be pushed around, as Lapford does, deserves to have his feelings hurt. When we left three weeks ago, we were his colleagues, his friends, and now what are we? Is he considering our feelings?"

"He might be. We don't know."

"You might not, Owen. But I do. And it's my belief he'll announce whatever Sir Leopold and the rest of 'em tell him to announce."

"Listen, Cosmo — I still say — "

"Sex — sex — sex!"

"I'm not thinking about sex — "

"You imagine you're not, but you are. It's the thought of the women on the other side that's worrying you and turning you soft. What will Mrs. Lapford feel — and Hazel Honeypot — and little Shining Eyes who was here last night? Well, if you must have women on your mind, then just remember Elfreda."

"What about Elfreda?"

"She's emotionally involved with this Foundation. And unless we're tough, somebody may get tough with her. We also happen to be living on her money. Not even on the Foundation money yet. *Her money.*" Saltana didn't enjoy glaring and shouting at his friend, but there were times — and this was one of them — when Owen Tuby just had to be glared and shouted at. His soft but rubbery obstinacy could be maddening.

"All right, all right, I guessed that and don't like it any more than you do." In danger of losing his temper for once, Tuby tried hard to control himself. He succeeded too, continuing now in his usual warmly persuasive tone. "Because Elfreda's in this difficult situation, then that's all the more reason why we should take it easy, try to make friends and not enemies, and not begin clouting people right and left. Cosmo," he added, almost plaintively, "you're too hard."

Saltana had to laugh. "And you're too soft, Owen. The East got into you. Believe me — if we don't hit them, they'll hit us."

Tuby had his pipe going again. "It doesn't follow," he said mildly. "We don't have to use our heads as battering rams, they've other uses. And one thing's certain in all this. If you and I start quarrelling, we're done for. And just when we're ready to make something together. That's true, isn't it?"

Saltana admitted that it was all too true. And he gave his friend a reassuring pat on the shoulder.

"Now once we do what you want to do," said Tuby, "once we tell O. V. Mere or anybody else who'll spread the news that we're through with this place, because it isn't good enough — then that's final — war's declared, as Elfreda said late last night. Right, Cosmo?"

"Certainly, Owen. We advance on all fronts."

"Then let's give Jayjay — and ourselves — one last chance. Remember, I haven't seen him since we came back. And you haven't. You're only guessing what his attitude is."

Saltana shook his head. "No, I'm not. He's just waiting to be told he must get rid of us. He'd do it himself now, only he hasn't the guts. And I'll tell you exactly when he turned against us. It was before the pressure began to build up. It was at that party of his, when his wife asked us to do what he didn't know how to do himself — cope with those students. And he's probably jealous of you and her — "

"He needn't be — "

"I know, I know. And in one sense, that makes it worse. No, no, never mind about her. What does this last chance of yours amount to, Owen?"

"I want to talk to him, find out what he's thinking and feeling, and discover, without giving too much away, if he might be ready to put out an amicable joint statement. We part — but part as friends. Damn it, Cosmo, we have to stay here, at least through the winter, so why cut ourselves off?"

"You're still thinking about all those women of yours," Saltana muttered, chiefly to gain time. He knew his resentment could be taking him too far, and that Tuby was arguing sensibly, and now he couldn't make up his mind.

"I don't have to bother about that. We can discuss the women — if you must — some other time. Now — do I go and talk to him?"

Saltana's mind was made up now. "Yes, but not alone. *We* go and talk to him."

"I'm not sure that's wise — " Tuby began uneasily.

"Yes, it is. And I'll tell you why. This is a very tricky situation, Owen. If you're alone with him and say too much, he just might rush out a statement ahead of us. Then I'll blame you. If we're both there, then we both know where we are with him."

"But if you lose your temper — "

"God in Heaven!" Saltana shouted, his temper well lost. "Why do you people think I'm like a charge of guncotton? You're like Elfreda last night on the way to Sir Leopold, warning me not to lose my temper when later I was calm and quiet and she was exploding. I know when to be calm and quiet," he thundered. "I am in fact a calm and quiet man. Ask Elfreda."

"I don't need to. She told me, shining with admiration. All right then, Cosmo. We both talk to him. Let's go down and give him a ring."

Elfreda and the two youngsters appeared to have finished re-arranging the files. "We need the telephone," said Saltana briskly. "But not for anything confidential. You two can stay."

"Yes, darling," said Primrose appealingly from far away. "But what — do I do — now? You really must — give me — something to do."

"Certainly. You ring Lapford, Owen. Now then, girl, a young man brought up in the country has just inherited half a million pounds. He's twenty-two years of age and not too bright. As soon as possible he wants to project an image of himself as an *in* and pace-setting type, like the young men he's seen in coloured advertisements. Tell him what he has to do. You too, Mickley. Try doing it first without referring to the files. Better clear out, we may disturb you."

"Yes, darling."

"Okay, Prof. After you, Beautiful."

As they went, Saltana turned round and discovered that Elfreda was at the telephone. He raised his eyebrows at Tuby, who whispered, "She insisted. Says she *enjoys* using the phone."

"Good God!" Saltana muttered and stared at Elfreda. He began to look at her as if they'd never met before. She was plumpish but trim and satisfying, worth a dozen narrow and elongated Primroses; her nose turned up a little and her mouth might be too full and wide for a severe taste; but apart from a hair-do that didn't become her — too fussy and frizzled, too much a hairdresser's fancy notion — she was an extremely attractive woman.

"Oh — what a pity, Mrs. Dobb! You did tell him Professor Saltana and Dr. Tuby wanted to see him — rather urgently? I see. Just a moment, please, Mrs. Dobb." She covered the receiver, glanced quickly at Tuby, and then concentrated upon Saltana. "Too busy to see you this morning, he told her," she said in a fierce whisper. "And she sounded a bit flustered. I know Mrs. Dobb fairly well now. What do I say?"

"Ask her — very nicely, as a favour — if anybody has an appointment with him during the next hour or so." This wouldn't be easy, Saltana knew, and Elfreda managed it very cleverly by not putting her question immediately, as Saltana would have done, but by sliding it in as one item in a lot of intimate feminine chitchat.

"A sweet little job, Elfreda my dear. Well, now he will have somebody with him during the next hour or so. He'll have *us*. You don't object to this move, Owen?"

Tuby didn't. "And we might as well walk there. No, Elfreda — good of you to offer the car — but we'll be better off on our feet with so much fog about."

"And we'll be back before lunch."

"You won't be too nasty to poor Jayjay, will you?" Elfreda said anxiously.

"Certainly not. No, not even when he's pretending he's too busy to see us. But why doesn't somebody ask anybody round here not to be too nasty to poor Cosmo Saltana?"

"Because you're not that sort of man," Elfreda replied promptly. Then she turned away.

The fog wasn't quite as thick as it appeared to be from the house, but even so it isolated them in a muffled and dripping world and brought them closer in spirit than they had been earlier. But they had been walking several minutes before Tuby spoke.

"I'll admit that his telling his secretary he's too busy to see us doesn't give me much hope of him, Cosmo. But you'll still give him a chance, won't you? Play it my way — one of us putting out a feeler about an amicable joint statement — eh?"

"I'll keep my promise to you, my boy. But in return I want a promise from you. If we obviously fail, if he won't accept your last chance, if it's clear they're ready to do the dirty on us, then you must let me play it my way — and no more objections. Agreed?"

"Yes, of course." Though Tuby sounded reluctant, anything but enthusiastic. "Perhaps we were wrong to go away. If we hadn't gone, we might have met every objection as soon as it was raised. But everything seemed all set. I'll confess I'm worried, Cosmo. We aren't anywhere yet. We're playing poker with about thirty bob in our pockets." Perhaps it was the damp white morning, but he seemed to shiver a little.

"We're a little further on than you think, Owen. While we were in London last week, you were seeing everything from this end — the wrong end. I don't think I told you that Primrose said her friends the Birtles were much impressed — that was after I began talking elementary *Social Imagistics* to them. She said that Simon Birtle didn't like me but admitted, grudgingly, that I was a very clever fellow who might go a long way."

"What about his wife?"

"She behaved at first as if she was Peter Rabbit's mother or somebody like that, but later, after some image talk, she began taking a fairly shrewd interest in it. The Birtle papers and magazines aren't what we want, of course, but the Birtles themselves get about and talk, and people listen to the rich. And it must be *Social Imagistics* and image talk all the time, day and night, with us now, Owen. The next two months are the testing time, my boy. If we haven't got anywhere by then, we're through. On our way to a lectureship in Tasmania."

"Or a warm chair in Sierra Leone, drinking equally warm bad bottled beer. By God — no, Cosmo! We're living in a world where there are no longer any standards where the money is. It's now all fashion, what's new, amusing, exciting, what might mean something when the rest of it doesn't mean anything. And if we can't make 'em take *Social Imagistics* just long enough, then we deserve what we'll have to take elsewhere — "

"Save some of that, apart from the cynicism, for the radio, Owen. You might be on the air fairly soon. It'll take longer to get me on television."

"Why not reverse it — you on radio, me on television?"

"No sense in that. You've the better voice, I the more attractive appearance. So I claim the visual medium."

Tuby thought this over for a hundred yards or so. "I'm not so sure about that," he announced finally.

"About what?"

"This attractive appearance you're claiming."

Saltana was astounded. "Hell's bells! There can't be any comparison. Ask anybody. Ask Elfreda — young Primrose — "

"No, no, no! We're talking not in bedroom but television terms. I know far more about television than you do. It can play tricks with certain people, and you might easily be one of 'em. Badly lit, you could look bloody sinister, Cosmo. And then where are we? Professor Saltana — the sinister image man! We're out. Before talking again to O. V. Mere, we ought to give this some thought."

"Balls! I never heard such dam' nonsense. I don't say I can't look sinister, just for effect. But when I want to please, I please. It's realized at once that I'm a well-built and attractive-looking man. In Latin America, where the masculine standard of good looks is higher than you've ever known, I was frequently referred to as a handsome man. It runs in my family. Now, my boy, just take a look at yourself, if you can stand it — "

"Certainly I can stand it," Tuby put in indignantly. "And so can everybody else. I look cheerful, friendly, lovable — yes, I'll say it, lovable.

And I couldn't look sinister if I tried. Women who've seen me on television — "

"Chinese, Indians, Malays," Saltana shouted. "With a traditional taste for little fatties. *Look out!*" For now they were crossing the road, near the main entrance to the university, and Saltana was only just in time to pluck his friend away from a lorry suddenly roaring down on them.

Then, safely across, Saltana was surprised to see Tuby's shoulders begin to shake. Then Tuby was laughing so hard he had to lean against one of the pillars at the entrance.

"What's the joke, if there is one?" Saltana grumpily demanded.

"Oh — there is." And he stopped there because he had to laugh again. "Two middle-aged scholars — never mind image men now — I say *scholars* — walking through a fog — angrily arguing about their appearance! Cosmo — for God's sake — laugh!"

Saltana obliged with something, hardly a laugh.

Tuby put out a hand to stop Saltana from moving on. "Cosmo my friend, I know what might be going wrong with us. We've almost stopped laughing. Solemnity is creeping in. Our faces are getting longer and longer. We're taking ourselves seriously — "

"That's me, not you, Owen. I keep thinking about Elfreda and the money. A man needn't take his own money seriously, but as soon as he starts laughing about somebody else's, he's in danger of turning into a crook. There's a fine line we haven't to cross."

"Cosmo, there are also bridges we haven't to cross until we come to them. The longer your face, the grimmer you are, the worse it'll be for Elfreda, who was having the time of her life before we went away. She can't help taking her mood and tone from you, my friend. For God's sake, let's laugh — first at ourselves, as I've just been doing — and then at everybody else, beginning now with J. J. Lapford, Vice-Chancellor of the University of Brockshire."

Saltana nodded, and then rewarded him with a grin. "All right, my boy. But if we're going to do that, you'd better stop your heart bleeding for him — "

"But we give him a chance — "

"We give him a chance."

They picked their way carefully — and there seemed to be more fog inside the university than there had been along the road — towards Refectory and Admin. and Jayjay's room. There were two entrances to it, one direct and the other by way of Mrs. Dobb's office. Not wishing to get that good woman in any trouble, they chose the direct entrance, even though it announced that it was *Private*.

"Good morning, Jayjay," Tuby cried. "And how are you?"

"Oh — I say — look here," Jayjay protested, rising from his table-desk, his dinosaurus aspect, the small head waving uneasily above the bulk of him below, strongly in evidence. Saltana was trying to look amiable, but couldn't help staring at that decaying cavalry moustache, which he'd forgotten. When and why had the chap grown that thing? But Saltana felt he must say something. "Busy, are you, Vice-Chancellor?"

"Indeed I am — yes, Professor Saltana. In fact, I told Mrs. Dobb I couldn't be disturbed. And really I must say — " But then there was only head-waving.

"We won't keep you long," said Tuby, smiling. "We'll even keep our overcoats on, though it's warm in here. Saltana?"

"Certainly. A short visit. We just want to know what's happening, Vice-Chancellor."

"Well, as you saw Sir Leopold Namp last night, I gather — "

"Sorry to interrupt you," said Saltana, not grim, not sinister, a nice friendly chap, he felt. "But how did you gather that?"

"Sir Leopold told me about it over the phone. I also gather he made our position quite clear to you, Professor Saltana."

"He did — yes. Quite brutally clear. Indeed, I — "

But Tuby did some hasty coughing. "Sorry, Saltana. But if you don't mind, I'll come in now. You agreed, you remember."

"Certainly, certainly. Take over, Tuby." And Saltana fumbled in his overcoat pocket for a cheroot, brought one out and lit it, and then sat down to enjoy it.

Tuby remained standing, kept Jayjay's head still with a long look, gave it one of his slow sweet smiles. "Jayjay, I know you're being pressed from inside and outside the university. And I'm sorry, especially as everything seemed settled before we went away — "

"No, no — I can't accept that," Jayjay put in hastily.

"I see." Tuby didn't change his tone. "We were all too hasty, were we? And you feel now you can't give our Institute your academic blessing?"

"I still think it's an interesting idea — so far as I understand it. And there's nothing personal in all this, you must realize."

Saltana nearly intervened now with a very personal remark about Sir Leopold, but, catching an appealing glance from Tuby, he checked himself.

"In the circumstances then, Jayjay," said Tuby, still all honey, "suppose we put out a friendly joint statement — and there'll have to be something after all that publicity — saying in effect that Brockshire and our Institute aren't quite right for each other?"

Below the neck Jayjay was no wriggler, but now it seemed to Saltana, watching him closely, that somehow he contrived to wriggle. And clearly he didn't know what to say.

Giving Jayjay's last chance a last chance, Tuby continued in the same persuasive tone, "After all, we'll still be here for some time. Academically and officially we part company, but we can do it as friends. Why not?"

Tuby waited. Saltana sat smoking at them. Jayjay had to say something now. His head waved desperately — a sea lion in a fishless desert — and when he found his voice, it soon rose to a squeak. "In the circumstances — such a joint statement wouldn't be possible. Question of academic standards — " He wasn't coherent now. "Attitude of the Advisory Board . . . prestige of Brockshire . . . many members of the staff naturally resentful," he stuttered and squeaked. "Not properly qualified . . . if you'd been frank with me originally — mistake would not have arisen — "

"Are you suggesting," said Tuby, no friend now, "that Professor Saltana and I are not qualified to teach in your university? If so — "

"No, no — excellent degrees, I know. But not in sociology. And I know the Board will say — "

"Damn your Board, Lapford!" Saltana couldn't keep quiet any longer. "Tuby and I are the men who understand *Social Imagistics* — the very essence of sociology — "

Tired of head-waving and squeaking, Jayjay was now sitting down again and doing the usual dismissive act, shuffling papers. "I see no point," he said to the papers, "in our continuing this conversation."

"No friendly joint statement?" Tuby enquired.

"Quite impossible. And now — I'm extremely busy — you'd no right," he added, with the sudden anger weak men are apt to display, "to come barging in here — "

"Dr. Tuby," said Saltana in a formal manner, "what facilities has Brockshire offered to our Institute?"

Tuby answered in the same manner. "Half a hut."

"Anything else?"

"No, nothing, Professor Saltana."

"And would you say its Department of Sociology was properly organized and adequately staffed?"

"I would not."

"Neither would I, Dr. Tuby. So now, let's go. Sorry to have taken even a little of your valuable time, Vice-Chancellor."

"So am I," said Tuby smoothly. "And I was leaning over backwards for you, Lapford — you silly man!"

Saltana set a brisk pace on the way back. "I want to catch O. V. Mere before he leaves his office for that pub. Now you'll admit, Owen, I gave you every chance."

"You gave me and I gave him every chance. And you won't hear a murmur from me, Cosmo. From now on, I'll be with you crying havoc."

"You leave the strategy to me, my boy, and you take over the tactics."

"And fairly dirty some of 'em'll be. Did I tell you about that student Trotsky — Jeff — Jeff — some name you don't expect — oh yes, Con-

voy? Jeff Convoy — the agitator, the demonstrator, the protester, the
leader, the Mao of the English Revolution. Wait till he hears about this.
And don't walk at such a hell of a lick, man."

"I must catch Mere." And he did, with Elfreda's help, though Mere
then explained that he'd thought of giving the pub a miss, this being
Monday with a week-end to recover from. "You go down there in a few
minutes, Mere," Saltana told him, "and find that columnist brother-in-
law of yours. I've news for both of you. We've broken with Brockshire. It
can't offer us reasonable facilities. And its Department of Sociology, in
which we were supposed to work, isn't adequate, in our opinion."

Mere made various noises not easy to interpret over a long-distance
telephone — they may have been chuckles, although hardly anybody really does chuckle — but when words finally arrived Mere seemed to be
asking if Jayjay knew yet.

"No, not yet. That's where the Mere family comes in. One of you
can break the news to him — in print. Tuby and I have just seen him.
What about *who?* Oh — young Primrose. Nothing decided there yet. But
she can cope with her own publicity. Any news about radio and television?"

"Radio's more or less fixed. Television uncertain yet, but this news'll
help." Both Mere and the telephone sounded brisk and cheerful now.
"Listen, Saltana, will you be in later today, perhaps early this evening?"

"It looks as if I'll be in for weeks. Talk to you later, then, Mere. Hop
down to the pub now. 'Bye!" He came away from the telephone.

"Talking of pubs," said Tuby, who'd been listening, "don't we need
a drink?"

"Certainly. But look, Elfreda, from now on Owen and I must buy
our own booze."

"Never mind about that now," said Elfreda on her way to the drink
cupboard. "You must tell me exactly what happened. And here's your
whisky. Yours too, Owen."

"Bless you, Elfreda!" said Tuby. "And I'd better do the meeting with
Jayjay, Cosmo. You may be handsomer but I do a livelier turn."

And Elfreda laughed and applauded so much that Saltana decided
that this wasn't the time to warn her that for all of them, and for her especially, this break with Brockshire might have serious consequences. Let
her enjoy herself. He remembered Tuby's appeal not to allow solemnity
to come creeping in. And he told himself again that it wouldn't have a
chance to if he could stop worrying about Elfreda and her money. So he
laughed, after his own quieter fashion, when they did. Let her enjoy herself — until things turned sour, which he was pretty dam' sure they
would.

It was Elfreda who announced gleefully to Primrose and Mike Mickley, over lunch, the break with Brockshire, and she and Tuby between
them answered their questions and filled in the details. It was all high

spirits. Saltana said little, though he took care — at least so he hoped — not to look dubious or glum. Having lived a strange academic life mixed with frequent political upheavals, he was well acquainted with this particular form of high spirits, faintly feverish, a trifle hysterical, that had Tuby clowning hard and Elfreda screaming with laughter. This was the hilarity of people who thought they were triumphantly outfacing a challenge, a crisis, when in fact they weren't — and knew it deep inside themselves, where they really lived. However, he kept these thoughts to himself.

Yet towards the end of lunch he found young Mickley, his grin gone, regarding him thoughtfully. "Look, Prof — I'm on your side and all that jazz, but this makes a hell of a difference to me. Primrose too, I imagine — "

"Don't imagine — not for me. I can — look after myself — Mickley — "

"Mike — you remember — "

"Shut up. I mean — about me — "

"Okay, I leave you out, Beautiful. But Prof — we'll have to talk, won't we?"

"Certainly. I had it in mind. After coffee, you and Primrose, Dr. Tuby and I, will get together in the big room. I'm not shutting you out, Elfreda, but you might have other things you want to do — "

"I have, Cosmo — and anyhow I can't leave the phone today to Alfred. So forget about me."

Later, as the four of them went into the big room, Tuby said, "What do you think, Cosmo? This end — hard little chairs — seminar atmosphere? Or the other end — armchairs — drawing-room atmosphere — gracious living?"

"This end — seminar style. We'll pull out four of these chairs — or six if the younger generation has to loll — two each."

"Pooh to you, darling!" For her, Primrose was quite emphatic. "You try being a model. Talk about self-discipline! You three'd collapse after the first morning."

Saltana took Tuby aside while the other two were arranging the chairs. "Owen, this could be quite a tricky little situation. We need these two but I must be honest with them. Follow my lead if you get a signal. Might turn out to be something of a test for us."

"Image work?" Tuby asked, hopefully too.

"Image work, my boy." They then joined the other two, and as soon as Saltana had sat down he gave them a hard look and began at once. "Dr. Tuby and I will be sorry if you two have to leave us. We like you and believe you could be very useful to us quite soon. But for you this break with Brockshire is no joke. You, Mickley, have a grant for a postgraduate course in sociology there. No University of Brockshire, no grant. And you, Primrose, as everybody's been told, came to Brockshire to take

a degree. No degrees here, they're all down the road. So you'll have to
leave us too."

She replied at first with a high wailing sound. "I won't, not if you
want me here. They can keep their bloody degrees. You say everybody
knows — but what they know is that I'm going to work here at the Institute. I've told everybody I'm a *Social Imagistics* girl now — even if I
don't really know what that amounts to — "

"And isn't that the point?" Mickley cut in sharply. "Now — look,
Prof! And don't take offence. I like you two. I like it here. But I've got
to earn a living and I want a good degree. Now Brockshire's out, I can't
afford just to have fun and games here. Let's not pretend. Why did you
ask Cally to let me join you?"

Saltana allowed Tuby to get in first. "Professor Saltana thought you
might be intelligent, Mickley," said Tuby, who could be icy if need be.
"I don't know what he's thinking now."

"It wasn't that. He saw at once I wasn't a solemn ass and was ready
to play *Social Imagistics* — or anything else you two were cooking up.
But now I can't afford it. Let's not pretend. I know — and you know —
as a serious idea the thing's all wet. Just a game you're playing so that
Elfreda can set up her precious Foundation."

He got up to go, but Saltana thrust out a long arm and shoved him
back on to his chair. Both Tuby and Primrose were beginning a protest,
but Saltana silenced them. "Leave this to me, please. Now, Mickley,
you've had your say, let me have mine. That is, if you don't mind listening to a man thirty years older than yourself — "

"Prof, you're angry with me now — and I'm sorry. I wasn't trying
to get at you — "

"What did you think you were doing, then?" cried Primrose. "Stroking him — idiot?"

"Quiet, both of you! Just listen, don't interrupt." Saltana waited a
moment or two, staring hard at Mickley, now crimson with embarrassment. "Let's play this *Social Imagistics* game then, if that's what you want
to call it. I met you for the first time, three or four weeks ago. You were
hard at it deliberately projecting a certain image, which you've modified
since, no doubt because you were sharply criticized by Miss East. Quiet,
girl — no interruptions! You were ready to modify it, because although
superficially it appeared to be bold, brash, challenging, it was in fact an
uncertain image, not sharply imagined, not strongly held, a fairly typical
*Halt at Crossroads* image, I'd call it. What do you say, Tuby?"

"I agree, Saltana, though with a *Reverse Family* effect that didn't
help it."

"You're right, of course. I ought to have spotted that. It explains to
some extent the over-emphasis. We were all his parents and close relatives, timidly conventional people who had to be defied. It was an image
that would be chosen by a youth, clever enough, a good scholarship type,

who spent his first two years at his university dressing rather more carefully, behaving rather more carefully, than the other lads. He feels freer
during his third year, when he feels he's going to do well and can begin
moving away from his parents. So he does well, gets a good degree, and
is offered various things. Among them is a post-graduate course — in his
own subject, naturally, sociology — at a small, new, raw university,
Brockshire. There, he feels, he can be somebody. But what kind of somebody? What does he want to do if and when he lands his Ph.D.? To
teach somewhere — a lively new-style young don? Or to go into industry, on the public relations or personnel side, at least at first. The money's tempting, because, whatever he may say, he likes money, wants it, so
long as it's *well above a certain level* — "

Here he was interrupted by Mickley yelling at Primrose. "My God
— you're the end. Why the hell did you have to repeat all this to him?"

"You idiot, I've never told him a single thing about you. Anyhow,
much too boring."

"I don't believe you, East. He's just repeating — "

"Don't be a dam' young fool, Mickley." Saltana was really annoyed
now. "I'm not repeating anything. I don't know and don't care what
you've told Primrose."

"You're behaving like a chump, Mickley," Tuby told him sharply.
"First you accuse us of playing a silly little game. Next, when we try to
prove we aren't, you tell us we're cheating. Carry on, Saltana. *Halt at
Crossroads* image — with at least a touch of *Reverse Family* effect —
um? "

"Yes, that partly explains the jeans, jersey, neglected hair and face.
It represents a break with the family. Also a somebody, a graduate of an
older, larger, altogether more important university, outdoing what he's
already seen to be the usual Brockshire style. At the same time it's obviously a *Crossroads Image,* a makeshift until he makes up his mind which
way he'll turn. And the cheeky manner goes with it, of course, a cover
for bewilderment, uncertainty, a deep doubt about what he is and what
he represents. I saw that at once, as you must have done, Tuby. Here was
a graduate in sociology who was also a folk-singer who couldn't sing, a
guitar player without a guitar, a beatnik not opting out of society but
wanting a Ph.D. and an entry into society. It was a pitiful image — but
revealing — "

"All right, say I'm a mess," said Mickley sulkily. "But all the same,
you asked Cally to let me join you."

"Certainly. I saw from your attitude towards Cally and that argumentative ass, Friddle, that you were intelligent. And you are. You could
be very useful to us. But when you haven't really given a moment's serious thought to it, telling us that *Social Imagistics* is just a game we're
playing is damned impudence."

"Never mind about him," said Primrose. "Let him sulk a bit. Do me now, darling."

"Oh — no. If you're to be looked at in image terms, then Dr. Tuby can do it. He's the one you don't call *darling*. Dr. Tuby — kindly apply *Social Imagistics* to our young friend Primrose."

"Why not?" Tuby turned towards her, smiling.

"And now we'll see how *you* like it," Mickley muttered.

"I shan't mind," she told him. "I don't deceive myself as you boys always do. So start on me, Dr. Tuby. And you needn't work that smile so hard. Though of course you may be the smiler with a knife."

"No, I don't think so, my dear. You're an interesting but not unpleasant case. Quite deliberately, I suspect, and very sensibly, you chose and then gradually projected what we call a *Situation-Coping Image* — with certain undertones from depth psychology. You were a student of sociology at Leeds," Tuby began, using his warm honeyed tone. "In a very short time you became a fashionable model, thanks to your exceptional face and figure and, I imagine, unusual self-discipline. No, my dear, don't try to correct me as I go along. I've undertaken this at a moment's notice and must concentrate. Correct me afterwards, if you must. The situation demanded a complete change of image from anything known to your friends in Leeds. We can ignore appearance for the moment. We'll consider speech. I don't know where you were brought up — I've no facts on which to work — but I suspect that as a student in Leeds you employed a fairly vigorous Northcountry manner and style of speech. That had to be dropped from the new image. The situation demanded something less vigorous, humorous, realistic. And so did coping with the situation, in which you had little time to yourself, had to deal with all manner of people, and felt you must conserve your energy. To cope you needed something that sounded right for the image and at the same time didn't waste energy. So you adopted a manner — a faint and languid tone — a trail of brief phrases — that not only suggested social superiority, as it always has just because it implies that the speaker needn't bother about other people, but also required, once the trick of it had been learnt, the least possible effort. So you could save energy to meet the various and exacting demands made upon you. Now you had an image not only right for your situation but also enabling you to cope with it."

Tuby stopped there but looked as if he hadn't finished yet. The afternoon was darkening fast, and they hadn't bothered to switch on any lights. Though not given to such fancies, Saltana found himself peering through the dusk at one of those little scenes, never consciously arranged, that seem to be mysterious and yet meaningful in some strange way, like certain pictures that remain in the mind to tantalize it. The two men — Tuby, a round shape, a dim moon face, innocent and childlike somehow; Mickley, darker, hunched, and brooding — and the girl, slender, pale, almost luminous, were now not entirely the individual persons he knew so well, they were also vague figures in a group from some half-remembered painting, poem, old tale, or dream. And this aspect of them brought him a feeling, which he didn't welcome, of some hidden pattern about to be revealed, some order of life outside his experience, all his calculations, his ideas about this world.

"Is that all, then?" asked Primrose.

"No, not quite. I'm afraid I kept you waiting because my thoughts went wandering away." Tuby hesitated for a moment but then continued in a brisk, impersonal tone. "When I was young we found *anima* figures in the cinema — Garbo was the great example. By an *anima* figure I mean a woman, usually young and beautiful, on whom men can project the *anima* archetype from their own deep unconscious, which endows the woman with a poetic and magical quality."

Mickley stirred, making his chair creak, and might have been about to say something.

"The *anima* figure," Tuby went on, "is never a real person, somebody you know all about. She's removed from ordinary life, never comes from the next street but always from far away or nowhere at all, is exotic and enigmatic. Poetry, of course, is full of her, luring men to their doom. And she survives, though in slightly different forms, just as myths themselves survive, again in slightly different forms. Now I have an idea that the *anima* figure has moved from the cinema to those higher realms of fashion and advertising where the best-known models display themselves. And not only to women but through endless photography to men, who begin to find them irresistible — as *anima* figures. Which explains why so many rich young men, under their spell, marry them. And though the models themselves may not understand this magical attraction, some instinct tells them — if they're not merely accepting the advice of their male agents and photographers — to look and behave like *anima* figures. They begin to appear indifferent and aloof, like captive strange princesses, exotically far removed from the worries and anxieties, the wistful hopes and irrational fears, of ordinary girls. So by the time you had adopted the *Situation-Coping Image,* you were already, consciously or unconsciously, adding touches to suggest the *anima* figure. We might test this, Primrose, if you don't mind. Just when you were perfecting that faint, high, trailing manner of speech, did you ever consider adding a slight foreign accent?"

"You really *are* a clever little devil, aren't you?" said Primrose, somewhere between admiration and indignation. "Yes, I did. Now tell me why I adore *him.*" And she turned to point at Saltana.

"Never mind about that," said Saltana sharply. "You wanted some *Social Imagistics* analysis — at a moment's notice too, a sketch of the real thing — and now you've got it." And as Primrose protested, the door opened to let in a flood of light, changing the scene at once, and with it the head of Elfreda.

"That man Mere's on the phone for you, Cosmo," she told him. And he hurried out after her, but not before he heard Tuby saying, "The answer is — you *don't* adore him."

"Saltana, we've decided at this end not to use the break story today." Mere's voice seemed to come from far away — but then it always did — but now at least the line was clear. "I'd like to know a bit more, and Fred — my brother-in-law, the columnist, remember? — says he needs the Primrose East angle, which we haven't got. Have you?"

"No, not yet. We're out of angles. I can't tell you any more than I did this morning."

"I'll tell you what I'm going to do," said Mere, almost cheerfully for him. "I'll drive down in the morning, if there isn't too much fog. May stay the night, may not."

"If you don't, you'll have a devil of a lot of driving to do, won't you, Mere?"

His reply proved once again that you never know about people. "Love it, old man. Drive one of the fabulous ancient green Bentleys. And I'll bring Eden — my wife. Make a change for her. And listen, Saltana, it'll save time if you can give us lunch — half-past one, say. How do I find your place?"

Saltana explained where they were in relation to Tarbury and ended by saying he hoped to see them both round about one-thirty. Then he had to tell Elfreda what Mere had said.

"A good substantial lunch, then. Will I like him, Cosmo?"

"No, I don't think so. And he won't care if you don't. Surprising fellow, though. I can't imagine him in the open air at all, let alone driving one of those old green Bentleys. Or having a wife called Eden, ready to come along with him at this time of year in that sort of car. All very surprising."

"That's the point about England," said Elfreda thoughtfully. "Other people think it's full of dull men wearing bowlers and carrying rolled umbrellas. But really it specializes in odd and surprising individuals, who wouldn't exist anywhere else, certainly not in America, which thinks it's exciting — and isn't, not in my opinion. All the men Judson knew looked and talked and behaved just like Judson. What was going on in the big room before I burst in?"

Saltana told her how he and Tuby had felt compelled to give a tiny improvised demonstration of *Social Imagistics*. "I'd like to keep those two youngsters," he went on. "But if Primrose really wants a degree, she must leave us. And we can't ask Mickley to sacrifice his grant, his possible Ph.D., his chance of security — "

"Women are supposed to be mad for security," Elfreda observed slowly, "but I've an idea all that's been overdone. I'm not sure we don't despise men who are always thinking about security. I think we prefer men who are ready to take chances."

He gave her a long look, then ended it with a brief laugh. "You're in the right company then, my dear. Well, do I go back to the other three — or stay here?"

"You stay here. Anyhow, it'll be teatime soon and then they'll have to come in. Let's just sit — and talk about anything."

## 6

A cosy man, Tuby loved teatime, the real old chattering thing, no disguised "conference," and though he listened smilingly to Saltana's account of O. V. Mere's decisions and movements, if it had been left to him he would have preferred idle talk — though it wasn't so idle because it could be both revealing and perhaps heartwarming — to any discussion of plans and business. But of course the others, with Elfreda a possible exception, weren't leaving it to him. Primrose began it.

"Darling — sorry, I mean Professor Saltana — I'm staying with you, if you'll have me. I'm a *Social Imagistics* girl, I am. And don't bother about money yet. I have some. Though I may have to collect expenses, if I start running around for you. But there's one thing we couldn't settle in there. Do I change my image or not? Dr. Tuby thinks not."

"I think not too," Saltana told her. "We'll need your well-known public image for some time. I notice you've been moving away from it recently. So please get back to it, even here."

"Yes, darling."

"What about you, Mickley?"

"Prof, I don't know what to say. I withdraw the games bit. But — so what? You know how I'm situated. The minute you've broken with Lapford, Cally, Rittenden, and Co. and I'm still here, they'll whip that grant away from me — and I haven't a sausage."

"Elfreda, Tuby, and I between us can easily arrange for you to have a few pounds a week, for the time being. All that's easy. The hard part is concerned with your future. If you want to play safe, better say goodbye."

"And don't forget to say goodbye to me too," said Primrose. "Hurry back to the safe girls."

"Now — look — have a heart," cried Mickley. "I've a living to earn, and I still don't know what the hell this is all about — "

Saltana glared at him. Tuby saw he was really angry, and decided to intervene.

"Mickley, an hour or so ago you told us we were playing little games. You've just wtihdrawn that. Now you're telling us our idea won't work. We think it will — if we make it. And we've our living to earn too. And we're twice your age."

"But you've got Elfreda — "

"Clear out!" And Saltana jumped up in a passion. "Go on — *out!*"

"Oh — you *are* a bloody fool, Mike," Primrose wailed.

"Stop it, stop it, stop it," cried Elfreda. "Sit down, Cosmo. *And* you, Mike. Owen Tuby, you were talking. Now keep on talking." She looked at Primrose. "Men! Like giant mad babies."

"Take it easy, Cosmo. I don't think he quite meant what you thought he meant. Now then, Mickley, your trouble is you're still living in an academic atmosphere. And you've given no real thought to this image thing. Saltana and I have. We came home to find politicians and editors, advertising men and manufacturers, forever writing and talking about images. So we began thinking about images. And if you're asking yourself if we're any cleverer than you are, the answer is — *Yes,* as yet, by a devil of a long chalk. Now we're not going to persuade you — "

"Certainly not." Saltana was emphatic.

"If you have to be persuaded, you're no use to us. You must take a chance. If we flop, then we're the clowns, not you. If we succeed, a score of good jobs will be wide open to you. So you're not taking much of a chance. But if you're really like those young men in the advertisements who ask at once what pension a job carries, then hurry down the road and try to make friends with Professor Cally and Dr. Pawson. Now then, are you staying or going?"

"Dr. Tuby," cried Primrose, "I nearly love you. So I'll kiss you." Which she did, probably to gain time for Mickley.

"Well?" Saltana growled.

"I'm staying," said Mickley, still looking uncomfortable. "And I apologize for the fuss. I know dam' well you're both much cleverer than I am. That's partly the trouble — you're too clever. I want to learn and you've got to teach me."

"We're going to," said Saltana, rather grimly. "The first seminar starts in ten minutes' time, up in my room. Bring that stuff you knocked off so quickly this morning. Crude answers to a crude little question, I know, but they'll serve as a basis for discussion. And then perhaps in about an hour's time, Dr. Tuby will join us and give you a general talk. All right, Owen?"

Tuby said he'd be delighted, and then after they'd gone he lit a pipe and enjoyed it in silence while Alfred cleared away the tea things.

"Cosmo's very sensitive about me and my money, isn't he?" Elfreda remarked rather too casually when Alfred had departed.

"Yes. Much more than I am. I've been waiting for years for a rich woman to keep me — "

"Stop that silly nonsense. Be serious. Why is he?"

"Because he feels we rushed things through too quickly here and oughtn't to have gone away to Dublin. If we'd stayed we could have bounced them out of their objections to us. Probably we could, anyhow.

And as things have turned out, then we've loosened your hold on the Foundation. And he feels, as he says, you're emotionally involved there. It's not a question of money but your feelings being hurt, Elfreda."

She shook her head. "I think I've overdone all that. I'll have to talk to him. And it was I who lost my temper with that horrid Sir Leopold. He didn't."

"It was the same this morning with Jayjay. I persuaded Cosmo to give him a last chance, to keep it all friendly, but I started shouting before Cosmo did."

"Yet he bellowed just now at poor young Mike. But that was really about me, wasn't it?"

"It was about you, Elfreda."

"He's a curious man. Do you understand him, Owen?"

"Yes — that is, as one man understands another. But not as a woman might understand him."

No more could be said; the telephone was ringing. It was Isabel Lapford asking for Tuby. "What I think might be rather a nice dinner party on Saturday here," she said. "Could you possibly come? Just you yourself, I'm afraid. No room for anybody else."

"Isabel," said Tuby gravely, "Jayjay can't have told you about a talk Saltana and I had with him this morning."

"No, I haven't seen him since breakfast. Why?"

"Ask him to explain it to you in detail — how I offered to put out with him an amicable joint statement, and he refused. Twice Saltana has been snubbed — by Sir Leopold What's-it last night, and then this morning by your husband — and as I told you when we first met, he's a proud hard man. No, thank you, Isabel, I can't be with you on Saturday."

"Is this one of your jokes, Owen Tuby? Because if it is — "

"It isn't, Isabel. I wish it was. Goodbye, Isabel. And thank you for playing for us last night." And he rang off.

"You sounded sad, Owen," said Elfreda, who was now sewing something. "Is that how you feel — about her?"

"In a way — yes. She'll come badly out of this row. You'll see. Whatever she feels privately — and she was always really on our side, if only because we didn't bore her and most of the other people here did — she's very much the Vice-Chancellor's wife. Jayjay is mostly her creation. When the row starts, probably the day after tomorrow, she'll be the angriest and most vindictive of the lot. And while she's slashing at us, she'll be also slashing away essential parts of herself. Not a pretty sight, Elfreda."

"You fascinated her, Owen. She as good as told me when we were doing this house together."

"Nothing much in that. I merely filled in a few empty spaces in her relationship with Jayjay. As for me, I have a nasty habit of trying to charm women just to prove that a man with my face and shape can do it. Time I grew out of it at my age. Though actually I was genuinely sorry for her. I'm sorry for a lot of people, but mostly women — who have the harder time."

"Are you sorry for me?"

"Not at all, my dear. No need to be. But like Saltana — though he takes it harder — I feel we owe you a great deal and must take some responsibility as your friends. Well, I must go up and try to explain to those kids about images."

She laid her hands in her lap, gave him a long look, then said in a troubled voice, "All this image business — is it *real?* I worry about it sometimes."

"Elfreda, they were all talking to one another about images when Saltana and I were thousands of miles away, thinking about other things. They started it, we didn't. Mark Twain once said that everybody talked about the weather but nobody did anything about it. We're doing something about images."

She got up. "I'll tell Alfred to listen for the phone, then I'll go up with you. After all, if Primrose and Mike have to know about images, then so have I. Isn't that right?"

"It is. And we ought to have thought of it first. Though you won't have time to work at it as hard as those two will have to do. But you don't have to talk to Alfred about the phone. Stay here — keep on plying your needle, my dear — and I'll bring the three down here."

Tuby woke next morning with the vague feeling that something peculiar, outside all routine, was due to happen. After rummaging through his mind, which offered him a chest of drawers that gradually enlarged itself, he came upon the thought that O. V. Mere, who couldn't even be imagined driving a car, would be arriving for lunch with an unimaginable wife called Eden. That is, if it was a fine morning. And it was: the fog had gone, there was even some faint sunlight. He and Saltana worked by turns with Primrose and Mickley, ending by giving them some elementary image analyses to do during the afternoon and evening. Just before half-past one, when they were all having a drink in Elfreda's room, they heard the approaching sound, flat and hard and something between a roar and rattle, of the old Bentley. Rushing to the front door, they saw the long high green bonnet, leather-strapped, behind which, low down but open to the weather, two bundles were sitting. Primrose and Mickley were as surprised and delighted as they might have been if a friendly sabre-toothed tiger or mastodon had just arrived.

"God, it's fab," cried Primrose. "Why don't you get one, Mike?"

"Where — and with what? Just tell me, then I will. But it's fab all right. It's fab's father."

One bundle, unwrapping itself in the hall, turned into O. V. Mere, looking and behaving exactly as he had done when Tuby had first met him, weeks ago, in that office of his — still untidy, ash-and-dandruff, with the same cigarette smouldering in the corner of his mouth. "Just over three hours — door to door," he mumbled. "Not bad — eh? Of course she's murder on petrol now. Can't afford to take her out — except off tax. Whisky? Lead me to it. Eden'll want some too, if I know her, soon as Mrs. Thing — Drake — has shown her the can and then she's tarted herself up. So you're the famous Primrose East, are you? Nice kid, no doubt, but you don't do anything to me."

"I don't want to do anything to you," said Primrose. They were now in Elfreda's room. "But I can give you some whisky — and that might."

"How do you get hold of one of those Bentleys, Mr. Mere?" asked Mickley.

"God knows. Got mine from my younger brother who went to Canada. Hates Canada. Told him he would. Well, Saltana, any developments? No? Rang up Jayjay after I rang you yesterday afternoon. No change out of him. Might have been ringing up the bloody Treasury. Cagey on a high horse — not his line and I know him too well. Began to tell him so, but he hung up on me. Not like Jayjay — somebody's been getting at him. We'll talk this over at lunch. Must work fast. A-ha — here's Eden. Miss East, Professor Saltana, Dr. Tuby, Mr. — er — Mickley — my wife. Whisky for you somewhere, my dear."

Mrs. Mere — and from that time on Tuby could never think of her as Eden Mere, which suggested some place in a breathless travel advertisement — was fairly tall, had indignant light blue eyes, a roman nose, a long chin, and might have passed as the great Duke of Wellington masquerading in a tweed skirt and a beige twin-set. Her voice was very clear and emphatic, not uninflected like her husband's but even louder. It was impossible to imagine an intimate conversation between the Meres. Without working on it, she gave Tuby the impression that she was a refugee from the aristocracy. He saw her riding, one morning years ago, into some schoolroom of Mere's, her horse foundering among the blackboards and desks, and then, after shooting it, deciding to remain with Mere. Her staccato and emphatic speech was punctuated by a sound like *Ger-huh,* which might be derisory, questioning, or sharply conclusive.

"Wasn't it cold riding in that open car?" Tuby asked her.

"Appalling — appalling! Blows your head off, too. Eyes and nose streaming. Bumps as well — Oswald won't buy new tyres. *Ger-huh!* All the same I enjoy it, I really do. It's life and go. Which is more than can be said for bedmaking, dusting, doing macaroni cheese again in Wimbledon. *Ger-huh!* Any children?" she shouted at Elfreda. "No? We've three — sixteen, fourteen, twelve. And one thing I'll say for the little brutes. They all adore stodge — macaroni cheese, baked beans, fried bread, suet puds. They'll empty a dish of cold mashed potatoes where civilized people would want a biscuit. *Ger-huh!* Lunch? Quite ready — damned hungry really. But I'll take a little whisky in with me, if you don't mind."

The lunch table had been arranged, probably at Mere's suggestion, so that he and Saltana were sitting together, to do some hurried plotting. This left Tuby sitting between Mrs. Mere and Elfreda, with Mickley and Primrose on the other side. With her formidable presence and loud voice, Mrs. Mere dominated the talk without appearing even to try.

"How have you got along with the Lapfords?" she asked, obviously not expecting a reply. "Had three years of 'em here when Jayjay was Chief Education Officer and Oswald his dogsbody. *Ger-huh!* Didn't mind her so much. We just boasted together and got little snubs in. No children, that's her trouble. Runs Jayjay, of course, if nobody else is running him. *Ger-huh!* Jayjay's a soft ambitious man — not a good mixture. Now Oswald's hard — though he may not look it — but unambitious — much better. What are you, Dr. Tuby?"

"Soft *and* unambitious. A poached egg."

"I won't buy that," said Primrose. "Poached eggs don't think they're poached eggs. You're a deep one, you are. What about Professor Saltana?"

"Hardish," Tuby replied promptly. "But only moderately ambitious. He wants to be where he can't be pushed around but he doesn't really want to do much pushing around himself."

"Nice and sensible, I call that," said Elfreda. "Do have another cutlet, Mrs. Mere?"

"Thank you, I will. But I ought to be made to eat the one my husband's dropping ash on. *Ger-huh!* Wherever he is, Oswald's really living in the back room of a squalid café. It's like sitting all day next to an unmade bed, being married to that man. *Ger-huh!*"

Primrose began to giggle. "Don't do that, my dear," Mrs. Mere told her. "It's out of character."

"It is, yes," said Primrose gravely. "Wrong image."

"We're instructing her in *Social Imagistics,* Mrs. Mere," said Tuby.

"Oswald mentioned 'em. I like the sound of 'em," Mrs. Mere declared, looking round defiantly. "Ever since Oswald told me I've been wondering and curious. Ask him. *Ger-huh!* Anybody like to instruct me while he's running round the university this afternoon? I'm keen to learn. What are they and what do they do? One reason why I came down with him, apart from the outing. Outing? *Ger-huh!* If you were in London, Dr. Tuby, you'd never be able to keep me away."

Tuby nodded and smiled. But he wasn't simply being polite. He'd suddenly had a hunch about this woman. "If we were in London I don't think I'd want to keep you away. You might possibly have a flair for our kind of work."

"That reminds me, Dr. Tuby — as Oswald's too busy plotting to tell you — you're broadcasting on Friday night. Seven o'clock, I think — "

"Quarter-past," her husband threw at them, without a glance their way.

"Quarter-past, then. A programme called *New Times* or *New* Something. Oswald got you in to take the place of somebody's who's ill, and you'll be talking about your *Social* What's-its. Are you any good on the air?"

"Yes, I am."

"Well, that's really that, isn't it?" Mrs. Mere appealed to the others. "No false modesty about *him,* is there? *Ger-huh!* Is he any good on the air? Yes, he is. Bang! But I wouldn't have thought you were conceited, Dr. Tuby."

"It isn't conceit," said Tubly firmly. "It's the plain honest truth. I play the piano badly, I dance badly, I dress badly. I'm no treat to look at. And so on and so forth. But I know how to lecture and I'm good on the air."

"Certainly," said Saltana, who must have now finished his private session with Mere. "And that's the right attitude of mind. Undue modesty and deliberate understatements about one's abilities are themselves a form of conceit, probably the worst."

"Now, please," Mere cut in, "if it's all the same to you. Got to co-ordinate our plans. Then I'm off, hoping to speak to Cally, Lapford, and the Registrar. If what they say doesn't satisfy me — and I'm pretty dam' sure it won't — then I hurry back and we get on the phone to the Press. Saltana and I have already agreed on a statement that can go out under his name. And there's a local man you've used before, I understand. Now, Miss East — or do I call you Primrose? Right. Now, Primrose, later this evening, after I've gone, they'll be all getting through to you. You're the peg for the news story. You were the famous model who abandoned her career to complete her sociological studies and get a degree — blah, blah, blah. Now you're walking out of the university and any chance of a degree, what are you going to say?"

"What am I going to say?" Primrose hesitated and seemed to droop, but then, watching her intently, Tuby saw her small round chin go up. "I'm going to say that the sociology that really interests me is being taught here at the *Institute of Social Imagistics,* and here I'm staying — degree or no degree. Something like that, anyhow."

"Good girl," said Saltana. "That'll do for them, won't it, Mere?"

"They may want more — so she can add a few compliments to you and Tuby — if she can think of anything — "

"Do you mind?" cried Primrose indignantly. "Why — I adore them."

"And also add a mysterious reference — and keep it mysterious, my dear — to the scope and future activities of the Institute itself — playing a part in our national life — blah, blah, blah — "

"That's what I married — blah, blah, blah. *Ger-huh!*"

"It'll all tie in with your broadcast on Friday, Tuby. By the way, your producer is a Mrs. Mumby and she'll meet you at Broadcasting

House about six-thirty. A contract's on its way. And, Saltana, this should definitely get you a TV spot — probably on *Every Other Day* — wonderful publicity. But I'll be in touch, of course."

"Oswald Victor Mere," his wife began solemnly, rising most impressively from the table, "I wish to make an announcement, and I don't care who hears it — "

"My God, Eden, three are quite enough. And what a time and place to tell me — "

"Idiotic and damned indelicate, Oswald. *Ger-huh!* The announcement I wished to make is this. If these people should ever move their Institute and Social Gymnastics to London — or anywhere within easy reach of Wimbledon — I propose to offer my services to them if there's any money in it at all."

"Doing what, Eden, for God's sake?"

"Not ironing underclothes or serving baked beans and macaroni cheese, you may be sure, Oswald. *Ger-huh!* But in some executive capacity, however modest. Dr. Tuby has already said I might possibly have a flair. And I believe he has a flair for flairs, if you see what I mean? I also believe him to be a man for whom — and I'm not sure yet for what reason — I could easily develop a warm attachment."

And she laid a hand on Tuby's shoulder that made him feel he was about to be press-ganged into the Peninsula War. Gently relieving himself of its pressure, he rose and said, "I'll take over this afternoon, Cosmo, as you may be busy. Elfreda, Primrose, Mickley, we'll continue our seminar on elementary *Social Imagistics,* and you're welcome to join us, Mrs. Mere, just to get a tasting sample. The subject will be: The Image as Reflection, Challenge, or Repudiation. My room in a quarter of an hour."

Mere's cigarette wobbled. "I'm just an old education wallah. And I'll be damned if I know yet whether you fellows are half-barmy or really have something."

"Don't be a fool, Oswald," his wife told him sharply. "*Ger-huh!* Of course they really have something. I can smell it. I have a nose." Which certainly couldn't be denied.

With Mrs. Mere asking questions too, the session upstairs lasted longer than Tuby had thought it would, and it was nearly teatime when they all came down to Elfreda's room. Mere was back from the university and busy at the telephone.

"Good thing he came," Saltana muttered to Tuby. "They annoyed him so much, he's with us heart and soul — if he has a heart and soul. He swears they won't know what's hit them in the morning. I've got the local lad — Morgan — on to it too. Brockshire, here we leave you!"

Apart from one popular daily that displayed a lot of Primrose East leg and was heavily facetious about her scholastic career, the newspapers next morning didn't give the Institute very much space — bottom of a column here, a paragraph there — but Mere on the telephone from London said he was delighted, assuring Saltana that the fat would now be in the fire. But when this was reported to Tuby, he said glumly, "Yes, but who wants fat in the fire?" And he insisted upon doing a morning's analysis-of-image work with Primrose and Mickley, leaving Saltana and Elfreda in her room by the telephone, ready for further moves in the campaign. During lunch, both of them accused him of a lack of enthusiasm for the fight, of even a trace of a defeatist spirit.

"No," he told them, "it's not that. The trouble is, I'm essentially a peaceful type. I enjoy making friends, not enemies. And though I think we're entitled to do what we have done — to break away from them before they announced they were kicking us out — I can't help thinking too we may soon run into difficulties you aren't yet taking into account."

But when pressed to say what these difficulties might be, he shrugged away an answer. And then, while the other four were talking away and he was keeping silent, he decided to make a move entirely on his own, a move that might have been denounced as disloyal or idiotic, a move that turned out in the end to be of the highest importance to the Institute. He decided to ring up Isabel Lapford and, no matter how furiously angry she appeared to be, to ask if they could meet. And as it was a reasonably fine afternoon, he announced that he needed a walk. He remembered a call box on the way to Tarbury, and it was from there he rang her up. She took the call, presumably to let him hear how angry she was and what a contempt she had for him and his "wretched friends."

"Just a minute, Isabel, please. It's not my fault that this has happened. I did everything I could to stop it. And I've never spoken a word to the Press. I'm calling you now because I think we ought to meet and talk as soon as possible — "

"My God — you've got a nerve! Why should we?"

"Because we're friends and we haven't to lose our heads like the rest of them — "

"You can't come into this house — "

"I'm in that call box on the left just before you reach Tarbury. Why don't you jump into your car, pick me up here, and drive somewhere where we can talk quietly?"

"I can't talk quietly — "

"Yes, you can, Isabel. Let's try, anyhow."

"I don't know — I must think — I don't promise — "

"I'll be waiting. *Please!*"

Twenty long minutes later she arrived, driving fast and coming to a screaming halt. Her anger had now been transformed into a cold disdain. "I might as well tell you that I think this is an idiotic waste of time," she said as soon as he was sitting beside her.

"If you'll go where we can talk, I'll try to show you that it isn't, Isabel."

She produced a fairly ladylike snorting sound, then drove very fast,

taking almost immediately a left turn up a side road that avoided Tarbury and soon took them out into the country. Another turn, slower now,
brought them into a lane that wound upwards towards a copse that had
no wall or fence round it, and she was able to halt the car in its misty
shadow. "And if anybody sees us here, God knows what they'll think
we're up to."

"What we're really up to is perhaps even better than what they'll
think we're up to. And that is — keeping hold of friendship and making a pact."

"That's all very well, but do you realize what you people are doing
to Jayjay and Brockshire? And I happen to be the Vice-Chancellor's wife,
you might remember."

"I'm sorry, my dear. I really am. But you must be patient with me
for a minute or two while I point out exactly what has been happening."
After describing the situation they found on their return, Saltana's and
Elfreda's interview with Sir Leopold, his own attempt to persuade Jayjay to issue a friendly joint statement, he went on: "There isn't anything
here you can blame me for, Isabel — "

"Except coming here pretending to be a sociologist," she flashed
at him.

"I don't accept that." He kept his tone calm and easy, knowing only
too well that it is the anger in voices that produces more anger. "Saltana
and I are up to our necks in what is essentially a sociological subject. I'm
hoping to explain some of it in a radio interview on Friday evening —
seven-fifteen, if you're interested — "

"Why should I be interested?" Sharp, scornful.

"Why not?" he asked her mildly. "If it's outside the academic field,
then no doubt you're well rid of us. But why be angry and bitter?"

"You know dam' well why. You're making Jayjay and the university
— *our* university — look silly. Saying our facilities are inadequate!"

"But why should that make you look silly? They *are* inadequate — "

"Of course they are. But that's not the point."

As she stopped there, he didn't press her to tell him what the point
was. That would make her angrier still. So, if only to relieve the tension,
he asked her permission to light his pipe and then smoked in silence for
some moments. "It's just possible, from now on," he began finally, "there
may be some sort of idiotic feud between us, the kind of thing that never
did anybody any good. What I propose is that you and I don't join in.
We're really a pair of secret fifth columns."

She twisted a little to offer him a scornful bright stare. "Oh, you're
afraid now you may have gone too far."

He answered that with a look that told her he didn't propose to
waste any words on that remark. "You could run into trouble, y'know, Isabel. For example, last week, just after I got back here, one of your stu-

dents came to see me, to tell me there was a move to turn us out and that he and his friends were all on our side."

"Who was it?"

"He'll be round again, tonight or tomorrow," Tuby went on calmly. "I can ask him to prove he's on our side, which is what he'd love to hear. Or I can tell him not to make an ass of himself. Now what am I to say? I offer you a sensible and friendly little pact — so that whoever plays the angry fool, we don't — and you tell me I'm afraid we may have gone too far. Remember what you felt on Sunday night when we had the music. We're all really the same people. But now some of us — though I don't include myself — are beginning to talk like politicians. Drop me where you turned off the main road, please, then we shan't be seen together and I can easily walk home."

She turned to face the dashboard and for a moment or two it looked as if she were about to start the car and move off without another word. But then, without looking at him, she said in a small muffled voice, "If you must know, I warned Jayjay not to let himself be pushed too hard, and to come to some sort of agreement with you people. He never told me about your offer. Which wasn't like him because he tells me everything and usually asks my advice. But even if I think privately he's made a fool of himself, my place is by his side."

"I never suggested it wasn't, my dear Isabel. But you and I can agree to remain not only on speaking terms but also on a genuinely friendly helpful basis. We don't do any feuding. On the quiet we exchange news and views, for our mutual benefit. We behave sensibly."

"I hate to admit it, but I don't really understand you and Saltana."

He smiled. "We're just a pair of wandering scholars — "

"Oh — fiddlefaddle! At least I know you're dam' clever, both of you, and have the cheek of the devil. And I suppose you're ambitious. Like me — I freely admit it — not like Jayjay, who really only wants a quiet life. You're tired of being a nobody. You want to be a *somebody*."

Tuby shook his head, though he was still smiling. "I don't want to be a somebody. I *am* a somebody. That is — to myself. But if you mean having my name in the papers, being recognized and on familiar terms with the great, I don't want it, I don't give a hoot for it, have a complete contempt for it. And this applies to Saltana too. We don't give a damn. The only difference between us is that he doesn't mind making enemies — if you hit him, he'll hit you back and *harder* — whereas I dislike making enemies and prefer making friends. With you, for instance, my dear Isabel." And he took her hands.

She didn't try to release her hands but she frowned at him. "I knew from the first you were the more dangerous one. But we'll have our little pact. Though I don't quite see what's involved in it."

"Nothing much. We meet occasionally. Or we simply use the telephone. To exchange news and views. Sensible fifth-column work without any serious disloyalty. Quietly avoiding any bull-headed glaring and shouting and feuding. You agree, my dear?"

"I agree, Owen." And this time she kissed him, not passionately but quite warmly, finding the exact level on which he felt their relationship should be.

He got back to what he felt ought now to be called Headquarters only to discover, rather to his disgust, a television van outside the front door. It didn't belong to the B.B.C. but to some other network, strange to him. Inside, all was uproar, lights, cables, excitement. Primrose and Saltana, who looked chalky but seemed to be calm and relaxed, were about to be interviewed in the big room. Tuby decided they didn't need him and went across to Elfreda's room, in the hope of finding tea there. There was a forlorn arrangement of about eight used cups, but not a clean one and no teapot. He went into the kitchen but it was empty, which meant that Florrie and Alfred hadn't been able to resist the dazzling goings-on of television, so he returned to Elfreda's room, gave himself a hefty whisky-and-soda, and took it upstairs. He felt the idiotic melancholy of the man who doesn't want to be in something and yet feels he oughtn't to be left out of it. Alone and quiet in his own room, smoking a pipe and sipping his drink, he ought to have sunk himself deep into a profound and perhaps creative reverie, but actually he did what he had often warned his students against doing — just idly attended to a meaningless procession of images and odd thoughts, like a man trapped in a fourth-rate film show.

Partly because he'd played no part in the newspaper interviews by telephone and the television performance, partly too because he said nothing about his talk and understanding with Isabel Lapford, he felt this odd-man-out sensation the remainder of that day and most of the next. He was with the others, pretending to share at least some of their excitement, but not *of* them. He didn't really come alive until after dinner on Thursday when he had to take a phone call from Lois Terry.

"I've just had an idea," she announced, gasping a little as if she'd just run to the telephone. "You see, when I'm in my bath I always listen to my transistor set. And I heard a man announce that Dr. Tuby of the *Institute of Social Imagistics* — famous already, obviously — would be interviewed tomorrow night on the seven-fifteen programme. Is it true?"

"It is. Somewhere in Broadcasting House. Why? Will you listen, my dear?"

"Oh — my idea's much more exciting than that. You see, I'd already arranged to go up tomorrow afternoon and stay the night. I need some books and must do some shopping on Saturday morning. I'll be driving up, and if you can take my little old brute of a car, then I could drive you too. And you'll have to stay the night, won't you?"

"I suppose so — yes. I hadn't given it a thought," he added, quite truthfully. "Stupid of me. I ought to have booked a room."

"Well, you needn't if you don't want to. This is part of my idea. My sister Audrey — she's three years older than I am and has been married for ages — has a nice large flat, in St. John's Wood, and she and her husband are away, so I'll be staying there — and you can too. Unless of course you're frightened of me, dear Dr. Tuby," she added, with something between a final gasp and a laugh.

"I am a little, Lois, naturally. But I'm even more afraid of trying to find some forlorn little hotel bedroom somewhere, probably in Bloomsbury. So, my dear, I accept your very kind invitation with enormous pleasure and gratitude — car, bed, and all — "

"As I said," she put in hastily, "it's quite a large flat — you'll have a room of your own — even your own bathroom — "

"But I hope you'll be free to dine with me after the broadcast — "

"Yes, of course — lovely! Could you please be ready just before three — and I'll pick you up? I must run now. I have two students coming and I can hear them at the door. 'Bye!"

It was a few minutes to three on Friday afternoon when Tuby put his small suitcase and then himself into Lois's car. She was wearing a deep yellow woollen coat and a little dark brown hat, and looked surprisingly smart and gay. Saltana and Elfreda were busy at the telephone, but Primrose and Mickley insisted upon seeing Lois and Tuby off, rather as if they were a newly married couple; and indeed some bawdy observations had to be checked by some noisy engine-running and gear-clashing. Before they had turned into the main road, Lois announced that she had had her car overhauled and that now it oughtn't to be too bad. After Tarbury, between any difficult bits of driving, they discussed the Institute's break with Brockshire. To his surprise, Lois condemned their move.

"It's chiefly because I hate this nasty sneering publicity," she confessed. "And I can't help feeling sorry for Jayjay, who's a bit dim but is trying hard. And he hadn't a chance against you buccaneers."

"I'm no buccaneer," Tuby objected mildly. "And their decision to turn us out, after accepting us, was very harsh — especially for Elfreda Drake." And he explained about Elfreda and the Judson Drake Foundation and the Americans.

But Lois was no fool, even though she might occasionally behave like one. "I don't see that what's happened is going to help her. I may be talking like an academic — and, after all, I *am* one — but it seems to me her position's weaker than it was."

"Actually it is," he admitted. "And they're so busy gleefully scoring points, back there, that this is being overlooked. But don't forget, Lois, that we didn't create this situation. While Saltana and I were away, some of your colleagues and Jayjay and his Advisory Board ganged up to clear us out. The one who's really to blame is Jayjay. Once he'd accepted us, he should have held on. You say he tries hard, but this time he didn't try hard enough."

"You rushed the poor old walrus, you buccaneers. And then," she added shrewdly, "feeling too confident, you went away — a great mistake. And the greatest mistake of all — and I'm being sensible now, not a jealous cat — was your having anything to do with Primrose East. I'm not against her — "

"Don't be. She's a likeable girl — "

"But she was bound to raise the temperature all round. But that's enough, don't you think? The poor old car's not doing too badly so far, is it? Do you like a journey by car?"

"Only when I'm with you, Lois my dear."

"The trouble about being a woman is you enjoy that kind of remark even when you know it doesn't mean a dam' thing. You insult your own intelligence. Perhaps I'd better stop chattering so that you can think about your broadcast. Are you feeling nervous?"

"No, not at all."

"You're lucky. I've just done it three times — and even then it was only regional, not national — and each time I felt petrified. Even worse than I do giving a public lecture. Any advice you care to give me, dear Dr. Tuby, will be gratefully received."

Tuby, serious beneath a mock-solemn manner, began: "Out of my much longer experience, dear Dr. Terry, I'll venture a little advice. When broadcasting, don't open your imagination, close it. Don't imagine a vast audience. It isn't really there. You're mostly talking to one or two nice ordinary people, passing the time. Then when you're speaking in public, try to remember that the audience — except perhaps at political and similar meetings — are just as anxious as you are for the occasion to be a success. They're on your side. And again don't multiply them into a collective monster. If you find yourself doing this, then pick out one person who looks sympathetic and talk to her — or, in your case, perhaps him. If I feel I have to concentrate on anybody, I choose a good-looking woman."

By now the day had gone, lights were flashing and dipping, cyclists were flirting with suicide, and the traffic both ways thickened and slowed up as they ground their way into London. Lois said she loathed this kind of driving and was bad at it, so Tuby kept quiet and began to wonder uneasily if he'd arrive at Broadcasting House in decent time. But six-thirty had seemed to him unnecessarily early — he'd often rushed into radio stations in the East a few minutes before going on the air — so he wasn't unhappy when Lois brought him outside Broadcasting House at twenty to seven.

"Now I'll take your bag," she told him. "I'm going straight up to Audrey's. Her married name's Slinger, but it's all here — address and phone number." She gave him a slip of paper. "I'll jump straight into a bath, listen to you, then be ready for that dinner as soon as you arrive. There's a not-bad restaurant in the same building. And no hanging round here after the broadcast, lapping up praise and booze, Tuby my pet. A taxi to Audrey's at once. 'Bye — and good luck!"

The producer in charge of him, Mrs. Mumby, was a thickset, heavy-chinned, schoolmistressy type who didn't like the look of him just as he didn't like the look of her. There was this difference, however, that while her appearance wasn't misleading, his was, for he was no ordinary chubby and smiling little man.

"You'll probably want to go through your notes," she told him.

"I haven't any. What I would like is a drink."

"That can be arranged. But it doesn't always make people less nervous."

"I'm not feeling nervous," Tuby said, smiling. "I just like a drink about this time. And I've been sitting in a car for nearly four hours."

A little later, when he was smoking a pipe and enjoying his whisky, she began instructing him in a routine fashion, as if she'd just been wound up to do it. "If you have to read anything, try to do it as naturally as possible."

"I haven't to read anything, Mrs. Mumby."

"Try to relax — "

"I am relaxed — "

"Don't think about all the people who'll be listening to you — "

"I shan't." Though by this time he was beginning to feel that he and Mrs. Mumby weren't in communication.

"Try to avoid coughing and that sort of thing, but don't worry about a few little slips — just correct them quite naturally."

Tuby gave it up, said nothing, drank some whisky.

"What did you say?" Mrs. Mumby enquired, rather suspiciously.

"I didn't say anything. Not that time." They were like two characters in avant-garde drama. Now she ought to tear her clothes off or shoot him.

"We'll go up to the studio in a minute," said Mrs. Mumby. "Harvey Bacon, who'll be interviewing you, is very good, but he can be naughty now and again and slip in a tricky loaded question."

"Then he may get a tricky loaded answer."

Mrs. Mumby regarded him with a deepening suspicion. "Dr. Tuby, am I right in thinking this is your first time here?"

"Not quite, Mrs. Mumby. But I've been out of the country for about twenty years."

"Have you indeed? Well, I think we ought to go up to the studio. Finish your drink."

They didn't exchange a word going up in the lift. Tuby felt that if it had gone up for miles, no further attempt at communication would have been possible. There was a certain science-fiction air about the corridor along which she led him: a couple or robots might be around. The studio was rather small and Harvey Bacon rather large. He was quite handsome in a smooth, empty way, and suggested an actor playing a cynical friend of the family in an Edwardian comedy. He greeted Tuby with a kind of central-heating-thermostatic warmth. Tuby didn't feel nervous — he hadn't been boasting there — but did feel alone and a long way from anywhere and would have welcomed another and stiffer whisky. Mrs. Mumby left them, after giving Harvey Bacon a real smile and Tuby a ghastly one, either out of avant-garde drama or science fiction. Harvey Bacon sat him across a table and explained his *slow-down* and *hurry-up* signals, kept an eye on the warning light, and then began the usual welcome-to-the-programme-now-I-tell-them-who-you-are routine, in a voice that was golden syrup spread on satin.

Tuby could do this voice too, but he realized at once there must be contrast. He would take all the honey out of his tone, keeping it steadily pleasant but crisp.

"Now, Dr. Tuby," said Harvey Bacon, "these last few days we've been reading or hearing about this *Institute of Social Imagistics*. And I believe you're the Deputy Director of it."

"I am — yes."

"Splendid! I wonder if you could explain quite briefly what this Institute proposes to do — "

"Certainly. We're making a close study and analysis of images. We're ready to decide in particular cases whether certain public images are unsuitable or suitable — and, if suitable, how they should be projected."

"I see," said Bacon, who didn't. "*Social Imagistics* — um?" He paused for a moment, artfully. "But honestly, Dr. Tuby, do you think this image thing of yours really necessary?"

"In strict terms, no, I don't," Tuby replied, quite pleasantly. "Life could go on very well without it — "

"A very candid admission — "

"Just as life could go on very well without this interview or this programme — "

"That's not very complimentary — "

"No, but your question didn't suggest we were about to exchange compliments." And Tuby smiled at him above the microphone. You load the question, laddie, I'll load the answer. "But allow me to expand my reply," Tuby went on smoothly. "For my part — and here I can't speak for my colleagues — I would gladly abandon any further work on *Social Imagistics* if everybody else would agree to stop writing and talking about images. But that's not likely, is it? We read and hear more and more about images — in politics, advertising and commerce, journalism, even in private life — so Professor Saltana and I decided to devote ourselves to a thorough study of them."

"But not entirely by yourselves, I gather, Dr. Tuby. You're already beginning to instruct and train some assistants, aren't you? Among them Miss Primrose East, the well-known model."

This mention of Primrose, even so soon, was inevitable, and Tuby was ready to deal with it. "Miss East was a student in sociology before she became a model. She decided to join us rather than return to a routine course in sociology. We're very glad because she's both eager and intelligent, and we believe she has a flair for this particular work."

"That's wonderful, Dr. Tuby. But — if you don't mind my being completely frank with you — "

"Not at all — so long as I can be equally frank with you — "

"Of course. Well then — I can't help wondering what this particular work of yours amounts to. I mean, is there *really* anything in it?"

"We think there's a great deal in it, as I've already suggested. But if you feel it's all too vague and generalized, let's take a particular example of an image. Your own, for example. You must know you're projecting a certain image — "

"Am I?" Bacon gave an uncertain little laugh to the listeners and a warning little shake of the head to Tuby. "I didn't know I was — but perhaps I am — "

"Of course you are," Tuby told him pleasantly. "And if you'd like me to prove to you I'm not wasting my time with *Social Imagistics,* then I'll be happy to analyse this image of yours, to explain why you decided to adopt it, to assess its suitability — "

"No, no, please! After all, the listeners are interested in you, not me."

"I doubt that. But can we assume, from now on, that this particular work of ours *really may* have something in it?"

"Of course, of course! I never actually doubted it. And what I'd like you to do now, Dr. Tuby, is to give us a rough idea — and I realize it must be a complicated subject — of how you approach this problem of images." And having got that out, Harvey Bacon looked relieved.

Tuby felt some relief too. This would be the smooth home stretch. He was prepared for it, ready to give a little away, to keep the more intelligent listeners interested, but not too much. Using an easy and informal seminar, not public-lecture, manner, he explained how and why public images were now so important, touched on their objective and subjective significance, described how they could be divided into main groups and sub-groups, giving a few examples of each, and was jogging along so pleasantly that Harvey Bacon's signal to close took him by surprise.

"Well, I don't know what Auntie Mumby's thinking," said Bacon as soon as they were off the air, "but if anybody wants my opinion you were bloody good, though of course an old hand. You had me sweating for a minute when you offered to take my image to pieces. Would you have gone through with it if I hadn't stopped you?"

"Yes, I wasn't bluffing. Sorry about the sweating but you rather asked for it, y'know."

Mrs. Mumby joined them. "Came over splendidly, Dr. Tuby. Quite one of the best in the whole series. But you're obviously an experienced broadcaster. Why didn't you tell me?"

"I kept trying to. Well, thank you, both of you. I wish I could stay for a drink but I promised to take a girl out to dinner and she'll be waiting impatiently."

He began to feel impatient himself by the time he'd waited several minutes for a taxi. Having acquitted himself manfully, he was eager now for food, drink, feminine admiration and cosseting. It was not very far to these mansion flats in St. John's Wood, but even so he found himself making silly little movements, as he sat forward instead of leaning back, to help the taxi along. The flats, an imposing block, had three separate entrances but he soon found the one he wanted, which would take him up to 14A, and he had just time to notice, on his left, an Italian-style restaurant, not too full, not too empty, that was obviously the place that Lois had mentioned. And in the lift he saw himself seating her cosily in there and had just caught a glimpse of her magnificent eyes, across the table in candlelight, before he reached the fifth floor. To his right were 14A and 14B, sharing the whole corridor between them, obviously fine large flats. 14A (Slinger) was the nearer door, on his left, and 14B was clearly at the end of the corridor and had its door open there. As he rang at 14A — and it was one of those very loud bells — he wished vaguely that Lois was waiting for him in 14B, so impatient she had the door already open. After ringing a second time, he took another look at Lois's slip of paper — and there it was — no B but a bold A. He was just about to ring a third time when he heard the 14B door slammed to, brutally killing any idea that Lois might have popped along there, passing a few minutes in neighbourly chat. And the third ring, longest and loudest, left him drearily convinced that wherever Dr. Lois Terry might be, she wasn't waiting for him anywhere behind that door. And the name Slinger proved it was the right door. Or would have been if she'd been there.

Hardly knowing what he was up to, he went along to 14B, which told him plainly that there he would find *T. M. O'R. Moskatt* — one of the silliest bloody names he'd ever struck this side of Suez. Bewildered and disappointed, hungry and thirsty as he certainly was, this was no time to offer him *T. M. O'R. Moskatt*. He went back to 14A and used Lois's bit of paper to write: *I am down in restaurant but where are you? O. T.*, and then wrapped the paper round a penny and pushed it through the letter slot.

Even if the restaurant had offered him the superb food and drink so often mentioned in advertisements and so rarely found outside them, he wouldn't have been an appreciative patron, if only because he sat where he could watch the door and thought Lois would come running in at any moment. As it was, he had a rather dismal starchy meal and the whisky seemed to have been watered. But he made a lingering job of it, simply because he saw no point in hurrying back up there, where if she had returned she couldn't miss his note. In fact it was well after nine when he found himself staring bitterly at that 14A door, which began to sneer at him after he'd idiotically tried another ring. And now, just to make him feel sillier, the 14B door was open again, and several people went past him, on their way to T. M. O'R. Moskatt. So — what next? He couldn't even get at his suitcase, which was somewhere behind that door. Moskatt might have a silly name, but there he was, welcoming his friends, not disappearing and keeping them shut out, like this crazy girl, the victim not only of illicit love but also of her close acquaintance with the incestuous lechers, poisoners, and madmen of Jacobean tragedy. Perhaps she drank hard now and again, as some odd girls did, and having gone early to look in at Moskatt's she had downed glass after glass of some infernal brew and had then passed out. It was a thought, though not much of one, but it served to take him along again to 14B. The door was still open and there was a devil of a din coming from somewhere inside. He didn't exactly walk in but he did step forward a pace or two. Then he was pulled further in by a large brown hand.

"I was wondering if — " Tuby began.

"This is it, this is it," cried the owner of the hand who was also large and brown, nicely sozzled, and somehow suggested a Middle Eastern Irishman — perhaps T. M. O'Reilly Moskatt. "Glad to see you. Everybody's here. What you drinking?"

"Oh — Scotch, thank you!"

"In you go, then! In you go! I'll find you a beautiful big Scotch."

And now Moskatt — if it *was* Moskatt — a quick mover in spite of his size and condition — adroitly changed from pulling to pushing, and the next moment Tuby was in the party, which was crowded, very noisy, and appeared at a first glance to be as sozzled as Moskatt. Tuby tried to edge his way round a group standing near the door, but he half-fell over the feet of a woman sitting in an armchair. "Oh — I'm sorry — very clumsy of me!"

"Not to worry," she told him. "I was keeping this for somebody, but you have it." And she indicated a short fat stool by her side. "Quite suitable, don't you think?"

Tuby nodded, smiled, sat down. Moskatt's hand appeared again, gave him a large Scotch, then vanished. "Is he Moskatt?" he asked the woman.

"You're supposed to know that."

"Well, I don't. I came to enquire about the girl in the next flat, who's mysteriously disappeared. I left her to do a broadcast, then we were to have dinner together — "

"Just a minute!" The woman twisted round a little and leant forward to be closer to him. She was a handsome woman, probably in her late thirties, with black hair, coldish grey-blue eyes, and rather hollow cheeks. Her voice was hoarse, not sexy-low in the film style but just plain hoarse. "Ju-u-st a minute, my friend. Now, I'm Ella Ringmore — Mrs. Ringmore, if you like. What's your name?"

"Tuby — Dr. Tuby — "

"That's it, of course — of course. I heard your broadcast while I was dressing. All about images — and — what did you call them?"

"*Social Imagistics?*"

"Right! And, Dr. Tuby, I was *fascinated*. If you'd gone on, I'd have stayed with you — party or no party. I made a note to talk about you on Monday."

"You did, Mrs. Ringmore? I'm flattered. But talk about me *where*, may I ask?"

"I'm in advertising, Dr. Tuby. With Prospect, Peterson and Modley." She seemed to wait for some exclamation from him. "You've heard of Prospect, Peterson and Modley, haven't you?"

Tuby smiled and shook his head. "Sorry! I haven't heard of anybody. I've spent the last twenty years teaching in universities in the Far East."

"For God's sake! Where are you now, then, doing all this fascinating image stuff?"

"Our Institute at present is at Tarwoods Manor, near Tarbury, Brockshire."

"And that's where you've got Primrose — um? You might give her my love — Ella Ringmore, remember?" She was now scrabbling in her handbag. "Look — be a sweet man — and you look and sound like a sweet man too — and write the address and phone number in this little book of mine. The truth is, I'm blind as a bat without my specs — and I won't wear 'em at parties. Too stinkingly vain! Nice clear writing, please, Dr. Tuby, dear."

After handing back her little book, Tuby drank some of his Scotch and then took a long thoughtful look at Mrs. Ringmore — of Prospect, Peterson and Modley — who was busy with her handbag. He couldn't really see how she was dressed, but her long earrings looked valuable, and the general effect of her didn't suggest she was one of the agency's humbler workers. She might in fact be only a step or two below Modley, Peterson or even Prospect. And she had gone well beyond polite party conversation when she had insisted upon having the address of the Institute.

"Are you thinking about me as a person or as an image?" she demanded, surprising him.

"I hadn't really arrived at either. I was wondering rather idly what your position was in your agency."

"Not too far from the top, even though it's much harder for a woman. Which is pretty dam' silly when you remember how much advertising is directed towards women. Now look, Dr. Tuby, I think we ought to talk about *my* image. You don't belong to this party and I've had enough of it, so why don't you finish your drink? Then we'll creep away. Do you like night clubs?"

"I detest them — even when somebody else is footing the monstrous bill — "

"Well, we could go to my place. By the way, there's no Mr. Ringmore there. You must have occasionally known men who were immensely conceited when they had absolutely *nothing* to be conceited about. Well, that was my Derek Ringmore. Couldn't keep a job. Always frittered money away. Always insulted the people you liked. And always immensely conceited and very dictatorial. So there had to be a divorce. But why am I telling you all this?"

"You want to get it in before I start examining and perhaps analysing your image," Tuby told her, smiling.

She thought about that. "You could be right. I'd love to hear you talking to our three directors. Prospect and Modley would hate your guts, but you'd have Alex Peterson gurgling with pleasure. Hello!" She was looking towards the door. "Who's the stricken deer?"

Tuby hastily finished his drink and got up. "That's my hostess who vanished. I'm here, Lois," he called to her. Then when she had seen him, he turned to Ella Ringmore and held out his hand. "I must go, Mrs. Ringmore. I hope we meet again."

"We're going to, Dr. Tuby. You'll see. Now go and comfort that poor girl."

Breathless and distressed, Lois clutched his arm as soon as they were out in the corridor. "The moment I got back and saw your note — I rushed down to the restaurant — and of course you weren't there. Then I didn't know what to do — and — oh God — I was so angry with myself and so ashamed and miserable — then I thought you might have asked Mr. Moskatt — "

"I tried to — but he simply pulled and pushed me into his party. Who and what is Moskatt?"

"Oh — I don't know." Lois's mind was anywhere but on Moskatt. "Audrey did tell me once. Something to do with advertising in Egypt and Syria and places. And he's always giving parties, Audrey says. Well, here we are at last," she continued, letting him in. "And here's your suitcase. Do you want to take it and tell me you never want to set eyes on me again? It would serve me right if you did."

"I don't think people should be served right, except in shops and restaurants. By the way," he added, giving her time to recover as they moved forward, "that place below is no good. Nothing freshly cooked, just heated up, and they water the whisky."

"Oh God — I'm such a fool. And I'm so sorry — so ashamed. Keeping you locked out like that! But when I went I thought I'd be back

quite soon, but of course he went on and on. And I don't love him —
haven't done for ages. I don't even *like* him now. But I had to stay — and
listen and listen to him — all bloody nonsense! And I missed your broadcast. *And* our dinner. I paid for my silliness — I really did. So don't —
*please* — be cool and detached — "

And then, as she ended in sobs, he gathered her into his arms and
began comforting her, with the right kind of noises and sundry strokings.
"Let's forget about it, Lois my dear. You need food and drink, don't you?"

"Yes, I haven't had a thing. Lend me your handkerchief, please,
darling. God — I must look a soppy mess." Then, as she dabbed away:
"Are you hungry? No? Thirsty though — um? Tea or whisky? I think
I'll have whisky too. Bob — Audrey's husband — always has lots. And
I'll find something to eat in the 'fridge. Audrey has an enormous 'fridge."

Tuby followed her round, collected the whisky and a syphon and
two glasses; then, leaving her to her various ploys, installed himself in
a sagging old armchair among the books, files, model yachts and planes,
bits of hi-fi apparatus, cigar boxes, that nearly filled Bob's room. And
with a pipe and a glass, he was content to wait there, guessing she would
be some time. Finally she arrived, carrying a plate of sandwiches, looking
younger, fresher, more hopeful, and apparently wearing nothing much
except bedroom slippers and a dark red well-used dressing gown. She reduced the lighting to one standard lamp behind him, sat on a cushion at
his feet, began eating a sandwich and accepted the whisky-and-soda he
mixed for her. Looking up at him, her eyes were enormous. He thought
again what a quivering vulnerable girl this was.

"Do you want me to explain *exactly* what happened tonight?"

"No, I don't, Lois. Instead, *I'll* tell *you*. That'll keep the temperature
down. It'll also show how clever I am, which is of course what I'm up to
half the time. You finished with this man. He accepted it — had to. But
a situation arose quite suddenly that gave him a chance to make a fresh
appeal. He rang up Tarbury. You'd left this number in case of emergency.
So he got you here. 'Now — listen, please, Lois darling.' he cried, as he
began his tale — "

"Yes, it's all quite true — and you *are* clever — but why did I go
running to him when all I wanted was to be here with you?"

"Our emotions can develop mechanical habits — except in Jacobean
drama. You ran because you'd run so often before — "

"But it's so disgusting — so *degrading*. I stopped loving him ages
ago. I tell you, I don't even *like* him any more — "

"You probably stopped liking him before you stopped loving him.
Indeed, it's just possible you never did like him. Think that over some
time — but not now. We've had this chap for tonight."

"We have. But don't imagine he had me. It wasn't that kind of session at all. Just argument and appeals and recriminations and Do-you-re-
member-what-you-said? and the old unmerry-go-round. Have a sandwich,

Tuby darling? I could say Owen but I like Tuby better — d'you mind?
— it sounds more like you. Sandwich?"

"No, thank you, my dear. I'm full of that stodgy pasta from below.
But you carry on. Those great eyes of yours have to be fed. The broadcast went pretty well, by the way. Anyhow, it seemed to impress that
woman I was talking to at Moskatt's. I don't know if you noticed her?"

"Of course I did — the moment I saw you saying goodbye to her.
Very handsome, very smart, probably ruthless. Let me do some clever
guessing now. My turn. She was so interested in this image idea, she suggested you should leave the party and talk at her place — um?"

"She did. But not because she'd any designs on me. She's in advertising — fairly high up and, I'd say, very ambitious. She realized how
useful our Institute might be."

Lois stopped her last sandwich in mid-air. "But you're not in advertising — "

"No, not yet."

Her eyes signalled alarm, probably catastrophes, despair. "Oh —
but you *can't* — "

"I didn't say we were going to be — "

"Wait — wait!" She put down her sandwich and had a drink. "Tuby
darling, it's all wrong your leaving the university. Oh — I know they
wanted you out, but you could have talked your way in again. I know it's
chiefly Saltana, not you. But though Brockshire's half-finished and pretty
dim, it gave you a respectable steady background. And you and Saltana
could have leavened the whole lump. You two were just what we needed.
And now it's all gone wrong and everybody's worse off. Which is something," she added fiercely, "that's always bloody well happening. And it's
mostly masculine conceit and pride and insane male aggressiveness. And
you can stop grinning."

"I wasn't grinning at what you said, Lois my dear. I've said it myself. It was your sudden fierce manner. Like a gazelle or some such creature suddenly turning and charging. Also — if I may mention it —
you're almost displaying your breasts."

"Well, they're quite good, so I don't care." But she pulled the dressing gown closer. "It wasn't intentional, though. Not a consolation prize
for a wrecked evening. At least," she went on slowly and thoughtfully,
"I think not. I'm never quite sure what the other me, the inside one,
might be up to. Are you?"

"Mine can still surprise me," Tuby confessed, "though of course
we've been together much longer."

As if to point and mock that difference between them, Lois sprang
up with an ease and grace that left Tuby divided between pleasure and
melancholy. She had to find a space somewhere among the clutter for her
plate and glass, and this took a little time, perhaps rather longer, Tuby
felt, than it need have taken. He was about to relight his pipe but stopped

when he saw her swing round, decision and fire in her eyes. A moment later, she was bending over him, kissing him. It was a long and deep kiss, not like anything between them before.

"Don't you want to make love to me?"

"I do," said Tuby, "but I'm not going to."

She thrust herself away from him. "Oh — I suppose it's got to be Hazel Honeyfield." She was furious.

"In one sense — yes — "

"Don't bother explaining, I don't want to know — "

"Because already you've missed the point. She's a joke. And you aren't. When a man makes love to you, he's into a relationship, not just rounding off the evening. Come here." And he pulled her gently down so that she was kneeling on the floor, close to his chair, and he could put out a hand to touch her cheek, her hair. "It was you who mentioned a con-solation prize, remember? It was in your mind. And that's not what I want, even though I'd enjoy it. And to begin a real relationship, this isn't the right evening, we're in the wrong atmosphere. We could make a bad start." And he went on in this vein, his voice as caressing as the hand that remained on her cheek when she pressed hard against it; and he re-flected how for once he was using more of his persuasiveness to keep a girl away from his bed than he had used so many times to talk girls into it. When he finally got into it alone, in a rather forlorn little spare room, he fell asleep fairly quickly but not deeply, and he thought he heard the door open and, after a few moments, close again. But he never mentioned this at breakfast or when he went shopping with her or during the long ride back to Tarbury, when they talked about almost everything except the opening and shutting of bedroom doors. In fact, he never did mention it, not ever, and neither did Dr. Lois Terry.

## 7

It was the middle of the week that followed Tuby's broadcast, Wednesday morning, in fact. Elfreda was doing her accounts. She was good at ac-counts and generally enjoyed doing them, especially here where there was so little for her to do: they made her feel busy and important. But now she was finding some of the bills rather worrying. Florrie and Alfred were good but they were inclined to be extravagant, and food prices in England were much higher than she'd expected them to be — daylight robbery, some of them. What it cost for seven of them — because of course you had to include Florrie and Alfred — to live well, as they did, in this big house was no joke at all, not even after years of housekeeping on the Pacific Coast.

She was able to consider her dismay because nothing else was happening. It was one of those mornings. Even the post and the papers hadn't been delivered yet; there was fog about. And anyhow this was one of those flat times that come after days and days of excitement. The previous week there had been all this telephoning and interviewing and searching the papers for pieces to cut out and paste in a book, which Elfreda had insisted upon doing. And now, so quickly, so surprisingly, all the excitement had died down. Nobody living more than three miles away — except, of course, Mr. and Mrs. O. V. Mere — seemed to care any longer about the relations between the Institute and the University of Brockshire. Moreover, there was now nothing to look forward to — and Elfreda was a great looker-forward-to — except Cosmo Saltana's appearance on television, in a week's time. And although Primrose and Mike Mickley sat together most of the day, taking instruction from either Saltana or Tuby (sometimes from both, as she knew they were doing this morning) and regularly spent some time alone comparing notes, no romance between them seemed to be blossoming. Elfreda attributed her disappointment to a natural warm-hearted interest in these young creatures, but she didn't like the way in which Primrose still kept on telling Cosmo Saltana that she adored him, even though he still laughed at her. You never knew with girls. And — my God — you certainly never knew when men might suddenly give in. So she couldn't help feeling uneasy.

Just before eleven, Alfred brought in the post and the papers — with his usual important flourish, as if they were dispatches from the front. The post, which Elfreda had to remind herself not to call the "mail," consisted of a few bills and circulars and one letter — addressed to Dr. Tuby from London. After Alfred had brought in the tray and she had begun pouring out the tea, she gave Tuby's letter to him as soon as he came in.

"It's from A. G. Peterson of Prospect, Peterson and Modley," he announced, more to Saltana than to her. "And it says: *Following your talk with our Mrs. Ringmore the other evening, will you make an appointment to see me here — any time during the day, at your convenience?*" He looked at Saltana. "That's the woman I told you about — the advertising woman — "

"I know," said Saltana, frowning. "And it's a nibble. Our very first nibble."

"What do we say to him?"

Elfreda was annoyed at being shut out like this. "But who's nibbling at what?" she demanded.

"An advertising agency wants to pick our brains, probably for fourpence." Saltana tossed it her way, impatiently. Then he concentrated on Tuby again. "It's a gamble — but I think we're polite but quite unresponsive. You don't actually snub the man but you don't particularly want to see him."

"Playing hard to get, are you?" said Elfreda, a touch of derision in her manner.

"How about this, Cosmo? I thank him for his suggestion, of course, but as I have no immediate plans to take me to London and am very busy here, it might be some time before I could call on him. Let's get that down, please, Elfreda."

She got it down and quickly typed it while they were muttering at each other over their teacups. "Now I want to say something to you two. Never instal a bar in your house. If you do, then as soon as you have anything like a party, you'll find yourself stuck behind that bar, working like hell as an unpaid barman and not even being thanked for the drinks. Am I making my point, gentlemen?"

"About home bars — yes," Saltana began.

"Come off it. What I'm asking you to remember is that I'm not an unpaid secretary round here. Just look at this Institute writing paper. I'm Mrs. Judson Drake, Assistant Director and General Secretary of the *Institute of Social Imagistics* — and though I don't mind answering the phone and doing the letters, when we've nobody else, that doesn't mean you can talk as if I'm not here, like two executives with some kid from the typists' pool."

"You're quite right, Elfreda," said Tuby, "and I apologize."

"And what about you — mastermind?" she asked Saltana.

"Of course, of course, my dear!" he replied hastily. "I'm trying to think how to make you understand — " But there he checked himself, looked at his watch, and went on: "Must start again on time. I'll take them for the next hour, Owen." And he hurried out.

Tuby passed his cup to be refilled, settled down with his pipe, and twinkled away at Elfreda. "Don't make me explain that remark of Cosmo's about making you understand. I'd only have to invent something."

"And I was being too touchy," she admitted. That was one thing about Owen Tuby, you could admit anything to him. With Cosmo Saltana it was all rather complicated. She was too often a bit on edge now when he was about. "I think I'm feeling let down and rather bored after the excitement of last week."

"Well, if you'd like something to do, I can give you two little telephone chores. Only do them when I've gone, Elfreda. We don't seem to have been by ourselves at all lately, and I'd hate to cut it short."

"So would I, Owen. I always feel cosy with you, even if you are an artful wicked little man no woman's safe listening to. Oh — no, I know you, Dr. Tuby. Now what are these chores — as you call 'em? Look — notebook all ready."

"Number one, then. Quite straightforward. Please ring up the Registrar's office — you needn't say who you are — and ask for the day and time of a public lecture, to be given by a Professor Steril, on Notes Towards a Reconsideration of T. S. Eliot — "

"Gracious me! Do you want to hear it?"

"No, Elfreda, I don't. I want to give a public lecture here in the big room on the same day and at the same time. And the title of my lecture will be *Not Two Cultures, Not Even One.* This isn't part of any feud with Brockshire, by the way. The point is, I'm against Professor Steril, from whom I've suffered in the past. As soon as we have this information about his lecture, then you and I, my dear Elfreda, will have to work fast and hard to let everybody know about mine. But we can talk about that over lunch. Now the next little job is trickier. You see, I think our friend Cosmo ought to have some more music on Sunday. It'll do him good — us too — after all these stratagems and spoils — "

"Oh — I'm all for this. But aren't you forgetting? Isabel Lapford arranged most of it last time, as well as playing herself."

"No, I wasn't forgetting — "

"Then how are we going to manage without her?"

"We're not." Then Tuby dropped to a conspiratorial whisper. "I'll tell you a secret, my dear. In the middle of the barney last week, I persuaded Isabel to meet me and then persuaded her not to join in any feuding. She and I would remain friends, if only on the quiet. And finally she agreed. Now nobody enjoyed that music the other Sunday more than she did — "

"No, Owen, this is out."

"You mean you're not prepared just to ring her up — "

"I certainly am *not.* You're the persuader round here. I wouldn't put it past you to persuade a duchess to do a fan dance. So if you want Isabel Lapford to organize another musical evening here, you just turn on your persuasion — "

But now he wasn't listening to her. He was rummaging through his pockets. "I'd clean forgotten — until you said *duchess.* Many thanks, Elfreda. Here it is. Now then, my dear, please ring that number and ask if Dr. Owen Tuby — and don't forget the *Owen* — can speak to the Duchess of Brockshire."

"Stop it. If you want to play little games — "

"No little games. I want to speak to the Duchess of Brockshire — yes, the one who'll be opening the Library early next month. She happens to be an old friend of mine. Now do you ring that number or do I?"

Believing him now, she did, remembering to put some stress on the *Owen.* And it worked.

"Yes, Owen Tuby, Petro my dear . . . Well, I thought having read about us, you might have got in touch, *if* you really wanted to see me again. Then I thought you might be away . . . Of course, Petro, as soon as you like . . . Oh, I remember that laugh. You've just had one of your ideas, haven't you? . . . Yes, I could, but I think it would be better if you came here and met my friends . . . Tarwoods Manor . . . No, the Thaxleys aren't. We rented it from them, and it's all differ-

ent . . . Friday lunch ought to be all right, but I must just ask. Hold
on a second." He looked at Elfreda, who nodded an almost violent affirm-
ative. "Yes, perfect! About one — um? . . . Yes, young Primrose is
here — and I'll tell her. Friday then, my dear."

"Well, you're old friends all right," said Elfreda, delighted that
things were about to happen again. "Just when I think you're bluffing,
you aren't. But how come? When were you thick with the aristocracy?"

"Never. She was Petronella Corby, a young rep actress, when I
knew her. When I was with the Bureau of Current Affairs, towards the
end of the war, we put on some documentary plays, Living Newspaper
stuff, and used a few young actresses. Petronella was one of them. Saltana
was with us and he'll remember her, though he never knew her as well
as I did. Then some time afterwards — I forget exactly when — she
married this chap, though he wasn't the Duke of Brockshire then."

"I'm just wondering," she said slowly, staring hard at him, "how
your powers of persuasion were, back in those days. You knew her *very*
well, didn't you?"

"We were fairly close friends — yes. Petronella — Petro, we always
called her — was a companionable sort of girl. I thought she might have
changed completely. But I don't think she has. By the way, I'll be out to
dinner on Saturday. I'm dining with Dr. Honeyfield, whose status re-
searches might be useful to us."

"She has a cousin staying with her, she told me — "

"The cousin is about to leave," Tuby announced gravely. "So Dr.
Honeyfield and I will be in no danger of boring her by our exchange of
notes on status and its relation to the acceptance or rejection of particular images."

She didn't see Tuby again before lunch. They were all at table when
she told him that Professor Steril would be giving his lecture at 6:30 on
the following Wednesday. "And this means," she added, "we've just got
a week to collect an audience for your lecture, Owen."

"What *is* this?" Saltana demanded sharply, giving both of them a
frowning glance. But after he'd been told, he concentrated upon Tuby.
"I don't understand you, my friend. For the past week or so, the rest of
us have felt you were strangely lukewarm about our quarrel with Brockshire. You weren't with us in spirit. You held yourself aloof. But now you
want to give a public lecture here just because this Professor Steril's giving one over there, hoping to take away some of his potential audience.
Can you explain it?"

"Easily, Cosmo. I've suffered under Steril, whose literary criticism
I dislike intensely, and as soon as I heard he was coming I decided to give
a lecture myself at the same time. So it's not part of our quarrel with
Brockshire. On the other hand, if you're now losing interest, you might
like to know that Steril's host here is Professor Brigham, one of the group
actively working against us while we were away."

"And thoroughly wet," Mickley announced. "One of the wettest, my spies tell me."

"Then these same spies," said Tuby, "might start spreading the news about *my* lecture. Assisted by Jeff Convoy, even though he's also wet."

"We must rush an advertisement into the local paper," said Saltana, no longer dubious. "There's just time, isn't there, Elfreda? Any other suggestions?"

"Mike and I could do a poster and sneak it into the students' Refectory," said Primrose.

Saltana nodded. "And there ought to be something I can do to help, though at the moment I'm damned if I can think what it is — apart from drafting the advertisement for the local paper."

"Elfreda," Tuby said, "I seem to remember Lois Terry telling me that the Brighams would be giving a party for Steril after the lecture. Couldn't we ask a few members of our audience to stay on — buffet supper and drinks? That is, if it wouldn't be too much trouble and expense for you, Elfreda?"

"Not a bit. And I'd love it," she cried, genuinely enthusiastic. "It's this lunch on Friday that's bothering me. Are you sure she'll eat *any-thing?*" But she looked at Saltana now. "The Duchess of Brockshire's coming to lunch on Friday, Cosmo."

"What — Petro?" Primrose was obviously delighted. "This'll be a gas."

"Cosmo," said Tuby, "you remember young Petronella Corby when we were doing those Bureau shows?"

"You mean the one you were always disappearing with?"

"The same. Well, she's now the local great lady, wife of the Chancellor of the University. Some time before the end of term, she's opening the Library and then spending the rest of the day here — dinner, seeing a play, party afterwards — "

"By which time," said Primrose, "Her Grace Petro will be climbing up the curtains. I remember once in Cannes, she and Tippy — that's the Duke — "

"No, no, girl," said Saltana, cutting in. "Save your reminiscences. I want to know what's going on." He looked sternly at Tuby. "Why is she coming here on Friday? This is a respectable institute, Dr. Tuby. Of course she may have changed during the last twenty years, though hardly anybody ever does, I've noticed. Has she? You've spoken to her?"

"Over the phone. And I'd say she hasn't. She told me she had an *idea* — and then began laughing. I don't know if you remember any of her *ideas*, Cosmo, but we'd better find out what this one is. If Jayjay and his friends are on the receiving end of it, all right. But as you say, Professor Saltana, this is a respectable institute — "

"Not when you say it, Dr. Tuby. No, no, quiet!" He looked round at them all now. "A programme emerges, my friends. Duchess Petronella lunching here on Friday. Owen Tuby's lecture next Wednesday. Then next day I go to London to make my first appearance on television — "

"Then I go with you," Primrose announced.

"I don't know about that. We'll see." And it was obvious from Saltana's tone that he didn't propose to discuss this subject.

Elfreda knew she was being silly when, just after lunch, she contrived to be alone with Saltana and put the jealous question to him. "Just tell me this, Cosmo. Why should Primrose go with you to London?"

He gave her a darkening stare. "I don't think you're really asking for information, Elfreda. Why Primrose and not you? Why not you? It's a cry, not a question."

She didn't know what to say, so she kept quiet. Her face was busy being ashamed of her. Then she went on without thinking what she was saying, everything coming out in a heated rush. "I don't dislike Primrose — don't think that. We've always been friendly. But I must tell you I'm sorry now you and Tuby ever bothered about her. She's caused all the trouble here. I saw that when you were away. All that silly publicity! She was never right for us — "

"Yes, she was, Elfreda. And still is. Now listen to me, my dear." They were in her room, and now he turned her office chair round, dropped on to it, then reached out and pulled her gently towards him, finally keeping his hands under her forearms. This made her his prisoner and she loved it. What next, what next? But clearly he wanted to talk.

"They were about to kick us out, not because of Primrose, but because Owen Tuby and I weren't officially qualified to teach sociology. We deceived them. And before that — and this is a dam' sight more important — we deceived you. And at present we're living on your money, not even Foundation money, because up to now you haven't had any, have you?"

"It's only a matter of form," she began, but he stopped her, tightening a little his grasp of her arms and very gently shaking her.

"It isn't, you know, Elfreda. And we may be walking a tightrope the next few weeks. It's going to be tricky as hell. You see, Owen Tuby and I, though we don't agree on everything, have come to a definite agreement about this — that if there's to be no Foundation grant for the Institute here, then we pack it up. You couldn't afford to keep it going — and anyhow we don't propose to live on your money. So what do we do? This is where it's tricky — and where young Primrose might be very useful — "

"Oh— shut up!"

"What?"

"For God's sake — either hold me or let me go." And she found herself — soft bloody fool! — starting to bawl. And without releasing her he contrived somehow to get up and hold her pretty close — and she made it closer — and fussed over her and comforted her, finally giving her a kiss, a very pleasant kiss too but not quite what she had in mind by this time. But she more or less lived on it, her memory nibbling away at it, for nearly two days, until in fact just before one on Friday, when, already on the alert, she saw a small sports car shooting up the drive. But she saw it through the window of her room; she had posted Alfred in the hall. And Alfred, announcing the visitor, was at least magnificent in manner and gesture, if not in words. "Issa duchessa. Now I bringa ize."

"I'm Mrs. Drake," Elfreda began.

"My dear, I know you are. Read about you. Just a quick dash to the loo and to patch up the face. This way? Lots of lovely drinks all ready, I see. And you're what, darling? Elfreda? Well, do call me Petro — everybody does," she continued as they went upstairs. "Longing to see Owen Tuby again — though God knows it's ages and ages — but a heavenly pet. And he sounded just the same on the phone. You just haven't to listen or you're gone. I was gone, though I was hardly out of the egg then. How about you, darling?"

"No, he's been waiting for you, Petro," Elfreda declared boldly.

"A gigantic sweet lie if I ever heard one, Elfreda darling. In here? Do go down and start mixing things and drinking and so forth — "

Elfreda on her way down decided confusedly that Petro was like an actress playing a duchess playing an actress. She was dressed all tweedy but was wearing a lot of make-up and enormous black false eyelashes. She might have been a very pretty girl seen through a window running with rain. She still had a neat little figure, though she must be now in her middle forties, Elfreda concluded enviously; and she had an amusing voice, throaty but with plenty of gurgles and swoops up. She told the other four, now helping themselves to drinks in her room, that she was quite ready to like Petro.

"Unreliable and wearing, I'd say," Saltana told her, "if she's anything like she used to be. Leave her to Owen. He knows how to handle her."

"They talk about the swinging young generation," said Primrose. "We haven't the energy to be as wild as Petro and her middle-aged chums."

"I'll try her with a vodka martini," said Tuby thoughtfully among the drinks.

"You can try me with one as well," said Saltana. "There won't be much work done here this afternoon."

Five minutes later, Petro came charging in, flung herself at Tuby, embraced Primrose, greeted Saltana and Mike Mickley with more reserve, and accepted a vodka martini.

"One of yours, I suppose, darling," she said to Tuby, giving him her glass to be refilled. She turned to the others. "He was always trying to get me reeling an' stinkin', even when I was a mere child. But isn't this nice? Isn't it, Primrose darling? So glad you all swept out of that boring Brockshire University. Can't imagine why they made poor Tippy Chancellor. Never read a book except three by Surtees and a few by Wodehouse. And Tippy's *straight out* of Wodehouse. Even that tedious grampus — what's his name — Lapford — couldn't see Tippy opening a Library. Oh — that reminds me — Tuby darling, could you write a solemn little library-opening speech for me? Then I can learn it as lines. You will? I adore you. Don't you adore him, Primrose?"

"No, Petro. I adore Professor Saltana."

"Do you? Yes — I can see you might. Tuby darling, if you insist I'll just take one more of your delicious martinis. Elfreda, we're not ruining your lunch, are we? Our food's so filthy now — Tippy just wants lumps of meat and anyhow we're broke — I try to forget about food. Thank you, Tuby darling. I did think of asking you over to our place, but it's so much nicer here. That hellish great house is freezing all the time. We can't afford to keep the central heating going — takes tons a day and relays of chaps at the furnace — and even then it's useless. It was installed before central heating was really invented. Oh — what about this play I have to see, darling?"

"Can't tell you much, Petro my dear," said Tuby. "All I know is that it's by one Ted Jenks, the writer-in-residence at Brockshire and a gloomy young proletarian, and that it's about an incestuous window-cleaner."

"Oh God — another of those, is it? And it won't even have any really filthy bits. They'll have been cut — so I can't even keep nudging Mrs. Thing — Lapford — "

"Careful now, Petro," cried Elfreda, who'd stopped worrying about lunch and was feeling mischievous. "Isabel Lapford and Owen Tuby are very chummy — "

"No!" Petro went whooping up. "He must just be keeping himself in practice. This doesn't sound like you. And after all that time in the East too? Acrobatic stuff — I've been reading about them. You must tell me about them after lunch. Do you mind, Elfreda? The point is, I must have Tuby to myself for a while after lunch because I must explain my *idea* to him."

"That could involve the police," said Saltana darkly. "I seem to remember one of your *ideas* did once."

"Twice, as a matter of fact," said Tuby. "However, my dear Petronella, I'm at your disposal after lunch. And isn't it time we had lunch?"

It was after half-past two when they left the dining room, and it was about half-past three when Tuby brought the Duchess of Brockshire down from his room. She was if anything more gurgly and whoopy than ever, but Elfreda, who joined them in the hall, being both sharp-eyed and intuitive on these occasions, decided at once they'd done nothing up there but talk. Petro embraced her so warmly that Elfreda could feel the monstrous eyelashes like insects on her cheek.

"Had the most gorgeous time, darling," cried Petro. "Do ask me again. I'd bring Tippy only he's off to thaw out — staying with friends in Morocco. I may join them once I've opened this wretched Library. But we're all to have fun in the evening. Tuby'll tell you about my *idea.* 'Bye now, pets!"

Tuby showed signs of shuffling off towards the big room, where Saltana and his pupils might have been working — and might not — but Elfreda led him to her own room. "You're going to tell me about this *idea* of hers now — remember?"

Tuby nodded, settled deep into the armchair, and lit his pipe. Then he asked her — between preliminary puffs — how she liked Duchess Petronella.

"On the whole I do. Yes, I *do.* Though as Saltana said, she's a bit wearing."

Tuby did a kind of puff-sigh. "At twenty-three she was dotty but entrancing to look at. I often think English girls never looked better than they did in the war. Now — at least with me — she's still playing twenty-three and being dotty, but of course it isn't the same."

"You needn't tell any of us. We *know.*"

"No, you don't, my dear. That's where you go wrong, making yourselves miserable. Take you, for instance. I'm certain you're more attractive now than you were twenty years ago. I'd bet on it. Women reach their best at different ages. You're a forties type. Poor Petro is an early-twenties type."

"I can never tell if you're just buttering me up — but bless you, Owen, all the same. Now — what about this *idea?*"

"It's pretty daft, of course," said Tuby out of a smoky calm, "though not to be compared with what she used to get up to. Her *idea* is that she should take us — that is, you and me and Saltana, not the youngsters — to the play and then to Isabel's party as friends of hers. Heavily disguised, of course. And she'll be responsible for the disguises. That's really what'll make her happy — superintending the disguising."

Elfreda stared at him. "I can't believe a word of this. You're making it up."

"I couldn't make anything up, not after forty-five minutes with Petro hotly pursuing one of her *ideas.* I'm to be an Indian. And I can do Indians — God knows! Saltana, who'll have to be talked into this caper, is to be a bearded Spanish landowner. Your disguise won't be quite so easy, though the wig and spectacles will make an enormous difference — "

"Stop it, Owen! I wouldn't dream of going there wearing wigs and spectacles, and anyhow Isabel Lapford would take one look at me and see who it was at once. No, no, you leave me out."

"Pity!" said Tuby calmly — and very cunningly, as she soon realized. "When it comes to the night, you'll hate being left out, I can tell you that now. A good part too. We saw you as one of those cast-iron blue-haired queer-spectacled American matrons who are to be found on all world cruises, never quite sure what continent they're in. You must know them."

"Know them? I've suffered for hours and hours from scores of them. All those photographs and souvenirs they bring back! *Mrs. Drake, just look at this one of Al and I in front of the Pyramids. And doesn't that guide we had look cute? Do I know them!*"

"Elfreda, you can't throw away a part like that. Your tourist battle-cruiser and my Indian — we can forget Saltana, a bit part, as they say — can be a triumph."

"It does seem a shame to waste it, I must admit," said Elfreda, who was already remembering a Mrs. Burney and a Mrs. Fokenberg. "If it was just Jayjay and the others, I might risk it. But I can't see myself fooling Isabel for two minutes. Can you? Honestly now, Owen — "

"No, you're right, of course. I was giving this problem some thought even while Petro was prattling away." He lowered his voice as he leant forward a little. "You and I, Elfreda, must secretly take Isabel into our confidence. It's only fair to her, and it protects us. She may object, of course — "

"You bet your bottom dollar she will!"

"Then if one of us can't succeed in persuading her — "

"That's your job — "

"She must be told that Petro, whose only interest in the evening is this caper, will call off attending the play and the party. Now we'll have to move warily here. It'll call for some neat bluffing. You see, my dear, Petro mustn't know that Isabel knows who we are. That would almost ruin Petro's evening. Besides, our enjoyment, your pleasure and mine, will be heightened by our knowing that Petro doesn't know that Isabel knows."

"But what about Cosmo? Suppose he agrees to wear false beards and things — and I doubt if he will — do we tell him that Isabel Lapford's in the secret?"

"I think so," said Tuby slowly. "Isabel would be our hostess, and I think Cosmo would object to deceiving a hostess. But I'll put Petro's idea up to him. He's certain to ask me what it was, knowing Petro of old. Once I know whether it's two of us or three who are in the caper," he continued, now speaking quickly, warming to the work, "I must ring up Petro to tell her. Then I must have a secret talk with Isabel to explain what we're up to, and if possible I must do this before Petro asks her if she can bring three guests."

"I love it when things are happening, don't you?"

"I think I do," said Tuby thoughtfully, "but then usually when they actually *are* happening I find I don't. The inconsistencies I discover in my inner world are appalling."

But the following afternoon, Saturday, something happened that Elfreda wasn't expecting. She had gone upstairs immediately after lunch to do some repairs on the loose hem of a skirt and one of her prettiest blouses. When she came down again, just after three, she found she had the house to herself. Saltana and Tuby, Primrose and Mike, even Alfred and Florrie, all had vanished into the fine if misty afternoon. She felt deeply aggrieved. She didn't mind being alone in the house, but she felt she might have been included in some plan for the afternoon, that *somebody* might have told her *something*. She didn't like going for walks by herself; she didn't want to drive into Tarbury on a Saturday afternoon; and anyhow it was now rather too late to do anything much; and when she turned on the television, all it offered her was rugby football, which had always seemed to her quite idiotic. So she was ready to welcome the car — and it sounded like a large car — that she heard arriving at the front door.

He was a very tall young man with little eyes and a long nose, and she knew at once he was American. "Good afternoon, ma'am! I'm enquiring for Mrs. Judson Drake."

"I'm Mrs. Judson Drake."

"Well, that's fine — just fine! I'm Barry Wragley, Mrs. Judson Drake, working at present in Ox-ford. You don't know me but you'll remember my uncle and aunt in Sweetsprings — Mr. and Mrs. Nat Wragley."

She remembered them only very vaguely, but this of course made all the difference. At first she had thought he was selling something. Now she asked him in and took him along to her office, glad to be able to talk to somebody, after being neglected by everybody else in the house. Soon Elfreda found herself telling him about the Judson Drake Sociological Foundation, the trouble she'd had with Professor Lentenban, how she'd met Professor Saltana and Dr. Tuby, and what had happened since they came to Brockshire. It all came gushing out, a hot spring, for this was the first chance she'd had to tell the whole story from her point of view and to somebody not involved in it, somebody who listened carefully too, not interrupting her, only prompting her occasionally with a sympathetic question. It was after four when she'd finished and had apologized for talking so much about herself, not giving him a chance; and she asked him to stay to tea, adding that it was more than likely that Professor Saltana and Dr. Tuby would be returning any minute. But he got up, shaking his head and smiling, then telling her she had passed the time so quickly that it was now later than he had thought and he must be getting back to Ox-ford.

Just as she was crossing the hall with him, to show him out, Saltana and Tuby walked in, but before she could start any introductions he had said "Hi!" to them and had hurried out to his car. After she'd waved him off, she found Saltana and Tuby still standing there.

"Tell us about that young American," said Saltana, very quietly.

"Oh — *him!*" As if he didn't matter. "His name's Barry Wragley, if you must know. He's at Oxford but he comes from Portland, Oregon. He has an uncle and aunt who live in Sweetsprings — and he's stayed with them a few times — so we talked about Sweetsprings — and then we got on to the Foundation and the Institute — and what's been happening — " She made her voice trail away to nothing.

Saltana was still dark and broody. "If you told this chap everything," he said slowly, "as I suspect you did, then there's just a chance that during the past hour you may have talked yourself out of the Judson Drake Foundation."

"Oh — what nonsense, Cosmo! How suspicious can you get! Here's a young man, the nephew of some people I knew back in Sweetsprings, and he comes to pay me a nice friendly visit, giving me a chance to talk for once — oh, it's just too ridiculous — isn't it, Owen?"

"No, Elfreda, I'm afraid it isn't," Tuby replied gently.

"To begin with," said Saltana, not angrily at all but in a calm detached manner that was worse, "why should a young man drive miles and miles to call on a strange woman just because she may have met his uncle and aunt?"

"Because they're like that — Americans. And what seems a long way here seems nothing to them. They'll drive for an hour any time just to visit with somebody. As I know — and you don't. You don't know and you don't care," she added wildly, fighting both him and her rising doubts, "just because you're always so dam' pleased with yourself, Cosmo Saltana."

"I put it to you, Elfreda," he went on, talking like a lawyer now, which made it even worse still, "that you knew nothing about this young American except that he might possibly be related to some vague acquaintances of yours in Sweetsprings. What is he doing in Oxford? How did he know where to find you? Why should he listen to all you had to tell him about the Foundation and this Institute and Tuby and me, and then hurry away without even being introduced to us? Try to find answers to those questions, Elfreda." He drank his tea in one great gulp, spluttered and coughed (which served him right), then got up, still making various noises. After a moment or two, he announced majestically, "I now propose to keep on being so dam' pleased with myself up in my room. And I don't want to be disturbed, as I shall be playing my clarinet."

Feeling wretched, anxious not to burst into tears, Elfreda filled her own cup and then Tuby's. "It was stupid saying that to him. But you know how it is, Owen? Suddenly we feel so mad, we'll say anything. You know?"

"Certainly," said Tuby, lighting his pipe. "I always make allowance for it. But though you let fly — apparently quite wildly — in point of fact you don't say *anything*. Without giving yourselves time to take aim, generally you hit a target. Saltana *is* pleased with himself."

"No more than you are."

"There's nothing much in it," said Tuby calmly. "We're both pleased with ourselves, Cosmo and I. It's one reason why we get on so well. Now your trouble, Elfreda, is that you're not sufficiently pleased with yourself. Inside you're too doubtful and humble. No, no, my dear, just think about it — don't protest." He took a sip or two of tea. "Now about that young American. I think you can assume he was sent here to collect some information. What they'll do with it over there, of course we don't know. Cosmo went too far when he told you that you may have talked yourself out of the Foundation — "

"I could have hit him when he said that — "

"You might try hitting him some time, but do it when nobody else is present — and preferably upstairs — "

"I don't know what you're talking about — but do shut up — " Elfreda, burning, could have slapped *him* too. She watched him finish his tea, in that neat catlike way he had, and saw that he was about to go.

"Always remember, please, Elfreda, that Cosmo Saltana is extremely sensitive about you and the Foundation. He's always on the alert because he feels very protective. If he's angry when I'm not, that's because he's really closer to you and feels everything more."

"You both think I did something silly this afternoon, don't you?" she asked in her smallest voice. She was only about a foot high, she felt.

"Frankly — yes, my dear. Though I think Cosmo — in his anxiety over you, his desire to protect you — made too much of the possible consequences. Not to worry, Elfreda. Oh, and one last thought, my dear. Please don't make a fuss about young Primrose going to London with Saltana next Thursday. It worries him, and as I've already told him, I think she ought to go."

"Why — for God's sake?" she snapped at him.

"Purely and simply — Institute tactics — or strategy — I'm not sure which. I could explain, but I'd rather not."

"All right, then — go away! *Go away!* Go on — before I throw something at you — "

Already at the door, Tuby opened it, turned to shake his head at her, then vanished. Elfreda threw a box of paper fasteners at the door, saw them burst out of the box and scatter all over the floor, and then began trying to pick them up through a blur of tears. A woman her age! Idiot — idiot — idiot!

## *8*

Late on Wednesday afternoon, less than an hour before Tuby's lecture, Saltana took a call from London but decided not to bother Tuby with it — though it would have to be discussed between them — until they were having a drink together, much later. Tuby never read a lecture, never even used notes, but he liked to concentrate beforehand on what he would say; so now he was up in his room and would stay there until Saltana, taking the chair for him, sent Mike Mickley or Primrose to tell him they were all ready and waiting. Saltana went across and looked into the big room, where the piano and the armchairs had been pushed against the far wall, and every upright chair in the whole house had been added to the little chairs already there; so that now, according to the two youngsters, who obviously enjoyed this public-entertainment kind of fuss, they had seats for nearly a hundred. There were no signs yet of nearly a hundred, but it was early, and a few of those people who are always early for everything, and usually sit staring defiantly at nothing, had already arrived. Saltana, not wishing to return to Elfreda's room where she was sitting all dressed up and so brightly polite it was just as if they'd met for the first time (she'd been working up to this for the last three days), slipped into the dining room, hoping that drinks might have been laid out there, for the little party afterwards, and was able to enjoy a quiet whisky, a thinking-man-chairman's whisky. It was all the more enjoyable because now he could just hear the sound, muffled by the solid closed door, of people arriving and chattering in the hall.

Just as some people must always come defiantly early, others, far more numerous, must stay away from their seats as long as they can, chattering away in halls, vestibules, anterooms, foyers. So when he finished his drink and ventured into the hall, he found it crowded. There were students of all shapes and sizes, still arriving too, but also a fair number of older people, more than he'd expected to see. Primrose, looking like a vastly elongated daffodil, detached herself from a group near the door of the big room and swiftly squirmed her way through to come hissing at him. "It's fab but awkward, darling," she hissed. "There won't be enough chairs. What do we do?"

"We've another ten minutes or so," he said, not hissing back. "Some students will have to stand or sit on the floor. Try to make all the older people take their seats. I'll help. And be ready, when I give you the signal, to nip up and tell Tuby we're all set."

No sooner had he asked one group of older people to take their seats please than he came face to face with Mrs. Lapford. He was so astonished that his tactless "Well, well!" came out before he could think what he was saying.

"Yes, I'm here, Professor Saltana." Her voice was cold; her cheeks looked hot. "I can only hope Dr. Tuby really *wanted* to give this lecture."

"He's been wanting to give it ever since we met again in London. And I suspect — he hasn't said anything to me — he asked you, perhaps begged you, to hear it. He'll be disappointed — and so will I, so will Elfreda — if you don't stay on afterwards. Now — in you go, please, Mrs. Lapford."

And moving around, ignoring the students for the time being, he ran into Tuby's girl friends, the delectable Hazel and the Terry one with the big haunted eyes, talking together, perhaps about Tuby. He had a good excuse for putting an arm round Hazel as he showed her the doorway waiting for her. She moved obediently, but the other one, her eyes enormous, detained him. "Professor Saltana, it's a *serious* lecture, isn't it? I mean — not just clever nonsense — I'd hate that — "

"You might have to smile at times," he told her rather sharply, "if you can bear it. But Tuby's a man who can be serious about serious things. You ought to know that by now. Go in — and sit where he can see you." He turned and caught sight of Elfreda. "Listen, my dear," he said hurriedly. "Run and get a notebook and pencil. We need some record of this — for Tuby's sake — "

"But my shorthand's so rusty," she protested. "And I don't suppose I'll understand what he's talking about — "

"Never mind. We can make do with rough notes. Hurry now!"

Between five and ten minutes later, all the chairs were occupied; there were students standing at the back and down each side; Primrose had brought Tuby down; and Saltana was standing on the small dais that young Mickley had cleverly contrived for them. An old hand at chairing lectures and meetings, Saltana avoided forced humour, time-wasting rambling, any anticipation of what the lecturer might say. After welcoming his audience to the Institute, he went on: "It is possible that a few of you may not know the title of Dr. Tuby's lecture. It is *Not Two Cultures, Not Even One*. It suggests a large subject but I can assure you — and I have known Dr. Tuby for many years — that he has the breadth of mind and range of interests necessary for such a subject. Finally, he asks me to say that while he enjoys answering questions, he believes they are out of place at the end of a public lecture. But those of you who have questions — please note that Dr. Tuby will gladly answer them at an informal discussion meeting — a seminar, if you like — at nine o'clock here on Friday night. And now — Dr. Tuby."

There was some applause while Saltana got down and settled into one of the armchairs and Tuby stepped on to the dais, carrying no notes, looking chubby and comfortable, smiling. "Mr. Chairman, Ladies and Gentlemen — *Not Two Cultures, Not Even One*. This title, I'm afraid, is misleading. I must find a better one. It suggests sneering and jeering, and I don't propose to sneer and jeer. It is in fact a clumsy but perfectly

serious statement of a belief I have held for some years now. But first,"
he continued in that curiously persuasive and winning tone which Saltana had often amiably envied, "I must first explain how I am using the
term *culture*. I am giving it the broadest and deepest possible significance. It is not something that comes and goes within a century. A culture in this sense will last several hundred years. So — that of the Middle Ages, based on a vision of God, declined during the fifteenth century, only to be succeeded during and after the Renaissance by another,
based on a vision of Man, which has lasted almost until our own time.
But no successor has yet emerged. We are not living with two cultures,
we are trying to live — and not happily — without one at all. This is
one reason why everything seems to move so quickly. The arts change as
rapidly as the fashions. And one kind of art seems as good as another.
There are no longer any commonly accepted standards. A book I read
with pleasure and some profit some years ago was one by William Gaunt,
the art critic and historian, who had previously written about the Pre-
Raphaelites and the later aesthetes. In the volume I have in mind he
turns to the art and literature of this century. And he calls it *The March
of the Moderns*. In terms of originality, talent, even genius, he shows us
a most impressive procession. But where are his marching moderns going? Are they really marching or are they just going round and round,
after kicking their way, sometimes exploding their way, out of what remains of the old culture? What vision is taking the place of that vision
of Man which succeeded the mediaeval vision of God? What foundations of a new culture are being laid, what pillars are going up? It may
well be — and this might come through the nuclear physicists and the
mathematical astronomers — that our age will arrive at a culture of its
own, based on a vision of the Universe; but what is certain, to my mind,
is that we have not arrived at it yet. Not two cultures, not even one! Mr.
Gaunt's Moderns are not marching anywhere. They have a vision of
Nothing. Again let me say that I am not denying the individual merit of
these artists, their originality, talent, genius. But I see no sign of a new
culture, with its own profound affirmations, its own certain standards,
arising out of their work. I remember listening, years ago, to a Hollywood film man who told me about some studio experts who were called
*distressers*. Their job was to make a studio set look broken-down, decayed,
dirty, thick with cobwebs, and so forth. And it seems to me that many
of these Moderns, not really on the march at all, are simply *distressers* of
the old cultural scene. They are breaking something down, not building
anything up. Here we might usefully compare two writers not entirely
unalike, being both verbal magicians and weighty humorists — Rabelais
and James Joyce — "

Saltana's attention began to wander. Tuby had explained to him before the essential difference between Rabelais and Joyce. Now he looked
at the people sitting in front of him, their eyes fixed on Tuby, as he

hadn't looked at them before. Most of them were being deeply attentive
so that their faces wore an innocent and vulnerable look — apart, of
course, from the usual few cocky students, who imagined they already
knew everything and now had only to pass an examination or two to
prove it. Saltana's thoughts went on roaming. And then, because somebody suddenly shifted a little, he caught Elfreda's face, determined but
looking rather baffled, a good woman doing her best, and he wished she
hadn't to look down all the time, doing her notes, so that he could catch
her eye and give her a comforting grin. He still had to offer her some
sort of explanation — and without saying too much, making her feel anxious about the Foundation — of why it was he had decided that Primrose must drive him to London in the morning. He was rehearsing what
to tell her when he realized that Tuby had now launched himself into
his final peroration — the Bomb, nihilism and pessimism, the confusion
and hopelessness of modern man, the revolt of the deeply frustrated
young, the blind acceleration of science and technology, the confusion
and bewilderment and emptiness in which sex was being asked to carry
too heavy a load — "No, ladies and gentlemen, not two cultures, not
even one."

Saltana let them applaud, which they did with enthusiasm, for
about a minute, but then, knowing that Tuby needed a drink even more
than he did, stepped on to the dais and held up a hand. Knew he was
expressing the feeling of the audience when he said how deeply grateful
we all were to Dr. Tuby — most fascinating and provocative and stimu-
lating lecture — those who had questions should return at nine on Friday evening.

Saltana and Tuby made for Elfreda's office room, where they could
have a drink or two without being interrupted by any guests.

"A great success, Owen. I'm not surprised, of course, but I do congratulate you." They drank some whisky and Tuby lit his pipe.

"Cosmo, I didn't know you were staying in London over Friday
night," Tuby said casually.

"This is what's happening and what I wanted to talk to you about,
Owen. Primrose has fixed me up at the Birtles', which saves a hotel bill
and gives me a chance to talk to them again. Now earlier this evening,
when you were upstairs, I had a call from that advertising woman you
met, Ella Ringmore — of Prospect, Peterson and Modley. She'd heard I
was going to be on television tomorrow night, and she suggested that if I
was free afterwards I might like to pay her a visit — with food laid on.
While I'm picking at her food, she'll probably try to pick my brains.
What do you think? You met her."

"Attractive — and more your style than mine — and ambitious and
tough, I'd say, Cosmo. I think you'll enjoy taking her on."

"I'll call her as soon as I'm in London, Owen. Apart from the television, I regard this trip — Birtles and all — as being cautiously explor-

atory. Just to see if anybody really wants us. We have to know, my boy, and pretty soon too. We can't stay here living on Elfreda's money."

Tuby didn't offer him a shrug — Tuby wasn't a shrugging type — but it was as if he did. "She can well afford it for a few more months, and she isn't getting bad value. What would she be doing if she wasn't here? Sitting in hotel lounges trying to make a few friends, that's all."

This didn't please Saltana. "How the devil do you know what she'd be doing? And that's not the point — "

"All right, I know how you feel. But I don't see how you can promise anything to anybody in London and keep her Foundation going here. And you're not proposing to walk out of it, are you?"

"Of course I'm not," Saltana thundered at him. "It's the very last dam' thing I'd do, and you know it." He took a drink, then continued in a lower and easier tone. "But we have to know how it looks in London — *now*. We may not have anything like the time we thought we'd have, Owen. This Foundation of Elfreda's looks shaky to me. What if it collapses under us and we still don't know where we are?" He tapped Tuby's dusty-pink tie. "I'm just trying to explain why I'm spending two nights in London."

"I gather that. Just."

"Owen, I'd be grateful if you'd be particularly attentive to Elfreda these next two days — perhaps take her out somewhere tomorrow night. I can't explain to her exactly what I'm up to in London — it would suggest I've no confidence in the Foundation — and she resents being left behind when young Primrose is going." He gave Tuby a hopeful look. "Take her out to dinner somewhere — and then you could give her some sort of explanation. You'll do it better than I can."

"This isn't like you, Cosmo."

"I'm often not like me. I have a complicated rich nature, my boy."

In exactly the same tone of self-satisfaction, Tuby said, "I have a simple nature but a richly complicated mind."

"You have, have you? Well, bring them both into the dining room, to amuse your lady friends. I'm hungry."

There were about a dozen people standing round the table. Saltana accepted some pâté from Elfreda. "I did what I could," she began. "I mean, about taking down the lecture. But a lot of those French names defeated me. Why are you staying until Saturday?"

"It's partly Institute business, Elfreda. I'm meeting some people at the Birtles' on Friday night. You know about them. By the way, Owen Tuby wants to take you out to dinner tomorrow night — partly for a change, partly to talk things over — hello, young woman!" This was to Lois Terry, who had used a glass to nudge him. "Was Tuby sufficiently serious for you?"

"He's a wonderful lecturer, isn't he?" Her eyes blazed away at him. "And I'm furious because I can't get to him to tell him so. My God! He makes everybody I've heard here sound like tuppence. And that makes me furious too. It's all such a waste. He ought to be here — running the English Department."

"At the risk of making you even furiouser, my dear girl," said Saltana dryly, "let me tell you that Owen Tuby wouldn't accept your English Department if it were offered to him on a plate."

"And let me tell you, Professor Saltana," she cried, breathless with indignation, "that I think you're a rotten bad influence on him. And I'm going to tell him so."

He moved away, and this brought him alongside Mrs. Lapford.

"Can I help you to anything? No? You're not about to lose your temper, are you, Mrs. Lapford? I ask because one woman has already been angry with me, and I'm feeling rather shaken. I hope you liked Tuby's lecture."

"Of course. He's quite extraordinary. Are you as good as that, Professor Saltana?"

"As a public performer — no. Tuby loves audiences and on the whole I don't. I've always been most effective handling small groups of students. This may help me on television, but I'll know more about that tomorrow night at this time."

"What I know now," she said rather bitterly, "is that Jayjay and the others were madly foolish not to keep you two here. On the arts side — the one I understand — we simply haven't got men like you and Tuby — "

"You certainly haven't."

"And you're not exactly modest, are you?"

"If a man my age is still creeping around being modest, then he deserves to be shoved into a corner."

"All right, perhaps he does," she told him sharply. "But I think it's infuriating and sickening when two men like you refuse to teach in universities, just to go on with this image nonsense."

"Mrs. Lapford, that's how people like you talk. But you might ask yourself where we found this *image nonsense,* as you call it. Did Tuby find it in India and Malaya? He did not. Was I familiar with it in Central and South America? I was not. We found it here, waiting for us. Images, images, images! Very well then, why not *Social Imagistics?* No, Mrs. Lapford — please! I can't take any more sharp-tempered ladies tonight. I'm going to talk about music to our friend, the old 'cellist. I didn't even know he was here — but there he is. Excuse me!"

Primrose landed him in Mayfair the following afternoon, in good time to take tea with Mrs. Birtle, who seemed genuinely glad to see him and to listen at ease to their gossip. Two hours later, a taxi hired by the B.B.C. took him out to Television Centre, sufficiently imposing outside, and inside quite terrifying, as if it had been suggested by Kafka at a séance. He was met by the assistant producer of the programme — a dreamy young man called Matson, Metson, or Mitson — taken aloft and then along Kafka corridors for a drink, taken back and then below to be shown the studio and just where and how he would sit, up and along the corridors again for another drink, then back again to the studio, where he met the man who would interview him, the celebrated Ben Hacker. Matson, Metson, or Mitson had told him not to be afraid of Ben Hacker, and now Hacker himself told him not to worry, and Saltana, who had admitted that this was his first appearance on television, said he would do his best. Hacker had a square face, square spectacles, a tiny upper lip decorated by a mini-moustache, and a hell of a great square jaw, which he began to set as soon as the lights were turned on. Sitting opposite him, Saltana felt he was about to be interrogated by an important member of the World State Secret Police some time between the years 1995 and 1998. The lights blazed away; a lot of mysterious youths gave instructions to a lot of other mysterious youths; Saltana said a few words and a microphone was moved; Hacker, not content with his squared square jaw, now produced a tremendous frown; and then they were on the air.

"Professor Saltana," Hacker began in an accusing tone, "you're the Director of the so-called *Institute of Social Imagistics* — "

"Certainly. But don't let us say *so-called,* which always suggests some shady kind of masquerade. What I'm Director of *is* quite simply the *Institute of Social Imagistics.*"

"But hardly quite simply," said Hacker, hard at it, frowning and accusing. "I think most of us can't imagine what you're attempting to do. Could you explain — briefly?"

"I can try. We're doing a close study and analysis of all manner of projected images."

"You think that's important?"

"It appears to be," said Saltana mildly. "We're always reading and hearing about images — not only in political and commercial circles but even in private life. If they aren't important, then a lot of people have been — and still are — wasting their time and ours."

"Quite so, quite so!" Hacker sounded impatient. "But after all it's just a manner of speaking." As Saltana didn't reply, he pressed on. "Don't you agree it's no more than that?"

"I don't agree or disagree. I think it's simpler to talk about images. But if to you it's a manner of speaking, then I can tell you we're doing a close study and analysis of a manner of speaking." And Saltana popped a cheroot into his mouth and lit it.

Hacker frowned harder than ever. This was, he obviously thought, all a bit much. "But I've been given to understand, Professor Saltana, that you actually undertake to examine and analyse individual images. At least, that was the impression left by your colleague Dr. Tuby when he was interviewed on sound radio. I believe he even offered to comment on his interviewer's image." Hacker unjawed and unfrowned himself for a moment, to produce a short barking laugh. "An offer that wasn't accepted. I suppose you'd say I was projecting a particular image — um?"

"Certainly. You're in the business."

"Very well, then. Out of your expertise, tell me about my image." The frown and set jaw were back, but somehow he also contrived a small teasing smile, like a gay awning on a battleship. "Ready when you are, Professor Saltana. What about *my* image?"

"On the spur of the moment? We don't improvise our analyses, you know — "

"Well, of course, if you reject my little challenge — "

"No, no, I'll do what I can." Staring hard at the other man, Saltana waited a moment. "I'd say it's no longer a good image, Mr. Hacker. Earlier, I imagine, it did suggest a man not too far removed from most of his viewers — but rather more sceptical, more stubborn, more intellectually honest, and of course more articulate. One of their rather superior neighbours, perhaps. And I've no doubt that for some time this image you projected made you extremely popular."

"Then there can't have been much wrong with it."

"No, not until you began — not consciously, I imagine — to overemphasise some of the qualities it suggests. Because you never thought about it, you overdid it. The mask, we might say, was coarser and harder — "

"Now steady, Professor — " A little bark-laugh.

"The image took on an inquisitorial appearance," Saltana continued calmly. "There was about it a suggestion of official interrogation. So that whereas originally you had the sympathy of your viewers, because you seemed to be representing them, behaving as they would have liked to behave themselves, now this sympathy began to move away from you, going to the persons you were interviewing. Your image suggested that you had naturally the upper hand, and a certain chivalry lingering among the ordinary English people puts them on the side of the underdog. That's why I began by saying that it was no longer a good image — "

"And you've made your point, Professor Saltana, though it doesn't follow we all agree with you." Hacker spoke very quickly. "Now tell me how you're organizing this Institute of yours. We've read in the Press that Miss Primrose East is one of your assistants."

"We're training her, she's working very well indeed, and we're hoping she'll stay with us. Her experience as a model makes her unusually perceptive about certain types of images — perhaps rather more perceptive than Dr. Tuby and I are — and if she stays with us, she's going to be very valuable indeed." And the rest was easy, Saltana smoothly telling him little or nothing about the Institute (and one sharp question about its immediate future would have meant a scurry across very thin ice), while appearing to tell him everything. And then the programme was over, the lights were off, and Saltana, not at all as relaxed as he looked and sounded, was able to get out of that damned chair.

"Went very well, didn't you think?" said Hacker.

"I haven't the least idea," Saltana told him, "never having done this before." A little later, moving ahead out of the studio, he overheard Hacker telling Matson, Metson, or Mitson that the next time they planted such a cool bastard in front of him, he'd like a word or two of warning. Having refused a drink — not that he didn't want one; the journey to it would waste too much time — Saltana was escorted to the main entrance, where a taxi would be waiting for him, by Matson, Metson, or Mitson, who came out of his dreaminess to say that Saltana had been dead right about Ben Hacker. "And I hope some of the big boys had their eyes on the box tonight. If so, Professor, you have it made."

Saltana had called Mrs. Ringmore at her office as soon as he had arrived at the Birtles' and, having nothing better to do, had gladly accepted her invitation to dine — "a little on the sketchy side, probably" — at home with her. She looked tall and very handsome in some sort of long housecoat, dark blue with some faint hieroglyphics in red. He saw at once what Tuby had meant; she was more his kind of woman.

"Mrs. Ringmore, this is extremely kind of you — and I'm sorry I'm late. I even refused a drink at the B.B.C. to come here quickly, but the taxi lost me."

"You've arrived just at the right moment, Professor Saltana." They were in a tiny hallway. "Along there if you'd like to wash. I'll be in the sitting room — here."

When he joined her there, the room, which was fairly large, surprised him. Instead of being severe, abstract, ultra-modern, it looked almost mid-Victorian. "It makes a nice change from the office," she explained as she gave him the whisky he'd asked for. "You can imagine what that looks like."

He told her he'd never been inside an advertising agency.

"It wouldn't take long to remedy that." And when he didn't reply, she went on: "Y'know, you were even better tonight than your friend Dr. Tuby was on sound radio. Of course, towards the end you were obviously just spitballing, but before that you'd put that idiotic Ben Hacker where he belonged. And don't think it'll go unnoticed. By this time the story will be flying round. And if you want to be a television personality, you're in now."

"I don't. But I might want to use it now and again."

"And I want to know a lot more about you, Professor Saltana. But you ought to be fed first. We eat more or less in the kitchen, which *isn't* Victorian." And it was indeed a spacious gracious-living-but-functional kitchen, with one end of it, behind a four-foot barrier, turned into a small dining booth. It was an arrangement that suggested intimacy; the chicken marengo was excellent; and Saltana was enjoying himself. Nevertheless, though he regarded his hostess with smiling approval, he answered her warily. He rather liked those coldish greyish eyes, which Tuby had mentioned, but he felt that as yet they were still within business hours, representing Prospect, Peterson and Modley.

But then, after a few minutes' dinner chat, she was quite frank with him about this. "Not knowing what on earth you were like, I took a chance inviting you here because Alex Peterson and I agreed that I ought to. He wrote to your Dr. Tuby, you know, and got a reply that was as near a snub as dammit. You knew, did you?"

"Certainly. We discussed it."

"And we think we're rather important people, Professor Saltana. Do I have to keep saying *Professor*? It's a bit off-putting, y'know."

"Just *Saltana* then. I have a Christian name but I keep it a secret until people are used to me."

"I'm Ella — and you don't have to be used to me."

"Not right for you, I'm afraid." He shook his head with mock solemnity. "Doesn't fit this kitchen or the drawing room — and not right even for Prospect, Peterson and Modley."

"I know that, of course." She replied quite seriously. "Wrong for my image, you'd say, wouldn't you? But it happens to be my name, part of the real me, which *Ringmore* isn't anyhow, so I've stuck to it. The surname I lost when I married, along with a lot of other things, was Scarp. Is that any use to you, Saltana?"

"Yes, I like it, Scarp."

"As I was saying when names came up — we're rather important people and we spend a hell of a lot of money every year. And of course images and advertising are very closely connected. You must know that, Saltana."

They were now ready to take their coffee into the sitting room. There she gave herself a hefty liqueur brandy, which he refused, preferring to keep to whisky. He was settling himself down into a big old armchair and lighting a cheroot when she sprang up from the sofa opposite him and tossed a portfolio into his lap.

"Saltana, tell me candidly what you think of that line of approach. It's entirely directed at women — a new cleanser — and the artist, one of our best men, has done a slight tongue-in-cheek return to the styles of the Twenties and Thirties."

He had indeed. Sketch after sketch showed the same white-haired, apple-cheeked, motherly type, really belonging to a children's picture book. "Well, my dear, I'm new to this — though I'm beginning to know something about images — but I'd say this idea wouldn't work. The faint suggestion of burlesque isn't any good. The sort of women you have in mind take advertising seriously. And if they take this seriously, then it's out because they know this smiling, sweet, pink-and-white image doesn't

belong to their world. The image of a fairly realistic contemporary housewife, rather grimly satisfied at last, would work ten thousand times better. You must know this, my dear Scarp."

She took the portfolio away. "It's more or less what Alex Peterson
and I said this morning." She returned to the sofa and stretched herself
out, either very carelessly or very carefully — and Saltana couldn't decide which. Rather long legs, of course, but shapely, indeed. There wasn't
much light — just a shaded lamp behind her, an occasional flicker from
the two logs in the fireplace, and a dim cluster on the opposite wall —
but Saltana could just see that she was beginning to frown across at him.
"Thinking it over, I'm surprised and rather disappointed that you like
Scarp. I know it simply means a steep descent, but as a name it suggests
somebody small, hard, and mean — perhaps a dwarf moneylender in a
Victorian novel. I'm against it, Saltana. I was called Kate at college."

He felt lazy, not disinclined to talk but not wanting to make much
of an effort.

"What about *my* image?" she demanded, after a pause he'd welcomed. An implacable sex.

"I was afraid of that," he murmured. "Tuby and I have had to attempt this, once or twice, but it's not the way we work, y'know, Kate.
It's like asking a soloist to play or sing something at sight. I'm no soloist
but I happen to play the clarinet and I'm a hopeless sight-reader. Do you
enjoy the clarinet?"

"I wouldn't know. I've no ear for music — and you're trying to
change the subject. My image, please."

"Well, just remember I'm a researcher into *Social Imagistics,* not a
fortune-teller. And you'd better bring a cushion and sit at my feet. . . .
You're off duty now, Kate," he began slowly and quietly, "so you're not
projecting the complete daytime image. But I can imagine it. Hard and
keen, hammered and then sharpened metal. You have to work with self-
indulgent and untidy men, so you're all self-discipline, strictly rationing
yourself with food and drink — "

"How do you know that?"

"Those attractive but telltale hollows in your cheeks. The taut and
slightly hungry look. And not only with food and drink, of course, but
also speech and behaviour — even emotions. You're proud as the devil.
You probably came — half-hurt, half-bewildered, all sloppy — out of an
unsuccessful marriage, took a job as a secretary, then enlisted in the army
of career women, and started carving your way through and up. You used
sex but wouldn't let it use you."

"You wouldn't be artfully talking me into anything now, would you,
Saltana?"

"No, that's Tuby, not me. You're with the wrong partner. So —
you bring to — what's it? — Prospect, Peterson and Modley, who aren't
worth it, the kind of determination, endurance and courage, and general

female unscrupulousness, that has enabled other women to bring six children out of a plague-stricken city. The severe hair arrangement, the erect carriage, the no-nonsense clothes and manner, the quick but thinnish smile, the cold watchful eye — "

"Oh — stop it!" She didn't scramble to her feet — too awkward a move — but leant far back, well away from him, with her hands behind her. "All right then — go on."

"The trouble is, my dear Kate," Saltana continued in a rather warmer tone, "it isn't really a woman's life. You're compelled to spend ten shillings of yourself to earn a shilling's worth of real satisfaction. You give to a business what it's no right to demand. Oh — yes, I agree, just because you're a woman and can't loll around and bluster and brag and booze like the men."

"You can say *that* again, Saltana," she cried, American-style.

"It's the image of a woman sharpened to too fine an edge, with no room to move, to sprawl, to let go. Mind you, Kate my dear, I'm speaking as a rather old-fashioned kind of man, who likes this room — "

"Well, it's *my* room, isn't it?" She was sitting upright now, not close but not determinedly far away. "And asking you here was my idea, not the firm's. And I liked your voice on the phone. But why did you accept my invitation?"

"Partly to pick your brains, which incidentally I haven't done. Curiosity too. And also because Tuby, a very good judge of women, said you were very attractive, but not his type — mine."

"And all you've done is to frighten me, Saltana." She folded her hands on his knee and stared up at him, looking as reproachful as she sounded. He leant forward and held her face in his hand, and kissed her. She pushed herself up and her arms went whipping round him, and the next kiss was a very long one.

It was after midnight when Saltana, still only half-dressed, returned from the bedroom to mix himself a drink for the road and to relight the cheroot he had left in the sitting room. When he went back to Mrs. Ella (Kate) Ringmore, she stirred sleepily and reluctantly.

"Why is it," she asked, "that you real men, who really do make love, are so damnably restless so soon?"

"It's a sex difference, my dear." He was tying his tie. "Some American has suggested we're two different species, but he goes too far. Now tell me — does your Mr. Peterson know you've been entertaining me tonight? And if he does, you can't just say you seduced me — "

"Shut up — and come here."

"I'm trying to talk a little business before I go."

"Oh — for God's sake! And why go?"

"Because I'm not staying in an hotel but with the Simon Birtles, Primrose's friends." But he finished his drink and then went over and sat on the edge of the bed. "It's for your sake, my dear Kate, not mine. I'll tell you all I can tell you. Tuby and I don't know yet what we're going to do. If the Foundation holds, then we must stay with it. If it doesn't, then we'll have to plan like mad. We're poor men."

"And that's all, is it?" She was really awake now. "No, I believe you, Saltana darling. Well, can you keep a secret?"

"Certainly. Don't I look as if I could?"

"Yes, you do — a silly question." She reached for his hands. "Listen — then. Alex Peterson and I are always disagreeing with old Prospect and Arthur Modley and it's more than likely we'll soon be starting our own agency. So why shouldn't you and Tuby come in with us? Forget the Foundation. No capital required. Peterson can supply that. What d'you think?"

"Sorry, my dear! Either we stay with the Foundation or we go into business on our own — as image experts and consultants. But which it's to be, I don't know yet. When I do know, I'll tell you, Kate my dear. If not for business, then for pleasure." He kissed her. "Now don't move. I can let myself out. You've given me a wonderful evening. Bless you, Kate!"

Saltana spent the next afternoon trying to find the scores of two arrangements for clarinet, piano, violin, and 'cello. He had a little session with Simon Birtle just before the dinner guests arrived. "They're more or less the same kind of people you met last time you dined here," said Birtle, "except for one man — Jimmy Kilburn." He paused for a cry of wonder or joy from Saltana, who couldn't oblige him. "Don't know about Jimmy Kilburn? Well, he's coming specially to talk to you, so I'd better tell you about Jimmy Kilburn. He's a little Cockney sparrow of a fellow — about sixty I suppose — who started as an underpaid little clerk in the City, with no advantages of any sort except his wits, and who's now one of the hottest but wiliest financial men round the town. I've done business several times with Jimmy — and you have to watch him — but all the same we're friends. You'll enjoy Jimmy, I think, Saltana."

"I'll try. But why is he coming here to talk to *me?* Unless of course he wants to give me a million or so. He has millions, has he?"

Birtle looked grave and dropped his voice to a whisper. "Five — eight — perhaps ten million. I doubt if anybody knows except Jimmy himself." Then, off the subject of money, Birtle raised his voice. "Met him yesterday and he was talking about this image thing — for himself — so I put him on to you, Saltana. By the way, I've been thinking about what you said to me last time you were here — and my wife's mentioned it more than once, you know how women do — no, this'll have to keep. People here."

This time Saltana found himself sitting among the editors and columnists while his former place at the end, next to Mrs. Birtle, was now occupied by Jimmy Kilburn. Saltana gave him a long look. He was a small droopy man, his face all predatory nose, who just nodded away, letting Mrs. Birtle do all the talking.

Not long after dinner, Birtle brought Saltana and Jimmy Kilburn together and then took them off to his study. "You don't want anybody listening in to this, I fancy, Jimmy," Birtle said on the way. "And some of the sharpest ears in town are back there tonight."

Saltana had spent part of the morning in this study, prowling round the bookshelves that covered its walls, but now, its heavy curtains drawn and just one big standard lamp alight in the middle, it looked quite different — huge, dim, secret, a place for a whispered exchange of stratagems.

"Now do I stay on?" Birtle asked them. "Or do you two prefer to be alone?"

"All the same to me," Saltana told him.

Jimmy Kilburn didn't share this indifference. "Yer don't 'ave it bugged or anything like that, do yer, Simon boy? No? Then leave us to it. Join yer when we're through." Kilburn had a husky Cockney voice; he sounded like a barrow man at the end of a very long day.

There were drinks and sandwiches on a tray. Saltana helped himself to a whisky. "Anything for you, Mr. Kilburn?"

"Drop of orange later, thanks all the same. Drinkin' man, are yer, Professor?"

"Certainly."

"I'm not. Never touch it. Simon Birtle isn't, neether. An' better without it, both of us."

"Well, I'm better with it," said Saltana firmly. No reply to that came from the little man, now half-lost in an armchair. As the silence continued, Saltana felt he had to say something, just to break it. "How does a man collect a gigantic amount of money? I've often wondered. Now you can tell me."

"Chiefly by 'avin' a nose for it. I'm not talkin' about this 'orrible big bonk of mine, though that comes in 'andy. But yer 'ave to know where the money is. Kind of instink, yer might call it. Y'aven't to be really clever. Compared to a bloke like you, I'm bloody stupid. No, no, I am, honest. But I can smell it where you can't. If somebody gave us a thousand quid each an' dropped us in a strange place, by the end of a year I'd 'ave twenty thousand an' you'd be wonderin' 'ow to pay the gas bill. No slur intended, Professor, I didn't say I'd be 'appier than you. We're just talkin' about money."

"And that's not what you wanted to talk to me about, is it? Obviously not."

"That's right." Jimmy Kilburn cleared his throat, then hesitated a moment. "Okey-dokey, yer get the lot. Strick confidence, mind. I'm gettin' married. First time — though I've 'ad plenty of the ol' rolypoly. A widow — big fine woman — give me thirty to forty pound. Classy, not like me — an' comfortably off, not marryin' me for the money — honest! Just enjoys me as an amusin' little sod, which I am when yer get to know me. But she says I oughta get into public life. Along with a nicer image, she says. Then we saw you on the telly las' night. Don't need to know any more, do yer?"

"No, that will do. You want me to talk to you about changing your image — um?"

"Right. An' don't think I'm cadging it, just 'cos we 'appen to be 'ere together. Name a fee an' I'll pay it. Jimmy Kilburn never wants something for nothink."

"Well, that's what it'll have to be, this time." And he explained briefly the relation between the Institute and the Judson Drake Foundation. "So there's no fee. If by any chance I should ever find myself working independently, outside the Foundation, then the fee would be considerable. But on the other hand, my assistants and I would then make a detailed study of your image problem, a very different thing from what I can offer you here tonight." He knew he sounded pompous but couldn't help feeling that this was expected of him, the specialist.

"Just off the cuff, like. 'Ardly doin' the subjeck justice. Would feel just the same meself. Well, do yer best." And Jimmy Kilburn, who'd been leaning forward for the last few minutes, now settled himself back expectantly.

"The idea is that you should prepare for public life by changing your present image. It would involve various changes, which I've no doubt you're willing to make, in your appearance, speech, general manner, style of life, bringing you closer to the kind of men your future wife knows best, the kind of men prominent in public life. Right?"

"Dead on! An' I expeck you could give me a list of these changes — "

"I could, but I'm not going to. You've asked for my advice, so let me tell you that I think the whole idea is wrong. No — I must explain what I mean, Mr. Kilburn. When you've made all these changes — what are you, who are you, where are you? You've already told me your fiancée enjoys you as you are. She herself doesn't want a different Jimmy Kilburn. But public life does, she imagines. And here she's wrong. You'd end up, after working hard at it, simply as a passable imitation of a general type we know too well already. Instead of standing out, you'd disappear among a crowd. No, no, if you really want some success in public life, you mustn't attempt a quite different image but must heighten and strengthen, even to a suggestion of caricature, the one you have now — "

"God's truth! I wish she was 'ere. What about some time tomorrow?"

"Sorry, but I must get back to the Institute. But let me explain about this public-life image. You wear, I see, rather unfashionable dark clothes. All right, wear some that are even darker and more unfashionable. You're a self-made Cockney type. Be more of it, not less of it. Be sharper and bolder still, speaking your mind. Give the smallest tips in the West End, appear to be consistently mean and grudging, but then suddenly make enormous and staggering donations. Be a *character,* an eccentric character, a miser on Monday and wildly generous on Thursday. We need some characters. People will talk about you. 'Have you heard the latest Jimmy Kilburn story?' they'll ask one another. And while you're achieving this effect, you'll have a devil of a sight more fun than drearily trying to turn yourself into somebody else. So my advice is — not less Jimmy Kilburn — but more." And Saltana, who'd not only been talking but also finishing a cigar, emptied his glass.

" 'Ere!" cried Kilburn, jumping out of his chair. "All that's right down my street — an' bloody marvellous. I wish to God she'd 'eard yer. 'Owever, I've a good memory. Listen — if she got in touch, would yer tell 'er or write 'er what yer've just told me? Yer would? I'd be very grateful. But I'll tell yer one thing, Professor Saltana." He was sitting down again now but more or less on the edge of his chair, leaning forward. "Yer out of yer mind givin' this image stuff away, Foundation or no Foundation. Yer wouldn't catch me doin' it. 'Ere, give me the address an' phone number of this place yer goin' to — yer Institute. An' listen. If y'ever want to do a deal — any sort — come straight to me." He leant further forward and spoke in a whisper. "Simon's a smart feller in 'is way but what 'e's got is all a bit dodgy — magazines an' that. A lotta women an' kids 'ave only to turn their noses up — an' where is 'e? Out on 'is arse. No, if y'ever 'ave a little deal in mind, yer come straight to me. I'm not in the phone book. Not me meself — otherwise I'm all over the bloody book. But my two private numbers — 'ome an' office — are on this card. 'Ere!" And he flipped a small card out of his wallet with such speed it was like a conjuring trick. "Ring me any time, Professor. Yer've done me a big favour — no, no, I call it a big favour, you can call it what yer like."

In the morning, Primrose asked him if he'd mind returning alone to Tarbury by train. They were having tea when he arrived. Elfreda gave him a reproachful glance and said he looked tired. Mike Mickley behaved as if Saltana had done away with Primrose somewhere en route. And Tuby, clean out of tact for once and possibly half out of his mind, announced that because of some daft whim of Petronella's he, Cosmo Saltana, would soon be expected to gum on crêpe hair and pass himself off as a rich Spanish landowner.

He put down his cup and stared hard at his colleague, now looking somewhat abashed. "I don't know if your friend the Duchess of Brockshire has a lake near her country residence. But if she has, then you can both jump into it." And he went upstairs, to play his clarinet.

*9*

There was a reason why Tuby had been so tactless, blurting out a plan that ought to have been put to Saltana slowly and stealthily, bit by bit. Petro's *idea* had grown in his mind and had begun to illuminate itself there. He had had a secret meeting with her on Thursday afternoon, when she was on her way back from some Young Farmers' official lunch — "My God, darling, they aren't even *like* farmers any more, just assorted clots talking about their Jags." They had settled a few details but had spent more time and energy exchanging wild fancies about Elfreda's American-tourist type, Saltana's grandee, Tuby's Indian. This was childish, he knew, but then Petro was one of those people, not unusually attractive, intelligent, charming, who are able somehow to create their own atmospheres. (Tuby didn't see himself as one of these people but then remembered that Isabel Lapford obviously thought he was, and probably the Denis Brighams thought Isabel was, and a dim somebody somewhere thought the Denis Brighams were, and so on and so on towards the outer darkness and the unimaginable spaces of the Universe.) And this daft atmosphere of Petro's lingered just like the flavour of her lips (a kind of chemical raspberry) after she had gone. So thoughts about the plan had blossomed and brightened.

They were not suffering, such thoughts, from any cheerful competition. Tuby had taken Elfreda out to dinner on Thursday, as he had promised to do, and they had watched Cosmo's appearance on television together with great satisfaction, but she had spent too much of the evening asking him questions about Saltana that he couldn't answer. Why two nights in London? What was he up to there? Why did he keep breaking off any talk about the Institute and the Foundation? If he had any ideas, then what were they? And so forth. And Tuby didn't want to suggest either that he knew but wouldn't tell her or that he wasn't in his friend's confidence at the moment. The result was that he began to feel and sound like a civil servant at bay. Not a good evening.

Then on Friday afternoon he had seen Isabel Lapford, to let her into the secret of Petro's plan and their impersonations. At first she didn't believe him, and then when she did she was furious, not amused at all. She was ready to cancel the whole evening's programme, the playgoing, the party, the lot, until Tuby pointed out that Petro, baulked of her plan and its disguises, was quite capable of washing out the whole day's programme, with no Duchess of Brockshire, wife of the Chancellor, to open the Library, for which, Tuby added, he'd written her an excellent speech that might be widely quoted in the Press. He also added that their three impersonations would be so convincing that everybody would be deceived, for after all they were not being attempted in broad daylight but only in the darkish confusion of the playgoing, then at the party, which, if she felt worried, she could keep rather on the dim side. Reluctantly, with no sense at all of the huge lark it might be, she agreed to play her part, asking for three extra seats for the Duchess's house guests, who would be described in a letter that Petro had promised to send. And this letter would seem quite straight because in fact, as Tuby was quick to point out, Petro didn't know that Isabel *knew*. This brought a faint gleam of amusement to Isabel's fine eyes, but then, going into the attack immediately after acknowledging defeat, a familiar stratagem in the battle of the sexes, she told him he ought to be ashamed of himself, not simply for this piece of clowning but for submitting to Saltana's bad influence.

It was no better when he went after dinner that evening to drink tea with Lois Terry, who took exactly the same line as Isabel had done. (To her disgust, when he pointed this out.) He was a marvellous lecturer, as she'd thought he would be, and he was just wasting himself on that cynical and rather sinister Saltana. No, she'd refused to go and look at Saltana on television, disliking as she did both television *and* Saltana, and knowing only too well that Saltana was clever enough not to make a fool of himself, which she might have enjoyed. And then she got back to the lecture and bogged them both down in one of those idiotic arguments, with one set of personal tastes opposing another, that every man past his twenty-first birthday should avoid like the plague. She was cross with him; he was sharply sarcastic with her; and he could feel himself getting redder and fatter and older, while poor Lois, who could look really beautiful when excited and happy, turned paler and plainer and then seemed to come out in blotches. He left fairly early; about fifteen seconds, he concluded, going downstairs, before she burst into tears. Anything — perhaps even an attempt at rape — would have been better than this evening of squabble. He walked back from Tarbury through patches of fog and a ruined friendship.

He conveyed some sense of these experiences to Saltana, late on Sunday night, over a drink in Saltana's room. It was the first time they had really got together, at ease with each other, not merely since Saltana had returned from London but for some days before that. "A time like this, Cosmo," Tuby went on, "makes me wonder why we don't believe in astrology. I feel fixed to some hidden pattern. Suddenly I'm trying to talk to my women friends through a glass wall."

"You could do with one, you Casanova of the lecture rooms and hostels," said Saltana, grinning. But then he looked stern. "Well, what about my first appearance on television?"

"I've told you, haven't I?"

"No, you haven't."

"Well, of course you were magnificent, Cosmo. We all thought that. Towards the end — and here I'm not blaming you, I know how you were situated — you were just letting it tick over — "

"What else could I do? Your Mrs. Ringmore called it spitballing — "

"Ah — yes, Cosmo. What about her?"

"A handsome woman," Saltana replied gravely, "and a most agreeable hostess. But just before I left — rather late — I had to tell her that whatever happened we'd no intention of joining an advertising agency. I spoke for you there, I hope, Owen?"

"You most certainly did, Cosmo. I'll go back to teaching first."

"Which way are we going — towards honest research, on Elfreda's Foundation money when it's secure, or towards bogus but profitable expertise?"

"Right, Cosmo. I'm beginning to feel I'm floating in mid-air somewhere between them. And my girl friends' accusations and reproaches, though I confront them boldly, are beginning to unsettle me. I'm willing to trust your judgment, Cosmo, to agree to any major decision you arrive at, but after all — what's happening — or going to happen?"

"I don't know — because Elfreda doesn't know *yet,* though I have an idea she soon will. And our first loyalty is to her. She *staked* us, pardner. And if I don't say much downstairs, that's not because I'm mysterymongering. I don't want her to feel uneasy. Oh — I know — she *is* uneasy, but I don't want to make it any worse for her. For instance, I had a curious session with a man at Birtle's place on Friday night. But before I explain this encounter, you'll have another, won't you? We might as well kill this bottle."

"I'll join you if you insist, Cosmo." Then, while the glasses were being filled: "By the way, do you ever tell yourself that you drink too much?"

"Certainly. I've been telling myself that since about 1933. And for months on end I've had to drink South American whiskies, with tartan labels, that would take the bristles off a badger. But now — about Friday night — " And he reported in detail his encounter with Jimmy Kilburn. Then when he had done: "Don't think we need mention it to Elfreda — um?"

"No," said Tuby. "Talking of Elfreda, d'you know she's quite a performer? The American tourist-matron she's doing for Petro will really be something. Pity you'll miss it, Cosmo."

"Why should I miss it?"

"Because when I mentioned it yesterday, you told us to jump in the lake — "

"I certainly don't intend to wear false whiskers — "

"You can't go as yourself. Come, come! Petro and I thought the part of a Spanish landowner would suit you admirably and wouldn't be too difficult, but of course if you feel it's beyond you — "

"Beyond me? Of course it isn't beyond me. And I've known scores of 'em. What are you? An Indian? Good God, man! — if you can be an

Indian, I can be a Spaniard. But what about false whiskers and wigs and clothes? Must do the thing properly, Owen."

"Petro already has a lot of gear and she's collecting some more, and she's coming to lunch next Friday, bringing everything with her. She opens the Library on Tuesday week, leaves after lunch, ostensibly to cope with her three new house guests. Actually she'll come here. We'll have what you might call a dress rehearsal. We'll dine — in costume — rather early, then we go with her first to the play and afterwards to the Lapfords' party."

"Bit risky — the party — isn't it?"

"The lighting there will be dimmish. And just think of the opportunities it'll offer."

"I am," said Saltana with a slow grin. "Even though my role has certain severe limitations. However, we'll see."

The week that followed was coldish, wet and dark, and largely uneventful, though Tuby had some enquiries from sound radio, Saltana from television, all three channels, and O. V. Mere, who appeared to have adopted them, perhaps because of his wife's new passion for image work, rang up several times. It was Petronella, Duchess of Brockshire, who saved the week for Tuby, arriving in the highest spirits on Friday, with sufficient theatrical gear to outfit a touring company, and getting rather pickled even before lunch.

After lunch, when the stuff Petro had brought had been spread out among the chairs in the big room, Primrose and Mike Mickley expressed their joint dismay and mounting indignation at being left out.

"Darling children," cried Petro, who was sorting out wigs in a sketchy manner, "I really couldn't be more sorry. But while I can just get away with *three* peculiar guests, *five* would sink me — not a hope! And Primrose darling, you'd have to be *very peculiar* indeed not to be recognized. No, no, no — deeply miz, ducks, but it's out."

"Oh — pills, darling! With that heavenly red wig, dark specs, and lots and lots of padding on the bosom and hips, nobody would have a clue."

"And with that bald wig and the droopy moustache," said Mickley, "I could do my village cricketer — a great success one time."

"We'll miss it, my boy," said Saltana. "But even the Lapfords would begin to wonder if a village cricketer arrived at their party."

"Or all this horsy black hair," cried Primrose, holding it up, "with a dead-white face and my cheeks bulged out somehow and a long shapeless dress — a kind of butch type! Petro — please — please!"

"Darling, three's the limit. Can't possibly risk any more. Not in my lot. Of course, if you want to borrow anything we don't need — "

"That's it," Mickley shouted triumphantly. "Primrose, we go on our own. We'll *crash* the Lapford party. Never mind the play. It'll be terrible anyhow."

"Mike, let's do that. Only you'll have to think of something better than a village cricketer — some sort of professor. And I'll be his hideous wife. A grey wig if there is one — and I'll bulge like mad. Oh — and wear those funny teeth."

While this was going on, Tuby had been quietly looking after himself. He had appropriated a wig of smooth black hair and had tried it on. He had found some tinted spectacles that would darken his eyes, even if they left him unable to see properly without his own glasses. And among the clothes was a light blue suit that looked as if it might fit him more or less, and would have to do, even though it was made of thin material never intended for an English December night. Already wearing a blue-grey wig and square spectacles, Elfreda seemed more than halfway towards Mrs. Irwin Appleglass of Seattle — or whomever she had in mind. Saltana was gravely investigating an outfit, which included several high stiff collars, that was probably last worn by a solicitor in a Galsworthy play. "I haven't been in Spain for thirty years," he said to Tuby. "Not since Franco took it over. I may have to switch to a Costa Rican Minister of Finance."

"You can't change now, darling," cried Petro, arriving at that moment. "I've told Mrs. Thing — Lapford — who you are — a rich Spanish landowner, a friend of Tippy's. Tuby sweetie, I'm furious now *I* can't be somebody else. It'll be so boring, just being me."

"No, it won't. You *are* somebody else — always were. Have you learnt my speech for the opening?"

"Word perfect. And it's heaven. Would you like to hear me do it, darling?"

"No, you might take the bloom off it. They won't want you to make another speech at the lunch, will they?"

"If they do, my sweet, all they'll get is one of those sickening little first-night jobs — what a wonderful audience! — God bless everyone! I'll come straight here — into your waiting arms, Tuby my precious — and have a nice little lie-down before we ring up on Petro's Brockshire Follies. Now I must fly — I really must. 'Byebye, everybody! Thank you, Elfreda darling — God! — you're beginning to look like one of those horrors, only your mouth's wrong of course, still human — lovely lunch — the only decent food I ever get — "

Not one of their minds was working properly during those next few days. The ancient fever of dressing up and performing was working in their blood. They began to address one another in strange accents. The creatures of their heated imaginations were beginning to take them over. The *Institute of Social Imagistics* was no longer a centre of calm and rewarding research. Outside, the weather had cleared and brightened; there were nights of frost and some blue sparkling days, so that afternoon walks were a pleasure; but inside, it was as if the strange lights and shadows of the playhouse were creeping nearer, together with all the unhealthy

excitement of impersonation and performance — not, as Tuby and Saltana agreed, a good atmosphere.

Tuesday was another of these crisp days. In the morning it was
decided that only Mike Mickley could attend the opening ceremony in
the Library, to report Petro's performance there. The others, it was felt,
would be recognized at once and perhaps told they were unwelcome on
the Brockshire campus. Even Mickley was uncertain, but Saltana told
him he had only to dress as he'd done when they'd first met, like a guitar
player on his way to a pop group, and nobody in authority would distinguish him from a hundred others. So off he went while the others
hung about or did odd jobs, never really settling down to anything really
worth doing. Primrose was practising wearing the funny teeth she'd
claimed, and she gave Tuby a series of shocks until he in turn went into
rehearsal too, trying out the tinted spectacles of his Indian role that left
him without his own glasses, half-blind. It was one of those mornings
when sensitive men are tempted to start drinking too early, as Tuby and
Saltana told each other several times, before deciding to have a drink.
They were in fact enjoying a second drink — when Mickley, who'd borrowed Primrose's car, returned just after half-past twelve. They all gathered in Elfreda's room to hear his report.

He was enthusiastic. "Honestly, she was marvellous. What a show!
They wanted a duchess — and she gave 'em one. Looked marvellous,
sounded marvellous. Hell of a good speech you wrote for her, Dr. Tuby,
and you ought to have heard her deliver it. Made Sir Leopold Who's-it
and old Jayjay and the Librarian, Stample, seem like buckets of sludge.
And the audience ate her up. They loved her. So did I. I hate to say so,
but you have to hand it to the Establishment — "

"She's not the Establishment. She's the Stage," Tuby hastily reminded him.

"Well, whatever she is, she knows how to do her stuff. Honestly, I
could hardly believe she was the same one who'd come screeching and
tarting it here, always half-stoned. Different woman altogether."

About half-past three, two cars arrived together. Though clearly not
dressed for it, Petro was driving her own car. Behind her was an enormous oldish Rolls in charge of a small oldish chauffeur, who proceeded
to bring out several pieces of luggage.

"Come to stay, Petro?" Saltana enquired dryly.

"No, you idiot, but I have to change here, haven't I? You men never
*think.* Carson, when you've taken those things in, you can go, but be
back about half-past seven, will you? You do realize, don't you, my
darlings," she cried as she swept them into the hall, "that the car thing is
quite tricky? I had to work it out most carefully. You see, I have to make
my entrance in the Rolls with Carson driving. And I'll have to do the
same tonight, taking you people. And he'll bring us back here. But then
he can go, and I'll go home, as late as I please, in my own car. Coming,

I followed him, then we stopped about half a mile from the entrance, and I parked my car in a lay-by, got into the Rolls to make my entrance. So that's that. The speech went terribly well, Tuby my darling, and I never dried — just fluffed once."

"Mike Mickley here told us you were marvellous," said Tuby.

"Oh — how sweet of you! I'd kiss you for that, Mike dear, only that lunch rather got me down — "

"Yes, Petro, you seem strangely sober to me," Tuby told her.

"Darling, I'm dying for a real drink. I wish to God I'd taken a flask. Let's go along to your office, Elfreda darling — lead the way. Just for one stiff swig. Tuby my sweet, they gave me two tiny glasses of very pale sherry and then during lunch just one and a half glasses of what must have been *blanc de blanc de blanc* — I was drinking *water* half the time." They were now in Elfreda's room. "Yes, darling, anything that's handy — and *strong* — brandy, whisky, vodka. Then I'll go up, get out of these damned eyelashes and into something loose — and have a rest before the evening show. How are your parts coming along, darlings? Costumes and make-up okay? Cheers dears!" She took a huge swig of the brandy Elfreda had handed her.

To pass an hour or so, Tuby and Saltana walked briskly to Tarbury and bought a few things they didn't particularly want. On the way back — it was inevitable — they discussed their parts for the evening. "I made a mistake leaving our names to Petro. I forgot, and she says she suddenly had to invent them when she was on the phone to Isabel Lapford. So I'm Dr. Ram Dass, which is just about as corny as they come. She must have been reading a 1908 volume of *Punch*. Who are you?"

"Don Fernandez — which is all my eye," said Saltana rather gloomily. "I could of course throw in a few other names if anybody's interested. I'm wearing a bald wig, a beard I have to make by gumming on a lot of hair and then trimming it to the required shape, and a damnably high stiff collar that may saw my head off before we're through."

"My wig and clothes are all right," said Tuby, "but I can't help wondering about this bottle of staining stuff that Petro brought. I have a suspicion that either it'll start coming off halfway through the evening, or it'll stay on for days."

"Do we know what we're doing, Owen, letting ourselves in for this caper?"

"The mood's wrong, Cosmo, that's all. We had the right idea when we started drinking before lunch. Then we didn't keep it up and now we're out in the desert."

"Our only hope, you believe, Owen, is from now on to be half-pissed — um?"

"I do, Cosmo. This is no programme for sober men of our age. Besides, as I know from experience, hitting the bot will improve my Indian accent. I don't know about your Spanish lisp, which might get rather sloppy."

"It might, but ten to one I won't know. Stride out now, Tuby."

They had two very large quick ones before going upstairs. Nobody else was around. What the three women and Mickley were doing, Tuby neither knew nor cared. No longer a victim of fresh air and the prosaic shopkeeping of Tarbury, he felt a sharp change of mood. The mad lights and shadows of the playhouse were returning; the ancient fever burned again in his blood; the evening no longer held any menace and was already bright with the promise of golden joys. He had a bottle up in his room and tilted it once or twice as an aid to his speedy transformation into Dr. Ram Dass. A deft man even at a time like this, he rapidly undressed, had a lightning shave, applied the stain to his face and neck and a weaker portion to the back of his hands, got into a white shirt and the light blue suit and added the palest of his ties, fastened the wig on carefully, took off his own spectacles and put on the tinted pair, finished his drink before triumphantly regarding his transformation, and then made two discoveries. The first and less important was that he'd forgotten to give himself any socks and shoes. The second confirmed his earlier doubts. Wearing these tinted specs and without his own, he couldn't even see what he looked like. Ram Dass, even if he were sober, would be falling over everybody. So now he tried wearing both pairs and stared hard at the image in the looking glass. It came straight out of a horror film. This was Dr. Ram Dass the mad scientist. And when he began laughing, the result was worse.

He crept into Elfreda's office below, where Primrose and Mike, who didn't need to change for some time yet, were busy mixing martinis. Using his Indian voice, he said, "What do you think of me please, Miss East?"

She turned round and screamed.

"Christ — they'll have kittens at the Lapfords'," said Mike.

"Of course it is true," continued Tuby, still Indian, "I have a peculiar line of research — "

"Don't tell me," cried Primrose, shuddering. "And stop looking like that. Take something off."

"It's the two pairs of specs that do it," said Tuby, no longer Indian, as he removed the tinted pair. "It's quite a problem. I'm not sufficiently convincing just with these. With the tinted pair, I simply can't see. And with both on I run the lab in Bombay where girls go and are never seen again. Thank you, my dear." He accepted what looked like an unusually large martini. Then, as the door opened: "Now — who is it? Ah — Don Fernandez. *Buenas tardes* — or whatever it is! You look like one of those old-fashioned doctors on a foreign mineral-water label, Cosmo." It was the bald wig and the longish beard that did it. "But are those pince-nez right? Why this last-minute touch?"

"I'm a scholarly Spanish landowner, old-world and eccentric," Saltana replied coldly. "I don't find you very convincing, Owen."

"I'm wearing my ordinary specs at the moment," said Tuby. "Not in the part."

"Drain a martini through that hair, darling," Primrose said to Saltana, holding out a glass. "Perhaps you ought to grow a beard. Without the bald bit and those ancient eyeglasses, you'd be fab."

"This collar's a mistake," Saltana grumbled, trying to loosen it. "I can see myself tearing it off before the evening's over."

"Prof, I can see us tearing everything off," said Mickley.

"They may not even let you into that party, my lad," Saltana told him. "What are you two going as?"

"Professor and Mrs. Rumpleton," Primrose replied, and then began to giggle.

"I doubt if the Lapfords know the Rumpletons," said Tuby. "But if you'll tell me what time you think you'll arrive, I'll try to be near the front door and bounce you in." He changed to Indian. "Good gracious me — yes! My very nice old friends — Professor and Mrs. Rumpleton — it is a very great surprise and pleasure indeed."

"You sound like a Welshman I used to know," said Saltana, still critical.

"Most of them sound like Welshmen you used to know. Oh — Elfreda — yes — very good indeed!" And so it was. With her blue-grey wig, with steel waves in it, square spectacles with red rims, a sallow aged face and a rat-trap of a mouth, Elfreda was now an indefatigable and implacable American matron touring the wincing world.

"Not bad, is it?" said Elfreda, not using the voice yet. "Petro says it's good and she's met dozens of 'em — "

"I got mixed up with fifty of them one time in Athens," said Primrose. "At least half looking just like you, darling. What's happened to Petro?"

"Down in a minute. The trouble now is that I don't know who I am — and Petro can't remember — "

"You're Mrs. Irwin Appleglass of Seattle," said Tuby firmly.

Looking magnificent and ducal in a dress of shimmering gold, Petro came dashing in, screaming for a drink, then going round exclaiming at her mummers, almost at once sending the temperature up and the drinks down. Nobody ate much at dinner. Florrie kept following Alfred in, to point and roar with laughter. Mrs. Irwin Appleglass, Don Fernandez, and Dr. Ram Dass began getting into their parts. Primrose and Mike, though not in costume, tried out the Rumpletons — and were terrible. Petro, who had easily caught up with Saltana and Tuby in the imbibing stakes, produced between shrieks of laughter wilder and wilder ideas of what they might possibly attempt at the Lapford party, ideas that even Tuby, feeling reckless and more than half-tight, rejected without hesitation. But then, after they'd hurriedly swallowed some coffee, and Alfred had announced the arrival of the Rolls, Petro — who really never ought to have left the Theatre, Tuby thought — suddenly turned into the Duchess of Brockshire about to take three guests to its university.

"We only think we're stoned," she announced solemnly. "Serious now — keeping well within your parts, you three — until at least we're safely inside the theatre, which incidentally isn't one, they told me this morning, but the large lecture hall in the Science Building. Come on, now. We'll see you two later at the Lapfords', if you get in. But don't forget — you don't know me." Wearing a long cloak now, she led the way out.

At the last minute, realizing how inadequate his thin blue suit would be against a cold night, Tuby had put on his overcoat, which was well outside the Ram Dass part, and could only hope that in the dark nobody would notice that it was an overcoat that had paid several visits to the university before tonight. He shared the two occasional seats in the Rolls with Saltana, whose thick dark suit needed no overcoat. When they were moving, Elfreda, huddling down in her fine mink coat — and it might easily be Mrs. Appleglass's — was heard to say in a small voice that she was already feeling scared.

"Nonsense, darling!" cried Petro. "They'll never guess. They're all so dim. All except Mrs. Lapford, who's not entirely a fool. But I can stick close to her — "

"No, Petro my dear," said Tuby. "Leave her to me."

"Darling, I'm not sure you're *that* good — "

"I am. You haven't seen me yet wearing my tinted glasses. They make all the difference. And my Italian voice is famous from Delhi to Hong Kong. You attend to Jayjay — blind him with glamour and charm — and please leave Isabel to me, Petro — there's a good girl. And you haven't heard that for a long time."

"You couldn't be more wrong, Tuby darling. Tippy never stops saying it. He's very sweet — but terribly, terribly tedious."

"I don't like the idea of this science lecture hall," Don Fernandez–Saltana growled. "No bar. No drinks in the interval. I could do with one now. All this hair on my face is making me feel thirsty."

"I know, darling. We ought to have brought a flask — or something. And we can't very well ask for drinks. We're a few minutes late already."

This was all to the good, Tuby felt, and so it proved to be. The rest of the audience was in and waiting. Jayjay and Isabel, Rittenden and some other dogsbody, were there to greet them, just inside the entrance; there were some gabbled introductions; Jayjay led the way with Petro, and Tuby followed close behind with Isabel. At the last minute he'd remembered to replace his own spectacles with the tinted pair and now could hardly see a thing, so he took Isabel's arm going up the stairs.

"You will excuse me, please, Lady Lapford," he said in a high clear Ram Dass tone, "but I am having great trouble with my eyes — especially at night time, when it really is jolly difficult."

"Please don't apologize, Dr. Ram Dass, I quite understand." But then she hissed in his ear: "Are you tight?"

"Tired? No, not at all, thank you." High and clear again. "It is just these jolly rotten eyes of mine. When I watch the play I will wear two pairs of glasses, if you don't mind." He gave a titter and squeezed her arm. "I ask if you don't mind because everybody tells me I look so horrible, quite putrid, in my two pairs of glasses."

"Along here now, Dr. Ram Dass. I've arranged for seats in the fourth row because they'll give us the best view. No, you go first, after the Duchess. I'm next to you, then Don Fernandez and Mrs. — er — Appleglass — isn't it — ?"

As soon as Tuby was seated between Petro and Isabel, the hall lights went out and two or three spotlights came on, focussed on the platform stage. Tuby put the tinted pair over his own spectacles, and then was able to see that there was no stage set, just a door and a window against some curtaining and in front of them a table and a few small wooden chairs. Though the spotlights were on and the audience quietly expectant, there was now one of those waits that so often precede rough-and-ready amateur productions. Somebody ought to say something, Tuby felt, and so it might as well be Dr. Ram Dass.

"I am looking forward very much to this play," Ram Dass told Mrs. Lapford and probably a dozen other people. "I have read — oh, goodness! — twenty times — you have now a great renaissance of English Drama. Angry young men! Kitchen sink! Very much sex and No Communication! Naughty language! It will be jolly interesting, I am sure."

Then three things all happened at once. A female character, not easily seen, made an entrance. Tuby's left hand, down by his side, was seized and squeezed hard by Petronella, Duchess of Brockshire. His right hand was hastily pulled down from his knee by Isabel Lapford, who then dug her nails into his palm. Was this in anger or loving friendship? Was she continuing their quarrel, possibly newly inflamed by his Ram Dass impudence? Or was she amused by it, after a rather wearing Mrs. Vice-Chancellor day, and giving him a signal that all was well between them? To decide this, he gently eased his left hand out of Petro's grasp, then made a stealthy little turn towards his right and Isabel — and, this being a lecture room not a theatre, there were no armrests, no separations, between seats — at the same time contriving to escape from the nail-digging and to entwine his fingers with hers. This move wasn't resisted, but he needed more proof, so he slid his right leg out a little until it encountered her left leg, then he increased the pressure, and, to his delight, this pressure was returned. This not only meant no war, an armistice, peace declared; they were into an entente. This promised well for the party.

Meanwhile, Ted Jenks's play was making no promises. The female character — young, it seemed — had gone off and then come back with two pans, which she put on the table, took off the table, put them on again, took them off again, and walked round with them, until another and older female character — soon established as her mother — made a very noisy entrance, yelling some low-life dialogue with a gasping and gulping violence, something of an achievement by the wife of the Professor of Botany. Then mother and daughter, after cursing each other heartily, were interrupted by a neighbour, very large, very fat (the wife of the Lecturer in German), who may have had some terribly violent and disturbing things to say but made little more noise, saying them, than a mouse. Then, after a lot of standing about (Petro whispered that they all kept *drying,* poor wretches), Alf, that bloody rotten sod of a window-cleaner who obviously had designs on his step-daughter, appeared and started shouting for his dinner, the greedy bastard, and, after some trouble round the door, was given the usual plate of sliced bananas. Defying him — the measly snotty twit — his wife and the giant-mouse neighbour went off to the local, telling the daughter to kick his testicles up into his guts if she'd any trouble with her step-father. And trouble, obviously, was on its way. Alf, not well cast, as he gave the impression of being a weedy student with a nervous jump in his voice, pushed aside the sliced bananas and began drinking from a bottle he had in his pocket. Rather foolishly placing herself as far from the door as was possible, his step-daughter, Marge, promised to "do him" if he tried it again, and then, while Alf was still working on the bottle, made a long confused speech about the younger generation, wages and incomes, industry and the cost of living, the hypocrisies of Church and State, the problems of identity and communication. This was too much for Alf — as indeed it was for Tuby, who found it hard to keep awake. After finishing the cold tea in the bottle, Alf went for Marge by slowly walking round the table, beginning with his back turned to her. It wasn't easy on that smallish platform for two people in movement to avoid bumping into each other, but in this relentless pursuit of Marge by Alf they contrived to have most of the platform between them for several minutes. Then Marge thought of the door and went out, with Alf now closely behind her. One scream from Marge outside and the act was over, the spotlights were off, the hall lights on.

"We thought you might like a drink during the interval," said Isabel across Tuby to Petro. "There's a little room above. I'll lead the way, shall I? Dr. Ram Dass?"

They climbed to the top of the hall, went along a corridor, entered some kind of little office, where drinks had been set out. The Duchess and her guests firmly declared for whisky. "Even you, Dr. Ram Dass?" Isabel enquired mischievously. "There *is* lemon squash."

Wishing she could see a wink through his tinted specs, Tuby said solemnly and for all to hear, "In Indi-yah the lemon squash would be very nice, very welcome, but here in England it is so beastly cold I do not object to drinking your whisky — thank you so much."

"My — my — you're just saying what I always say, Dr. Ram Dass," said Elfreda as Mrs. Irwin Appleglass. But then she took him on one side and whispered, "Jayjay keeps giving me some puzzled looks. D'you think he's spotted me?"

"Not to worry, my dear," Tuby muttered. "He's given me puzzled looks since the first time we met. He's a puzzled man, that's all." Don Fernandez approached them, so Tuby went into loud and clear Ram Dass specially for him. "You are liking the play very much, Don Fernandez? Very nice piece?"

"*Lo siento mucho.* For studenth — perhapth tho." He put an arm round both of them and bent his head between them. "What about this damned beard?" he whispered. "Feel it's coming off any minute. No? Are you sure?"

Petro's voice, very gay, rang through the room. "Oh — no, Vice-Chancellor, I'm adoring it. So *stark* — and all that! I suppose he's raping her now in the next room, if there *is* a next room, because that door seemed to be the front door, didn't it? Perhaps he's having her in the street. It's that kind of *district,* I imagine, isn't it? Just one more act, is there? Good! Oh — Dr. Ram Dass!" And she took him clean outside into the corridor. "Must find a loo before we go back to that bloody play. I know — I'll ask Mrs. Thing. But what I wanted to say, darling, is this. You seemed to me to be doing a bit of stealthy snogging and footsie work with Mrs. Thing. Don't tell me she starts misbehaving at once with the first Indian who comes along — looking like you too! Now then, Tuby darling — give!"

"I'll confess, Petro my dear. I *had* to tell her beforehand. Otherwise she'd have spotted us in the first twenty seconds."

"Perfectly true — and I forgive you, darling. But you'll have to pay more attention to me or I'll never possibly *endure* this other act. My God — what a play — and what a production! How *can* they?" But now the door opened and Isabel appeared with Elfreda. "Dear Mrs. Lapford," cried Petro, "I was just wondering if I might possibly — " And they went to their loo. Jayjay and Rittenden took charge of Saltana and Tuby, marching them further along the corridor.

"I hope you're enjoying the play," said Jayjay in that falsely hearty but clear tone kept for foreigners. "The author, Ted Jenks, is our writer-in-residence this year. Do you understand that term, Don Fernandez?"

"Never at all," the Don replied promptly.

"You'll have a chance of meeting him later, at my house, Dr. Ram Dass."

"Tophole! I will tell him it is a jolly good play."

"A little on the crude side, perhaps," said Rittenden.

"Good gracious — yes! All very much on the crude side," cried Dr. Ram Dass with enthusiasm. "Filthy talk! All new angry style! Ripping stuff!" And received a sharp jab in the ribs from Don Fernandez. Saltana evidently thought he was overdoing it.

Tuby returned reluctantly and rather sleepily to his seat at the play, and indeed, not long after the second act opened on a stage that was almost dark, he fell asleep. He was vaguely conscious of various nudges from Isabel and Petro, but some defence mechanism in his unconscious enabled him to avoid taking in any more of the play. However, at the end not many people there clapped longer and harder than Dr. Ram Dass. The play in fact got what is called in show biz "a mixed reception," but Ted Jenks, wearing a special dirty new jersey, took a call and made a speech — thenking one an' dall for their unerstanning nappree-shee-yshun of what he inevitably called "ma work." Dr. Ram Dass — all jolly ripping tophole — led the applause, and was told by Mrs. Lapford, under her breath, that he really was a monster and she couldn't think why she ever bothered her head two minutes about him. Which to Tuby, who'd heard this kind of talk before, set the tone and pattern of the party. This, he decided, was to be Isabel's night.

Now the four of them were in the Rolls again, on their way to the Lapfords'. And Petro, free at last to speak her mind, spoke it. "My God, darlings, did you ever *ever* sit through such a play — and such a production?"

"I must say I didn't think it was very good," said Elfreda, out of her lay innocence.

"Good, my dear? It was utterly unspeakable. All right for you, Tuby, you just snored all through Act Two. You still snore, you know, darling?"

"He *still* snores?" This was Elfreda again, no longer speaking out of lay innocence. "When did you hear him before, dear?"

"Oh — darling, when we were all working together, ages ago, we were all kind of mixed up — "

"Speak for yourself, Petro," said Saltana severely. "I'm worried about this dam' beard. I can't see it surviving this party. And anyhow we're going to be spotted — all at close quarters."

"I'm sure we are," said Elfreda, worry in her voice.

"I thought of that," Tuby told them complacently. "So I told Isabel Lapford to keep the lighting dim — and perhaps throw in a dark corner or two."

"Good as far as it goes," said Saltana. "But I hope you reminded her that some of us can't keep going on cider and Yugoslav claret cup. She may fix *you* up properly, my boy — "

"She'll do that all right," cried Petro. "You weren't sitting next to them. That one, mind you. All starch and prunes, I'd have said. I'm keeping my eye on you two, Tuby darling. Now — look — we ought to make them play games, otherwise it'll be all snuffly university talk. What d'you suggest? Of course there's always *The Game* — "

"You mean, Tuby's — " Saltana began.

"Shut up. I mean the one we all used to play night after night, ages ago — one from each group being told a title and then having to act it — you remember? Well, I could *start* them on that — just to loosen them up, don't you think? After all, it's *my* party. I have an *idea* already but I just can't get hold of it."

"Don't try, Petro," Saltana told her. "One *idea* of yours has already landed me with this grotesque outfit. The next will probably see me, dressed in nothing but this beard and my underpants, reviving the Apache dance with the wife of the Professor of Geology."

"I've just thought of something," said Petro. "If I tell Carson to go home now with this car, how do we get back to the Institute?"

"We cadge lifts home," said Tuby.

"Assuming we're still on speaking terms with somebody," said Saltana, obviously inclined now towards a dark view of the evening ahead.

"I'll tell you what," cried Elfreda. "Petro can't go back to the Institute to bring her car. She couldn't drive it in the dress she's wearing — and anyhow she must go straight to the party. But if the chauffeur takes me back, then he can go home and I can drive to the Lapfords' in my car. Then it'll be waiting for us."

"A sound idea," said Saltana. "And the only one that's come my way during the last day or two. I'll come with you, Elfreda. And we'll make sure of at least one decent drink. Besides, I'd be glad to lose half an hour or so of Don Fernandez, a boring character."

"Oh — I wish you would, Cosmo," Elfreda told him. "I feel the same about Mrs. Irwin Appleglass. When I'm not talking to anybody, I can think of dozens of funny remarks for her to make, but then when somebody's looking at me I can't remember one of them. But don't think we're running away from the party, Petro dear."

"I'll try not to, darling. Though how the hell I explain where you've gone, seeing that you're supposed to be house guests of mine, I can't imagine. You can think of something, Tuby darling, can't you? You're not trying to dodge arriving at the Lapfords' with me, are you?"

"Certainly not," Tuby replied cheerfully. "I enjoy being Dr. Ram Dass, and I propose to exploit him to the full at the party. Where, in fact, we are now arriving. And lots of other cars already."

Five minutes later, the Duchess of Brockshire and Dr. Ram Dass made an impressive entrance into the hall of the Lapford house, where Jayjay and Isabel were waiting to receive them.

"Oh — where are your other two guests?" cried Isabel. Her manner was perfect, but Tuby caught the glint of mischief in her fine eyes.

"I promised to offer you many apologies from Mrs. Appleglass and Don Fernandez," he said hastily, though in the Ram Dass silkiest tone. "They will be here very, very soon, but Mrs. Appleglass wished very much to send a cable to Mr. Appleglass — "

"Really? I thought she was a widow — "

"Mr. Appleglass is her brother-in-law. Very nice man. I met him in Indi-yah — Agra — Taj Mahal." He gave both Lapfords an enormous smile.

"But — look here," said Jayjay, his head waving, "I'm afraid the Tarbury post office won't be open now. She could have telephoned it from here, y'know — "

But Isabel now swept the guest of honour away, to tidy herself up somewhere, and Tuby indicated to Jayjay that other people were waiting to be welcomed, and then moved on to the drawing room. Isabel had kept her promise about the lighting. It was all comfortably dim. He was now wearing both pairs of spectacles, which meant, however horrible he looked, he could just recognize anybody he knew. A girl, probably a student, gave him a startled glance but offered him a glass of some muck from the tray she was carrying. He refused, with a smile and little bow, and then found himself facing Donald Cally and his wife, the scrubbed Scots nurse.

"Dr. Ram Dass," he told them, putting his hands together just below his chin. "Who are you, please?" He felt this was too good to miss.

"Professor Cally, head of Sociology here." It came in a shout, of course. "And this is Mrs. Cally."

"You're staying with the Duchess of Brockshire, aren't you, Dr. Dass?" said Mrs. Cally. "I'm told they have a lovely old house."

Tuby moved nearer and attempted a very confidential tone, not easy in the Ram Dass style. "Very cold house. No nice comforts. Food very bad. Always cold meats. If she asks you to go to her house, you say 'Very, very sorry, but some time perhaps.' Then you don't go."

"Oh — dear! Still, I'm not altogether surprised," said Mrs. Cally. "I have heard rumours. But plenty to drink, from all accounts."

"No — no — no. This is very untrue, if you will pardon me." This was coming too near the truth. "All very false — such accounts. Yes, Professor Cally — please?"

"Want you to meet one of my assistants," Cally shouted. "Dr. Honeyfield."

Would Hazel spot him? She was giving him a peculiar look, but that might be the horror-film effect. "A great pleasure to meet you, Dr. Honeyfield. You look so very nice, so very pretty, if you will excuse a personal comment. In Indi-yah we are very outspoken, you know." She murmured something, no longer looking straight at him. Now he drew her to one side, away from Cally. "I have a little secret for you, Dr. Honeyfield," he confided. "I am staying with the Duchess of Brockshire. We met in Indi-yah. Also as a guest is a Spanish gentleman, Don Fernandez — old-fashioned gentleman but jolly nice fellow. He is coming here a little later. You will notice him at once, I think. He is tall with not much hair but plenty of beard. And I know he will wish to talk to you — Don Fernandez — "

"But how does he know about me?" And was she giving him a peculiar look again?

"Oh — goodness! That is such a boring long story — "

"What is, Dr. Ram Dass?" But this was Isabel, suddenly at his elbow. "Or mustn't you tell? I'm taking him away, Dr. Honeyfield, because I want him to meet some of our English Department." The hand moving him away gave his arm a little squeeze. Tuby gave a quick glance round; the room was filling up; and Petro had made her entrance and was already suggesting *The Game*. He brought Isabel to a halt for a moment between two groups, exclaiming loudly, "This is such a very nice room," then muttering, "but get me out of it soon. I need a drink."

She brought him up near the door. "Dr. Ram Dass — Professor Brigham and Mrs. Brigham — Dr. Lois Terry — and Mr. Ted Jenks, our writer-in-residence and the author of the play you saw tonight — "

"Very good play — very comical," cried Dr. Ram Dass.

"*Comical?*" This came from both Jenks and Mrs. Brigham, who looked like an angry clown again.

"No, no, no — wrong word, of course, and please pardon the mistake. *Anatomical.* Very good play — very anatomical — "

Lois Terry gave a little shriek of laughter, then looked apologetic, her eyes deep pools of repentance.

Ted Jenks was about to say something, but Brigham got in first. "What you're really saying, Dr. Ram Dass, is that you feel, as we all do, that in this play Jenks is being deeply analytical, trying to show us the *anatomy* of a certain section of our society. You'd agree with that, I think, wouldn't you?" Brigham enquired earnestly.

"I would agree with that very much indeed. Anatomical *and* analytical as you say." Tuby now realized that Isabel had vanished and that Brigham was about to continue droning away. But he was rescued by Lois.

"Dr. Ram Dass," she said sharply, "I have an urgent private message for you." And she almost pushed him out of the door into the hall, where a few people were hanging about but a quiet dim corner could still be found.

"Owen Tuby, what do you think you're doing?" The eyes were now immense accusations.

"How did you guess?" he whispered.

"Don't be silly. To begin with, you have a funny little lump on the left corner of your chin. I've often noticed it."

"Nobody else has."

"I'm not nobody else. And I'm not stupid. I may behave stupidly sometimes — I did the last twice we've been together — but I knew it was you at once. *Dr. Ram Dass!*" But then she began laughing, just when he expected either solemn apologies or reproaches. She was still laughing when Isabel found them.

"Oh — here you are, Dr. Ram Dass — " Isabel began.

"Owen Tuby, you mean, Mrs. Lapford." Lois was serious, rather indignant or scornful, having changed in a flash. An extraordinary girl. "I knew him at once. And I also knew at once you were well in the secret. But I won't say anything, if that's what you want."

"I hope not, Lois," said Tuby gently. "It wasn't Mrs. Lapford's idea. Nor, strictly speaking, mine."

Dim as it was in that corner, he saw the two women throw him a glance and then regard each other intently, as if they'd now withdrawn into some female world of mysterious defiances, challenges, battles of eyes, and fragmentary phrases, which he heard them begin to exchange. From the drawing room came a shriek or two from Petro, now starting to organize *The Game*. His attention returned to find the two women looking enquiringly at him. As if, before anything more could be said or done, they expected him to choose between them. And it wasn't Lois's night, not with him in this getup; the whole mood, tone, feeling of it were wrong for her. Hadn't he already decided it was Isabel's night? So he turned to her. "Sorry, Isabel!" As if his mind had been wandering. "You were wanting me, weren't you?"

"Thank you!" Lois spoke very sharply indeed. "And — goodnight!" She almost ran.

Isabel made almost the same speed, taking him through the side door and along the corridor and into the little pantry place, the whisky department, where they'd been before. She locked the door behind her, then poured out a large whisky for him and a smaller one — though not as small as last time — for herself. "Have you been making love to that girl?" she enquired abruptly.

"Certainly not, Isabel my dear. If I had, I wouldn't tell you, but I'm prepared to swear I haven't."

"I think she's in love with you, Owen."

"No, no, no! She's just recovering from one of those long messy affairs. Well, bless you for this!" He held up his glass. "I'd had several earlier — too many, perhaps — and was just beginning to feel melancholy. All wrong for Dr. Ram Dass — a cheerful type."

"I don't believe Indians talk like that now."

"Of course not. Petro saddled me with Ram Dass, so I had to be

Ram Dassy — about fifty years out of date. Still, I've enjoyed the part so far."

"And poor Jayjay's completely taken in." She put a finger to his cheek. "Does this stuff come off?"

"I borrowed a bottle of it from Petro, who swears it doesn't. By the way, she'll be screaming inside — and outside soon — for strong drink. And as she's probably keeping the party going while we lurk here, we owe her something. I'll go while you hold the fort here." He finished his whisky. "I'll take her a tumbler of gin. They'll think it's water."

"But does she like gin?"

"Petro likes anything seventy proof and over."

"She was very impressive this morning," said Isabel as she poured out the gin. She told me upstairs you wrote that speech for her. She adores you. She told me so."

"An old friend. A lovely young madcap, years ago. Well, she'll bless us for this gin. Keep the door locked while I'm gone, Isabel. This is our place and our night. I'll give two slow taps on the door, then three quick taps. And you attend to our glasses in the meantime, my dear."

*The Game* was in progress, with three groups hard at it. Petro must have volunteered to give out the titles, to get the game going, so she was standing alone, away from the groups.

"Tuby darling," she muttered, "for God's sake bring me a real drink."

Dr. Ram Dass replied, holding out the glass. "Very special nice water for you, dear Duchess of Brockshire — "

"*Water!* And you at least half-loaded already — " But then she took a sip of it and gave him a wide sweet smile. "Marvellous, darling! But don't stay lurking with Mrs. Thing all night. I need you."

She might have said more, but at that moment Mrs. Cally came bounding across, hissing like an enraged serpent. "*Tale of Two Cities.*"

Crossing the hall, he saw two strange figures standing just inside the front door, and he took off his tinted spectacles as he went nearer. They looked horrible. Mike was wearing a black suit too small for him, a grey wig, a walrus moustache, and very thick spectacles he'd borrowed from somebody, adding a final sinister touch. In a shapeless long dress, a black wig, with a chalky make-up and those funny teeth she'd tried on earlier, Primrose looked like Dracula's sister.

"Ah — Dr. Ram Dass," cried Mike in what he thought was a voice unlike his own. "Professor and Mrs. Rumpleton — you remember?"

"Good gracious me!" And Dr. Ram Dass shook hands with them, to get closer. "This is a tophole nice surprise, Professor and Mrs. Rumpleton."

"How do we look, Doc?" whispered Mike.

"Academics from another planet. Don't venture near any light."

"Mrs. Appleglass and Don Fernandez are here too," Primrose announced in a deep Mrs. Rumpleton tone.

Tuby just gave himself time to nod and smile, then fled. Over his new drink, he explained the latest development of the masquerade to Isabel, who had a high colour now and a sparkle in her eye. He thought she would resent this really impudent Rumpleton invasion, but she didn't seem to care and was more interested in what was happening in the drawing room.

"They're up to their necks in *The Game* just now," he explained. "And by the time Petro's finished that gin, she'll have them playing something really wild. You're not being missed, if that is what's worrying you, my dear."

She smiled rather vaguely. "They probably think I'm in the kitchen, helping those girls to cut sandwiches. And in the kitchen they think I'm in the drawing room. And I'm here — with you. Do I sound a bit tight?"

"I wouldn't know, being in that state myself. But I wish I wasn't looking like Ram Dass. It must be putting you off."

"No — no — it's putting me on. Not that I've ever been in the least attracted by Indians. But somehow — just because I know it's really you — and yet at the same time you look quite strange — and everything's ridiculous tonight — quite mad. I'm feeling quite mad too. Oh — and — but what's the use of talking?" Abandoning speech, she wrapped herself round him, pressed herself close, and kissed him long but not hard, her lips opening at once. And because it was this woman, usually so stiffly self-conscious, so proud, no Hazel Honeyfield melting at a touch, it was very exciting indeed.

But then she held him at arms' length, looking very solemn. "Oh — of course this is quite mad, but for once I don't care. There are two things I want to ask you, though. Will you answer me truthfully, Owen?"

"Certainly, Isabel." And he meant it.

"Do you think you'll be leaving here soon?"

"I don't know, my dear. We really don't know where we are just now. But if you'll take a guess, I'd say it's unlikely we'll be here very much longer. And I'm not saying this because I feel it's the answer you'd like."

"Well, it is, of course. No long messy Lois Terry affairs for me. Now for the other question, which you've probably heard many times before. I'm not just a woman to be had at a party, am I? You care about me a little — as a person — don't you?"

"Of course I do, Isabel. I did from the first. You must know that, my dear."

"Well — listen," she began in an urgent whisper. "If you turn to the left at the top of the stairs — I mean on the first floor — the door at the end belongs to a little spare room we hardly ever use. Be there in about ten minutes' time. If you should happen to run into anybody on the stairs or the landing, just be lost and stupid, looking for a bathroom. Don't knock, go straight in — it'll be dark — and lock the door behind you. Oh — and before you come up, make sure everybody's busy in the drawing room." She gave him a quick kiss and hurried out.

He waited a minute or two, finished his drink and decided against having another, then went along to the little side door and peeped out. Shouts of laughter were coming from the drawing room, which seemed to be full now, and there was only one person standing in the hall. Tuby went *pssst* at this tall melancholy figure. Don Fernandez was trying to look like Don Quixote.

"And about time too, my boy," said Saltana as Tuby took him into the little pantry place. "I'm tired of this beard, I don't like party games, and I'm a cup or two too low to make any of your lecherous advances. That's right, fill it up. But aren't you having one?"

"No, I've already had two in here. And in a few minutes I must leave you, Cosmo. You can stay here if you like."

"It'll depend on how I feel when I've refreshed myself. I never ought to have allowed myself to be talked into this Fernandez part. It offers no scope. The women don't like the look of me. I ought to have come as a gaucho straight from the pampas — dark, picturesque, exotic — appealing to the worst in Brockshire womanhood. Yes, my boy, a gaucho."

"But what would a gaucho be doing here?"

"What are we all doing here? Guests of the Duchess of Brockshire. And don't tell me Petro wouldn't entertain a gaucho if she could find one. He'd stand a dam' sight better chance than this miserable Don Fernandez. Another whisky — and I'll stay to have one — and I may tear off this beard and this hellish collar, then go bouncing in there as myself, either plastered or half-barmy. You're going then, are you? Anything I can do for you, Owen?"

"Just keep the beard and collar on, and go along to help Petro. Show them an old-fashioned Spanish landowner in his wilder moments. *Olé — olé!*"

Tuby crept up the stairs unnoticed. Then he turned to the left, clearly away from the master bedrooms, and because there was no light at all along this part of the corridor he had almost to grope his way to the end of it. He could feel his heart thumping, as if he'd leapt back thirty years, doing his first creeping towards a waiting girl in a bedroom. He also felt curiously divided, one part of him, still excited by her embrace, wanting to get on with it and take the woman, and another part feeling oddly reluctant, wishing itself out of this stealthy and rather squalid business in the dark. However, the room was not in fact completely dark; the curtains, though drawn, admitted some light from outside; and a naked Isabel was just visible. Like other women he had known, having once committed herself to the adventure she had discarded caution with her clothes, so that now he was apprehensive and she was quite reckless. She made love as if she'd just heard about its possibilities. He felt he was pleasuring her rather than indulging himself, which was fair enough — for he was certain she'd never done anything like this before, not at anybody's party, let alone her own — and he ended feeling vaguely sorry for her and fond of her and generally rather sad. He also began to feel cold, putting on that thin suit again.

Slipping down the stairs past several solid ladies going up, he could hear Petro shrieking instructions from inside the drawing room and then saw that some kind of grand-chain antic had spilt out into the hall. He had just time to catch a glimpse of Don Fernandez, who was jigging away but keeping hold of Hazel Honeyfield instead of handing her on. In great need of a whisky now, he made for the side door and the little pantry place. And who was in there, taking a quick nip? None other than Vice-Chancellor J. J. Lapford, whose head began waving at once at the sight of Dr. Ram Dass.

"Vice-Chancellor, I am sorry but I am feeling jolly cold. This suit I am wearing is only right for Indi-yah. I think some nice whisky would make me feel much better — "

"Yes, of course, Dr. Ram Dass. Help yourself, won't you? Had the idea you Indians didn't care for whisky — brandy — that sort of thing."

"In my case this idea is all tommyrot, Vice-Chancellor. Yes, please, I will help myself as you are so kind." And he poured out a stiff one very quickly. "Cheers to you!" And then, having downed half of it, he continued: "You are wondering something, I know, Vice-Chancellor. You are wondering how I knew there might be something warming for me here. So I will tell you, though it is not an interesting story. When I felt cold I went into the kitchen and your wife was very kind although so jolly busy there and told me how I could find this little room where there was whisky."

"I see. Yes, yes, of course. Is my wife there now? I was wondering what had become of her."

"Oh — good gracious me! No, I cannot tell you that, Vice-Chancellor. This was some time back because at first I was very stupid — I am rotten about directions — and I went upstairs but then I saw that could not be right and did not like to ask anybody — "

"No, no, quite right. Glad you didn't mention it." Jayjay's head was still now, and he seemed to be staring rather hard. "Getting rather boisterous in there, I'm afraid. Bit too much for me."

"Our friend the Duchess can be very lively, you know, at times, Vice-Chancellor. Oh — my hat! — you should have seen her at Jaipur. You have been to Jaipur?"

"Haven't been to India at all, I'm sorry to say. But you know, Dr. Ram Dass, I can't help feeling we've met before."

"I think so too, Vice-Chancellor. I had this feeling when I first arrived and saw you, but I must tell you I have a putrid memory — absolutely putrid."

"Some education conference, perhaps — ?"

"That is a very clever idea. I have attended some jolly big conferences — in London — in Paris — all expenses paid from Indi-yah and back — and many ripping times. And now Vice-Chancellor," he added gravely, "I ask a very great favour from you. Not for myself but for our gracious friend — the Duchess of Brockshire. I know she will be wanting very much to have a quiet little talk with me — about when we go and our plans and so forth — and I think this is a tophole place for such a little talk. So the very great favour is only that you tell her where I am — very quiet, very secret — "

"Yes, I can do that, Dr. Ram Dass. And you might drop a hint — just the merest hint — that we've all had a long day and the party does seem to be getting rather out of hand — you know?"

"Of course, of course — a very tactful hint. I can drop such a hint in here alone with her. But if you say it out there it could be merry bloody hell. So, thank you, now I will wait."

And Tuby was glad to be left alone. He was beginning to find the Dr. Ram Dass part rather wearing in all its aspects. Not that Petro would be restful, but the poor dear did deserve another strong drink. He left the door slightly ajar for her and put a glass by the side of the gin bottle.

Petro burst in, flung herself at him, locked the door, pounced on the gin, all in about thirty-five seconds. "My God, that's better. A life-saver! I'll forgive you for lurking all night, you devil." She gave the place a measuring glance round. "Very cramping, of course, but we've done it in worse places, darling."

"But years and years ago, Petro my dear. No doubt you're still young enough for such antics, but I'm too old and too fat."

"Not too old and too fat to have been lurking — "

"I was trying to dodge the party. What are they doing now?"

"Having a little romp, darling. We found a record of those jiggly old tunes — y'know, gathering peasecods or fumbling petticoats or whatever they did — so everybody under fifty-five and fifteen stone is jiggling and romping. Poor old Lapford's terrified. He can see an orgy looming. Darling Tuby, even though you do look so bloody sinister as Dr. What's-it, I still adore you. Don't you think we might — "

"No, I don't, Petro. It simply wouldn't work and then we'd be furious with each other and what's been a wonderful reunion would turn into a disaster. Finish your drink. Then if you're not too plastered, we'll go and jiggle and romp for a while and then pack up."

This is what they did. *Diddy-up-a-doo-doo* went the peasecods or petticoats tune, and Tuby swung Petro over to her next partner. *Diddy-up-a-doo-doo,* and he was facing Mrs. Cally, still neat, scrubbed, ready for the operating theatre. *Diddy-up-a-doo-doo,* and now he was out of the

hall and into the drawing room and with a pink horse of a woman; and
then it was Hazel Honeyfield and, forgetting he was Dr. Ram Dass, he
squeezed her hand hard and was surprised when she jerked it away.
*Diddy-up-a-doo-doo,* and then it was a tall thin girl he didn't know who
was trying to rock 'n' roll, and following her was a square Central European type grimly determined to enjoy Old English Customs. *Diddy-up-
a-doo-doo,* and now his hands were squeezed hard because this was Isabel
Lapford, who cheated to stay with him an extra turn, and this made him
feel suddenly sad again, and the gaiety never returned to the *Diddy-up-a-
doo-doo* of the next few minutes, when against his will he found himself
wondering about Lois Terry. And then Elfreda, who hadn't enjoyed being Mrs. Irwin Appleglass, drove them home, where there was a little
scene because Petro, who wasn't fit to drive yet, wanted to lie down
somewhere and be looked after by Tuby. Elfreda, stern for once, would
have none of this and attended to Petro herself. Left below to wait for
the women, Tuby found a filled pipe of his near the drinks in Elfreda's
room and began to enjoy the smoke he'd been missing all night. Saltana
took off the horrible high collar and most of the beard, gave himself a
small whisky as a nightcap, sank into a chair and stretched out his legs,
and said slowly: "It was Voltaire, I believe, who declared that life would
be tolerable if it were not for its amusements."

# *10*

It was the following Saturday morning when Elfreda took a personal call
from Oxford. The man who spoke to her, in a deep American voice, gave
his name as Orland M. Stockton and said he was an attorney. He had
spent the night in Oxford with a friend and now, if Mrs. Judson Drake
were free and willing to receive him, he proposed to rent an automobile
and call upon her during the early afternoon. No, he was sorry he could
not explain over the telephone exactly why he wanted to see her — he
made a point of never doing this in professional matters — but he assured Mrs. Judson Drake that this was fairly urgent legal business, and
that he was giving himself the trouble of calling upon her because this
would be more tactful and considerate than simply writing her a letter.
Orland M. Stockton sounded an immensely solemn man, even for a
lawyer, and Elfreda rather shakily told him she could see him about half-
past two, and then explained how and where he could find her.

Later, as soon as they were available, she told Saltana and Tuby
about Orland M. Stockton, and it was agreed that she should have about
ten minutes alone with him and that Saltana and Tuby would then,

though apparently by accident, arrive on the scene. Nothing more was said because it was now lunchtime and they were joined by Primrose and Mike. At the table they were led by Elfreda into talk about Christmas, which was already putting dabs of cottonwool on the shop windows of Tarbury. Mike was going home for Christmas, and Primrose, who had no home, was spending it with the Birtles. Elfreda, who loved Christmas and felt she must do something about it, announced she would stay right here in the Institute, but spoke vaguely about inviting an old aunt and a certain cousin, even though she couldn't help remembering that she'd never liked either of them. Then to her dismay she discovered that both Saltana and Tuby, corrupted perhaps by their long years in Latin America and the East, were Christmas-haters. They even went so far as to declare that they had gone away just to escape it.

"Largely arrived here with the Prince Consort," said Tuby, "and ought to have departed with him. Now, of course, it's been taken over by the various associations of Wholesale and Retail Trades."

"Whenever I used to receive a specially big and expensive Christmas card," said Saltana, "with a lot of guff on it about Old Friendship and Auld Lang Syne and so forth, it was invariably from some scoundrel."

And of course there was much more to this effect, both men being clever and cynical, showing off, and Elfreda could have slapped them. She didn't stay for coffee, telling them she wanted to change before Orland M. Stockton arrived, and it was nearly half-past two when she came down again.

Mr. Stockton was a big fat man, very American in type, with a yellowish giant face on which dwarf features were holding a huddled conference. He was as immensely solemn as he had sounded over the phone. And he began to frighten Elfreda even while he was still talking about the weather and his journey from Oxford and was bringing documents out of a briefcase.

"Is it — something — about the Foundation?" she enquired timidly as he stared in silence at his documents.

"It is indeed, Mrs. Judson Drake. You will hardly believe it, but these came from Portland — airmail, of course — in four days. Very remarkable — *very* remarkable!" And then, without a word of warning, he went straight into some gabble about Judge Somebody in the Something Court, until Elfreda begged him to stop. Couldn't he just tell her what it all meant?

"Willingly — willingly! You want the gist of it, I guess, Mrs. Judson Drake. Most ladies do, I know. Well, the gist of the judgment is — you are not entitled, under the law of the State of Oregon, to set up, finance, control, here in Britain, a Judson Drake Sociological Foundation — "

She was furious. "Oh — I'm not. Well, who is, then?"

"Strictly speaking, I am under no legal obligation to answer that question, Mrs. Judson Drake. But we're not in court now. This could be considered a social call and I will try to answer your question later. What I wish you to understand now, Mrs. Judson Drake, is that this — er — *Institute of Social Imagistics* cannot attract, for its maintenance, any funds belonging to the Judson Drake Sociological Foundation. It has been agreed by the Court, replying to an appeal in the name of Mr. Walt Drake, that this Institute does not comply with the terms and conditions of the Foundation — "

"No, I'll bet it doesn't," cried Elfreda angrily. "Walt and his mother, on the spot, have fixed that all right. And I've already spent thousands of dollars on this place — "

"So I imagine, Mrs. Judson Drake. But in this matter the Court — in spite, I believe, of some sharp protests — has ruled in your favour. In view of the fact that your adviser — er — Professor Lentenban — suffered some sort of breakdown in health, so that you felt compelled to act hastily, without being fully aware of the terms and conditions of the Foundation, the Court has ruled that you should be given the sum of five thousand dollars from the Foundation, to reimburse you — "

"Well, that's very nice of the Court and I appreciate it, but it's not the money. It's the slap in the face that's so hard to take. I've been deliberately humiliated by that pair of stinkers — "

It was at that moment that Saltana and Tuby walked in, pretending to look surprised. She gave them one wild look, cried, "They've taken the Foundation away from me," burst into tears, and ran out of the room, hardly slowing down before she banged the door of her bedroom behind her.

She kicked off her shoes and got out of her suit and then cried and cried on the bed. Losing the Foundation was of course simply the start of it, a signal for the floodgates to open, then out came the lot. She was no use to her friends; she was forty-two, had no husband, had no child and never looked like having one now; nobody loved her and why should anybody love her? After all, she was no use to her friends, she was forty-two, no husband, no child — and this misery-go-round, once started, wouldn't stop. But finally she fell asleep.

It was dark when the knocking wakened her. The door was opened and then she heard Florrie. "Mrs. Drake, Ah felt Ah'd better tell yer — tea's in — scones an' all. If it'ud just been three chaps, Ah wouldn't 'ave bothered yer, but as there's these two ladies besides — "

"Ladies? What ladies?" Elfreda was sitting up now but still in the dark, not wanting Florrie to see what a sight she must look.

"Alfred says they've both been 'ere afore but can't remember their names. Trouble with Alfred is — 'e just *won't bother*."

"All right, thank you, Florrie." Plenty of light now, with a face to be attended to — and uninvited ladies — blast them! — taking tea below. She wasn't long, however — she never dawdled doing her face and dressing — and quite soon she was hurrying downstairs. But there on the half-landing was Saltana. He rather startled her, and anyhow she was feeling irritable. "What on earth d'you think you're doing?"

"Waiting for you, Elfreda." It was his no-nonsense tone.

"Well, what's all this about? Florrie says two ladies have come to tea. What's happening? I never invited two ladies — don't want two ladies — "

"*Drop it,* girl." Saltana didn't raise his voice, but he made it sound terrifying. He also held her very firmly by the shoulders, pushed his face down close to hers, and continued in a fierce low tone. "We've no time for half-hysterical questions. Tuby and I have been working hard and fast since you ran away. We've kept Stockton here and we're selling him the idea of Brockshire taking over the Foundation. Tuby got Mrs. Lapford here to sell her the same idea. She's mad keen to keep this house. And we've got little Hazel Honeypot here to sell them both the idea of her running the Foundation — "

"What — *her?* They turn me out — and now you want them to take *her!*" Elfreda's voice rose almost to a scream. Then she thought Saltana was going to shake her.

"Not so much noise, woman. And try to *think.* Little Hazel's got a doctorate in sociology. *And* she's doing the kind of research the Americans like. *And* we could use some of her stuff. *And* our friend Stockton, like most of 'em, is a very susceptible man and Hazel's a dish, a baby doll, a sweetie-pie — "

"Oh — I know, I know, but what are *we* going to do?"

"Later, later! What we aren't going to do is to go in there and balls everything up because we're losing our temper. For God's sake, do understand we're doing this even more for you than for ourselves. We're trying to cut your losses." He gave her a quick kiss. "Now come along, Elfreda my dear. Show 'em you don't care about losing the Foundation and you're all in favour of our plan."

"Yes, but don't you see — we must be going to do *something,* otherwise I can't pretend to be in favour of leaving here."

"Oh that, yes. Certainly. Well, you can tell 'em the Institute's moving to London."

"But is it?"

"It's going to have a dam' good try. But that'll keep until tonight. Come on now. All smiles. Gracious hostess." And he put her arm through his and kept it there until they entered the room.

"Hi, Isabel — Hazel! Sorry I'm late! I was busy upstairs and didn't hear the bell. Mr. Stockton, is anybody looking after you? Good!" She sent a bright glance round. "Well — isn't this *exciting?*"

Tuby, who knew a brave effort when he saw one, said, "I always want to say *No* to that question, but not this time."

"A very interesting situation has developed here, Mrs. Judson

Drake," said Orland M. Stockton, every word weighing several pounds. And obviously he had tons in stock.

"Yes, I know, I know," Elfreda cried hastily. "And it would be wonderful if both of you could use this house — Isabel — Hazel — "

"It would be Hazel's really," said Isabel. "I'd only want the big room occasionally. I think we might run a music club. But I hate the idea of your having to leave it, Elfreda."

"Yes, dear, but we can't work in London and still live in Brockshire, can we? And really we always saw the Institute working in London, didn't we, Cosmo?"

"Certainly," said Saltana.

Isabel got up. "Elfreda, I'm sorry about this. But I've just rung up Jayjay to find out if he's free for an hour, and as he says he is, I feel I must take Hazel and Mr. Stockton away now — to explain our plan to Jayjay. So do please excuse us."

As each of these three had a car, a kind of motorcade set out for the Vice-Chancellor's house. Feeling hungry and thirsty now, Elfreda went straight back to her room to swallow some stewed tea and eat a scone or two. It wasn't easy to do this while trying to appear dignified and rather melancholy, but she did her best.

"I know you must have been busy this afternoon," she said to Saltana and Tuby, as if regarding their activities from a great height. "But hasn't all this telephoning and plotting and introducing people to other people been useless? As far as I could see, this Stockton was only a lawyer delivering a message. What's he got to do with setting up the Foundation in a different way?"

"A good deal," said Saltana. "And stop sounding so grand, Elfreda. There was a chance to do something quickly, so we took it. Stockton told us how he stood after you'd gone. He's been instructed to set up the Foundation in collaboration with an American Professor of Sociology in London — Steinberg or Steinway or something. Now this man's dam' busy — he's doing a series of lectures and a series of broadcasts — and it's about ten to one he'll accept any suggestion of Stockton's that's academically respectable. So why not the University of Brockshire? And why not — as Director — Dr. H. Honeyfield from the Department of Sociology? Especially as it looks like a tremendous public snub to Owen and me. No, no, Elfreda — we might have had to think and work fast, but we're rushing along the right lines."

"And, Elfreda dear," said Tuby, smiling, "you mustn't be prejudiced by the fact that we were depending a little on Hazel's dimples. I won't say Orland M. Stockton's muddy little eyes lit up when he saw her — they're not lighter-uppers — but there was a faint suggestion of animation on that moon face. I think she'll land the job, but only after she's had several intimate talks with Orland M."

"And I think you're disgusting," said Elfreda, just to keep in opposition and not be too easily won round. She looked at Saltana. "I brought in that London bit for you. But I don't see what on earth we're going to do there. All I really know is that I've lost the Foundation. That's the solid fact. The rest is just a vague muddle."

Saltana nodded. "We'll tell you how it looks to us after dinner. Now I have to do some telephoning." He consulted a small card, then dialled what seemed to Elfreda, keeping a sharp eye on him, a London number. "Mr. Kilburn, please. Professor Saltana here. . . . Jimmy Kilburn? Yes, Cosmo Saltana, you remember? . . . Yes, and I'm keeping my promise. Now is there any chance of my seeing you on Monday, if I come up to London? . . . Yes, of course. One o'clock then — your office. Yes, I have the address. 'Bye!" He looked at Tuby. "Doesn't waste any time, friend Kilburn. I'm lunching with him at his office. If he's trying out the image I suggested to him, it'll be either jellied eels or fish and chips. I must ring up O. V. Mere shortly." And then, without even a glance at Elfreda, he stalked out.

"Owen, what am I supposed to have done? What's the matter with him?" she demanded, blinking away angry little tears. "When he met me on the stairs, he was quite ferocious and gripped my shoulders so hard it hurt. Is he blaming me for losing the Foundation?"

"No, no, no, my dear! You've got it all the wrong way round. He's sorry for *your* sake about the Foundation, that's all. From our point of view he's glad we're out of it. If we were still in it, he wouldn't be able to do what he wants to do — set up the Institute in London. He's the ambitious one, don't forget — not me. And now he's in his great man-of-action and man-of-destiny mood, which I can't share, though I'll go along with him. And when he's in this mood, he's impatient with feminine irrational likes and dislikes. It won't last. We'll all be able to talk properly after dinner. Why don't I run us down to The Bell? I know it's Saturday but it's early yet, and we could be cosy for an hour in that little bar."

They had a pinkish little corner to themselves. There were three loud men standing at the bar counter, telling one another the same thing over and over again (nitrogen and pasture came into it), but this heightened rather than diminished their feeling of cosy intimacy in their corner.

"But this time," said Tuby, smiling, when their drinks were in front of them, "unlike the other night when you dined with me, my dear, we don't go on and on about friend Cosmo."

"You then," said Elfreda, not at all annoyed by his warning. "Do you want to leave here — to go to London? Honestly, now!"

"I'm reluctant to leave here, but for an ignoble reason. When my better nature asserts itself, I'm eager for London. Don't you find that surprising, my dear? Say you do, even if you don't."

"Well, I do, without any pretense. I'd have thought it would be the other way. Here — for duty. There — for pleasure, enjoyment, fun and games."

"Not at all. Here for comfort — because you've made us very comfortable, Elfreda — and, if you like, fun and games. All of which I'm going to miss in London, at least for some time. And London's the worst city I know to be poor in. And I've no lady-loves there. On the other hand — and now we come to my better nature — unless we've no luck at all, I do hope to be *working* there, which I'm not really doing here. Better nature? Yes. Oh — there's vanity in it, there's greed. But there *is* something else, something different. That one talent which is death to hide. Men feel this very strongly, my dear, and that's why most of 'em now also feel damnably frustrated. We need another drink. No, no — I'll do it. Same again?"

Elfreda watched him fondly as he went across to the bar. In a way, she felt, she was really *fonder* of him than she was of Cosmo Saltana, who could so easily turn rough and nasty, and anger or frighten her. She couldn't imagine Owen Tuby doing that. But then — and yet — and then — but yet —

"Thank you, Owen dear. I was thinking nice things about you. No, never mind! You're spoilt already. But do you realize that all your adoring girl friends here think you're wasting yourself in this image business, having been led astray by your wicked friend Saltana?"

"Yes, I've heard them on this subject, Elfreda. Expressing themselves with some vigour. And I always tell them they're quite wrong."

Elfreda now arrived at the question she'd had in mind for some minutes. "Who's the one you'll miss the most?"

"What a question! You're making me feel I'm sitting out at my first dance, about 1932. However, if you'll risk a guess, I'll give you a truthful answer."

Enjoying herself, Elfreda didn't hesitate. "Hazel Honeyfield first — and we all know why. Isabel Lapford next. And not so far behind, not after whatever happened at that party last Tuesday. I don't know where Duchess Petro comes in, though she undoubtedly adores you. Then somewhere in the procession, trailing well behind and looking sad, poor little Lois Terry. So there you are," she added, not without a touch of complacency.

"The famous intuition at work." Tuby shook his head. "And all wrong. The truth is, your minds are too firmly fixed on bed work. Constantly editing a sort of *Who's Having Whom*. On my list — and, after all, I ought to know — Lois is an easy first. I'm really going to miss that girl. And the devil of it is — we're out with each other since last Tuesday. End of friendship before it even began to ripen. Isabel comes next, after a considerable interval. Then sweet delicious Hazel. In terms of things to eat — you might say that Hazel's some mixture of ice cream and chocolate sauce, Isabel's plum cake, and Lois, crisp new bread. Or put it another way. I always know what dear Hazel will say or do. Isabel is capable of a few surprises. Lois is entirely unpredictable; I never have a clue what she'll say or do next. And that's the one I'm going to miss — and especially, as I said earlier, as I've nobody in London to look forward to. Even at my age, I'm ashamed to admit, I'm still a great looker-forward-to — being idiotic enough to believe all too often that life's nothing now but will blaze up again gloriously next Wednesday."

"Oh — but so am I," cried Elfreda. "But is that bad?"

"Certainly it is. You rob yourself of experience. You cheat yourself out of the present moment. You think life's nothing, when it's still something, really all you have, because of next Wednesday. But then next Wednesday's not what you thought it would be — "

"Because you expect too much. That's what happens to me, nearly all the time. Then I tell myself what a fool I am. But I never thought you'd be like that."

"In theory I'm not. In practice I often am. But it's partly the fault of our civilization, which encourages us to look back and look forward at the expense of the present moment. But isn't it time we went?"

"I was just going to say so. Let's go." But on their way out to the car, having been ruminating, she said, "I can't help wondering if images come into this, somewhere. D'you think they do, Owen?"

"I know they do, Elfreda. They're part of the unreality that's swindling us."

"And yet you and Cosmo — "

"Yes, yes, yes, I know. We're going into the business, you might say. But that's the kind of world we found when we came back here. So if it's images they wanted, we'd give 'em images — and do it properly — *with knobs on,* as chaps used to say."

She said very little going back; she didn't like driving at night, and anyhow she'd had two fairly strong drinks; and below her immediate anxiety about the car and the road she felt a continued flutter of apprehension concerning Cosmo Saltana. Would he be in the same mood? But when they found him still sitting by the telephone in her room, she saw at once that he was in a good temper.

"Out boozing, eh? Well, not a bad idea. And I've had a rather hefty one myself. Two things to report," Saltana continued, in a more business-like manner. "Mrs. Lapford rang up — asking for you, of course, my boy, her little sweetie-pie — but she condescended to tell me that Lapford's very keen on keeping the Foundation here, with Honeypot in charge. And he's having a word with Sir Leopold Thing — Namp. That man'll be ringing up his Sir Leopold soon to ask if he can change his pants. I also gathered that our little Honeypot is willing to go up to London next week to meet Stockton again and with him the American Professor — Steinberg, Steinway, whoever he is. It's my belief we'll swing this, Owen. And don't pull a face, Mrs. Drake."

"I don't care who they put in charge," Elfreda declared, "I've said goodbye to the Foundation already, except I'll make sure I get the five thousand dollars I've been promised. I want to know what's going to happen to us. And it is *us,* isn't it?" She looked at Saltana. "You're not thinking of leaving me out now the Foundation's gone?"

Saltana shook his head but it was Tuby who spoke. "Certainly not," he told her, getting up. "But you can both leave me out until dinner. I'm in need of various kinds of *mod. con.*" And off he went.

"The most tactful man in Brockshire," said Saltana, "if that means anything. Yes, Elfreda my dear, it's very much *us* if that's what you want. Quite apart from the fact that we're fondly devoted to you, and speaking quite selfishly now, we're going to need you badly in London. You can organize things. You understand business — in a way Tuby and I don't. And the *Institute of Social Imagistics* must now either go into business or vanish into limbo." He came over and stood close, resting his hands lightly on her shoulders and looking down on her as she sat upright. "What worries me, my dear, is that you're comparatively well off and we're poor men. No, no, Elfreda, listen, please! We'll have to spend money — I'll explain how later — but this means bringing in an outsider, who may in the end make more than the three of us put together, doing all the work." He took his hands away now rather sharply, as if he suddenly felt that touching her wasn't fair, as if he guessed that his hands were more significant than his words. "So why not make use of some of your money? And if you were a man, I wouldn't hesitate. But you're a woman — "

"And I suppose nobody's ever told you that women dislike hesitating men. Worriers and ditherers!" She pushed her chair back and sprang out of it. "Well, where do we go from here? It's nearly dinnertime and I must tidy up." She sounded as cross as she felt. How idiotic! What a waste of a promising moment! She could have been in his arms now.

"I wanted you to be thinking it over," he went on rather lamely. "Before we really got down to it, after dinner. You're a businesswoman — "

"A businesswoman! You can't ever have seen any." She was almost shouting. "And what am I supposed to be thinking over? I don't *know* anything. And if you do, then you've kept it to yourself. All I've had from you is *Later, later.*" And though he began saying something, she didn't stay to listen.

When they were settled in Elfreda's room after dinner, Saltana said, "I suppose one of us ought to take charge of this little meeting," and was obviously taking charge himself while he said it.

"I suggest I do that," said Elfreda firmly. "I ask the questions, and you two supply the answers — if you can."

And as Tuby declared at once that this was a good idea, Saltana couldn't very well say it wasn't. What he did was to sink back into his chair and light a cheroot in a very patient and forbearing manner.

Not looking directly at either of them, Elfreda began, "Moving the Institute to London may be quite expensive. What is it going to do there?"

As Saltana didn't reply at once, Tuby said rather hesitantly, "Well — I imagine — it will act as a consultant — give advice on image problems — "

"You don't sound very hopeful or confident," Elfreda said severely. "Are you?"

"I must confess I'm not."

"Neither am I. Saltana?"

"I don't know enough," Saltana began, "but I know a great deal more than either of you. I've been keeping it in mind, and you haven't. It's my belief — and O. V. Mere agrees with me — that we could soon have the Institute in business."

"You'd have to find somebody better than Mere to persuade me," Elfreda told him, adopting a fairly lofty tone. "He'd never talk me into investing ten dollars in anything."

"All right, forget him." Saltana was rather curt. "But remember, there's been a lot of useful publicity about us already, and there could be plenty more if we were on the spot, making use of television, radio, and the Press. Then again, tough financial men like Jimmy Kilburn — who immediately fixed up lunch for Monday — and Simon Birtle are interested and take us seriously. And Owen, you remember that advertising woman, Mrs. Ringmore, invited us to join her new agency. Of course there's no question of our joining her or anybody else. We must be independent consultants. But I believe that as soon as it's widely known that the Institute's in business, ready to be consulted, the patrons, the clients, the customers will begin to line up. The advertising people, the manufacturers and industrialists, men who live in the public eye, they all have image problems, and we're the image experts. How much money there'll be in it, that of course I don't know yet. But we'll be going to work where the money is, that's a certainty."

"It's an even greater certainty," said Elfreda, now the cold businesswoman, "that quite a packet will have to be spent first. The Institute can't operate from a couple of hotel back bedrooms. It'll have to have its own premises — fairly central and handsomely furnished. It'll have to pay out salaries and wages right from the start, long before it's earned a penny. I doubt if you realize what you're letting yourselves in for, not being businessmen."

"If we'd been businessmen," Saltana growled, "we'd never have had this idea."

"Nor have been able to carry it out," said Tuby cheerfully. "But a business head has got to come in somewhere. Now I'm not sure about these Jimmy Kilburns and Simon Birtles. I want to be fleecing them, not having them fleecing me."

"You've never set eyes on either of them, Tuby," said Saltana sharply. "Leave all that to me."

But for once, Tuby was openly rebellious. "Just a minute! I've something to say to Elfreda you won't bring yourself to say. Elfreda, you must help us. We can't start unless you do. Now don't misunderstand me — "

"She couldn't," Saltana shouted. "Not when you're asking her to keep you — "

"Don't be a bloody fool. I'm not." Tuby could shout too. "We'll go shares in what the Institute earns, but until then I don't take a penny of Elfreda's money. I'll keep myself — radio, journalism, lecturing, anything — even if I have to live in a back attic on stewed tea and baked beans. That's what I meant when I asked her not to misunderstand me — and you had to put your dam' great oafish oar in, Cosmo. No, no, shut up, man! If she wants to help us, then she must go to London with you on Monday, she must be in it up to the neck, she must plan and work out figures and look at possible premises and talk to people who have to be talked to and be from now on completely in your confidence with every fear and hope plainly shared — "

"Oh, Owen Tuby," she cried, jumping up, "how right you are! I must kiss you for that." Which she did, and then looked defiantly at Saltana.

"Don't look at me like that, woman. I kept some things from you because I didn't want you to feel uneasy about the Foundation. I'm not taking a penny from you either — as that artful little devil knows very well, because we talked it over earlier. And of course come to London on Monday — plot, plan, calculate, as hard as you can — and I'll keep nothing from you. A lot of this is going to be in your territory, not in mine. Give me a lead — and I'll follow. Now we need a drink. Stir yourself, Tuby."

"No, I'll do them." Elfreda always wanted to be doing something for somebody when she felt happy. "But will you be all right here, Owen, while we're away?"

"Certainly, my dear. I can take care of anything that turns up at this end. I can do some work and keep the youngsters at it."

"To say nothing of enjoying a series of farewell sessions with lady friends," said Saltana. "By the way, reverting to Primrose and Mickley, I suggest we don't put the London proposition to them until we know more. Agreed? Good!"

"You're sure you don't want Primrose with you this time, Cosmo?" Elfreda was handing them their whiskies.

"Positive! Thank you, my dear. No, you and I between us can do all that's necessary."

"I'm sure you can, Cosmo, Elfreda," said Tuby, so bland, so smooth, that both of them gave him a look. He raised his glass ceremoniously. "I now give you the toast of the *Institute of Social Imagistics* — coupled with Robinson's Hotel and the commercial, social, and political life of our great capital city."

It was an awful lot to get coupled. But they drank to it.

*Volume II: London End*

## 1

Owen Tuby, Doctor of Literature and Deputy Director of the *Institute of Social Imagistics,* 4 Half Moon House, Half Moon Street, W.1, walked back to the office after lunch. It was a raw day in early February, no weather for loitering, but he walked slowly, smoking his pipe. He had had two ham sandwiches and a bottle of stout in a pub, and the pub had been crowded and had charged him far too much for the sandwiches. His friend, Professor Cosmo Saltana, Director of the Institute, had that morning asked him and the three women on the staff — Elfreda Drake, Primrose East, and Mrs. Eden Mere — to attend a meeting in the Director's room at 2:45. It was 2:50 when Tuby signalled the lift to take him to the fourth floor, entirely occupied by the Institute. He didn't like this lift, which pretended to be automatic but obviously had a whimsical and slightly malignant personality of its own.

Once inside the Institute, Tuby rather gloomily returned the greeting of Beryl Edgar, who combined the duties — very light so far — of typist and receptionist. Beryl was a girl in her early twenties with not much of a nose, a loose mouth, a receding chin, all suggesting, together with her conversation, a kind of young female village idiot; and yet, so strangely are we put together, she had large and really quite beautiful eyes, burnt sienna flecked with copper. Tuby always felt she must have borrowed them from somebody. Now he made haste to leave his hat and overcoat in his own room and then went along to Saltana's. But Saltana wasn't there, only the three women, sitting close together, with a feminine-huddle look about them. Tuby guessed at once that they had just been talking about him and not about Saltana. And told them so.

"Well, yes, that's true, Owen," said Elfreda Drake. "We were agreeing that you don't seem happy these days."

"We were being very sympathetic, darling," said Primrose East. She didn't smile because now she was made up and dressed to look like those girls, right there in the trend, who wouldn't know how to smile.

"Remember, dear Dr. Tuby," said Mrs. Mere, frowning at him — and she now had a hair-do that made her look like the Duke of Wellington gone mad — "we love you. So what's the matter?"

"Are you wishing you were back in Brockshire?" Elfreda added.

"Just now, my dear, I'm afraid I am." He thought for a moment. "I think it's chiefly the Underground. Not being able to afford taxis, except on rare occasions, I find myself using the Underground twice a day. And I'm not an Underground man. Often I feel trapped in the ruins of a civilization. Better food and more drink would help me, but I can't afford them."

"Also, darling, you're probably missing those doting women of Brockshire," said Primrose.

"Possibly."

And then Saltana was in the room. There had been no sound of the door opening, so that Tuby felt he must have left it ajar. He also felt there could be an awkward situation here.

"Sorry I'm late," Saltana began briskly. He was inclined to be brisk these days. "Not my fault. Elfreda, Eden, Primrose, you'll have to wait a little longer for the meeting. I must talk to Dr. Tuby. I'll let you know when we're through. And I won't take any calls, Elfreda. Ask Beryl to put them through to you."

As the women went out, Tuby reflected that his old and close friend, Cosmo Saltana, was now deep in a role. That speech didn't belong to Professor Saltana, who for years had taught philosophy in Guatemala, Bolivia, and other places round there. It came from Saltana's new role as a busy executive.

But then Saltana turned into himself again. "Owen, I'll admit I was eavesdropping out there," he began as he sat down. "It's working out badly for you so far, isn't it? You were being a bit fanciful with the women, of course, but how bad is it?"

"Much worse if I stop being fanciful, Cosmo," Tuby replied dryly. "You and I agreed to live at first on what we could make outside the Institute. I've done three broadcasts and four articles, two of 'em for Birtle's horrible magazines — "

"And that's about enough," Saltana put in quickly. "Not our field, our public. We mustn't cheapen ourselves."

"Quite so. The last thing I want to do is to write any more of these imbecile pieces. But I've kept my promise not to borrow from Elfreda. Now it's possible I've been spoilt, but on what I'm making, it's a miserable existence. I don't want to start whining, but I'm worse off at present than anybody here. Elfreda — who can afford it and good luck to her — is comfortably settled again at Robinson's Hotel. Primrose lives with the Birtles. Eden Mere goes home to Wimbledon. You're here on the spot — no damned Underground morning and night — cosy and rent-free just because Jimmy Kilburn had an empty furnished flat on his hands. And as far as I can gather — because you haven't been telling me much lately — you're always dining out — the Kilburns, the Birtles, Elfreda, Ella Ringmore — with what the boys now call *crumpet* thrown in. Whereas I pay eight pounds a week to the Ilberts for bed and breakfast. Then I have to feed myself, and half the week I'm eating horrible food. That wouldn't matter so much — and I'll even throw in the Underground — if I could afford to buy enough whisky to make it all a bit hazy. But just when I need to drink steadily, I find it's costing too much."

"I know, I know." Saltana sounded impatient. "I live here too, Owen, and I'm only a few pounds a week better off than you are. But look — if it's so bad you could move in with me. That would save something and you wouldn't have the Underground."

"Thanks, Cosmo, but it wouldn't work. And this isn't a general grumble. I have a point to make. I gather you've already turned down various offers to the Institute. All right, I'm not saying you ought to accept them, whatever they are. I trust your judgment. But when you're turning business away, I'd just like you to remember the fix I'm in — bored or irritated, with no real work to do, no real money coming in, eating rubber ravioli, sitting in the Underground wondering if I can afford a couple of large whiskies — "

"Owen my friend," cried Saltana, jumping up, "I'll admit I've been leaving you out of my calculations. You're having a worse time than I thought. I'm sorry, my boy. But now *I've* a point to make, and it's one I was going to make anyhow at the little meeting I called for this afternoon. So we'll have the women in. No, I'll do it."

He sat down behind his desk, back in the executive role now, and switched something on. A great squawking noise came out of it. Annoyed, Saltana did something else with switches. Tuby, who'd refused to have any fancy office equipment, any labour-saving devices that wasted time, sat smoking and grinning. The women arrived at last. They wore those sceptical and faintly mocking smiles that either mean nothing or belong to some ultimate feminine secret.

"Two things," Saltana began in his new brisk manner. "Is it true that during the last two or three weeks I've been turning down various offers to the Institute? Certainly it is. As Elfreda already knows, though the decisions have been mine. I've refused to consider these enquiries because they didn't seem good enough. They might have brought us a few hundred pounds but at the same time they could have been robbing us of thousands of pounds. We'd have been in on the wrong level. They'd have damaged our image. Either we provide a top service, which means an expensive service, or we pack up. Now the kind of commissions we want will be arriving any day. It's not that I merely believe this, I *know* it. What is it today? Tuesday? Then I'm willing to bet fifty pounds that by this time next week we'll have sufficient work on our hands — and the right kind too — to begin keeping us all busy."

"Professor Saltana, I'm not going to bet anything," said Mrs. Mere severely, "but I can't see how you *can* know."

"I move around," he told her solemnly. "I hear things. And now the time's about ripe."

"Wish I could move around and hear things," said Mrs. Mere. "So far haven't moved at all — *Ger-huh* — except to and from Wimbledon; heard nothing. I'm not counting my husband. He shares your optimism, Professor Saltana. Attribute that to the fact that you stand about in bars together, drinking too much. So far I'm finding it very dull here, so dull that sometimes I switch on the mock computer just to make something happen. And the little lights are rather pretty. *Ger-huh!* Sorry, Professor Saltana. Do go on."

"Thank you," said Saltana rather dryly. "Now if we're about to offer images to people, then we ought to consider our own images."

Tuby nodded, without smiling. "Quite right. I've been thinking about this."

"It's really a question of how we divide up the work — in terms of our own temperaments and images. Some clients will obviously demand sympathy. They will need reassurance, courage, hope. Others, who think they're tough, who take advantage of other people's weaknesses, may have to meet icy severity here. I propose to handle these clients myself, and if I need any feminine cooperation — and that will be inevitable in many cases — I shall call on either Mrs. Mere or Primrose — perhaps at times on both of you."

"Very good!" cried Mrs. Mere. "Look forward to this. If they come blustering in here, we treat them like dirt. Or if they want to be treated like dirt in their own offices, I'll descend upon them. Excellent!"

"I can see you doing it, darling," said Primrose. "But I'm not sure how good I'll be with the icy severity bit. What do *you* think, dear Dr. Tuby?"

"It depends on what's needed to create a feeling of inferiority," said Tuby, enjoying himself. "A figure representing youth, beauty, fashion — together with a rather detached but faintly amused manner — would soon reduce some men to a jelly — "

"Not you and Cosmo, you devils!" cried Elfreda.

"Oh — but they're quite different," Primrose protested. "I know the men he means."

Tuby ignored them and continued calmly: "Other clients — and I'm still thinking of the tougher types — who might not respond to Primrose would need Mrs. Mere. She'd be the haughty, implacable, all-demanding figure of expertise — the specialist who says in effect *Take it or leave it*. That's what you have in mind, isn't it, Director?"

"Certainly. On the other hand, where sympathy, encouragement, optimism are needed, then you, Primrose — and, where necessary, you, Elfreda — take over. When prospective clients arrive, Beryl will first hand them on to you, Elfreda; then if they seem to you worth while you'll hand them on to me. I decide then if they're soft or hard cases, tough or tender. Agreed?"

They did agree, though Elfreda still looked doubtful. "I'll never be able to tell if they're right for us — "

Saltana stopped her. "Elfreda, you persist in underrating your ability and shrewdness. I've complete confidence in you."

"We all have," Mrs. Mere declared in her emphatic way. "Don't sell yourself short, dear."

"It's only this." Elfreda looked at Saltana and sounded apologetic. "Even supposing I *am* shrewd and all that — which I doubt — how am I to judge if they're right for us if I'm really not quite sure what you're after? So just tell me that, Cosmo Saltana."

"Certainly." Saltana settled back in his chair so that Tuby knew at once he was about to enjoy himself making a speech. "My dear Elfreda, we're about to enter the world of commercial enterprise and advertising. It's a world in which, we're given to understand, what is all-important is public service. Whenever its leaders hold a conference, they declare with such eloquence as they can command, their desire, their determination, to serve the community. All they ask, it seems, is to be able to do this. In the larger world we all know, a selfish and materialistic world, darkened by predatory motives and greed, such men shine like beacons. But this will not be the light that will guide you, Elfreda. Here we're on a lower plane altogether. Apart from doing an occasional favour for a friend, what we want here is — *money*. We leave public service, the good of the common weal, to our clients. What we propose is to screw as much out of them as we can. So — again of course excluding friends — if they look like money, we want them. If they don't, turn them away."

"Professor Saltana," Mrs. Mere shouted sternly, "I call that very cynical."

"That's what I call it, Mrs. Mere." He got up. "Well — I must do some telephoning. End of meeting."

Tuby went along to his room, which was at the end of the corridor going to the left from the entrance hall. As Saltana's room was at the end of the corridor going to the right, their two offices were as far from each other as it was possible to be. Saltana had objected to this, saying they would waste time, but Tuby had insisted on claiming the room he now occupied. It was not quite as large as Saltana's but had bigger windows than the rooms allotted to Elfreda, Primrose, and Mrs. Mere. The room facing the entrance, where Beryl did her typing when she wasn't playing receptionist outside in the hall, hadn't any windows at all, but then it also housed the mock computer, which they had bought from a theatrical company. With the door left wide open, as it generally was, the mock computer in there, when all its little lights were flashing and changing, looked most impressive.

But though Tuby had some fine windows, there was not much to see out of them. That was the trouble about the fourth floor, which was too high to offer a street scene and not high enough to provide a wide prospect of roofs and distant buildings. For the fiftieth time he told himself it wasn't his kind of room. It had been designed, decorated, fur-

nished, for a jet-age executive, not for Dr. Owen Tuby, Lecturer on English Literature in India and the Far East for the last twenty years. But
its pale but hard shades, its suggestion of plastics combined with high-
duty alloys, might easily belong to an *Institute of Social Imagistics,* and
after all, Tuby was here as its Deputy Director. However, as he was also
here to supply sympathy, empathy, a cheery optimism to clients who
might need them, he decided that as soon as the Institute could afford
them he would demand a few changes in this room. As head of the Sympathy Department here, he hadn't to look as if he were running an air-
craft factory.

To persuade himself he wasn't doing nothing, he drew the curtains,
also pale but hard, switched on a few lights, all uncosy, and took from
a shelf one of the image-analysis files. He opened it on his desk, stared
hard at a page for about a minute, then filled and lit a pipe and began
to wonder where he could afford to go for dinner. It was like starting to
edit a Bad Food Guide. He knew he had only to say the word and his
landlady, Marion Ilbert, would provide him with a dinner far better than
most of those he ate — her breakfasts suggested she wasn't a bad cook
— and charge him little or nothing. And that would lead straight to
trouble. He liked Marion — her nonsense of a nose, hint of freckles,
smudgy grey eyes, her mixture of apologies and saucy exclamations —
and he knew she was rapidly growing too fond of him, of his voice and
talk and direct interest in her as a person, for like many wives of her
standing she was really very lonely. Paul Ilbert, a steady civil servant,
higher executive grade in the Ministry of Housing, wasn't a bad husband. He was good-tempered, reliable about money, devoted to their children (now away at school, which was why they welcomed Tuby's eight
pounds a week — off tax too), but he was very much a hobby man —
and a continuing interest in his wife wasn't one of his hobbies.

Marion, Tuby reflected, had begun by giving him one egg for breakfast; now it was two; and he had only to make one decisive move and
then if he liked he could have half a dozen. Not that he thought of her
in terms of eggs, rashers, sausages, though he could save on lunch by
starting with a dam' good breakfast. (Even on week-ends he only took
breakfast with them, and it was a nuisance eating out, especially on Sunday. However, he and Paul Ilbert had kept to their original agreement, in
spite of Marion's frequent — indeed, increasingly frequent — protesta-
tions.) The trouble was that while he had thought her rather unattractive at first — a bit dumpy, rather worn and worrying — now he was
beginning to feel he'd been quite wrong, that here was a desirable woman.
No doubt this was partly because now he knew her and liked her as a
person. But there was another reason, of which he was fully aware, avoiding as he always did all self-deception. He hadn't made love to a woman
since he'd taken Isabel Lapford at that party two months ago. He was no
chaser who had to have it, but even so — two months? And now this

made him think about that party, and he didn't want to think about it. With an effort he closed the shutters on it, and then felt something he rarely felt — a touch, a sour taste, of self-contempt.

He relit his pipe, picked up a pencil as if about to put down a few ticks and queries, and stared again at the image-analysis file. But he needed people now, their actual problems and questions, and not this abstract stuff, which was beginning to bore him. It bored Saltana too, though he'd never admit it.

"Hello, Elfreda!" She had just come hurrying in. "It's just occurred to me that while Cosmo imagines I'm better at the theory of this image thing than he is, but not so good when it has to be applied to actual people, I think — I know — he beats me in theory but isn't quite so good in practice."

"Owen, you can tell me about that tonight," she said hastily. "That is, if you're free to dine with me at Robinson's. Are you?"

"I am, my dear, and I'd love it. But tell me — and be quite truthful — did Saltana put you up to this?"

"Not really. We were talking and we both had the same idea at the very same moment. And you and I don't seem to have had a good natter for ages. About half-past seven then — in the bar." She said this very quickly and appeared about to go, but then she thought of something. "Don't bother going home to Belsize Park to change or anything. You look just right as you are, Owen." And now she did move.

About four hours later, he was smiling at Elfreda across that same old table in the far corner of Robinson's dining room. "Perfect! I was hoping you'd be able to book this table again. Remember our first dinner here when Cosmo and I had just met you?"

"Now *really,* Owen! Don't be silly. It was only a few months ago."

"Yes, of course. The truth is, my dear, I'm a nostalgia-monger. I can feel nostalgic even about places I thoroughly detested. I think it's the flavour I enjoy. Though I prefer the flavour of these shrimps Newburg or whatever they are." And while he listened to Elfreda chattering away, he thought how solid, dependable, civilized, Robinson's seemed now after most of the places he'd eaten in lately. But he knew that at any moment Elfreda would work the talk round to Saltana; then he would have to pay attention. The moment came just before the pepper steaks.

"Tell me something, Owen," she began. "Do you think Cosmo's changed at all since we moved to London?" Like many blue-eyed women, she looked particularly blue-eyed and as innocent as a summer's day when she was about to play detective.

"Yes, I do. But remember, my dear, I've not been seeing much of him lately."

"Is that because he's spending a lot of his time with some woman?" There was a touch of scorn here. No man worth being called one, it hinted, should waste his hours on *some woman,* always a contemptible creature.

Tuby waited until the steaks and vegetables had been served, but he did smilingly shake his head, to bring her out of suspense. Then when they were alone: "You're on the wrong track there, I'm sure, Elfreda. My impression is that Cosmo's using his evenings — a cocktail party here, a dinner party there — showing the flag of the *Institute of Social Imagistics.* Because he's refused small business, he's looking for big business. Cosmo Saltana isn't womanising, he's *working.* If he doesn't want to talk about it, that's because he's a proud man and he's accepted a challenge in a way you and I haven't. He thinks we'd weaken his resolution. And he's quite right — we would. For example, I'd accept any tinpot business just in the hope of taking a few taxis and not filling myself with *potage du jour* every other night. Coming to London has softened me and hardened Cosmo. We're really still close friends, but at the moment we're not on the same wavelength."

Elfreda didn't look relieved, because she'd contrived in the first place not to look anxious. But relief was there in her voice when she went on to talk about the Institute and its chances. Then she changed the subject quite sharply. "I had a letter yesterday from your friend Lois Terry."

"Good God! I didn't know you were on those terms. Just bare acquaintances."

"Don't be silly, Owen. You must know very well she's only writing to me because she feels she can't write to you. It would be all the same to her if I dropped dead."

"The last look she gave me — this was at the Lapford party — *told* me to drop dead."

"You've never written to her?"

"Certainly not. Too difficult, too delicate," said Tuby thoughtfully.

"But you're still interested in that girl, aren't you? She is in you. Sticks out a mile, poor dear."

"What sticks out two miles, Elfreda, is that Lois Terry and I were destined to be always at cross-purposes. Every time we got together, something went wrong. A remarkable girl. Not pretty but sometimes quite beautiful. Sensitive and very quick. A sharp original mind. I think we were fascinated by each other but — alas, alas — never in the same way at the same time. So remember me to her — but rather distantly."

"Can't you do better than that?"

Tuby chewed a little, then gave her a hard look. "She hates Cosmo, y'know. She believes he's lured me away from educating the young, probably from the lowest motives. Let's forget about Lois."

It was her turn to give him a hard look. Then she nodded and smiled. "Well, who are you fascinating now, Owen? Perhaps your landlady — Eden's cousin, isn't she?"

"She is. But there's no family resemblance." He sketched Marion Il-bert for her. He went on: "Her husband, Paul, is a decent fellow but he's passionately devoted to two hobbies. One is snooker, at which he's so good that he plays for his club. The other is philately — you know, collecting foreign stamps. So if he's not out playing snooker, he's out talking about stamps somewhere, and when he's in he's probably show-ing some other maniac his stamp collection. He's about fourteen years old, you might say. And there's poor Marion — "

"I know," cried Elfreda. "You needn't go on. Eden ought to have thought of that before she sent you there, unless of course she did it on purpose. So what's happening?"

"So far nothing's happened except I've had a lot of compliments, little attentions, and two eggs for breakfast. And I assure you, Elfreda, I don't *want* anything to happen. She's essentially a serious little woman with two children away at school. She's no sexual tough getting in and out of bed while still talking about sociology, new French fiction, or the Academic Advisory Board."

"Then it wouldn't be fair — unless you were serious — "

"I know, my dear. But while I'm no Casanova, there she is — all available, under the same roof, while her husband's playing snooker in Bromley or swapping stamps in Islington. And at the moment I'm lead-ing a very dull life, Elfreda, as you can imagine. And she has my sym-pathy. And I *like* her. Which at once eggs me on and puts me off. I could leave, of course — "

"Just what I was going to suggest — "

"But that might be hard on them — all of 'em, including the two kids at school — and equally hard on me. I wish to God you and Cosmo would make something happen in the Institute — or outside it, for that matter." Then he stared at her. "Anything wrong, Elfreda?"

"No, no, not really," she answered, her eyes wide. "I just had one of those sudden feelings I sometimes get. So don't worry, Owen. A lot of things are going to happen — quite soon." She was immensely solemn, delphic. "I just *know* they are."

After dinner they took coffee in the Small Lounge, where they'd first met, and later Tuby had a whisky or two and talked to her about the East. Having saved the price of a dinner, he felt he could afford a taxi to Belsize Park. There he'd no sooner opened the front door than Marion came out of the sitting room to welcome him. Having been to some party, she was all tarted up, determinedly gay and coquettish.

"You're not to go straight upstairs, Dr. Tuby," she cried, almost pushing him into the sitting room, which he disliked because it had too many small pieces of furniture and too many knick-knacks. "You never see me properly dressed with all my warpaint on. Just slopping around in the morning wearing any old thing. Now then — see!" She stood in front of him, smiling, asking to be admired and desired.

"Charming, Marion! Really delightful! Thank you for a pretty sight!" She'd never believe him if he told her that in fact she looked much better slopping around in the morning wearing any old thing. At least half the women he'd ever known had seemed more desirable when they'd taken no trouble with their appearance than when they had, and had looked all wrong, like poor Marion at this moment. Her naturally appealing little face, freckles and all, had gone; this best dress, a lilac affair, didn't suit her; she had merely turned herself into an unappealing somebody else.

"And thank you, kind sir! Now if I make some tea, won't you stay and talk? Oh — *do!* Paul's snooker team's gone to Amersham or somewhere tonight. Somebody's driving him back but they'll be *ages.*" And off she went, humming away.

He ought to have said he was tired and gone straight up. But — o dear, oh dear! — in she came with the tea, ready to be gay again or the quiet thoughtful listener; she switched off half the lights, sat on a pouffe close to him and then closer, touched his wrist with a finger, let her hand fall on his in an absent-minded fashion, finally rested an elbow on his knees and stared up at him, her lips parted, as he talked and talked — about anything, nothing — just talking himself out of it. Then as he was about to fake a yawn, he found himself with a real one. "I'm sorry, my dear, but I must go to bed. A long day, a heavy dinner, too much to drink." He struggled out of the chair.

"I know — you're tired," she said, moving with him towards the door. "You've been so sweet. Having you here makes such a difference." And as he halted in the doorway she flung her arms round his neck and gave him a clumsy lipsticky kiss. "Goodnight!" Oh dear! Oh dear! And he went oh-dearing all the way up to the second-floor front, his room.

About eleven o'clock next morning, Wednesday, just after Tuby had accepted a cup of coffee from Beryl Edgar — it wasn't good coffee but it helped to pass the time — Saltana came through on the intercom. (Tuby felt that Saltana was turning into an intercom type and might soon be feeding programmes into the mock computer.) Could Tuby lunch with him upstairs in 9B where there was some eatable cold stuff? Yes, Tuby could. Next, could Tuby keep his afternoon free? Yes, yes, Tuby could — and would — but why? "Explain over lunch, my boy," Saltana told him in his grating intercom voice. " 'Bye now!"

*'Bye now!* too, God help us all! And was he to have this performance all through lunch? Nothing happened until Mrs. Mere looked in, rather like a ship arriving.

"Ever heard of something called Lacy Pieces?" she demanded.

"Never — and I'd rather not, Eden."

"Quite so. But they were enquiring. By the way — meant to ask you yesterday," she shouted. "You making love to my cousin Marion?"

"Certainly not. If I were, I wouldn't tell you. But I'm not."

"Believe you. Not attracted?"

"Vaguely — but not seriously. If it stops being vague, I'd prefer to move."

"Pity in a way. She'll have to find somebody. A woman can't live on reports of snooker matches and transactions in foreign stamps."

"What about her children?"

"Better but not enough. Letters every Sunday and a cake for half-term. Why send 'em away to school? Dam' silly! But then Marion *is* silly, always was. Better leave her alone."

"I intend to."

"*Ger-huh!*" And she vanished.

Just after one, he and Saltana persuaded the lift to take them up to the ninth floor. They took their whisky into the little dining room, where there were sardines, a pork pie, and Russian salad in a cardboard container. The table, apparently so much scrubbed and uneven wood, looked at first as if it had just been brought from some foreign village tavern, but then turned out to be made of plastic. Half Moon House wasn't going to be left behind.

"Do you know anything about a comedian called Lon Bracton?" Saltana demanded, over the sardines.

Tuby thought for a moment. "I saw him once in a film — in Singapore, I think. Tall thin fellow. Funny sometimes, not always."

Saltana looked pleased. "I was right to see that this was your job. You'll be taking another look at him this afternoon."

"Why — what is all this?"

"Institute business, my boy. He has an agent called Wilf Orange who came through this morning. Apparently Lon Bracton's one of his most important clients and can earn enormous sums. But he's a difficult man — indecisive, moody, probably quite neurotic. Now he's heard about us and he's wondering if we couldn't help him to change his image. This is entirely Bracton's idea, nothing to do with Wilf Orange, who obviously thinks this is just another of Bracton's crazy notions. But Orange has to act as go-between, and when I pressed him he admitted we might be able to ask a socking great fee, if only because it can be charged against taxes. So I've arranged for Orange to call for you here at half-past two, take you to the cinema where Bracton's last film is being shown, then pick you up there afterwards so that you can go and see Bracton himself. If you don't want to do it, Owen, then you needn't, but it seemed rather more your kind of job."

"I agree, Cosmo." Tuby took a chunk of pie. "I'm looking forward to it." That seemed to be all, so Tuby asked, "Tell me, Cosmo, are you enjoying all this?"

"What d'you think?" Saltana growled. "Bloody silly question, Owen!" He brought a hand down hard on the plastic tabletop. "But I'm in it now, right up to the neck. This move to London has to be successful. Quickly too — or in six months we're a pair of bankrupt academics who've clowned and failed. So for Christ's sake, Owen, don't stand on the side, wishing you were back in Brockshire or Hong Kong. Jump in and join me. It's our only chance."

"I know it, Cosmo. Sorry if I've been rather down. It must be this London life on a low budget." He continued in a brisker tone: "So — this actors' agent, Wilf Orange, at two-thirty. Right? Well now, if there's no coffee, I'll take a touch more whisky."

To save time, Tuby went down to the street entrance to meet Wilf Orange, who arrived, ten minutes late, in a large car with a chauffeur. He was a wiry energetic man who was wearing, among other things, a bow tie the colour of his name. His speech was hoarse-voiced, staccato, conspiratorial, and, like many show-business types nowadays, he seemed neither English nor American but a kind of Cockney New Yorker.

"Can't make it with you to the picture, Dr. Tuby. Must get back to the office. Things have come up. But not to worry. Sam — driver — has it all taped. After you've seen the picture, I take you to see Lon. All his idea this, not mine, with all due respect ot you, Dr. Tuby."

"I'd better know the title of this film I'm supposed to see," Tuby told him. They were moving out to the car.

"*Lon Don*. Spanish setting — that's the Don bit. Lon's the star. So — *Lon Don*. You got it?"

Tuby nodded and smiled. "I've got it. But I doubt if I'll grow fond of it."

"Nice line. Lon could use it. Well, you won't like the picture neither. Just between us, it's been a crap-out, a flunkum, a muffaroo. Lon knows it. Doesn't kid himself. But it's the last one he did. You have to catch it, then tell him straight — "

"But look here — I'm no film critic — "

"Who is, tell me that? It's this image idea that's hooked Lon. Or it was at two o'clock this morning." Tuby was in the car now. "Sam knows where to take you. Second-run house Chelsea way. Maybe twenty people there. See you later, then."

There may have been more than twenty altogether but he shared the circle with only three other people. As in the earlier film Tuby had seen, Lon Bracton had his funny moments, but all too often he just missed the mark, and Tuby began to think he understood why this happened. Unequal as Lon Bracton might be, when he was absent from the screen the film was trifling and tedious, and several times Tuby dozed off. It was just after five when he went down to the entrance, to discover that it was raining hard but that Wilf Orange and Sam were waiting for him.

"Worse or better than you expected?" Orange asked in the car.

"Neither, I'd say, Mr. Orange — "

"Look — make it Wilf, will you? I'm not trying to force the

chummy bit. But how would you like to be called Mr. Orange? Always makes me feel ridiculous. Think you've anything you can tell Lon?"

"Yes, if he insists — "

"He never does anything else. Boy, can he insist!"

"But I'd prefer a little more time, Wilf. I'm talking now in image terms. Tell me about Bracton."

"I'll do that. But where have you been?"

"If you mean I ought to know about him — "

"Well, everybody does. Notorious!"

"I've been out in the Far East for years and years."

"Say — listen! There's no what's-it — yoga — in this thing of yours, is there? No? Glad to hear it 'cos he's already tried that. Tried nearly everything, Lon has. Been analysed twice — the lot. Look — half the time — no, say a third — he's a wonderful hard-working comic. For two years they worshipped him on the box — television, I mean. They rolled over soon as they heard his name. Then suddenly he couldn't do it — broke his contract — doctor's orders, of course. Same with pictures. Same with live shows. The money's been enormous, but even so I've had more trouble with him than any other three clients put together. 'Cos the other two-thirds of the time Lon's beany, foofoo, nutty as a fruitcake. It's not the sauce, the hard stuff, though he can lap it up. It isn't even the women, though there's always one around, sometimes married to him, sometimes not. It's Lon himself. He's several people. He goes to the can a good sweet guy and comes back a lousy bastard. You help yourself to a drink, turn round, and it isn't the same fella. He'll keep you up and you'll be falling about laughing, and the very next day he'll tell you he can't work. For weeks on end he can be more dippy-batty than half the people put away in mental homes. Yet when he's really working and it's all coming through, I tell you, Dr. Tuby, this is a great comic — the best we've got."

They were now in the roar and glitter of the West End. Tuby rather liked Wilf Orange and was quite ready to talk to Lon Bracton, yet he found himself being invaded by vague feelings of mistrust and melancholy. Perhaps it was the rain, the meaningless blurred lights, the sense rather than the actual sight of the rush-hour masses. "There's just a chance I might be able to help him. But remember I'm neither a psychiatrist nor an expert on television and film comedy. All I can offer him is an image analysis. But it just might work — just — " Tuby's voice trailed away.

This didn't depress Wilf. To Tuby's surprise, it aroused his enthusiasm. "You know what you are, Dr. Tuby?" he cried. "You're refreshing. No kidding! Listen! I'm surrounded by people — all day, half the night — who say they have everything. You name it, they have it. Big, big deals, all of 'em! Every man a genius! Every girl a wonder! They start selling themselves in the doorway. You'd think the place was flooded with talent instead of running out of it. And I thought you'd be another of 'em. But no, I'm wrong. You're quiet, you're not sure, you haven't got it all made. It's refreshing — it's lovely!"

They stopped somewhere up Portland Place, hurried indoors, and were taken to the top floor. "Back again," Wilf groaned as they went along the corridor. "I might as well live here."

The door was opened by a burly fellow with a battered face, who scowled and said, "No, no, no!"

"Come off it, Leslie. We're due here. This is Dr. Tuby — "

"Lon says *No* so I say *No*."

"Now listen, Leslie, you've got the message wrong — "

"No, I 'aven't. Lon mentioned you an' 'im specially. Now bugger off!" And then they were looking at the door, not at Leslie.

"Well," said Wilf wearily as they turned away, "see what I meant? Knew there'd be trouble as soon as I saw that Leslie was back on the job. Always sends for Leslie when he suddenly decides he can't see anybody." They walked back to the lift. "Lon had a piece of Leslie one time. An egg. A turkey. Leslie can slam doors, that's all," he went on bitterly. "Never had any defence and his big punch never connected if the other heavy could move at all. Two hundred pounds of cat meat. And telling me to bugger off!"

He brooded over this until they were back in the car. "Dr. Tuby," he then began, "this shouldn't have happened to you. I'm mortified. And you must be mortified."

"No, Wilf, just rather annoyed." Tuby took care to sound calm and clear. "Bracton has wasted my afternoon and most of my early evening. I shall charge him only a nominal fee of fifty guineas, but if he makes any attempt to avoid payment I'll sue him at once."

"He won't. Anyhow I'll be paying it. Send you a cheque in the morning, Dr. Tuby. I tell you, I'm mortified. Why don't we have a drink? Okay? Fine! I'm a member of a drinking and dining club not fifty yards from your office. Come Into The Garden, Maud. Know it?"

"Good God — no! Do you mean it's really called — "

"That's right. Have to keep changing the gimmicks. Used to be called The Bulldog Breed — with stuffed bulldogs all over the joint. Now it's Maud and the garden. You'll see. Sam," he called, "stop at the club."

"Murder for parking," Sam called back.

"Then come back in an hour for me." He leant back. "What were we saying?"

"I've just been wondering why Lon Bracton's not seeing anybody. What's he doing?"

"You'd think he was lushing it up — or had three girls in there — wouldn't you? Or a poker game, maybe. No, sir! My bet — and one gets you five — all he's doing up there is reading books. Some days you can't stop him. He just has to read books. Can you beat it?"

"Perhaps I could. I've read a lot of books. You might say, I was in the business."

"Ah — that's different. You're not a comic. And you've got the brains to stand it. Lon hasn't. I don't think he knows what the hell he's reading. He's a nut case."

In the club they found a corner in a room transformed into a bower of artificial leaves and flowers. Close to their table were plastic roses as big as cabbages. The black-bat night had flown: all was brilliant moonlight with a hint of dawn over the bar. Both the waitress and the barman (who had thick side-whiskers) were in mid-Victorian costume. Tuby felt better when he'd had some whisky. Meanwhile, Wilf continued to describe Lon's eccentricities and then, after more whisky, touched upon his own desperate commitments and responsibilities as a successful agent. After some young acquaintance had tried to join them and had been rebuffed ("You're interrupting business here, Mac"), Wilf and the whisky together began praising Tuby. "You know something, Doc? I've got confidence in you. And that's a lot coming from Wilf Orange — ask anybody. And I'll tell you why I've got confidence. First, like I said, you didn't give yourself the big buildup. Second, you weren't mortified. Nice and quiet, going there. Nice and quiet, coming away after we're told to bugger off. You're cool and easy, Doc. And if anybody's going to put Lon right, it'll be you. And I'll tell you another thing. You put Lon right and I'll have another image job for you. Big money and lovely work!" He'd been talking quietly, in his hoarse conspiratorial manner, but now he dropped to a whisper, his mouth not six inches from Tuby's ear. "Meldy Glebe."

Tuby hadn't room to turn his head and felt as idiotic as the room looked, as he whispered back staring straight in front of him. "What? Who?"

"Meldy Glebe. Not seen her? I'm not surprised. She's in pictures. One of my clients. There's half a million invested in her, pounds not dollars. Shacked up with one of the big boys on the other side. And she's not right yet. They know it. I know it. She knows it. And ten to one it's an image job. That's my thinking now, Doc. But I can't sell you to 'em till I can quote Lon at 'em, you follow?" Orange was still whispering, but now Tuby had moved away a little so that he could turn his head.

And he did. "What's she like — this Meldy Glebe?"

"Darkish redhead — scrumdoodle — knock your eyes out. But mixed up. Booked for a sex symbol and doesn't like sex. Doesn't like anything so far except riding in fast jets, money, and fancy drinks. And," he continued, raising his voice, "we've just time for two more non-fancy drinks. Hey — Maud!"

## 2

"It's about this cheque for fifty guineas from Wilf Orange," Elfreda said to Tuby two days later.

"Ah — he's stumped up, has he? Good! And Cosmo said you'd know how to deal with it." Tuby sat down and smiled across her desk.

Elfreda was about to frown, but then remembered she'd decided not to do any frowning. Bad for the forehead. She must keep any looks she still had. "This money's really outside any arrangements we worked out. If you'd gone on with this comedian — Bracton — and earned a fee of five hundred pounds or a thousand pounds, that would have been quite different. As it is, you'd better have this fifty guineas, so I'll let you have a cheque for it."

Tuby stopped smiling. "No charity in this, I hope, Elfreda?"

"No, no, really not, Owen. I'm letting you have it all because I don't see what else to do with it — all too confusing. Look — I've already made out a cheque to you on the Institute. The cheque from Orange was of course made out to us. Here!"

"Well, thank you, my dear!" Tuby was smiling again as he took the cheque. "I won't pretend I don't need this."

Elfreda felt that no tactful reply to this was possible. "I suppose this is the end of this comedian thing, isn't it?"

"I don't think so," said Tuby thoughtfully. "When he rang me yesterday afternoon, wanting me to go round again, I was tough with him. If he wants to go on with it, he has to come here first. And I'm willing to bet three to one that he will, especially as Wilf Orange is now on my side. He was against the idea at first, but somehow he came round to it."

Tuby didn't sound confident and conceited but faintly surprised, and that was why Elfreda felt a sudden rush of affection for him. "Everybody's on your side, Owen, sooner or later," she declared, almost with maternal pride. "Cosmo may be the boss of this show — and at the moment he's being very bossy, I must say — but I don't believe he'd have a hope without you — "

"And I couldn't even start without him. The other afternoon, when Saltana told us that within a week we'd be getting the kind of enquiries we wanted, from big business, I didn't believe him. And I thought he was wrong turning down smaller jobs — "

"So did I," she put in hastily.

"And now I've changed my mind. I haven't the tiniest bit of evidence. I'm being quite irrational. But then I didn't believe him, even though I pretended to, and now I do. Elfreda my dear, we're just about to turn a corner. Loins must be girded, whatever that implies. And now, Mrs. Drake, before the rush of business sweeps us away, let us testify to our confidence — our pride — in our Director, Professor Cosmo Saltana, who, on our behalf, is poised over the brilliant idiot world of commerce and fashion like a great eagle — ready at any moment to fall, as Tennyson said, like a thunderbolt." He got up, twinkling away at her.

"Owen dear, I'm sure you'd much, much rather be lecturing and talking somewhere than waiting here to argue with people about their images. That girl, Lois Terry, is right."

"That girl, like so many girls, makes judgments before she's considered the evidence or indeed really knows what evidence there is. I never told her or anybody else that I proposed to spend the rest of my life in the image business."

"Can I tell her that?"

Tuby hesitated, which was unusual for him. "You tell her what you like, Elfreda," he replied finally. "Only — no matchmaking, please! Marry off Primrose to some formidable young man. Entangle our Mrs. Mere in some appalling liaison. Push our Beryl's boy friend, if she has one, towards the altar and the horrible bedroom suite. But allow Dr. Owen Tuby to dree his own weird, which incidentally isn't a bad description of travelling in the Underground towards another helping of pasta left over from lunch and hastily warmed up for dinner. And thank you for the cheque, my dear. Some of it will be spent on coq au vin and taxis."

Before she could think of a reply, he had gone. Oh dear! What a pity it was Cosmo Saltana she wanted and not this sweet little man, so cosy, so lovable, with the voice you could listen to forever! And she reflected, not for the first time, that the trouble about being a woman was that it was both hard and ridiculous. You knew what you wanted but didn't exactly know why. Unlike men, who had reasons by the score, long lists for and against, and still didn't know what they wanted. She did a bit of office work, which was better than thinking, but was interrupted by Primrose, who was wearing her grey sack thing again with yards of lilac stockings.

"You're criticising me, darling," cried Primrose. "I saw it in your eye."

"I was just thinking how absolutely ravishing you'd have looked in the clothes that were fashionable when I was your age."

"But now I look a mess — "

"No, you couldn't look a mess, Primrose. But still — "

"I know, darling, I know. But fashion isn't just silly," Primrose continued earnestly. "Not just a commercial trick. There's something *behind* it. Every complete change of fashion has a *meaning,* I believe, darling. Perhaps Professor Saltana or Dr. Tuby could explain it. We must ask them some time. But I came in to remind you that Phil Rawbin's coming in this morning."

"Phil Who, dear?"

"Oh — darling — I'm sorry. I thought I'd told you — and of course I haven't. Professor Saltana said we needed somebody — working part-time — who could do photography and also some sketches, perhaps, to show the sort of image we had in mind. So then I remembered Phil Rawbin, who's a photographer just to earn a living, and an artist as well. All he *really* cares about is doing landscapes in water colour, but he can do fab little sketches. I've watched him doing them. He always has a sketchbook with him — oh yes! — and he always has in his pocket the sweetest little water-colour box you ever saw, only about four inches long — heavenly! And he's just the person we need. So I arranged for him to come in this morning — to see the boss."

"What's he like?"

Primrose looked solemn. "I think he's the most *beautiful* man I've ever seen."

"Oh — *is* he? Are you — ?"

"No, no, no, no — I'm not, he isn't, we aren't. Not like that at all." Primrose sounded rather cross. "Now listen — Elfreda darling — once and for all! Just belt up on this sex bit with me. You tried your hardest to crowd me into bed with Mike Mickley, when you ought to have known I *despised* him — he was so weak and wet and *abject*. Darling, when I trot obediently bedwards with a man, he'll be the sort of man who won't need any help from you or anybody else. He'll just say 'Bed, Primrose!' and off I'll go. A sort of younger Cosmo Saltana — oh yes, darling, I'm cured of *that,* so don't worry. But Phil Rawbin's quite different. He's beautiful, sad, all by himself a long way off. He ought to be just standing in a cathedral."

Elfreda had never met anybody who ought to be just standing in a cathedral. Feeling rather bewildered, she was about to ask a question, but Mrs. Mere came in with a tray and three cups of coffee. "Beryl's busy telephoning for Professor Saltana, so I'm doing the coffee. It's something to do while I wait for somebody to be haughty with, to snub, to cut down to dwarf size. The trouble is, I keep practising on my poor husband who wonders what he's done wrong. Though that doesn't matter because he always *has* done something wrong. What are you talking about?"

"Phil Rawbin, Eden darling. You remember, I told you about him — "

"You did. And I meant to tell you this morning that Oswald knows him. No, don't exclaim. The fact is," Mrs. Mere continued, not without a touch of pride, "my husband knows almost everybody. Men, I mean — not women, thank God! It's because he's spent so much time in saloon bars — "

Following this sombre thought, they drank their coffee in silence. It was broken by a signal from Beryl in the reception hall. Mr. Rawbin had arrived.

Mrs. Mere hastily collected the coffee cups. "I'll go. But of course I'll take a peep at him. No more. No naughty stare. He's one of us."

Phil Rawbin was rather tall and thin, and was wearing a black corduroy suit and a crimson scarf. His hair, moustache, and short beard were very dark; he had hollow cheeks, and the general effect of the hairless part of his face suggested it had been carved out of old ivory. Elfreda saw at once what Primrose had meant by her remark about a cathedral. It was as if an Early Christian martyr had arrived with a portfolio.

Primrose took the portfolio away from him as soon as she had introduced him to Elfreda. "I'll tell Professor Saltana you're here, Phil darling, and perhaps he'd like to glance through this, if you don't mind."

"Okay by me, Primrose. Go ahead."

Elfreda found this rather startling. He ought to have had a deep sad voice and to have said something deep and sad, about the Second Coming or something of that sort. Now she didn't know whether to talk to his appearance or talk to his voice.

Primrose looked in. "Come on, Phil. The great chief's waiting." Phil nodded and got up.

Primrose returned a moment later. "What's the matter with you, Elfreda darling?"

"Nothing. How's Cosmo Saltana this morning?"

"In one of his short-and-sharp, rough-and-tough moods, as if we were turning down wealthy clients by the score. No, darling, don't be indignant. I'm not really being bitchy. I know just how he feels. And anyhow Simon Birtle swears we'll be doing terribly well any week now. He says everything always comes with a rush, and he ought to know. If you want my opinion, darling, nearly all the people who have a lot of money to spend — in business or not — are like mad sheep. They all rush together. Now — what's this?"

Beryl was calling through. "What's his name again?" Elfreda asked. "Rolf Tenzie?"

"Oh — I know him," cried Primrose. "Tell her to send him in here." And as soon as Elfreda had done this, Primrose continued in a hurried whisper: "He's in public relations — or used to be. A deluxe smoothie — you watch!"

Thank goodness Primrose was with her! Elfreda felt she'd never have been able to cope if she'd had to receive Rolf Tenzie by herself. He swept in, a hand outstretched, crying, "Primrose — how perfectly *marvellous!* Where was it? Antibes? Cap Ferrat? A *fun* time, I distinctly remember."

When Primrose introduced him, he behaved as if he'd been waiting for this moment all his life. It was easier to see his clothes, which were exquisite and expensive down to the last detail, than it was to see Rolf Tenzie himself. His voice, rather high but resonant, seemed to Elfreda to come out of a sort of blur, rather as if a clever middle-aged actor were playing a charming young man in a colour film not quite in focus. And when he did anything, such as produce a cigarette case and a lighter, it was all so smooth and fast it was like conjuring. At any time there might be a pair of doves or a string of flags. In an office he just wasn't quite *real*.

"Are you still in public relations, Rolf?" Primrose was asking.

"Now, now, sweetie ducks — no *teasing!*"

"I'm not. I'm really asking."

"But I've been with Jacques Nazaire for the past year. And Jacques *is* P.R. At least you know *that*, Primrose. Don't you, Mrs. Drake?"

"I don't know anything," Elfreda announced comfortably.

"I see, I see," cried Rolf Tenzie, quite happily. "I'm just a plaything round here this morning. Go on then — have fun! I can't complain, can I? You didn't ask me to pay you a call, did you?"

It was at this moment that Tuby twinkled at them round the door. "Oh — I'm sorry — "

But Primrose and Elfreda insisted upon his joining them and being made known to Rolf Tenzie, who exclaimed in wonder and delight.

"Dr. Tuby, Dr. Tuby, as soon as I told Jacques I was about to pop into the *Institute of Social Imagistics* — we're only three minutes away, you know — he said I must make sure I met Dr. Tuby. D'you know why?"

"I can't imagine," said Tuby, smiling.

"Well, it's all rather exciting. I occasionally take a peep at TV — and I've seen your Professor Saltana — very impressive, as I told Jacques. But he won't go near the goggle box — hurts his eyes, he says — but he's always buying transistors — smaller and smaller, incredible! — and turning them on at odd times. And he's listened to you, Dr. Tuby — and he says you're marvellous — but marvellous! He says he'd put you on the team any day — and lovely money! Means it too. And just remember, please — this is *Jacques*."

"Very gratifying, Mr. Tenzie," said Tuby calmly. "But who is Jacques?"

Primrose started to giggle, though she knew it was bad for her image.

"It's a plot of course," Tenzie declared emphatically, though still keeping his voice and manner as smooth as cream. "All you naughty people in it — beautiful teamwork, I must say — a conspiracy to drive me out of my little mind, just because I never asked for an appointment. Confess, Dr. Tuby — now confess!"

"What I'll confess, Mr. Tenzie, is that although I'm a specialist in imagistics, I'm also an academic who's just returned from a long exile in the Far East. So please accept the fact I know nothing about this Jacques of yours and tell me about him."

"Of course, Dr. Tuby — a pleasure! Jacques Nazaire — French

father, mother American — is the top public relations man in Europe. And there are only two in America in his class, perhaps only one. Started in Paris — still has a branch there — then began operating here. Taken on a few wealthy prominent individuals. Changed the public image of a number of great combines and groups. Does it for whole countries now. Take that African place — Bezania — for instance. Marvellous job! Half of 'em are supposed to be cannibals, but any week now one of the colour supplements will be publishing some of their favourite recipes — "

"You mean," said Tuby, "dress and marinate with herbs the leg of a well-grown child of four — "

"Stop it, Owen!" cried Elfreda.

"Two other new African countries are nibbling — well, no — are *considering* offers to Jacques. I can't mention names, Dr. Tuby, but you can probably guess — "

"No, I can't," said Tuby firmly. "Now tell me what we can do for you, my dear sir."

"I don't know yet, Dr. Tuby. This is a sort of neighbourly call and I wanted to meet Primrose again. But *we* have to change images, and *you* are experts on images. We ought to be able to do business. But of course that's up to Jacques — "

"And our Director, Professor Saltana," Tuby put in hastily.

"And he's got somebody with him at the moment," said Primrose. "*And* I ought to warn you, Rolf, he's hardly at his smoothest and sweetest this morning. You see, darling, Professor Saltana and Dr. Tuby aren't the kind of men you're used to dealing with — *quite* different — "

"I'm aware of that, Primrose my sweet. Now here's an idea. Why don't you three come and meet Jacques about half-past five or so this afternoon? There'll be people looking in for drinks — quite informal, not social, not a real party — you can come just as you are — and you'll meet Jacques and some of the team. Can do? Lovely fun!" He went round shaking hands and distributing cards. "The card thing's rather squalid, but it tells you where to find us and you have to show it to the man be-low. Jacques still behaves as if somebody might have a plastic bomb — Paris, of course. But he's a supersonic sweetie — you'll discover. 'Bye for now!"

"It might be quite fun, at that," Primrose declared after he had gone.

"And Saltana might want to know about this Jacques," said Elfreda, who tried to sound businesslike. "Don't you agree, Owen, it might be useful?"

Tuby looked from one to the other in mock solemnity. "It may not be fun. It may not be useful. But to a man of my age and tastes, with my financial resources, any offer of free liquor from five-thirty onwards is irresistible."

It was just after five-thirty when the three of them started off through the drizzle along Curzon Street, towards Jacques Nazaire's address. Saltana had left earlier, not telling anybody where he was going: it was part of his new tycoonery act and it left Elfreda feeling rather cross with him; he might be popping off to see some woman. Moreover, she was now feeling less confident about this Jacques Nazaire thing. It was all right for Primrose, who was always ready to go anywhere and meet anybody. And Tuby of course never cared what he looked like, just didn't give a damn. But Elfreda felt she wasn't looking smart enough and wished she'd been strong-minded and had rushed back to Robinson's to change. And this initial feeling of uneasiness, of inferiority, as she realized later, played an important part in all that happened afterwards.

A commissionaire passed them in and then they took a lift to the top floor. There seemed to be about a dozen people in the long and very expensive-looking room — dim rose and old gold but with pictures clamouring to be stared at — where Rolf Tenzie greeted them as if they were his oldest friends. Jacques Nazaire wore a beautiful charcoal-grey suit and a pale-yellow tie, which did nothing to restore Elfreda's confidence, and he had one of those French faces that seem to be all a sharp bony ridge you could almost use as a paper-knife. He also had the one-deep-look-into-the-eyes-then-kiss-your-hand technique, which Elfreda always felt she ought to despise but never quite managed it. Three young men surrounded Primrose. Jacques Nazaire took Tuby away into a far corner. Elfreda accepted a gin-and-tonic from a man in a white coat who looked like an elderly French general, and then, feeling if anything even more inferior and unworthy, went to stare at a painting of a great golden nude in a bathroom, by somebody she'd vaguely heard about, called Bonnard. She drank most of the gin-and-tonic — it was a big one, too — but it didn't do her much good and she began to wonder if she couldn't quietly slip away. Then it happened.

"Sure is quite a painting," the man said, "but why don't I ask Alphonse over there to freshen that drink for you?" As she turned, he gave a delighted yelp. "Well, well, well! Now don't tell me it isn't a small world. You're Mrs. Judson Drake — Elfreda, isn't it? Remember me? Frank Maclaskie. Used to do business with Judson. Met you in Sweetsprings, and you and Judson had dinner with me one time at the club in Portland. And here we are — a hell of a long way from dear old Oregon. Say — this is great. Now — don't move. Just give me that glass and I'll get us refills from Alphonse. Gin-and-tonic, isn't it? And if you'd like to nibble something, there's a guy wheeling in a trolley. I'll send him right along. And don't move, Elfreda. Mustn't lose you now."

He gave her a broad grin — he had the face for it — and off he went, obviously delighted. But then, in spite of herself, so was she. All right, all right, she'd met dozens of him with Judson — broad-faced and ruddy, broad-shouldered but paunchy for all the golf they played, all doing and saying the same things, laying down the law about everything

after a few drinks and after a few more getting you into a corner for a
heavy pass — and when she'd left Oregon she'd hoped never to meet
one of them again. And she remembered Frank Maclaskie more clearly
now. Judson had called him a *sharpshooter,* and he was quite rich, probably about fifty, and had been divorced, she seemed to remember. The
very type she'd had quite enough of, thank you! A noisy clown, compared with Cosmo Saltana and Owen Tuby! And yet — and yet — he
was genuinely delighted to find her here, wasn't he? He was ready to
make a *fuss* of her, which nobody else had done for some time. And
though she'd told herself she didn't want any more of that Western
geniality and slapdash generosity, knowing quite well that these spenders-
and-chasers were the very men who didn't understand and didn't really
like women, for all that it was pleasant just for once to warm and preen
oneself in that atmosphere they so quickly created. In short, if this Frank
Maclaskie wanted to be attentive for a few days — and he might be
feeling a bit lonely too — she wasn't going to snub him.

So when he came back, bringing the drinks himself, and begged
her to dine with him, she told him he could call for her at Robinson's
just before eight, but added she would now slip away from this party,
to give herself plenty of time to change. He had to stay on, he said, not to
lush it up but to talk some business with Nazaire, but he insisted — and
this was typical, and Saltana and Tuby would never have thought of it —
on going down to the entrance with her, putting her into his hired Rolls,
and telling the driver very solemnly, as if she were a beautiful precious
package, to deliver her to Robinson's Hotel. All this — and after two
large gins — was a bit heady, and she couldn't help feeling just a little
beautiful and precious all through a long hot bath and some careful
changing, even though she kept telling herself she knew all about the
Frank Maclaskies, and what their attentions were worth. But wasn't
there a nice *silly* side of her that never got much of a chance with Saltana and Tuby?

As soon as the Rolls was leaving Robinson's, Frank Maclaskie, who
was now a trifle high, told her triumphantly they were on their way to a
very special restaurant where against heavy odds he'd been able to book
a table. She'd never heard of this restaurant before, but she'd listened to
too many Frank Maclaskies describing their travels not to know that for
them there always *was* one very special restaurant, hard to get into, just
as there was always one particular hotel, in London or Paris or Frankfurt
or Rome, where they must stay at all costs. And the fact that they always
wanted the same kind of room and ordered the same kind of food didn't
worry them at all. This very special restaurant was thickly carpeted and
curtained, hushed, solemn, with head waiters tiptoeing about like under-
takers. And Frank Maclaskie of course wouldn't even look at the enormous menu but asked at once for a big steak rare, French fried potatoes
and a salad, and Scotch-on-the-rocks. However, he was quite patient

while Elfreda hovered over the menu and also rather blindly chose a half-bottle of claret. And they weren't jammed up against other tables but could talk freely.

Looking back afterwards on this Maclaskie episode, Elfreda realized that the talk they had then was the only sensible thing that came out of it. Apparently Jack Nazaire, as Frank called him, had said something to him about the Institute, and this had roused his curiosity. So he wasn't just being polite when he asked her to tell him about it. And much to her surprise, he took it seriously.

"You've got something there, Elfreda," he told her. "Jack Nazaire thinks so — and he's one smart cookie — and *I* think so. And I'm talking to you now as a businessman. Okay, we all talk about images — so how about making 'em a speciality? Clever — very clever! I wish I'd thought of it myself. What d'you call it again?"

"It's the *Institute of Social Imagistics,*" she said rather proudly.

"Kinda long-haired maybe — but I dunno — got class. The big corporations would go for it. 'Gentlemen, here's a special report from the *Institute of Social Imagistics.*' They'd lap it up like cream. How you fixed there, Elfreda? You incorporated — limited company, as they say over here? Like to tell me how you've split the shares?"

"I'd prefer not to, if you don't mind, Frank. I'll bet *you* wouldn't in my place."

They were sitting side by side, and he turned to give her a broad grin. "You can say that again, baby! I might have known Judson would have you trained right. Left you over half a million, didn't he? No, no, I'm not changing the subject. Point is this, Elfreda — you've got a big new idea to sell there, but you're also stuck with these two professors — Director and Deputy Director — with enough shares between 'em, I'll bet, to outvote you every time. Okay — don't say it. I know — it was their idea and they're the experts. But you're not playing around in a college now, you're in business. And when you're in business, you don't want professors, you want businessmen."

"Well, I'm a businesswoman — "

"You might be at that. And I've known a few very smart businesswomen, Elfreda, though none of 'em looked like you. But with an idea like this to sell, you need, first, a real hot promoter, and behind him a cool long-headed fella who can handle figures and work out contracts. And all you've got is a couple of professors — "

"Who happen to be friends of mine — close friends — "

"Fine — fine! And of course you keep 'em on — they're the experts. Good salaries — for *them* — even some commission. But I'm talking to you as a friend now, Elfreda. And it's nothing for me — though I'd buy a piece of it tomorrow if the management was right." And then, without mentioning any facts and figures, he began to boast how he and his friends and business associates were moving in and quietly taking over, especially here in poor old half-ruined Britain. But then she stopped him.

"Frank Maclaskie, you're forgetting something. And I'd better remind you before you tell me any more. I'm not American, you know, I'm English. Born here. Brought up here. And now back here. And after America, it's small and often stuffy and a dirty mess. But I love it. You've just made me realize that. I love it. And I never really loved one single bit of America — never, never, never!"

"Elfreda," he declared solemnly, "I liked the way you said that. Straight from the heart, that was — and the good old British spirit. And if I opened my big mouth too wide — really just because I was feeling good — then I apologize. And if I was feeling good, that's because whenever I saw you in Portland or Sweetsprings I wanted to know you better — and then — why, for God's sake — there you are at Jack Nazaire's — and now here we are — " And he covered her hand on the table with his, hot and heavy, a kind of big steak rare among hands.

They had been sitting a long time over dinner; now they ought to leave. All Elfreda wanted to do was to return to Robinson's — alone. But this was the moment when all the Frank Maclaskies demanded to go on the town and take a look at the hot spots. She was just wondering whether to plead a long tiring day or a headache when he spoke again.

"Tell you how I'm fixed tonight, Elfreda. Have to see a man at some night club — forget the name right now but have it in my diary — and if you'd like to come along — well, he'll only take ten minutes — "

"No, Frank, if you don't mind. I'm feeling rather tired and all I want to do is to take a taxi back to my hotel — "

"I know — you want to call it a day. But tomorrow's different — Saturday — no office all day. Now why don't we double date with Charlie Murch tomorrow night? He's a friend of mine over here from Seattle — smart as a whip and lots of laughs. Now he goes around here with a woman he knows, British, Vi Somebody — met her for a minute the other night. So why don't I call Charlie in the morning and fix a double date? If you've already got a date, call it off, Elfreda. You'll like Charlie and this Vi — and it could be a million laughs. What d'you say?"

She was doing nothing the next night — Saturday too — and though she was dubious about all those laughs, at least another woman would be there. "All right, Frank — if you can arrange it with the other two — "

"Sure thing! Call you in the morning."

And he did, just after ten o'clock, and said he would pick her up in the Rolls about seven. They would eat fairly early, he said, in the Grill at the Savoy, where Charlie was staying. Twenty minutes later, she took a call from Cosmo Saltana, who was in his room at the Institute. Nobody else was there, of course, as it was Saturday, but then Saltana had only to go down five floors.

"Elfreda, let me give you dinner tonight. Several Institute things I want to talk about — "

"Oh — Cosmo, I'm sorry but I can't, not tonight." She tried to sound sorry but it wasn't easy. "You see, yesterday at Jacques Nazaire's I met a friend from Oregon." And she explained about Frank Maclaskie. "And he told me at dinner," she continued hastily, feeling nervous but trying to sound cool and teasing, "that he thought our Institute was a great idea, and he'd be ready to buy what he called *a piece of it* if it had the right management — "

"Very good of him," Saltana put in dryly. "He knows exactly how to run it, I suppose?"

She gave him a little laugh, rather fluttery. "He says we need businessmen — not *two professors,* as he called you and Tuby. Of course I told him — "

But Saltana wouldn't let her go on. "Yes, yes, you can tell me the rest on Monday. And try to keep him fairly sober. Some of 'em turn nasty when they're plastered. Now I've another call or two to make. 'Bye!"

Even when she knew he'd rung off, Elfreda still found herself holding the receiver, trying to decide if it had happened at last. Was he simply annoyed, the grand Director, because he couldn't talk to her about the Institute whenever he pleased? Or was he just plain jealous? For the rest of the day, her mind hesitated between these alternatives, one so boring, the other so deliciously heartwarming.

Saturday evening started badly and never recovered. First of all, the programme had been changed, without anybody asking Elfreda what *she* would like. Instead of dining quietly and sensibly in the Savoy Grill, they were to have a few drinks up in Charlie Murch's suite and then eat at some place that ran a big cabaret show. Only somebody like Charlie Murch who knew all the ropes, Frank explained in the Rolls, would have been able to book a table for four on Saturday night at this place. Elfreda wished Charlie had known fewer ropes, but didn't say so, not wishing to hurt Frank's feelings. There was no more talk about the Institute and business, and already Frank was sitting too close, pressing against her two hundred pounds of rare steak. Then up in the suite among the few drinks, Elfreda realised almost at once she wasn't going to like Charlie Murch and his Vi — a Mrs. Tarriton or Farriton or something. Charlie was a thinner and darker and faintly sinister version of Frank. Vi was thin and dark too, restless, a great arm-tapper and -slapper with the men and given to sudden high screams of laughter that convinced Charlie and Frank, though not Elfreda, that they were irrepressible comedians. The off-colour stories came out even faster than the drinks. Elfreda wasn't prudish but she'd always found this atmosphere of generalised sex, a kind of extension of fourteen-year-old curiosity, very boring. And Vi wasn't going to be any help to another woman. She was obviously a

strictly competitive and bitchy type, and after she'd closed her eyes for
one of her screams of laughter, to please the men, she'd open them to
give Elfreda a cold and calculating look, assessing the competition.

The other thing was that Elfreda was beginning to feel very hungry.
Her stomach wanted food and not the Scotches-on-the-rocks and the very
strong martinis that Charlie was handing out. So she soon refused to keep
up with the other three, who were all getting high, and this did not improve her relations with Vi, who clearly suspected that either Elfreda
was a spoilsport or was working some competitive line new to her. And
when the men did at last suggest a move, Vi didn't exchange the usual
feminine smile or nod but made for the bedroom and bathroom as if
they were for her exclusive use. However, Elfreda followed her, aware
of her own needs even if this dam' woman wasn't. But not a word was
spoken between them. War had been declared. Then the Rolls, which
seemed to be full of pressing legs and wandering hands, took them to the
cabaret place.

It was packed, hot, and already thick with cigar smoke. Their rope-
pulled miracle of a table was small for four, even if it had had any space
around it, which it hadn't; and it was close to the stage and the band.
Nothing was happening on the stage yet, though the lighting was being
changed, but Charlie and Frank proceeded to give a performance, noisily
throwing their weight about to demand instant service of food and two
bottles of champagne. Waiters sweated, implored, pushed, and cursed
under their breath in various Mediterranean languages. Just before all
light went off their table, Elfreda saw that she had in front of her a
smear of soup and — thank God! — a roll and a pat of butter. The
champagne arrived and was splashed into glasses by a Sicilian assassin almost ready to reach for his knife. Coloured lights flooded the stage. The
band produced a brassy chord. A white light illuminated a microphone
and then a man who pulled faces, told a dirty story about a homosexual,
and announced that the eight most beautiful girls in London would open
the cabaret. The girls, who seemed to be wearing bikinis made of sequins,
kept their fine legs moving briskly and moved their mouths as if they
were singing, though Elfreda couldn't hear a word. Frank and Charlie
gazed in wonder and delight, even though one of them — and she never
could decide which one — was also fondling her knee. Having finished
the roll and butter, Elfreda impatiently awaited the next course. It arrived just when two men on the stage began to throw a girl about, and it
consisted of three inches of some grey mysterious fish, which she tasted
and then pushed around, fearful all the time that one of the men, glisten-
ing with sweat, might slip and send the girl crashing down on the table.
She drank all the champagne that came her way but it didn't make her
feel gay, only hungrier, and as Charlie's untouched roll was so close to
her right elbow, she stole it. A boring veal dish, with peas, rice, and
flour paste, was now banged down in front of them, and Elfreda ate al-

most all of it, together with Charlie's roll. By this time the man had returned to the microphone half out of his mind with importance, the stage lighting was dizzy with excitement, the band was blaring away, people were standing up and being told to sit down, and even Vi, though now apparently facing some real competition, was clapping with the rest. Vi, Charlie, and Frank told one another at the top of their voices that this kid, only nineteen, was the biggest hit in London, was going to New York next month, then out to Las Vegas and the Coast — boy oh boy oh boy! — Merleen Jacobs.

So far Elfreda had really known only discomfort. With Merleen Jacobs came agony. She was nothing much to look at, except that she did contrive to look overdressed and yet untidy and rather mucky. But when she confided her private joys and sorrows to the mike she held a few inches away, with a great deal about *ma lerve for yew,* she went right into the eardrums with a gimlet and never stopped turning it. Elfreda had heard plenty of noisy singers in her time but they had merely assaulted the ear, whereas Merleen went right through it, twisting deep into the head, turning herself into migraine or neuralgia with band accompaniment. When she stopped, Elfreda applauded with the rest, out of sheer relief. But then of course that started her off again, and it was impossible to get used to her; and indeed each time she was *worse;* and Elfreda discovered that putting her hands to her ears was no good because Merleen was on the other side of the hands, drilling away into the brain. And when at last the audience let her go, for a few minutes it seemed wonderful, just to have no Merleen.

But now of course Vi and Charlie and Frank, dropping ash on ice cream, had had enough of this spot and wanted some other, hotter spot, and after a noisy argument — they were all three half-stoned — Vi had her way. They were to go to Jeff & Betty's club because Vi actually knew Jeff and Betty. Frank had let the Rolls go and they had to take a taxi to some mysterious address in South Kensington. At least it seemed mysterious to Elfreda. And this was the odd thing. Unlike the other three, she'd really had very little to drink, but their behaviour and the evening itself, with all its coloured lights, noise, smoke, muttering waiters, and the Merleen agony, together had created an atmosphere in which she just might as well have been high as a kite. There was no longer any *sense* in anything. Idiotic things just happened.

They went down some stairs to Jeff & Betty's but even after a lot of argument just inside, by the bar, with Vi proclaiming her friendship with Jeff and Betty, no table, no chairs were available for them, so they had to stand, along with a number of other people, between the bar and the two or three steps going down to the main floor of the club. This gave them a good view of the small spot-lighted space where there was a white piano. Nothing was happening there yet, but apparently Jeff and Betty — a fab act, they were all telling one another — would be on any moment.

Three girls and two young men greeted Vi and joined in. Frank and Charlie bought whiskies. A tall gaunt woman — Betty was no beauty — sat at the piano and was loudly applauded. All the people standing around Elfreda crowded forward to hear better. The peculiar-looking Betty was now playing the piano. Frank had a heavy arm round Elfreda and put his other arm, the arm with a glass at the end of it, round one of the three girls, who turned to twitch the glass away and empty it. More applause now, because there was Jeff, small and neat in a white tie and tails. They began singing a peculiar duet, and after a minute of it Elfreda realised that it was Jeff who was at the piano and that Betty had the white tie and tails. And then quite suddenly she knew she'd had enough of this night out. She squirmed out of Frank's embrace, pushed through the people standing behind, claimed her coat upstairs, and went looking for a taxi.

It was close to noon and she was still in bed, looking at the Sunday papers, when Frank called her. "Hey, Elfreda, what happened to you last night?"

"Sorry, Frank, but I'd a terrible headache so I just sneaked off — "

"Didn't miss a thing except a hell of a hangover. Party got a bit rough, too. Reason I'm calling though, Elfreda, is that a fella's been on the line to me from Paris and I'm flying over for a couple o' days so I won't be around. See you when I get back, though. Try an' stop me!"

"And that's just what I'm going to do, you big ape," she muttered at the receiver as she put it down. Quarter of an hour later, as she was running her bath, there was another call for her. Saltana perhaps? Or Frank Maclaskie again — wanting her to go to Paris — and a hope he had! But it was Owen Tuby — thank goodness! And if she was free tonight, then would she dine with him for once? He knew a decent little French place, only five minutes' walk away, and he'd go round and book a table if she were free. She was — and blessed him. About seven-thirty then — and he gave her the address.

"I like it here," said Elfreda. They were drinking Chambéry in a corner of Tuby's decent little French place.

"Good! So do I. It hasn't been open long, of course," Tuby went on. "Soon it'll be ruined. But now it's still plain and simple — no chi-chi, no *flambé* rubbish. It represents that no-nonsense aspect of French provincial life. We might start with vichysoisse. It'll be out of a tin — it always is — but it's an honest tin. And if you don't want meat, they do a superb omelette Gargamelle. Somebody in the kitchen must have been to Chinon, where I stayed once — before the war. And if you'll join me, I'll drink wine for once instead of whisky."

Over the soup she described all that happened the night before with Frank, Charlie, and Vi. "But please don't tell Saltana, Owen. It'll make me look such a fool. Where is he tonight — do you know?"

"For once — I do. He's gone out to Wimbledon, to be *en famille* with the Meres." He twinkled at her. "All quite safe. No beautiful designing women, Elfreda. Just whisky, conspiracy, boasting."

She hesitated, giving him an apologetic little smile. "I understand men like Frank Maclaskie and his friend Charlie drinking so much. They're empty inside — and rather frightened. But you and Saltana aren't at all like that. So why do you two drink so much? It's always puzzled me, Owen."

"We're not the same, of course. Two quite different men. And in point of fact Saltana doesn't drink as much as I do. Often does it to keep me company. You really want to know about *him,* my dear, not about me — "

"No, I don't. And anyhow he's not here and you are. So why do *you* drink so much, Dr. Tuby?"

He waited a moment or two before replying. Then he began quite slowly. "I think — possibly — to soften my ego. Perhaps to creep a little nearer enlightenment. Unfortunately I never know the exact amount necessary to release the mind from egoism, negative emotions, the blinkers of self-love, the bleaching and deadening processes of self-interest. And too much is as bad as too little. But I must admit that at parties I often drink hard to rescue myself from boredom. That's because the party level of relationships is nearly always tedious. I drank rather too much — after you'd gone, I think — at Jacques Nazaire's on Friday night."

"I saw him take you away to talk. What did he want?"

"To offer me a job, my dear. A large salary and a lot of expense money too. So of course I had to explain that I didn't want to work for him or anybody else. Only for and with the Institute." He didn't go on because now the great omelette had arrived.

It was delicious. Elfreda was happy to eat in silence for a while. Then she told Tuby what Frank Maclaskie had said about the Institute on Friday night. Tuby's reaction was of course quite different from what Saltana's had been on the telephone. He was merely amused. "What your friend doesn't understand — and perhaps you don't, Elfreda — is that Cosmo Saltana and I have never intended to build up a business in the ordinary way. This isn't our life. And — this may surprise you, my dear — Saltana hates it even more than I do. He thinks I don't know that," he added rather complacently, "but of course I do. And you must bear it in mind, Elfreda. It explains why he's so touchy these days. He's not himself." He gave her a long look.

She had never meant to confide in him — certainly not here, eating omelette and cheese sauce — but that look seemed to demand a confidence. "Owen, I'll tell you something you may have guessed already. I love Cosmo Saltana. I'd marry him tomorrow. And if that's no use, I'd gladly live with him, just anyhow he likes. Now — that's out. Do you think I'm a fool?"

"I'd be a fool if I did, my dear. I'm very fond of you both. If you two were happy together, I'd be happy too. I dislike matchmaking, but I'm ready to make an exception of this one."

"You're sweet. But why — why — I mean — oh, just tell me about him! You understand him much better than I do. Please, Owen!"

"We'll drink a little of this wine first. Comes from the same region as the omelette. Not grand but very pleasant."

This was maddening, of course — how men went on about things that didn't really matter, far worse than women — but she obeyed him. She even accepted a little more of the omelette, but inside she was all impatience and anxiety.

"If you imagine that Saltana's not deeply interested in you, not sharply attracted to you, then you're quite wrong. He has been from the first. And this has complicated our plans for the Institute all along, down in Brockshire, now here. You must accept that, Elfreda," he ended, rather sharply for him.

She nodded but didn't say anything, not knowing what to say. Instead, she gave him what she hoped was an appealing, questioning look. It worked too.

"Now there are several things to remember about Cosmo Saltana," Tuby told her, not in his usual companionable fashion but rather as if she were one of his students. "For example, as he spent years and years in Latin America avoiding marriage, he's still — so to speak — not geared for it. Then again, unlike me, he's a proud man. You're well off and he's still poor, and he never forgets that for a minute. Now comes sex."

Elfreda just stopped herself from saying *Ah!* But as he hesitated, she did say, "Yes, go on, Owen. Sex?"

"Here Cosmo and I are more or less alike. You may think we're just a pair of sexual buccaneers, hurrying any desirable woman into the bedroom. This isn't true of me and — though I don't know any details — I'm certain it isn't true of him. We divide desirable women roughly into the tough and the tender. The tender are those who after they've successfully made love with a man begin to feel they belong to him. The tough are those who enjoy it but then pass on, thinking about something else. To make love to the tender, just to round off an evening, is to behave like a cheat. Saltana and I may be disreputable but we aren't cheats."

"I know that, Owen." Then she had a little struggle with herself. "But after all, physical sex doesn't mean so much to a woman." As she saw him staring at her, she added hastily: "At least not in my experience."

He was still staring but then he smiled. "Elfreda my dear," he said softly and without any suggestion of superiority and patronage, "as you're obviously a warm-hearted, generous, sensuous woman, I can only conclude you've never really had any experience. You only think you have. You've only walked round the water, dipping a toe in here, a hand there. You've never been *in* it, taking as much as you can possibly bear, hardly knowing where you are, who you are. But I'm embarrassing you, my dear. Let's talk about the Institute."

"Not yet. What happens if I make Cosmo jealous?"

"I don't know," he replied slowly. "I wish I did — but I don't. It isn't anything a man knows about another man. Except that it wouldn't work if it was all too obvious. He's a proud man, remember. And this is where we have to talk about the Institute. We can't leave it out. Saltana wants to make a lot of money quickly. I agree in principle but I don't feel as passionately concerned as he does — and anyhow I'm leaving the major decisions to him. Now at the moment poor Saltana is walking a tightrope juggling five oranges. If he turns down small consultant jobs, we aren't making any money, just when we need some. But if he accepts them, he feels — quite rightly too, I think — we'll never land the big jobs and the big money — "

"But meanwhile Primrose and Eden and I sit around wondering what to do with ourselves. It's boring and sometimes quite depressing." Elfreda couldn't help sounding rather bitter.

"I knew what you women were feeling. Saltana and I dined last night. I told him it wasn't fair to you and that we might soon lose Primrose. So I forced him to compromise. This is what we agreed — and I ought to add that I took your agreement, knowing what you felt, Elfreda, for granted. If we have an enquiry, with the possibility of a reasonable fee, that we'd naturally hand over to you three women, then we don't turn it down, even though it's not in Saltana's big-money league. This means the Institute has a chance of earning something and you girls won't be just twiddling your beautiful thumbs. There, Elfreda!" he concluded triumphantly.

"I'm all for it, of course, Owen. But when is it going to happen, when do we make a start?"

"Tomorrow morning," he replied coolly. "Saltana likes to pop down on Saturdays to see if there's anything in the post. And yesterday morning there was. Two enquiries, in fact. No, no, no — my dear — I sternly refuse to tell you. Love should come before curiosity. We can't rob Saltana of his little surprise, can we? Come, come, the man's having a hard time." And not another word, though she was burningly curious, could she get out of Tuby on this subject, though he was eloquent over the coffee on many others.

At about quarter to eleven next morning, word came through from Saltana, whom she hadn't yet seen, that she must ask Primrose and Mrs. Mere to join her. He would be shortly handing over a Mr. Rod Bruton to them.

"The point is," Elfreda explained proudly, "there's a new policy.

Tuby told me about it last night. Certain possible clients, who might otherwise be turned away, will be taken on if we three can handle them. Or two of us — or even one of us, of course."

"In other words," said Mrs. Mere, looking and sounding displeased, "we females are to be the bargain basement of the Institute. *Ger-huh!*"

Primrose protested against this attitude. "It's perfectly sensible, darling. It may bring in some money and it means we'll have something to do. And it *doesn't* mean we won't be working with Professor Saltana or Dr. Tuby on bigger things afterwards. Does it, Elfreda?"

"Of course not. It's perfectly reasonable and sensible — "

"My dears, I withdraw my remark," said Mrs. Mere grandly. She sat down and then changed her tone. "The truth is, I only made it because it sounded rather good. Nobody believes me, not even Oswald, but the fact is I often talk for effect."

Saltana marched in his Rod Bruton, who appeared to be trying to make some objection. "Mrs. Drake — Assistant Director." Saltana was topping Bruton's protest. "Mrs. Mere. Miss Primrose East. And I leave you in their very capable hands, Mr. Bruton." He was now ready to go.

"But lo-look here, Professor S-Saltana," Bruton stammered, "I'm cer-certain our per-per-proprietor and per-per-publisher assumed that either y-you or Der-Der-Doctor Tuby would der-deal with our — our — "

"My dear sir," said Saltana in his severest manner, "I have already dealt with your enquiry. I've handed you over to the members of my staff best able to consider your problem and then solve it for you— in image terms. Good God!" he continued, warming up now. "You're in search of a suitable image for your new magazine — *Trend* or *Lure* or *Whim* or *Craze* or whatever you propose to call it. Who buys and reads such magazines? Women of course — "

"And y-y-young men," Bruton said hurriedly.

"Very well then — young men. But am I a young man? Is Dr. Tuby? No. We're middle-aged men. And damnably crusty, cynical middle-aged men too, who couldn't be paid to read your kind of magazine. Come, come, my boy, even if your proprietor and publisher is an idiot, *you* don't have to be one. I leave you with these ladies. You couldn't be in better hands. And Mrs. Drake will explain why." And out he marched.

"*Do* sit down, Mr. Bruton," said Primrose sweetly, and moved as if to put him into the chair.

"Th-thanks! He's really s-s-something, isn't he?" Bruton was wearing one of those rough short overcoats and looked very hot in it. He was an odd young man because he was stocky and broad-faced and chinny, with a quite formidably determined appearance, and yet had this light uncertain voice and stammer. Moreover, now that he was sitting down he didn't seem to know where to look.

Elfreda felt it was up to her — Saltana had said as much — so she made an effort. "Professor Saltana was quite right, you know, Mr. Bruton." It was coming out quite calm and clear, and now he was looking at her. He had dark and swimmy eyes. "Let me explain. We all three know about images, of course, but otherwise we're all quite different. Mrs. Mere is also a wife and mother — and her husband's a well-known educationist and editor. Miss East — Primrose — was a top model — but then you must know that." Bruton nodded rapidly. "And I'm a businesswoman and I've spent most of the last twenty years in America." And ten to one he'd be impressed by that. These types always were.

Then Mrs. Mere came crashing in. "Now then — who wants to publish this magazine — and why?"

With less stammering than before, Bruton explained that he represented a company that published a number of successful trade papers. Its boss man, Charry, wanted to bring out a fashionable magazine, partly to make fuller use of some new machinery, partly for prestige reasons. The magazine would be a monthly, using plenty of colour. It would appeal to both sexes, with not too much emphasis on youth. It would aim at a quality readership but on a broad base, with not too much London *in* stuff, only just enough to make a big audience feel it was a small select one. And there was a good deal more of this from Bruton while the three women stared at him, not saying a word.

But when he had done, Elfreda and her two assistants exchanged glances charged with meaning. "Well," said Elfreda, drawing it out, "I don't believe — but no, you tell him, Eden."

"Probably it's not your fault, Mr. Bruton," Mrs. Mere told him severely. "I can well believe your Mr. Charry is to blame. But I don't think you know what you want yet."

"Perfectly true, darling," said Primrose, "but perhaps that's why they feel an image might help them." She turned a deeply sympathetic look on to Bruton, who at once looked more hopeful.

"An image of *what?*" And Mrs. Mere's *what* was terrifying.

Elfreda felt it was her turn. She held Bruton's dark swimmy eyes and smiled at them. "We're not clear about this, you know, Mr. Bruton. Do you want an image for the magazine itself — a simplified figure, easily recognizable? I seem to remember several quite famous ones. Or do you want — to use in your advertising campaign — an image of your reader, the kind of image that would attract other readers?"

"Or don't you know what you want? *Ger-huh!*" Again, Mrs. Mere of course, who was working hard at throwing the other two into pleasant relief.

"We don't mind which it is," Primrose told him in an encouraging tone. "We might do a little preliminary work on both, don't you think, Elfreda?"

Bruton came to the surface. "That would be m-m-marvellous. B-but I th-think one of you ought to s-see Mr. Ch-Ch-Ch-Ch — "

It was as if he was off in a train, Elfreda thought. "Mr. Charry? Well now, why don't you phone and see if one of us could see him as soon as possible — perhaps this afternoon? And I suggest Mrs. Mere."

Bruton's eyes stopped swimming — to gleam. He even managed a grin. "S-s-so do I. But I'm r-rotten on the phone."

"Give me the number and I'll talk to him," said Mrs. Mere, rising majestically. "And I'll do it from our room — not here. And if he has a direct private number, give me that — write it down, Mr. Bruton — I don't want to be passed around among a lot of little secretaries."

When she had gone out, Bruton said that the trouble with Charry was that like so many boss men he didn't really know his own mind, except about money.

"Well, he'll discover that Mrs. Mere knows her own mind," said Elfreda.

"You're t-t-telling me!" cried Bruton, quite happily for him. Then of course he kept looking at Primrose, who pretended not to be aware of him, while Elfreda reflected how cleverly cunning Tuby had been to realize so early, when they first met, that Eden Mere might be very useful to them. Or was it Saltana? She found she couldn't remember.

Eden sailed in like a battlecruiser. "I see him at three o'clock," she announced. "He was already engaged for lunch, which is a pity because I like expensive food and don't get enough of it. *Ger-huh!* But from three onwards I hope to discover what Mr. Charry has in mind — if he *has* a mind and not merely an acquisitive instinct."

"So there you are, Mr. Bruton," said Elfreda, getting up. "We can't do anything more for you at the moment, but while Mrs. Mere is talking to your chief, Primrose and I will be doing some preliminary work on both types of image."

Goodbyes were said. Boiling now in that thick overcoat, Bruton took a last look at Primrose and departed.

Just before three, when Eden had already left for her appointment with Charry, and Elfreda and Primrose had settled down cosily to discuss magazine images, the two of them were summoned by intercom to Tuby's room. There they found him smoking a pipe at a slim young man with a pink face and pale-blonde hair, eyebrows, and eyelashes, who gave them a startled glance as he jumped from his chair.

"Mrs. Drake and Miss Primrose East — and this is Mr. Alan Axwick, Member of Parliament." Tuby rolled it out richly. "Sit down, ladies, please? And you, Mr. Axwick." Tuby sank deeper into the chair behind his desk, smiled at Axwick, then looked at Elfreda and Primrose. "You may remember, ladies, that Mr. Axwick, though a member of the party in opposition, gained a surprising victory in a recent by-election. Moreover, his family business — something to do with biscuits — accepted a take-over bid by one of the big food combines, and now he has the right to consider himself a wealthy man. So here he is — a comparatively rich new M.P. *But* — you'll forgive me, Mr. Axwick, but I have to mention this — he can't help feeling disappointed. Both politically and socially he is not attracting the attention he had hoped to attract. Or am I overstating it, Mr. Axwick?"

"Well — yes, I think you are a bit, Dr. Tuby," said Axwick apologetically. It was impossible to imagine him dealing with hecklers at street-corner meetings. On the other hand, Elfreda decided, he was rather sweet. "The point is," he went on, now taking in Elfreda and Primrose, "I just can't help wondering if I wouldn't do better if I changed my image. To something a bit more out of the ordinary. For instance, there's one of our chaps — only a backbencher like me, though of course he's been longer in the House — who has these side-whiskers and wears a stock instead of a tie — and he's not specially bright, really, though lots of confidence by now, of course — and he's in demand all the time — on the telly, public dinners, giving the prizes, and what-have-you — and it's all really because he stands out — image of course. Wouldn't you say, Miss East?"

"I *would* say, Mr. Axwick." She opened her eyes very wide, one of her tricks, instead of smiling. "And we know all about that here — naturally."

"Of course, of course! As soon as I heard about this Institute, I was on to it like — like — a knife. As I told you, Dr. Tuby."

"You did. And you're offering us an interesting little problem." Tuby did some thoughtful pipe-work. Then he pointed the stem at Axwick, who looked startled again. "By the way, I think you're wondering why I've asked Mrs. Drake and Miss East to join us. No — no apologies, Mr. Axwick, please! This is business — not social life. You couldn't help feeling that your image problem — " and Elfreda felt that nothing could be deeper and more solemn than Tuby's tone now — "had a political background — not entirely, of course, but largely — so why should I need feminine assistance? This *was,* I think, passing through your mind, wasn't it, Mr. Axwick?"

"Well yes — I suppose it was — in a way — though only for a moment — " He did something to his tie, a silvery grey, but this only called attention to the deeper pink of his cheeks.

"But who can say where political life ends and social life begins?" Tuby demanded of nobody in particular. "Who can decide the breadth and depth of feminine influence upon the choice of television performers? Or indeed upon journalism? And who knows how many public dinners, open to both sexes, are organised by women? And is it the headmaster or the headmaster's wife or daughter who suggests the public figure for Speech Day? I could go on and on, Mr. Axwick, but I trust I've made my point."

"Oh yes — you have indeed, Dr. Tuby. The fact is, I hadn't really thought — "

"Quite so," Tuby cut in rather severely. "But we *have* to think — here in our particular field. You think for us in the House of Commons. We think for you in this Institute, where we know, among other things, that women on the whole are far more image-conscious than men."

"No doubt about it," said Elfreda, who felt she'd been silent too long.

Axwick gave her a few rapid nods, tried a couple on Primrose, made a noise that suggested he was about to say something, was checked by Tuby.

"But now you're thinking," said Tuby very smoothly, "I've argued myself out of the picture. Why should you consult me when these two far more attractive and more image-conscious creatures are available? Why not leave yourself entirely in their sensitive hands? The answer is — I'm rather more creative, more articulate, and far, far more impudent. But who wants impudence? We do, you do — it's essential for image work. Now Mr. Axwick, you can't leave us to begin our research before you've agreed with us about one or two elementary things. For example, we reject whiskers, beards, eccentric hair styles — eh, Elfreda?"

"Of course, Owen. Settled that almost at once." Which in fact was quite true.

"And fancy dress is out," said Primrose. "And I'll bet you're not sorry, are you, Mr. Axwick?"

The pink deepened. "Well — no, I'm not really — I must confess. In fact — I was hoping you wouldn't want me to change my appearance much. On the other hand, one has to catch their eye — I'm thinking now particularly of the Press — " He gave Tuby a bewildered look.

"But we could throw the whole thing into reverse, you know," said Tuby thoughtfully. "He's before your time, but when I was a youngster, Barrie the dramatist could always command the maximum publicity by being the shyest man in London."

"A-ha!" cried Primrose, widening her eyes at Axwick.

"But I want to be able to go places — make some speeches," Axwick protested.

"So did Barrie. Of course his work made him well known — I don't want to overdo this — but the legend that he was unapproachable and unavailable helped him enormously. What we must avoid is an average so-so attitude. You must either run towards publicity or appear to run away from it. I suggest we work on this *Reverse Image*. You are dedicated to some mysterious pursuit, hobby, research. Why do you arrange to destroy all photographs of yourself? Why do you meet your constituents only at strange hours? Why do you keep going to Grenoble? Are you married or aren't you?"

"Well — I don't know — that might be rather awkward — I mean, I'm practically engaged — "

Tuby rose and came round his desk, holding out a hand. "Leave this to us, Mr. Axwick." He shook hands. "Primrose will see you out and you could tell her a little about your girl friend. And remember, please, that when, in a few days, you feel we're working on the right lines, you will pay the Institute a holding fee, to be followed by the final fee when you've agreed in detail on the image we'll have worked out for you."

"And how much do you think this final fee ought to be?" Elfreda asked as soon as the other two had gone.

"That's up to you, my dear," Tuby told her. "But he's rich — he wouldn't know where to start without us — oh well — you'd better talk it over with Saltana — "

"No, Owen, I don't want to go running to him as soon as we have a client to deal with. What about a hundred and fifty guineas for what you call a holding fee — and that's new, isn't it?"

"Yes, I just invented it. Rather good, I thought — "

"And then — say, a thousand guineas when he's completely satisfied — um? If you're sure he can afford it, Owen. He's rather sweet, isn't he?"

This was Primrose's verdict when she returned. "Really a little sweetie-man, a kind of toffee-apple M.P. Can he go far, as they say, in politics, Dr. Tuby?"

"About as far as three lamb cutlets in a tiger's cage. Did he tell you anything about his girl?"

"Yes — and she sounds the end. Do we *have* to bring her in?"

Tuby looked at his watch. "Try working something out with her — and then without her. On the lines I suggested, my dears. You'll have to start on your own. I've a famous comic — Lon Bracton — due here any time now — "

"And you can have him," said Primrose. "Come on, Elfreda darling, back to your room — and a little cosy image work."

They had been exchanging ideas — most of them bad and only fit to giggle over — for about half an hour when Eden Mere marched in. "This man Charry began by trying to bully me but in ten minutes I reduced him to a bleating jelly. He doesn't really know what he wants, of course — he's a blown-up bookkeeper like so many of these men — so I told him we'd do some preliminary work along both lines — image of the magazine — image of its reader."

"Holding fee then," said Elfreda, and then explained it. "I ought to have thought of that. Or Saltana. But actually it was Tuby's idea. He's not supposed to bother about money but for all that, he produced this idea straight out of the blue. He *is* a clever little man."

Elfreda kept Primrose with her on the Alan Axwick job. They stayed with it until about six o'clock; started again next morning, Tuesday, and had sorted everything out, ready for Tuby, when they were interrupted by Saltana. It was now just past noon.

"If that folder's for Dr. Tuby, Primrose, run along with it now.

He'll be able to go through it with you before he goes out to his show-business lunch. And I want to talk to Elfreda." And he sat down, stretched out his long legs, and lit a cheroot. Elfreda fiddled with things on her desk. She felt self-conscious, nervous, vaguely apprehensive. Now what?

"It's time we talked, Elfreda," he said at last. "Why don't we have lunch together, if you don't mind just a drink and a sandwich?"

"All right, Cosmo. Only not in some noisy pub, please."

"If they aren't noisy, they're apt to be damned expensive. There's a lunch problem as well as a traffic problem in this city." He sounded gloomy.

"Aren't you enjoying London, Cosmo?"

"No, I'm not, Elfreda."

She waited for him to add something to that, and when he didn't she began to tell him what was happening about the magazine and what she and Primrose were trying to do for Alan Axwick. But it all came out badly, the kind of nervous female prattle he probably hated. And then, without any announcement, any warning, in came — larger and noisier than life — Frank Maclaskie.

"Hi — Elfreda! Only got back an hour ago. Say — I'm sorry — must be interrupting something — "

"Professor Saltana — this is Mr. Frank Maclaskie — from Oregon — " She got it out somehow.

"Pleased to meet you, Professor! Heard about you from Elfreda. Nobody at reception out there — so walked straight in — but if you're talking business I'll walk straight out. Just looked in to see if you might be free for lunch, Elfreda."

And Saltana cut in sharply before she could reply. "Consider yourself free for lunch, Elfreda, please. Good day, Mr. Maclaskie." And he went out, stiff-backed, stiff-legged.

Now she wasn't even taking in what Frank was saying. *Saltana was jealous.* Hip-hip-hurray!

### 3

Saltana wasn't conscious of feeling jealous. But he was certainly suspicious, as he told Tuby over the drink and sandwich he'd promised Elfreda. "I don't want these American businessmen nosing around, Owen. I don't trust 'em. I've watched 'em operate in Latin America. One of us must warn Elfreda."

"Then you do it, Cosmo. I'm a poor warner. Nobody believes me. I haven't the face and voice for it. I'm a persuader."

Saltana took a large bite out of his ham sandwich and munched away at it rather drearily. Two young men in dark suits got up together, as if they were about to do a step-dance, and put on narrow-brimmed bowler hats. Their departure gave Saltana a glimpse of a girl who had a white face and lilac lips and looked like a mad clown. Further along, two middle-aged men laughed like hell, probably about nothing. Saltana drank some stout and wished he'd ordered whisky. Outside it was darkish and wettish.

"Say it, Cosmo," said Tuby, smiling. "Denounce something. Spit it out, don't swallow it — and I'm not referring to that sandwich, my friend. You listened to my complaints. Now I'll listen to yours."

Saltana didn't reply at once, just nodded. He began to put his thoughts in order. "Very well, Owen. Now there's going to be nothing wrong with the Institute as a business. With any luck at all we'll soon be earning a lot of money, far more than we thought. I'm worried about myself — not about the Institute."

"I realized that, Cosmo. Spare me nothing. Tell all."

"Apart from the music I can occasionally listen to — and its music is good — I hate this bloody great sodden city. And I need to make some music myself. I've hardly touched my clarinet. In this respect I was better off in Brockshire — "

"In other respects too, as I told you — "

Saltana ignored that. "But I'm beginning to suffer from starvation of the mind, the soul. I'm having to spend more and more time with people I dislike. I can take — and I've enjoyed — peons, peasants, simple people, satisfying their natural appetites. I welcome — as you know — men and women who really think, really feel. But I'm having to move around more and more in a kind of underworld full of people who are neither simple nor subtle but idiotic, people who think they think, imagine they feel, who are armoured in self-deception — " But there he broke off, saying, "Which reminds me, Owen. We must be more and more careful how we divide up our clients. If it's sympathy and tactful handling they need, you must take 'em over immediately. It seems as if they'll get less and less from me."

Tuby looked and then sounded rather anxious. "My end of it, with Elfreda and Primrose ably assisting, what we might call the Sympathetic Department, will soon be taking on almost everybody — unless of course you're expecting enquiries and commissions from some tough types — "

"And I am, I am, Owen. Any day now they'll be arriving. And with them we have a chance of demanding enormous fees, and the Institute really begins to make money."

"And you and I really begin to drink ourselves to death — "

"No, we don't — "

"So — to what end? '*What then?*' sang Plato's ghost. '*What then?*' "
But Tuby was smiling.

Saltana didn't return the smile, though he noticed it. He'd had an idea — or at least the hazily shining nucleus of one. At this moment he didn't even want to work it out himself, let alone talk to Tuby about it. He was content to know it was there, waiting for the mood and the hour. Already he felt different.

They said very little, trudging back to the Institute. Saltana was aware of his idea but not really thinking about it, rather like a man walking round and round an enormous gift-wrapped package. But then, just as they were in sight of Half Moon Street, Tuby apparently felt he had to say something.

"Elfreda's not interested in that American, y'know."

"I never suggested she was. Why should she be? He looked the usual loud-mouthed clot. The point is, we don't want any of these fellows sniffing round the Institute."

"Not yet, certainly," said Tuby rather dreamily. "Not until we're ready to sell it to them." They were now entering their building.

Saltana stopped, clapped a hand on Tuby's shoulder to make him stop too, then bent down and whispered. "You little Welsh sorcerer! Leave my mind alone. You must have other things to read."

Tuby grinned but said nothing. It was just like him, Saltana reflected gratefully as they went towards the lift, to know intuitively when not to pursue a subject. While neither imitating nor admiring it, Tuby respected now a certain half-secretive, half-dramatic element in Saltana's temperament, which made him keep things to himself and then bring out sudden startling announcements about them. Just as he, Saltana, smilingly tolerated Tuby's fairly frequent outbreaks of English-Lit. eloquence. They understood each other, even if this London life hadn't kept them as close as they'd been earlier. And they were now, Saltana told himself, a powerful little team.

Inside the Institute and before they separated to go to their opposite ends of the corridor, Tuby said, "A week ago I was wondering what the devil to do with myself. Now I must work on this Lon Bracton puzzle. And I must also see how the women are going on with the magazine and with our little M.P. By God, Cosmo — *I'm busy*. What about you?"

"Two appointments, both here. A Brigadier Rampside at three — and at four a Mrs. Nan Wolker, representing Pennine Fabrics. Don't know what either of 'em wants. Probably see you before you leave, Owen."

Saltana was glad to see that someone had switched on the bogus computer. Perhaps it could do with a few more green and blue lights. Then, passing Elfreda's door, which was ajar, he caught her voice and Primrose's. So if Elfreda *had* gone out with her American friend, it hadn't been one of those long intimate lunches. But what, if anything, did that prove? He hurried along to his own room, put his feet on the desk, lit a cheroot, and began to think about women.

Brigadier Rampside was a man about fifty, pink and spruce but with rather angry bloodshot eyes, as if he were furious with himself for drinking too much at lunchtime. He explained that he was employed by the Ministry of Defence to do public relations for the Army. "Seen you two or three times on the goggle box, Professor Saltana. Very effective. Put up a poor show myself on television, don't know why. My wife says I look popeyed and sound as if I'm barking, but she could be taking me down a peg or two. You know how they are?"

"Not after marriage, I don't."

"Quite right. I was forgetting. Had you looked up, y'know. Wounded in Western Desert, weren't you, then transferred to Education Corps, then Bureau of Current Affairs? Good record. Just what we want."

"Want for what, Brigadier?"

"This image thing. We're about to spend every penny we can afford on an advertising campaign. Badly in need of the right kind of recruit. Want to offer him an image that'll tempt him. Question is — what image? I said we ought to consult a specialist. Had to argue it for hours. But now — here I am." He smiled, displaying some unusually large white teeth, but then, as Saltana said nothing, looked noble and stern. "You'd like to do something for the old country, wouldn't you, Professor Saltana?"

"Beside the point, isn't it?" Saltana gave him a grim smile. "What you really mean is this. Would I like to do something for nothing for the Ministry of Defence? And the answer is — No, I wouldn't, Brigadier. Are there any newspapers that publish your advertisements for nothing?"

"No — but we do sometimes get a reduction — "

"Then I'll offer you one. I'll go far below the Institute's usual rates. A fee of two hundred and fifty guineas if you accept and decide to use the image we finally work out for you. Meanwhile, what we call a holding fee of fifty guineas. We have to demand a holding fee to protect ourselves against merely frivolous enquiries, people who have some vague idea and want us to work for nothing on it."

"Quite so. Well, I can guarantee your holding fee here and now. To confirm your final fee I'll have to go higher. Wouldn't take a further cut, would you? I'm asking because they will."

"Certainly not," Saltana told him severely. "If you were an ordinary commercial firm, we'd be demanding at least four times as much. I won't even listen to any attempt at bargaining."

"Quite so. I like a fella that knows his own mind. Should be all right, but I have to go through the motions. Now we're pressed — " and he dived for a briefcase — "so I'll leave some of our department bumf with you — advertising and image stuff." He didn't put the file on Saltana's desk but handed it over to him rather solemnly. "Supposed to do it this way. Confidential file. Security — and all that. Balls of course. But Commander Crast's as hot as mustard these days."

"Who's Commander Crast?"

"Now, now, now!" cried the Brigadier playfully. But then he saw that Saltana was serious. "My dear fella, Commander Crast is in charge of *all security*."

"Is he indeed?"

"He *is* indeed."

"Then he's in charge of a lot of expensive rubbish," Saltana declared.

Brigadier Rampside couldn't decide whether to look shocked or delighted, so pulled a face or two, then held out his hand. "I'll be in touch. Press on, much as you can, Professor Saltana." He marched to the door, but once there, he turned. "I'd pay a fiver to hear you tell him that." He chortled, vanished.

Saltana looked rather idly through the file the Brigadier had left. It consisted mostly of reports of meetings, in which men who didn't want to be left out of anything also didn't want to be committed to anything. He pushed the file away, gave a possible army image some thought, made a few notes.

At five-past four Mrs. Nan Wolker, representing Pennine Fabrics, arrived like a pretty little projectile. She was in her late thirties — or might even be forty — and was smallish, smart, fair, and she partly redeemed an aggressively decisive manner by opening wide at him a pair of fine greyish-green eyes. Before he could ask her to sit down, she had drawn up a chair to his desk and was using the eyes at him.

"I imagine you know about Pennine Fabrics, Professor Saltana," she began at once.

"No, I don't, Mrs. Wolker. I only know about images."

"Not a bad line to take if you don't overdo it. Try it on our Sir Herbert — and that might easily happen — and he'd hit the ceiling. And Sir Herbert," she went on, at a great speed but quite clear, no gabbling, "is Sir Herbert Ossett, head of Pennine Fabrics, a West Riding group that produces everything from old-fashioned woollens to the last word in synthetic fabrics. Like this — the latest and not on the market yet." She had pulled some stuff out of a capacious handbag and now spread it on the desk. "What do you think of it? No, don't tell me yet. I must explain why I'm here. I'm in charge of advertising for Pennine Fabrics and I have to work out a campaign for this new product — it's very important and the men up there are already thinking big — and I had an idea I might come direct to you instead of working through our usual agency — " And she had to stop there because she had run out of breath.

"Take it easy, Mrs. Wolker. Our time isn't so valuable. I take it you're here because you're wondering if we might find a suitable image for this fabric. But there's no point in asking me what I think of this stuff. My opinion's worthless." He held up a hand to prevent Mrs. Wolker from starting again, and asked through the intercom for Miss East.

"Oh — of course — Primrose East," cried Mrs. Wolker. "I'd forgotten she was here — and of course — this makes it better still. Very clever of you. That — and not even pretending to know anything about it yourself. I'm surrounded by men who pretend to know everything. Oh — Primrose — hiya! Remember me — Nan Wolker — Pennine Fabrics?"

"Certainly I do, Nan. Lovely to see you. Yes, Professor Saltana?"

"How busy are you along there, Primrose?"

"Up to our necks, all three of us, with that mag — you know — "

"Darling, don't tell me you're finding an image for a new magazine," cried Mrs. Wolker, at once all excited curiosity.

"She's not," Saltana told her severely. "We don't give out that kind of information, Mrs. Wolker. You wouldn't want me to tell the next client who walks in about your new fabric, would you?"

"My God — no! Crushed — and serves me right! Sorry, Primrose dear!"

"Take this stuff along, Primrose, and all three of you have a good look at it. Mrs. Wolker can join you in a few minutes." As Primrose went out, the telephone buzzed. "Yes, she's here," he told it. "For you, Mrs. Wolker."

Whatever the message was, it annoyed Mrs. Wolker. "Oh — what a nuisance — the stupid man! I was probably a fool to ask him anyhow — but now what am I going to do? Look, dear, I won't come back to the office. Hold the fort and phone me at home if anything urgent turns up — no, I'll try to get hold of somebody. 'Bye!" As soon as she had put down the receiver, she did some big eye work on Saltana. "Y'know, if you happen to be free tonight, Professor Saltana, you could do me an enormous favour. I'm giving a tiny dinner party — two couples coming, both the men from the agency that has our account — and now the wretched third man has had to go chasing off to Frankfurt, and I loathe being a man short. Can you take pity on me? *And* eat a dam' good dinner? Can you?"

"I could — yes." Saltana made it slow and thoughtful, like a man about to get out of several pleasant engagements. "What time and where?"

"Oh — bless you! And you mightn't be wasting your time business-wise. Eight o'clock — and here's the address. Black tie if it isn't a nuisance. I don't insist as a rule but I like to keep these agency men up to the mark — and it gives their wives a chance to dress up — poor dears!"

"Black tie then," said Saltana. Then he gave her a hard look. "Just one thing before you go along to talk to Primrose and the other two. We have a strict rule here against anybody being allowed to pick our brains

— for nothing. Dr. Tuby and I may be a pair of simple unsophisticated academics — "

"Stop that! I've heard both of you on the air — and there's a lot of buzz about you going around. If you're just a simple pair of men, then I'm a goose girl. Let's say there's no free brain-picking, then what happens?"

"You pay us a holding fee to start us working on your problem, then a proper fee if you accept the image we've produced for you and decide to make use of it."

"Fair enough! But when it comes to paying out money — real money — then I ought to warn you it won't be just me you'll have to deal with — and oop there in t'West Riding, tha knaws, there's some reight rough tough chaps come into t' picture — "

"Thanks for the warning," said Saltana coldly. "But I think we can look after ourselves here. Before we set up the Institute in London, we had some expert advisers — Jimmy Kilburn for one — you may have heard of him — "

"Of course I have. Now do I go along and talk to the girls? Good! And you'll be there at eight? Lovely! Well, I won't come back because I'll be seeing you then. But will you do one little thing for me before I go, dear Professor Saltana? It'll please me and won't cost you anything. Just stop looking at me like that for a moment — and give me one little smile."

He nodded gravely, looked deep into her eyes, then slowly, slowly smiled. "And if that gives you any pleasure, my dear, you should try my friend and partner, Dr. Tuby, some time. A plump spectacled little man — but in five minutes your senses would be reeling."

"No, no, no, I don't like charmers. But you — my goodness! So don't get run over — or anything. Eight o'clock, then."

Saltana worked for some time on possible Army Images, then decided he ought to consult Owen Tuby, who, though he might not look it, was another old soldier. However, Tuby was still out on his Lon Bracton job, and it was nearly six when he came back. "Tired of sitting in my office, Owen," said Saltana. "Let's go up to the flat. I can give you a drink there."

"No, thank you, Cosmo. We'll have to drink somewhere else. That airport look upstairs does something to me. We'll go to a pub."

"If we can find a quiet corner. Perhaps we ought to join a club."

"Perhaps you ought," Tuby told him. "But I'm not. My experience of clubs is that while pretending to keep out undesirable characters, they wall you in with all the ruthless bores. And I know a quiet corner, not five minutes' walk away."

Once in it they described their afternoons. "I propose to leave Lon Bracton alone for a week or so, then go and polish him off," Tuby concluded. "His chief trouble — and it applies to a lot of other people —

is that he has far too much money for the sense he's got. It's as if a child were given a full-sized locomotive to play with. On twenty pounds a week Bracton would probably be a sensible fellow. With hundreds and hundreds of pounds a week he's insufferable."

"I've often thought that about most of the Americans I've met," said Saltana thoughtfully. "Not the academics, of course. The others. They have more money than they know how to spend properly. Like an adolescent with five pounds a day pocket money. But let's get back to this army thing, Owen. Any preliminary ideas?"

"I've never really concentrated on their advertising, Cosmo. But I'd say, at a venture, they've been appealing too much to self-interest — good pay, good prospects, that sort of thing. As if they were Imperial Chemicals or Shell Oil. I'd be inclined to go the other way. Give the lads an image of a chap who doesn't give a damn — almost a Foreign Legion touch. *He's not afraid* — this is our image chap — *even if you are* — that approach. I'll give this army image some thought. We might insinuate some feminine appeal too, Cosmo. I suspect that girls read all advertisements. It's the important news that they skip. By the way, not much money in this, I imagine."

"Very little. But it might be useful. On the other hand," Saltana continued, "there could be barrels of it from Pennine Fabrics." And he explained about Nan Wolker. "And even if I don't bring it off with them, I assure you, my dear Owen, the money is moving in our direction — you'll see. Now, just one for the road — um?"

Like many another man who has had time to waste before an engagement, Saltana wasted too much of it, so that he didn't arrive at Nan Wolker's place, the upper half of a house in Islington, until nearly quarter-past eight. "I'm very sorry indeed, Mrs. Wolker," he told her gravely. "But I have to depend on taxis and they are hard to find in or near Half Moon Street. Please accept my apologies."

"Not to worry, dear Professor Saltana!" She was wearing a pinkish dress wtih some pale-blue shapes in it — perhaps a triumph of Pennine Fabrics — and was looking much prettier than she had done in the afternoon. "You'll have to hurry over your cocktail, that's all." She led the way into an elaborately Early Victorian sitting room, where an elderly hired-butler type was mixing and handing out drinks. "This is Professor Saltana — at last, and he's very sorry. Sam and Betty Peachtree. Archie and Sara Prest. And I'll leave you to get acquainted while I make sure we're having some dinner."

Saltana was able to swallow two large but rather watery martinis before she reappeared, and to exchange a few blah-blah remarks with his fellow guests. The Peachtrees were Americans about his own age. Betty, who ought to have changed both her names, was tall and gaunt and already waiting to go home. Sam Peachtree, though cleanly shaved and smartly dressed, was one of those Americans who look as if they have been taken out of an Abe Lincoln mould that has been used too often, so that all the fine lines are blurred; and he was immensely solemn. The other two, the Prests, were very different, English and much younger. Sara was a thinnish angry brunette, wearing a scarlet and black dress like a flag she was carrying into battle, for she was obviously in the middle of a quarrel with her husband, Archie. This didn't prejudice Saltana against her, if only because he didn't like Archie's face, which was broad, pink, and owlish — there was enough tortoiseshell on his spectacles to make a jewel case — and he didn't like Archie's voice, which was both nasal and conceited, as if he were a kind of Oxbridge-don-adman.

Just before she took them into the dining room, Nan Wolker pretended to show Saltana a picture and whispered rapidly: "You can't sit next to me at dinner. It won't work out. And I daren't monopolise you after dinner. So stay on. They'll all go fairly early. And we've lots to talk about, haven't we?"

"Certainly," said Saltana.

So he sat between Mrs. Peachtree and Sara Prest, who started on him as soon as they were spooning away at their avocados. "I saw you twice on the telly, Professor Saltana, and I thought you were absolutely fab. And I can't understand," she continued, raising her voice so that Archie might hear it, "I simply *can't* understand why you're going in for advertising. Why — *why?*"

"If you mean advertising myself and the Institute, Mrs. Prest, I do it simply because it has to be done. We're new, we may not be around very long, so we have to be talked about."

"No, that's all right. I understand *that*. I mean the ad business." Another shot at Archie, no doubt.

"We're not in the ad business. We're in the image business. Most of our clients at the moment have nothing to do with advertising. But of course if agencies and advertisers want to make use of our expertise, they can do so — that is, if they're ready to pay the fees we ask."

Glancing across the table, Saltana caught an enquiring look from Nan Wolker. He wasn't quite sure what it meant so he gave her a smile, to which she made an immediate dazzling reply.

Archie, who had been listening, took charge now. "If you want to put it like that, Professor, that's okay with me. But I think you'll agree with me and my colleague Sam Peachtree here that quite apart from what we do for commerce and merchandising, we admen today are responsible for a great public service. That's right, isn't it, Sam?"

Sam waited a moment and then made his announcement in a deep hollow tone, quite impersonal, as if he had turned himself into a talking town-hall clock. "With an aggressive outreach — chance of major breakthrough with new programming thrust." There, without looking at anybody, he stopped, as a clock might stop striking the hour.

Making nothing out of Sam's performance, not even sure he had heard him properly, Saltana now looked at Archie, who was staring at him expectantly. "Dr. Tuby and I aren't like you. We aren't responsible for any great public service. We're just in it for the money."

Sara Prest gave a triumphant little yelp and cried, "Professor, I love you."

"None of that, Sara!" This was their hostess. "I found him — and he's mine."

Archie frowned on them. "We're trying to have a little serious conversation here. Values — and all that — eh, Sam?"

After another pause, Sam struck again, announcing something that sounded to Saltana like "Dynamic progressiveness and educational-awareness experience."

"Finish your alligator pear, Sam," his wife told him. "The man wants to clear." And indeed the hired-butler type was now hovering around. There was nothing but blah-blah until the duck with orange sauce had been served, and Saltana found himself drinking some excellent claret. He raised his glass to Nan Wolker, as a tribute to her taste, and she sparkled back at him.

But Archie insisted upon some serious conversation. "I couldn't go on if I didn't believe I was performing a great public service — "

"It does you credit, Mr. Prest," Saltana told him smoothly.

"And neither could Sam, I know — "

"More tie-in and feedback incremental." And if Sam didn't announce this, Saltana seemed to hear something like it. He began to feel that Sam must be quietly and solemnly out of his mind.

"Hold it a minute, Sam." Archie looked accusingly again at Saltana. "Look here, has my wife put you up to this? No, no, leave that. But don't tell me there's nothing in it for you but the money."

"No, I must modify that — "

"Oh — no, Professor, you're disappointing me now." And this came, at his elbow, from Sara Prest.

"Then I'm sorry." Saltana gave her a small smile. "But there is something else. Tuby and I, just a pair of obscure academics, have managed to acquire a certain amount of new knowledge and a specialised skill, and we like to show off. Perhaps Tuby enjoys it more than I do, but then I'm rather more conceited than he is."

"Haven't you a wife?" Sara demanded.

"Not yet — no."

"What a waste!" She appealed to Nan Wolker. "I mean, fancy having a husband who could just talk like that — instead of pretending all the time!"

Archie was about to make an angry reply, but Nan came in smartly with a question addressed both to him and to Sam. This made it possible for Saltana to talk quietly to Sara Prest.

"My dear, you're obviously in the middle of a domestic quarrel," he told her, "but that's no reason why you should use me as a stick to beat your husband with. You've made him thoroughly dislike me now — and that could be a nuisance. I may have to collaborate with him."

"If you mean — about Pennine Fabrics, you haven't to worry. If Nan likes you — and she obviously does — she can go right above Archie's head. And he's terrified they may lose the account. He's always terrified about something, and then he pretends and boasts harder than ever. But I oughtn't to have said what I did — and I'm sorry. I know it's all wrong, but when I'm really angry I'll hit anybody with anything. But I was talking to Nan as well. And she knew what I meant all right, because Ronnie Wolker was even worse than Archie. I don't suppose you knew him, did you?"

"Never heard of him. I only met Nan Wolker this afternoon — she came to see me on business, heard that a man had dropped out of this party, and begged me to take his place. Is she widowed, divorced, separated — what?"

"She divorced him, then he went out to join an agency in Australia. Nan's not really a friend of mine. She's too much the businesswoman, never letting go, working all the time, and of course she has to be tough as an old boot with that Pennine lot. They may even frighten *you*, Professor Saltana."

Saltana stopped listening after this and began to feel a weight of boredom, which never left him even when they returned to the sitting room for coffee and brandy and he enjoyed the cigar that Sam Peachtree presented him with, as a kind of prize for listening without protest to the Peachtree solemn imbecilities. He answered politely when spoken to but ventured nothing himself, except to exchange a few glances with his hostess. And though he accepted every drink he was offered, emptying his glass fairly quickly, all that happened was that the boredom soon came to be darkly tinged with melancholy. Not for the first time, for during the last weeks he had sat through many dinner parties of this sort, he asked himself bleakly what the hell he thought he was doing.

Sara and Mrs. Peachtree took their husbands away at about ten-thirty. After seeing them out, Nan didn't return for a few minutes. The cigar Sam had given him was really too large and now was getting soggy, so Saltana threw it into the fire, then stayed on his feet and stared with disgust at three simpering china cows on a corner shelf. Nan came in wheeling a little drink trolley; she was wearing a greenish-blueish house-coat and slippers now, and looked different for the second time that evening; and as soon as he had taken in her new appearance she switched off all the lights except one standard lamp, well away from the fireplace.

"I can't call you Professor, it sounds ridiculous. So what, then?"

"Just *Saltana*. But as I find Wolker awkward, I'll take leave to call you Nan. A drink?"

"A very weak whisky, please! And do help yourself to a much stronger one." She settled into the armchair like a cat. He gave her a nod and went to the drink trolley. She waited a moment and then called out, "Well, you helped me out — and you were bored. I'm sorry, Saltana."

"And I'm sorry if it was so obvious. You promised me a good dinner and you gave me one. Thank you, Nan. *You* weren't boring me, of course. It was the company. Mrs. Peachtree had nothing to say. Sam seemed to me a kind of solemn imbecile. And the Prests were too busy continuing the quarrel they'd begun probably while they were dressing."

"They've been at it on and off for months and months. It's not doing Archie's work any good. He's a fool but he knew how to handle his accounts. I gave Sara a strong hint about not making him feel she despises him. After all, she enjoys spending the money he earns. What was she saying to you about me, Saltana? I know I was being mentioned."

"Yes, but nothing really hostile, no malice. You were rather too much the businesswoman for her, working all the time, toughened by Pennine types. That line, but no spite in it. She also said that your ex-husband — Ronnie, isn't it? — was even worse than Archie."

"About the same," said Nan coolly. "But I got rid of him whereas Sara, with two children, is stuck with Archie. But either she ought to leave him or stop despising him. Women oughtn't to live with men if they can't respect them. You agree, don't you?"

"Certainly." Saltana stretched out his legs towards the fire, now very much alive in the half-light, drank some whisky, and felt rather sleepy.

Nan probably noticed this because now she spoke quite sharply. "Saltana, I'm not objecting to those women of yours at the Institute. They may come up with some interesting ideas. But let's get this straight. I'm not going to ask Pennine to pay you a whacking great fee on *their* work. You mentioned your knowledge and skill at dinner — well, if any big fee's going to be demanded, it'll have to pay for *you* and not simply for something the girls may cook up. Is that understood?"

He sat up and stared at her. "Tuby and I know more about images than the women do, though by this time they know a good deal about them. But because your enquiry begins with a new fabric, you talk to the women first. They know about fabrics, we don't. But at some point — that is, if you don't find us too expensive or if we don't consider you too troublesome and demanding — I'll take over. Or if I'm too busy, Tuby will. It's really more his kind of thing — "

"No, it isn't. I don't want a charmer — "

"Or we may do some work on it together," he went on, as if she hadn't spoken. "Incidentally, as you've mentioned a fee, I must tell you that it will be decided by Mrs. Elfreda Drake, who's responsible for all the Institute finances. So then you'll be back, whether you like it or not, with your own sex. Well — now — " And, rather slowly and impressively he got up.

If she had been sitting like a cat, she now sprang like one, and before he could make any further move she was pushing him back into his chair. "No, you're not going like that, you devil! You know very well I only talked like that because you were beginning to look bored again, and I wanted to wake you up. And I was loving it just before that. Being cosy for once — talking about anything — with a real man. Look — will you do something for me? And this isn't a bitchy pass — I'm not that type at all." He was now leaning back in his chair and she was sitting on the arm of it. "Just hold me in your arms — and talk — about anything — where you've been — what you've done — anything. Just talk — not sex. Will you — please?"

She made a move but he checked her gently. "It's all very well to say *No sex,* my dear — " and he spoke gently too — "but you're an attractive woman and I have the normal male reactions. In a way you're insulting both of us."

"Oh — if you must have sex," she cried impatiently, "then take it, grab it, get on and get done with it! But we'll be different creatures — sweating and panting and moaning — and I want us as we are." She had found an appealing tone now. "Please — Saltana! I'll never forget it if you do this for me. Just hold me — and talk — about anything — it doesn't matter."

And though he would have betted against it, that was exactly what he did. In half an hour she was asleep, and he would soon have been sleeping too if his arms and legs hadn't ached. Finally he had to try to disengage himself. She opened her eyes, smiled dreamily, and murmured her thanks. She was now lying in the chair and he was standing up, moving his arms and legs out of their cramp. He told her it was time he went home.

Then suddenly she was out of the chair and apparently wide awake. Her manner and tone were as briskly impersonal as they had been when she had first walked into his office. "I'll ring your Mrs. Drake some time tomorrow and unless your preliminary fee — holding fee, isn't it? — is outrageous, I'll pay it so that you can go ahead. I want you to work fast because Sir Herbert Ossett, head of Pennine Fabrics, may be in London towards the end of next week. Meanwhile, I'll be in touch."

He let that pass, not reminding her, not even by a look, that they had been so closely in touch for the last forty-five minutes that his arms and legs still ached. He merely nodded. "Excellent! And thank you for an unusually good dinner. By the way, who cooked it?"

"I did. I always do."

"I can see you're an extremely capable woman," Saltana told her, smiling. "Thank you again — and — goodnight!" It would have spoilt the odd little scene to have mentioned transport, ringing for a taxi, that sort of thing. So he had plenty of time, trying to find a taxi on a raw midnight in Islington, to wonder both at Nan Wolker and at himself —

the last man, he would have said of himself, to agree to some platonic
nonsense late in the evening, arriving too in a period of abstinence. Did
he only tell himself this woman was attractive? Was there a lack of that
mysterious but essential polarity? Or was there now something wrong
with Cosmo Saltana?

He was kept busy all next morning. He spent the first hour with
Tuby, working on the army image and then telephoning Brigadier Rampside. A man called Lingston, advertising manager of Bevs Ltd, rang up
to make an appointment, because he was planning a campaign for a new
drink, Bobbly, that might need a special image. Then he summoned the
women to tell him what they thought of the Pennine Fabrics material
that Mrs. Wolker had left with them. They were enthusiastic about the
stuff, were unanimously agreed that any image associated with it would
have to be feminine, but couldn't decide if the appeal should be directed
to the twenties, the thirties, or the forties. Finding this altogether too
feminine for him in his present mood, Saltana told them to take their
problem to Tuby, this in spite of their protests that Tuby was fully
engaged.

"I know Owen Tuby better than you do," he told them sharply, facing their accusing gaze with his conscience pricking him. "And he loves
it. He was grumbling only the other day that he hadn't enough to do."
Fortunately, just as Mrs. Mere was about to be severe with him, he had
to take a call on the phone and was able to wave them away.

It was from Radley, a television producer he had worked with once
before. "We need you tonight if you can make it, Professor Saltana. And
I hope to God you can — we're rather stumped. We're doing the first of
four monthly programmes with Professor Cally of Brockshire University,
who's very good value on the box. I think you know him, don't you?"

"I know him — yes. Does he want to talk to me on your TV?"

"He talks to three people, different types, and one of tonight's three,
a psychologist, rang me this morning to say he couldn't make it — thinks
he has 'flu. I've spoken to Cally, and as we're in a fix he says he's ready
to take you on about this image thing — and of course we'd love it, especially as the other two tonight are on the dull side — "

"A hundred guineas."

"Oh — well — I don't know if our contracts people could wear
that. The other two — "

"A hundred guineas," Saltana repeated firmly. "I won't be shouted
at by Cally, who's an ass, for anything less."

"I'll call you back."

So about ten o'clock that night, Saltana, accompanied (at his urgent request) by his friend and colleague, Dr. Owen Tuby, who had already almost hypnotised Radley's pretty assistant, Clarice Something, was
drinking large whiskies at Television Centre. They were there for some
preliminary talk before the programme, which went on the air at 10:35.

The other two people who had to face Professor Cally were a female iron-side who was an authority on housing, a Mrs. Prake, and a Dr. Sittle, who was a Medical Officer of Health for somewhere; and they were now talking as eagerly to Cally as if their lives depended on it. Saltana was standing apart, drinking steadily and smoking a cheroot, and was telling himself how important this place was and how fatuous it was. He was also trying to listen in to some whispers between Tuby and the pretty Clarice, who were not far away and seemed to be arranging to see the programme together in a small viewing room. Then Radley, who had been buzzing around the place like a lost bumblebee, settled on to Saltana.

"Sure you wouldn't like to work things out with Cally before we go down?" Radley sounded anxious, but then he always sounded anxious.

"No, he's very happy with those two," Saltana replied carelessly. "But you oughtn't to have made him up. You ought to have made him down. All that bone! More than ever, as Tuby was saying. It'll look like a programme on Death."

"Look here — is it true that you and Cally were at loggerheads down there in Brockshire? It is, isn't it? Well, I think I ought to warn you that he's ready to go for you on this image thing. Of course we all like a ding-dong on the box — it's good TV — "

"No, it isn't, Radley," said Saltana quite pleasantly. "You people and the journalists may enjoy it. I don't believe the average viewer does. Why should he? There he is in his slippers with a beer or a cup of co-coa, longing for a quiet life, and suddenly, just off his hearth rug, there have arrived a couple of fellows interrupting each other, shouting at each other, getting angrier and angrier. He doesn't want that at work or in a pub, let alone at home, late in the evening. I suggest you people look into this. And don't imagine I propose to behave like that on the air, whatever that ass Cally says."

"Quite so," said Tuby as he joined them. "I gather you propose to keep your temper, Cosmo."

"Certainly. Cally can do the shouting. He shouts, anyhow."

Under the studio lights, which always made Saltana feel idiotic, the three of them sat in a row, with Ironside Prake in the middle and Sal-tana on her right, facing Cally, now so much gleaming bone. The first programme in the Professor Cally series, *One Man Wants To Know,* went on the air. Cally shouted some preliminary nonsense at all three of them — and at several million viewers — and then concentrated on Dr. Sittle, a good choice because he was nervous and even duller than Cally. Saltana listened idly, still feeling idiotic. The duet with Mrs. Prake was far more entertaining. She was much tougher than Dr. Sittle; indeed she was tougher than Cally, probably tougher than anybody else in the build-ing. And because Cally shouted, she shouted, probably under the impres-sion that everybody, except poor Dr. Sittle, shouted on television; and the pair of them made so much noise that a young man with a beard and an orange shirt arrived, just outside the cameras' range, to flap his hands at them. This didn't worry Mrs. Prake — perhaps she never noticed him — but it rattled Cally, who lost any chance he might have had of talking Mrs. Prake down.

Turning to Saltana, Cally began by telling Saltana who Saltana was. "You are Professor Saltana, Director of the so-called *Institute of Social Imagistics.*"

"And you," said Saltana quietly and smoothly, "are Professor Cally of the so-called University of Brockshire." And Saltana stared at him, hoping he'd challenge this *so-called.*

Cally hesitated, then avoided the trap. "Now then, Professor Saltana, with all due respect," he shouted, not showing any sign of respect, due or otherwise, "I must tell you I'm opposed to all this fuss about images."

"I don't blame you."

"You *don't?*" And Cally wasn't pretending to feel astounded.

"Certainly not. Too much fuss about images. Too much fuss about advertising. Too much fuss about television." And wearing a rueful little smile, Saltana shook his head.

Cally looked annoyed. A mistake. "We can leave out television — "

But Saltana cut in, not by raising his voice but by sharpening its tone. "Not if we're discussing images, we can't." Again, the rueful little smile.

"Television," Cally shouted, "is merely another means of communication. Images don't necessarily come into it. We can have television without all this talk about images."

"Professor Cally," Saltana told him rather sadly, "you and I seem to be living in different worlds."

"If you mean that I still live in the academic world and now you don't, I'll agree with you, Professor Saltana. And in *my* world we don't think it necessary to pretend to have any expertise about images."

"Not even when you use television, Professor Cally?" Saltana's manner and tone were quiet and courteous, that of a man trying hard to understand and be helpful.

Cally had either to adopt the same manner and tone or bluster away and obviously be more offensive. The trap was there and immediately he fell into it. "A means of communication is one thing," he shouted, "and nonsense about images is something very different. I'll admit we read and hear a lot of rubbishy gossip about them — "

"You're referring chiefly to the Press now, are you, Professor Cally?" Still quiet, courteous, trying to be helpful.

But Cally avoided that trap. "What I'm saying is that to any conscientious sociologist or social scientist, any pretense of making a special study of images, of creating an expertise of images, is nothing more than pretentious nonsense."

"You mean that my colleagues and I at the Institute," Saltana told him, smiling, "are simply so many charlatans — um?"

"I'm not going as far as that. You're putting words into my mouth."

"I'd hate to do that, Professor Cally. But of course in one strict sense, we *are* charlatans — "

"You're saying it, Professor Saltana, I'm not — "

"But then in the same strict sense, belonging to an intelligent world fast disappearing, you're a charlatan too — we're *all* charlatans." Here Cally tried to interrupt but Saltana, glaring and thundering now, stopped him. "*You* ought to be with your students. *I* ought to be teaching philosophy. But in a world that insists upon writing and talking about images, my colleagues and I are prepared to offer for sale some expert advice." He caught sight of the orange-shirted young man gesturing again. "And that's all I have to say to you, Professor Cally."

And Cally had to wind up, promising another interesting discussion in a month's time. *And until then* — whatever that meant — *goodnight!*

They had been asked to talk to each other until the picture faded out, and while Cally leant forward to nod and jabber at Dr. Sittle, Saltana and Mrs. Prake exchanged a few whispers. "I say, you gave it to him hot and strong, didn't you, Professor Saltana? Man's rather a fool though, don't you think?"

"I do. But then we'd met already, down in Brockshire. Are you going back to the Hospitality Department for another drink, Mrs. Prake?"

"Can't have another because I didn't have one before. But I'm not going up there again. Late for me — must be toddling along."

Saltana found his own way back to the whisky. Tuby was already there, with a rather flushed and bright-eyed Clarice. "Oh, Professor Saltana," she cried, "Dr. Tuby and I loved it."

"Loved what?" Saltana enquired gravely.

Tuby jumped in. "Cally asked for it, of course. Where is he? Or have all those three gone home? Where they belong, of course. Clarice says I ought to leave sound radio for television. I've pointed out that I'm easier to listen to than to look at. Ah — here's Radley. Are you happy, Mr. Radley?"

"The usual please, Clarice. Fairly happy, Dr. Tuby. By the way, I've never heard you on steam radio — never listen — but I'm told you're wonderful. Now why don't you come over to the box — team up for a series with Professor Saltana?"

"Running short of cross-talk comedians, are you?" said Tuby, smiling. "Well, I'm willing to try."

"Any time — for me," said Saltana.

"Let me think about this. Oh — thank you, Clarice. If I could set up a series for you both, it would have to start some time late in the autumn — or early next year. Why — what's the matter?" For Radley saw that both men were shaking their heads.

"We can't guarantee to be available late in the autumn, my dear fellow," Saltana told him very quietly. "Can we, Owen?"

"I'm afraid not, Cosmo."

"Oh — now — come off it," Radley protested. "Not joining the brain drain, are you?"

"No, no," said Tuby gently. "But perhaps coming off it. Clarice my dear, just another touch of whisky for Professor Saltana and me before we venture into the cold night."

When they were in the taxi that had been provided for them, Saltana said to Tuby, "Owen, did you happen to notice that bulky fellow in the raincoat — the one with the large ginger moustache — "?

"You mean the one with the cap and the car too small for him? Yes, why?"

"He was in the pub at lunchtime. Now he's here. It could be a coincidence, but something seems to tell me it isn't. I'll try a different pub tomorrow — and if he's there I'll ask him what he thinks he's doing."

Saltana had a busy morning and it was only at the last moment, when he and Tuby left the Institute together, that he remembered they had to try a different pub. He mentioned this to Tuby as they turned into Curzon Street.

"Oh — he'll be there, I think," Tuby replied. "Don't look now, but I noticed his little car. I've been followed before, Cosmo, haven't you?"

"Weeks on end. I've taught in places where anybody wearing a collar and tie is liable to be shadowed by the secret police. However, it's a new experience in London."

Ten minutes later, in a pub that wasn't too crowded, they took their drinks and sandwiches across the room to where, in the far corner, the bulky-raincoat–ginger-moustache–cap-too-small man was gloomily nursing a half-empty glass of bitter.

"Finish that," Saltana told him pleasantly, "and have a drink with me."

"Ta very much, old boy!" And he called at once for a double whisky. "Don't even like beer — but what the hell are you to do? Cheers!"

"Cheers! But isn't it rather stupid, giving you this job? You're so conspicuous, y'know."

He winked at them. "Stick out a mile, don't I? Tried a silk hat and wedding gear one time, but, as I told 'em, this is just as good and a dam' sight cheaper. More convenient as well, naturally." And he winked again. Saltana raised his eyebrows at Tuby.

"They were rather more subtle in the East, Cosmo. I've come across this one before. Our friend's job is to attract your attention. But also to *distract* it. Because he's around, you never notice the one who's *really* keeping you under constant observation. It's an old Chinese trick."

"Never been near China." But he winked again.

"Let's forget about China," said Saltana severely. "I don't care if there's one of you or two of you following me around, I know it's intolerable. Who employs you?"

"I'm not talking, old boy. But — " and he went into a hoarse whisper — "I can set your mind at rest on one point. It's not divorce business." He ended with an enormous wink.

On their way back to Half Moon House, Saltana suddenly remembered what Brigadier Rampside had said when he had handed over that file. "Owen, I've got it," he declared. "It's this dam' *security* nonsense. Commander Thing — I've forgotten his name. Secret Service — for God's sake! Counter-espionage! I'll ring up Rampside and tell him either he stops this nonsense or creates an army image himself."

"Quite right, Cosmo. Pity if we have to drop it, though," Tuby went on. "Only waiting now for young Phil Rawbin to provide us with a photograph or a sketch — the recruit who doesn't want to be a bank clerk or an insurance man. So try to keep your temper, Director."

Half the afternoon had gone before Saltana was able to speak to the Brigadier. After he had described, with sardonic emphasis, their encounter with Ginger Moustache, he continued: "Now Dr. Tuby and I think we have what you need — and we're only waiting to show you a photograph or sketch. But you won't get a dam' thing from us, Brigadier, unless these idiot bloodhounds are called off."

"It's this security thing, of course." Rampside sounded weary. "All bull and balls, I agree. But that's Commander Crast — "

"Get me an appointment with him as soon as you can," Saltana demanded. "You can go with me, of course — "

"You couldn't stop me." The Brigadier sounded livelier now. "Tomorrow morning, perhaps. Anyhow I'll see what I can do."

Next morning they were kept waiting nearly half an hour, to Saltana's increasing annoyance, before being admitted into the presence of Commander Crast, M.P., who was directly responsible to the Cabinet for all security. He was a short broad man with no neck, a bald head, and a face in which everything appeared to have been folded away, like a draper's shop after closing time. He knew Brigadier Rampside, of course, and greeted him with some faint approach to cordiality. But so far as he acknowledged Saltana's existence, it was chiefly to suggest he didn't like the look of him. It seemed improbable that he would ever consent to listen to anything that Saltana might say.

While Commander Crast was busy cleaning a pipe, the Brigadier explained what the Institute was doing for him. "And Professor Saltana has discovered he's now under surveillance, strongly objects to it, and has told me that if it continues he won't finish the work he's started for us — "

"And undertaken, as a favour, at an exceptionally low fee," Saltana put in.

Commander Crast, now blowing through his pipe, didn't even glance in Saltana's direction. "Routine security measures, Brigadier Rampside. Very properly you reported handing over to this man a Ministry of Defence confidential file. We have no security check on him. We can't help wondering if a Professor Saltana should be in possession of a confidential file. So we put into operation certain routine measures." He was filling his pipe now, and not as a routine operation but carefully, lovingly.

"But, Commander, this file only contained minutes of meetings about army public relations and advertising — "

"No doubt. But suppose one of these newspapermen took a look through it. Can't you see the headline — *How They Waste Their Time And Our Money?* And what if the agent of a foreign power read it? *You* don't know what they might get out of it. *You* don't have to think in terms of our national security — I *do*."

"Could you possibly take your mind off it for a moment or two?" Saltana asked in a dangerously quiet tone. "I am *here,* you know. So perhaps I might be allowed to say something."

The Commander's pipe was going well. "Go ahead. But don't bother wasting sarcasm on me. Water off a duck's back. I have a big job to do — and you ought to know as well as I do how important it is."

"I don't, though. How important is it?"

The Commander took out his pipe, perhaps to help him to stare harder at Saltana. "I'm talking about *national security*."

"So am I," said Saltana quite pleasantly. "And as I've already told Brigadier Rampside, I think it's a lot of expensive rubbish."

"Then I haven't to waste any more time listening to you, have I? You can go out that way — it's quicker." The Commander turned to Rampside. "Well — now, Brigadier — "

"He can't tell you anything." Without shouting, Saltana, once he was roused, could produce a curiously penetrating tone not to be topped by anything short of a bellow. "*And I can.* It's this. In five minutes I shall go back to the Institute, immediately cancel the work we've done for Brigadier Rampside, and then ask all our staff to tell their friends in the Press, radio, and television exactly what has happened. In fact, we'll set up a press conference — "

"My God — no — Saltana!" The cry came from the Brigadier's heart.

The Commander tried to say something, but Saltana was too quick, penetrating, impressive.

"No, you'll listen to me, my friend. I've thought for years that all this security and espionage and counter-espionage and shadowings and passwords and disguises was just so much damned nonsense. I object to being taxed a shilling to pay for it. Keep it where it belongs — in paperbacks, on cinema screens. The only security worth having is the common belief that you're living in a civilized country under a sensible government."

"*Shut up!*" It needed a bellow and now the Commander jumping up, had produced one.

"Certainly not. I thought I'd done with these imbecilities when I left Latin America. But you're even more extravagant and stupider than they are. Having me followed by these idiots! Wasting the money we give you! When I remember you've already had Russian agents helping to run the Foreign Office — "

"That's why I'm here, you fool," the Commander bellowed. And slapped his desk.

Saltana leant over and gave the desk a harder slap. "If I'd more time to waste, I'd ask you what difference it made. Why don't you get into films and paperbacks? Then you'd earn some money instead of spending ours." The Commander was pressing buzzers and ringing bells now. Saltana, upright again, turned to Rampside. "I'll give you half an hour, Brigadier. After that, I spill everything."

And he marched out, deliberately ignoring the door that Crast had indicated. He had to stalk through three different offices, and he muttered in Spanish all the way to the front door, just to give them something to report to the Commander, the little fat spider in the web of lunacy.

## 4

Tuby was working on some notes the women had given him about the new magazine, when Saltana burst in, triumphant.

"Our Army stuff won't be wasted, Owen," he announced. "Rampside just called me. But I must tell you the whole story." And Tuby delighted in every moment of it. "So there we are," said Saltana, getting up. "And we ought to celebrate this victory over the forces of darkness and imbecility. Are you free for lunch? Good! Well, for once we'll have a dam' good lunch, Owen. I can afford it. After all, I earned a hundred guineas the other night, just for rebuking that portentous ass, Cally — something I'd have been glad to do for nothing. So we lunch. What are you doing this afternoon? Nothing that calls for strict sobriety, I hope?"

"On the contrary," said Tuby, smiling. "I'm going with Wilf Orange, the agent, to attend — for the last time — to Lon Bracton, the comedian. I propose to finish him off. I'm tired of him. So not only is sobriety not called for, it would amount to a serious disadvantage."

And Saltana went bustling out, leaving Tuby to think — rather idly now — about the new magazine. The women were rather vague about an image for the magazine itself — after all, so far they had seen only a half-empty dummy. But each of them knew what she wanted for an image of the magazine's ideal reader. Mrs. Mere saw her as a tall and rather stern wife and mother; Elfreda preferred a well-to-do woman of about forty, with no obvious domestic background; and Primrose demanded a fashionable youngish girl, unmarried, independent, perhaps a model. Grinning, Tuby added a note of his own: *What about a smallish, plumpish man about fifty? He might even wear spectacles.*

He and Saltana ate and drank very well indeed, and not five minutes' walk from Half Moon House. Tuby strolled up just in time to see Wilf Orange arrive in the same large car he had used before. Wilf knew a man who'd had a good lunch when he met one. "You've been doing all right, Doc," he declared at once. "Lotsa good stuff been going down the hatch, eh? I can tell. As for me — a glass of milk and two bananas. But I'm not bittter. Nobody can say Wilf Orange is bitter. But what are you going to tell Lon this afternoon?"

Tuby was smoking an expensive cigar, which Saltana had compelled him to accept because pipes were not allowed where they had been lunching. He always felt self-conscious when he was smoking this kind of cigar, belonging to another world; he saw himself as halfway towards being a rich and cynical man of affairs, perhaps yawning on a yacht after a £35,000,000 take-over bid.

"Wilf, I'm going to tell your friend Lon Bracton that I'm seeing him for the last time. Now he must take it or leave it. If he doesn't accept the advice I give him, then I'm through with him."

"Never works with Lon. Can't make him accept a straight *either-or*. I gave it up two years ago. Might as well ask a jellyfish to toe the line. He'll never wear it, Doc. Sorry — 'cos of course I'm on your side — right from the start I was."

"Well, we shall see, Wilf. But I do beg you to back me up, show him you're on my side. And — believe me — I wouldn't ask this if I didn't feel that what I'm going to suggest is the only way out for him. Best for him, for you, for me, for everybody." And Tuby, half-closing his eyes, puffed away, feeling richer than ever, more cynical, more the razor-sharp man of business.

"You're making sense to me, Doc, even if I don't know what you have in mind. And another thing. You settle Lon this afternoon, you leave him happy, and I take you straight to Meldy Glebe. Remember me telling you about her, first time we met? Well, I have her lined up for you as soon as Lon's out of the way. I've mentioned you and she's already curious. And don't think that's not remarkable. You don't run a jet, you don't talk money, terms, and deals, and you don't mix fancy drinks, yet she's innarested. And if you knew Meldy, that would surprise you."

"It does. Though you're wrong on one point, Wilf. I *can* mix fancy drinks. Picked it up out East. But let me concentrate on Lon Bracton." And closing his eyes, Tuby almost immediately went to sleep.

Bracton's flat, on the top floor of a new block in Portland Place, was nearly all sitting room. It was an enormous and detestable room, very sparsely furnished but very untidy, littered with television and radio sets, record-players and records, unread books and all manner of gadgets and rubbish. The last time, the very last time, Tuby told himself, surveying it with disgust. Lon Bracton — very tall and lean with a crooked nose, mouth, and chin — was wearing a gaudy but rather dirty dressing-gown, and was attended by a young blonde, also looking rather dirty; and Tuby couldn't decide if this was the fourth he had seen here or if Lon had now gone back to the first one, for they all looked alike. The blonde, who held Lon's hand, looked as if she had just been hypnotised and told to keep her mouth wide open.

"I know, Dr. Tuby, I know," said Lon in his usual grunt-and-squeak voice. "Written all over you, man. Give poor old Lon up as a bad job. Nothing to be done with him. Can't straighten the poor sod out to make a good image. Eh — eh — eh? Not blaming you — not blaming you at all."

"No, Lon," Tuby began calmly. "Your intuition isn't working this afternoon. You're a mile out. I haven't come to give up your case. I've come to settle it." He gave both men a confident smile. "Lon, we never got anywhere because we were moving in the wrong direction. Partly your fault, but mostly mine." Tuby waited a moment. "I ought to have ignored the fact that you'd had two analysts working on you — "

"But I told you they didn't do me any good — didn't I — eh — eh?"

"Certainly you did, Lon. But they made me look in the wrong direction. Suppose they had succeeded and turned you into a solid decent reliable citizen — how long do you think *you'd* have lasted at the Palladium? Thank God they didn't succeed! So — you're not quiet, not well behaved, not reliable — you're neurotic. Most artists and performers are. Otherwise, they'd be doing something else — something quieter, solider, more dependable. But you're in the one market where a neurosis fetches a high price — "

"Okay, okay, I've got your point. But I don't *want* a neurosis. I don't *enjoy* being neurotic — eh — eh?"

"And that's where you sent me off in the wrong direction, Lon. That's why I couldn't find the right image for you. But I have it now. It's that of a *very neurotic man*. On the stage and screen or off them. You're a neurotic man who plays an even more neurotic man. Instead of trying to fight it, you go right along with it. Any audience you have will always have its share of neurotic people, but you, Lon Bracton, will never fail to

seem a dam' sight worse than they are. And they'll tell one another —
not just the neurotic types but the whole lot of them — that Lon Bracton's
just as barmy off the stage as he is on it — crackers — bonkers! And as
long as you watch your timing — and you know all about that, Lon —
you can go on and do almost anything you like — and they'll love it. You
could eat your supper and read the evening paper on the stage — and
they'd still love it — "

"Eh — eh — eh — eh!" He grinned at Tuby in his crooked fashion, his mouth going one way, his nose another; then he looked at Wilf
Orange. "It's here, Wilf. He's got something."

"Of course he's got something. Knew he would have, right from the
start. Anything else, Doc?"

"Certainly." This was decisive enough, but then Tuby hesitated a
moment. "Lon, I wonder if Miss — er — could leave us for a few minutes — ?"

"Why not — eh — eh? Budgy, go and wash your hair— or something — "

"Oh — Lon —I wanta listen— "

"Go and have a bath— not dangerous and might do you good —
try it — "

There was a little more of this. Tuby waited patiently. He had to
convince Bracton now or give it up, taking back to the Institute the story
of a defeat. "Now let me make this quite clear, Lon. You go along with
the neurosis instead of trying to fight it. You're the neurotic comedian.
That's your image whether you're performing or not. From now on, you
don't suppress your neurotic condition, you exploit it. You don't try to
behave normally and rationally and then do something enormously silly
— like breaking a contract — you indulge your whims and fancies all
the time. And if you do that, you'll probably be quite sensible about
important things."

"That'll be the day," cried Wilf. "Sorry, Doc!"

"Shut up then — eh? I'm with you so far," he told Tuby. "But why
turn Budgy out? Sex coming into it now — eh — eh?"

"It would help this image," said Tuby carefully, "if you stopped
messing about with these kids and married a real woman — "

"Oh — no, no — never! I know me — and I'm a lecherous sod. I
like plenty of it — and all young and tender — eh?"

"Lon, I know a lot more about this than you do," Tuby told him
sternly. "One night with a real woman— and I'll bet you've never had
one — would be worth more, even lecherously, than a hundred nights
with these flipperty bits, who aren't your size and weight. There's no
genuine polarity, Lon. And that's where making love really starts. Two
persons, not one person and just a squeal and wriggle. And then there's
the image to be considered. A very neurotic man needs a solid sensible
wife. If she happens to be an actress, all the better; she'll know how to

play her part, exactly what to say to interviewers. If I were in your place, Lon, I'd begin looking around for an attractive, good-hearted but solid character actress about thirty-five — and then marry her. And the wedding can be as eccentric as you like."

"This is it — " Wilf began.

"Dry up!" Lon regarded Tuby thoughtfully. "I can see where you're taking me — and it's great. But I'm not sure about this sex-and-marriage bit. For instance, are you certain that's how it works — in bed, I mean?"

"Of course I am, Lon."

"Isn't it keeping a cow when you've a dairy round the corner — eh — eh?"

"It would be if making love had anything to do with the milk business," Tuby replied rather coldly. "But that's just stupid. It hasn't. It's a psychological act as well as a physiological one. You can't satisfy yourself pretending to be a teenager. Enjoy being neurotic — that's the image — but stop feeding a neurosis on a really deep and dangerous level." Tuby got up and this time he looked at Bracton without a smile. "I can't do any more for you, Lon. I promised to find you a reliable image, and I've offered you one. If you'd like it all in writing, you can have it."

"Okay, I'll have it. One or two things there I need to mull over. Wilf, you said we could take it off tax, didn't you — eh? Okay, then you pay Dr. Tuby his fee, whatever it is. Guess he's earned it — eh — eh? And now you can both push off — I want to think — if I *can* think. Dr. Tuby, come and see the next show I do — Wilf can get you seats — then come round and tell me how I'm doing — eh — eh? And if in the show you see me eating supper and reading the paper, start the applause — eh?"

As they went towards the lift, Wilf was exultant. "He'll wear it, Doc. I can tell. You've done it, you've really gone and done it. Let me have a carbon of what you send him in writing. So I can remind him — if I have to. You're a marvel, Doc, but then I knew that from the start, didn't I?"

Nothing more was said until they were in the car, apparently on their way to the Baronial Hotel. "By the way, Doc, what's the damage?"

"A thousand guineas," Tuby told him quietly, trying hard to play it cool. "The cheque to be made payable to the *Institute of Social Imagistics* — you have the address, Wilf."

"I have, Doc. Now let me tell you — where I'm taking you now — straight to Meldy Glebe, as I said — you can walk away with more than that if you bring it off. Mind you, it may be a much tougher job. Lon's on his own but Meldy isn't — she's a *property*. But they can't push her around any more. She's digging herself in, young Meldy. Told you before, didn't I, what an eyeful she is? Studio booked her into this Baronial Hotel. Just 'cos it's the latest, silliest, and costs the most. Built by American money. And they sent a pair of nancies from the Coast to doll it up. You wait! It's the Sunset Boulevard idea of the Oldy Englishy style."

It wasn't easy to gain admittance into Meldy Glebe's suite on the top floor of the Baronial Hotel, but while Wilf attended to all that, Tuby hung about and then trotted along with him half in a dream, wondering if he was losing all contact with reality. Meldy's suite, which was called Wars of the Roses and defied any credibility, was an insane mixture of 1968, 1568, and 1268. Together with the latest electronic devices, it offered plastic Tudor beams, imitation tapestries, suits of armour, and neat arrangements of broadswords and battle axes. In the very large sitting room, Meldy was having a business conference with three men who looked so much alike that Tuby couldn't bother to notice any possible differences between them. The subject under discussion, in which Wilf promptly joined, appeared to be "percentages of the gross." Tuby couldn't even pretend to have any interest. Briefly acknowledging Wilf's introduction of him, Meldy had waved Tuby towards a genuinely ancient oak chest, to one side of the vast fireplace. It had one knob different from the others, and small white lettering said *Press Here*. So Tuby pressed, and at once the oak chest transformed itself into an illuminated little bar, and Tuby helped himself to a whisky. Sugary background music was dripping into the room all the time, and after he had taken a good pull at his whisky Tuby discovered that these sounds were coming out of a small fat mortar on the other side of the fireplace. After that, without making any attempt to listen to the talk coming from the group in the middle of the room, Tuby moved so that he could take a long look at his possible client, Miss Meldy Glebe.

He decided that she wasn't beautiful, but then he never used this term apart from character and spirit. A woman like Lois Terry, for instance, could look unattractive, quite plain, almost ugly, but then in a flash of the spirit, the depths inside suddenly lighting up, she could be beautiful. Meldy Glebe didn't belong to this rare series. On the other hand, she was so delectably pretty, so immediately and voluptuously attractive — and would retain this attractiveness under all conditions — that it was easy to understand why she was regarded as a princess of sexpots. She had shortish hair that was almost a dark Venetian red; widely spaced eyes of a coppery hue; and though she was wearing loose lounging pyjamas, which mixed yellow and brown ochres, it seemed more than likely that she had an exceptionally fine figure; and for the rest, she appeared to be still in her early twenties, was probably about five-foot-six, and had a hoarse and uncultivated voice, not quite ugly but certainly not pleasing. And whatever this percentages-of-the-gross business might be, it was undoubtedly something in which she took a passionate interest.

But suddenly she'd had enough of it. She waved away the three men, who all moved at the same time as if they were really a triple appearance of the same man. Then for the first time she really took in Tuby.

"What kind of a doctor are you?"

"Not a medical one — a Doctor of Letters — Literature," Tuby replied, smiling.

"Then what are you doing in this image racket that Wilf's going on about?" She frowned at him but still looked ravishingly pretty; she had that kind of face. "Don't tell me it isn't just another racket."

"All right, I won't, Miss Glebe." Tuby was still smiling.

Wilf, who was helping himself to a drink, snickered. "You won't get any change out of him, Meldy. I told you."

"Give me a tonic, Wilf. And then when you've swallowed that drink, dust off. If I'm going to talk to this man, I don't want you in a ringside seat. And you've got to write that letter to the front office — don't forget."

"I'm on my way," Wilf told her, and hastily finished his drink and departed.

The girl sipped her tonic water for a few moments, saying nothing, then pointed to a chair close to where she was lounging. Tuby sat down rather carefully on another chair.

"What's the idea? I pointed at this chair — not that."

Tuby smiled at her. "That's why I didn't sit in it, Miss Glebe. I shan't be any use to you if you point and I sit. A bad beginning, don't you think?"

"I get it. And don't call me Miss Glebe. It isn't my name anyhow. So just make it Meldy. Even if this isn't a beginning at all but a sudden ending. Because I haven't made up my mind about you."

"Quite right, Meldy." Tuby began filling his pipe.

"What d'you think of this place?" she demanded rather sharply.

"It's terrible. At first I felt I must be going out of my mind." He held up his pipe. "All right to smoke this?"

"Why not? I've a couple of little pipes myself somewhere." She waited until he had his pipe comfortably going. "D'you think I'm beautiful?"

"No."

The coppery eyes — green-flecked, he saw now — opened wide. "No? Why the hell not, Dr. Tuby?"

He gave voice now to the thoughts he'd entertained when he'd taken his first good look at her, being careful to explain himself slowly and impressively. And rather to his surprise she listened without giving any sign of impatience.

"You really talk, don't you? Have you seen any of my pictures?"

"No, I haven't."

"Well, why not — for God's sake?"

"I don't see many films, Meldy. But of course if you decide to become a client of the Institute, I'll try to see as many as I can. What do *you* think of them?"

"I think they're a load of horseshit. But then maybe your Institute is too."

To this he made no reply but regarded her amiably, just keeping his pipe going.

"When I smoke one of those things it always gets too goddam hot. I pull too hard at it, I guess. I must try your way next time. Fix yourself a refill, Dr. Tuby. Nothing for me." Her curiously hoarse voice went on and on as he returned to the old-oak-chest bar. "I don't do this steady drinking. I just like something new and fancy now and again. Can you think of anything I might like to try? Wilf told me you'd lived in the Far East. Any ideas from there?"

"Let me see what you have here, Meldy." Tuby worked hard for a couple of minutes, then gave her a glass of a darkish pink liquid. "Try this. It's called a Kuala Lumpur Special," he lied calmly. "Three different liqueurs with rather a lot of angostura bitters."

"Looks fine! Do *you* drink it?"

"Not if I can help it, my dear. It's a disgusting concoction, in my opinion. But try it, try it!" He went back for his whisky.

She was frowning over it when he returned, to sit this time in the chair — leathery and baronial — she'd pointed at. "Well?"

"When I've downed this, either I'll be half-stoned — or sick. I don't really like drinking. And I don't like sex. What about you?"

"The question's too general, Meldy. I like making love to certain persons. And I like drinking certain drinks. You won't feel sick, by the way. The bitters will attend to that. And the colour suits you." He smiled at her.

She took another sip and then stared at him thoughtfully above her glass. "Dr. Tuby, I'm beginning to see what Wilf Orange meant. There *is* something about you. Not like all those empty bastards who keep coming round — those three, for instance, *And* my father — he's American and Mother's English — and they split up years ago — and now you seem to me to be just what he never was. I was a mixed-up kid from the start. I've got these looks, so I'm important to a lot of people and there's money tied up to me — but I never feel the looks are *me*. Where am I now? What am I? A pin-up the boys stare at when they want to play with themselves," she continued bitterly. "I just sit behind these looks of mine, which aren't *me*, wondering what it's all about. And if you don't know what I'm talking about, tell me now so we aren't wasting our time." Her tone was harsh, but the look she gave him was appealing.

"I think I saw most of that, Meldy," he told her gently, "when I watched you talking to Wilf Orange and those three men. It was like looking at the front of an exquisite house and seeing somebody staring and glaring out of one of the windows." She gave a little cry but Tuby decided to ignore it. "There's at least one thing you enjoy — talking business, battling with the men of figures on their own ground — "

"I do, I do, I do!" she cried. "But that's because there's so little else. If I'm not staring out of the window of that house, then I'm walking up and down the bloody empty rooms. And that's really *me* — not what they see outside. Understand?"

He nodded, smiling, and then murmured more to himself than to her:

*"Never shall a young man, Thrown into despair . . ."*

"What are you muttering about?" she demanded, rather irritably.

"I was reminded of a poem by Yeats, addressed to a girl who had beautiful hair. It's quite short. Listen!" And she did.

She said nothing for a moment or two, just stared at him. "For Chrissake! I never knew there was anybody who thought like that and could write it down. I've had poetry sent me and tried to read some — all new stuff, you bet — and it all seemed a pile of manure. Do me a favour, Dr. Tuby. Get me this book — this Who's-it — Yeats — please!"

"Yes, I'll do that, Meldy. Even if you decide not to be a client of our Institute — "

"I don't know about the Institute, but if being a client means that you keep coming round to talk to me, then nobody's going to stop me. Unless of course you don't want me." And she looked and sounded quite wistful.

"I want you as a client, Meldy, for two good reasons. I want to earn a big fat fee. And I like you."

"Yes — and when you say that, you're not licking your lips and stripping me with your eyes. So I believe you really *do* like me — *me*." Smiling at him, she sat up as if she might spring across and embrace him. "Do you think you can do something for me?"

"Why, yes, Meldy, I do." He was brisk and cheerful. "I'll start thinking about you — in image terms — and I'll arrange with Orange to see one or two of your films. But now you must have things to do, and I must hurry back to the Institute, to catch my colleagues — Professor Saltana and Mrs. Drake — "

"Bring them to brunch on Sunday." She was very eager. "Just you three and me. And that would help, wouldn't it? But if they can't come, you will, won't you? Please, Dr. Tuby!"

"Delighted, my dear! Of course I don't know if Saltana and Elfreda Drake are free, but I'll telephone a message in the morning. What hour is brunchtime with you? About eleven-thirty, do you think? Good! By the way, we're all fond of food and eat heartily, but the kitchen shouldn't be too baronial — sides of beef, venison pasties, that sort of thing. But I must go. And I believe I left my overcoat on that suit of armour in the corridor. Incidentally," he continued as they went out of the room to-gether, "do you live alone in this huge suite, Meldy?"

"No men, if that's what you're wondering, Dr. Tuby. I've a maid — a coloured girl who came over with me — but I gave her this afternoon off. She'll be back soon to begin tarting me up for this goddam party." She insisted upon helping him into his overcoat, and gazed at him before letting him go. "Y'know, you're nothing to look at, are you?"

"I am not. Unlike you, Meldy. Everything to look at, you are."

"And I'll tell you now, Dr. Tuby. When I first saw you, I was dis-appointed. How you do it, I don't know — maybe what you say and how you say it and being *with* me as these bastards never are — but you make all these big handsome leading men I act with seem like hunks of flesh in a meat market. After half an hour I couldn't care less how you looked. Man — you're a honeypot."

He thanked her gravely. "But that reminds me, Meldy. We'll have to decide quite soon if you ought to speak American or English. You're mixed up there too, aren't you? Be thinking it over, my dear."

"I've done it and got nowhere. You'll have to decide."

"Until Sunday then, Meldy — and I'll let you know about the other two — "

"What if they don't like me and I don't like them?"

"I can't imagine it happening. Oh — and thank you for that ex-cellent whisky!"

The pageboy he shared the lift with appeared to be wearing a dou-blet and hose. The porter outside, who offered to find him a taxi, ap-parently belonged to the Yeomen of the Guard. Tuby decided to walk to the Institute, less than half a mile away, if only to clear his head. The door of the Institute was still open, but Beryl had gone and so had Prim-rose and Mrs. Mere. He thought Elfreda must have left too, but then he found her sitting in Saltana's room, the pair of them looking cheerful and rather cosy, and — if he could believe his ears — talking about a savoury cereal.

"We've had an enquiry from Albion United Foods," Saltana ex-plained, with a touch of his senior-executive manner. "They're planning a big campaign to market a savoury cereal — new type of breakfast food."

"Then you'll take charge of that, Cosmo."

"I intend to, Owen. Have you any news?"

"Very good news. I settled Lon Bracton — and Wilf Orange has agreed to pay us a thousand guineas. Note that, please, Elfreda!"

"Owen, that's wonderful," she cried. "Why, that's — "

Tuby stopped her. "Later, my dear. We've now been given the strange case of the sex symbol who doesn't like sex — namely, Meldy Glebe. I've already had some talk with her, high up in an insane hotel called the Baronial. That's why I wished the savoury cereal on to you,

Cosmo. I may feel better tomorrow, but at the moment I'm half out of my mind and a savoury cereal might just take me round the bend."

"But Meldy Glebe — she's a lovely girl, isn't she?" Elfreda sounded excited. "I've seen her in several films. Haven't you?"

Both men assured her promptly that they hadn't. And Saltana added that he'd never even heard of her. So Elfreda concentrated on Tuby. "That hair — those eyes — and her figure — didn't she absolutely bowl you over, Owen?"

"No, she didn't, my dear. Though she is an extremely attractive girl. And I like her."

"Did she like you?"

"I think she did, you know. But she's an odd girl." And he went on to tell them about Meldy Glebe. "I'll have to see at least one or two of her films, so you must allow me time for that, Cosmo. According to her agent, Orange, she's a valuable property — that's his term, not mine — and as they're finding her very difficult, if I can succeed in pleasing both the property and its owners we may be very handsomely rewarded. More than a thousand guineas, Elfreda. Now you have a chance of meeting my new friend Meldy yourselves. She's asked me to bring you both to brunch, as she calls it, on Sunday — about eleven-thirty — "

"Oh, I'd love it. You're free, aren't you, Cosmo?"

"I could be — yes." Saltana displayed no enthusiasm, but then he hadn't quite got down from his senior-executive perch. "Yes — I'll come along. Perhaps you could pick me up here, Elfreda — "

"Just what I was going to suggest," cried Elfreda happily. "I read she has a suite in this new Baronial Hotel, and I'm longing to see it — "

"Even though it's already threatened Owen's sanity?" Saltana was very dry, as he often was when Elfreda began to gush. Now he looked at Tuby. "Just the four of us? No male film stars? No press agents? No photographers? Well, well, well! You seem to have made an impression on this young woman very quickly."

"Oh — really — Cosmo, why do you sound so surprised?" Elfreda was almost indignant. "You ought to know what he's like by this time. The girl's probably all confused and unhappy — and he goes and smiles and twinkles at her and uses that voice of his — and she's mesmerised. And she's not the only one," she added, with a meaningful look.

"You're overstating it, Elfreda," said Tuby mildly. "But it's just possible she sees me as a father figure."

"Wait until Sunday," Elfreda told him, "and then I'll let you know if it's just father-figuring. Oh — Owen — that sweet little Alan Axwick, the M.P., called this afternoon, and I said you'd see him in the morning. He's arranged this big party — as you told him to do — for next Thursday, and that's all set up, but he doesn't know what's going to happen — y'know, to help his image — "

"Neither do I," said Tuby. He'd forgotten about little Axwick, and now tried to look and sound as if he didn't feel guilty. "But I'll think of something before I see him in the morning."

Saltana frowned at him. "He's your client, Owen, and I don't want to interfere. I've never met an innocent little member of Parliament, but Elfreda assures me that's what he is."

"Innocent as an egg — and rich."

"So I gather — " Saltana was still the senior executive — "and we'd like some of his money. Nevertheless," he went on sternly, "I'd also like to believe the Institute can offer a genuine service to this Axwick, even if he is more than half a fool. After all, this isn't a confidence-trick establishment — "

"Strictly speaking," said Tuby sharply, resenting Saltana's manner, "that's exactly what we are. No, no — let's leave that. Axwick came to us. We didn't approach him. He wants to be noticed so he asked me to find him a noticeable image. And so long as he's reasonably cooperative — and I shan't demand much help from him — he'll soon have all the attention he wants. And as I've had a long day, I'm getting more attention from you — and of a kind I resent — than *I want*." And he got up and was about to turn away when Elfreda grabbed his arm.

"Owen, you can't go like that. What's the matter with you two men? I can't bear it when you suddenly stop being friendly. You started it, Cosmo. Say you're sorry. Go on — say you're sorry."

"Certainly." And Saltana gave both of them one of his rare grins. The senior executive had vanished. "Sorry, Owen! It's this big-business atmosphere we're moving into."

"And a fat lot you'll see of that if you two start quarrelling now. Owen, *you* say something."

As he smilingly added his own apology, Tuby suddenly felt that this tiny quarrel scene would sooner or later be repeated, but immensely enlarged; and this feeling was so strong that instead of rambling on he said no more.

However, Elfreda took charge of them. "Why don't you both come and dine with me at Robinson's? You're free tonight, aren't you, Owen? And if you're dating some woman, Cosmo, you'd better put her off — just for once. If only for the sake of the Institute."

So less than an hour later, when Elfreda had gone up to bathe and change, Tuby and Saltana sat once again in the bar at Robinson's, and Tuby, improvising rapidly, began to explain what he had in mind for little Alan Axwick.

Next morning, just as Tuby had finished dictating his report, as promised, to Lon Bracton, in came the pink and pale-blonde Alan Axwick, smoking a pipe as if it didn't really belong to him and might be taken away at any moment.

"Mr. Axwick, I'm delighted to see you. I feel I owe you an apology.

The truth is, I've been desperately busy, chiefly with demanding show-business types — and you know what they are."

"Matter of fact I don't, Dr. Tuby." He sounded far more apologetic than Tuby had done. "And I've been thinking that if I had a better image — "

Tuby cut him short. "It's on its way, Mr. Axwick. Now you've arranged the evening party for next Thursday, haven't you?"

"Oh — yes — that's all right. Lot of chaps from the House are coming, some of the lobby correspondents, wanting to pick up a bit of gossip, and a few columnists that Miss East put me on to — and it ought to be a jolly good party. But then — if you don't mind my saying so, Dr. Tuby — so what? Where do we go from there? That's what's worrying me — frankly."

"Not to worry, my dear Mr. Axwick. Now let me see," Tuby continued, deeply thoughtful. "We agreed we should all work on a *Reverse Image*. You obtain publicity by apparently trying to avoid it — remember?"

"I made a careful note of what you said, Dr. Tuby. I'm dedicated, you said, to some mysterious pursuit, hobby, research. Why do I arrange to destroy all photographs of myself? Why do I meet my constituents at strange hours? Why do I keep going to Grenoble?"

"Grenoble — yes, of course." Tuby was still so deeply thoughtful, his face was quite stiff. "Have you been there yet?"

"Well — no, I haven't — not yet. I've been trying out some of the other things — being mysterious and all that — but so far nobody seems to notice it. I've mentioned Grenoble to various chaps, but they didn't seem particularly interested. And I feel I can't go there until I know what I'm supposed to be doing there. So you'll have to tell me, Dr. Tuby."

"No, no, no! You're missing the point. If *you* don't know what you're doing in Grenoble, then you can't possibly tell anybody else, so it remains a mystery."

"I can see that. But if nobody cares — "

"Mr. Axwick, I'll attend to that. Already you've sprinkled a few Grenobles around and have been mysterious. Good! You've done what I wanted you to do. Now I take over. I'll compel them to pay attention to you. That's why I asked you to arrange this party. It's there we fire the Axwick rocket. Now then," Tuby continued impressively, "you must arrange — or we'll do it for you, if you like — for a car to be waiting outside your house on Thursday night. You must have a bag packed. You must book a seat on the first plane going to Paris any time after about eleven-forty-five that night. Once in Paris you find your way to Grenoble — by plane, train, car, whichever is most convenient — as soon as you can — "

"But couldn't I just go to Paris — and leave it at that?"

"Fatal! You could wreck the whole scheme. You really must leave this to us, Mr. Axwick. But Miss East knows more about the way the Press works than I do, so I'll put it to her. Excuse me!"

When Primrose floated in, she smiled at Axwick, who turned a deeper pink at the very sight of her; then she pulled a face at Tuby. "Is it urgent, Dr. Tuby? We're hellishly busy along there."

"We're all hellishly busy, Primrose. But you've had to work a great deal with the Press, so I want to put a question to you, for the benefit of Mr. Axwick. Let us suppose — and I believe this will happen — he suddenly arouses the interest and curiosity of the Press by making a dramatic dash to Grenoble. *But* — and this is his suggestion, not mine — he actually goes no further than Paris. What would happen?"

"Well, if the boys were madly involved, darling, the minute he'd gone they'd be phoning Paris, and the boys at that end would be looking out for him. Grenoble would go down the drain. Of course if he could do a convincing mystery-man performance in Paris — "

"I couldn't, Miss East. Wouldn't know where to start."

Primrose nodded and smiled. "My view entirely. No, you'll have to keep to the script. And trust Dr. Tuby. This is for Thursday, isn't it?"

"It is, Primrose. And I'll explain what I have in mind later. That's all now, thank you, my dear." And out she went.

"Mr. Axwick," Tuby began, rather severely, "remember now — the car, the packed bag, the plane seat — and after that the simplest possible cooperation with us. Just do what you obviously have to do, without making any protest. And if you haven't attracted any attention by Friday morning, you can forget about us — and we'll not charge you a penny." Axwick tried to say something, but Tuby stopped him. "But if we succeed — and I'm confident of it — then the Institute will demand a substantial fee. Agreed? Good! One last thing. Eleven o'clock will be the time, and before that you must make sure that drinks are circulating freely — champagne perhaps for those who like it. Good, good, good!" Tuby felt he was suddenly sounding like a clergyman, as he went round to shake hands with Axwick, who was blinking between bewilderment and dawning hope. Then, left to himself, Tuby remembered to telephone Meldy Glebe about the three of them going to brunch on Sunday. Meldy was still asleep but her coloured maid — whose name was Dorothea, perhaps out of *Middlemarch* — carefully repeated the message.

It was because he thought Meldy might be sleeping late again that Tuby took care to arrive at her suite on Sunday morning about a quarter of an hour before Elfreda and Saltana were due there. But Meldy, wearing emerald-green pants and some kind of dusty-pink coat, was already up and in command. And Dorothea, a pretty girl done in milk chocolate, was there too, tidying the room and humming to herself. There were also two waiters setting the table, both dressed as if they had just been brought back from the Forest of Arden.

"Would pineapple juice help you to mix something fancy?" Meldy asked him. "Because I have some."

"Excellent! I might try a Singapore Tease — I think I can remember the ingredients. Would you like one now, as a bracer before the other two arrive?"

"Yes, please — mix me one, Tuby dear. I've decided to call you *Tuby dear*. Okay?"

"Okay, Meldy." He was on his way to the old-oak-chest bar. "I must add that not being a bruncher and having gone without breakfast, I'm devilish hungry. I hope Elfreda and Saltana aren't late."

"I talked specially to the head waiter about this brunch. Man, it's a hell of a brunch — and I'd hate to be paying for it myself. But they dumped me in here. Okay, boys." She was now looking at the table and talking to the Arden foresters. "Is everything here? And the hot stuff keeping hot? Fine, fine!"

The foresters departed. Tuby decided against giving himself a whisky; he was too hungry. Moreover, he already felt rather light-headed, being empty inside and trying to cope with the Baronial Hotel. He poured out a little of the Singapore Tease he had just invented, and tried it. Disgusting. "I think you'll like this, Meldy." He took the glass across to her. "Half a cocktail, half a longish drink. All the planters, the old Malaya hands, loved it. They'd sit for hours in the Raffles Hotel, rows of 'em, swigging their Singapore Teases."

"Thanks, Tuby dear." She tasted it without pulling a face. Then she gave him a wide coppery look. "But you're not fooling me, y'know. Not one bit." Tuby twinkled at her.

Elfreda, comely, smiling, and very smart, and Saltana, in a new dark suit Tuby had never seen before, made an impressive entrance. The way Saltana lit up at the sight of Meldy worried Tuby, not for any sexual reason, at least not on Tuby's part, but simply because the girl was his client and he didn't want to lose her to Saltana. And the threat was there as soon as Meldy took Elfreda out of the room, with Dorothea in tow.

"I can't help wondering, Owen," said Saltana quietly and very solemnly, "if your sympathetic and persuasive treatment is right for this girl."

"You saw at a glance, didn't you, Cosmo, that something more authoritative and incisive might be better? Well, you're wrong. I know Meldy and you don't. You'd have her fighting mad in ten minutes."

"Nonsense! However, we'll see."

They sat at the table at once, as soon as the women returned. "Well, Professor Saltana," said Meldy when they began eating, "what d'you think of this hotel? Dr. Tuby thinks it's a great joke."

"Then I don't agree with him, Miss Glebe." Saltana gave her one of his dark piercing looks. "It's not a joke, it's a calamity. It's one more expensive piece of evidence that we've come to the end of the civilization that followed the Renaissance. No taste, no standards, no values! A place like this mocks the past and sneers at the present. Or don't you agree with me, Miss Glebe?"

"Oh — don't ask me. I'm just a bad actress trading on her looks."

Elfreda hurried to the rescue. "You're not a bad actress, Meldy. And as for your looks, as you call 'em, they're just wonderful. Dr. Tuby saw one of your pictures yesterday morning — private showing — and I don't suppose he's told you — "

"There hasn't been time, my dear."

Meldy, who had been looking sulky, now looked wary, though still bewitchingly pretty. "Which one was it?"

"The one in which you pretend to be a girl hipster, in order to rescue your brother. *Your Eyelashes Are Hurting Me.* In a few scenes — all with the brother — you weren't lousy at all, Meldy. You were quite good." Tuby smiled at her. "But in your scenes with your handsome lover, your private contempt for him and the script came through."

"Well, I loved it," Elfreda declared defiantly.

After a longish pause in the talk, though not in the eating and drinking, Meldy, who had been brooding, opened her eyes wide and gave Saltana a challenging coppery-emerald look. "Okay, Professor Saltana, we're in the horse-manure trade. But what about you and your Institute and your images? For all I know, that could be just a lot of bamfoozle and flubdub. No, Tuby dear, you keep out of this. I'm talking to the Professor, the boss man."

"You're talking, Miss Glebe," Saltana told her sharply, "but you're not really saying anything."

"Of course I am — and you know it. I'm crazy about Dr. Tuby, but that doesn't mean I'm ready to believe in you and your Institute and this image flamdoodle — "

"Miss Glebe," Saltana began, very sharply indeed, "I understood from Dr. Tuby that you'd already agreed to consult the Institute — "

"If it's the money you're thinking about, that's all okay." She was almost contemptuous. "That's all between my agent Wilf Orange and the studio bosses. But I'm talking about *me* now — what *I* feel — and I say you haven't sold me this image bambosh."

Saltana's manner was suddenly freezing, and Elfreda was looking unhappy. But a warning glance from Meldy told Tuby he might do more harm than good by jumping in now. Clearly she wanted to have it out with Saltana.

"As Dr. Tuby will tell you," Saltana went on, "we've had to defend our image research and expertise on many occasions, both in public and in private. But, Miss Glebe, you're the last person who ought to challenge our activities. You *are* an image. Take away your function as an image — and what are you? An extremely good-looking girl who might be working at a milliner's and sharing a cheap bed-sitting room. We think you can be improved as an image; otherwise Dr. Tuby wouldn't have accepted your case. It's too early yet for him to say exactly what ought to be done. But I imagine that however it may be modified, your image will have to be highly charged with sex — "

"Oh — turn it off!" Meldy's low hoarse voice couldn't rise to a scream, but she did her best. "I might have expected that — in spite of all this now-you're-back-in-the-classroom line of yours, Professor. I want the sex taken out of it. I don't like sex. All that God-awful puffing and panting and bloody fuss — " She cut herself short. "Why the grin? I'm serious, y'know, Professor."

"Miss Glebe — Meldy, if I may — sex is something between persons." Saltana was speaking slowly and quietly. "If it isn't, then it's mostly what you say it is. But I doubt, for all its potency, if it can turn half-persons into whole persons. Yet that's what it's expected to do nowadays, when there are so many frustrated half-persons. As frustration builds up, sex is being asked to carry too heavy a load. Get on to the bed or in it — and all will be well. But if it isn't, then there's more frustration still."

Meldy, responding to this change of manner, nodded and then turned to Tuby. "Is that what you believe too?"

"More or less, my dear, though I might express it differently. But I don't agree with Saltana in thinking that whatever we do with your image it will have to be highly charged with sex. And remember, you're my case, not his. It ought to be possible," he continued dreamily, "to create an image — and one that wouldn't drive you off the screen or even considerably lower your value in the film market — of a girl who ought to be a sex symbol, because she looks it, but very obviously isn't. There could be a certain piquancy in that. And I have an idea that the young, who now prefer films to television, could appreciate such an image, both on and off the screen."

"If this is a situation," Saltana muttered, "in which sex is about to be repudiated, I no longer know anything about human nature."

"Cosmo, you've never really understood my slice of it."

"And that could be true," Elfreda observed. "I'm not sure you *do* understand people, Cosmo."

"He doesn't understand *me*," said Meldy, "though I don't hate his guts as I did a few minutes ago. But even so, if he tries to take me away from you, Tuby dear, the deal's off."

"Then I won't try, Meldy," said Saltana, showing no sign of resentment.

Tuby told Saltana and Elfreda gravely: "As Meldy and I can't spare very much time for each other, we must make the best use we can of the next hour or two. I want her to talk about herself." He spoke as if she weren't there at their elbow, but now Meldy had had enough of that.

"I'm still here, folks. *Me*." But she returned Tuby's smile. "If you don't go to sleep — and I'll bet you do — I'm ready to talk about myself for hours and hours."

She was — and she did, at least for an hour and a half or so, until in fact Tuby, who'd been nodding and then jerking himself awake for ten or fifteen minutes, went to sleep. When he woke up he didn't know where he was for some moments, possibly in bed in a haunted house, but then he realized he was stretched out on the long settee, with a cushion under his head and some kind of rug over him. Beneath a solitary light, Dorothea was sewing but also keeping an eye on him. When he struggled up and was about to speak, she shushed him.

"You went to sleep," she whispered, "so Miss Meldy went off to lie down — and now she's asleep. And she needs some rest. She has to go out tonight — and she sure needs all her strength, the way she goes on, objecting to everything, fighting everybody."

They were standing close together now. "Quite so, Dorothea. And thank you for looking after me. Good God — it's after five o'clock. I'll creep away quietly."

She went with him towards the outer door and helped him on with his overcoat. "When I say Miss Meldy's fighting everybody, I don't mean you — no, sir. She's just plumb crazy about you. And after never giving all them handsome young men never even a little smile. But then you're a sweet-talking man, Doc Tuby — "

"And not much to look at, you must admit, Dorothea."

"Some girls — and Miss Meldy's one — they don't want to look, they just want to listen. 'Bye now, Doc Tuby!"

This was more or less Elfreda's theme when she came into his room at the Institute next morning. "I hope you realize, Owen," she began at once, "that Meldy Glebe's falling in love with you."

"Nonsense, my dear!" And Tuby was rather sharp, genuinely believing it *was* nonsense. "The girl's been longing to talk to somebody, that's all."

"I'm not so sure about that — "

"I am. And I'm about to turn myself into what is sometimes called a *socialite*. I've accepted an invitation from our Meldy to attend a film première tomorrow night, wearing a dinner jacket now too small for me and greenish in certain lights. Then there's little Axwick's party on Thursday, at which the Institute will begin to earn its fee — rather dramatically. I forget — are you going?"

"You bet, Owen! He asked me specially. But I doubt if Cosmo will go. Anything else, Owen?"

"Well — no," Tuby admitted. "Wilf Orange has arranged for me to see another of Meldy's films this afternoon. He says it's called *Darling, How Can You?* and is one of those offbeat romps in which the actors, making it, had a much better time than any audience will ever have with it. Full of *in* jokes, Wilf says, and as I've never been *in*, I'll be just gaping like a bewildered peasant. However, it may give me a useful tip or two about young Meldy." But he was being buzzed. "Yes, Beryl? — well, send him along." He gave Elfreda one of his slow wide grins. "You must stay for this fellow. Cosmo's out, Beryl says. And his name is Ezra J. Smithy. So fasten your seatbelt, Mrs. Judson Drake."

Ezra J. Smithy seemed to come into the room sideways, as if invisible men might try to bar his way. There wasn't much of him apart from his nose, which was very long, starting too high up and ending too far down, overshadowing his mouth. Though he could see quite well, he appeared to have no eyes, just slits. He was strange rather than repellently ugly: he had a kind of friendly insect look.

"I hear plenty of talk about this Institute," he began, hardly moving his lips — if he had any lips. "Even so, I'm taking a chance. And you can say that again."

"Very well, Mr. Smithy," said Tuby, smiling, "you're taking a chance. Go on."

"Dan Luckett's coming over. Maybe next month. Maybe the month after. Who knows — with Dan?"

"I don't," Tuby told him. "But then I don't know Dan. Who is he?"

"Just a minute!" Elfreda sounded excited. "Do you mean the Dan Luckett who owns all those cheap restaurants? Eat At Dan's?"

"Eat At Dan's," Ezra J. Smithy repeated solemnly. "Right from Maine and across to San Diego."

"Everybody knows them in America, Owen. You can't miss them. They're everywhere. And everybody knows about Dan Luckett too. Lots of publicity all the time. Are you connected with him then, Mr. Smithy?"

"Personal assistant. Trouble-shooter. Running boy," Ezra J. ended modestly. "Now this is how it is — in confidence, strict confidence." But now he looked at his watch, as if he'd already spent hours with them instead of about two minutes. And apparently his watch told him to speed up. "Dan's breaking into the British market. All planned except the publicity campaign. You work with an agency?"

"No, we don't," said Tuby. "We're consulted by agencies but whenever possible we prefer to work directly with our clients. I take it that Mr. Luckett might want to make use of an image for his British restaurants — "

"Either an image representing the Luckett places," Elfreda put in eagerly, "or an image of the ideal British Luckett customer — "

"A matter to be discussed," said Tuby hastily. "We can offer you either kind of image. And we're the only experts in this field."

"That's what I've heard," said Smithy, talking even faster than they'd been doing. "Makes sense to me. Should do with Dan. Anyhow I'll take a chance. Talk to Dan later today. If he likes it, talk to your Director, the Professor, tomorrow. Now do me a favour. Dan wants a sociological survey — habits, tastes, prejudices, status symbols — of any typical British community. And he wants it quick. Can you give me somebody?"

"I can," Tuby replied at once. "Dr. Hazel Honeyfield, Department of Sociology, University of Brockshire, and Director of the Judson Drake Foundation there. She's done several surveys of the West Midlands."

"I'll phone her. No, don't need it on paper. Keep everything in my head. Have to — with Dan. Tell her you recommended her, Dr. Tuby. All for now. Must go. Pleasure meeting you both. 'Bye!" And confident now there were no invisible men lurking round the door, Ezra J. Smithy didn't trouble to turn sideways but shot straight out of the room. Tuby could hardly believe he'd really been with them.

In a large crowded cinema, full of people laughing at anything, *Darling, How Can You?* might just have been tolerable. But taken alone, in a tiny viewing place, and all in cold blood, it could only be endured, like two hours of threatening neuralgia. It was in dazzling colour and the action was divided between Southern California, the west coast of Mexico, and the French Riviera — mostly Palm Springs, Acapulco, and Antibes. Succeeding after a time in taking his mind away when Meldy was off the screen, Tuby was able to hang on to the end. But whenever she appeared, rather like a talking poster of a very pretty girl, he gave her all his attention. And he began to arrive at certain conclusions that he sketched for her, the following night, when he dined in her suite before they went to the film première. He was wearing his too-small greenish dinner jacket, in which he looked, he thought, like the house manager of a minor provincial theatre about to go bankrupt.

"I don't want to dwell on the obvious, my dear," he began, while they were still eating, "but of course you're hopelessly miscast in these films. They're based on your looks and not on your personality. Even if I didn't know you, I'd be aware of your contempt showing through. Cast as a sexy girl, you simply cancel yourself out. We don't get the character, such as it is, and we don't get you. It's hopeless casting you as a sexpot adventuress or a dumb husband-hunter. We don't believe a word of it. You ought to be a girl stockbroker or lawyer, not thinking about sex at all. The more alluring you appear to be, the more the men stare and lick their lips, the more you concentrate on the business deals or legal decisions you're describing to them — "

"Yes — yes — yes, Tuby dear!" Meldy looked at once eager and bewitching. It was the first time he'd seen her really dressed up. She was wearing an elaborate confection — it seemed to be a pale apricot shining through some kind of vague silvery mist — that had been specially designed for this occasion.

"And of course you project this new image into your life off the screen. You don't give a damn what all the others do. You're going your own way." He waited a moment, then looked hard at her. "And you start tonight, Meldy."

"Doing what?"

"Not wearing that dress. Going in a sweater and pants — or something — "

"My God — Tuby dear — I couldn't do that. The studio men 'ud go up in flames. Besides, Princess Who's-it's going to be there. They mightn't even let me in — "

"All the better," Tuby told her coolly. "If you were barred, the story would go round the world in a few hours. We're living in that kind of world now, and it's one reason why it can't last much longer. But if you really want a new image and the maximum publicity for it, nothing could be better. Instead of being one of a number of overdressed tarted-up pretty girls, all trying to catch the eyes of the photographers, you will be as noticeable as a fountain in the desert."

"I know, I know — but Tuby dear, I can't do it. You don't know what it's like — "

Tuby nodded. He finished his whisky, flicked the napkin across his lips and then threw it down, and pushed himself up from the table. "Thank you for dinner, Meldy. Now I'm going home." He spoke quite coldly, in the sharpest contrast to his usual warm honeyed tone. "Professor Saltana may decide to keep the Institute working for you, but so far as I'm concerned — you're out. From now on you'd be wasting my time."

But she caught him as he moved — really, very slowly — away from the table, and she flung herself at him. "You can't — you can't — Tuby dear! It would be worse than ever now — I wouldn't know where I was — and you ought to know I'm crazy about you. Wait — wait — I'll do it." She gave him a hurried kiss and ran into the bedroom. He could hear the voice of Dorothea rising in protest. A few moments later, Dorothea appeared, to stare at him accusingly.

"That beautiful dress! Telling her to take it off! Man, what you doing to Miss Meldy?"

"I'm helping her to change her image, Dorothea. It's what I'm being paid to do. And if she'll work with me, she'll be happier — and in the end be far more successful." He went a few steps nearer, still looking hard at her, but smiling now. "I want you on my side, my dear. And I ask you to believe that I know what I'm doing."

Dorothea shook her pretty head. "Well, I just hope you do. My — my — you're the sweet-talkingest little man — for a white — I ever did listen to — " But a call from the bedroom cut her short.

A minute or two later, Meldy appeared. She had ruffled her hair, and was wearing a fur coat over a high-necked grey sweater and black pants. "Okay, will I do now?"

"Perfect, Meldy my dear. Thank you! And you're looking even more ravishing — and I mean it — than you did in that dress."

"Tell that to the front office men when they start spitting at me. My God — you're the only man on earth I'd have done this for. And I'm not going to fasten this coat. It'll be all loose. I won't cheat. Let's go. The car's waiting."

It was a weeping cold night but the patient imbeciles were packed thick round the cinema. There seemed to Tuby enough policemen on duty to have prevented, if they had been elsewhere, a score of burglaries, a dozen cars from being stolen, probably four or five old people from being bashed. After much crawling, waiting, and crawling again, they were released from the car with a flourish, as if they were a present to somebody and made their way into the decorated and highly illuminated foyer of the cinema. It was crowded with dressed-up show-business types, all pretending to be looking around for acquaintances when in fact they were hoping to catch the attention of press photographers, TV cameramen, and commentators who were jabbing microphones into people's faces. A sudden swirling movement — cause unknown — separated Tuby and Meldy, and he found himself being pushed into a corner, where a radio man seemed to be yapping ecstatically into a mike. "And it certainly looks like being a great night — yes, a great night — here tonight — " But he was drying up, when he noticed Tuby and insisted upon sharing the mike with him. "Wouldn't you say it's a great night, sir?"

"No," said Tuby.

"Really! And — let's see — you're — er — "

"I'm Dr. Tuby of the *Institute of Social Imagistics*."

"Of course — Dr. Tuby — *Social Imagistics* — and may I ask — "

"I'm the guest of Miss Meldy Glebe, who is one of our clients — "

"And — my word — what a client — eh? But I don't see her — "

"I didn't — but now I do. Those are her black pants going up the stairs. Excuse me!" And he had just time to hear the radio men crying *Black pants!* behind him, in a further fit of ecstasy. When he finally found Meldy, she was near the entrance to the circle, listening to the furious whispers of a smallish, plumpish, spectacled man, who might have been Tuby's older and unhealthier brother.

"You ask Dr. Tuby," said Meldy. "This is Dr. Tuby. Mr. Brimber. One of my studio bosses."

"Then I ask you, Dr. Tuby — why — why — why?" Mr. Brimber was heating up and seemed to smell of all those toilet preparations that make men more manly.

"I'm changing her image."

"And does that mean that on an important occasion like this, she has to come looking like — looking like — "

"Yes. Part of the new image." Tuby was smiling, cool, entirely unruffled. "And not only does she look wonderful, but everybody's talking about her — " As if he really knew this.

"Don't worry about Mr. Brimber," said Tuby, when they were in their seats. "If it's publicity for you he wants, he'll soon be a happy man. That is, if he *can* be a happy man."

"He can't, Tuby dear. Oh — and I must warn you we'll be having supper with him — and some of the others — afterwards."

"I'm delighted to hear it. By the way, am I rotten with egoism — or does he look rather like me?"

Meldy giggled. "Of course, Tuby dear. I noticed that when I first met you. Only — he looks as if he'd been living under a stone for the last ten years. And you don't."

Now the seats on each side of them were being filled by film people. And not only was Mr. Brimber one of them, but so was Mrs. Brimber, who took the seat next to Tuby. She was short, broad, and pug-faced, and as the house lights were fading, she whispered. "How are you on arthritis, doctor?"

"I'm against it," said Tuby.

The film had been produced by the people who had Meldy under contract, but she herself was not in it. The film seemed to belong to that horrible world which reveals itself when we have a high temperature. It was so brightly coloured that Tuby's eyes ached at it, and when he tried to close them the relentless screen images forced them open again. Worse still, it was excruciatingly noisy, as if determined, no matter the cost in pain and suffering, to force itself upon the attention. Striking a match sounded like sawing a house in two, and any car beginning to move off suggested the opening of a tank battle.

"Well, Tuby dear?" And Meldy squeezed his arm while the others were applauding. "How about that?"

"Horrible, horrible!" he muttered in her ear, as they were leaving the auditorium in a cloud of toilet preparations, male and female. Tuby told himself — not for the first time, but now with more evidence to hand — that he liked Western women least when they were all dressed to kill. And the thought of the supper party didn't please him at all now. He longed to sneak away, free of all Brimbering, but felt he couldn't leave Meldy to face them alone. He joined her as they all went down the great staircase together, allowing Mrs. Brimber to go on talking about health to a complete stranger, and he saw that the mass media were still lurking in the foyer. A breathless girl, gasping that she was from *During The Week,* a television programme, compelled Meldy and Tuby to stop and listen to her, only because she looked as if she might collapse if they didn't.

Supper, for about twenty, was served in a private room of a large and expensive hotel not far from the Baronial. Tuby sat between an eye- and teeth-flashing brunette and Mrs. Brimber, who was now trying to talk to him about sciatica. Tuby felt tired so he drank a good deal; the waiters were probably tired too and they exchanged angry hisses; and the food was very tired, as if it had been hanging about far too long. Idiot speeches were made, at the command of Mr. Brimber, who appeared to be delighted to hear people say the same fatuous things in exactly the same way, as if speech had just been invented; and finally, as Tuby, dreamy now, had got himself back into Kashmir, he too found himself called upon to say a few words.

"Mr. Brimber, ladies, and gentlemen," he heard himself saying, wondering what the hell to say next, "I must thank our host — or hosts — for this very agreeable supper party — as I do now, most warmly." And now what? "I am — as I hope you know — an image expert. I am here in good company — because, after all, most of you deal in images, in one way or another." Some took this well, others badly. He had to check an impulse to burst out laughing. "We at the *Institute of Social Imagistics* are proud to have Miss Meldy Glebe among our many clients," he continued with immense mock-gravity. "But you will forgive me if I say no more on this subject here and now. The truth is, Miss Glebe and I have agreed to appear tomorrow night on the very popular television pro-gramme, *During The Week*." There was applause here, led by Mr. Brim-ber. "So I will say no more — except to thank you again for your delight-ful hospitality."

"Very nice, Doctor," said Mrs. Brimber as soon as he sat down. "But be careful what you say about her health. Alfred — Mr. Brimber — likes people to think they're all very healthy."

"Quite so, Mrs. Brimber, but if you don't mind my saying so, Mr. Brimber himself doesn't look quite up to the mark."

"Oh — he's not — he's not, Doctor. I keep telling him — "

But Tuby, after emptying his glass, was back in Kashmir, lolling among delectable girls and roses. Later, there was a car waiting to take Meldy a hundred yards or so to the Baronial. As soon as they were in the car, which couldn't move off at once, she turned impulsively, embraced and kissed him. "Don't go," she whispered. "Come up. I have a feeling this time it'll be all different."

"It might be, my dear. But — I'm sorry — it's too late, it's been too long a day, and it would be all wrong if you were disappointed. And we have to be together tomorrow night."

"Yes, Tuby dear — tomorrow then. You must come to dinner — we haven't to be at the studio until half-past nine — and tell me how I ought to look and what I ought to say. Television always terrifies me — and you don't care about anybody or anything — you're *wonderful*, dar-ling. Now I can slip out here" — for they had already arrived at the Baronial — "and you tell him to take you home." Which Tuby did, promptly.

"And I simply couldn't tell the girl," he said to Saltana next morn-ing, "that I'd never been on television in my life. If I could have handed the thing over to you, Cosmo, I would have done, but because I was there with her last night, naturally with all this publicity it's me they want."

"Certainly. And now you need a little advice. Well, the first thing is not to give a damn. Just talk as you would anywhere. The second thing

is involved in that. Don't try to please the viewers. They're always looking at people who are trying too hard to please them. Politicians behaving like secondhand-car salesmen. But they'll be looking at the girl, not
you. Will she have much to say for herself?"

"No, but I'll suggest a few remarks. I'll remember about not really
giving a damn. But I'd feel stiff and unnatural if I didn't try to please
the audience — not myself at all. I'll have to work something out. Any
chance of your watching us, Cosmo? I wish you would."

"I can easily do that. Elfreda tells me she has a little sitting room
now, with a television set. Even if she can't be there herself, she'll let me
use the place. But it's ten to one she'll be there. She doesn't seem to be
making many friends, so far as I can tell, Owen."

"And one day, Cosmo, I'll explain why."

"A detestable, insufferable kind of remark! What the devil — " But
Tuby had gone.

## 5

Elfreda had asked Saltana to dine with her before they watched television together, but he said he wanted to do some work at the Institute
after hours, when it was quiet, and then eat at a pub as soon as he felt
he'd done enough work. She told herself that she believed this and didn't
believe he was going to see some woman — that Mrs. Wolker, for instance, the Fabrics woman, who was for ever phoning him — but even
so, just after dinner, she invented some excuse to ring him at the Institute — and there he was, sounding rather weary. But then she'd known
all the time, hadn't she, that he would be there and had told her the exact truth?

Pleased with him and rather displeased with herself, and generally
feeling rather flustered, she changed a few things round in the sitting
room, made sure the whisky was all ready for him and a box of his cheroots (she had asked Primrose to find out where he bought them), and
switched on the television set, if only to be certain it was working properly. Then she tried her two armchairs at various angles to the set, unable to give her attention to whatever it was hoping to show her, then
suddenly decided to wear another dress.

He arrived about ten, a quarter of an hour before *During The Week*
would be on, and he really did look rather tired. "And I'll bet you didn't
get anything fit to eat at your pub, Cosmo."

"Rather stale stuff, I must admit, Elfreda." He looked too tall and impressive, too much like a great dark hawk, for this small room, but he took it in appreciatively. "You have a touch with rooms, my dear. I'd never imagine this was an hotel sitting room. It's alive — and they're always dead." And while he took the whisky for granted, he was almost embarrassingly surprised by the box of cheroots she offered him. "Why, this is uncommonly kind and thoughtful of you, Elfreda. I'd only a couple left too, and I could see myself having to nurse them. Thank you!" He said nothing about Primrose having asked him where he bought them, but Elfreda felt she knew, from the dark but warm look he gave her, that he understood exactly what had happened but thought it better not to mention it. Instead, she risked a rather tricky question. "Are you wishing you were on tonight instead of Tuby? I mean, it's easy for you — and quite new and strange to him — and there's been all this publicity."

He nodded. "I'm feeling a little nervous for him. Owen can talk, of course — nobody better — but he's very self-conscious about his appearance. I told him this morning everybody would be looking at the girl, as well they might, but it's not strictly true. And he'll feel it isn't, when he's sitting there under the lights. Perhaps I ought to have told him to keep his eyes closed and imagine he's still on radio. Well, here's wishing him luck!" After drinking, he continued, in a deeper tone: "Elfreda, I *feel* — and I'm putting it like that because it's not rational and I've no evidence yet — I *feel* that last night Owen gave the Institute the greatest lift and boost it's had so far — "

"I wouldn't be surprised, Cosmo — "

"And I must confess to feeling a trifle jealous. I'm the Director, but up to now he's ahead of me. My birds aren't coming home to roost as fast as his are, and I'm not even sure they're bigger birds."

They had to wait a few minutes for *During The Week*. With it came a face and a voice that Elfreda now knew very well, those of its master of ceremonies, Povey, with his handsome head of grey hair, neat beard, carefully friendly smile. He announced, not unlike a man running a children's party, that tonight *During The Week* would interview a cabinet minister, produce two research doctors who believed they had something new about heart disease, give viewers a glimpse of a man with a very strange hobby, and talk to Meldy Glebe and her image expert, Dr. Tuby. Something for everybody, Povey contrived to suggest.

Elfreda was sorry for the cabinet minister, interviewed by one of Povey's severer colleagues, who behaved as if he were running a police station and had found the politician there, under arrest. Saltana refused to be sorry for him, saying that senior ministers didn't have to go running to the television screen as often as they could. The two doctors said they were greatly excited by the recent result of their research, but as they didn't look or sound excited, Elfreda lost interest in them. The strange hobby, which belonged to a man who was very tall and thin and looked dotty, was teaching white mice to play a very rudimentary game

of football. When the mice were shown running about, Povey himself
made an appearance, shouting and blowing a whistle. It all seemed just
as dotty as the owner and trainer of the mice. Then Elfreda and Saltana
found themselves staring hard at Meldy Glebe, who was wearing a high-
necked grey sweater and black pants and looking quite lovely too, Elfreda
thought, and of course Owen Tuby, who was smoking his pipe and offered no sign of nervousness. They were being interviewed by a bustling
aggressive kind of man called Murch. And this worried Elfreda, who had
seen Murch in action before.

"He can be quite nasty and sneering," she told Saltana, while
Murch was asking Meldy a few routine questions. "I feel anxious for
Owen."

"I don't. A clever smoothie would have been much more dangerous. With any luck, Owen can make this fellow seem bad-mannered and
oafish. And just because he's giving the girl an easy ride," Saltana continued, "his change of manner when he tackles Tuby will be all the more
obvious — and won't help him."

And certainly there could be no doubt about the change of manner.
"Now then, Dr. Tuby, according to various statements in the Press, you
were responsible for Miss Glebe's rather startling appearance last night."

"I was indeed," Tuby told him, smiling. "I found Miss Glebe wearing a beautiful new dress for the occasion, and I asked her to take it off
and wear some careless old clothes."

"She can't have liked that. Didn't she protest?"

"Of course. Any girl would — and especially an extremely pretty
girl getting ready to be stared at and photographed." Tuby relit his pipe.

"Her *new image* comes into this, doesn't it?" There was a sneer im-
plied in Murch's heavy accentuation. The first shot had been fired.

Tuby offered him a smiling nod. "It does indeed."

"But, Dr. Tuby, some of us can't help feeling this image business of
yours is really a joke thing."

"Do you mean," Tuby enquired blandly, "that whenever you use the
term *image* yourself, you're merely being funny? No — allow me, please!"
Murch was trying to interrupt him. "And that perhaps when it's being
used, over and over again, hundreds of times each week, on television,
radio, and in the Press, everybody's being funny?"

"No, of course I don't, Dr. Tuby. That's quite different — "

"You mean, then, that when I and my colleagues talk about images
it's a *joke thing,* but that when you and your colleagues talk about them,
then it isn't — um?" And Tuby gave him a wide warm smile.

"I mean that we don't pretend to be experts, giving advice on images, whereas you do. And that this image-expert thing seems to some of
us rather bogus — just a stunt. What's your reply to that, Dr. Tuby?"
And Murch leant back, as if ready to spend a minute or two watching
Tuby wriggling out of this situation.

"Mr. Murch — I have that right, I hope? — thank you! — we live in an age of images chiefly because our world has now discovered various ways of projecting them widely. This is probably something it has always wanted to do. In the past, emperors, popes, kings, famous statesmen, and soldiers have chosen images for themselves and have tried, with limited means, to project them. Now we can do much better. You and your colleagues are in the image-projecting business — as you know very well. My colleagues and I have chosen to concentrate on what is being projected — the images themselves, to which, I can assure you, Mr. Murch, we have given much time and thought. And it seems to me that if *we* are bogus, then *you* are bogus, and it's *all* bogus."

"Now, wait a minute, Dr. Tuby. That sounds plausible, but I can't accept it. We aren't doing the same thing — and it's a matter of degree — and the claims you make — "

"But how much do you know about images, Mr. Murch? Would you agree with Collard and Pleyel on the dwindling significance of the objective correlative of the image? Do you know the discussion between Broadwood, Erard, and Bluthner on the frequent urgent necessity of the *Reverse Image?* And what about Steinway's analysis of the underlying sexual element in all images — "

"Well, I agree with some of it, of course — "

"But they're all pianos," cried Meldy. "I know because I worked in a music shop one time. How can they be all pianos, Dr. Tuby?"

"Because I had to think of some names very quickly, Meldy," said Tuby, smiling. "And they were the first I thought of. So if I was going to talk a little solemn nonsense — "

"Miss Glebe, Dr. Tuby," Murch broke in desperately, "Thank you for coming along — "

And then they were looking again at Povey, who was nodding and smiling as if he had indeed given them the great treat he had promised. "And that's all for tonight from *During The Week.* We shall be back again — "

But Elfreda had switched him off so that she could be enthusiastic about Tuby. "He was wonderful, wasn't he? I loved every bit of it, didn't you?"

"No, I didn't."

"Cosmo, what's the matter with you? I believe you *are* jealous of Owen Tuby — "

"Not at the moment. May I help myself, Elfreda?" He sent out a long arm towards the whisky and the cheroots. "Of course he'd known at once that fellow was against him, so he made him look foolish."

While Saltana was still busy with his whisky and cheroot, Elfreda turned her chair to face the fire — she'd had one lit specially, not for warmth but for the look of it, for cosiness — and now she motioned him to do the same. Only one weak light was on and she left it at that, again for cosy intimacy. The setting was just right, but of course Saltana in his present mood was ruining everything. Even so, she thought his sombre face in the firelight looked marvellous, like that of some great prince.

"That's what I did, you remember, when I first went on television — "

"But Owen Tuby mustn't do it — "

"Don't snap at me, Elfreda. You don't know yet what I'm talking about. The point is, we're in a very different position now. And Owen was too mischievous. He let his sense of humour run away with him. You and I enjoyed it — and possibly a lot of other people did too. But what about the men who might want to consult us? The money-and-power men, not as a rule able to understand and appreciate intellectual mischief, academic whimsicalities. Even if they aren't solemn themselves, they like solemnity in the experts they consult. So I feel very dubious about Owen's clever little performance."

"And you're also talking to me as if I was one of your students in Guatemala or somewhere." She spoke quite sharply.

"Then I apologize, my dear. I may have been feeling somewhat nettled because you imagined I was jealous of Owen's performance tonight. I assure you, I'm not."

The telephone cut into her question. A personal call from Tarbury, Brockshire. "Elfreda, this is Lois — Lois Terry. Don't think I'm being idiotic or too nosy, but I feel I must know. So you must tell me — honestly — "

"About Tuby?" But that was just a fill-in. It had to be Tuby. "Did you see him on television tonight, Lois?"

"Yes, of course," said the urgent little telephone voice. Elfreda could see her huge eyes almost lighting up the receiver. "And it's about that film girl that all the boys here drool over. Surely she's absolutely doting on him, isn't she? Either I don't know how to look at telly people — or every look was adoring — "

"I said that last Sunday, Lois, after we lunched with them — "

"Well, that can mean only one thing, I suspect!" Lois managed a little laugh, false as teeth in a bowl. "So if you know what's going on, Elfreda, I wish you'd tell me."

"Well, I don't, Lois. But Saltana's here — and he might know — "

"Oh — I wouldn't trust him — "

"Just a minute!" She cupped the ear of the receiver and looked at Saltana. "It's Lois Terry — "

"And she wants to know if they're busy copulating," said Saltana heartily, as if he wanted Lois to hear him. "Well, she won't believe me — but my answer is *No*."

"I could hear some of that," Lois told Elfreda. "How does he know they aren't? Men always say they never tell one another such things. And anyhow — "

But Saltana, who could move very quickly when he wanted to, took Elfreda by surprise, and had the receiver now. "This is Saltana — you remember? — the man you accused of debauching poor Dr. Tuby, snatching him away from a pure academic life. And I'm ready to bet a hundred to one that Owen Tuby isn't making love to Meldy Glebe. Be quiet — and I'll tell you why he isn't. She's a client. She's too young. She's been bewildered and miserable, and he wouldn't want to take advantage of a temporary infatuation. There's honour among lechers, Dr. Terry. Do you want to speak to Elfreda again? Here she is."

"Elfreda, that man always makes me feel so damned angry. But do you think he's right? After all, she looks a ravishing creature — and if she adores him — "

"No, Lois, I believe Saltana's quite right. But if by any chance he isn't, I'll tell you, my dear. But what are *you* going to do?"

"Ring off — and many thanks, Elfreda — "

"But — wait a minute — you can't keep — "

The little false laugh again. "Yes, I can. Goodnight."

"And that's another one," said Elfreda as she sat down, "who adores our sweet little man. Which reminds me, Cosmo, that you promised to take me to Alan Axwick's party tomorrow night. And don't look like that. This is *business* — you know, that thing you're mad about these days — so you can hardly think and talk about anything else." She was immensely scornful, though she had to work hard to keep her voice from trembling.

"I'll make one point," said Saltana coolly, much to coolly, "and then we'll drop the subject, Elfreda. I want to get into business in order to get out of business." And she had to be content with that. They talked idly about something and nothing for several minutes, and then Saltana left her. She didn't try to make him stay longer; she wanted him to go so that she could think about him.

With Phil Rawbin there, making sketches for them, she and Primrose and Eden Mere worked rather desperately all Thursday morning on that wretched magazine image. All four of them were tired of that magazine, even before it came into existence — if it ever would.

"I think we ought to tell Saltana," said Elfreda, "that we're wasting too much time on these people. After all, we can't please people who don't know their own minds."

"It's what one has to do most of the time, darling," said Primrose. "But I agree about this magazine lot. They're wet. Will you tell the boss?"

But before they had decided when and how, the man himself stalked in, almost sparking, and crackling with urgency. "If you're not working on that fabric, then drop whatever you are doing, all of you. Nan Wolker has just telephoned to say that their great man, Sir Herbert Ossett, comes to London on Monday, and we must have something ready to show him — or else."

"I met him once," Primrose put in hastily. "An' 'e shouts yer bloody 'ead off, 'e does, Sir 'Erbert. Sorry, darling, go on!"

"If he tries to shout my bloody head off, I'll shout his bloody head off," Saltana declared. "And whatever image you decide on for the fabric, I'll stand behind you so long as you explain why you've chosen it. But if you're still arguing about it, then come to a decision as soon as you can. Also, decide who'll speak for you."

"If the man's a bully," said Mrs. Mere grimly, "then I hope it'll be me."

"You can have him, darling," said Primrose. "I wouldn't have enough voice, anyhow."

"Settle it — and everything else — between you, ladies." Saltana's manner was easier now. "You can tell me how far you've got, Elfreda, when we meet tonight. But — to work, to work!" And out he went.

"That's the Axwick party, isn't it, darling?" said Primrose. "I'm going too — because I'm dying to know what'll happen — and I'm being taken by a man — an M.P. — called Rupert Pickrup. He has rather short legs but a huge solemn head and says everything as if he was having to declare war on Brazil. But with any luck, I'll lose him once we're there."

"You heard the boss," cried Elfreda. "To work, to work! Who's got the Pennine Fabrics file?"

And they never stopped arguing — not even during lunch, which they ate together — until six o'clock.

It was well after nine when Elfreda and Saltana arrived at Alan Axwick's house, which was just off Knightsbridge and quite large and imposing.

The room into which they were ceremoniously ushered was very large indeed — perhaps a ballroom once — and there seemed to be about a hundred people already there, some crowding round the buffet, the rest of them scattered around, mostly near the walls, talking hard and drinking champagne. But because so many of the guests were M.P.'s, there was no evening dress. However, Alan Axwick himself was wearing a beautiful dark blue lounge suit, and a tie nearly as pink as his cheeks. He greeted Elfreda with modest enthusiasm and Saltana with awe. "I suppose you know about me, Professor Saltana?" he enquired in an earnest whisper.

"Of course, Mr. Axwick." Saltana contrived one of his piercing looks. "Extremely interesting little case. And, as you know, Dr. Tuby has it in hand."

Axwick brightened and then faded, like a faulty electric light bulb. "Oh yes — I quite understand that. But he doesn't seem to be here yet. And I must say, with all due respect, I wish I knew what he's planned to do tonight. I mean — you know — it makes me feel uneasy."

"Quite wrong, Mr. Axwick, if I may say so, with all due respect,"

Saltana said gravely. "I *know* that Dr. Tuby is doing some brilliant planning on your behalf. So — not to worry, my dear fellow!"

"Jolly good! And I'll try not to. And thanks very much, Professor Saltana. And do get some drinks and things." He hurried away to greet some new arrivals.

He really was rather sweet. And Elfreda felt anxious for him. "Cosmo, what *is* Owen going to do?"

"I haven't the faintest notion, my dear. Let's eat and drink. This kind of party can't be endured unless one's constantly eating and drinking."

A few minutes later, near the buffet, Primrose wormed herself towards them. She had just time to hiss a warning when her escort caught up with her. He had rather short legs, a big head, and poached eyes; and Primrose introduced him as Rupert Pickrup, M.P., and then vanished.

"You're running this image thing, aren't you, sir?" Pickrup had a deep hollow sort of voice, as if he might be talking in a zinc tank.

Elfreda caught a glint of mischief in the dark look Saltana gave him. "Certainly. And you're in the House. Government or Opposition?"

So far as poached eyes can express astonishment, Pickrup's did. "Why — the Opposition, of course. As a matter of fact — and I thought you might have seen it somewhere — I've just been given a leg-up in the party — "

"You have? I've missed that, Mr. Pickrup. So what are you now?"

"I'm Parliamentary Private Secretary to the Shadow Minister of Possible Developments." And Pickrup followed this with a deep short cough.

Saltana nodded gravely. "You've a responsibility there, Mr. Pickrup. And still young, I imagine." Elfreda felt Saltana was overdoing it now, but Pickrup nodded back, just as solemnly.

"Just thirty. And only two years in the House," he said. "Now where's Miss East? I'm supposed to be looking after her." And he asked them to excuse him.

"I'll leave you a moment, if you don't mind, Elfreda," said Saltana. "I must enquire if there's any whisky. What about you? No? Back in a moment, then."

Elfreda finished her champagne and was wondering what to do with her glass — there was no waiter near her — when a man said, "Allow me" and deftly substituted a full glass for her empty one.

"Oh — thank you — " And though he'd startled her, she knew at once that something about her looks attracted him. He was a powerfully built man, perhaps about fifty, and he had a big old-fashioned black moustache, an enormous blue chin, and a nose and cheeks that seemed purplish: he was like a man made out of big bones and blackberries. "Name's Tenks. Sir James, actually. Not interested in politics, perhaps?"

"No, I'm not. And I'm Mrs. Judson Drake. Oh — and this is Professor Saltana — Director of the *Institute of Social Imagistics* — Sir James Tenks — "

"President of the Board of Trade," said Sir James in his brisk and rather barking style. "At the moment."

"I know," Saltana told him. "I read the papers." He was short and sharp too, very different from what he'd been with Axwick and Pickrup. Elfreda, who had often watched boxing on television with Judson, felt this was a meeting of heavyweights.

"Heard about you. Image stuff, eh? How about my image?"

Saltana gave him a hard look. "You can find the Institute at Half Moon House, Sir James."

"No time, no inclination — "

"Then I'll offer you a brief but free demonstration," said Saltana, with a small smile. "In confidence, are you happy where you are?"

"Also in confidence — no. I want the Ministry of Defence."

"Wrong image."

"Oh — come, come, man! Do I look like the Board of Trade?"

Saltana stopped being short and sharp now. "Let me explain — in my expert capacity. Your present image — and I doubt if you could change it now — is that of a rather hard, semi-military, swashbuckling type — "

"I know that. Defence then. You must tell me something I don't know, Professor — "

"I'm about to do that, Sir James. Your image is wrong for Defence because we're not expanding it but contracting it, cutting it down, in fact retreating. And you look as if you want to lead a cavalry charge and not beat a cautious retreat. Everybody would suspect every statement you made. But somebody made a clever move — putting you in the Board of Trade. We want our trade to be expansive, aggressive, even rough and tough. Our traders ought to behave as you look. So your image is exactly right. End of free demonstration, my dear sir."

"And you're no fool, are you?" said Sir James slowly, staring at him. "And I also observe you've found some whisky, which is what I now propose to do. But tell me again." And he turned to Elfreda.

"Tell him what?" Saltana sounded suspicious.

But Elfreda knew what he meant. "This is Professor Saltana — Director of the *Institute of Social Imagistics,* where I am too. And it's at Half Moon House, Half Moon Street."

"Many thanks!" He gave them both a nod and turned away.

"I don't think he needed all that, Elfreda," Saltana grumbled.

"I dare say I was overdoing it," she told him, "but somehow I felt like that." She had in fact felt more than she could explain to Saltana — or indeed explain properly even to herself: as if this odd little encounter was quite unreasonably important, in some way not directly connected with Sir James Tenks himself, though she had enjoyed his first admiring glance. Months later, when she looked back at this brief scene and felt that it had led to a complete change of direction and style in her life, she believed that somewhere deep down she had known this at the time.

It must have been at least half-past ten when Owen Tuby joined them. He was followed by Primrose, and then, at Tuby's urgent request, the four of them held a quick meeting at the far side of the grand piano, out of hearing of the other guests.

"The point is," Tuby began, "by eleven o'clock I need a fairly clear space in the middle of the room. It's not too bad now — it might do as it is — but I'd rather it was clearer and it certainly mustn't be allowed to fill up. So you three must help me."

"Doing what?" demanded Saltana. "We can't go round pushing people nearer the walls."

"But — in effect — you can." Tuby was obviously in earnest about this. "For instance, if you notice a group that's encroaching, you join them from the middle and gradually ease them back. And I don't need to tell Elfreda and Primrose what to do. They're well up in all these tricks."

"I'll love it, darling," said Primrose. "A new kind of party game — *Get 'em out of the Middle* — and one could have marks and prizes." She looked at Tuby. "But couldn't the waiters help?"

Tuby nodded. "I've already bribed two of them. All drinks served on the wall side. I must now get Axwick into position. Show starts at eleven, remember."

Elfreda found she hadn't much to do — this party seemed to prefer a doughnut shape — and if Primrose seemed to be much busier, that was because she'd now turned it into a game. By the time it was nearly eleven, Elfreda, with Saltana in reluctant attendance, had worked her way round to be near Axwick, who had been placed by Tuby on the edge of the middle space furthest away from the door. But Tuby himself she couldn't see anywhere. What on earth was going to happen? She put the question to Saltana.

"I think Owen's going to shoot up through a trapdoor," Saltana muttered, "wearing ballet dress and waving a magic wand."

"You're just jealous, darling," said Primrose, who had appeared from nowhere. "Now what? Every party ought to have something like this. A *happening* instead of dreary old cabaret." But even Primrose stopped talking for the last half-minute.

"Mr. Axwick! Mr. Axwick!" Tuby had come hurrying in, calling urgently and making good use of his voice. "Mr. Axwick!" And when Axwick, scarlet now, not pink, went forward to meet him, Tuby began whispering in his ear and pointed to the door.

The woman who entered slowly and most impressively was tall, wore a fur coat over a long black dress, was crowned with a lofty silvery hair-do, and had a very pale face and inky dark glasses. She held out her hands, and Tuby, still whispering, swept Axwick towards them. They went into a brief huddle and then the woman took Axwick's arm and led him out of the room, with Tuby, apparently flustered now and dithering, close behind them. But then as the buzz of speculation rose all round the room, Tuby returned and, like the cunning old hand he was, soon commanded everyone's attention. "Ladies and gentlemen! Ladies and gentlemen — one moment, please! Mr. Axwick begged me to offer you his apologies. He has had to leave you but he hopes you will stay and keep the party going. There is more champagne on ice and some of it is being opened now. And the chef tells me that hot food will soon be delivered to the buffet. Again, he sends his apologies to you all — only a most urgent call — "

A voice cried "Grenoble?" and there was some laughter and applause.

Tuby, who had baited the hook for this interruption, held up a hand, produced an enigmatic smile, and said, "It might be Grenoble. Mr. Axwick didn't tell me where he was going. He asked me to apologize — and you to enjoy yourselves."

At once then he beckoned his three friends to follow him, hurried out, and as they reached the hall they saw him holding open a door for them. As soon as they had entered the room there, a small study, he closed the door behind him and locked it.

"Drinks and food here," he announced. "Arranged it with Axwick. Help yourselves. Had to have a bolt-hole." He was triumphant, if rather out of breath. He sat down, and when there was some knocking at the door and they looked at him enquiringly, he shook his head. "We ignore it. Probably the Press. A drink, please, Primrose, Elfreda."

Elfreda got there first. She liked the four of them being in this little room, with everybody else locked out. It was dramatic, conspiratorial, and yet snug. "Here you are, Owen. You've earned it. But who was the woman?"

"Don't tell her, darling," cried Primrose. "Let me, because I guessed at once. Meldy Glebe plus very high heels and that enormous wig. And looking like Dracula's sister."

"Of course — how stupid of me!" said Elfreda. "But where's the poor girl now?"

"On her way to the airport with him. Then the car takes her back, looking like herself, to the Baronial Hotel." Tuby stared at the table. "Are those hot sausage rolls?"

"They are, Owen," said Saltana. "And very superior hot sausage rolls too." Then, as he handed them round: "But is Axwick actually going to Grenoble? He is? To do what?"

"He doesn't know. I don't know. Nobody will know," Tuby replied, as complacently as the sausage roll would allow him to sound. "That's the beauty of it, Cosmo."

Saltana looked dubious. "Too impudent, I'd say, Owen. Very risky. You and I could get away with it — "

"You two could get away with murder," Primrose put in quickly.

"But little Axwick might break down under pressure. And then not only will he look silly but he can make us and the Institute look silly too — just at the wrong time."

Tuby took a drink, put down his glass, and for once looked defiant. "I gave this a little thought, you know, Cosmo. It happens to be *my* case. And you didn't even want to discuss it."

"Oh — don't spoil everything, you two," Elfreda cried, genuinely distressed. "It seems to be always happening now — "

"Darling, it's something that's wrong with men," said Primrose. "I believe they can't help it."

"Possibly, my dear." Tuby no longer sounded annoyed. "But I owe our Director an explanation. Now then, Axwick won't be under any real pressure. The story's not important enough. It's just an overnight curiosity, worth a paragraph here and there — probably rather sly — in the morning. But he had to go to Grenoble — I insisted upon that. Now he'll be remembered as the fellow who had to leave his own jamboree, as a fellow who has more in him than meets the eye, a whimsical or rather mysterious little fellow, not at all an ordinary if well-to-do backbencher. That's the kind of image he wanted, Cosmo, and instead of pottering around with him for weeks, I've changed his image overnight. Of course I'll give him a little advice when he comes back, but the real job's done."

"Owen, you may well be right." Saltana's tone was very different now. "As Elfreda knows, I've been feeling rather jealous — "

She had to interrupt him. "He isn't really, Owen. He's only feeling a bit frustrated — with all this big business stuff — "

"While I've had the quick and easy cases that I've enjoyed handling," said Tuby, smiling.

"Especially Meldy Glebe, darling," Primrose threw at him.

"I'm a father figure there, Primrose — "

"And I've known some very funny work go on with father figures, darling — "

"Not in this instance. I assure you." Tuby didn't smile.

"That's what I said last night, isn't it, Elfreda?" Saltana was triumphant. "Now do I tell him about that call?"

"No, you don't." Elfreda found herself shouting at him. There were times when women had to protect one another against men, all of them. "Just shut up about last night."

"Very well then — *business!*" And Saltana shouted that too.

"Business? What business?" They stared at him.

"Institute business — of course. Here we are — four of us — in a quiet room and well supplied with food and drink. It may be late and we may be all half-plastered, but it's at these times that creative ideas rise and take wing — "

"You sound like an advertising man," Tuby told him.

"Because I'm having to think like one. As you know damned well, my friend. Now then, let's make ourselves comfortable and then exchange a few ideas about that fabric, which should come first, and then the savoury breakfast cereal and that new drink Bobbly — "

"Ugh!" Primrose made a face like a stricken monkey. "Can't we choose something not so sick-making?"

"The fabric then. That's really urgent. Have you girls decided anything?"

But the girls hadn't, and Elfreda had not only to advance her own opinions but also those of the absent Mrs. Mere. By the time she had done this and had disagreed with Primrose not only about what Primrose thought but also about what Primrose thought Eden Mere thought, midnight had come and gone, and though Saltana, in a slightly glazed fashion, was still attentive, Tuby was already gently snoring. And then Elfreda fancied she heard a knocking on the door, and silenced Primrose and Saltana to make sure. It was quite unlike the earlier demanding and loud knocking of the Press. It was persistent but somehow tentative, appealing, almost wistful knocking. Elfreda told Saltana he must see who it was.

"Primrose," came from the figure that didn't enter the room but seemed to fall into it.

"My God — it's Rupert Pickrup. Hold him up, darling."

Tuby was struggling out of his doze. "What — who?"

Elfreda was giggling, something she'd tried hard to stop doing. "It's Primrose's escort, Owen."

"An' she's been lurking," Pickrup declared, reproachfully and with some difficulty. "Lurking! Knew hadn't gone home. Asked butler fellow."

"Darling," cried Primrose, "we've been having a meeting."

"Meeting? Meeting?" He glared round accusingly. "Not informed. Why not informed meeting?"

"Pickrup's a politician, Owen," said Saltana solemnly. "In fact, a coming man. He's already Parliamentary Private Secretary to the Shadow Minister of Possible Developments."

"Good God!" cried Tuby. "We must take him home."

Elfreda had to take some aspirin next morning — why did she drink champagne when she knew it didn't agree with her? — and Primrose looked peaky and was cross and argumentative; and as Eden Mere, who felt she ought to have been invited to that party and didn't want to hear about it now, was always delighted to disagree with anybody and everybody, the three of them, still using endearments but drenching them in vinegar, went on and on all day about the best image for that dam' fabric. It was all so wearying that Elfreda, who'd admired the stuff at first, began to take an increasing dislike to it. She went to bed early that night, tried to read a novel about one of those dim damp characters who couldn't tie his shoelaces properly and wondered if he'd committed a murder or not, and made up her mind, just before going to sleep, to give herself a very quiet, not-doing-anything-in-particular Saturday. And this she did, and nothing happened until she was having tea in her sitting room and was asked if she could take a transatlantic call.

It was from Frank Maclaskie, who was staying with some friends in Westchester, New York, and after some hearty but rather routine questions about her health and general state of well-being, he arrived at what she guessed was the purpose of his call.

"Just wondering how that Institute of yours is going, Elfreda. Doing good business?"

"Yes, we are, Frank. More work than we know how to deal with, a lot of publicity, and bigger and bigger fees are rolling in. I know — because I'm in charge of the finances."

"And you keep right on doing just that, Elfreda," he chuckled. "You've got a great idea there — a great idea — and that's not just what I think, Elfreda. But have you still got the long-hairs and eggheads hanging on — that couple of professors?"

"Of course, Frank. Don't be silly. They *are* the Institute. It couldn't exist without them."

He did some more chuckling; he might have been here in her sitting room. What marvels we made — and how silly we still were! "Don't you believe it, Elfreda. Not blaming you — know how these fellas can talk — specially to a woman. But once they're out and some businessmen are in, you'll be rolling. And — listen, Elfreda — don't do anything without telling me first. I'm your friend — and you have a great idea there. Keep in touch, eh? Fine, fine, fine! 'Bye now, Elfreda."

She rang up Saltana, to ask him if she'd said the right things and what she ought to say the next time Frank Maclaskie called her. But of course there was no reply. He was out somewhere, and she couldn't imagine where a man like Cosmo Saltana would be at five o'clock on Saturday — unless of course he was with some woman.

But she hadn't long to wait on Monday morning before she saw him. Just as the three women were beginning their fabric arguments all over again, he marched in, curt and commanding. They had an hour to decide on the best possible image for the fabric, and then Phil Rawbin would have to be there, be given his instructions and told not to stop working — lunch or no lunch — until he had what they wanted. And what this Sir Herbert Ossett *ought* to want, Saltana added. Mrs. Wolker had rung him to say that Sir Herbert would be at the Institute at three sharp. And Sir Herbert apparently was doing them a great favour by agreeing to come there at all; generally he expected people working for him in any capacity to go and see him. Then Saltana, just when all three of them were fed up with him, so sharp and bossy, suddenly changed his tone completely.

"And now I'll talk like a man and a brother — "

"And about time too, Professor Saltana," said Eden sharply.

"Yes, but save that for Sir Herbert. And he'll be difficult." He offered them one of his rare grins. "Now this job's important — and I'm in your hands. What do I know about fabrics? I'll stand up to the man for a few minutes, but then I must hand him over to you three. You have to sell him your image. I can't even try because I don't know enough about fabrics for women. Elfreda — Eden — Primrose — I'm depending on you." Even artful little Owen Tuby, Elfreda reflected, couldn't have done it better. And now, of course, being appealed to, depended upon, they really set to work.

They knew that Sir Herbert and Mrs. Wolker arrived promptly at three because Beryl told them. She also said he looked like one of those fiery old dads who seem as if they're going to burst. Primrose went a few steps along the corridor and returned to say that a shouting match had already started. "But then I told you about him, didn't I?"

"Yes, dear." Mrs. Mere was so far the dignified matron, but then she added: "Shouts yer bloody 'ead off, you told us, dear." And Elfreda was still giggling when she was summoned to join Saltana and the two visitors.

"And no more giggles, darling," Primrose warned her as she left them.

The two men were standing up, glaring at each other, while Mrs. Wolker, whom Elfreda disliked, seemed to be cowering in a corner.

"And just you listen to me," Sir Herbert was bellowing.

But Saltana, who had the voice and manner for it, cut sharply through. "If you'll stop shouting for a moment, I'll introduce you to Mrs. Judson Drake — "

"Oh — beg pardon!" And a warm meaty sort of hand closed over Elfreda's. Sir Herbert was rather short but very broad and fat, had a warm meaty face too, and did look as if at any moment he might burst. But he was quite beautifully dressed, which surprised Elfreda until she remembered that after all he was head of Pennine Fabrics. He had the kind of voice she hadn't heard for a long time.

"Now there's nowt wrong wi' you, Mrs. Drake." He was still holding her hand. "I like a nice-looking woman — an' allus try to 'ave a few workin' round where I can see 'em. Just ask Nan Wolker if I don't. So I'm pleased to meet yer, Mrs. Drake." But then he dropped her hand, turned to look at Saltana and, his face swelling and reddening, he started shouting again.

"But I did yer a favour — comin' 'ere instead of tellin' yer to come to my place — but now yer tryin' to take advantage — I say tryin' to take advantage."

"Nonsense!" Saltana was sitting down now, and had just lit a cheroot.

"Nonsense?" Sir Herbert seemed to be staggered by this cool treatment. "What d'yer mean — *nonsense?*"

"I mean that I'm not trying to take advantage of you, Sir Herbert. To be candid, I don't know what you're talking about."

This sent Sir Herbert into a rage. He hadn't sat down; he didn't look as if he would ever sit down again. But as soon as he raised his voice he seemed to do a furious little dance, as if he must either move his feet or explode. "Yer don't know what I'm talkin' about? I call that bloody cheek an' impudence. Well, I'll tell yer what I'm talkin' about. First, I come an' see yer instead of makin' yer come an' see me. A favour on my part. An' right off yer take advantage. Now listen. When 'Erbert Ossett does business 'e does it wi' the top man. No exception — top man — boss. But I'm not 'ere five minutes afore yer tellin' me I must go an' start arguin' wi' three of your women. An I tell yer I don't do business that way. Boss — top man — every time, without fail." He seemed to like the sound of these last four words, because as he sat down he repeated them, enjoying them more: "Ev-ery ti-ime, with-out fai-ai-ail." Then he looked round, as if for applause. Elfreda glanced from him to Saltana in despair. This would be like having a two-hundred-pound three-year-old on your hands.

"Sir Herbert," Saltana began quite calmly, "first I must point out that Mrs. Drake here, Miss Primrose East, and Mrs. Mere have had careful instruction in image work from Dr. Tuby and me. They don't know as much as we do — that's not to be expected — but they know a great deal more than you do — "

"They might — an' then again they might not," Sir Herbert declared. "But that's not the point."

"Secondly — " and Saltana went on as if Sir Herbert hadn't spoken — "being women, they understand far more about fabrics — their nature, their appeal, their use — than I do."

"I dare say — but when I do business, then I want — "

"Don't tell me all that again," Saltana cut in sharply. "I'm not deaf — and I'm not an imbecile. Elfreda, after days and days of research and discussion, you and Primrose and Mrs. Mere have agreed on an image for this fabric — "

"Yes, we have." Then she looked enquiringly at Sir Herbert, who seemed prepared to listen to her quite amiably. "We can explain exactly what we have in mind — and can show you some sketches — "

"All right, luv — then do it 'ere — boss's room where I belong. I don't 'ave to be pushed down passage, do I?" His temper was rising again.

Elfreda risked smiling at him. "No, of course not, Sir Herbert. But there are four of us, with the artist, and all his sketches and our notes — so if you wouldn't mind — "

"Yer askin' me to do yer a favour, are yer?"

"Well — yes, I am." Another smile.

He didn't return the smile. "That's the second favour I've done on this job," he told Saltana. "An' it's the last. Lead on, Mrs. Drake. No, you stop 'ere, Nan luv. I can trust me own judgment." He gave the room a general glare. "I say — I can trust me own judgment."

Primrose and Eden were waiting for them. Phil Rawbin, who disliked showing his work, had slipped away; he might be talking to Tuby. Sir Herbert had met Primrose before and said so — it was somewhere, he remembered, "on Riveera." And he added, "A lot o' slap an' tickle goin' on, I'd say — eh, luv?" Primrose said there was but she hadn't been involved, being dead against slap and tickle and all that jazz. Eden appeared to be taller than ever as she acknowledged Sir Herbert's existence; she was formidably beaky and stately but was condescending for a few minutes to a far lower social level, as if a king's older sister were receiving a small provincial mayor. And Sir Herbert, in spite of his enormous opinion of himself, couldn't help being somewhat impressed.

"I wouldn't 'ave thought this would 'ave been in yer line, Mrs. Mere."

"My husband — O. V. Mere, the educationist, editor, and consultant — met Professor Saltana and Dr. Tuby just after they had decided to establish, first at a university, an *Institute of Social Imagistics,*" she told him loftily. "Later, when I met them, I realized, as my husband had done at once, that here were two original and brilliant minds. I asked to be able to take some part in their image research. Fascinating, of course! And now, we three here together make a very strong team of feminine researchers." As Sir Herbert tried to interrupt, she checked him. "Kindly allow me to explain. It will be to your advantage, Sir Herbert," she continued severely. "I am not wasting your time. Mrs. Drake, who has spent many years in America and is in fact the widow of an American millionaire, represents the sophisticated, cosmopolitan, well-to-do woman of forty. Primrose, as you must know, is the young girl but a highly sophisticated, experienced, fashionable young girl. And I, Sir Herbert, am not sophisticated in this sense of the term. I am not fashionable. I am not well-to-do. What am I, then? I am the British matron, Sir Herbert, the wife, the mother, condemned to think hard before spending a few pounds on anything, and in that capacity I may be considered the balance wheel on the — *Ger-huh!* — whatever it is that has a balance wheel." She ended rather lamely, but even so it was an impressive performance. And Sir Herbert acknowledged this by keeping quiet and nodding a great deal.

"I get yer point, Mrs. Mere. So let's get down to business. Now we at Pennine are about to put on market the best synthetic 'ard-wearin' fabric we've manufactured for many a year. Yer've 'ad a piece — an' it's an honest sample, no jiggery-pokery — yer've seen it, yer've 'andled it. Now

it'll cost a fortune putting it on market — an' we're ready to spend a fortune — but not on any bit o' nonsense. If it's an image job, as our Nan
Wolker seems to think, we've got to 'ave the right image — just one, but
one that's dead right. Now then — 'oo starts?" And he looked from one
to the other of them. But they had already worked this out. Primrose
would begin.

"Well, darling — "

"No soft soap, lass — "

"I call everybody *darling* but you can be an exception," Primrose retorted coldly. She stared so hard he stopped wriggling in his chair. "We
decided early on we needed only one image — and that it should be not
a *Maker's Image* — this is the man who makes this lovely fabric for you
and all that — but a *User's Image* — she always chooses it, why don't
you? We agreed about that, and then of course I said it must be a girl —
someone rather like me — "

"Could *be* you, I'm thinkin'," Sir Herbert shouted. "Any road a right
nice-lookin' girl. We're all with yer there, for a start."

"Certainly not," said Eden contemptuously. "Elfreda, you first."

"Girls like Primrose can wear anything, Sir Herbert," said Elfreda,
who found herself speaking quite firmly, now that it was up to her. "And
women can't. As we know only too well. If I saw a colour photo of Primrose wearing a new fabric, I'd admire Primrose or feel envious, but I'd
hardly notice the fabric. All right for her, whatever it is, but what about
me? I'm forty, not twenty. She could be wearing dishcloths and lengths
of old rope — and nobody cares. But me — I've got to be careful. I can't
depend on any stuff that's lying around or cheap. And I'm looking for a
new dependable fabric for *myself,* not for a girl younger and prettier than
I am. Eden?"

"An' when do I get a word in edgeways?" Sir Herbert demanded.

"Later," Mrs. Mere told him severely. "You must listen to me first.
Otherwise, what are we doing? We must now translate Elfreda's argument into image terms. It was a question, as we soon realized, of preferring the *Under Image* to the *Over Image*. As both Professor Saltana and
Dr. Tuby have pointed out to us, considerable resistance — especially
among reasonably intelligent women — has now been built up against
the *Over Image,* obviously suggesting superiority, an ideal but distant target. What is needed at the present time is the *Under Image,* not unpleas-
ing in itself — it would be absurd to offer a hag — but an image that
the average woman could identify herself with — or believe she could
improve upon. Both Professor Saltana and Dr. Tuby have stressed to us
the importance of the *Under Image* — "

"Oh — shut it!" And this came out at the top of Sir Herbert's voice.

*"What did you say?"* And Mrs. Mere, who hadn't sat down, looked
about eight feet high — and terrible.

But Sir Herbert, now apparently in a rage, wasn't easily quelled. "I didn't come 'ere to listen to a lecture on *Over Images* and *Under Images*. I'm a busy man. If yer've got owt to show me, then let's 'ave a look."

"Well, here are some rough sketches, Sir Herbert," said Elfreda, who felt anything but calm and confident now. "Of course in a good colour photo, showing a model just like this, actually wearing a suit or a dress made of your fabric, it would be far more effective — "

Sir Herbert hurled the sketches away and pushed himself out of the chair. "Just wasting my time, that's all yer doin'. 'Oo'd look at 'er? 'Undreds just like 'er in any train or bus or down the nearest street! Don't try an' come it over me," he shouted. "I'm off." But he wasn't, because Mrs. Mere, now as angry as he was, stood in front of the door.

"Sir Herbert Ossett," she began, her great nose quivering, her eyes flashing, "some men working for you — chemists or engineers or whatever they are — must have had to *think* — in order to produce this new fabric. Don't you ever think? Because so far you seem to me one of the stupidest men I've ever known." And she stepped aside, opened the door, and glared him out.

They listened to him stamping along the corridor, clearly about to tell Saltana it was all off, and then Eden closed the door quite gently and they looked at one another. Elfreda, who was always surprising herself, began crying. What would Saltana think of them — of her — and after he'd told them he depended on them?

"All my fault, I imagine," said Eden, embracing Elfreda and squeezing out a few tears herself.

"Darling — don't — don't!" said Primrose, joining the damp huddle. She was also tearful, but declared fiercely she would get even somehow with that old so-and-so.

Ten minutes or so of squashy misery, with the three of them still huddled, went crawling by; they knew Sir Herbert had gone for they had heard him go, even behind their closed door; and all they could decide was that if Saltana sent for one of them, the other two would go with her. But that didn't happen. He came to them.

Elfreda loved the man but didn't know yet what he might do or say next, and now he surprised her — and won her heart forever — by not being angry at all, not even cross, annoyed, irritable, never even looking as if he might reproach them. He merely said rather casually, "Well, that didn't work, did it? Tell me what happened."

"You must blame me," Eden began at once, but Elfreda and Primrose rushed in, and it was several minutes before Saltana, unusually patient, was able to persuade each of them to report in turn exactly what she had said to Sir Herbert.

"I don't know what else you could have done or said," he told them. "It's my opinion now that Ossett never intended to take us seriously. I think he'd been talked into coming here by Nan Wolker." He may have heard faint sniffs. He stopped, looked round at them, and then continued: "I have an idea Mrs. Wolker isn't popular here."

"No, Cosmo," said Elfreda, "we don't like her."

"Such a snappy and suspicious little woman," Mrs. Mere added.

"I'd say — a typical business bitch," said Primrose.

"I thought that myself at first, but now I know her better, I don't agree with you. Now this is much harder on Nan Wolker than it is on us. We've wasted some time and lost a possible client, but she may have lost the confidence of her boss — he was very short and sharp with her as they left — and put her whole position into jeopardy. And if you're wondering why I'm making a speech about Nan Wolker, it's because we ought to feel sorry for her — and then we shan't feel so sorry for ourselves. And now let's push on with some other work," he concluded rather lightly.

As soon as he had gone, Elfreda saw that the other two were raising eyebrows at each other. "I know what you're thinking," she told them. "I'm thinking the same thing. Either Cosmo Saltana's changing or he put on a very special performance for us. He *sounded* quite different from our usual Professor Saltana — "

"I know, darling," said Primrose. "But of course he may really be making mad love to ratty little Wolker — "

"I doubt that," said Eden.

"And I'm sure you're wrong, Primrose," Elfreda declared with some warmth. "I think Saltana meant what he said — and that he wanted us to stop feeling sorry for ourselves."

Later, in her bath, Elfreda decided that Saltana's speech was intended not only to make her feel easier but also to remove any suspicion she may have felt about him and Nan Wolker. And this it had done, except of course if he was now feeling so sorry for poor little Nan, then poor little Nan, probably one of those blondes who can shed a few tears without ruining their faces, might soon seek and find consolation in his arms. Any poor little Nan, really working at it, could have any man, even a Saltana, tied to the bedpost. Then she reproached herself for being so cynical, and thought how wonderful Saltana had been with them — with her, really — not being angry at all. She was still wobbling between these two lines of thought when she was drying herself and had to take a telephone call.

It was from Saltana. "I don't know what's happening, but Ossett has just rung up to ask if we — that's you and I — could go and see him at his flat at nine o'clock. It's above their London office in Baker Street — the address is in the phone book. I hope you can make it, Elfreda. You can? Good! Well, I'll pick up Rawbin's sketches and bring them along, and wait for you down below just before nine, so we can march in together. He's no objection to Primrose being there — though I don't think it's worth while trying to get hold of her now — but he won't have that bloody huge Mrs. Mere, he says, not even over his dead body. No, I don't know what he wants. Probably *he* doesn't. But he's leaving in the morning, so we ought to give him a chance — if it's only to apologize."

"Yes, of course, Cosmo. Is Mrs. Wolker going to be there?"

"I don't know, Elfreda. She didn't call me. It was some secretary who put me through to the great Sir Herbert. Look out for me then, about nine, down below."

Nan Wolker *was* there, looking very small and rather wan, as Elfreda saw at once when Sir Herbert admitted her and Saltana into his company flat, which looked like all the company flats — or, rather, corporation executive apartments — she'd ever seen, and, like most of them, carried a strong flavour of cigars and whisky. Perhaps because of the cigars and whisky, which he immediately shared with Saltana, Sir Herbert seemed far more amiable than he'd been in the afternoon.

"An' yer've got them sketches? Good! Now — I want to give yer a fair do. I was a bit 'asty this afternoon, I know, but when that Mrs. Mere, talkin' to me as if I was a school lad, started lecturin' me on *Under Images* and *Over Images,* I'd 'ad enough and 'ad to bugger off. If yer'll pardon me French, Mrs. Drake. Take me tip, Saltana, an' get rid o' that woman. She'll ruin yer. She's bloody murder."

"Not everybody likes her manner, Sir Herbert," Saltana told him coolly. "But she was talking good sense. If you come to our Institute, you can hardly object to somebody wanting to discuss images."

"Well, 'appen that was me mistake, callin' on yer instead of askin' yer to come an' see me. Now look! These are yer sketches an' 'ere's what our regular advertisin' chaps 'ave come up with. I think you met two of 'em — at Nan's. Now just look! There's no comparison, is there?"

He was showing them some colour-photographs of a very pretty girl draped in the new fabric.

"They're excellent photographs of the fabric," said Saltana coldly. "But with the same facilities, we could display it just as well. In fact, better."

" 'Ow d'yer make that out?"

"I'll explain that in a moment."

"I dare say. But yer can't deny that this lot catches yer eye an' yours look nowt beside 'em." And Sir Herbert sat down, swallowed some whisky, then complacently puffed away at his cigar. Nan Wolker stared at nothing in particular, didn't speak, looked as if she might never speak again.

"Elfreda?" And Saltana raised his eyebrows and almost smiled at her. "Any comment?"

She had been dreading this but now that she couldn't escape the appeal, she contrived to suggest a cool, offhand but expert manner. "A typical *Over Image,* of course. I see scores of them, just like this, every week. Sometimes it's this same girl."

"I dare say, Mrs. Drake," said Sir Herbert, still complacent, "but she catches yer eye, doesn't she? Can't get away from that."

"But that's just what I do — get away from it. If I were a man, I might not, but I'm a woman — and I'm tired of this girl — and all the other girls. They can't sell me anything to wear. They're putting me off, not bringing me on. And it's my kind who'll buy the fabric. But the *Over Image* won't persuade us. We resist it. We've had too much of it."

"An' I think I could easily 'ave too much of this *Under Image* and *Over Image* stuff, Mrs. Drake — "

Saltana took a deep drink and then looked hard at Sir Herbert. "All right, then — in plain terms — no images. We want to show you a colour photograph — probably several, of course — of a woman who'll look like those sketches. She isn't young, she isn't beautiful. She's a pleasant, intelligent, young middle-aged woman, who might be the wife of a doctor, an engineer, an accountant. There are hundreds of thousands of women like her, some who look less pleasant and intelligent, some who feel at once they are more attractive. But most of them will believe — if the new fabric appeals to them — that they can *do more with it than this woman can.* They haven't to make a despairing attempt, after failing over and over again, to be like her, as they have with that pretty young girl you showed us. Envy breeds a self-protective cynicism. They no longer believe in that girl. They know she's a highly-paid professional model who's not even interested in your fabric. They've built up a resistance — as Elfreda suggested — against this superiority, this wouldn't-you-like-to-be-me? advertising. I'm sorry, Sir Herbert, but you're out of date in your image thinking. The *Under Image,* which says in effect 'I'm like you but perhaps you're more promising,' is driving out the *Over Image,* saying 'What would you give to be like me?' And the curious thing is, as we've recently discovered, that people have seen so many *Over Images* that the *Under Image* often acts as what we call a *Feedback Image* — that is — "

"No, it isn't," Sir Herbert cut in sharply. "Yer promised there'd be none o' that. Mrs. Drake, yer don't 'ave to agree with yer boss — not tonight, any road. 'Alf the time me lot won't think way I think. Now tell me straight, luv, did yer agree with all that?"

"But of course! I know he's right. And Primrose, Mrs. Mere, and I went to work along those lines."

"Nan, luv? 'Igh time yer put a word in."

"Very well, then." And Mrs. Wolker, sitting up and trembling a little, sounded almost passionate. "I agree with every single thing Professor Saltana has said. As far as I'm concerned, that routine pretty-girl image they've just cooked up for you — is *out.* But I don't propose to argue about it. Not tonight. It's late and I'm tired."

"So am I, luv, for that matter. 'Ave to make an early start in mornin' an' all." He pushed himself up, and the other three rose with him. "Now make a note, Nan luv, to get that length o' fabric back from agency an' send it straight away to this Institute lot. They'll 'ave to make do wi' this length 'cos I can't 'ave pieces o' this stuff all over the place. Y'understand — it's secret yet," he shouted at them all. "*Secret.* 'As to be. There's people in our bloody trade would take milk out of yer tea. Now then — Professor an' Mrs. Drake — I want yer to get crackin' an' find right model for this woman yer 'ave in mind an' do some colour photos sharp as yer can. Could you come up North if yer 'ave to, Professor?"

"I'm extremely busy," said Saltana, "but if I thought you were giving our ideas serious consideration and wanted me to explain them to your associates up there — "

"That's just what I'd be after," shouted Sir Herbert. "But I'll let yer know. I say, I'll let yer know. Got yer sketches? Right! 'Cos I don't want 'em an' you do — eh? It's photos we want. Can't talk me out o' *them.* I say, yer can't talk me out o' *them.*"

Nan Wolker was with them as they waited for a taxi. When one drew up, Elfreda was immensely relieved to hear Saltana say, "Nan, we'll drop you first, then I'll take Elfreda to her hotel." And indeed when, a week later, Saltana left for the North and Sir Herbert, and Elfreda learnt that Nan Wolker was not going with him, she began to feel quite friendly towards Nan, who after all had been very helpful, and invited her to dinner.

## 6

Saltana returned from the North on a Sunday — Sir Herbert didn't believe in free Saturdays for directors if they hadn't made up their minds by Friday night — and was given a hair-raising lift to London by one of the younger directors, who had a fast car that was never allowed to stay long behind any other car. It was April now but still damnably cold in West Riding, and Saltana, who hated cold weather, was glad to go roaring out of it. Though it was late evening when they got there, London by comparison seemed to be already enjoying spring. Saltana telephoned Elfreda to announce his return. No, he wouldn't go round to see her. After a drink and a sandwich — he'd had an enormous lunch — he was going early to bed, after three nights of Yorkshire hospitality. But he'd talk to them all in the morning. So would she see that everybody was in his room not much later than ten o'clock?

"I'm doing it this way," he began, first looking at Tuby, then at Elfreda, then at Primrose and Mrs. Mere, "so I can tell you what happened to me, and then you can tell me what's been happening here. This will save time and avoid any misunderstandings."

"Certainly," said Tuby.

"And rests on a sound democratic basis," said Mrs. Mere. "Proceed, my dear Director. Were you successful — and did you enjoy your trip?"

"On the whole, I didn't. I seemed to spend an interminable time arguing with *royds* — Ackroyds, Boothroyds, Murgatroyds — who either shouted, like Sir Herbert, or talked through clenched teeth. And I could never decide if they were profoundly insecure or intolerably conceited. But they made me fight every inch of the way, though as soon as each battle was over they pressed food and drink upon me in staggering quantities. As for the chosen image, they compromised. They'll use ours *and* the pretty-girl image supplied by the agency. However, they've agreed to pay us two thousand pounds for the use of our image for three months, and then if they decide to keep on using it they'll pay us a further two thousand for the next six months. It might have been better, but we don't come out of it too badly."

The others made those vague committee noises suggesting agreement.

"And now — what's been happening here? Dr. Tuby?" Saltana liked a certain formality in these meetings.

"I'll take my own cases first, Director," said Tuby, who, as Saltana knew very well, cared nothing for formality himself but was ready to indulge his friend. "Alan Axwick insisted upon paying his fee, telling me he was completely satisfied. I offered to round off and highlight his image, but he implored me not to do anything else. He's been noticed, talked about, had some paragraphs in the Press, and has been asked to take part in a television programme. Case closed, then. That of Meldy Glebe is of course far more complicated — "

"I'll bet," said Primrose.

"On the other hand," Tuby continued smoothly, "the fee should be considerably higher — according to her agent, Wilf Orange. At present, she's on location in Italy — starting a new film, in which she's demanded certain changes, as the result of our discussions of her image. She wanted me to go out there for further talks — "

"And you know why?" said Elfreda. "She's crazy about you — "

"But I told her I was much too busy. However, I've agreed to continue our image discussions when she comes back. Meanwhile, she's told Wilf Orange I ought to be paid half the fee at once — that is, two thousand five hundred — "

"Five thousand altogether?" Saltana couldn't help feeling envious. All that for lolling around with a pretty girl! And he'd just had a three-day shouting match in the bleak North for far less! "Was that your figure, or Elfreda's?"

"No, Wilf Orange's. He's told the studio people that Meldy has only to sulk for a day and they'd lose twice that. He's almost certain they'll pay. Now what's the rest? Ezra Smithy — that's the man who represents Dan Luckett — "

"Eat At Dan's," Elfreda reminded Saltana.

"He's agreed to a holding fee of five hundred and has asked us to do some work on a few possible images. He doesn't know when Luckett may suddenly decide to come to London, so we must have something to show him. And Smithy also says that if we came up with something that excited Luckett the fee might be very large indeed. So the ladies and I have been exchanging a few ideas. Elfreda — your turn."

"We're also working on Bobbly — the new drink — you remember? — that Bevs Ltd badly wanted an image for. They've now paid a holding fee, but as they're your clients, not Dr. Tuby's, we haven't gone very far yet — "

"And it smells and tastes like a mixture of soda water and furniture polish," said Mrs. Mere.

"Darling, it really isn't too bad," said Primrose.

"My dear child, after the life you've led the last few years, you no longer know *what* you're drinking. And don't tell me again *it looks gay.*"

"Quiet, you two! I'm talking." Elfreda glanced at some notes, then looked up to give Saltana a rich slow smile. She was very smart, very attractive, he thought, this Monday morning. "Albion Foods rang up on Friday," she told him. "You know — the people who want to market a savoury breakfast cereal. I told them you were away and that you'd talk to them today or tomorrow."

Saltana made a note. "Anything else?" And while Elfreda hesitated, he saw that all four of them were exchanging odd looks. "Come on, now. What is it?"

"Two enquiries over the phone sounded nutty to me," she told him. "One was a girl, who stammered and stuttered and didn't seem to know what she wanted. The other seemed to be an oldish man — a sort of angry prophet. I felt I couldn't turn them down when you weren't here, so I simply put them off for two or three days. You *might* be interested — "

"I might — and I'm very glad you didn't turn them down flat. That's my prerogative. But I don't think those two calls explain your hesitation, Elfreda, and the glances you four were exchanging a minute ago. So now — what?"

"I'll take over if you want me to, Elfreda," said Tuby.

"Bless you! But I feel it's my job, Owen." She looked at Saltana, and he knew she was being very brave. "On Thursday we had an enquiry — a man actually came to see us — on behalf of a new German-American firm. They're about to put on the market here a range of packaged food substitutes, and they're ready to pay us a lot of money if we can find a really attractive image for them."

"Well, that's our business, isn't it?"

"Not mine, it isn't," cried Mrs. Mere. "He left some samples. I tried them. And they're rubbish."

"So that's it," said Saltana, looking hard at Elfreda and ignoring Eden Mere. He was the captain staring down from the bridge at what might prove to be a mutinous crew.

Blinking a little, Elfreda stared back at him. "Yes, that's it. I told him you weren't here — I had to, of course — but I must tell you that all three of us are dead against accepting this commission. We simply can't bring ourselves to produce bright tempting images to sell innocent people this rubbish."

"And I think they're right, Director," said Tuby.

"Oh — you do, do you, Deputy Director?" And Saltana felt he was looking and sounding sufficiently grim.

"Yes, I do." Tuby spoke very quietly. "We may be here to make money — and as quick as we can — but not anyhow and in any way. We don't have to help these fellows to swindle and corrupt the public."

"No doubt we don't. But who's to decide that that is what they're doing — or about to do? I'm still supposed to be in charge of this Institute. I have to make the decisions, Dr. Tuby."

"Not all of them, Professor Saltana. What you and I know about packaged food substitutes," Tuby continued, still not raising his voice, "wouldn't be worth tuppence of anybody's money. But the women *do* know about them. In this instance, they're *our* experts. You can't ignore their opinion — "

"You're missing the point. I'm not questioning their opinion of dehydrated cabbage or instant lamb chops or whatever the stuff pretends to be. What I am most sharply denying is their assumption that they can make decisions for the Institute — "

"Oh — don't be so stuffy," cried Primrose. "We don't want to run the Institute — and you know bloody well we don't. Just creep round here like mice. But not only won't I do any work for that muck, I won't work for an Institute that takes any of its money." And she hurried out, not even closing the door behind her.

"And neither will I," cried Mrs. Mere as she left too.

"Oh — my God!" Elfreda, all a wild blue look, jumped up. "Perhaps I'd better — " And out she went.

Tuby closed the door carefully, returned to his seat, and relit his pipe, and then said, "Well, Cosmo?"

"Did you know they were going to do that, Owen?"

"No, I didn't. But then I also didn't know you'd take such a high line — "

"It's a matter of principle — "

"The women aren't much interested in matters of principle — "

"Nonsense! It's the only defence they have for their own behaviour — "

"No, no, no, Cosmo! They try the muck and then they imagine thousands of other women saying to their husbands, sons, lovers, friends, 'Darling, I'm trying something new and rather fascinating' — and then being horribly disappointed. So they feel disgusted and furious. However, there are still a few samples left, and you could leave early for lunch, go upstairs, and try the stuff yourself. It will ruin your lunch but could save your face. And you want to save your face, don't you?"

"I want to save this Institute, Owen." And Saltana announced this in all sincerity. "The money's just beginning to roll in, but if I start allowing them to make decisions — "

"No, no, no again, Cosmo! You see this as a kind of power test, but that's not how their minds are working. You've only to say, 'You're quite right, girls. It's rubbish and we won't touch it,' and they'll be more deeply devoted to you than ever. I know them better than you do. And don't forget I'm as anxious as you are to make money."

"No, not quite, I think, Owen. I want much more money than you do — " But Saltana looked at the expression on Tuby's face, and he laughed. "All right, you go along and tell the women I'll accept their verdict on that packaged substitute stuff — I'd have hated it anyhow — and that we're all friends again. And then come back — unless you've something urgent — and we'll do some work together on the bigger jobs looming up. Unless of course you'd rather work on your own."

"Come off it, Cosmo. I'm a better persuader and soft-soaper than you are, but that's all. The truth is, of course, that all that rough-and-tumble in the North and having to accept a compromise have shaken you a little — "

"And all because I'm too bloody conceited, Owen," said Saltana earnestly. He now felt more open, more expansive. In suggesting that he and Tuby should work together, he had exercised what his mother used to call his *better nature*. Egoism, probably green-rotten with jealousy or envy of Tuby's easy successes, had demanded that he should, if anything, widen the distance between them when working; and egoism had been defeated, negative feelings had been banished, the sun of his better nature had risen. In its warmth he worked, lunched, then worked again with Tuby until the end of the day. Then, over a drink, they decided amiably it would save time if they concentrated separately on their own clients.

Later in the week, Saltana lunched with Simon Birtle at one of Birtle's clubs. They hadn't met for some weeks, and Birtle explained that he'd been in Canada and the States. The club was one of those huge and solemn institutions where the food seemed all the more horrible because of the pomp that surrounded it, portions of shepherd's pie being served as if they were wild duck brought by helicopter.

"Primrose says you're all very busy," said Birtle as soon as they were settled in the great sad dining room, "and doing very well. Are you?" And his hottish red-brown eyes looked suspicious. "Or is it mostly bluff?"

"Only one part bluff to two parts busy," Saltana replied cheerfully.

"You're getting a devil of a lot of publicity," said Birtle, almost making a grievance out of it.

"We are indeed. But then people come to us in search of publicity, and some of it rubs off on us."

"Anybody wanting to take you over yet?" Birtle sounded very casual this time, thereby signalling his interest to Saltana's sharp ear.

"One or two advertising agencies — and of course we've turned them down. And Elfreda Drake, who appears to have some rich and powerful American friends, has had to answer several enquiries from them over the transatlantic phone." Saltana's manner was casual-lofty. Would Birtle be taken in by it? Probably not. It might save time and trouble, he concluded sardonically, if they both talked like honest men.

"Don't consider letting the Americans in, Saltana, before you talk to me." Birtle suddenly stopped sounding casual, looked hard at Saltana, and said, "What d'you know about high society?"

Surprised, Saltana stopped buttering a biscuit and stared back at him. "Nothing at all. I didn't know it still existed."

"Well, it does. I wouldn't say Gladys and I are in it, but they offer us a peep now and again. They have nephews and nieces who might be ready to do a little work for our papers and magazines. They'll always use you, y'know. You've heard of the Sturtletons, of course?"

"No, I haven't."

Birtle frowned at him. "This isn't a pose, is it?"

"Certainly not. I can and do pose, of course, but this is neither the time nor the place for posing. So tell me about the Sturtletons."

"He's an earl. Oldish dullish chap, but filthy rich and has a lot of political influence. His wife — Lady Harriet — daughter of a duke — is a very different type. Much younger, wonderful looks, famous smart hostess who's generally supposed to have slept around a lot, and she's always turning up in the gossip columns and the glossies."

"I don't read 'em, don't see 'em."

"Anyway, she wants to meet you. She's seen you on the telly and read about you and the Institute, and she's curious. I know this because she told me so on the phone yesterday. They're giving one of their big grand dinner parties next Thursday, and Gladys and I are going, and she asked me if I could persuade you to go — with Primrose, who doesn't know about it yet. Say *Yes* — and I'll tell her and she'll send cards, of course. And you'll be a dam' fool if you don't go. New experience — fascinating woman — and you'll meet a lot of very influential people. Great chance, Saltana! Don't miss it."

"Very well, Birtle — and many thanks! Shall I mention it to Primrose?"

"Do that. And she can probably fill you in — at least on Lady Harriet."

And Primrose could — and did, that very afternoon. "Fab, darling — I'm all for it. I met her at a party in Cannes and then at one they gave in London. Not a dinner party — they're much grander — but a buffet supper do. I don't remember meeting him — perhaps he wasn't around — but — my God — *she* was around, all right. She's quite beautiful — in a kind of enamel-finish style — old, of course — "

"How old? About forty?"

"About that — yes," said Primrose, impervious to irony on this subject. "And I'd say — a cold-hearted bitch. A left-over *femme fatale*. A man-eater, everybody says. So if she asked the Birtles to bring you — watch it, chum!"

"Nonsense! I'm too old, too poor, and have no social graces. Now if it were Owen Tuby — "

"No, she'd never be interested in *him*. She's too physical. She'd take one look at him, mentally undress him, and drop him out — all in a couple of seconds. But you're like an older and cleverer version of those Italian types she used to run around with on the Riviera. So I say, darling — *watch it*."

Saltana laughed. "Very well, Primrose. Just to stop you worrying, if she gives me a chance — though that's unlikely — I'll not only be blunt and ungracious, I'll be downright rude to her."

"Oh no — you won't!" Primrose was genuinely horrified. "She's had so much flattery, she'd be fascinated at once, wondering how to make you crawl. No, no — lay off the rude bit!"

"You take some pleasing, girl. All right, I'll just be an open-mouthed peasant, touching an imaginary forelock."

"I'll bet! Anyhow — just watch it!"

Sometimes Primrose still stayed at the Birtles' and at other times she didn't, and Saltana and Tuby had given up trying to understand her domestic arrangements, though they accepted Elfreda's repeated statement that as yet no man was involved in any of them. However, that night she was staying at the Birtles' and Saltana called for her there. It was only eight o'clock and Simon Birtle offered them a drink. "Won't take us more than ten minutes — and the Sturtletons dine late." He looked reproachfully at Saltana. "They also like a white tie, I'm afraid, old man."

"So I see," said Saltana, smiling. "But a dinner jacket is now as far as I'll go. This is oldish but rather elegant. The coat, you may have no-

ticed, is made of very fine black velvet, designed and executed by an elderly Indian in Guatemala City."

"It's a fab coat, darling," cried Primrose, who was wearing a long
dress for once, composed of mysterious shades of grey and green and faint
rose, and looked splendid. "Isn't it, Gladys?"

"You look very distinguished, Professor Saltana," said Mrs. Birtle.
"And I never know why Simon worries about black ties and white ties.
As if there wasn't enough to worry about!"

"Doesn't matter to me, my dear," said her husband. "Only I happen
to know that old Sturtleton's rather a stickler."

"Well, pooh to Stickler Sturtleton!" cried Primrose, who could respond at once to a champagne cocktail. "The representatives of the Institute are going to knock them cold. But now you look so handsome and
distinguished, Professor darling, don't forget — watch it with Lady
Harriet!"

"Now that's silly, Primrose," said Mrs. Birtle.

"Well, I don't know about that," said Birtle. And he began to re-
count some of her ladyship's exploits, known to but not used by the Press.
But then he remembered the time, said they'd be late, and bustled them
into the waiting limousine. It took them to a very large corner house in
Belgravia, where there were footmen in uniform, ancestors on the walls,
much grand illumination, and the Sturtletons and about twenty other
people in a drawing room that was like a museum.

By chance Saltana was greeted first by his host, a red-faced old
buffer with very blue popeyes, who said, "Glad y'could come," and obviously neither knew nor cared who the hell he was. But when Birtle,
conscious of that black tie and coat, and embarrassed, presented him to
Lady Harriet, she gave him a sharp look, then a sweet hostess smile, and
cried in a rather high and slightly nasal voice, "But of course — how
marv'lous! You're the *image* man. And you must promise not to go tonight
before we've had a private little talk about *my* image — which I'm sure
is absolutely *foul*." Another smile, and then she had to greet somebody else.

Saltana took a drink from a tray offered to him, without noticing
what it was, and moved nowhere in particular, trying to look as if he'd
really had too much of this kind of thing. But then a squeal made him
turn, and there at his elbow was Petronella, Duchess of Brockshire, in
pillar-box red, too much make-up, and probably already half-sloshed.

"Darling Primrose told me you were here," Petro began, doing tremendous false-eyelash work. "And of course wonderful to see you! But
where oh where is my sweet little Owen Tuby? You ought to have *made*
Hatty rope him in. I read about him and that film star, Meldy What's-it,
who can't act for nuts. Having her like mad, I suppose, the wicked little
man?" She grabbed a drink from a passing tray.

"No, Petro — a strictly platonic relationship. But where have you been since you stayed with us in Brockshire?"

"My dear, you'd never guess. With Tippy — in Africa. Not in Morocco, where he was before — you remember? — but much further down, somewhere in the middle of the bloody great place. Tippy's still there. Can't tear himself away from all those animals. Listen — an *idea!* Why don't we phone Tuby and tell him to put on a boiled shirt and blow in after dinner — say, about ten-thirty?"

"Wouldn't work, Petro. To begin with, he lives in digs — somewhere Belsize Park way — and he eats out, so he wouldn't be there to answer your call — "

"Then as soon as dinner's over — and Hatty won't care, she only asked me to make up her table — I'll push off, jump in a cab, and give him a wonderful surprise — the pet. What's his address, for God's sake? And don't just tell me — I'll forget by the time dinner's over, and I'm nearly stoned — be a love and write it down for me in big letters. Use that dam' great invitation card the Sturtletons always send — I haven't one, being a last-minute fill-up."

"Are you sure you want to go up there, Petro?"

"You mean — he has a woman already installed there?"

"No, Petro, I know he hasn't. But still — are you sure?"

"I'm not quite sure now — this minute — but I'm sure I'll be sure by the time I've had dinner. So be a sweet lamb — and very large letters, please! I can't wear my specs unless I take off these eyelashes — "

He wondered if she would be able to read anything at all by the time she had drunk her way through dinner, but he felt rather mischievously that Tuby might as well be given a taste of high life, so he carefully followed Petro's instructions. And no sooner had she put the card into her handbag than they were summoned ceremoniously to dinner. He had to take in Gladys Birtle, no great treat, though she was a sensible woman and he liked her. Moreover, she might be able to tell him about some of the other people there, so far all of them unknown to him. They processed slowly and solemnly into a huge gold and white dining room, where more uniformed footmen were standing at attention behind the chairs. In his innocence, Saltana found himself moving in a world he had thought had ceased to exist. It was as if the Empire still reddened world maps, as if balance of payments and desperate borrowings and severe taxation belonged to some other Britain, as if the Sturtletons lived in dreamland but somehow made it come true. With Mrs. Birtle on his right and Primrose on his left, all of them far removed from their host and hostess, he took his seat feeling like Cosmo through the Looking Glass. And, if only not to be overcome by the sense of dreamlike unreality, he kept asking himself where the hell all the money came from. To that he had no reply — and never really tried to find one — but even so, and in spite of his talk about being an anarchist and a republican, he lost a certain innocence that night and was never the same again.

It promised to be a very good dinner, and indeed it was magnificent, with the various wines — and Saltana refused none of them — on the same high level as the food. As Primrose was being very talkative and gay with the young man on her left — the only young man in the room — Saltana was able to question Mrs. Birtle about the other guests. Some of them she didn't recognize at all, but she indicated several senior members of the Opposition — and one of them was the Leader himself, Sir Henry Flinch-Epworth, a square-faced frowning man with an untidy moustache. There were several aristocratic personages too, whom she thought she recognized, and two courses came and went while she was trying to sort them out and kept on correcting herself. Saltana listened dreamily and occasionally looked down the long glittering table at Lady Harriet, who was glittering away too. Once she caught his enquiring look and answered it with a nod and a sudden wide smile that seemed out of character. He began to wonder about her image. However, he felt he couldn't neglect Mrs. Birtle — and the old boy on her other side seemed to be deaf — so he thought of a non-recognizing question for her.

"A small point," he said, "but why, when you and I and Primrose have been seated together, has your husband been moved away from us?"

"Oh — that often happens at dinners like this," she told him. "The ones who are in the know — the women as well as the men — want Simon closer. Because of his papers and magazines, of course. They think he has a lot of influence, just as he does. Though I'm not sure, as I tell him sometimes. After all, he's Opposition too, like them, but they're out, aren't they? Sometimes I think that he and all his editors are influential only about things that don't matter much."

"I'd like to believe it," said Saltana, who was eating a prune ice that had had Armagnac poured over it. "But I've often thought that it's these things that don't matter that *do* matter in the end."

When the women had gone, the men didn't stay round the table but went up some stairs, into a library. And for the first time, Saltana felt envious. It was high, softly lit, darkly crimson, furnished with old leather armchairs and with plenty of low tables, and there must have been about twenty thousand books round the walls. After staring about appreciatively, Saltana found himself sharing a cigar-cutter with a tall haughty-looking man, probably in his sixties.

As soon as their cigars were alight, this man said, "Ah lah wah tah gah fah mah lah bah rah." At least that is what Saltana seemed to hear, and the man looked very English too. And not tight. Was he asking a question?

"I've no idea," said Saltana pleasantly. "Sorry!"

The man nodded solemnly, gave Saltana a little pat on the shoulder, and wandered away. Saltana drank some coffee, some brandy, more coffee, and enjoyed his cigar, which was superb.

He saw that Sturtleton, with whom he had not exchanged a word since he was first greeted by him, had now gone into a huddle with the Leader of the Opposition and the man who talked ah-lah-wah-tah; and the rest of them were dismissed to join the ladies in the drawing room. Saltana sought out Primrose. "I don't see Petro. Has she gone?"

"She's dashed off to call on Tuby. She told me you gave her his address. And it isn't entirely mischief, darling. She really does adore him. Isn't it queer," Primrose went on, slowing up now, "how you two put us girls neatly into two camps? Petro still adores Tuby. So did those three Brockshire women — Mrs. Lapford, tarty little Hazel Thing, and the English Lecturer with the huge eyes. Then Meldy Glebe. Elfreda adores *you*. So did I but it's wearing off. Then that Ringmore advertising woman — and little Nan Wolker of Pennine Fabrics — oh, I know about you — *and* Tuby — "

"Not as much as you think, girl. And that's enough. There were about three women trying to listen in. And here are the Birtles. Do they want to go? I promised our hostess — "

"I'll bet!" cried Primrose, cutting him short. "And now — look — there are some new people coming in. It always happens at these parties. If you're waiting to get *her* alone, you could be hanging about half the night. Hello, darlings," she said to the Birtles, "have you had enough?"

Gladys Birtle said she had and Simon said he hadn't, because he knew Sturtleton still wanted a quiet word with him. Then Primrose's smooth young dinner partner joined them, and insisted upon telling them three funny *in* stories that Primrose and Birtle had obviously heard before and Mrs. Birtle and Saltana didn't understand. Birtle was beginning one of his own when he was interrupted by their hostess.

"Sorry — but I'm taking this clever and rather sinister man away from you. He promised to tell me something about my image, and now he'll have to keep his promise."

"Yes, darling." Primrose smiled sweetly but didn't keep the protest out of her voice. "But we do run an institute, you know, to explain about images."

"And I'd like a little advice for nothing."

"Well — "

"My dear, I do it all the time. Doctors, lawyers, City men — I've picked their brains for hours here. Most of them love it. So come along, Professor Saltana, and we'll find a quiet corner."

They found it well to the left of the great fireplace and not far from the first window, where two small armchairs faced each other below an enormous eighteenth-century family group, in which the children all looked like midget and rather desperate adults. He said that to Lady Harriet, but she only nodded indifferently. "I don't *see* these dam' pic-

tures any more," she confessed. "Love your coat, though. At dinner, Lord
Withamstone — rather sweet but an imbecile — told me you were a
violinist he'd met at one of Dotty Ironbridge's week-ends. I didn't correct
him. Just said he ought to tell you. Did he?"

"No. But if he had, I'd have confessed I play the clarinet."

She laughed but then said, "But you don't play the clarinet, do
you?"

"Certainly I do."

"But I read somewhere you'd been a Professor of Philosophy."

"I was a Professor of Philosophy who played the clarinet. Still do,
though I'm rapidly deteriorating. It's an instrument that demands constant practice."

"And now you're too busy with images. Tell me about mine." And
she sat up a little, keeping a small set smile, as if offering herself for
inspection.

"This isn't the way we try to do it, you know," he told her, though
he stared hard at her. "I can only offer you a little quick guesswork."

"I'm hardly entitled to anything else, am I?" she murmured. "But
you make me feel you're such a clever man — " But then she moved. He
didn't know why, because she was facing the room and he wasn't. "Oh —
hell! Some people going. Stay there. Don't move. Back in a moment. Have
a whisky — and take one for me."

A footman had arrived, wheeling up a kind of grog cart. Saltana
accepted two whiskies from it, and had just tried his when her ladyship
returned and settled down with her drink. "Perhaps we ought to finish
these before you begin," she said. "Then I won't lose my temper and
you'll be braver. Are you brave?"

"Certainly not. I just managed to get by in the desert. But it's something your class *really* has — courage."

"I think so too. But that *really* of yours suggests we claim a lot of
things we haven't got."

"That's how it looks to me." He tried to sound easy and pleasant,
not too professorial. "From the outside, of course, reading memoirs and
occasional pieces about you. Perhaps because you no longer feel quite
secure, you seem to me — and it's persistent if not entirely deliberate —
to overrate one another." He wondered whether to stop there, but as she
looked at him, over the glass she hadn't quite emptied, with calm ex-
pectancy, he went on. "So in your circles, a fairly handsome woman is an
astounding beauty. Anybody who makes a few amusing remarks is a great
wit, the author of a book or two a literary genius. A tolerant hostess is a
wonderful darling of darlings. And any man who has about as much insight into public affairs as the average party agent or town councillor is
credited with awe-inspiring political wisdom."

"You devil!" But she said it quite calmly. "And I suppose I'm one
of those fairly handsome women who — you know — "

"No, you're better than that." He was trying to be as cool as she seemed to be. "But I'm wondering about this firmly rooted class quality — courage — "

"Me?" Now she was genuinely indignant. "My dear man, where have you been? Over and over again I've been called *reckless*."

"I'm thinking and talking now in image terms. That's what you want, isn't it? But I can stop, you know."

"My God — you can't, not now. I'm too curious. Oh — damn! More people wanting to say goodnight." She was up now. "And Doggy's bringing his politicians in. Look," she continued in a hurried whisper, "just hang on. I'll tell Doggy he'll have to cope for a few minutes — that I'm consulting Professor Saltana — he'll think it's medical. And I'll tell your friends to wait for you. *And* send along some booze — make you braver still."

Saltana gazed dreamily at the eighteenth-century family, the man so stolidly pleased with himself, his wife, still slender and fair but anxious, wondering about her next pregnancy, the five children who looked like midget adults but who were waiting to spring to life again somewhere else. He felt sad, but he knew he had eaten and drunk too much. Her ladyship glided back to her chair. "Now then, Professor!"

He roused himself and looked hard at her before he spoke. "When I first saw you — and then watched you at the dinner table — I told myself that here was a very handsome woman, a very attractive woman, possibly a fascinating woman. But why did she have to look so hard and glittering?"

"I can tell you that. To compete with that dam' great dinner table and all our chandeliers and gilt and ancestors and heirlooms."

"I realized that of course, but it wouldn't do. If you really wanted to compete, you'd have tried to appear soft and blooming, not hard and glittering. But all these diamonds, the hardest of the stones! The metallic look of your dress! Then hair that might be some sort of beaten bronze! The eyes too — even the eyes — fine eyes of course — and a most unusual dark blue, but not windows, not pools, like a pair of sapphires. Then the make-up, giving the face a porcelain effect! Kissing that cheek, I thought, would be like kissing a Chinese vase. Why an image so hard, so coldly glittering, so metallic? What is the woman who's projecting such an image armouring herself against?" He waited a moment, then rose quickly. "And that's all, Lady Harriet. You're needed elsewhere. I must go home. And thank you for a really magnificent dinner!"

She had risen too, and now she put a hand on his arm. "You've all kinds of tricks, haven't you, Professor Saltana? That sudden break, and then the change of tone! Very clever! I shall look at my book and then ring you at your Institute. Could you bear it?"

"Certainly." And that was his last word to her that night.

The next morning, Tuby wandered into the Institute, stifling yawns.

"If you're expecting any bright ideas from me this morning, my friend, kindly remember that last night you told Petronella, Duchess of Brockshire, lit up and ready to give a gala performance, where to find me. I can only talk sentences like that when I'm feeling worn out." He yawned himself into a chair, took out his pipe, put it back again.

"She insisted, Owen. And I know you're fond of her. You're not being turned out of your digs, are you?"

"Good God — what a way to talk at our age! Takes me back nearly thirty years. No, fortunately the Ilberts are away — school holidays now. Petro left about five, after a non-stop talking jag. She was very eloquent about that woman — Hatty, she calls her — who entertained you in such grandeur last night. How was it?"

"Like suddenly walking into one of Disraeli's novels."

"You surprise me, Cosmo. Have you ever read any of Disraeli's novels?"

"Two or three, years ago, in a nursing home after having my tonsils out. When I arrived, last night, Lord Sturtleton said 'Glad y'could come,' and when I was leaving he said 'Glad y'could come,' and that was all from him — except a dam' good dinner and unlimited expensive booze. But his wife, Lady Harriet, wanted to know about her image, so I obliged, briefly. We haven't a client there, Owen. Nor, I'd say, the beginning of a beautiful friendship. She said she was going to ring me here, but my guess is — her curiosity being satisfied — Lady Harriet will allow me to sink back into the nameless and faceless masses."

"I wonder," said Tuby slowly. "There are times, Cosmo — not many of them, I admit, but they exist — when you underrate yourself."

And indeed, Saltana guessed wrong. Late next morning, Thursday, Lady Harriet telephoned. They were having a few people down for the week-end. She knew he would be too busy to come down on Friday, but perhaps he could arrive in time for lunch on Saturday and put up with them at least until Sunday afternoon.

Unlike Tuby, who was capable of wearing rather loud tweeds anywhere, Saltana had no country clothes, and he left for Paddington on Saturday morning wearing his best dark suit. He guessed it would look out of place, but then he was going to be out of place anyhow. He had packed his clarinet, together with Brahms's Sonata in F minor, opus 120, for piano and clarinet or viola, seeing himself in some remote bedroom, running through the sonata while the others were playing bridge or inspecting the stables or the piggeries. He was met at the station by a gloomy elderly chauffeur, who drove him slowly through the early spring drizzle to Queningford Castle, a horrible and enormous place that cried out to be turned into a teachers' training college. It was now about half-past twelve. Neither host nor hostess, nor any fellow guests, could be seen or heard: hothouses, stables or piggeries, ancient keep, some long portrait gallery — where? His bag vanished, probably never to be seen again, and then he followed a man, who might have been the chauffeur's equally disenchanted brother, up the great staircase, along a corridor, then up a shorter and much narrower flight of stairs, into a fair-sized bedroom. It didn't suggest a castle at all, neither mediaeval nor Victorian, being brightly decorated and furnished in the Scandinavian modern style. It had a large low bed, and a door in each side wall. One door led into a bathroom, he was pleased to discover, but the other, as he soon found out when he was left to prowl, refused to lead anywhere, being locked on the other side. A maid out of a musical — for she was youngish, had a lingering look and splendid legs, and might start a song-and-dance at any moment — arrived with his bag and insisted upon unpacking it, so that to cover his defeat he went into the bathroom and did some rather noisy splashing work at the wash-basin there. When he emerged, to find his hairbrush and use it, the maid had gone. It was now nearly one o'clock, and he went slowly downstairs, wondering if he'd been a fool to accept the invitation.

But now there was a lot of noise coming through an open door to the left of the enormous armoured, tapestried, portraited entrance hall. About a dozen people were in there, drinking this and that. Lord Sturtleton shook his hand and said, "Glad y'could come," still neither knowing nor caring who the hell he was. Lady Harriet was in tweeds and looking quite different from how she had on Tuesday night. She seemed quite genuinely glad to see him and at once conjured up a whisky for him. "I'm wondering if you know anybody here," she said.

Saltana heard two voices and, by moving a little, saw two faces he recognised. "I know those two," he told Lady Harriet. "The Lapfords — he's Vice-Chancellor of Brockshire — "

"Oh — yes, they're just here for lunch. Doggy wanted to talk to him about something," she replied carelessly. "Are they chums?"

"They are not. He turned Tuby and me out of his university — or he would have done if we hadn't resigned first. And she doesn't like me, though Tuby was rather thick with her."

"She isn't bad-looking in a rather dreary way. But she'd be difficult to be thick with, I'd have thought."

"Yes — but you don't know Tuby."

"Really?" She smiled. "Perhaps I've invited the wrong man down. No? Not my style, perhaps. By the way, do you like to be taken around and shown things?"

"No, I don't. I've always hated sightseeing."

"Thank God for that! But I hope you won't be bored."

"I shall retire to my room and practise the clarinet."

She laughed. "You really are a character, aren't you? Look — I'm going to run and change my place cards for lunch. I shall put you next to the Lapford woman — just to see what happens."

He and Isabel Lapford talked to their other neighbours during the first course. Her husband, Jayjay, was sitting across from them, talking hard, his body a motionless bulk but his little head waving away, more like a dinosaur than ever. Saltana felt it was time to turn to Mrs. Lapford. And she was ready for him.

"Well, Professor Saltana, this is quite a surprise," she began, with a small cold smile. "I didn't know you moved in these exalted circles."

"I don't. Lady Harriet was curious about me — *and* her image — so she invited me to dine the other night. And as her curiosity was left unsatisfied, she suggested the week-end here."

"Oh — you're staying?"

"Tonight at least. And I'd say — my first and last appearance."

"Leaving Brockshire doesn't seem to have done your Institute any harm. You're doing very well, aren't you? Though I must tell you I still believe it's all impudent nonsense."

"So do I." And that takes the wind out of your sails, Isabel dear, he added silently. "And so of course does Owen Tuby. He's even more impudent than I am."

She ignored that and continued hurriedly: "However, I must confess I enjoyed your encounter with our Professor Cally on television."

"That's because you dislike Cally even more than you dislike me, Mrs. Lapford. By the way, did you see Tuby with his film-star client, Meldy Glebe?"

"I heard about it and read about it," she said as if from a great height. "But I don't sit watching television every night and I'm not interested in film actresses."

"Neither are we. It's just the money. Incidentally, if anybody should ask you, we have a strict rule at the Institute against sleeping with our clients."

"Now really, Professor Saltana!" But then she suddenly stopped being indignant and even laughed. "For sheer impudence, you two men — !" But instead of finishing the sentence, she drank some wine.

He drank some too. "If I put a question to you, Mrs. Lapford, will you answer me quite truthfully?"

"I don't suppose so, Professor Saltana. But you can try me. Go on."

He waited a moment, then said softly, "Don't you miss us at Brockshire? The truth, now."

"Our feelings are mixed. I must admit," she went on, lowering her voice, "now that you've had so much publicity, I think Jayjay regrets your leaving us. Publicity's rather a weakness of his, and one I don't share. How is Elfreda Drake?"

"Very busy and reasonably happy, I think. She's still at Robinson's Hotel and I'm certain she'd be glad to see you there. I'll tell her we met and talked. You should write to her. I believe she exchanges letters with Tuby's friend, the girl with the eyes, who thinks I'm debauching him — you know the one I mean — Lois — what is it? — Terry. How is she?"

"I see very little of Dr. Terry." And there was no regret in Isabel Lapford's tone. "Jayjay and Professor Brigham think highly of her work in the English Department — and indeed they've been persuading her not to accept an invitation to spend a year in America, at Vassar — but I've never cared for her personally. Deliberately eccentric — and rather raffish, I've always felt."

"Well," said Saltana thoughtfully, "there are people — in Brockshire too, some of 'em — who seem to imagine that Tuby and I are rather raffish — "

"That's quite different," she broke in hastily. "You're *men*. And I must say — very strange men too. I simply don't understand what you're doing and why you're doing it. I gave you a truthful answer. Now give me one."

"Certainly. We're trying to make a lot of money very quickly. We're even using a mock computer too. We tell everybody it's just a lot of little lights switching themselves on and off, but nobody believes us."

She laughed. "I do. But what's the point of it all?"

He waited a moment or two. "Tuby and I aren't entirely without a plan. But you might say that at the moment we're trying to make sure we don't have to ask people like your husband for a job. And that remark, my dear, is not meant to be offensive."

"I'm not your dear — thank God — but somehow I believe you."

Later, after coffee had been served in an adjacent room, which had too many pictures and too much bric-a-brac and looked as if it were waiting for an auctioneer, both Lapfords cornered Saltana. They were about to leave, but Jayjay felt he had to put a question to Professor Saltana. "Not about yourself. I gather your Institute is rapidly establishing itself in London — eh! Splendid, splendid! But we — I — have been wondering about Dr. Tuby. Is there any chance he might like to return to academic life? I ask this because we're enlarging the English Department — and —" here he lowered his voice — "there might soon be a chair for him there."

"I'll tell him that," said Saltana. "Though you could always write to him — care of the Institute, Half Moon House, Half Moon Street — "

"Well no, I could hardly do that, you know." Jayjay did a little head-waving. "Not unless I knew he might be ready to welcome such a proposal. Have to feel my way first. But I've always been under the impression — and several people have mentioned it — my wife, for example, and Lois Terry of the English Department — that he was considerably more reluctant to leave Brockshire than you were, Professor Saltana."

"Possibly," said Saltana dryly. "Tuby enjoyed himself there rather more than I did. But though I'll tell him what you've said — it wouldn't be fair not to — I know you've no hope of getting him back to Brockshire. So if you have a vacancy — a possible chair, perhaps — in your English Department, I advise you to find somebody else."

It was then, as Saltana told Tuby and Elfreda afterwards, that Vice-Chancellor Lapford, the fatuous Jayjay, said something that Saltana couldn't ignore, couldn't forget, something that soon helped to shape and to colour all his plans. "All very well, Saltana," said Jayjay. "But have you anything really solid? Couldn't it be, with all the publicity you've had, just a nine days' wonder? To keep in business, mightn't you have to turn yourselves into just another advertising agency?"

"I don't think so," Saltana replied promptly and briskly, apparently all confidence. "However, I'll pass that on to Tuby too." He gave them both a small farewell smile. But later he found it impossible to remind himself that Lapford was a foolish empty man.

He took such thoughts upstairs with him and was able to dismiss them by going through the Brahms sonata several times. He put his clarinet away at about half-past four, feeling that he ought to make an appearance down below at teatime. There were only half a dozen people in the small drawing room. Sturtleton himself, he learnt, had departed on some political business and would not be back until next day, just in time for Sunday lunch, which would be a full-scale affair. Lady Harriet was deep in lively chat with a youngish couple called Inchture, but a few minutes later Saltana had her to himself. "You were disappointing with that Lapford woman," she said. "I kept an eye on you, and no feathers were flying. You even made her laugh. She was almost sparkling."

"She was thinking about my friend Tuby. He's the charmer, not I."

"You don't really believe that. How's my image? No, we'll save that until after dinner. What are you going to do until then?"

"Play billiards with Sir Emery."

Saltana had plenty of time to wonder about her in the billiard room, where his partner was a handsome and excessively polite Sir Emery Clavering, a boyish fifty-five or so, a baronet, he was told later, belonging to a very old and distinguished family. Saltana didn't play too badly — he still had a good eye and a steady hand — but he was kept waiting and watching on the raised leather settee because Sir Emery played superbly well. "Rather lucky there, I'm afraid," he would murmur as he built up breaks of thirty and forty. And when, after two games of billiards, they tried snooker, he was politer still, murmuring all manner of apologies while being murderously efficient. By the time they had cleared everything away and had covered the table and were sharing the whisky and soda, Saltana found it possible to hold a conversation with Sir Emery. He began by explaining that he had promised to talk to Lady Harriet after dinner about her image and was feeling rather bewildered. "It seemed simple the other night, when I was dining with them in London, but now I'm not sure where I am."

"Well, you're here, aren't you?" said Sir Emery. "Hatty herself ask you down? She did? Well then, where are you? I mean, which room are you in?"

Saltana described as best he could the location and style of his room. And something that might have been a flicker of amused interest disturbed Sir Emery's pale-blue earnest gaze.

"That one, is it?" he said. "I'm not surprised. Good for images, that room. So I wouldn't say too much tonight, old man. And thanks for the game. Go up and start dressing, don't you think?"

Two new couples, one quite young, the other middle-aged, were drinking cocktails when Saltana, wearing his old black velvet coat again, joined the party. These people had names, of course, but Saltana couldn't bother remembering what they were. However, at dinner he found himself sitting between the two women. The younger one, not long married, had a button nose, a pouting mouth, a chin in retreat, and three subjects — horses, roulette, and My Husband. The older woman had a carefully sweet expression which never varied, and a tongue that dripped vitriol into Saltana's ear, everybody else at the table being in turn the victims of her untiring malignity. Bored by the one on his right, depressed by the one on his left, Saltana drank too much and began to feel sad.

After coffee and much loud chatter, he wandered, poised between boredom and melancholy, into a neighbouring room, where some lights were on and a log fire was sleepily burning. It was a library, though smaller and less impressive than the one in the town house. There were several shelves of eighteenth- and early nineteenth-century travel books. He found one on Latin America and settled down by the fire with it. Perhaps he could read himself out of his present mood, even though the old foxed pages suggested more boredom and melancholy.

He had left the door open — it was the least he could do — but now he heard somebody closing it. He rose and turned, to see Lady Harriet advancing towards him.

"So here you are — lurking. Tired of us already. You don't want to play poker, do you?"

"No, thank you. Not that I object to the game — played it often at one time — but I can't afford to play here." He sat down, as she was now sitting in the opposite armchair.

"I've got them playing. Poker's been *out* for ages, but now it's *in* again."

"Who decides if things are *out* or *in?*"

"About six of us — not counting a royal or two," she replied carelessly. "If you've got one of those little cheroots to spare, I'll smoke one with you." He went across with one and then she guided the hand holding the lighted match. "Did anybody ever tell you, Professor Saltana, that apart from not having premature white hair — and there you've slipped up — you're any sensible person's idea of a clever good-looking charlatan?"

"Not until tonight, Hatty. But if you want to reverse our roles, ex-

amine and analyse my image, go ahead. It's Saturday night and I oughtn't
to be working."

"Oh — no! On Tuesday you said I was all hard, glittering, armoured to protect some mysterious self, and I invited you down specially
to examine my country image and to tell me more. And I've even started
a poker game in there so that we should have more time alone. So get
on with it, man — do your stuff." And she sat back, crossed her legs —
perhaps carelessly, perhaps not — and clearly offered herself for further inspection. Her cheroot was still alight.

So was his, and he pretended for some moments that he had nothing to do but enjoy it. "Here in the country," he began finally, speaking
slowly, "instead of glittering Political Hostess, we have Gracious Chatelaine, just as elsewhere — yes, I've been asking about you — on the Riviera or in the Bahamas they have Ultra-Smart Reckless Hatty. Now for
Gracious Chatelaine, most of the hardness, glitter, armour, has gone. A
minimum of jewellery. Soft tweeds during the day, and now this dress
— what? — a kind of French mustard shade? — and incidentally very
charming. Even the hair is no longer metallic. As for the eyes — "

"Any windows, pools? You see, I remember."

"No longer another pair of precious stones, anyhow. Softly shadowed, we'll say, with occasional glints of mischief. A complete change,
certainly, partly for your guests — a mixed political-social lot on a low-
ish level, you think — but a change carried further than usual chiefly for
my benefit, just to show me."

"My God — has anybody ever told you how conceited you are,
Saltana?"

"Yes, *I* have — frequently. Which ought to suggest I can't be altogether bogus and a charlatan. There must be honesty and integrity somewhere. But what about you? Isn't this deliberate projection of very different images in itself suspicious? Here are the roles, but who's the actress? What's the sign of a fully mature integrated personality — that he
or she talks and behaves more or less the same everywhere, in all companies?"

"Oh — don't be such a bloody fool. To begin with, I'm a woman.
And a woman born, brought up, married, in a small narrow class — "

"Still highly privileged, wealthy, feeling socially secure," he told
her. "And please don't keep breaking in. Listen — and then tell me at
the end it's all moonshine — but first — *listen*. Just allow me to do what
you invited me here to do." He looked hard at her.

"Yes, Professor," she said with obvious mock humility. And he
caught that glint of mischief in her eye.

"Being a woman," he continued, realizing that he was about to lecture her and not caring — she could like it or lump it — "is socially
more complicated than being a man. But you're so placed — this country being so riddled with and befogged by tradition — that you're in a

better position to project steadily an image that does justice to your real and total personality. But somewhere along the line you've thrown all this away. You don't steadily project anything. I can't discuss your image because you haven't got one. What you have — and I've seen two already and I know there must be several more — is a series of masks and rapidly improvised character parts. You're a one-woman repertory company. Behind all that you may not be clever, may not be attractive, may not even be a woman — a female, yes, but not a real woman." She was about to protest, but he checked her. "You say you remember what I told you on Tuesday night? What was the last thing I said before I broke off our talk?"

"You ended with a question the other night. What, you asked, is the woman who's projecting such an image armouring herself against? So, still curious, I arranged for you to answer Tuesday's question on Saturday — here and now. But you're not doing that. You're saying something quite different."

"Of course I am. I'm considering two images now, not one. And I don't need any more. The situation is regressive," Saltana continued, quicker and less emphatic than he'd been earlier. "But tell me something — and I'm not really changing the subject. Why — after marrying Sturtleton — didn't you follow him into politics?"

"I did — for the first few years. I could have shown you my political image then. But I simply couldn't go on saying the same dam' things and listening to other people saying them. Now let's talk about something else. I must attend to the poker players soon. A few nearly always drop out and then have to be amused. Look — ask me something you oughtn't to ask me — and dare me to tell you the truth."

"Certainly. When did you go to bed with Sir Emery Clavering?"

In her indignation she jumped out of her chair. "What — after all this blah-blah about English gentlemen never telling! You and Emery there in the billiard room! Talking it over!"

"Nonsense!" He was on his feet too. "Of course he never said a word about it. You're miles out, my dear Hatty. It was a remark he made about the house, together with a faint something in his manner, that sent me jumping to a conclusion — and then a question I oughtn't to ask."

"All right. It was about three years ago — a week-end like this, only he happened to come alone. And I was curious. Then I soon learnt why his wife looks like hell — and goes to bed wondering if she ought to have called five no trumps. And it seems to me, Saltana, you're much cleverer as a kind of conversational detective than you are with your image talk."

"It looks, then, as if our Institute is going to be *out*, never *in*," he said lightly. "However, it's probably easier for us charlatans to fool businessmen."

"Well, my dear man, you can't fool me, not when you suggest I'm just a lot of images with nothing real and alive behind them. Take a look at me. Closer. Now then!"

She took his cheeks between her hands, raised her mouth to his, and then, to his astonishment, almost savagely kept her tongue, which was hot and curiously hard, darting rapidly between his lips. Before he could make a move, she had stepped back. "*Something* there, surely? No, don't tell me. I must go. Do my duty."

"Better not rush in. You're looking too excited."

"And you don't look as cool as you sound, Professor. But I can manage my image. You'll find some whisky in your room, but don't drink too much — for various good reasons. And don't go up yet — settle down to smoke and read for a while — if you can. Then if nobody looks in and finds you, I'll wonder where you are and I'll send somebody."

"What a conspirator you'd make!"

"I love it." She opened a door in the wall of books. "I'm going out this way. Try not to fall asleep — later, I mean, upstairs." She quietly closed the door behind her. He was staring at the wall of books again, as if he had been visited by a phantom. Perhaps he had.

Lady Harriet's intuition must have been working; no more than five minutes later, somebody came in, rather noisily too, and it was, of all people, the malevolent woman who'd sat on his left at dinner. "Oh, it's you, Professor. Studious, I see. We're wondering where Hatty — Lady Harriet — is."

Saltana shook his head. "I've no idea where she is." Which was the exact truth. "I'll return this book to its shelf — and join you. What's happpening?"

"Lady Clavering and two men are still playing poker. The rest of us are beginning to yawn."

So they were too, he found. The grog cart was in, but Saltana kept away from it. The button-nosed bride was holding on to My Husband as if he might suddenly try to vanish or turn into somebody else. Their hostess came hurrying in, declaring that she was furious, and then told a long and complicated story about a call she'd put through to Antibes. She was a good liar and obviously enjoyed displaying her talent — probably, Saltana concluded, that most dangerous type, the creative artist who can't create any art. After two or three of the women had left, Saltana felt it was time he went too, and he approached his hostess rather formally but added that he'd had rather a long day.

"Oh — poor you! Well, do have a good night, Professor Saltana." Their handshake was a brief formality — and yet conspiratorial, Lady Harriet's method being a quick pressure on the palm by her middle finger. How long and how many times had she done this, Saltana wondered as he went upstairs. Quite sure that he had plenty of time, he undressed slowly, took a shower, began to sip a whisky while still drying himself, decided against pyjamas as his old dressing gown was woolly and thickish, turned out all the lights except the bedside lamp, added a little more whisky to the weak mixture of his original drink, lit a cheroot, stretched himself out luxuriously. But his mind, if it could still be called a mind, raced away, not consuming but enlarging and slowing up the time he would have to wait. He wanted and yet didn't want the woman. He hadn't felt like this for many a year; he didn't like what he was feeling; she might not keep her promise — for that was what it amounted to — being a devious specimen of a notoriously perfidious class, and if that locked door was never opened, then his night would be slowly ruined; and yet if she did visit him, curiosity meeting curiosity, he half-dreaded what would happen, having drifted into a sexual situation that for once he hadn't deliberately created. So his mind raced and time crawled.

He had almost given her up and was feeling angry when he heard the key turn in the lock. She slipped in and locked the door from the in-side. She was wearing some kind of Chinese robe and somehow seemed an utterly strange woman, to whom he would have to introduce himself. And for a moment or two, that was all he felt.

But she wasn't sharing this feeling. "Well now, my dear Professor, let's see if there isn't *something* — *somebody* — behind all those images you talk about. And get rid of that terrible dressing gown, for God's sake." And as soon as he had done this, she flung away the robe, stood naked before him for a moment, a magnificently challenging figure of a woman, and then hurled herself at him.

He knew what it was going to be as soon as she had spoken — sex as a battle, with the male, so triumphant in the early stages, inevitably having to suffer defeat. She knew everything and did everything, making use of all tactics in the campaign of nerves and blood, mucus and gristle, and doing it with increasing ferocity and hostility, so that even before his virility, spurred by instinctive vanity, was quite exhausted, he was be-ginning to loathe this sweat-slippery voracious creature. Then — though after how long he was never able to discover — he was putting on his dressing gown while she stayed, still naked and panting, on the bed. "Give me a drink," she said.

He gave her a drink and then threw the robe over her. She sat up with her glass, gave him a sidelong mocking look, and said, "Not bad, Saltana. Not for a man of your age. How do you feel?"

"Like a young whore who's been entertaining three sailors. And that's intended to change the subject."

"Don't even want to talk now, do you? Not even about images — with nothing real behind them. But now you know there *is* something, there *is* somebody, don't you?" She finished her drink and began putting on the robe.

He waited until she was ready to go. "I'll tell you exactly what there is. And I'm not trying to be offensive. There's an intolerable itch, combined with immaturity and a hatred of men. And if you're going to describe what the riding master did when you were fourteen, please don't bother."

"My dear man, you're tired. So don't work so hard trying to be bloody rude. I've heard too many of you just about this time of night. It's boring. By the way, I'm not visible until late on Sunday mornings, but no doubt you'll stay to lunch — and be nice and polite."

"I'll be polite if we meet — and delighted if we don't."

"And I still think you and your images are bogus. 'Night!" But before she had opened the door he had turned away, making for the bathroom, to have another shower. He felt badly in need of one.

It was nearly seven o'clock on Sunday evening when he was back in Half Moon House. He dozed for an hour or so, called Elfreda and was immensely relieved to find she was in and ready to welcome him later, had a drink and a sandwich, and then took a taxi to Robinson's. He knew she would question him closely about his grand week-end and Lady Harriet, and in the cab he roughed out a heavily edited and rather boring account of it.

"Did she make a pass at you, Cosmo?" And Elfreda was staring hard. The trouble was, too, that he'd never felt more deeply fond of her — at once so comely and sensible and affectionate, so clear-eyed, such a *real woman*.

"What — after calling me a charlatan and telling me our Institute must be bogus! Elfreda, I dislike that woman intensely."

"But very attractive, isn't she?"

"Elfreda, I was just thinking — at the very moment you asked about her — how infinitely more attractive in every way you are. Indeed, I was already thinking that when I rang you to see if I could come round — to take a good long appreciative look at you. Though there was something I wanted to talk over," he added hastily, "something that Lapford surprised me by saying."

And now Elfreda surprised him. "Cosmo, give me a kiss — just a kiss — a friendly kind of kiss — not — not sexy."

He kissed her full on the lips, but gently. It was a very good kiss, so rewarding that he felt at once it would have to be repeated now whenever they first met in the morning or parted in the evening.

"Well," Elfreda began uncertainly when he was back in his chair, "what — what — did Jayjay say — that surprised you, Cosmo?"

"He warned me — this was after he and Isabel said they wanted Tuby in their English Department — that we might not have anything solid here, just a nine days' wonder after all the publicity we'd had, and that to keep in business we might have to turn ourselves into just another ad agency. And I'll admit, Elfreda, though of course I gave no sign of it, that this shook me. And coming from that pompous empty windbag too! Perhaps a man's a fool ever to dismiss another man as a fool."

She nodded and then after a moment or two said, "Have you thought that he might have been telling you what somebody else told him, somebody who knows a lot more about business than he does?"

"Elfreda, your mind's working — and mine wasn't. You're right; it's more than likely he was repeating what somebody had said — perhaps that tough industrialist, you remember, Sir Leonard Ramp or Namp — dismissing us. And that's why the Lapfords felt they might make a bid for Owen Tuby."

She looked bewildered. "But — Cosmo — you know it's not true. I mean, we *are* solid, we *can* stay in business just as ourselves — image people. Can't we?"

He felt so close to her, even dependent now, that he had to be honest with her. "I wouldn't say this in the office, my dear." Then he continued slowly: "But the answer is — I don't know, I really don't know."

"But why should somebody like Frank Maclaskie ring me up — from America too — to ask if we're doing good business, and keep telling me we have a great idea — if only — " and she began laughing — "if only the Institute would get rid of those long-haired egghead professors? I had to tell him you *were* the Institute." Then, after a pause: "What's the matter?"

"I was just thinking." He waited a moment. "Could you write to him if necessary, not now — later? Do any of his business chums — associates, I ought to say — come here? And if one of them wanted to talk to you, do you think you could hand him over to me?"

"Of course I could — and would — though they wouldn't be the sort of men you'd like."

At lunchtime on Monday, Saltana gave Tuby a brief — and not uncensored — account of his week-end, and then reported the Lapfords almost verbatim. "And I told them they'd no hope of getting you back there. True, isn't it, Owen?"

"Of course. Just like Jayjay too not to approach me directly himself. An empty poltroon."

"It's your women down there who've been working on him, my boy. They want their darling Dr. Tuby back." As Tuby made no reply to this, Saltana went on to explain what he'd said to Elfreda the night before, ending with Maclaskie. "The point being, Owen — and I didn't say this to Elfreda — that Maclaskie and his friends wouldn't dream of running the Institute separately. They'd see it as a gimmicky addition to a new American-financed advertising agency. The name's what they want. Elfreda told me earlier that Maclaskie was fascinated, kept mentioning it. Anyhow, that's my guess. What's yours?"

"If you mean about this business plotting, I haven't a guess. I leave it all to you — *and* Elfreda. You ought to be frank and open with her on these matters, and not bother about me. She knows about business. I don't."

"Leave that alone, Owen," Saltana muttered darkly. "I want to be frank and open with her — but can't yet — very personal reasons — "

"No doubt. The only time I agreed to be responsible for some accounts and entangle myself in figures, the result was a hell of a mess. And it was in Singapore and I was surrounded by Chinese, who *invented* business. Anything happen this morning?"

"Three new enquiries — two of 'em quite promising. What about you?"

"Young Meldy's coming back from Italy, with a new problem or two. She writes — all on a picture postcard of Roman fountains — that she'd like me to see her with her producer or director." He produced something between a sigh and a groan. "The only film people I've ever met — it was in India, though they were American — could talk on and on and on for days. Indian film people — and I kept clear of them — could probably go on for months."

On Wednesday afternoon, Saltana took a call from Sir James Tenks, President of the Board of Trade, the hefty fierce-looking fellow he had met at Axwick's party. "Got an idea, Saltana," Sir James barked. "Might be important. Rather not see you here. Nor at the House. What about a drink at my club? Sixish — eh?" And he mentioned the same huge solemn club where Saltana had lunched with Simon Birtle.

As soon as their whiskies were on the little table between them, Tenks crooked a finger beckoning Saltana to lean forward, leant forward himself, his purplish, bony, black-moustached face looking enormous and very formidable, and said, "Didn't forget what you said about my image, that night. Told a few people. Dam' clever, we all agreed. Now then — " and he dropped into a hoarse whisper — "this has to be off the record. Understood?"

"I haven't a record for it to be on," said Saltana.

"Strict confidence, then." And Tenks jerked himself upright, gave the room a commander-of-cavalry look, then leant forward again. "We go to the country in October. Yes, general election. Now then — what about the P.M.?"

"You mean the Prime Minister? What about him?"

"Given any thought to his image, Saltana?"

"Certainly not. Why should I?"

"Fair enough. As a busy professional, why should you? Take your point. Well, very much between ourselves, some of us are worried about his image." And Tenks picked up his whisky, frowned at it, sank about half of it.

Saltana followed his example but kept silent.

This compelled Tenks to try an exasperated hoarse whisper. "Come along now. Not trying to pick your brains. But — damn it — you must have looked at and listened to our dear Ernest Itterby often enough on the telly. Can't keep him away from that box. So you must understand why some of us are worried about his image — what?"

"I've never seen him on television, never heard him on radio, never given his image a moment's thought. So my brains wouldn't be worth picking, even if you started trying. However, thanks for this excellent whisky. Enjoyed seeing you again." And Saltana, who found Tenks's manner infectious and could hear himself beginning to bark, rose to go.

Tenks's meaty hand shot out to stop him. "No, no — hold it! Not at the bone yet. All the better if you haven't given Ernest's image a thought. Begin with a clean slate if you went to work on it."

"But I'm not going to work on it."

Tenks bent further forward so that his face took on an alarming hue, threatening apoplexy. "But suppose we could persuade him to let you work on it? A definite commission, dead secret of course. What about that? There's a summit for you, Saltana. The P.M. himself — think of that! You stay close at hand — some time late in the summer recess — have his new image all ready for October. What a chance!"

"It might be, I don't know," said Saltana, determined to keep cool while Tenks was heating up — dangerously too. "It could take a lot of time. And that would mean I'd want a lot of money."

"Money? Money?" Tenks could not have sounded more horrified if Saltana had demanded human sacrifice. "You can't be serious."

"Certainly I am. I do this image work for money."

"Yes, yes, naturally — but have a heart, man! We're talking about the P.M. now. You'd be doing a job for your country." And Tenks pushed his colossal blue chin even further out. "Important to you, isn't it?"

"No, it isn't. I don't know enough about Ernest Itterby. Improving his image might be helping to ruin the country, for all I know. I'm sorry, but the patriotic appeal won't work. All that will is a very substantial fee."

"But think what it would mean to your Institute — "

"What? As a dead secret?"

"Ah — take your point. Well then, what about an honour? One of those Order of the British Empire things — eh?"

"What British Empire? Might as well be Captain of Archers or Keepers of the Dodo. And anyhow I don't believe in honours."

"Only care about money? I'm surprised at you, Saltana."

"Then don't be, Tenks. Six or seven months ago, I was almost broke, wondering where to turn next. None of those City directorships you'd be offered if you lost the Board of Trade, were kicked out of the Cabinet, perhaps turned out of your seat at the next election! Fail in academic life and you could find yourself correcting papers for a correspondence course for fifteen pounds a week. Fail in politics and they make you a Companion of Honour and you collect five thousand a year from the City. And talking about five thousand, that's what I'd want."

"Not a chance! Party wouldn't wear it. Think again, man!"

"No, no, it's your turn to think. There might be a rich man some-where who'd like to do the Prime Minister a favour."

"Same thought occurred to me. Luckily, ample time to find such a chap. No more time now, though. Must get along to the House. Final point. All this in the strictest confidence, of course."

"Certainly. Except that I must say something about this to Dr. Tuby, who's both my partner and my closest friend."

"Is he reliable?"

"He's even better than I am. I look rather secretive whereas Tuby looks as if he'd tell you anything and everything, when in fact he only lets out what he wants you to know."

They were standing now, and Tenks put a heavy hand on Saltana's shoulder. "Tell me frankly," he whispered. "Would he be better for this particular job than you?"

"Depends on your man," Saltana replied. "I dominate. Tuby per-suades. We divide our work on that basis."

"Stick to *you,* then. That is, if we can bring it off. And with respect, Saltana, seems to me you're a bloody artful pair. Must go now."

It was a fine evening, with a yellow sky and a fresh breeze some-where above the diesel fumes. Saltana tried to walk briskly towards Half Moon Street, wondering when he would be able to find his way out of this city.

## 7

May, which had now arrived, began to disturb Tuby. It could be discov-ered, blossoming a little, even in Belsize Park, and there were a few vague traces of it, for a noticing man, in Half Moon Street. It made Tuby feel restless and almost painfully conscious of the fact that for the first time for many years Woman, in all her various aspects and roles, tempt-ing or healing, complementary or even disciplinary, was absent from his life. Even on a lower and narrower level, there was still this absence. He had resisted — and now almost checked — the advances of his landlady, Marion Ilbert. On the sound principle that the Institute did not make love to its clients, he had also resisted the temptation to prove to Meldy, who would do anything he asked her to do, that she was condemning sex too early and hastily. There had been, of course, the unexpected daft en-counter with Petronella, but that could be forgotten; and they had made no plans to meet again. The Lapfords' suggestion that he should go back to Brockshire didn't tempt him at all, but all the same, ever since Saltana had told him, he had been wondering about spending a few days, perhaps just a week-end, down there; he had some excuse, even if it was rather thin, because Smithy had announced that Hazel Honeyfield was now working on the survey for Dan Luckett. So there would be Hazel; there would be Isabel Lapford, obviously still interested; and there might — if he wanted to defy bad luck again, to take a chance on something either much better or much worse than an evening's amusement — there might be Lois Terry. But still he hesitated to go back there. And now it was May, rustling and shining and promising, his first in England for many years, and where there should have been Woman there was a blank.

It was not a blank that could be happily filled by Americans, whom he met or *contacted* in the way of business and the Institute. And he seemed to be always meeting them. There was Dan Luckett's Ezra J. Smithy, who clearly preferred visiting the Institute to telephoning, probably because it was really quicker, for he would slide in, announce that Dan was coming or not coming, and then shoot out, all in about two minutes flat. And there was the morning when Tuby had a message from Saltana asking him to go along there, to meet a visitor.

As soon as he saw the man, Tuby knew that he was an American and that they had met before. But where and when had he seen this outsize Humpty-Dumpty? He was still wondering when he shook hands and heard the man say, "Dr. Tooby — it's a vurry great pleasure."

"You remember Mr. Stockton, Owen, don't you? He came down to Brockshire — "

"Oh — yes, of course," said Tuby smiling. "You told Elfreda she couldn't have the Foundation — "

"An Oregon court decision, Dr. Tooby, not mine, I must remind you."

"And now Hazel Honeyfield's running it. How's she doing, Mr. Stockton?" They were now sitting down, not far from each end of Saltana's desk.

"Doing vurry well indeed, I understand, Dr. Tooby. But I haven't visited the Judson Drake Foundation this time over. I hope to go there the day after tomorrow. But Dr. Honeyfield and I got well acquainted the last time I was over. She is a lovely person."

"Certainly," said Saltana. Then he continued briskly, as if determined not to allow Stockton's slow and solemn manner to waste any more time: "I asked you to come along, Owen, because Mr. Stockton, on behalf of Mr. Maclaskie and his associates, is here to make a few formal enquiries about the Institute — "

"Without prejudice, Dr. Tooby. On a friendly basis, presooming on our acquaintance."

"Even so, Mr. Stockton, I've asked Dr. Tuby to join us to support me — or to correct me, if he wishes to — in what I'm about to tell you

And that will be, so far as I know it, the exact truth. First then — this *Institute of Social Imagistics* is rapidly showing itself to be commercially successful. We have never spent any money advertising ourselves, but — thanks chiefly to Dr. Tuby — the Institute has had an enormous amount of publicity — "

"I am aware of that, sir," said Stockton. "And so are my clients. We think it's a great idea, gentlemen — a *great* idea."

"Thank you, Mr. Stockton," said Saltana. "I'll only add under this first heading that we are now successfully demanding fees far larger than anything we had in mind a few months ago." Stockton, squeezing his features even closer together on the vast expanse of his face, nodded gravely several times.

"I now come to my second point," said Saltana, looking hard at Stockton. "And again I am going to tell you the exact truth. It's a point Elfreda — Mrs. Drake — has made at least twice in discussing the Institute with Maclaskie. She has told him — and now I'm telling you, Mr. Stockton — that not only did Dr. Tuby and I create the Institute but that, in effect, we *are* the Institute. Owen?"

"It's not quite fair to the women, Cosmo. They've now had some training and they come up with a few ideas. But still — in effect, as you said — we *are* the Institute."

"I want you to remember this, Mr. Stockton," said Saltana, looking hard at him again.

"You may be sure of that, Professor Saltana, Dr. Tooby. You have made it plain, gentlemen, that you feel you are indispensable. A claim, I must add, that I am not hearing for the first time." His features were spreading out a little, apparently in order to produce a smile. "Now permit me to put to you two questions — and two questions only. First, Professor Saltana, Dr. Tooby, do you see yourselves as businessmen?"

"Good God — no!" cried Tuby at once.

"And that's your answer from me too, Mr. Stockton," said Saltana.

"Excellent! It's a pleasure to deal with men who know their own minds. My second question. What would be your attitude towards any proposal to incorporate the Institute into a large-scale advertising agency? Professor Saltana?"

"Wouldn't consider such a proposal for a moment."

"Dr. Tooby?"

"I'd rather play the piano in a pub."

"In other words, another emphatic negative. Thank you, gentlemen! No more questions." He didn't rise, but looked as if he might accomplish this feat very soon. "I have taken no notes of our conversation, as you see. I have in fact a vurry good memory. But I would take it as a favour, Professor Saltana, if you would dictate the substance of our conversation — your two points about the Institute, then your answers to my two questions — and then send a clear typewritten copy to me at the Con-

naught Hotel. And I suggest that Dr. Tooby reads it too, and then adds
his signature to yours. Is that too much to ask?"

"Not at all," said Saltana briskly. "In fact I was about to suggest it
myself. You agree, Owen?"

Tuby said he did, though he was still wondering what the fuss was
all about. Saltana insisted upon showing Stockton out, and he gave Tuby
a wink as he passed.

"I'm being stupid about this, Cosmo," he cried as soon as Saltana,
his face alight, showed in the doorway. "Why the fuss, the growing eagerness, the undercover jubilation?"

"My dear Owen, it's possible, just possible, that these Americans —
Maclaskie and his friends — might want to take over the Institute and
buy us out. Maclaskie has told Elfreda more than once that if we could
be got rid of — "

"But we *are* the Institute," Tuby cut in, feeling exasperated. "And
we've just told Humpty-Dumpty so — told him the plain truth — "

"Certainly. It's one reason why I wanted you here — to witness that
I was speaking the exact truth. But didn't you notice that Stockton didn't
believe us? Oh — we thought we were indispensable — and he'd heard
that before. Now I must dictate all this to Elfreda — but listen, Owen!
Don't say anything to Elfreda about any possibility of a take-over. There
may be nothing in it. And I'd rather start explaining everything to her
when you and I can make a few plans of our own."

Tuby nodded, but for once didn't smile. "All right, Cosmo. But if I
felt as you do about Elfreda, I'd begin taking her into my confidence."

Then there was Meldy, now back from Rome and with a suite in
the Baronial Hotel again, this time in a sitting room crowded and dazzling with newly painted heraldic shields. He had had one rather unsatisfactory session with her — she had found herself at odds with the producer and the director of her film, and was feeling uncertain of herself
— so now he had agreed to see her with the director, an Italian-Ameri-
can called Tasco. And in fact Tasco was already there, among the glis-
tening shields, when Tuby arrived.

Meldy, who had been filming earlier, was wearing a dark green
sweater and black pants, and looked rather tired but still ravishing. Tasco
was wearing cherry-red pants and a horrible sports coat, about the same
yellowish shade as Stockton's face; and he looked as if he had been tired
for years, and was very thin, wriggly, given to jumping up and down and
knotting himself into different chairs, and was probably thoroughly
neurotic.

"You'll have whisky, won't you, Tuby darling?" said Meldy, opening two steel breastplates to reveal a small illuminated bar. "I'm not
drinking anything. And Tasco only drinks milk and vodka."

"Good God!" cried Tuby. He looked at Tasco, now knotted in a
chair. "What's it like?"

"Terrible, terrible! But it expresses my personality. And everywhere — in Hollywood, Rome, London — people say, 'Here comes Tasco — where is the milk and vodka?' I'm neurotic as hell, Doctor. Nearly a nut case." He untwined himself, leapt out of the chair, and stood in front of Tuby. "You think I look neurotic?"

"Yes, I do," said Tuby cheerfully. "Thank you, my dear!" This was to Meldy, for the whisky.

"Okay, okay, okay! But I make pictures — good pictures. With Meldy I can make a good picture," he cried passionately.

Tuby nodded and smiled, found a reasonably comfortable chair, put his glass on a small table that was once a drum, and lit his pipe. He then looked up, only to find that Tasco was now sitting on the floor, three or four yards from where he had been standing. This was going to be like arguing with a troupe of acrobats.

"You hear what she wants?" cried Tasco. "British accent! British manner! This is what she wants now. Talk like British mum, not like American father. Producer objects. I object. No good. This is what she wants. This is what her dear darling Dr. Tuby wants. We give in. And the front office has told us you do a great job with her — and give her publicity at the premeer money couldn't buy. It's great. You're great. Okay, okay, okay! We take the British accent. Say-ettle dee-own and smay-oke yor pape, Tuby dahling."

"Oh — shut up! I don't talk like that — and you know it, Tasco. And another thing. Dr. Tuby didn't tell me to be British, so don't blame him. He told me to try to be myself, to do what I wanted to do, that's all. So I decided I'd speak better English — the kind you can read poetry in. And I don't say *smay-oke yor pape, Tuby dahling*."

"She doesn't, you know, Mr. Tasco," said Tuby mildly. "I'm afraid your ear's at fault there."

"Or mebbe I'm kidding, Doctor. I'm a great little kidder, aren't I, Meldy?"

"No," said Meldy.

Ignoring that reply, Tasco jumped into a chair and looked as if he might be working himself into the Lotus position. "But now I'm not kidding, Doctor. Not with three million five at stake. *And* my rep. So I ask you — what's with Meldy Glebe? British accent? Okay, okay, if she must — no skin off our noses. But what's next?"

Meldy interrupted, obviously impatient now. "No, Tasco, let me explain. It'll take less time."

"Okay, okay, okay!" And Tasco, now more or less in the Lotus position, took his head between his hands and wagged it as if it were turning into a metronome.

"In the two sequences we shot down there," said Meldy, "I'm enigmatic. But now I have to turn into somebody. And I refuse to be a sexy nothing. Like you said, I want to be a girl lawyer or financier or scientist or somebody like that. It means some scenes will have to be rewritten, but I've talked to the two writers — and they don't mind. They even offered to come here — "

"This is serious, Doctor," Tasco continued, now squatting only about eighteen inches from Tuby's knees. "Three million five and my rep. Now Meldy's a sex symbol. Sex image, if that's how you like it. Okay, she don't like sex. In private, I mean. So what? But Meldy has to make with it on the screen. If she doesn't, what's she doing? What's the big money for? Now look — Doctor — you're pulling the wires with Meldy. She won't listen to us. You have the tight hold. Okay, *you* don't like sex — "

"Stop there, Mr. Tasco!" He didn't, but leapt up and flung himself into a chair. However, Tuby was in command now. "What makes you imagine I dislike sex?"

"Now look — Doctor — you tell her to ditch the sex image. And she'll do anything you want — and she says you haven't been laying her — "

"Oh — shut up!" Meldy was furious.

"So that's it," Tasco muttered, retreating from Meldy's fury and Tuby's sharp change of tone. "You don't like sex. So she's all against it. And we're out on a limb."

"Mr. Tasco, I am Deputy Director of the *Institute of Social Imagistics*," Tuby began sternly, "and the Institute has a strict rule against *laying* its clients, however desirable they may be. And now before I go on — and I propose to go on at some length, my friend — I must ask a small service of you. Assume any posture you like — draped round a chair, kneeling or lying on the floor, or even standing on your head — but please *keep still*, otherwise I can't talk and you can't listen properly. Now decide where and how you want to be, Mr. Tasco."

"Oh, Tuby darling," Meldy sighed, "I love you."

"Now you are wildly wrong when you imagine I dislike sex. And you are thinking mainly of its physical side, I suppose. Now as far as that is concerned, I know fifty times more about it than you do — "

"Me? Aw — wait a minute, Doctor — "

"My dear sir," Tuby thundered, "I am a persuasive, warm-blooded, sensual, and self-indulgent man. And where have I spent the last twenty years? In the East — surrounded by women, Indian or Chinese, to whom love-making is an art, based on ancient subtle traditions and practices — highly trained women, mistresses of the erotic, who would regard you, my friend, as a clumsy, ignorant, contemptible barbarian, quite incapable of bringing any satisfaction to an amorous woman. You dare to talk to me about sex! I would as soon listen to a boy of fifteen. Sex — good God!" And Tuby, still looking indignant, drained half his whisky. Then, noticing Meldy's fixed gaze, he smiled at her.

"Doctor — you win. I'm wrong. I've heard about some of them —

out East. Read some hot bits too. Seemed to me, though, you'd have to
be an acrobat."

"Well, that shouldn't worry you," Tuby grunted as Tasco sprang up
and hurled himself into another chair.

"Say — Meldy — I don't laugh at you any more about your Tuby
darling. This guy's *something*."

"What did I tell you? Now shut up and listen to him."

Tuby, who always knew exactly when to do this, now changed his
manner completely, not forcing anything, talking easily and pleasantly.
"When I first met Meldy I realized she was unhappy and feeling rebellious. I liked her, accepted her as a client because I felt I could help her,
and believed I could reasonably demand a substantial fee because I might
prevent enormous losses on her contract."

"And you can say that again, Doctor," said Tasco.

"I saw two of her films and reported on them to her. Her appearance in them was unsatisfactory, and there were obvious good image reasons. She was being asked to project a simple sexual image — of the type
you still have in mind. But it was too simple and wasn't even being
sharply projected. It was being blurred by what we call the *Unconscious
Counter-Image,* coming from her own idea of herself. I saw that what
was needed was a conscious and definite *Counter-Image.* If she had this
to project, then she could afford to sharpen and heighten the original sex
image, knowing that it would be replaced by the *Counter-Image.* In film
terms, we meet a deliciously attractive girl, apparently ripe for a husband
or lover, but then we find that what she wants to do is to use her brains,
in some professional capacity, being far more concerned about that than
making use of her looks. And if you can't see the story possibilities there,
then you're not the director I take you to be, Mr. Tasco."

"But about this image thing — "

"Don't interrupt him," said Meldy sharply.

"We have now projected the *Counter-Image.* But we don't leave it
at that. We begin alternating, with increasing rapidity, the two images,
until finally we achieve the bewildering but fascinating *Double Image.*
And that's not all. As you know, I advised Meldy to go to that première
in her oldest clothes — and to make all public appearances like that,
looking as if she didn't care a damn. Now this is the *Reverse Other Image,* which haunts the minds of audiences as they watch the superb creature on the screen. Whether she did it deliberately or not, I don't know,
but Garbo used the *Reverse Other Image* very effectively, thirty years
ago — "

"But I'm no Garbo — let's face it, Tuby darling — "

"That's not the point, my dear. We must consider your images. We
could have now the *Double Image* on the screen haunted by the *Reverse
Other Image,* not present on the screen but floating in the minds of audiences and adding its own fascination — "

"Are you getting this, Tasco?" demanded Meldy with some severity.

Tasco leapt out of the chair. "Jeesus — look at the time! That agent — Orange — was right. Meldy's right. I was all wrong. Work on *me* some time. Be seeing you. Ring you later tonight, Meldy. No, don't move — I'm on my way. Kiss him for me too." And he bounded out.

"All right, I will." And she wrapped herself round Tuby and began kissing him. "Tuby darling, couldn't you," she murmured between kisses, "couldn't you — please — teach me — you know, some of those things — I mean, when you were talking to Tasco — about Eastern women — "

Tuby was no great resister of temptation— and this was terrible. Moreover, he was genuinely fond of the girl. But this cut both ways, and more for her sake than his own, he was able gently to release himself.

"No, my dear, it wouldn't work. We haven't the right kind of relationship. We'd both be sorry afterwards. We mightn't feel guilty but we'd feel silly."

"I wouldn't have but now you've said that, I might." She sat down and gave him a long speculative look. "Is it because of this girl — well, woman really — quite old, over thirty?"

"What girl — woman really — ?"

"I meant to tell you, but Tasco got here first. It was yesterday and I'd just got back from the studio. Then she was here — knocked and walked in. How she did it, I don't know. But this woman just came up and walked in. I was going to ask her how she did it, but there wasn't time. I never even got her name. But she certainly knows you."

"But do *I* know *her?*"

"Well, she's about my height but rather thinner — her face is, anyhow — and she wouldn't be much to look at — hair and face needed attention and her clothes were boring — if it wasn't for her eyes, though she had a lovely voice too. But the eyes were the knockout — "

"Unusually large and expressive," said Tuby, pretending to be cooler than he felt. "A light hazel when she's amused, darkening to a sepia when she's feeling tragic. And her name is Lois Terry."

"And she's very clever, isn't she? I knew at once she was."

"She wasn't very clever yesterday, bursting in on you. But she can be brilliant at six o'clock and be utterly daft at nine o'clock. Even so, I can't think why she'd want to see you, Meldy."

"Well, she started straight off and asked me if I'd tell her the truth, looking at me with those eyes. And I said I'd try to, what did she want? I may say I felt a bit scared, thinking she might be round the bend. She didn't sit down or anything, just stood there looking at me with those eyes — and she had this lovely voice as well. So then she asked about you and me, and I said you'd been a great help to me, and you liked me and I adored you, which you know I do, Tuby darling. But then I guessed what she was after, so I said there wasn't any sex between us, nothing like that, though I also said that was our business, not hers. And she said that was quite true and she apologized for charging in and asking me questions, gave me a very nice smile, then went straight out, before I could ask her what it was all about. Did you make love to her when you were down there?"

"No, I didn't."

"Don't you ever — unless they're brown or yellow and know fifty-five positions? Is that it, Tuby darling?"

"It is not. And you're oversimplifying something that is really very complicated. And I must go now, my dear. And you ought to rest. You'll probably be up half the night arguing with Tasco and his two writers."

"I know." She said it with a sigh, but then brightened up. "But we won, didn't we? Thanks to you, Tuby darling!" And she kissed him, but affectionately this time. He was really fond of Meldy now, he told himself after leaving her; but on his way down and then out of the hotel, he thought in a rather confused fashion about Lois Terry.

This American procession was broken by a very British interlude — Jimmy Kilburn's dinner party for the Institute. Jimmy Kilburn, the eccentric Cockney millionaire, was Saltana's friend, not Tuby's. It was Saltana, meeting him at the Birtles' in the autumn, the Brockshire time, who had advised Kilburn, then about to marry and possibly enter public life, not to change his style and habits but to project a sharp and striking image based on them; and of course it was Kilburn, out of gratitude, who had made it possible for the Institute, which he and Elfreda had modestly financed, to be installed so quickly in Half Moon House. Tuby had only met him twice, and then briefly, and now, at this Institute party, was meeting Mrs. Kilburn for the first time. And the Kilburns made a rum pair. He was small, droopy, all nose, and talked like a Cockney character comedian, whereas she was immensely genteel, an upholstered kind of woman, with a large white face, a rosebud mouth, and washed-out blue eyes, who greeted Tuby graciously like minor royalty opening something in Coketown. The drawing room, where cocktails were being served from a portable bar, had so much plush and gilt in it that it might have been part of an old music hall. Elfreda, Primrose, and Saltana were already there. The men had been told not to dress, but the women were having none of that nonsense and were looking splendid.

Jimmy Kilburn took Tuby to one side. "What'll yer 'ave, Tuby? Never touch it meself but like to push the booze around. An' that Spanish sod we 'ave is so bloody slow. Martini — whisky — fancy Italian stuff — what?"

Tuby took a martini, already mixed and too weak, and asked if Eden Mere was expected.

"She was asked, all right. An' 'er ol' man — "

"O. V. Mere? I haven't seen him for a long time."

"I 'ave — just on the telly. Gets 'em talkin' about politics an' education. 'E just sits, fag in 'is mouf, then says time's up an' 'bye for now. Easy money, if yer ask me. Bit of a cunnin' bugger, isn't 'e?"

"Artful in his way — yes. I think this needs a little more gin. May I?"

"That's the idear. Now what 'ave we got? 'Scuse me!"

The Meres had arrived. Eden was wearing a long dress of vertical red and white stripes and had her hair piled up, and looked about eight feet high. O. V. had made no concessions to the dinner party. He looked just as ashy and dandruffy and crumpled as ever, and the eternally half-smoked cigarette still hung from his lower lip. And as soon as introductions were over, he dodged the white-coated houseman and joined Tuby at the portable bar, where he helped himself to a whisky with such speed and dexterity that it seemed like a conjuring trick. "All here, are we, Tuby?"

"Not quite. You'll see. But how are things with you, Mere? I keep hearing about you on television."

"Wangled a little series. Sold the Redbrick mag since I saw you last. To a pair of young chumps who'd found some money somewhere. Gives me time to look around — politics perhaps. No electioneering — none of that dam' nonsense." He wobbled his cigarette at Tuby. "Eden says you're all very busy and making money. I don't tell her what I think. Never pays. But between ourselves, Tuby, when are you selling out?"

"I didn't know we were."

Mere may have winked but it was hard to tell, his eyes never looking more than about one-third open. Certainly his cigarette wobbled. "All right, old boy, play it like that. Not blaming you. But of course, I've *heard* things."

After a minute or two of O. V. Mere, Tuby always found he began to feel cunning too, though exactly about *what,* he never knew. "Never believe all you hear, old boy. There are rumours and *rumours.*" Tuby wasn't proud of this, though he did feel it had the right O. V. Mere cadence and flavour, though of course it needed the smouldering cigarette, the two-thirds closed eyes.

Tuby settled down comfortably to enjoy his dinner, which promised to be excellent. The dining room was almost as large and imposing as the drawing room, and was not quite the Baronial Hotel but had moved in that direction.

At first he exchanged chitchat with his hostess, who talked rather like a duchess in a fairly good repertory production, and quite unlike the only real duchess he knew, Petro, who'd come from some fairly bad repertory companies. But then she turned to Saltana, and he could talk to Eden, who looked as if she had had enough of her other neighbour. Tuby hoped he would be able to avoid any very personal topics, if only because Eden could never moderate her voice, which rang out from her

Wellingtonian profile as if it were sending into the line a brigade of light infantry. But he hoped in vain.

"As you know, Tuby dear," she said after a minute or two, "Elfreda is no tittle-tattle. But from certain things she's let fall — and putting two and two together as I can't help doing — I gather you're behaving extremely badly to this clever young woman at Brockshire University."

Tuby tried to tell her quietly that if she meant Lois Terry, then he was not the one who was behaving badly.

"Speak up, please, my dear," she commanded from her great height. "You're mumbling so I can't catch what you're saying. *Who* is behaving badly? One of you must be."

"That doesn't follow," said Tuby, feeling it would be safe to speak up on this statement. But he soon realized he had made a mistake.

"That's better, Tuby dear. But of course it must follow — if, as I gather, *you're lovers.*" And this came ringing out.

Tuby was desperate and it made him rash. "Let's talk after dinner, Eden, then I'll explain everything." He had to be loud and clear too.

"And what about me?" said Elfreda, leaning forward and smiling. She was probably feeling bored, which explained her rather stupid intervention.

"What *is* all this, Dr. Tuby?" said Mrs. Kilburn, clearly bewildered.

"A little Institute joke, really," Tuby told her. And he made no effort to keep his voice down. "When people work together they seem to find it necessary to bounce these little jokes among themselves, no matter how tedious they may seem to other people."

"Nonsense!" Eden Mere exclaimed. Tuby could have kicked her.

"Certainly not," said Saltana, coming to Tuby's rescue in his most authoritative manner. "It was one of my greatest trials working for so long with Latin Americans — " And on he went, dominating his end of the table.

Tuby thanked him as soon as the women had gone and then they moved up to be nearer their host, but for the time being he was deep in talk with O. V. Mere, now himself again, with the cigarette dangling.

"Mere asked me, before dinner, when we were selling out," said Tuby. "Have you been talking to him, Cosmo?"

"I have not. In fact I haven't seen him for weeks."

"Then where could he have picked up this idea?"

"O. V. exists in that kind of atmosphere — like Jimmy Kilburn, though he exists on a higher level of it. They see everybody selling out, taking over, merging, splitting up, doing good turns and bad turns, bluffing, double-crossing — "

"Yes, yes, yes, Cosmo, I know what you mean. I'll put a little question to you, if I may, my friend?"

"Go ahead, Owen."

"It's this." And Tuby stared hard at his friend but spoke very softly. "*Are* we selling out?"

"Not yet, of course. And I want to talk to Jimmy about it. You try to keep Mere occupied. Or take him to join the women."

"Harder, I think. Our O. V. isn't a ladies' man. No, no, whisky and plotting for him — and whisky without plotting for me."

A few minutes later, Saltana had Kilburn to himself, and Tuby had Mere. "And I might soon have something for you, Tuby," Mere was saying, his eyes almost closed, the cigarette smouldering away. "That is, if I think the money's there. Political."

"No, O. V. I'm the great exception to the rule that man is a political animal — "

"Quite — but this would be an image job for you — "

"Ah — that's different. Except I'd have to read all that stuff in the Press about politicians' images — and attend, God save us, to their horrible appearances on television. No, it would never be worth it."

"Only," Mere murmured — and no man could do more with a murmur — "if it were either the P.M. or the Leader of the Opposition." And he nearly opened one eye.

Tuby could now feel the cunning infection beginning to work in him. He closed one eye and went down to a meaningful murmur too. "Big game, certainly. Very big game, undoubtedly." He felt a bit tight, but that might be the cunning effect and this corridors-of-power talk. "But, after all, they're very different kettles of fish, aren't they?"

Mere's cigarette wobbled. "Who says so?"

"Well, *they* do, don't they? Kettles of fish at daggers drawn. That's the way they talk. I don't. What I'm trying to say is — you could have some influence in only one party. And which party are you proposing to work with?"

"Both." And Mere removed the cigarette to finish his whisky.

Still feeling bewildered, Tuby finished his whisky too. "Perhaps we ought to leave Saltana and Kilburn and join the ladies."

"Why? You'll only have my dear wife asking you about your private life at the top of her voice."

"There is that, certainly. But that seems to be her voice, not the top of it. Doesn't she ever talk quietly?"

"She decided, about twenty years ago, I wouldn't listen if she did — she was right too — and now she can't talk any other way. Otherwise, a first-class wife."

"Why don't you do me a favour, O. V., and make sure your wife doesn't shout questions at me? Keep talking to her yourself."

"What about?" Mere enquired gloomily.

"Ask her how she enjoyed the dinner — that sort of thing."

"She'd think I was going out of my mind — "

"Well, there's a topic. Come on!'

They went along to the drawing room. Elfreda seemed ready to pounce upon Tuby, who offered no resistance and allowed himself to be taken into a corner. Under one of those pictures of cardinals and another, which Tuby felt he had seen before, of a young man in a gondola about to receive a flower tossed out of a barred window, they were able to sit close and undisturbed, and to talk freely. Which was something, Elfreda confessed, she found it hard to do in the office. "And now you can tell me, Owen, why you're behaving so badly to that poor girl, Lois Terry."

"That poor girl, as you call her, burst into Meldy Glebe's hotel room, the other evening, to ask her — "

"I know, I know," Elfreda cut in hastily. "She told me."

"Good God! I no longer have the least idea what's happening under my very nose. Perhaps you can tell me how Lois managed it. Meldy's supposed to be guaranteed against invasion."

"Lois has a cousin who's secretary or assistant to the manager there." Elfreda was beaming. But then she gave Tuby a solemnly reproachful look. "You're always so sweet, Owen, yet you've cut yourself off from poor Lois, just as if you thought she'd done something terrible to you. And I'm sure she hasn't. It can't be just because she doesn't like the idea of the Institute and thinks you ought to be teaching at a university. Or can it? And please be serious and truthful, Owen."

"Not so easy, Elfreda. I'd have to tell you things about Lois she mightn't want you to know — "

"You couldn't. She's told me everything. I know far more about her than you do."

"From her point of view, not mine. Lois is very much a real person. She has some remarkable qualities, chiefly wasted in Brockshire. But we've had no luck together. And I realize now it wasn't really a matter of luck."

"You mean — being entangled so long with that man. Oh — I know all about that — "

"One of those messy unrewarding affairs that go on and on," said Tuby sadly, "that unusually sensitive girls so often find themselves landed with. They're too soft-hearted either to break it off or to force the men into a divorce and then a remarriage. No, Elfreda — I know what you're going to say. She's broken it off, never wants to see the man again."

"And I know that's true, Owen. She swears it is, and I believe her."

"I don't blame you — or her. But has she really disentangled herself from him *inside,* where she really lives? I don't think so. A lot of women can't help having one *magic man,* who might be any kind of clot they've gone to bed with and have built up in their imagination, and, whatever Lois may say or do, this fellow's still the magic man — "

"Oh — rubbish!" Elfreda cried impatiently. "Would she — when you never give her a sign — keep asking about you, really chasing after you, feeling jealous — ?"

"Yes, she would. Not for myself. After all, look at me, for God's sake! No, she's trying to prove to herself she really has finished with that fellow. She's trying desperately hard to shatter that image of the magic man — "

"You silly man! It's all quite simple, and the poor girl's in love with you. And now I'll tell you something about yourself, Owen Tuby. You have the sense to know she's a serious sensitive person — not like these Hazels and Petros you amuse yourself with — and deep down you don't *want* such a person to be in love with you. It's a responsibility. And you'll invent any theory just to dodge it."

"Very neat, Elfreda. Quite wrong. But excusable because a certain suggestion of irresponsibility is part of my persona. The fact is, however, that Lois is precisely the rare kind of woman who would soon make me feel deeply responsible, and it's that mistake I'm avoiding — "

"Oh — fiddle-faddle! What has the poor girl got to do to prove she's free of that man — come crawling on her knees — ?"

"The last thing to do, I'd say. No, Elfreda dear, enough's enough. Time we joined the party." He got up. "Look — Saltana and Jimmy Kilburn are here now."

"What have they been talking about?"

"Settling our future, I suspect. But you could ask one of them."

About ten busy days later the American procession began again. It was restarted by Ezra J. Smithy, who slid in one morning to announce that Dan Luckett, Big Dan himself, would be with them the very next day. Moreover, Dan, who liked to see for himself where and how a man worked, would set aside all tycoon status and privileges by calling himself on Tuby. "So brace yourself, man," said Ezra, and shot out, leaving behind him, to spread throughout the Institute, curiosity, wonder, excitement. Big Dan, they all knew by this time, did everything in a big way, which meant that if they could find the right image for him, as Elfreda kept pointing out, he would be their most valuable client. Smithy had already given the Institute five hundred pounds as a mere holding fee. The final fee, if they were successful, Elfreda declared, might be anything up to ten thousand pounds. And it had been decided almost from the first that Saltana, to avoid any clash of imperious temperaments, must leave Dan Luckett to Tuby, the persuader, and to Elfreda, who understood Americans.

Tuby, who had been bracing himself ever since nine-thirty and was getting tired of it, felt more relief than apprehension when at last, two hours later, Ezra Smithy came in sideways as usual but then opened the door wide, to allow Dan to make a big entrance. He did this, holding out an enormous hand.

"Hiya, fella! I'm Dan Luckett — and Ez tells me you're Doc Tuby.

And I'm glad to meetya. Now take a load of this." And instead of advancing to shake hands, he stopped about four feet from Tuby's desk, still with the hand outstretched, like a man about to pose for a photograph. He was indeed a big man, probably about sixty, and he had rumpled white hair, a large and deeply tanned face, and a wide toothy grin. But why was he standing like that? Tuby looked enquiringly at Ezra Smithy.

"Dan's got a hundred and fifty thousand full-colour bills out, all over the States, showing him just like that — with *Eat At Dan's,* nothing else, printed underneath."

"And just ordered another fifty thousand, Ez." Dan had now dropped his hand and his pose and was about to sit down. "Whatya think, fella? Let's get down to business. What'ull that do for me among you British?"

"Kill you stone dead," Tuby told him.

"Ya wouldn't be just beating up business, wouldya?"

"Yes."

It looked for a moment as if Dan couldn't decide whether to be angry or amused. Then he produced a very loud though rather mechanical laugh, slapped his thigh, and said, "Whatya think of that answer, Ez?"

"I told you, Dan. Dr. Tuby's a character."

"Sure! But so am I. So are you when your hair's down, Ez. About every New Year's. All righty, you want some business. So do I — though it'll cost me thirty-five million dollars just to get off the ground over here. But now ya going to tell me why that poster would kill me stone dead on this side. And if ya can't, fella — I'll be gone before ya could scratch ya ass."

Tuby stood up. "I'll be glad to explain what I meant, Mr. Luckett — "

"Dan— Dan. I keep calling ya *fella,* don't I? So it's Dan."

"All right, Dan. But if you don't mind, I'd like to bring in my colleague, Mrs. Judson Drake — Elfreda, if you prefer it. She's English but has spent years in America and married an American — in fact an Oregon millionaire — who died about two years ago. She knows your restaurants, Dan."

"Fine — bring her in. Call her on the intercom. No? Don't ya have an intercom?"

"Yes," said Tuby on his way to the door. Then he turned and smiled. "But I might want to say something to her I don't want you to hear, Dan." And he could still hear Dan's loud but mechanical laugh as he went along the corridor.

"I feel you ought to join us, Elfreda."

"If you think I'll be useful — of course." She found her bag and took a hasty look at herself. "What's he like?"

"Larger than life," Tuby whispered hurriedly. "Giant folksy performance — but shrewd and rather hard, I suspect. I'm going to stand up to him, though I'll take it easy while you're with us because he's the type who'll be vain and touchy if there's an attractive woman around. Your face is fine — so come along."

"And ya'll call me Dan or I just won't listen to ya," Dan was declaring a minute later. "And I'll call ya — what is it? — yeh, Elfreda. Nice name — and ya the first I've ever known. Wouldn't ya say that's right, Ez?"

"Not quite, Dan. Manageress of our older place in Cleveland, Ohio, one time was called Elfreda — remember?" Smithy seemed almost to blossom under the sun of Dan's presence.

"Think ya're wrong, Ez. But let's get on. Now that's a durned fine poster I described, fella, big hit everywhere, so why's it going to kill me dead — no, *stone* dead — over here? And ya better be good." Dan laughed.

Tuby detected a threatening undertone there. And it seemed to him that Dan's eyes looked out of some other world, not the hand-offering, wide-grinning, hiya-fella world at all. There was a half-smoked pipe on his desk, and Tuby, to settle himself, lit it carefully. "A big, handsome, friendly man holding out his hand," he began, "then *Eat At Dan's* — yes, I can see that it might be very effective. What we call a *Warm Image* and just one simple and probably familiar statement — excellent! But for America, not for this country."

"That's what y'already said, friend. Now make me believe ya."

"I'll try. Let me say that such an appeal would be fatal here for two very good reasons. In the first place, it's too American. Here we associate America with advanced technology, labour-saving devices, domestic gadgets, and so forth, but not with food. We have innumerable French, Italian, Chinese restaurants — but how many American? Once you're established, it won't matter if you're known to be American. But if you start by beating that particular drum, you never will be established."

"Ya buy hamburgers," Dan protested. "Ya buy hot dogs. Ya buy *ice* cream — "

"But they're not your idea of eating at Dan's, surely?" said Tuby. "And our own popular restaurants already concentrate on steaks, chicken, ham and eggs, that kind of thing. You may do them better, may offer more value for the money, may have a more efficient large-scale organisation — "

"I'll say we have — "

"Quite so. But you have to attract the public and establish yourselves — to prove your superiority, if it exists."

"It does. Leave that to me, fella."

"Of course, Dan. It's the original approach we're discussing — the first all-important image. Now not only would yours be too obviously American, it would also be too personal. Yes, here's Dan with his wide welcoming smile and his big outstretched hand — but who the hell is this Dan? Now who are the people here you want to attract?"

"Lower-income groups," Dan replied promptly. "White collars and good blue collars."

"So I imagined. And most of them are very suspicious. They don't want any Dan telling 'em he's their pal. After ten years it might be 'Good old Dan!' But most of them object to love at first sight. They're very suspicious, cynical, and not outgoing, not obviously extrovert. They live in an overcrowded little island and want to keep themselves to themselves. If I stand next to the average American in a queue, he isn't happy until he's told me he's John Smith, has a wife and three children, works as an electrician, and drives a Chevrolet or whatever it is. But if it's an average Englishman, he's hoping to God I won't speak to him. Isn't that true, Elfreda?"

"Yes — except for these youngsters we have now — "

"Not the trade I want, Elfreda," Dan told her. "Ya've nearly made ya point, Doc Tuby. Want to stick it right into me now? I'm running out of time."

"I said that kind of approach would kill you stone dead," Tuby declared emphatically, "because you'd be charging head first into a solid wall of prejudice. If you want to use an image — and I'd advise it — you just find the right image for our public. And what might work for a razor blade or ballpoint pen, something comparatively simple, won't work for a chain of popular restaurants. But you know that — and I mustn't waste your time. Now then," he continued briskly, "we've already been working on your case. Elfreda and her two assistants have some ideas — a few of the more promising are embodied in sketches by our artist — and now I suggest that Elfreda and perhaps one of her assistants, Primrose East, call on you at your convenience to discuss these ideas, which I can explain later in image terms. All right?"

"Fine! Elfreda, how about five o'clock — my suite at the Baronial Hotel? Know it? I'm there because I own a piece of it."

Elfreda said that she and Primrose, together with the material they'd been working on, would be there at five. This brought Dan out of his chair.

"One thing though, Ez," said Dan. "What about that survey some professor was doing for us?"

"Dr. Honeyfield says she could bring it up early next week. But she wants to go through it with Dr. Tuby. And I thought they could be getting together on that while you're in Paris."

"Why not? And it's ya baby. Pleased to have met ya, Doc Tuby. See ya at five, Elfreda — you'n Rosie — "

"Primrose, please," said Elfreda, smiling.

"And a dish," added Smithy without smiling.

The next time Tuby heard Smithy say that was on Friday morning, two days after his first encounter with Dan Luckett. "And a dish," but now he was describing Hazel Honeyfield, not Primrose. "I know because I went down there to see her, and she was all for the job and for talking over the results with you, her dear Dr. Tuby. How the hell you do it, I don't know, but she lit up like a little lighthouse. Now this is how it stands. I'm going over to Paris this afternoon with Dan and we won't be back till Tuesday. She can come up Monday evening, bringing her survey, so this is what I've fixed for you, pulling a string or two at the Baronial because Dan's got a piece of it. I've booked you into two single rooms — you're in 264, she's in 266 — with a communicating bathroom. Monday night. And you could take that without any pain, couldn't you? Yes, well that's what I thought." And there might have been a flicker of something passing across Ezra J. Smithy's dark sad face, at the end of this, his longest speech — the ghost, perhaps, of a conspiratorial wink or leer.

Tuby was on a radio programme at seven that night, and Saltana, for once at a loose end, went along with him, and then they dined together at an oldish French restaurant in Soho, rather smelly and overfurnished and decorated in a Nineties style, as if Toulouse Lautrec was expected to come creeping in at any moment. Though they ate and drank heartily enough, they were both in a heavy mood. The notes they compared on their work might have been tablets of lead.

"The truth is, Cosmo," said Tuby, after twenty minutes of this notecomparing, together with a generous helping of *pâté maison,* "and let's hope nobody's listening — we're bored. I am. And now I know you are."

"Certainly," said Saltana. "Yes, Owen, and we ought to be ashamed of ourselves. Out of a lot of dam' nonsense, we've created an institute which almost everybody takes quite seriously. It flourishes. The money rolls in, more in a week than we used to earn in a year. I've turned down three enquiries today. Have you ever heard of a new African country called Bezania?"

"No, I'm delighted to say. Did it want something from us?"

"Image for a Bezanian Air Line. I told the man — politely, of course — they were wasting enough money without wasting any more on us. I was right too. All the same, Owen, we ought to be ashamed of ourselves."

"Possibly, Cosmo. But I'm not very good at being ashamed of myself. And God knows I've been told to be, often enough. If I'm bored, I'm bored — and there it is. I'm almost yawning now when I trot out my images, even though I keep inventing new varieties on the spur of the moment. The *Reverse Softened Edge,* for example."

"But why don't you get out of Belsize Park, take a little furnished flat nearer Half Moon Street? You can afford it now."

"I know — but I'm too lazy." Tuby drank some wine, and then, still holding his glass, gave Saltana a long enquiring look. "Besides — is it worth while? We're getting out of this, aren't we, Cosmo? You and Jimmy

Kilburn have plans, haven't you? Don't say you haven't. I'm counting on you."

"Certainly we have. Shall I explain what we decided, the night we were dining with him?"

"No. But you ought to tell Elfreda."

Saltana scowled at him. "I can't yet. Strictly personal reasons — sorry, Owen! But we've probably three or four months yet, so you can leave Belsize Park, come much nearer. You don't have to find a place yourself. Put the women on to it. They have this built-in nest-finding faculty. And young Primrose lives in a world of flat-taking, flat-subletting, flat-leaving. Her friends move around like so many gipsies. Or tell Elfreda you need a place where her Dr. Lois Terry can spend the night with you. She won't think *that* disgusting — that's quite different — and she and Primrose will find a cosy little nest for you in a couple of days, probably sooner."

"Possibly. But unfortunately for that plan," said Tuby, with that great deliberation which so often sets unknown but fateful machinery in motion, "I don't propose to entertain Lois Terry at any hour, let alone a whole night."

"I hear you, Dr. Tuby," said Saltana gravely. He raised his glass. "And I looks to you."

It was just after half-past six on Monday evening when Tuby, in room 264 at the Baronial Hotel, stared around with a deepening sense of relief. The mediaeval-cum-Tudor theme was not so obvious on these lower and less expensive floors; no armour and stands of spears and axes down here, no walls of heraldic shields; apart from two idiotic plaster beams, this was a sensible hotel bedroom. After unpacking his small overnight bag, he went to the door into the bathroom. He didn't try to open it, but just listened. Water was running out of the bath in there, and then other sounds suggested that Hazel was in occupation. Good! After killing a little time examining pictures of Alnwick Castle and Kenilworth, he heard a click that told him Hazel had unlocked the bathroom from the inside; so she was now in 266, beginning to dress, and he was at liberty to attend to his own more modest toilet. But first he satisfied his curiosity by examining the bathroom door's mechanism: it could be locked on either side — a point to remember. There was a separate shower — no mediaeval-cum-Tudor nonsense about the Baronial bathrooms — and he used it, put on a clean shirt and the same suit he had just taken off, and then asked Room Service for two large dry martinis. Taking his time, he brushed his hair, tied his tie, changed from slippers to shoes, and was then ready to welcome the martinis, which were brought by a forester from either Sherwood or Arden, together with a monstrous bill for two pounds fifteen shillings. He gave the forester half a crown, and signed the bill. After all, Dan Luckett, who would have to pay the bill, owned a piece of the hotel. He took a sip of one martini, poured a little of the other into that glass, to keep the level equal, ate a potato chip, and then knocked on the bathroom door on Hazel's side. It was opened almost at once — and there she was, in a dress of dark green and light green, sparkling and dimpling away. She came straight into his arms, kissing him rapturously. "Darling Dr. Tuby! Isn't this *exciting?*"

"Wonderful, my dear! But come into *my* room. I have some martinis waiting for us."

"How clever of you! I daren't order a thing. Everything must cost the earth here, doesn't it? But then I suppose Mr. Smithy — or his great Dan Luckett — can afford it."

"You can say that again, baby." He passed over her martini. "We ought to dine soon. Are you hungry, Hazel?"

"Ravenous, darling. Two egg sandwiches for lunch, nothing since, and I've driven up from Tarbury. Yes, please — potato chips. Oh — I'm loving this — aren't you? Before I had my bath I read the hotel's description of itself — quite a booklet. I shall take mine away with me. It's absolutely crammed with fascinating status symbols. Haven't you got one here?"

"Haven't noticed one. Perhaps the last man in here took his away, though it's unlikely he was also a sociologist. What does it say about dining rooms?"

"There are two, darling. Ivanhoe and Twelfth Night. Which do you think?"

"Twelfth Night for me. It may be awful, but Ivanhoe could be a nightmare. I know what this hotel can do when it really tries. A client of ours had a suite here — two, in fact — "

"Meldy Glebe," cried Hazel triumphantly. "I know. We all know about you in Brockshire. But I can tell you about that at dinner. Let's go down to Twelfth Night." She finished her martini, gave him a brief excited hug, then cried, "Meet you outside my door, darling," and darted through the bathroom.

Left to himself these few moments, Tuby felt strangely uneasy, almost a trifle guilty. Somehow the mood of that Brockshire night, when he had made love to her and she had talked about "group-institution feedback" so solemnly, refused to return. Had he changed or had she? He couldn't decide, told himself to enjoy this luscious bit of luck, but the uneasiness persisted. When she joined him outside 266, she was carrying a formidable-looking file. "The survey?" he said as they went along the corridor. "We don't have to dine with that, do we, my dear?"

She squeezed his arm. "In a way — yes, we do, darling. But I'll tell you why, later, when we've eaten something and I feel stronger."

Twelfth Night was idiotic, of course, Elizabethan-Illyrian, with sketchy attempts to suggest a formal garden, waiters and waitresses in costume, boar's head and venison prominent on the menu. But there were other dishes more to their taste, and their table, in an imitation arbour, encouraged confidences.

"I've brought down the survey, darling, because before we — well — before doing anything else, I want you to take it up to your room, just forgetting about me, and really go through it very carefully." She offered him a wide appealing look.

"You do, Hazel, do you?" She was clearly so much in earnest that he couldn't be too flippant, though studying a social survey of the West Midlands had been no part of any plan of his for the evening.

"Please! And do be serious about this. It's terribly important for me and for the Foundation — our first commissioned survey. We've put a lot of good work into it, we really have."

"I'm sure you have, my dear." He lifted his glass to her, smiling.

She drank too, but then, after a rather anxious look, she went on: "I've heard so much talk about you ever since you left, I understand you much better than I did when — well, when you gave me dinner that night. Oh yes, I loved it, don't think I didn't. But I know now you're very clever and very mischievous, quite cynical, not really believing in any- thing — "

"Stop there, Hazel. Saltana and I hold some beliefs very strongly. However, go on."

"What about these famous images of yours?"

"Well — " and he smiled.

She had to smile too. "Yes — *well*. But I don't care about that. I adore you anyhow. But I do care about the Foundation and the work I'm trying to do. And you must help me just this once, please, darling. Even if you think you don't really need our survey — and I believe you do — you must spend some time with it so that you can bring it into your dis- cussions with Smithy and Luckett when they come back. I'll make it up to you afterwards." And she reached across and pressed his hand. "That's fair, isn't it?"

"It is, I suppose. But then — so are you, Hazel my dear." He pro- duced a mock sigh. "However, if that's what you want, I'll take your sur- vey straight up to my room — and do my homework."

"You're sweet."

He told her about the Lapfords meeting Saltana at the grand Sturtleton lunch, and what they had said about him, Tuby, returning to Brockshire to join the English Department.

"Oh — couldn't you?" She was all eagerness.

"Sorry — impossible! We have other plans, though I can't talk about them because they're far from settled yet." Then, after a pause, at least in talk though not in dining: "Tell me, Hazel, my dark and dimpling peach, have we been missed at all in Brockshire?"

"My God — yes! Terribly by some of us — including a lot of the students, who didn't really know you but were somehow excited by the *idea* of your being there. *And* Primrose East, of course." She laughed. "The story of that party at the Lapfords' for the Duchess goes round and round, getting wilder all the time. It's a legend already, so far the only one we have. Of course many of the staff, the drearier types, were glad you'd vanished. But there are some of us who miss you all the time, even though we know you were laughing at us. You're a wicked man." And she regarded him fondly. "Darling, you *know* we must miss you. And even Professor Saltana, though none of us really liked him — and I thought he was wickedly unfair to Donald Cally on television — "

"Never! It isn't possible to be unfair to Cally. And the man was trying to take the bread out of our mouths — on public money too!"

"Don't be silly. You and Saltana and Mrs. Drake must be raking in a fortune. Tell me how you do it — and about Meldy Glebe — and everything."

Answering her questions — and making her laugh — took him through the rest of dinner, and indeed he had had three cups of coffee before he had brought her up to date and had described Big Dan. It was now time for him to retire to his room with the survey. She was going to remain below, chiefly because he must not be tempted to invade her room but must settle down and do some work. So up he went with the formidable file, took the bottle of whisky out of his bag, decided against changing at once into pyjamas and dressing gown, gave himself a peg of whisky, lit a pipe, exercised will-power, and then buried himself in the survey. And it was not as hard going as he'd expected it to be; it was sensible, full of facts, and easy to read, Hazel, far less solemn than she'd been during his Brockshire days, having left out most of her sociological jargon. He read it through three times, then actually made some notes for possible image use. It was now about quarter to eleven and the delectable image of Hazel herself began to drive out any Eat-At-Dan's nonsense images. He filled his glass with a longish whisky-and-water, slowly undressed, got into pyjamas, dressing gown, slippers, and then thought how foolish he'd been not to set a time with Hazel. But then she'd never stay down there after eleven — surely? So now — what? He wasted a few minutes more or less now-whatting. Then he made a slow move towards the bathroom door, but before he reached it he heard the tapping. It was not locked on his side, and now it was flung open, dramatically revealing a flushed face, loosened hair, a kimono. But they didn't belong to Hazel Honeyfield.

"But — how — why — what — ?" Tuby stammered, stepping back.

"I ought to have known," Lois Terry said as she moved in. "You're disappointed."

"No — no, Lois," said Tuby, now recovering himself. "That wasn't my disappointed face — my astounded face. After all — "

He stopped, realizing this was no time for a lot of talk beginning with *After all*. She was trembling a little, she was biting her lower lip, the great eyes were filling with tears. And then he saw what he'd been refusing to see for months. Great God in Heaven! Why, *he loved this woman*. And he immediately told her so, taking her in his arms.

"And there's going to be no dam' nonsense this time," Lois declared as she released herself. "If I'm not made love to, I'll scream. I'll lock this bathroom door. You turn off that terrible top light — the bedside lamp'll do us. I hope you haven't been having a lot of women lately — "

"I haven't been having any. I must have been waiting for you, Lois."

"Unless of course this reputation of yours for lechery and raging lust is a fraud. And wouldn't *that* serve me right!" But then, very soon: "Oh darling — darling — yes, yes, yes!"

An astonishing and wonderful half-hour later, nuzzling him lovingly, she murmured, "It was a wild and desperate chance — I was leaving myself wide open to the worst snub a woman could possibly have — but I had to take the chance, after what Elfreda told me — y'know, that you thought I was still tangled up — "

"No — no — no, my sweet puss, now I know you're not. And what luck for me! A small point, though — and with respect, as the politicians and civil servants say — do you women tell each other everything?"

"Only when love really comes into it — and it's an S.O.S. Otherwise, if we're at all sensitive we don't. Now you want to know about Hazel, don't you?"

"Good God! Do you know, I'd clean forgotten about her — "

"That's the way to start — and you keep going along those lines, Tuby my love. I've decided I like Tuby better than Owen, by the way. But about Hazel. There's a night club here — As You Like It, up on the roof — crikey, this place is insane — and I arranged for a man to take Hazel up there. Through my cousin, who works here. And I hate to think what I'll have to do for that girl — in return for these favours. Now I'd better dash in there and rescue my clothes. Be back in a flash."

She wasn't quite as quick as that, and Tuby had time to taste not only a sip of whisky but a wonderful sense of happiness, expanding into all manner of extravagant feelings but having as its base a deep, deep satisfaction. Here at last was the woman for him. And he told her so as she slipped back with an armful of clothes and her bag and locked the bathroom door after her. "So drink to us, Lois my love. I'm afraid there's only one glass."

"If there were two, I'd want to drink out of yours. That's the state I'm in, already besotted," she added with some satisfaction. "Though I mustn't have much. I have to drive back to Tarbury some time tonight. I've a lecture at ten, and — though I don't look it, not at this moment — I'm a very conscientious teacher. Now about poor Hazel. She's half in love with you, I'm afraid, but in five minutes I made quite plain the difference between being half in love and looking forward to a pleasant sexy romp, and being really in love, with or without romps. And talking of romps — and being quite shameless — I wonder — well, let's see, shall we?"

At eight-thirty next morning, about six hours after Lois had gone, Tuby was sitting up in bed with the tea tray he had ordered the day before. His telephone rang. It was Hazel. "Good morning! If you're not breakfasting in your room, I thought we might have it together downstairs — "

"Yes, of course, Hazel. In about half an hour — "

"Then we could discuss the survey — "

"What survey?"

"My God — do you mean to say — "

"No — no — no — sorry! Did quite a lot of work on it. Excellent survey— and going to be very useful. Yes, yes — very, very useful indeed, and I congratulate you, Hazel." And he didn't add that he was ready now to congratulate everybody — about everything.

## 8

This was the first June that Elfreda had spent in London or in England for many years — a fine one, moreover — and she ought to have been enjoying it. She was trying hard enough, not only on the week-ends and in the evenings but even during lunchtime, when she would eat sandwiches and some fruit and then cut across to Green Park and then watch the birds in St. James's Park. But it was no use; she couldn't help feeling restless and dissatisfied. She was glad about Tuby and Lois, of course; so far that was working out wonderfully. They obviously adored each other, and he would be off to Tarbury on Saturdays and she would come dashing up in the middle of the week, sometimes calling at the Institute if they happened to be working late, as they often did now. And although nothing was being said about marriage, at least not as far as Elfreda could discover, clearly this was no mere affair. But being on the edge of it did nothing to make her feel less restless and dissatisfied. If Saltana had been an ordinary sensible man he would have followed his friend's example, would have turned to *her;* but not being an ordinary man, and in some ways not sensible at all, being obstinate and proud and *contrary,* he made her feel he had more or less turned away from her, was always busy with something or other, day and night, so that she was actually seeing less of him than she had done for months and months.

She had said as much to Lois one evening, when Lois had called for

Tuby and had to wait in her room because Tuby still had somebody with him. "I don't know what's the matter with the man, Lois. Has Tuby ever said anything to you about him?"

"He's talked to me about Saltana, of course," said Lois. "Trying to make me understand him. Because they're such close friends and he thinks I'm unfair to him. He won't admit — no, not for a single moment — that Saltana lured him away from academic life. Swears it's absolutely untrue. Even hints they have some sort of plan, but won't say what it is — immediately talks — like an angel, curse him! — about something else. You know how they are — even Tuby? Confess anything one minute — and then the next minute so *guarded,* downright *secretive* — isn't it odd? Almost from another planet, my dear."

"And nothing about me — ever?"

"Well yes, darling — *once.* And that's better — you looked so miserable just then. Oh — I know — you've seen me looking much worse — I've really got the face for it. But Tuby was telling me how much keener Saltana was on business and making a lot of money and playing the big busy executive. And I said it wasn't a type I admired, and I was glad *he* wasn't like that. And he said Saltana wasn't really, that Saltana was doing it partly for the plan but also — and this is where you come in, Elfreda dear — partly for you — "

"For me? Are you sure, Lois?"

"Absolutely. Let's see if I can remember it exactly. Yes — he said, *But it's partly because of Elfreda.* There! Then of course he maddeningly changed the subject. Look, my dear, couldn't you — all or nothing — take a chance — you know, the way I did — ?"

"If it had been Owen Tuby — yes. But with Cosmo Saltana? Can you imagine it?"

"Well no, I can't," Lois replied hurriedly.

"Neither can I. Oh dear!"

And *oh dear* it remained. Even their most successful case — for Dan Luckett had finally accepted a *Customer Image,* which showed Phil Rawbin and a friend of Primrose's, not too glamorous or sexy, simply with the words *They Eat At Dan's Now* — she had shared with Tuby and not at all with Saltana. And it wasn't until Mr. Greenleaf called — and Saltana interrupted them — that she felt for a few minutes that Saltana had come closer again.

Frank Maclaskie had asked Mr. Greenleaf to see her, and one look at Mr. Greenleaf told her this was business and no nonsense about going on the town and taking in the hot spots. It was impossible to imagine Mr. Greenleaf buying drinks in a night club. He was just about the narrowest man she'd ever seen: shoulders, head, eyes, mouth, all very narrow. Listening to him was like watching a ventriloquist rehearsing without his dummy. He should never have gone on calling himself Greenleaf: he might have been a man made out of biscuits.

He began by telling her that she was a businesswoman and that he was a businessman, reckoned to be successful in his own field, the agency game, being now executive head of Fritch, Birg and Greenleaf, of New York, Chicago, and Los Angeles, with some of the biggest accounts in the country, including that of her friend and his — Dan Luckett. He rested for a while after saying this, though it had come out slowly and without emphasis.

"I see, Mr. Greenleaf," she said finally. "Well — ?"

"If you tell me something, I tell you something. How about that, Mrs. Judson Drake?"

"I don't know, Mr. Greenleaf. What do you want me to tell you?"

"There's a certain agency over here we're interested in. Now this is what you can tell me, Mrs. Judson Drake. Has that agency made you an offer to take over your Institute?"

"Several agencies have suggested we should work in close association with them. And we've turned them down. But *no* agency has made us a take-over bid, if that's what you mean."

"That right?" Mr. Greenleaf hadn't much room in which to show surprise, but he did what he could.

"Of course. I might have invented one for you — but I didn't."

"And I appreciate that, Mrs. Judson Drake. Way I like to do business myself. Cards on the table every time."

"And is that the something you're telling me in return for my something?" She smiled at him, even though there seemed so little to smile at.

"Indeed it is not, Mrs. Judson Drake. Cards on the table — and now you'll see my whole hand. Fritch, Birg and Greenleaf are moving into the British field. We're nearly ready to make a take-over bid for a certain British agency. But we don't want them to acquire your Institute first. We want it ourselves if the price is right."

"Good gracious — do you? And has this anything to do with that lawyer, Mr. Stockton, who came here some weeks ago?"

"It has. And I have read the report signed by your Director and Deputy Director, the scholastic gentlemen. This is why I've come straight to you, Mrs. Judson Drake. You're a businesswoman. They are *not* businessmen. And I am wondering what is their voting position in your company — what stock do they control?"

Elfreda laughed. "You've told me twice I'm a businesswoman, Mr. Greenleaf. If I'm not, then you're just trying to flatter me. If I am, then I'm not going to answer your questions."

Mr. Greenleaf didn't laugh, but he gave Elfreda the impression that if he'd been able to, he would have. "Too-*shay!*" he said.

"But, Mr. Greenleaf, why should we want to sell this Institute to you or anybody else? We're making money. We're enjoying ourselves — "

It was then that Saltana came marching in. "Elfreda — oh — sorry!"

"No, don't go." She introduced them and then explained briefly why Mr. Greenleaf had come to see her. "And I was just asking Mr. Greenleaf why we should want to let his company take over the Institute when we're making money — and enjoying ourselves — "

"If we *are* enjoying ourselves," said Saltana rather sharply.

"You have a point there surely, Professor," said Mr. Greenleaf, quite quickly for him. "Why should two scholastic gentlemen like yourself and your friend want to remain in the business world when you might be pursuing your ideals elsewhere?"

"Quite so," said Saltana, to Elfreda's surprise.

"But you know very well you're indispensable to the Institute, Cosmo," she cried. "You and Tuby said so to Mr. Stockton in that memo I typed out."

"Yes, but he didn't believe us," said Saltana, smiling. "And you don't believe it, do you, Mr. Greenleaf? Now don't spare my feelings. Tell the truth now. You and Stockton and Maclaskie — and perhaps half a dozen more of you — all believe that Tuby and I are a liability, not an asset, to this Institute, don't you?"

"Well, we're businessmen — and this Institute is in business — "

"But this is silly," Elfreda protested. "*We* know — even if *they* don't — that there wouldn't be an Institute — "

"Hold it, Elfreda," Saltana cut in sharply. He looked at Mr. Greenleaf, who appeared to be ready to leave them now. "Offer us enough and you can take over the Institute and buy Tuby and me out at the same time. Think it over and name your price to Mrs. Drake, who looks after our finances."

"But Cosmo — "

"No, Elfreda, please! I think that's as far as we can go this morning, isn't it, Mr. Greenleaf? Let me see you out." And Elfreda was left there, boiling.

"Cosmo Saltana," she began at once as soon as he reappeared, grinning, "are you going barmy or were you just being funny or what? And don't stand there, looking like that. You can't want those people to take over the Institute — *our* Institute — "

"Why not? If they'll pay us enough, of course. And it'll take time, naturally."

"But it's all so ridiculous. They won't know what to do with it — "

"That's their lookout. We've warned them that Tuby and I are indispensable, and of course they don't believe us. I've just been reading the life of that extraordinary Victorian, Richard Burton," he continued in an easier tone, "and a short entry in one of his diaries pleased me so much that I copied it into my pocket book. Here it is. *It is a very curious, and not altogether unpleasant sensation, that of not being believed when you are speaking the truth. I have had great difficulty in training my wife to enjoy it.* There you are, Elfreda."

She was furious with him and his Richard Burton. "My God — do you mean to tell me that you and Owen Tuby are ready to be bought out and just slip away, leaving me with a lot of Greenleafs and Stocktons and Maclaskies — ?"

"Are you out of your mind, woman?" And this was in his really terrible voice, and he had come closer to glare at her.

"No, it's you, Cosmo — not me — "

"Rubbish!" He leant across her desk and seized her hands. "Don't you understand? When we go, then of course you go too. We don't have to tell them that yet. You know very well what's in their idiotic minds. It was you who first told me. Get rid of these long-haired egghead professors! They'd want you to stay on, but of course when Tuby and I go, then you go — "

She pulled her hands away. "How do you know I'd want to go?"

"God's jumping Moses, girl! You've just said you don't want to be left with a lot of Greenleafs — "

"Stop swearing and shouting at me, Cosmo." Her voice was beginning to crack and sound silly, and that was his fault too. "I won't be taken for granted like that. I don't have to trot after you and Tuby like a little puppy-dog. And I don't even know what you want to do if you did leave the Institute. You don't tell me anything." And, to her disgust, she began to cry.

He was round the desk, by her side, bending over her, before she knew what was happening. "Elfreda my dear — " and now of course this was quite a different voice, a deep appealing whisper — "we can't tell you because we don't know ourselves yet. Tuby and I haven't planned anything. We don't even begin to discuss our future. What would our resources be? We haven't a notion yet. Even if these people really want to take us over — and are ready to pay us what we ask — it'll all take time. The only thing that's certain is that if we do go, then we want you with us, my dear. Whatever the plan might be, we couldn't do without you. Ask Tuby."

And she did, that very day, after they'd discussed a very strange enquiry, from an old and rich Canadian, who looked part-Indian, on behalf of his granddaughter, a lumping nineteen-year-old who believed they could do something with her image. "Tell me this, Owen. If you and Saltana left the Institute — let's say because some Americans gave you a nice golden handshake — would you want me to go with you?"

Tuby stared at her, astonished. "I call that an idiotic question, Elfreda. Unless some plan we had seemed to you quite insane, of course we'd want you with us. We came into this together, you and I and Saltana, and we go out of it together. That's understood — surely? My dear Mrs. Judson Drake, what's been churning away behind those clear eyes, that smooth forehead? I think you must be tormenting yourself with thoughts of Primrose and her useless young man — um?"

Elfreda certainly didn't torment herself with thoughts of Primrose and her useless young man; but this affair, at first astonishing, then irritating, then depressing, offered no help when Elfreda was feeling restless and dissatisfied. There were times indeed when she could have slapped Primrose. The young man's name was Eric Chetsweth, and he was tallish and thinnish and droopy, had rather long fair hair, a silly moustache, pale and puzzled eyes, and a voice that was peculiarly maddening because it wavered between condescension and whining. After five minutes of him, Eden and Elfreda agreed afterwards that this was a useless young man. Even little Beryl for once wasn't impressed. Saltana and Tuby dismissed him with a shrug. Yet it was for this miserable Eric Chetsweth that Primrose, who could regard unmoved the beautiful sad face of clever Phil Rawbin, who was pursued by all sorts of attractive men, who calmly accepted their attentions and laughed at them afterwards, that Primrose East herself, no less, fell like a lunatic ton of bricks.

"He's rather marvellous, don't you think?" Primrose had said.

"No, I don't think," said Eden Mere severely. "Just a typical mass media dogsbody — there are hundreds of them. And they've all written half a novel or one act of a play, or they've lost their aunt's legacy in a one-third share of a boutique or a bar in Ibiza. No, Primrose dear, I'd say — " and this was the first pronouncement of the verdict — "a useless young man."

Tuby said to Elfreda and Eden, not long afterwards: "He's *Eric: or Less and Less.*"

But for no sensible reason anybody could discover — it really was ridiculous — Primrose soon became completely infatuated with this useless young man. It was as if she'd gone out of her mind. It was Eric this and Eric that; she was forever phoning him or taking calls from him; they would lunch together and she would be waiting in the evening for him to pick her up at the Institute; and then after two or three weeks it became clear that not only had he lost his television job but that he had also moved into her flat.

"You're not surprised, are you, Elfreda?" said Eden. "I'm not. Inevitable with that kind of young man. The next thing we'll learn — you'll see — is that he has a wife and two children living with her parents at Worthing or somewhere. Mark my words."

"And the trouble is, Eden, because she knows we don't like him, poor Primrose is changing — really becoming rather difficult."

And indeed the very next day she told Elfreda it was time her salary went up, she was being shockingly underpaid. Elfreda took this demand to Saltana. "We're paying her twenty-five pounds a week, Cosmo, and of course we could afford to pay her more. But I know very well it's only because she's having to keep this useless young man of hers. If we agree to give her thirty or thirty-five, it's *him* we're really paying, not poor Primrose."

Saltana frowned. "Perhaps I ought to talk to this fellow — "

"Oh — no! Please don't do that, Cosmo. You'd upset him, then he'd upset Primrose, then she might walk straight out. And it would soon be in the newspapers that she'd left the Institute — "

"No, we don't want that," Saltana said hastily. "This isn't the time for bad publicity. We've two groups already nibbling — your Americans and, so Jimmy Kilburn tells me, some people here. Raise the girl's salary then, Elfreda."

"Another thing. She told Eden we ought to take Eric on here. We needed somebody, she said, and of course her dear Eric would be perfect. But I wouldn't have him around if he paid us to work here. He'd be worse than useless."

"Certainly. Though, when one comes to think of it, he can't be useless everywhere or she wouldn't dote on him as she does." He gave her a sly look.

Elfreda really was beginning to feel bewildered and rather depressed. First, of course, this Primrose thing. And though she and Eden Mere liked each other, even now she never knew quite where she was with Eden, who could be very shrewd one minute and utterly daft the next. Then the Institute itself, which had appeared to be securely anchored only a few weeks ago, now seemed to wobble and be about to drift, what with these Stocktons and Greenleafs and Kilburns and nibbles and take-overs. Finally — and this was really the worst of all, far worse than Primrose's useless young man — she couldn't escape the feeling, though she tried hard enough, that both Saltana and Tuby were no longer being completely open and frank with her. It was all so vague that she couldn't challenge them. It was as if she smelled something cooking but could never catch them at it. There was never a sign, never a piece of evidence she could brandish in their faces, yet the feeling persisted that somehow she was being *left out*.

However, she did tackle Tuby, one warm and airless evening just after they'd finished work. She and Eden had found a furnished flat for him not ten minutes' walk from Half Moon House. 3A Darvil Court was expensive and they'd had to persuade Tuby he could afford it now. It was so designed, decorated, and furnished, as Tuby told them, that it was rather like a flat in a bad dream, but it was convenient, it was surprisingly roomy, and — this was Eden's point — it was a good address. Lois said it was horrible but didn't really care, so long as Tuby was waiting for her there: together they made grisly Jacobean-tragedy jokes about it, rolling round the place, she told Elfreda, half-dressed and laughing. And this evening Tuby had asked Elfreda to have a drink with him and to suggest how 3A Darvil Court might be improved, swiftly, tastefully, and at no great expense. And over a gin-and-tonic she did offer a few suggestions.

"By the way," she added, "you must have noticed it's all rather dusty."

"Is it? I hadn't noticed. The truth is, I'm rather dusty myself. But I think Lois pulls a face at it sometimes."

"It's supposed to be a service flat. Who cleans it?"

"Mostly, I think, a young and tender Irish maiden who goes dreamily around. She's probably writing one of those sexy novels that become 'starkly revealing,' and 'shocking exposures' for the paperback trade. I met her current boy friend, the other day. He's Primrose's useless young man's working-class cousin — if you know what I mean."

She felt that this was the moment to tackle him. They were sitting more or less at ease, fairly close and companionable. "Tuby dear, you know something? I'm beginning to feel *left out.* I mean, at the Institute. What's happening?"

"Nothing much — and that's why." Tuby smiled. "So we all feel left out. But I have Lois, Primrose has *Eric-or-Less-and-Less,* and Eden has her family and O. V. Mere — and just imagine that!"

"And Saltana?"

"No woman, if that's what you're thinking."

"He wouldn't tell you if he had, would he?"

"No, but I'd know. As I've told you before, I'm an intuitive type, besides being an old Saltana hand. At the moment, I'd say, he's wandering among schemes and dreams, and being a proud man he doesn't want to talk about them because he'd look silly if they all flopped. And that's all I can tell you, my dear."

"You mean, it's all you're going to tell me, you artful man. Well, I came here feeling dissatisfied. And I'm still feeling dissatisfied. I have my intuitions too, Dr. Tuby, and they're telling me I'm being left out of something I oughtn't to be left out of. So what do you say to that?"

"At this moment, sitting here, I'm not conscious of concealing anything from you, Elfreda my dear. Of course almost anything *could* happen. I take that for granted nowadays."

Saltana's room at the Institute might just as well have had a bomb hidden in it, ticking away, waiting for them. As they were now into July, when Saltana summoned them to his room they'd been talking about holidays. Eden had said she was taking the children to Brittany — and damn the expense — though she wasn't sure that O. V. would be able to join them. Primrose announced proudly — she took a pride apparently in all Eric's demands and whims — that Eric was mad keen for them to go to Sardinia, where he knew a man. (Eric knew men everywhere but they never helped to keep him.) And Elfreda and Eden were just exchanging glances charged with meaning, and Primrose, who never missed these glances, was about to be furious with them, when Saltana's summons came. Big executive stuff this morning, eh? They filed into his room demurely, but all scepticism and thinly disguised female mockery; and found Tuby, for once without a smile, already there.

It began quietly enough. "This is something I felt I ought to explain to all of you," said Saltana. "It's about this man, Jacques Nazaire, the public relations wizard. As some of you know — you met him before I did — he lives and works just round the corner. This means you may easily run into him or be invited to one of his parties — or meet him at other people's parties. Nazaire has approached me several times, directly or indirectly, and I've turned him down. This Institute doesn't have to supply images to Nazaire and his clients. It's not the kind of work we want to do. Nazaire, my friends, is *out*. I don't enjoy exercising my authority as Director, but in this particular instance I feel I must. That's why you're here this morning. From now on, you are not to entertain — or even appear to consider — any suggestion coming from Nazaire or any of his assistants. You can reply at once that the Institute is not interested. Now — is that understood?"

The women murmured vaguely. But Tuby, looking annoyed, spoke out. "It's understood, Director, but speaking for myself, not for these ladies, I must tell you that it's also sharply resented."

Saltana stared at him. "I don't see why it should be, Deputy Director."

"Because it seems to me intolerably high-handed, altogether too authoritarian. You are Director of this Institute, not Louis the Fourteenth. I must remind you that this *Institute of Social Imagistics* was as much my idea as yours, that we thought of it and then planned it together — "

"Oh — this is silly!" cried Elfreda, who was always irritated by this stiff unreal way of talking that men seemed to enjoy. "We're all friends — "

"We *were*. But I've just been *ordered* to behave in a certain way. I don't care about Jacques Nazaire, but I strongly resent being told I must immediately jump on any suggestion he happens to make, tell him in effect to shut up."

"So do I, for that matter," said Primrose sulkily.

"This is between Dr. Tuby and myself, Miss East," Saltana told her with icy severity.

"In that case," said Eden, rising — and it was always something to see her rise — "we girls can go."

"Certainly not," said Saltana sharply. "Sit down, Mrs. Mere. I don't want to have to explain to you afterwards what Dr. Tuby and I had to say to each other. Dr. Tuby has been feeling restive for some time — "

"You mean *you* have, Saltana." And Tuby's manner, as he cut in like that, was much less formal, far more real, and therefore important, Elfreda felt disturbingly.

"And you've been restive, anxious to give orders," Tuby continued, "simply because I happen to have had the more interesting and valuable cases, the more rewarding clients, and you've been feeling increasingly jealous and envious — "

"Oh — no — please, Tuby!" Elfreda heard herself pleading.

"I'm sorry, Elfreda, but it's the real reason why we've had this hoity-toity performance this morning. It isn't Jacques Nazaire — who cares about him? Saltana wanted to give his authority an airing. Do this, don't do that! Well, I refuse to obey his commands. The limit has been reached, Herr Direktor. I shall please myself how and what I reply to Jacques Nazaire or to anybody else."

"Not while I'm Director of this Institute, you won't, Tuby."

"Stop it — stop it — you two!" Elfreda was compelled once more to make some protest, if only to turn these two back into themselves again. It was like listening to two strangers. And neither of them gave her even a look, just glared at each other.

"If you think you're calling my bluff, Saltana, you're wrong." Tuby spoke very quietly now, making it seem, Elfreda felt, all the more sinister. "Unless you're prepared to offer an apology — "

"Apology be damned!"

"Then I take no more dictatorial nonsense from you — "

"But you can't *leave* us!" Eden shrieked.

"If he doesn't mean that, Mrs. Mere," said Saltana coldly, "then what does he mean?"

"Allow me the floor for a minute." And Tuby got up and looked at Elfreda and the other two, not at Saltana. "The *Institute of Social Imagistics* is as much my creation as it is Saltana's. Indeed, if anything, rather more. Naturally I'm not going to say goodbye to the idea just because Saltana thinks he ought to dominate everybody. And unless he's half-insane with rage, even *he* can't claim a monopoly of *Social Imagistics* — "

"I'll grant you that," Saltana growled. "But what are you suggesting? There can't be two Institutes."

Still standing there, Tuby thought for a moment or two. "This will do. The *Society of Social Imagistics*. Director: Owen Tuby. Address, for the time being — 3A Darvil Court. I wasn't bluffing, you see, Saltana?"

"No, just getting ready to make a gigantic ass of yourself, Tuby. All right. Go ahead."

Elfreda and the other two, who had been looking at one another with widening and fearful eyes, could keep quiet no longer. They exploded: "But you can't possibly do this — " . . . "You're both absolutely mad — " . . . "What will everybody think? And the Press — ?"

Tuby must have caught the last word. "I shall tell the Press as much as it ought to know. It's essential that I should. Just a dignified but informative statement. I've nothing more to say here, so I'll set to work now. And no interruptions, ladies please, for the next hour." And he left them.

They rushed together, loudly protesting, towards Saltana's desk. But he wasn't listening to them. He got up, looked at his watch — doing this very deliberately and somehow quietening them — and said, "I have an appointment. I must go." And he left them too.

Eden immediately took a line of her own. "I'm not surprised, my dears, not surprised at all. It's happened with all the men I've known well — my father, two uncles, and Oswald, of course. Quite suddenly, without warning, they go out of their minds. Elfreda dear, it must be tea this morning, not coffee, and I'll make it — and we'll have it — the big pot — in your room. Decide nothing, say nothing, of any importance until the pot and I arrive."

As they went along the corridor, Primrose said, "If Tuby really is telling the Press, then I must phone Eric. He knows lots of newspapermen, and they'll believe Eric." And she hurried ahead.

"That's all we need now — Eric," Elfreda muttered bitterly, and then as she turned into her own room she felt relieved to have it to herself for a few minutes. Oh — those two idiots! My God — Men! Eden was right — suddenly they could go straight out of their minds. They could turn into different people — not her Saltana, but a sneering monster — not lovable little Owen Tuby, not like him at all, but a lump of resentment, pride, obstinacy, and lunacy. And now she ought to think because somebody ought to start thinking, and she couldn't think. As she sat down at her desk, a great tide of feeling rose and washed over her. And she wept.

Eden marched in with the tray. "I know, I know, Elfreda dear. Even I feel shattered — and of course you were much closer to the wretches. Let's curse all of them over our teacups. They pretend that all they want is a quiet life. But as soon as they're within sight of one — what do they do? Start a quarrel and go banging about. Here's your tea. I think both of us ought to take sugar this morning."

Elfreda didn't feel like talking; she enjoyed her tea and the large sympathetic presence of Eden, tactfully silent now though at other times she could be monumentally tactless. But after she'd finished her second cup, Elfreda looked at her watch. "As soon as Tuby's had the hour he asked for, I'm going along to talk to him."

"Arrangements now, no recrimination, I suggest," said Eden loftily. "For example, we can't all stay here with Saltana. Poor Tuby must have somebody."

"I've been thinking about that. What do you want to do, Eden?"

"I believe I ought to go with Tuby. We complement each other very neatly. He's a charmer, I'm a bully. I can be severe whenever he's inclined to be too easy. Saltana will have to make do with Primrose, who's not very helpful at present, I must admit, but will be splendid again once she's ditched that useless young man. Which she's bound to do soon, unless of course she finds herself pregnant. And I'm afraid that's quite likely. Useless young men impregnate their girls almost without fail. Perhaps this explains why there seem to be more and more useless people in the world." And Eden awarded Elfreda, as if it were a medal, her Duke of Wellington smile.

Elfreda was trying to think again. "What do you feel I ought to do?" she asked finally.

"Oh — no question about that at all, my dear. I didn't consider it worth discussion. It's your duty to remain with the Institute *and* join Tuby's Society, looking after all our finances. If there's one person who's really needed, it's you, Elfreda. Without you we'd be all floundering in chaos."

And Tuby made the very same point when, a little later, she ventured into his room. He was calm, gentle, very sweet, quite unlike the obstinate and angry little man who had denounced and defied Saltana.

"I'm very sorry indeed this has happened, my dear, though you must have seen signs of its blowing up for some time." He gave her a slow sad smile. "I don't want you to take my side — or of course Saltana's either. He needs your help. And I need it too, desperately, because I'm hopeless with accounts, money, all that part of it. And Eden wouldn't be much better. No, my dear, you'll have to divide yourself between the *Institute of Social Imagistics* and the *Society of Social Imagistics*. Put like that it sounds a hell of a job, but of course it won't be. Just popping along to Darvil Court every other day or so. Don't imagine that Saltana will object. He's not that kind of man — nothing mean, nothing small and spiteful about him." He waited a moment. "You're hesitating. You're uncertain, aren't you? Now don't be — for God's sake, Elfreda!"

She had gone to the window, though she hadn't seen anything through it, and now she came back. "It's not what you think. Something quite different. The trouble is," she went on slowly, frowning at him, "I still can't really believe it's happened — that you and Cosmo have quarrelled and split up and that you've finished here. There's something — I don't know — *unreal* about it, Owen."

He took the pipe out of his mouth and looked into the bowl as if something in there might help him. "You were there, my dear. You heard us. And if you feel it's all too sudden, you ought to remember some previous occasions when we were already at odds. Don't imagine I dislike Saltana as a man. We might be friends again one day. But I can't work with him any longer. And for the time being we're better working — or playing — apart."

So much for Tuby. Now for Saltana. But he didn't come back before lunch and was still missing during the afternoon. However, he phoned in about five o'clock to ask if there were any messages and she was able to speak to him. He had a dinner engagement he couldn't get out of, he told her, but he hoped to be able to join her, up in her sitting room, round about ten. So that was all right, ten not being very late; but then it was, with a lonely dismal evening merely crawling towards it; but then again it wasn't, not for the last twenty minutes, because she went into a flurry of changing, with this one too stiff and formal, that one — yes, well perhaps too intimate; and she was nearly out of breath when he arrived.

He wasn't tight — certainly not — but wherever he'd been he'd done his share of drinking. And perhaps plenty of talking too, because as soon as he'd settled into his armchair and had stretched out his long legs, he gave her the impression that he would rather listen than talk. So when his cheroot was drawing easily she told him what she'd arranged with Eden Mere and then with Tuby. "All to my utter astonishment," she concluded.

"Really? Now *you* astonish *me,* Elfreda. Come, come — Owen's always been an unusually thoughtful and considerate fellow — "

"How can you talk like that?" she demanded furiously.

He stared. "I'm afraid you don't understand him."

"No — and I told him I didn't understand him," she raged. "And now I'm telling you I don't understand you, Cosmo Saltana."

"That's quite possible — "

"Shut up! You two men are driving me up the wall. You've stopped making any sense. First you suddenly start insulting each other and say you can't work together any longer and bust everything up. Next you're poor-chapping each other and you're all thoughtful and considerate — so, if it's like that, why in hell's name don't you get on the phone to Tuby — *now, this minute* — and tell him it's all a mistake and you're sorry and he must forget about this morning — ?"

"Ah — no, Elfreda," he said quite coolly, "I couldn't possibly do that. He goes his way, I go mine. Finish!"

If he'd been angry too, it wouldn't have been so bad. But he was so cool and calm about it, like a kind of quiet lunatic, that he made her feel there was no sense in anything any more, and she couldn't talk — only cry. And then when she knew he was getting out of his chair, she told him to go away but went away herself, hurrying into the bedroom and in the dusk there flinging herself on to the bed.

Again she said, "Go away," when she knew he had followed her in, but — thank God! — he ignored her wretched mumblings and, wonderfully strong, lifted her up into his arms and told her how badly he'd behaved and how sorry he was and how much he loved her; and first there were comforting little kisses, and then longer kisses with all manner of variations new to her and terribly exciting; and then hands were here and hands were there, melting her very bones, and somehow he was fierce and demanding and yet gentle too (poor Judson hadn't had a clue), and they were making love.

Another difference — and she soon came to know this very well — was that while poor Judson after grunting over her for five minutes had gone straight to sleep, Cosmo, in spite of spinning everything out so miraculously, was suddenly quite wakeful and eager for drink, a smoke, talk. He dressed quickly and left her, but of course just to go into the sitting room. Droopy and dreamy, she slowly put on some night things, briefly attended to her face, sank at his feet, and drooped herself dreamily round his legs. He handed her his glass and she took a sip just because he wanted her to drink with him.

"Cosmo, I could never understand what the sex fuss was all about," she murmured. "I said so — more than once. Now I think they didn't make enough fuss." She heard her voice trailing away.

"Sleepy, my love?"

"Not exactly sleepy, darling. More — sloppy. But if you want to talk, I'll listen. I'll take in every single word. I love you. And I know you're longing to talk — aren't you?" Voice trailing again.

He was brisk, almost businesslike. She didn't mind, though it never ceased to surprise her. "I'm going to clear things up, my love. I'll ask the questions you'd be wanting to ask in a few hours' time. And give you the answers. You only have to nod if you agree with the questions and then understand my answers." He waited a moment. "Why, if I was in love with you, have I wasted all these months?"

"I'm nodding to that one, darling. Going with other women too. I knew. Why, then?"

"Because I didn't want an affair with you, Elfreda. This was serious. There was a real relationship here, and I felt responsible. I wanted to marry you, of course."

Nodding wouldn't do now. She made a little move so that she could look up and see him properly. "Then why didn't you ask me? Ask me now. Will I? Yes, I will. Next week. Bend down — kiss me." And he did. "I loved you before — months and months — ever since you came back from Ireland — but not like this. I think this is wonderful — and terrible. Let's get married next week, my darling."

One hand moved gently between her neck and shoulder, caressing them, before he replied. "You're not going to like this," he began slowly.

"My God, Cosmo, don't tell me you have a wife — "

He laughed. "No, my dear, that isn't — and hasn't been — the obstacle. It was — and still is — simply this — that you've too much money and I've too little — "

"Oh — pooh to that old stuff! That's not important. I don't care. Why should you?"

"You know, Elfreda my love, thousands of women must have said that to their men — and they were wrong. It represents one of the great illusions of women in love. They talk like that because they imagine that marriage simply means having their lovers with them all the time. And it doesn't. A dependent lover and a dependent husband aren't the same. When I marry you I don't have to have as much money as you have, my dear, but I do have to have enough to make me financially independent, so that I don't have to call for your support before I go ahead with my own plans, my own work."

"Oh — but Cosmo, I hate this. You sound as if you're shutting me out — "

"Then I'm not explaining myself properly. Perhaps I need another drink — "

"I'll get it. Don't move, darling." But this time, after returning his glass, she decided to curl up in the opposite chair so that she could watch his face as he talked. "Now, go on," she said. "You were going to tell me — or at least I hope so — that you didn't mean to shut me out."

"Certainly I was. I'd want you in with me. I wouldn't feel happy if you weren't — so as soon as we talk about marriage, I must think about money. That's been the trouble all along. That's one reason — there is another but we can leave that — why I've worried, connived, bullied, to push on with the Institute and all this image nonsense. It explains the difference between Owen Tuby and me. He's never felt the same urgency I've had spurring and whipping me. I've had to hold myself back from you because I still hadn't the money. Elfreda, it's your job from now on to discover who'll pay the biggest price for the Institute, including rich handshakes for Tuby and me — "

"But you idiots have parted — and now there'll be a Society as well as an Institute — "

"It doesn't matter — and there'll be all the more publicity. You sell 'em both, of course. They buy *Social Imagistics* lock, stock, and barrel. Now I may have to be away a good deal — never mind why at the moment, but there won't be any women involved in it — and I want you to tell Jimmy Kilburn everything that's happening — and he's a friend and very knowledgeable and hellishly shrewd. Yes?"

"Professor Saltana," she began, lightly covering her earnestness with a mock solemnity, "you are telling me that our marriage depends on my selling *Social Imagistics* for every cent it's worth — and indeed a dam' sight more. Well, I'm a woman screaming to be married. I'm also a businesswoman. So leave these Greenleafs, Stocktons, Maclaskies, or any other possible buyers to me. I spent over fifteen years with some very tough operators. So, Professor, you can now forget it all until the contracts are ready to be signed. If love and marriage are involved, it's the female who can be really hard. Boy! I'll drain the last cent out of somebody." She was already up, to make that speech impressive, and as he was up too, it was easy to wind her arms round his neck and press her cheek against his. "I love you, Cosmo. Now tell me."

And he did, then left her a few minutes afterwards. As she prepared for bed she felt she would never go to sleep, having so much to think about, to wonder at, so much she ought to be planning. But in fact she went to sleep almost at once.

## 9

A week before he had that scene with Tuby and then, later, made love to Elfreda, Saltana had at least set a foot in what he afterwards called the Labyrinth. First, he had another drink with Sir James Tenks, President of the Board of Trade, in that same corner of that same club. And Sir James was even more confidential, top-secret, conspiratorial, than before, sitting closer than ever and, with an obvious purpling effort, keeping low a voice never designed to be lowered.

"Two ends to this, Saltana. P.M.'s end — will he play your image game? Must leave that. Your end — where's your fee coming from? Found the fellow, I think. Good man for a life peerage. Now, Saltana, your end's open. Money could be there. But not just round the corner. Long way off yet. One move at a time."

"You're not making it sound very enticing," Saltana told him. "I'm inclined to say tedious and time-wasting."

"Not a quick and easy-money job, I agree. But forget all the big fees you might otherwise be earning. Sooner or later we'll take most of the money away from you."

"You won't if the money and I aren't here," Saltana muttered. "But I've no plans yet, so don't call the inspectors and the dogs. And I still say it sounds tedious."

"Won't be if you look at it differently. Like a good politician. It's making these moves that's fascinating. That's why we need so little outside entertainment. Chess on a grand scale. Pawns that can talk — knights and rooks that give interviews and collect press cuttings. *Enjoy* the dam' thing, man!"

"I may not have sufficient patience, Tenks. But I see what you mean — and I'll try. How many moves between me and the Prime Minister?"

"Haven't worked it out. Probably about ten — no, perhaps eight, if they're good moves. Itterby's very conscious of his place and position and also very touchy and suspicious. If it comes to that, we're *all* touchy and suspicious. As you'll soon discover, when you're making the moves. And you'll have to make 'em. Can't march into Number Ten and say, 'I've come to do your image.' Even so — if you'll play it my way — that's just where you're going next — Number Ten. Downing Street, I mean, of course. Chap called Jadson — P.M.'s press man. Dogsbody on public relations. Had a quiet word with him. All strictly confidential. You could see him in the morning — about twelve. Has a room in Number Ten — Jadson. Manage it?"

"Certainly. At least I'll be able to say I've been there."

"That's better, Saltana. You're a clever fellow — cynical as the devil too, I'd say — so enjoy it — enjoy it."

But in fact Saltana felt nothing when he walked into Number Ten next morning. However, there may have been something self-protective about this lack of reverence: after all, if your ultimate object is to change a prime minister's image, you gain nothing by thinking about William Pitt, Gladstone, Disraeli. He told himself this while waiting in a kind of entrance hall, where various types — some in uniform, some in mufti — regarded him amiably, as if they had known at once he couldn't be carrying a bomb. Then he was conducted along a winding corridor to Jadson's room, which looked as if it had been made out of a fairly large linen cupboard.

Jadson didn't look like O. V. Mere — he had a very long nose and thick glasses — but somehow he suggested a slightly younger, cleaned-up specimen of the Mere series. And he wasted no time on chit-chat. "How are you on the P.M.?"

"I know nothing about him. As I've already told Tenks."

"Not done your homework yet, Professor?"

Some catchphrases always irritated Saltana, and this was one of them. "I gathered from Tenks that various *moves* will have to be made and that you'd be able to tell me about them. I hope this is true."

"It is indeed," said Jadson with some complacency. "I ought to warn you that you're not going to find the P.M. easy. He doesn't know about you, of course — that'll come later — but he's quite satisfied with his image — still thinks it's dead right — in spite of a good deal of criticism both from inside the party and in the Press."

"What *is* his image?"

Jadson made a noise like some animal, perhaps a seal, barking. "You really will have to do your homework, won't you, Professor?"

Saltana had to smother an impulse to tell him to shut up about his homework, but actually replied quite mildly. "I've found there's a certain advantage in taking a fresh approach to an image problem, coming to it almost innocently from the outside. However, there's no harm in your telling me how he regards this image that he likes and the rest of you are feeling dubious about."

"Can do, briefly. Well, originally, a long time ago, Ernest Itterby was a young solicitor in a small country town. And his idea is to be still our country solicitor. 'We ought to get Mr. Itterby's opinion' — that's the idea. A super-solicitor — that's the P.M."

"I see," said Saltana, slowly and dubiously. "Well, I've been out of England for many years, but when I used to live here I never remember liking solicitors — or, for that matter, anybody else liking them. But perhaps people feel more insecure these days."

"Most people don't know what the hell they feel." Jadson sounded bitter. "A lot of 'em don't feel anything, I often think. But we must push on with this. First then, you ought to go along to party headquarters and see the General Secretary, Bob Brodick. That's chiefly for homework. They have a viewing room there and they can run through the P.M.'s television recordings for you — party political broadcasts, conference speeches, and so forth. But you'll have to clear that with Bob Brodick or you won't see a sausage. Great sense of his own importance, Bob has, and likes to keep everything in his own hands. I'll give him a ring and tell him about you."

"I'd appreciate that," said Saltana. "Especially as you obviously don't like him."

"This is all between ourselves, isn't it, Saltana?"

Saltana nodded. "If it became any more confidential, I'd be afraid to open my mouth at all."

"Well, I think he's a disaster — a stupid ignorant bastard. But I'd advise you to play up to him a bit."

"I'm not very good at playing up to stupid ignorant bastards. But I'll do what I can. Next moves?"

"My choices here — and I hope Tenks agrees because he'll have to fix it — are Frank Angle and Ken Stapleford." He brought out these names so triumphantly that Saltana was sorry to disappoint him, so long as nothing more was said about homework.

"And who are they?"

Jadson didn't sigh, but he did breathe heavily through his nose for a moment or two. "Frank Angle," he began with maddening patience, "is the Chief Whip. He's not specially close to the P.M. — in fact, I doubt if they like each other, but he carries a lot of weight in the party. Frank would be a very good man to have on your side."

"And not, I hope, another stupid ignorant bastard?"

"Not at all. Frank's a sensible steady fellow. Now Ken Stapleford's quite different. He's very close to the P.M. They're old friends, and in fact he's married to a cousin of Itterby's. You know about Ken Stapleford, surely? He's Minister of Possible Developments — "

"Good God! There is such a ministry, then?"

"There is. And some people — in fact, quite a lot of people — think Itterby created it to give Ken Stapleford a job, just to keep him around."

"And how would you describe him?"

"He's all right — means well — but I never know what the devil he's talking about. He's always very emphatic and rather long-winded but nobody knows what he's saying. Very useful at question time in the House, though. And if you can persuade him you ought to give the P.M. this image treatment, you're more than halfway there."

"And how do I arrive all the way there, Jadson?"

Holding up a forefinger and leaning forward, Jadson replied in a lowered voice: "Ethel — Itterby's wife. Once you've enlisted the others and you can talk her round — you're home."

Saltana took out his pocket book and a pen. "You're beginning to make me feel as if I were applying for the post of Chief Eunuch at the Court of Byzantium. Now let's see if I have this right. Bob Brodick — General Secretary at party headquarters. Frank Angle — Chief Whip. Ken Stapleford — Ministry of Possible Developments — God save us! Then, somewhere in the remote distance, Ethel — Mrs. Prime Minister — "

"And you'll have to tackle her when they're on holiday — during the recess. And either she'll take to you at once or hate the sight of you. She hates the sight of me, so I can't help you there. All I can do is to talk to Brodick about you. Tenks can arrange for you to meet Angle and Stapleford. Oh — and give me your phone number — at this Institute of yours."

Saltana did this, and then got up to go. "You've been very helpful, Jadson — more than you need have been — and I'm much obliged to you. If some of my remarks haven't suggested that, it's because I don't know where I am yet in your world."

Jadson, also standing now, nodded, grinned, then removed his spectacles and turned himself into somebody else. "I'm a political journalist," he said softly. "I've not had a year yet of this Number Ten caper and even if Itterby gets back in October I'm not having much more of it."

"I oughtn't to ask this," Saltana began, keeping his voice down too, "but — really in the strictest confidence — what do *you* feel about Itterby?"

Jadson was still polishing his spectacles and didn't look up. "I think he might have been a very decent fellow about twenty years ago. He *might*. My predecessor here took the line that Ernest Itterby had his faults but also had a magnetic personality. He's about as magnetic as a sack of damp oatmeal. But if you ever get to him, don't underrate him, Saltana. He knows nothing about most things worth knowing about, but he understands politics. That's why he's here, even if his image is frayed round the edges. Oh — and if you have any trouble with Bob Brodick, let me know."

It was the day before the quarrel with Tuby that Saltana went to party headquarters to meet Bob Brodick, whose room was on the second floor of a building that might have been a small factory, perhaps manufacturing clockwork beetles. Brodick was a shortish thickset Scot, bald, with a ginger moustache, a lot of chin, and a busy-and-angry look. And he had a busy-and-angry trick of repeating phrases, which Saltana found extremely irritating.

"Now then, Professor Saltana, this is without prejudice, without prejudice." And he did some busy-and-angry work with papers on his desk.

"What do you mean, Mr. Brodick?"

"Caught you on the telly — talking about images — and you didn't convince me — no, didn't convince me."

"I'm sorry about that," Saltana told him, and nearly said it twice.

"Another thing. I don't think you're a party member, are you?"

"No, I'm not a member of any party. I think I'd describe myself," Saltana continued, trying to slow down this exchange and make it sound more companionable, "as a philosophical anarchist."

Brodick dismissed this with a snort of contempt. "Out of date and not practical politics." And he added, wishing to do himself justice, "not practical politics. Get you nowhere."

"Perhaps that's where I want to be — I mean, politically speaking."

"Then you've come to the wrong shop, haven't you, Professor? What d'you think about the P.M.?"

Rather tired of answering this question, Saltana explained how little he knew, but then added pointedly that he was there, at Jadson's suggestion, to look at any recordings they might have of the P.M.'s television appearances.

"I know, I know, I know," cried Brodick with astonishing rapidity. "And you'll be shown some. All arranged." He rang a bell and a sad middle-aged woman, a permanent widow, looked in. "Tell Dave or Cliff, whichever it is, that Professor Saltana's here — and ready when he is." He waved her away and frowned at Saltana. "But in my opinion — and I know what I'm talking about — you're not going the right way about this. You don't get the essential quality of Ernest Itterby on the screen. You want him there — alive. Listen to him at a meeting or in the House. Then you have the man himself — the man himself." And both his tone and his look defied contradiction.

But Saltana didn't shrink from the challenge. And anyhow he was tired of Brodick. "I don't agree with you. I'm concerned with his image. And where do I find his image? I find it where the electorate find it — on the screen. If he has some essential quality that doesn't appear there — "

"I take your point, take your point. After all, that's why you're here, though that doesn't mean I'm convinced — not at all. Though nothing's settled yet, of course, and I can tell you here and now, Professor, you're a bloody long way yet from convincing Ernest Itterby — and I've known him for thirty years — that there's something wrong with his public image and you can put it right. And another thing. If you're not a member of the party, why do you want to bother with his image?"

"That's quite simple, Mr. Brodick. It's my profession and I'm expecting a substantial fee."

"Now wait a minute, wait a minute, wait a minute!" This was his quickest yet, like a machine gun. "Nothing's been said to me, and I'll tell you straight, Professor, I've no funds here for any fancy work with images. Oh — maybe — three or four guineas — "

"Five thousand pounds," said Saltana, just to see what would happen. "That's what I'm asking."

Brodick didn't even try to speak for several moments. Instead, he drummed on his desk. Then, perhaps to save himself from a complete explosion, he poured some water from his carafe and swallowed a pill, without even a glance at Saltana, as if his visitor had just vanished.

"I'll tell you something," he said finally and, curiously enough, with less emphasis than usual. "That's the most ridiculous bloody thing I've heard this year. Who d'you think is going to pay you five thousand pounds?"

"I haven't been told his name," said Saltana casually. "And of course I don't get it unless I'm successful — "

"Easily the most ridiculous bloody thing," Brodick continued, as if Saltana hadn't spoken. "I don't believe it. You're having me on — having me on. Yes, what is it?" he called. "Oh — it's you, Cliff. Well, this is Professor Saltana — and you know what he wants. And watch it, Cliff — he'll start telling you fairy tales."

Cliff was a type Saltana hadn't met before, though he'd seen and heard some of them in pubs. He looked like a garage hand but spoke with the slightly nasal precision of an Oxford don. "I hope you've no objection, Professor Saltana," he said as soon as they were out in the corridor, "but there's this man who's doing special part-time research for us now — we're frightfully lucky to get hold of him — and he wants to take a look at the P.M. too. So he's joining us."

"Not another image man, I hope?"

"Well, we're all image men to some extent," Cliff continued as they walked along, "but he doesn't pretend to have your expertise, naturally. He knows you, by the way. His name's Mere — O. V. Mere."

"Oh — yes — I know him well," said Saltana, compelling himself to speak with enormous gravity. "Mere's a first-class man. As you say, you've been lucky to get hold of him, even if only as a part-time researcher."

"I'm so glad you think so. We go up these stairs, Professor Saltana. All of us in the mass media section were keen on his coming to us. He was responsible for that TV series on politics and education, you know. Very contemporary sharp mind, we think."

"Quite right." Saltana was enjoying himself. "I think we can say that O. V. Mere is switched on."

"You're so right. Here we are." They turned in to a small projection theatre. "Best we can do at the moment, I'm afraid. Bob Brodick's so terrified of spending money. Ah — Mr. Mere — here already — good! And I needn't tell you this is Professor Saltana. Now do try to make yourselves as comfortable as possible. I thought about an hour of the P.M. might be enough."

"Rather more than enough," said Mere, slumped down with his smouldering cigarette. "What do you say, Saltana?"

"Certainly."

"Well, I must confess," said Cliff, "much as I admire the P.M., that an hour of him, without any relief, does rather tend towards the kiss of death. All right, Charlie," he called, "we're ready when you are."

It seemed to Saltana one of the longest hours he'd ever known. Ernest Itterby — a rather tall thin man about sixty, with a high-bridged nose and a cropped grey moustache — was of course never off the screen. His range was narrow indeed, from a faint smile to a faint frown. He never laughed, never scowled and glared, never spoke with passion. He read from his notes or the teleprompter a series of political clichés that bored the hell out of Saltana and apparently sent O. V. Mere to sleep. About two-thirds of the way through, Saltana began to feel he ought to tell Tenks he couldn't possibly go on with this: it would be like trying to build up a heroic and attractive figure out of lead weights. However, when it was all over, and so perhaps out of sheer relief, he suddenly decided he must go on with it. There was a challenge here, perhaps the last that *Social Imagistics* would ever have to face, and Cosmo Saltana couldn't run away from it.

"Well, what do you think?" Cliff asked them. He had ducked out as soon as the grim show had started, but now that the screen was empty he was back with them.

O. V. Mere had been cursing because his cigarette had fallen out of his mouth and burnt a hole in his shirt. "Why ask?" he grunted. "I can tell you later. And you've no right to ask Saltana. He's not on the job yet."

"Stupid of me, of course." But he looked and smiled at Saltana. "Still — perhaps just a hint. It would help us when we're arguing with Bob Brodick."

"Very briefly then," said Saltana. "He's projecting what we call a *Frayed Image*. And a particularly bad specimen of one. It's possible to use a *Frayed Image* when you've already prepared the *Emergent Image* beginning to show through. This can be effective in certain situations where *Image Transition* is necessary. But here with Itterby, nothing is coming through. He's merely like an actor who's been playing a country solicitor far too long — "

"Oh — marvellous! You're so right, of course. May I quote you?"

"So long as you also repeat exactly what I propose to say now. Itterby can't successfully sustain a conference and then a general election with that image. Could I persuade him to abandon it completely and then project a far better image I would prepare for him? I could. It wouldn't be easy but I could do it *if* — and everything hangs on this *if* — I had his confidence and could spend some time with him. But an analysis and advice merely on paper or during one hurried interview would do more harm than good. Can you remember that, Cliff?"

"Every word, Professor Saltana. And I'll pass on the message — very discreetly, of course. I have to see the Leader of the House this evening, in point of fact."

They were going out now. "I've something private I want to say to my friend Saltana, Cliff. So I'll show him out if he's through here."

"I am. Must get back to the Institute. What is it, O. V.?"

Mere had started another cigarette and was coughing to show that he was enjoying it. He stopped halfway down the main stairs, then went at once into one of his conspiratorial sessions. Saltana felt they ought to be wearing cloaks and covering their faces as they whispered together.

"What about friend Tuby?" Mere muttered. "Has he a pipeline into the Opposition?"

"A very small one. Young Axwick was one of his clients."

"Of course he was. And thanks to Tuby, little Axwick's moving up in the party. He's recently been appointed Parliamentary Private Secretary to the Shadow Minister of Transport. And he's now engaged to the daughter of the new Chairman of the party. She'd almost broken it off, but then when there was all that talk about some woman in Grenoble, she nailed him. So Tuby has a pipeline there." O. V. paused for a moment, bringing his face three or four inches closer. "Worth mentioning to Tuby, don't you think?"

"Certainly. As soon as I get back to the Institute."

"Just in case — "

"In case — yes, O. V."

And Saltana kept his word, telling Tuby exactly what Mere had said. But then next morning there was the quarrel, and the *Society of Social Imagistics* sprang into existence, and there were paragraphs in the Press, where Dr. Tuby was quoted as carefully announcing that no difference existed between himself and Professor Saltana in the theory and practice of their joint creation, *Social Imagistics,* but that they had no longer been able to agree on certain administrative matters. And the following week, Saltana and Elfreda had the Institute to themselves, except of course for young Beryl, who didn't want to take her holiday until the end of August. Eden had joined Tuby at 3A Darvil Court, where Elfreda now spent occasional mornings or afternoons. And Primrose had gone to Sardinia with her Eric, insisting upon taking her holiday at once, in a huff too — she would have flounced out if she'd been wearing the right kind of skirt — simply because she couldn't persuade Saltana and Elfreda to employ Eric.

"I wouldn't have that useless young man about the place," Saltana declared, as they were talking late one night in Elfreda's sitting room, "if he paid us to work here."

"I know, darling," said Elfreda. "And if they haven't started a baby already, it'll happen in Sardinia." She then gave him what was for El-freda a hard look. "What's all this about politics?" she enquired darkly.

So here it was, the question he'd been dreading. To tell her the truth, which he longed to do, would be to break his word, given not once but already half a dozen times.

"What about politics?" He knew this was idiotic, but it was the best he could do.

"Now don't be silly, Cosmo darling. I'm very vague about a lot of things but I'm not a complete idiot. Besides, there's Tuby too."

"Owen Tuby? You amaze me, my love. Unless of course he's turning into a different kind of man. And there were signs of it — beginning months ago, I'd say, not long after we came to London — "

"No, there weren't. Stop it, Cosmo. I know you're hiding something from me — and I hate it."

"And I hate it too, my love." He was quite serious now. "I'll tell you all I *can* tell you. There's to be a general election in October, and one or two people in the Government are asking my advice about im-ages. And that's as far as I'm committed, my dear. But I have to go and talk to some of them. And that's it."

"Then what's so secret about it?"

"Well, you know what politicians are — "

"No, I don't. And what about Tuby?"

"Tuby?" He laughed — and a bogus little job he made of it too, he felt. "You know very well I haven't spoken to him — never even set eyes on the little man — since he marched out of the Institute. You're the one who sees Tuby, my love, so you must ask him."

"I *have* asked him. *And* Eden, who's crazy with curiosity, especially as her husband seems to be mixed up in it — "

"O. V. — really?"

"Yes — O. V. *really*. She agrees with me that all you men have be-gun acting very strangely. But she says that's what happens as soon as it's politics. But after all, there are women in politics as well. Oh — dear, let's change the subject. What's happening tomorrow, Cosmo?"

"I expect to be working in my room most of the day, Elfreda, but I'll be out in the late afternoon. I have to see a man."

"Yes — and it's politics. Oh yes, it is. I can tell by your tone of voice. All deliberately vague — *I have to see a man*. And it doesn't suit you, darling."

The man Saltana was going to see was Frank Angle, the Chief Whip. Tenks had fixed this and had also arranged for one of his young men to meet Saltana at the House and take him up to the Chief Whip's room. Unfortunately, this arrangement was all too popular; there seemed to be lots of other people waiting for other people; and nearly ten min-utes were wasted before Tenks's young man and Saltana finally discov-ered each other. This didn't improve Saltana's temper; he found himself disliking almost everything he saw on his way to the Chief Whip, and he knew he might now find it all too easy to dislike the Chief Whip too. What a name anyhow — Frank Angle! And though he might well be — as Jadson had said he was — a sensible steady fellow, there were times when Saltana didn't warm towards sensible steady fellows.

Angle certainly looked the part. He'd done a reliable job on his own image. There was no possible appeal to *Social Imagistics* here. The general effect was nineteenth, not twentieth century — the hint of grey side-whiskers, the steel-rimmed spectacles halfway down the nose, the pulled-down wide mouth, the black coat and tie and stiff collar, all suggested duty and discipline and Victorian rectitude. If Itterby was a country solicitor, Frank Angle was his great-uncle, the founder of the firm. Yet Saltana, after taking a closer look at him, concluded that Angle was only a few years older than himself.

"Well, sit down, Professor Saltana." Angle's manner was quite pleasant. His voice was perhaps rather too light to be a perfect accompaniment to his visual image. "Roger Belworth, Leader of the House, may be looking in for a few minutes. No, not on public or private business, just to meet you. Roger," he added dryly, "likes meeting people, especially if they've been in the news. And you've not done badly there, I think, Professor Saltana."

"Possibly not, Mr. Angle. But it's no pleasure to me, and I don't employ a publicity agent. However, our Institute had to be written about, talked about, to find any business."

"And you're making money, are you?"

"Certainly. And far more than we expected to make."

Angle awarded him a small tight smile. "Both Jimmy Tenks and the P.M.'s man, Jadson, have talked to me about you. The idea still seems to me far-fetched, with all respect. We all write and talk about images, I know — but an image expert, called in like a physician or a surgeon — that's a bit steep, isn't it? I'm being quite frank with you, Professor Saltana, you see."

"Then I'll be equally frank with you, Mr. Angle. I've been telling myself what a good job you've done on your own image. Visually it's perfect. The only suggestion I can make — speaking as an expert — is that you might try to deepen your voice a little."

Angle stared above his steel rims. "I call that pretty cool, my dear sir. I've never given a minute's thought to my image. I've more important things to think about. So you're very wide of the mark there."

"Conscious attention isn't always necessary," said Saltana, determined to carry on as a cool customer. "An unconscious response to an urgent image situation — that of finding oneself Chief Whip, for instance — is often most effective, especially when no expert opinion has been sought."

"Nor, in my view, needed." Angle didn't look annoyed, but his tone was very sharp.

"In your case, perhaps not. But you must remember that Tenks, who began this, only wanted me to consider — and then improve — Ernest Itterby's image — "

"I'm aware of that. And Tenks also told me you can be trusted to keep this to yourself — all strictly confidential — um?"

"Certainly. I gave my word. But I must point out that if I can't get near Itterby without making a number of moves — explaining myself to this one and that one — complete secrecy will soon be impossible, even though I keep my promise."

"I realize that, Professor Saltana. But if you confine yourself to senior members of the party, I assure you we can keep a secret or two if a general election's coming up. You've been told about that, of course — um?"

"Yes. And I'll risk a prophecy. If that election depends to a large extent on your Leader's image — and he makes no attempt to change that image — then you'll be defeated."

"Oh — come, come! We have a programme — policies — "

"And millions of people who don't understand what they are, who stare at and listen to Ernest Itterby because there are no cowboys on the screen — "

The man who came in then was very fat, all ripe and rosy and smiling. Angle, who didn't seem pleased to see him, introduced them. And this, of course, was Roger Belworth, Leader of the House. His smile broadened and he shook hands enthusiastically, as if he had been waiting for this moment for years. A continuous chuckle is hard to keep going, but Belworth could do it. Yet his eyes, as Saltana observed, although they were difficult to see clearly, embedded as they were in so much pinkish fat, seemed to glitter rather than twinkle, like fragments of green glass.

"I don't know if Frank's already told you, Professor Saltana," Belworth said through his chuckles, "but he doesn't believe in you. And I do. Oh — most certainly I do. Whether our friend Jimmy Tenks does, I don't know."

Saltana stared at the great fat smiling mask. "Why shouldn't he?"

"Well, let's put it this way. Jimmy has a nice safe seat — he'll be back whatever happens — and he and Ernest have never got on. So it wouldn't worry Jimmy Tenks if Ernest made a fool of himself." And Belworth did a hum with his smile.

"So you believe in me, Mr. Belworth, but think I might encourage Ernest Itterby to make a fool of himself."

"No, no, no, my dear chap," cried Belworth. "I was referring then to our friend Jimmy Tenks, whom I've known — and much admired — for a long, long time."

"But you're not making sense, Roger," said Angle. "We all know Jimmy's ambitious and looking for a plum, not the Board of Trade. So he wants us back in office. Which means he'll do nothing to make Itterby look foolish."

"Frank — Frank — " and Belworth was reproachful but, of course, gigantically affectionate — "you're the best Chief Whip we've ever had — and I keep saying that to all the grumblers — but you don't always know what's going on." He began wagging his head and spoke very softly. "Dear old Jimmy doesn't want us to get back into power. At best, he thinks, we'll only scrape home and won't last long. And having had the Board of Trade, dear old Jimmy knows there'll be two or three very good things lined up for him in the City. And if we're out, he can enjoy the perks while making our poor Ernest look silly as Leader of the Opposition. Very much between ourselves, Professor Saltana."

"But you don't have to believe all that," Angle said to Saltana.

"I don't think I do," Saltana told him. Then he looked at Belworth, who was still one enormous smile. "Do you or do you not believe I could improve Itterby's image — and his chances?"

"My dear chap — I do — of course I do." Belworth chuckled. "You can't have forgotten that the very first thing I said was that I believed in you. And if you want a good word from me to our Ernest — not immediately, but as soon as we've risen for the summer — you've only got to say so. But I'll leave you now — to convince Frank, who has some old-fashioned prejudices. Unlike me. Professor Saltana, I'm entirely on your side and I'll back you to the limit." And off he went — chuckle, chuckle, chuckle.

"Well, there you are, Professor," said Angle rather dryly. "Leader of the House — and entirely on your side. What do you say to that?"

"Can you take my candid opinion, Mr. Angle?"

"Why not? Go ahead."

"He's worked hard on that image. An overweight Santa Claus without whiskers. But even so, it's a poor image, obviously over-emphasized and self-defeating. And he's not on my side. He's not on anybody's side. If he's a friend of yours, then I'm sorry — but in my book he's artful and treacherous and cold-hearted — a real stinker."

The Chief Whip neither smiled nor frowned. "Quite so. But he's a good Leader of the House. And a very good senior party man. He can chair what looks like a hopeless meeting and turn it into New Year's Eve, especially if they don't really know him. But that's enough about Roger. You're probably a busy man, and I know I am. So just tell me this. If you get through to the P.M. — during the recess — what can you do for him?"

"Give him a different image. What he's got now is in tatters, and even if it weren't, it would still be wrong. He shouldn't look and sound as if he's just been called in to offer a little good advice. It'll bore the hell out of the mass of voters. They can't think about politics. They can't amuse themselves. And they lack confidence — in themselves or in anything else. So what do they want? They want to be *told,* not advised. They want to be entertained. They — "

"Just a minute. I'm not saying you're wrong. But Ernest Itterby's where he is chiefly because he's a good party manager and has never had many downright enemies. And you're starting to outline a programme for a Lloyd George or a Churchill — "

"I don't think so. It's now chiefly a matter of adapting yourself to that little box. Which means being able at once to project an attractive image — attractive, that is, in terms of your particular situation. I'll find one for Itterby, well within his range, so long as he'll listen to me and give me some time. But I'm taking too much of yours, Mr. Angle." He stood up, but gave the other man an enquiring look.

Angle responded to it. "I want to think this over, Professor Saltana. But I'll tell you this — now. I didn't expect to be impressed, thought I'd soon have you out of here, your tail between your legs. But I *have* been impressed. If such a job could be done — and that's where I'm still uncertain — then you're the man to do it. I'll be in touch — either with you or Jimmy Tenks."

On his way out he ran into Jadson, the P.M.'s press man, and this was no great coincidence, because Jadson spent much of his time going in and out of the House. Saltana explained briefly what had happened so far, adding that only Ken Stapleford, Minister of Possible Developments, remained on Jadson's list of people to see.

"But the most important," said Jadson. "Closest to Itterby, as I told you. And I happen to know he's going to Washington very soon." He whipped out a pad and made a note. "I'll fix it for you to see him. But not at the Ministry, if I can manage it — at home. I think I told you Ken's wife, Ruth, is Itterby's cousin, and she might be really more use to you than Ken. Besides, you can understand what Ruth's talking about. With Ken you're lost in a fog more than half the time. How d'you get along with women, Saltana?"

"Not badly as a rule. And the image idea fascinates them. I'd be deeply obliged, Jadson, if you could arrange for me to see the Staplefords at home. But not miles and miles away, I hope."

"They've a flat not ten minutes' walk from here. Also, of course, a house in the country, not far from Itterby's. All right, leave it to me." Then he grinned. "The buzz from headquarters is that you didn't get on with Bob Brodick, but that young Cliff was greatly impressed after he'd shown you all that Itterby stuff on the screen. His present image wouldn't do at all, you thought, didn't you?"

"Certainly. If he won't improve his image, I'm ready to bet — and I mean to bet with real money — that his majority will go down the drain in October. Ten pounds, Jadson?"

"No bloody fear! That's why I'm running round, trying to help you. Final point. Be patient when Ken Stapleford ties himself into knots. Try not to ask him what the hell he means."

"I'll do my best," said Saltana, "though I've no great store of patience. Certainly not enough for politics."

Nearly a week later, a busy week too at the Institute, Saltana had an appointment to drink a glass of sherry, about seven-fifteen, at Stapleford's flat, between Westminster and Victoria. Their talk wouldn't have to last very long, he was told, because the Minister was due to dine with a group of industrialists at eight. Moreover, to his annoyance, when he did arrive at the flat, dead on seven-fifteen, it was only to be told by an apologetic Mrs. Stapleford that her husband wouldn't be available for some minutes, as he was still making notes for his speech to the industrialists.

"But at least I can give you some sherry, Professor Saltana," said Mrs. Stapleford. She was a woman about fifty, with grey hair but very dark eyes and eyebrows and a rather indignant kind of high colouring, as if somebody had just insulted her. But she seemed quite glad to see Saltana. "I must tell you that I'm quite curious. I've read and heard a lot about you and your images, and I've seen you twice on television."

"I feel flattered, Mrs. Stapleford," Saltana said, smiling. He tasted the sherry, which was terrible; there was no whisky in sight. The room they sat in was less attractive than his hostess, being almost as impersonal as the window of a not very enterprising furniture store. Probably the Staplefords were just camping here. "I imagine," he continued, "you're longing to get back to your house in the country, aren't you?"

"How clever of you to know that!"

"We charlatans have to be quick good guessers."

"Now, now — I'm sure you don't think of yourself as a charlatan, Professor Saltana." And when his only reply to that was an amused look, she went on: "But don't you feel sad at having lost your friend and partner, Dr. Tuby? You see, I know all about you. I've plenty of time — too much, in fact — to read the gossip columns, Ken being so busy at his Ministry and in the House. But you do feel sad, don't you, about that quarrel? Dr. Tuby seems such an amusing and attractive little man."

"Oh — he is, he is, Mrs. Stapleford. And a brilliant image man. Far better with some types of clients than I could ever be." Saltana tried hard to sound both regretful and modest. "But we found we couldn't work well together. Just one of those things," he concluded idiotically.

"You men! Ken — my husband — is just the same. He simply can't work with some people. And here he is — at last."

Ken Stapleford was about the same age as his wife and looked rather like Tenks, except that he had no moustache, military or otherwise. He began speaking most emphatically as soon as he came in, and he didn't stop for a moment even while he was shaking hands with Saltana, who felt glad almost at once that Stapleford would be taking his voice elsewhere very soon.

"I learnt in a roundabout way what you felt about Ernest's image and I'm sure from your own point of view as an expert Professor Saltana you're perfectly right and we senior members of the party after giving your opinion serious consideration should take it into account in any serious discussions we have concerning Ernest's image both in respect to the Party Conference and to the election but yours isn't the only point of view and though entitled to be treated with some respect as I assure you I am only too willing to do we must take into account not only the risks attending any last-minute change of image on the part of the Leader of the party and the present Prime Minister but also the larger question of the part to be played by the image and especially in connection with the prejudices not yet fully understood although we are doing some special research on this particular problem that is the prejudices of the floating voters who may or may not be far more responsive to one type of image than they are to another or may on the other hand be indifferent to the P.M.'s image and may prefer to concentrate upon a strong and easily understood programme and for my own part though ready to wait upon further developments especially those following the results of our special research I am inclined to take this view." He stopped there to toss down a glass of sherry as if he were taking medicine. "Dam' good sherry if you ask me and quite equal to the stuff we have to import from Spain and I'm delighted to have had this talk with you Professor Saltana and we must continue it another time, and don't wait up for me dear as I'm expected in the House after I've made my speech to these industrialists who are trying to make mischief but I hope to put a stop to that if it's the last thing I do. 'Bye — 'bye!" And the door was closing behind him.

"Poor Ken! He's so dreadfully rushed, these days." She sighed. "Another glass of sherry, Professor Saltana? No? I'm afraid some people find Ken hard to follow."

"And I'm afraid I'm one of those people, Mrs. Stapleford. And I also can't help feeling that a talk with you about Itterby's image might be far more rewarding."

She smiled and then replied almost in a whisper. "I can't help feeling that too. After all, Ernest *is* my first cousin. And we needn't make speeches at each other. But — " and she sketched a helpless gesture and raised her voice — "dinner's the problem. You must be a hungry man — and wives left to themselves too often make do with rather pathetic snacks on trays — "

"Mrs. Stapleford, I have no engagement this evening, and I was about to dine alone in a new little Italian restaurant — Roman style — just off Curzon Street, not far from our Institute. If you are free, then take pity on me. They know me there, and if I telephone while you're getting ready to come and dine, we'll have a table where we can talk at ease. The food's excellent and the wine isn't too bad. What do you say?"

He had seen her hesitating until he was about halfway through his little speech, but after that she began to light up. "Why — this is very kind — and I'd love it. An unexpected treat for a political wife. The telephone's over there. And I'll be ready in about ten minutes."

Half an hour later, she was fairly sparkling at him across their little corner table. "They do that Roman-style roast chicken very well here — the one stuffed with all manner of things. What do you think?" he asked her.

"I don't want to think. Wives and mothers — we have two enormous sons and a ravenous daughter, Professor Saltana — get tired of thinking about food. You order what you'd like — and I'll like it too. Oh — this is *fun*."

He encouraged her to talk about her two sons and her daughter and the house in the country, and Ernest Itterby and images were never mentioned until they were about halfway through dinner. And even then he left it to her to mention them.

"I'm sure — though you've been very sweet about it — listening to my chatter — you're dying for me to tell you something about Ernest Itterby, to help you with your image thing. And of course I've known him all my life. I believe you don't know him at all. Is that so?"

"Quite true. All I know is that his present image is very poor and that he's likely to prove rather touchy and difficult. So please tell me about him."

"I'm not changing the subject, but I must tell you this chicken dish is marvellous. I wish I knew how they do it. Now — about Ernest — in confidence, please — "

"The strictest — and I mean it — "

"Ernest isn't a great man, of course. He isn't a very good man. But neither is he a bad man, as so many people seem to think." She thought for a moment or two. "If you were abroad, you probably don't know what happened in the party a few years ago, when Ernest was elected to the leadership."

"I don't," said Saltana, "so please tell me."

"Two rivals — one a strong man, the other quite brilliant — cancelled each other out — and let Ernest in. He was the quiet unassuming man, not too strong or too brilliant, not hungry for power as the other two obviously were, good for the party and good for the country. That's what they believed — and still believe. Even Ken, who ought to know better, still half-believes it. But I've known Ernest Itterby for a long time, and I know that he's always been vain and always very ambitious. It's not as a private person he's unsatisfactory, even dangerous — he's always been good with Ethel and their children and he's been a good friend to Ken — it's as a public figure, raised high on the political platform. For instance, his modest optimism and his suggestion of deep feeling for the

English people are all humbug. In secret he's deeply pessimistic and
thinks the people are now mostly thoughtless and selfish riffraff." But
now she stared at him in sudden alarm. "Ken would be furious if he
knew I was talking like this. Being here with a strange attentive man
and this lovely dinner you've chosen are going to my head. You won't tell
anybody what I've said, will you?"

"Mrs. Stapleford, I hope to be married soon to a woman I'd very
much like you to know. Unfortunately she's dining with some American
friends tonight. But when I assure you — as I do — that I won't even
tell *her* what you've said, then I hope you'll feel safe."

When they were smoking over coffee Saltana returned to the subject of Ernest Itterby. "I can see he won't be easy. There'll be a clash between his vanity and his ambition. He won't want to change his image
just because I tell him it's no good. On the other hand, being ambitious,
he won't want to risk place and power. I'll be dealing with a divided
man, probably rather short on temper. And as I am too, there could easily
be a flaming row. It's been suggested I shouldn't go near him until he's
on holiday in the country. He won't be going abroad, I trust?"

"Oh no, he hates going abroad, except on official missions. And he
only stays at Chequers when he feels he ought to, for conferences. Their
place in the country — it's in Oxfordshire, not far from Burford — is
only ten miles from ours, so we see a lot of one another during the summer recess. I'd ask you to stay with us, so you could meet Ernest that
way, but I have an idea Ken might be against it. And you might too. I
won't ask you about *my* image — though I'll bet most women do — but
what about Ken's? And you can be quite frank. I love the man but I
know a lot of people find him hard to take."

"That's because he tries to combine two things that don't work together," said Saltana, adopting his usual professional image manner. "I'd
say he tries genuinely hard to see all round a subject, all sides to a question. But instead of being easy and rather hesitant, tentative, he tries
equally hard to be very emphatic. It's an impossible combination and it
must have done him great harm, certainly in public life."

"Oh — how right you are! And I wish you'd tell him that — very
tactfully. Though I suppose it's difficult being tactful if you're dealing
with images."

"It's impossible. But I'd like to work it so that I meet Itterby socially and don't begin talking about his image. *He* asks *me*. Now then —
it seems to me that I ought to be staying in the neighbourhood, spending
a week or two in some pleasant country hotel, and then you could introduce me to Itterby — not forcing it, of course, if he tends to be suspicious — "

"And he does. But I'm lunching with Ethel Itterby the day after tomorrow — we're great friends — and I'll tell her about you. No, don't
look like that — nothing about Ernest's image, of course. But I'll talk

about a possible hotel for you, and tell her she'll like you. And never mind
what I'll say — you're probably sufficiently conceited already."

"Certainly. Possibly one of the most conceited men you've ever
met — "

She laughed. "What? And all those politicians! Look — I've loved
it, Professor Saltana — you've no idea what a delightful surprise this has
been — but I think I ought to be going home now. Ken sometimes dashes
back from the House, bringing two or three men in for a drink, quite
unexpectedly. So, if you wouldn't mind putting me in a taxi — "

He did this before paying the bill, which might have held them up
another ten minutes, but then when she was inside the taxi and was
thanking him again through the open window, he remembered to give
her a card that had both his telephone numbers on it. This pleasant
woman, he knew, was worth more to him than all the politicians added
together; she was the key that would open the door to Itterby, and it had
been an inspiration to ask her to dine with him. A little later, he drifted
— it was a warm night — along Curzon Street towards Half Moon
House and his clarinet, which would help him to celebrate a successful
evening. And as he drifted, he wondered. Had Elfreda enjoyed meeting
her American friends again? And what was happening to Owen Tuby?

# 10

Tuby opened his political campaign by telling Alan Axwick over the
phone that he'd like some talk with him, and then accepting an invitation to lunch with Axwick and his fiancée, Daphne Nugent-Fortescue.
And now here they were, sitting at a table near the window at the Ca-
ligula, a small, fashionable, and extremely expensive restaurant, which
Tuby had already decided was dam' bad value for the money, like the
emperor himself. Daphne Nugent-Fortescue was one of those boring girls
with a classical Greek profile, and she did a lot of eye-opening and -shut-
ting, and either exclaimed or wailed. However, Axwick, now pinker and
more exquisitely dressed than ever, obviously regarded her as a kind of
miracle, a triumph of our biological productivity. A lover himself now,
spending every possible hour with the delectable and astonishing Lois,
Tuby accepted this strange infatuation — for Daphne really was a boring girl — with a tolerant smile, but Axwick's interest in transport was
much harder to take. Now that Axwick was Parliamentary Private Secretary to the Shadow Minister of Transport, he would insist upon explaining to Tuby — while Daphne closed her eyes — what was wrong with

British Railways and motor roads; and lunch was nearly over before Tuby could make his next move in his political campaign.

Finding an opening at last, he addressed them both. "Now you must help me, please. I am very anxious to have a short confidential talk with the Chairman of the Opposition party — "

"That's Daddy," Daphne exclaimed, her eyes wide open.

"Yes, Dr. Tuby," said Axwick. "Sir Rupert's now Chairman of the party. Jolly good move too, we all think."

"So I gather," Tuby told him gravely, trying out his new political persona. "Well, I have an extremely important piece of information for him."

"Couldn't you tell us?" Daphne was still keeping her eyes wide open at the risk of wearing herself out.

"I wish I could, Daphne, but it really is impossible. As Alan will tell you, so much that happens in politics can't be openly discussed — "

"Absolutely true, darling," said Axwick. "It just can't — that's all. The things I know already — as a P.P.S. — " And he shook the repository of so many secrets — his head. Daphne gave it a quick look, tasted some ice cream, then closed her eyes.

"So this is where I need your help. I must have this talk with Sir Rupert Nugent-Fortescue as soon as possible. I suppose he spends a great deal of time at party headquarters as well as in the House of Commons — "

"He's hardly ever at home," Daphne put in, wailing rather than exclaiming. "Mummy's furious."

"Sir Rupert's a tremendous worker," said Axwick. "And it won't be easy fitting you in, Dr. Tuby."

"I realize that. But you and Daphne, between you, ought to find a little space for me. I leave it to you, only adding that I want to speak to Sir Rupert in my capacity as Director of the *Society of Social Imagistics.*"

"It's not political, then," said Axwick. "An image thing."

"Alan — Daphne," Tuby began impressively. "It's political *and* an image thing. And that's all I can tell you, and even so I hope you'll keep it to yourselves. I must get back to Darvil Court — "

"I have your address and phone number," said Axwick.

"I know you have, my dear fellow. Daphne — what a pleasure it's been — meeting you at last! Alan — thank you for a magnificent lunch! And I'll now hope to have ten minutes of Sir Rupert's valuable time — preferably — and note this please, Daphne — not at party headquarters but at home."

"I'm for that, too," exclaimed Daphne, eyes at their widest now. "Mummy would adore you. She would, wouldn't she, darling?"

Axwick said that he saw what she meant, but gave Tuby the impression that he had his doubts about Lady Nugent-Fortescue as an instant adorer. Tuby then left them, but when he reached the street he was surprised to discover that he had left only half of them, because a rather breathless Daphne was at his elbow.

"It's about this Grenoble-woman thing," she exclaimed.

"Ah — *that* — yes indeed — yes." Tuby spoke very slowly because he was wondering what line to take with Daphne about Grenoble. Would she prefer her Alan to be an innocent or the kind of man capable of driving a Grenoble woman to despair and madness?

"He pretends it was all nothing — while I'm dying for him to describe — in detail — scenes of unbridled lust — "

"Daphne, you got that from the cover of a paperback," Tuby told her. "Now, my dear, at another time — and in a more suitable place — I'll tell you all I know. But I really must go and do some work." He gave her a little cheek-peck and hurried away.

However, this hurrying soon dwindled to a saunter. It was a warm afternoon; there was too much rich food and wine inside him, and already, while still on his feet and even moving them, he was beginning to feel sleepy. Once stretched out anywhere in 3A Darvil Court, he would lose consciousness in two or three minutes. Was anybody coming to see him? He couldn't remember. There was only one solid commercial job left to finish, and Eden Mere had it in hand. Because Meldy Glebe and Lon Bracton had talked about him — and probably Wilf Orange had recommended him to various clients — he had had a number of enquiries from show-business types, a few quite promising but far more of them quite hopeless, an assortment of alcoholics, nymphomaniacs, fetishists, and the rest, who didn't need an image expert but either a depth psychologist or three strong male nurses working eight-hour shifts. It couldn't be said, Tuby told himself dreamily, that the *Society of Social Imagistics* had at present a keen and resolute Director. If it weren't for the grimly conscientious Eden, occasionally abetted by Elfreda, he would do hardly any work at all.

"Eden," he told her at once, "I must have a nap. I hope nothing's happening."

"No doubt you do." No smile; all severity. "What has already happened is that you've been eating and drinking too much. *Ger-huh!* Very well, go and lie down for an hour. Then I'll call you."

"Why?"

"I'd call you anyhow — on principle. But in any case that film producer — the one with the horrible tic — is coming at quarter-past four."

"Yes, yes, yes — of course — yes." But then he remembered something. "Eden," he began hopefully, "what about Brittany? When do you go?"

"On Tuesday week — and God knows what will happen here when I do go. But I owe it to the children. Oswald won't be with us, except perhaps for a few days. I've never known him so busy — and most of it seems to be working, not drinking, though of course, as always with Mr.

O. V. Mere, there's somehow a constant dribble of drink into the work, whatever that is — all political, I believe. But don't stand there yawning at me, you silly man — go and have your nap."

It was two days later, at eleven in the morning, when Tuby presented himself at a house in Cadogan Square and asked for Sir Rupert Nugent-Fortescue. He was conducted to a study, where Sir Rupert was drinking coffee and immediately offered Tuby a cup. And here, Tuby thought, was undoubtedly the father of Daphne; a resemblance lingered, even though Sir Rupert was in his fifties, bulky and thoroughly male, and probably pickled in port and brandy. His eyes were like Daphne's, but instead of opening and shutting them he kept his most of the time in a curiously fixed round stare, in which there seemed to be both astonishment and exasperation, as if his last visitor had tried to sell him a mermaid. But his manner was more amiable than his stare.

"I'm due at party headquarters in half an hour, Dr. Tuby. You needn't explain who you are and so forth. We can save time on that, because I know about you."

"You realize, then, Sir Rupert, that the only two image experts in this country are Professor Saltana and myself, and that we are now working quite separately? You do? Good!" Tuby waited a moment, facing the stare, like two indignant blue moons. When he began again, he lowered his voice. "What I'm about to tell you now is very confidential indeed — top-secret information. You accept that, Sir Rupert? Thank you." Tuby paused again. "I have reason to believe," he continued softly, "that Saltana has had various consultations with members of the Government, and will shortly make a close personal study of Ernest Itterby — "

"To improve his image?" Sir Rupert broke in because he was obviously alarmed.

"Yes, indeed. And don't imagine he can't do it. He wouldn't have accepted the job, for which he'll ask a fee of several thousand pounds, unless he felt he'd be successful. I hope you weren't counting on Itterby's image damaging his party — "

Sir Rupert broke in again. "Of course we were — of course we were," he cried impatiently. "Itterby's personal popularity ratings have gone down and down. But — my God — if he turns up after the holidays with another and much better image — "

It was Tuby's turn to cut in. "And he will, of course, Saltana will see to that. He's not a better image man than I am — we're about equal — but each of us is more effective with certain subjects. Saltana dominates; I'm more persuasive."

"Yes — yes, but I'm trying to work this out. You say Saltana will be asking several thousand pounds — eh? Well, that's where your story breaks down, Dr. Tuby. If you can believe that Brodick and his party funds will cough up several thousand pounds for some image advice, then you can believe anything, my friend. No, no, you've swallowed some idle rumour. And we can smile again." And to prove that he could, he did.

Tuby smiled too, but also shook his head. "I wouldn't have come here with an idle rumour, Sir Rupert. Why make a fool of myself? I happen to know that Saltana's fee — " But he broke off to answer that stare with a hard one of his own. And now he spoke sharply too. "I'm sorry, but I must have your definite promise to keep this entirely to yourself. Otherwise, I can't tell you any more."

"I give you my solemn word, Dr. Tuby. And I apologize for suggesting you'd believe anything. Stupid of me! Now go on about Saltana's fee — though I think I know what's coming."

"I can't prove this," Tuby told him rather casually, "but to the best of my belief Saltana's fee will come from a well-to-do private member of their party, who no doubt will expect to be rewarded afterwards. Ah — that's what you guessed, isn't it? And if you decide to employ me," he continued blandly, "I suggest you raise the fee in a similar manner."

"Wait a minute — you're taking a devil of a lot for granted, aren't you?" The stare was hard at work now.

"No, I said *if*. But consider the position you're in now. Itterby's image is to be changed and vastly improved by a brilliant expert. Now I'm no student of politics, but even *I* know, after merely glancing at the Press, that you're not satisfied with the image of your Leader — Sir Henry Flinch-Epworth. Why, it's notoriously inadequate."

"Perhaps it is," said Sir Rupert hastily, "but it's got a damned sight better political programme behind it." He was over-emphatic really because he was feeling flustered.

Instead of replying at once, Tuby lit a pipe. Then after a puff or two he said very carefully, "If you can believe it will be a policy and not an image that will swing the floating vote, then *you* can believe anything." He stood up. "However, I mustn't waste any more of your valuable time."

"No — no — wait — wait!" He was up too. "This is more important than anything I was going to do this morning at headquarters. My trouble is, I don't really know how much you so-called image experts can do — "

"Not *so-called* please — that's always an insult. We *are* image experts. Saltana and I created *Social Imagistics* — "

"I know — but it's a bit fancy — "

"It's so fancy that it's been bringing me about a thousand pounds a week on an average — "

"Yes, I dare say — from manufacturers and advertising men and film stars — but we're hard-headed politicians — "

Tuby took his pipe out. "Hard-headed? Politicians? Since when? Come, come, Sir Rupert! You're not addressing a meeting now. I know nothing about your Sir Henry Flinch-Epworth, have never seen him, never heard him. Take me along to your headquarters, ask somebody there to show me some screen appearances of Flinch-Epworth, and I'll tell you frankly what I think of his image. Though not, of course, how it could be improved — that's my professional service. But if you feel I'm talking sense about his image, you will pay me an immediate hold-ing fee, as we call it, of five hundred pounds. I then go to work improv-ing Flinch-Epworth's image, and if I'm successful you pay me the re-maining four thousand five hundred pounds to make up the total fee of five thousand."

"Pretty stiff, aren't you?"

"I believe it's what the other people have agreed to pay Saltana. And I don't rate my services below him."

"Fair enough. But suppose you go to work on Harry Flinch-Epworth — and he's the most obstinate man I know — and then we tell you it's not a bad job but not good enough for that extra four thousand five hun-dred you want — where are you then?"

Tuby smiled. "Talking to the microphones and reporters — and I'm quite good at it. And then where will *you* be?"

"Sunk, probably. But you wouldn't do that to us?"

"Certainly I would if you tried bilking me." Then he changed his tone. "And after all, Sir Rupert, what's an odd five thousand — and not even coming out of party funds — against what you must be ready to spend between now and the general election? Come, we're both wasting time now. Take me with you to your headquarters and let me examine your Leader's image."

"Quite right — sensible thing to do. But I'll phone first — tell 'em to have the leader-image stuff ready for you. Then we can talk in the car."

It was that kind of car, very large and with the chauffeur screened off. It took them through a sunlight already hazy with petrol and diesel fumes, past hundreds of people who ought to have looked happy on a fine July morning but somehow didn't. Sir Rupert was obviously thinking hard — his face might have been at the dentist's — and Tuby didn't want to disturb him.

"I've been thinking, Tuby." They were now motionless in a traffic block. "I can't handle this alone. I've an appointment this morning with Geoff Wirrington. He's Deputy Leader and Shadow Home Secretary — he's at the Bar. Geoff hardly ever stops making speeches — notorious for it — but even so he can be depended upon to keep a secret. Now while you're looking at Harry Flinch-Epworth, I want to tell Geoff Wirrington what you've told me — in strict confidence, mind you, and of course with your permission. All right?"

Tuby made his consent very grudging.

"Don't trust politicians too far, eh? Well, I'll tell you a secret," Sir Rupert went on. "Neither do I. Tuby, I have to work with some of the biggest loud-mouthed asses in the country. And the fellows on the other side are even worse. But I happen to be a man of my word. And so is Geoff Wirrington, for all his speechifying." They were on the move again. "Well, here we are, and we'll go straight up to my room."

There was a sleek young man called Reg Something — Tuby never caught his surname — waiting for them just outside Sir Rupert's room. "And if you're all set along there, Reg, don't let's waste any time. I'll see you later, Dr. Tuby."

"I'm afraid our viewing room is down in the basement, Dr. Tuby," said Reg as they moved away together. "And it's really quicker to walk, if you don't mind. We really need another lift." When they were going downstairs, Reg produced an apologetic little cough. "By the way, there's another man joining us down there, if you don't mind, Dr. Tuby. He did a very successful television series, and though he's only doing part-time special research for us — he has other irons in the fire, of course — it's been a great stroke of luck getting hold of him. And he's interested in this image thing, though he doesn't pretend to be in your league. You *have* met, I think. His name's Mere — "

"O. V. Mere?" And Tuby had to work hard now to sound as solemn as Reg. "It is? Well done! Yes, I met O. V. Mere when we were both doing — er — educational work, and of course he's an absolutely first-class man — in his own field. Yes, Reg, you can congratulate yourselves on grabbing O. V. Mere even if he can give you only part of his time."

"These stairs now, Dr. Tuby. Rather slippery, I'm afraid. I'm delighted you feel that about Mere. We're finding that he's tremendously aware of trends."

"I can well believe that, Reg. Yes, I'd say that O. V.'s very much a trend man. He's an intuitive type. He has — shall we say? — antennae. He knows early what's in the air or just round the corner."

O. V. Mere was leaning against the wall, under a *No Smoking* sign, looking thoughtful, and with the usual cigarette smouldering away. Reg left them to talk to the man working the projector.

"These people are supposed to have all the money," said Mere, "yet it's bloody awful down here. The seats'll torture your arse." Then he went into the essential Mere act, the deeply conspiratorial, the muttering behind invisible cloaks: "Fixed yourself up with these people yet, old man?"

"Not definitely — no, O. V." As usual, Tuby now found himself in the act. "Only broached it to the Chairman this morning."

"You won't have to do as much running around as Saltana had to do. You told Nugent-Fortescue that Saltana was on the job for the other side, didn't you?"

"Indeed I did. If I hadn't, I don't think I'd be here."

"And if they give us an hour of Flinch-Epworth, you'll be wishing you *weren't* here. And these seats won't let you sleep."

Tuby went down to a very low mutter. "What's he like — this Flinch-Epworth?"

"You can divide all these senior politicians into crooks and chumps," Mere whispered gloomily. "Flinch-Epworth's a chump."

"Ready when you are," cried Reg, reappearing. He sounded as if he were about to distribute sweets and oranges at a children's party. 'About forty minutes, we decided — everything cut except the Leader himself. But it will give you a good idea of Sir Henry in various situations — facing up to all manner of challenges."

But what appeared on the screen didn't give Tuby this good idea at all. Sir Henry Flinch-Epworth may have found himself in various situations, may have faced all manner of challenges, but he seemed to Tuby always exactly the same — with the ghastly exception, probably making a speech at some social occasion, when he struggled with a little joke as if it were really a very big joke, like a man battling against a six-inch octopus. For the rest he always suggested a farmer desperately worried about something he didn't like to mention — foot-and-mouth disease, perhaps — who went on and on talking about things he knew he had to mention. He was as entertaining and inspiring as a helping of underdone boiled turnip. And even though Tuby seemed to be sitting upon a very large screw, he began to doze off before the end.

"Well, that's that," said Reg when the lights went up. "And I think you'll agree that the fundamental decency and honesty of the man come through."

"I dare say," Mere grunted. "But he's not asking for a job as a bailiff, but to be Prime Minister. That's your trouble. What do you think, Tuby, image-wise?"

"He projects an image all right, one he's fixed into with concrete. In fact we call this type the *Fixed Opaque Image*. And as it's wrong anyhow, it's death, of course. But I promised to join the Chairman and the Deputy Leader upstairs as soon as I could. Be seeing you soon, I hope, O. V. Thank you, Reg, and will you please act as guide again?"

Geoffrey Wirrington, the speechifyer, was waiting with Sir Rupert. They were having a drink and Sir Rupert, not a bad fellow, was civil enough to ask Tuby to have a drink too, before they questioned him. Wirrington, Deputy Leader and Shadow Home Secretary, had a long body, short legs, a large pale face, and the kind of wide mobile mouth designed for speechifying. But so far his manner was pleasant and easy.

"I've been put in the picture, Dr. Tuby," he said, smiling. "And now you've seen and heard our Leader in action. So what do you think?"

"I'll only say that the image your man is projecting so strongly and monotonously would now be disastrous. It's that of a farmer. And who likes a farmer? Not even another farmer."

"Well, Harry *is* a landowner," Sir Rupert began.

"And who likes landowners? Most of the people whose votes you want have a traditional mistrust and dislike of landowners. Half the time, Flinch-Epworth sounds as if he's about to order somebody off his property."

"Something in that, Rupert," Wirrington threw in. "But go on, Dr. Tuby."

"If I were handling this man, I'd first persuade him to break out of this fixed image. It's like a caricature of your party. Then I'd persuade him — and I know he's obstinate, but it could be done — to change his appearance. For example, to trim that moustache, tone down his complexion, wear different clothes. Then I'd show him how to *discover* thoughts and opinions as he speaks, instead of announcing them mechanically and trying to cover his boredom with bogus over-emphasis. His audiences, especially on television, are mostly incapable of giving serious consideration to such thoughts, opinions, conclusions, because they're not really politically-minded and anyhow most of the problems we have to solve are now far too complicated. But — these same people — and particularly the women — though intellectually stupid — are extraordinarily sensitive to nuances of appearance, manner, tone. Politically they may be idiots, but as nightly viewers of television they are in their own way expert psychologists — "

"But Harry Flinch-Epworth, I can assure you," Sir Rupert protested, "is fundamentally an honest and decent man — "

"So our friend Reg told me," said Tuby. "And I'm sure he is. But as the Leader of a great party? As a potential Prime Minister? Clamped into his present image, he talks about 'burning issues' when we know he isn't even striking a match under them. When he told me this country was facing ruin, I merely wondered what was really worrying him — whether to refence the hundred-acre or to buy another Guernsey bull. And he should never be allowed to attempt jokes, as he obviously has no sense of humour. The voters are constantly entertained by talented and highly professional comedians. You politicians forget that your standard of wit and humour in the House is so low. The men who amuse you wouldn't be allowed three minutes on the screen or in a successful workingmen's club — "

"We are not entertainers, Dr. Tuby," Wirrington came in, sharply.

"Then don't pretend to be, Mr. Wirrington."

Sir Rupert had been summoned to the telephone. "Who? Lord Sturtleton? I'll take the call in your room, Madge." On his way to the door, he said hastily, "Might get Doggy Sturtleton into this, Geoff."

"No, no — that tailor tycoon's your man," Wirrington called to the door. Then he gave Tuby a long grave look. "Shall I tell you what this country wants?"

"In a moment," said Tuby, getting up. "What *I* want is a little more whisky to put heart into this soda." As he returned to his chair he saw that Wirrington was now on his feet, standing stiffly, his face frozen, no longer the pleasant new acquaintance of a few minutes ago. The Deputy Leader and Shadow Home Secretary was about to make a speech.

"What this country wants," he began, his manner and tone quite different now, "is New and Inspiring Leadership based on Our Sound Traditions and yet irresistibly Moving Forward into the Modern Age — "

"Or what used to be known as having your cake and eating it." But there was no sign that Wirrington had heard this. He semed to have hypnotised himself.

"I am proud to represent a party that has never pretended that there was An Easy Way Out. We have not hesitated — " and Wirrington, who had the voice for it, was now reproducing the old Churchillian cadences — "at all times and in all places — to declare that Sacrifices Must be Made to rescue This Great Old Country of Ours. These Sacrifices must be borne — and I believe they will be borne eagerly and gladly, under the Right Leadership, by All Classes, from the greatest and wealthiest in the land to the humble toiler, the weary housewife, from the young student, beginning his adult life, to men who have grown grey in the service of their professions — "

"Hear, hear!" Tuby shouted, not to encourage Wirrington but in the hope of stopping him.

"Irony, was it?" And Tuby *had* stopped him, for now he was a man and a brother again, not an orator.

"A touch, perhaps," Tuby told him. "Not that it wasn't going to be a fine speech, but it demands a far larger audience and a town hall somewhere. Quite unsuitable for going on the air, of course."

"You think so?"

"I *know* so, Mr. Wirrington."

"Ex-academic, aren't you? I wonder if that explains your extremly dogmatic manner?" But Wirrington said this quite pleasantly.

"For which I very sincerely apologize," said Tuby in his most honeyed tone. "It's not my usual manner. The truth is, I'm out of my element here."

"Possibly. And yet I was thinking, when you were discussing Harry Flinch-Epworth — a most unfortunate choice as Leader, I've always thought — that the party ought to ask you to take all our new candidates through a crash course. You'd want a fairly stiff fee, of course— "

"About a million pounds. In other words, I'm not interested."

"Not interested in *what?*" This was Sir Rupert, back and curious.

"No party political job except working on your Leader's image. That's a real challenge. Moreover, it brings me into sharp competition with my former friend and partner, Saltana."

"He's working on Ernest Itterby, you remember, Geoff?"

"I do," said Wirrington gloomily. "I do indeed. Today's bad news."

Tuby stood up. "Well, I could be today's good news. And now I'll make two points. If ever I saw an image that demanded immediate attention — probably with a mental pickaxe — it's Flinch-Epworth's. I'm willing to bet a hundred pounds you can't win the election with it. Final point. I'm responsible for the *Society of Social Imagistics* — with enquiries from potential new clients coming through all day — and I must make my arrangements for August. So unless I hear from you within the next forty-eight hours, Sir Rupert — and here's my telephone number on this card — you can forget you ever set eyes on me. And now I'll leave you — and if I can find my friend O. V. Mere, I'll take him out to lunch."

"Oh, he's a friend of yours, is he? Clever chap. We're lucky to have him working for us here. And I can phone through for him to meet you below." Which Sir Rupert promptly did. Then he looked at Tuby, rather wistfully. "I don't know about forty-eight hours. What do *you* think, Geoff?"

"Thingummy — tailor tycoon. You could nail him in twenty-four hours, Rupert."

"Not if he happens to be abroad."

"We could risk that — but you want to be off, Dr. Tuby. Great pleasure — fascinating experience — "

"Did he begin making a speech at you?" Sir Rupert asked.

"He did," said Tuby, now outside the door. "But I stopped him. A nice fellow, but he wants to be careful of that speech-making complex — might develop into a psychosis."

O. V. Mere was waiting below. "How's it going, Tuby old man?"

Tuby found himself muttering too. "Chiefly now a question of raising the money, I fancy. Gave 'em a sharp ultimatum — within forty-eight hours — or else. Showing off, of course — but this big-money talk goes to my head."

"They'll raise it all right. And I have to talk to Nugent-Fortescue this afternoon — so I'll give him a shock if he needs one. Where are we going?"

"I thought — somewhere round here — "

O. V. moved even closer and more ash fell on to his ruined lapel. "No, we'll take a cab, old man. Terrible round here. Bars packed with C.I.D. men, Special Branch types, the secret bloody service, mass media reporters, hanging on to light ales and hoping to listen in to somebody's conversation. Come on. Hey — taxi!"

## 11

It was a close, thunder-haunted August night. Saltana was sitting in a small and rather shabby study, smoking a cigar with the Right Honourable Ernest Itterby, First Lord of the Treasury, etc., etc. Ruth Stapleford, accompanied by a son and a daughter, had picked him up at his hotel (Ken was away, discussing Possible Developments somewhere in the Commonwealth), to take him to the Itterby house, ostensibly to play tennis. But he had been told to shower and change there, then stay on for drinks and dinner. Itterby hadn't been visible before dinner, still being monopolised by P.M. and party duties, with secretaries and messengers and dispatch boxes coming and going, private telephone lines kept hard at work, and so forth. But now, much to Saltana's surprise, he had Itterby to himself. The Stapleford and Itterby youngsters had gone roaring and shouting into the night, to dance somewhere; Ruth Stapleford and Ethel Itterby, who had plotted all this together, were in the drawing room, not expecting to be joined by the men; and Saltana, while pretending to be idly enjoying his cigar, was thinking hard about Itterby's moustache. Itterby himself had frowned into his coffee cup, as if one of his problems were still disturbing him, and Saltana had respected his silence.

"You play a surprisingly good game of tennis, Professor Saltana. My youngsters were delighted."

"I played a lot of tennis in Latin America, especially in the early morning, Prime Minister."

Now came the tiny bomb, tossed into his lap. "Do you play your image game equally well? Because I think that's what my wife and Ruth had in mind."

"Quite true, sir." Saltana never tried to dodge and hedge at such moments. "But how did you know?"

Itterby smiled. "I'm a fairly cunning old hand, Saltana. Often I have to sniff what's in the air — and guess right for survival."

It was well said but there was vanity in it. Ruth Stapleford had been right there. "That I can imagine," Saltana told him.

"I don't know who put you up to it," the great man continued, still looking and sounding amused. "Jimmy Tenks and Roger Belworth, I fancy, but it doesn't matter. The fact that you're here, staring rather hard at me, suggests that as an expert — and I know all about that — you don't like my present image."

"No, I don't, Prime Minister. And you must allow me to make a point here, before we go on. An image may seem a very personal affair. But to us, working in *Social Imagistics,* it's quite impersonal. If after carefully considering your image I report on it adversely, I'm not criticising *you* but simply the image you're projecting."

"I'm not sure I agree with that, Professor Saltana, but if you tell me what you said about my image quite frankly, I promise not to be offended."

Deciding at once it would be safer to be highly technical, as impersonal as a surgeon discussing a tumour, Saltana explained about a *Frayed Image,* the apparent lack of any prepared *Emergent Image,* the danger of attempting at short notice a necessary *Image Transition.*

"All very impressive, no doubt," said Itterby, with a faint smile. "But let's come down to ordinary terms and political life, where *I* can play the expert. Of course I'm quite aware of the image I'm projecting to the electorate. And it doesn't seem to me at all a bad one. My father was a well-respected solicitor in a small country town, Saltana. And I worked with him as a junior partner until after I'd been several years in the House. So it came easy to me to look, talk, behave, like a small-town or country solicitor. Let's say a steady sensible man. Now most people are confused and bewildered, somewhat suspicious of politicians, and at heart rather fearful. They need advice, they need guidance, just as they do when they consult a solicitor. So I appear before them and talk to them as a rather unassuming but very sensible solicitor might do. It makes them feel safer. They can entrust the country to such a man, as of course they have done."

Saltana now spoke slowly and very carefully, tiptoeing along a path of eggs. "I take leave to doubt, Prime Minister, if it was your solicitor image — as distinct from the general image of your party — that brought you into power. The mass of people either know nothing about solicitors or dislike them. They mistrust rather than respect or admire the Law. By the way, I can show you the result of a little popular opinion poll on this subject. A friend of mine, O. V. Mere, who's been doing special research at your party headquarters, organised it for me. And now I must remind you again, Prime Minister, I'm being quite impersonal and you really mustn't take offence —"

"I've given you my promise already," said Itterby rather impatiently. "Go on, man."

"Then I must tell you that it isn't a part they want, and that you've played it too long for them already. The result is they suspect — quite unfairly, no doubt — insincerity — "

"Good God, man! What nonsense! Sincerity — and quite rightly too — is above all what I'm credited with — "

"We're not talking about *you,* but about your *image.*" Saltana had now abandoned his slow and careful approach. "These televiewers, whose votes you want, base their judgments not on policies or men, but on images. And there are more of these viewers now than there were a few years ago — "

"I'm inclined to agree with you there," said Itterby heavily, probably just to impose himself.

"Now the gaps in your image, with nothing they can recognize coming through, suggest insincerity to them. They want a complete dependable image, but not of a country solicitor. They don't want to be advised, they want to be *led.* Not persuaded, not exhorted — but *told.* So, Prime Minister, with all respect, I wouldn't be doing my professional duty if I didn't warn you against your present image. You must adopt another one as soon as possible. And it's all the more urgent because I understand that my former colleague, Dr. Tuby, who created *Social Imagistics* with me and is an extremely clever image man, has been commissioned to advise the Leader of the Opposition."

But this announcement, which left Saltana out of breath, fell disappointingly flat. "Has he indeed? I doubt if he'll make much headway with Harry Flinch-Epworth, who's notoriously obstinate and pig-headed. No, Saltana," Itterby added, smiling, "that leaves me unruffled."

"Yes, but you don't know Tuby. It's common knowledge," Saltana went on, coldly, "that Tuby and I broke up our partnership, so that I'm not prejudiced in his favour. But he's both intuitive and immensely persuasive. However, let me return to my point — "

"Yes, yes, that I need a new image — and as soon as possible." Itterby wasn't smiling now, but his manner and tone were still light, too easy, condescending. "But all this is very negative, Saltana. What kind of image, if any, have you in mind? And I'm afraid you'll have to be brief. I may be called away at any moment. I still have to run the country, even if I don't look it." And he added a smile, a little too tight, rather forced.

Having been warned, Saltana spoke quickly and indeed was somewhat vehement. "Then if you don't look it, sir, change the image and *do* look it. Banish the quiet professional advising type. They don't want it. They won't vote for it. Come closer to the ordinary man but of course enlarge yourself. You're one of *them* but the big one, the leader. Change your public manner — be more confident, more expansive. Change your style of dressing, let your hair grow longer — and your moustache, don't look so pale, careworn, quietly anxious, legal. This is of course the roughest briefest sketch of what I would advise — "

He was interrupted by a knock followed by a sleekish, faintly supercilious fellow Saltana hadn't seen before. "The Foreign Secretary's coming through, sir. And I've been warned to expect the Washington call in half an hour."

"Yes, Ben." Itterby was already up. "Goodnight, Professor Saltana — and all very interesting. Ben, stay here a minute and work out with Professor Saltana when he and I could get together quietly — an hour here, half an hour there — you could do it with your own little diary — " And he went out, leaving Ben to release the door, bring out his diary, look from it to Saltana and then back again to it, all with what appeared to Saltana a faint suggestion of distaste.

"Even now, when the P.M.'s supposed to be on holiday," Ben murmured, not looking at Saltana but at the diary, "he's frantically busy — so it's not going to be easy fitting you in. It's really important, is it?" But he still didn't look up, not for a few more moments — and then he did. "Sorry! Did you say something?"

"No — it was a little laugh," said Saltana. "I don't often do that — you know, really to myself. It came out quite unexpectedly. By the way,

I'd say these little sessions could be quite important — unless you don't care who wins the election. And I'm sorry I laughed."

About the time, later that August, when Saltana was having his third session with Ernest Itterby, seventy miles or so in a north-easterly direction Tuby was sauntering round a well-kept lawn and smoking a pipe with Sir Henry Flinch-Epworth, Leader of Her Majesty's Opposition. Tuby, who had been invited to stay for a few days, had arrived that morning at the Flinch-Epworths' just after twelve, had eaten a hefty lunch in the company of Sir Henry, his wife Mildred, and his daughter Sally, who had just left her husband, one Dermot Nulty ("rotten to the core" in Lady Flinch-Epworth's opinion), for the third and last — but *last* — time. It was a hazy, warm afternoon, and Tuby was wondering whether to begin work on Sir Henry or to make some excuse and find a deck chair for a nap. However, it was Sir Henry himself who compelled Tuby to set to work.

"I'll tell you now, Dr. Tuby. I didn't want you down here. And I usually get my own way. But Geoff Wirrington and Rupert Nugent-Fortescue put some party pressure on me. Came down themselves to talk me into it. Then when Mildred — my wife — heard who you were, she was curious and keen to meet you. And so was Sally — poor girl! Finally, I gave in, not a thing I often do. Now don't get me wrong here, Dr. Tuby. Nothing personal in this. In fact, I'm jolly glad now you're here, after the way you talked to the women about the East at lunch — had 'em hanging on every word. They'd give me hell now if you didn't stay a few days. But the point is — and I must make this clear — I don't believe in this image business."

"But you can't have led a political party, these days, without hearing and reading a lot about images — surely, Sir Henry?"

"No, of course not. Even been told I haven't the right image myself. But I'll tell you frankly I think it's all a lot of poppycock. And no offence intended, my dear fellow. Not getting at you. Might be doing something very useful for film stars or breakfast foods. Clever chap, obviously. Don't blame you. But politics — no, not on your life! State of the country — fate of the country — very serious urgent matters! Take me, for example. All I really want to do is to look after my estate and potter around the home farm. If I'm in politics — leading the party now — it's because I feel the old country's going to the devil unless we rescue it in time. And we shan't do that, sitting about wondering how to project images. With all respect. But I'm a plain downright sort of chap, who always tries honestly to speak his mind, and I must tell you I don't give a damn about images."

"Are you sure, Sir Henry?" Tuby enquired gently.

"Of course I am, my dear fellow. Don't see why you should doubt it."

"I'll tell you. And if I haven't taken any offence, then you mustn't.

That's only fair, isn't it? Good!" Tuby halted, turned, looked the other man in the eye. Still using an easy detached manner and gentle tone, he continued: "You're busy projecting an image at this very moment. This image suggests you're really a simple country gentleman who's rushed into politics to save the country as if it were a house on fire."

"And what's wrong with that?"

"It's an image that insults my intelligence. You've been a politician for many years, Sir Henry. You've held office under a previous Government. You're now the Leader of the Opposition. So how can you make believe you're just a plain-spoken, simple country gentleman who happens to have found his way into the House of Commons? If that's what you were, then at the best you'd still be one of your party's anything-but-brilliant backbenchers."

There might. have been a grin lurking behind Flinch-Epworth's large and untidy moustache. "Oversimplified, I dare say. I may have had to acquire a few tricks and dodges during the last twenty years. And I happen to know how to keep the party balanced but on the move, chiefly because I don't try to be too clever. In that respect I'm rather like the P.M. But if you're talking about images, Ernest Itterby — doing his family-doctor-cum-solicitor turn — has flogged his to death."

They moved on again, past the late August borders of tall blazing flowers. "Quite so," said Tuby rather casually. "But I must remind you — because I think you must have already been told — that my former partner, Professor Saltana, is already working on Itterby's image."

"He won't have much luck, if you ask me. I've known Ernest Itterby for a long time now. He's very obstinate — and behind that bogus modesty he's very pleased with himself, always."

"And I've known Saltana a long time too. And he's not only very clever, he has a strong compelling personality. So don't count on winning in October because Itterby, as you said, has flogged his image to death. Before then he may be projecting a new image." But the moment after he had said this, Tuby knew he had been careless and had made a wrong move.

"You're overdoing this, Dr. Tuby," Sir Henry said stiffly. "In our party we don't depend upon images. We have a sound policy, a sensible programme we're ready to carry out. We're not afraid of dealing honestly with the electorate." His colour, always high, was now higher still. His jaw was obstinately set. "I ought to go down and have a word with my pigman. Come along if you like, but I can't promise you any amusement — no images down there. Mildred and Sally will give you tea. I never have any. My party Secretary ought to be here by five and I'll be working with him until dinner. See you then, of course."

Feeling temporarily defeated, Tuby went slowly in search of a deck chair, sank into one, tried to think but began to doze. He didn't mind

losing sight of the August afternoon. He had never liked August afternoons. He was a June and September man.

"Dr. Tuby, I'm sure you'd like some tea," Sally was saying. "And
we're having it outside — on the terrace. Just us — thank God!"

"And very delightful." He scrambled out of the chair, feeling hot
and untidy. "I'll join you in a minute or two."

The women, probably rather bored with each other, eagerly welcomed him to their Earl Grey and cucumber sandwiches. In spite of their
difference in age and style of dress, mother and daughter were so alike
that it was almost comical, as if they had done it on purpose to amuse
him. They had the same large, rather fine grey eyes, absurd little snub
noses and heavy chins; not sexually appealing, at least not to Tuby, but
attractive in the way that some dogs are. Now they were curious, especially Sally, about Meldy Glebe and Lon Bracton and any other show-
business types he could find for them; and for the first half-hour he kept
their eyes alight with curiosity and amusement, until finally he had to
mention it.

"I feel I must tell you," he said, smiling, "that I find your eyes fascinating. They're so alike — and they're so magnificent — "

"Flatterer!" This was Lady Flinch-Epworth, Mildred, obviously enjoying herself.

"No, no — I'm a connoisseur. Some men concentrate on foreheads,
noses, mouths, necks — "

"And legs — my gosh!" cried Sally.

"We all *look* at legs, naturally. But rarely concentrate on them as we
do on various features. And I'm an eye man. So I was paying you more
than an idle compliment, Lady Flinch-Epworth — "

"Oh — no, not that. She's Mildred — I'm Sally — and what are
you, please?"

"Not Dr. Tuby, please. Just plain Tuby." Tuby lit his pipe in rather
a flashy way, like an actor, to keep their attention on him, for now it was
time to make his next move. After a few puffs, he looked appealingly
from mother to daughter, adding a wistful little smile. "I want to ask for
your help. And in order to do that, I must explain exactly what I'm trying
to do here — "

"Something about images, isn't it? That's what Daddy said."

Apart from not making any mention of a fee, which he felt was
no concern of theirs anyhow, he gave them a fairly truthful account of
what had happened at party headquarters, what he had felt, what he had
said, after those forty minutes of Sir Henry's screen appearances. Then
he went on: "Now when we were strolling on the lawn together after
lunch, after first warning me that he didn't believe in what he called this
*image business,* he did allow me to make one or two points, but then
quite suddenly he made it plain that he didn't want to listen to anything
more about images, and then, though not offensively, he more or less dis-

missed me. In spite of his initial warning, this came as rather a shock. I'm feeling baffled. There's much to do, and it looks as if I can't even start. And as I feel — and I hope I'm not assuming too much — that we three are friends already, I'm venturing to ask for your help." And he smiled at them. Mildred was looking — or trying to look, for she hadn't the face for it — thoughtful. It was Sally who spoke first.

"But that's what he really *is*, y'know — I mean a landowner and farming type. Then he's happy."

"That's not quite true, dear," said her mother. "That's what he *thinks*."

"Quite so. And as I've already pointed out to him," Tuby continued, "he is in fact an experienced politician, who's held office, and is now the Leader of his party. And he's chosen an image that a large number of voters will reject. They don't like landowners, they don't like farmers. And these people don't seriously consider policies and programmes. They're not politically-minded, they're image-minded."

"And I'm becoming midge-minded," said Sally, getting up.

"Yes, we'll go in. I'd quite forgotten. Would you like a whisky-and-soda? Or is it too early?"

"Not for me, I must confess. But of course if *you* feel it's too early, Mildred — "

"It is — but I shall have a gin-and-tonic. And I know where everything is, so you just sit here alone for a minute or two and think about images."

By the time his hostess returned, carrying the drinks, Tuby was thinking about her. And he told her so. "Yes, about you, Mildred. And I was wondering if I was being quite fair. Have I any right to try to enlist you into my side, probably dead against your husband's wishes?"

Lady Flinch-Epworth — for she seemed nearer to that than to Mildred, at this moment — glanced at her daughter and then looked hard at Tuby. "I don't think you're being unfair. But without going into images, because I'm sure we wouldn't be able to follow you, tell us quite plainly and frankly what you feel my husband ought to do — to improve his image. Can you?"

"I can." Tuby waited a moment. "He must get rid of anything that suggests he belongs to a narrow class. He must be less ordinary in one sense, more ordinary in another. He must both spread himself and enlarge himself. These viewer-voters want to be able to identify themselves with a man, yet want him to be a *leader*. They must feel he's one of them but on a larger and bolder scale, ready to do some thinking for them and then — not advising, not vaguely exhorting them — *telling* them what they must do. All right so far, ladies?"

"All right," said Sally, "but a bit dim about what he actually ought to do."

"I'm coming to that now. To do what I've suggested, Sir Henry must make certain quite definite changes. For example, in his speech — and this will be the hardest part. Like most members of his particular class, he's bad on vowel sounds. It shouldn't be *weathah* but *weather,* not *Ampah* but *Empire,* not *nartcharallay* but *naturally.* The point is, these very limited and lazy vowel sounds suggest condescension, a man who isn't going to bother to talk to you properly. Now — appearance, much easier to change than speech. Different clothes, but you'll understand about that. Hair rather longer. Moustache shorter, trimmer but not over-trimmed. He must just take the wildness out of it. He must also take down that high colour of his. Suggests hunting, fishing, and shooting, not long deep thoughts for the nation. Besides, on colour television he'll look like a beetroot, and then he's back to the bad old image. Any questions?"

"What *sort* of man have you in mind?" demanded Mildred. "Give me a type I've met and would easily recognize."

"Offhand I'd say a successful managerial type who's probably come up the hard way. And now he's thinking about the nation, not about machine tools. Remember, this isn't for his friends, his party colleagues, the people he has to meet when he's opening a garden fête. It's a screen image, for viewers who are also voters. Now, Mildred, Sally, you discuss this between you, because, if you'll forgive me, I'm feeling warm and scruffy and I need a bath. But one last thing, please." On his feet now, he smiled at Sally and then gave her mother a long look. "I don't propose to raise this image subject either at dinner or afterwards. I refuse to be snubbed in front of you two. And I can promise, if Sir Henry is with us, to keep the talk going briskly on other subjects. But if I hear nothing encouraging at breakfast — "

"Harry won't be with us," Mildred said quickly. "He gets up frightfully early and sees our farm manager — "

"I don't know if that helps or not. But though I love it here, if I know it's hopeless then I must catch the 10:35 to Town and get on with some work."

They both exclaimed at this, and Tuby felt it wasn't mere politeness. And Sally said, "I just adore listening to you, Tuby dear. It's absolutely fab after Dermot and his lot — my God! Oh — no, you *can't* go."

"I don't want to," said Tuby, smiling. "But if there's not the least sign of progress, then I'm afraid it's the 10:35. Sorry, my dear!"

He kept his word, and at dinner and after it — and Sir Henry remained with them — he never once mentioned the term *image.*

There are some men — perhaps a majority in this decadent age — who don't want and can't enjoy kidneys and bacon for breakfast on a warm morning in late August. But Tuby belonged to a more robust tradition and was down in good time, to help himself. Then Sally burst in, not wearing very much, pulled a face at the kidneys and bacon, kissed Tuby on the top of his head and said she loved him, and so had to be told she was too late, because he loved another. Mildred arrived a few minutes later, gave herself a cup of coffee and a piece of toast, and told Tuby very quietly that it wouldn't be necessary for him to catch the 10:35 — at least not that morning, perhaps about five mornings later. And she and Sally both declared he would have to go with them to a garden fête that afternoon; and he did and it was terrible, full of women with big hats, faces powdered until they were lilac, and angry eyes. And later, Tuby rang up Lois and told her he'd just been to a political-party garden fête and that it was terrible and he loved her, to which she replied he didn't love her, otherwise he'd tell her where he was and what he was doing and wouldn't keep her hanging about in Tarbury, worse than ever in August, and any fête — worse than death — served him dam' well right for being such a miserable secretive imitation lover. "Plastic men now we're getting," she told him, "to go with the plastic flowers. Tuby, I hate you." And because seriousness was creeping in — and there might be tears after he'd rung off — he said she was his love and always would be, that she must forgive him and be patient for a week or two more, and then everything would be different and wonderful.

About the middle of that *week or two more,* an afternoon in early September, Elfreda was sitting in her room at the Institute, looking across her desk at Jimmy Kilburn's man, Foster. And Elfreda was dismally in need of a real companion. She was alone in the Institute. Primrose was still in Sardinia with Eric. Even Beryl had gone on holiday now. And Saltana — oh, that maddening man she missed so much! — was still away somewhere, deep in political nonsense, and though he rang her up fairly regularly he still refused to tell her where she could ring him up — or better still, go and grab hold of him. And for the last two days he hadn't even rung up, just when she had so much to tell him. Nor could she feel any less lonely and deserted if she went from the Institute to the Society (these silly men!) at 3A Darvil Court. Eden was still with her children in Brittany. And Tuby — who might have had a little more sense — was another one playing boys' games; he had vanished, utterly vanished, so that poor Lois, hanging on at Tarbury, was half out of her mind, even though Tuby did ring her up — but even then, Lois said, only to talk nonsense about garden fêtes.

"Mr. Foster, I'm sure it's the best bid we could hope for, far better than we expected," said Elfreda, giving the man a warm smile that was wasted on him. "But the truth is, as a businesswoman, which is what Saltana and Tuby imagine me to be, I'm a fraud. So — please — instead of working so hard pencilling away, would you mind explaining how it would come out — in rough round figures, and if possible, please, in pounds and not in dollars?"

"I've anticipated that request, Mrs. Drake," he told her, in a kind voice though without a smile. He rummaged through his mass of papers.

"I just want a kind of rough picture," Elfreda added apologetically, "showing me who gets what."

"Yes, indeed — and it's not an unusual request." Foster cleared his throat, perhaps preparing it to talk about money, then glanced from Elfreda to the sheet of paper he had selected. "To the nearest round figure, then — in sterling. The total bid amounts to £150,000. This means that you and Mr. Kilburn, each of you with a thirty-five percent holding, will each receive £52,500 — still a rough estimate, of course. Professor Saltana and Dr. Tuby, who are entitled to fifteen percent each, will come out at £22,500 — yes, Mrs. Drake?"

"My God — it really is monstrous." Elfreda spoke with some heat, but was even angrier inside than she sounded. "Just look at it! Jimmy Kilburn and I invest £5,000 between us — and he lets us have these offices and the flat upstairs at a nominal rent, and I work here for less than a nominal salary. But that's the lot. And what do we get — £52,500 each!"

"A very profitable investment, certainly," said Foster, who obviously didn't understand what was boiling up in Elfreda's mind. "As I said earlier, the circumstances were particularly favourable. This American group is shortly to offer a take-over bid for the largest advertising agency in London. Before doing this, they wanted your *Social Imagistics.* And I don't think Mr. Kilburn would object to your knowing now, Mrs. Drake, that he apparently entered into competition with this American group, both for the agency and for your *Social Imagistics.* I may add," he went on in a deeper tone, suggesting awe, "that Mr. Kilburn is a master of these tactics."

"I dare say," said Elfreda rather impatiently, "and I've no doubt we owe a lot to him. But this is what infuriates me. We get £52,500 each — and Saltana and Tuby only get £22,500. And they did it all. They thought of *Social Imagistics.* They created all the publicity. They dealt with the clients. You and Kilburn and I would have had nothing at all to sell — not a sausage — if it hadn't been for them — "

"I realize that, of course, Mrs. Drake. But as you pointed out to Mr. Kilburn yourself, this American group didn't want Professor Saltana and Dr. Tuby, so Mr. Kilburn at once arranged for them to have three-year contracts. The termination of those contracts is included in the total bid, but in addition, as a severance bonus, Professor Saltana, as Director, will receive £11,500 and Dr. Tuby, as Deputy Director, a rather smaller sum — £10,000. So they will receive altogether £34,000 and £32,500 respectively. Handsome, surely, for two professional men?"

"No, not enough! We'll leave Tuby out of it for the moment, but I say that Saltana should get far more than £34,000. I don't care if we divide the total differently — and after all, I'm well off and Kilburn must be a millionaire several times over — or we make them give Saltana a far bigger bonus or whatever it is — but he has to have more than

£34,000. And if you're phoning Kilburn later, you can tell him this — you can pile it on — say I'm furious. And just remember that Kilburn's a friend of Saltana's and admires him."

"I'm well aware of that, Mrs. Drake. But you must understand that Mr. Kilburn in private life, where he can be very generous, and Mr. Kilburn in a business deal are two very different persons. And it's not clear to me, Mrs. Drake — so that I can't make it clear to him — why you should feel so strongly that Professor Saltana's £34,000 is simply inadequate."

"It isn't? Then I'll explain," Elfreda told him rather wildly. "Mr. Foster, have you ever been in love?"

He wasn't good at looking startled, but this question, almost obscene, undoubtedly shook him. "I believe so — yes, Mrs. Drake. My wife and family — three children — are now staying in Frinton, where I hope to join them this week-end. But are we still discussing Professor Saltana's £34,000?"

"We certainly are. He and I are in love and we want to get married. But he's ridiculously obstinate about not marrying me until he thinks he's sufficient money to feel independent of *my* money. It's absurd, of course — it's old-fashioned — it comes straight out of corny old novels, plays, films — but that's Cosmo Saltana for you — "

"And I must say," Foster declared surprisingly, "though I can see this may be troublesome, I admire his attitude. In his place, I should feel the same. But if £34,000 won't change it, what would? £50,000? A good round sum."

"I think £50,000 might just do it. But how we manage the extra £16,000, I don't know. I can't just give it to him. You understand that. He'd go up in flames — "

"I'll put it to Mr. Kilburn." He began putting all his papers into the briefcase. "I'll give you a call in the morning, to explain any suggestion Mr. Kilburn may have made, and then we'll meet again shortly, when I may have something for you to sign. And I much appreciate your confidence in me — I mean, regarding your marriage difficulties — which of course I will keep entirely to myself." He was ready to go now, but he lingered. "I'd like to mention it to Mrs. Foster, though, suppressing names of course. She often complains that my office stories are so dull. I think she'd enjoy this one. Goodbye for now, Mrs. Drake."

Elfreda thought for a few moments about Mr. Foster. The odd thing about him was that while he sounded like ninety, he couldn't be much more than forty. Perhaps Jimmy Kilburn *wanted* him to be like that, as a kind of foil. Then, arriving at Jimmy Kilburn, she thought about the American bid and the money and the division of the money, and she wondered if there were any way in which she could transfer some of her money to Cosmo without his knowing about it. And then naturally she wanted to talk to somebody about the whole fantastic thing — and who *was* there? She decided to give herself a pot of tea.

It was when she had just poured out her second cup that Primrose staggered in. Perhaps she didn't exactly stagger, but that was the general effect. She looked tired, crumpled, miserable. "Oh — Elfreda darling," she croaked — yes, croaked; no clear high voice now — "let me sit down and give me a cup — before I have to speak a single bloody word."

So Elfreda attended to her without asking a question. She guessed at once, of course, that Eric the Useless came into this and that poor Primrose had just flown from some Sardinian disaster.

It was Primrose who asked the first question. "What's happening here, darling?" Less of a croak now. "Nobody but you around?"

"Right, dear. And I'm busy selling the Institute."

"You're *not*?"

"I *am*. Lock, stock, and barrel."

"Oh — Christ! This just ends it all." But Primrose didn't burst into tears. She simply stared and stared at Elfreda while tears, really enormous, rolled and rolled down her cheeks. Moved with compassion and feeling rather conscience-stricken — Elfreda went across and comforted and fussed over the girl and finally made her drink another cup of tea.

"Thank you, darling. You're very sweet," said Primrose, hardly croaking at all, her voice rising every few words. "All the same, though — why didn't you people — older people — you and Eden and Saltana and Tuby — why didn't you warn me against that foul and useless Eric? Why the hell *didn't* you?"

A huge ignoble I-told-you-so asked to be shouted, but Elfreda suppressed it. "Primrose dear, we did try to — did hint we weren't keen on him. What happened? Or don't you want to talk about it?"

"No, not much. Not just yet. Everything happened. You name it, then it happened. And I've come straight from the plane. My bags are in the hall. I'd just enough money to pay for a taxi between the airport bus and here. All my clothes are filthy. And I just couldn't face that bloody flat — and trying to turn out two awful people he's installed there — " And Primrose — or this damp wan caricature of her — began weeping again.

"I'll tell you what we're going to do, Primrose. We'll hang around here a little longer — in case anybody phones — then we'll go straight to Robinson's, and after you've had a bath and a drink and then some food, you can tell me all about it and I can explain what's been happening here. And if there isn't a bedroom free, you can easily manage in my sitting room." Elfreda was very brisk, no more *there, there!* stuff. "Now go and freshen up, as we used to say in Oregon. You'll feel better, dear."

Nodding and trying to smile, Primrose stood up. And at that moment, as if trying to hurry her out of the room, the telephone rang. Cosmo — at last? But it was Lois.

"Have you any news?" Elfreda enquired eagerly. "I'm bursting with news — mostly financial, though. And I'm dying to tell Saltana but I don't know where he is. What's your news, Lois?"

"Elfreda, I think we've tied ourselves to madmen." And Lois — though of course it may have been a bad line — seemed to be gasping. "This one of mine — this Owen Tuby — this now-invisible man — has sent me a telegram, saying he can't reach me by phone but loves me and will send more telegrams. And, my dear, do you know where it was sent from? You'd never, never guess — and it would cost too much to try. But unless this telegram has been sent by one of his secret agents, this honey-tongued madman of mine is now — of all places — on *the Isle of Man*. And don't ask me why, dear, because I don't know — probably he doesn't know — only God knows."

Then Lois rang off. Oh — well — now Elfreda had to face an evening with Primrose, who would, she knew, insist upon telling her all those awful things about Useless Eric that she, Elfreda, could have told her, Primrose, if she'd only been ready to listen, weeks and weeks and weeks ago.

A few days later, Elfreda had spoken over the phone herself to Jimmy Kilburn in France, had been told how it could all be fixed up to satisfy her, and had finally signed everything, under Foster's guidance. And on that very afternoon she did her signing, Saltana was rattling across the country in a large touring car at least thirty years old. It belonged to Cliff, the young man he'd met at Itterby's party headquarters, but Cliff wasn't driving, he was sitting in back with Saltana. One of the two young technicians Cliff had brought down, either Ed or Pat, was driving, as a special favour he'd begged, and the other one, Pat or Ed, was up in front with him, making rude remarks. In the car with them was a recording in sight and sound — though how it had been done Saltana neither knew nor cared — of a speech Itterby had made the day before at a large private meeting of all the party's agents in the Midlands. And they were on their way to a mansion owned and occupied by one Ilbert Cumberland.

"I find it hard to believe," Saltana had said to Cliff, "that I'm going to stay a night with somebody called Ilbert Cumberland."

"Quite," Cliff had replied. "Not his real name, of course. Came here originally from somewhere in Central Europe. Now he's made a gigantic packet, getting control of hundreds of shops. Only met him once. He threw a big lunch at the last party conference. Genuine party member. Though I don't know how he comes into this image thing. Do you?"

"Yes, I do, my boy. And I think by this time you ought to be let into the secret. Cumberland's the man Sir James Tenks persuaded to put up the money for my fee. Tenks had to tell me that, over the phone yesterday morning, otherwise I wouldn't be with you now. But it's still very much a secret, you understand, Cliff. Don't whisper it even a hundred yards away from a reporter. I've had a devil of a job dodging them in Itterby's neighbourhood. But then I've had a devil of a job altogether, I can tell you, Cliff. It's been a dog's life — a talking dog too."

"Well, I'd like to be the first to congratulate you, Professor Saltana," Cliff had cried, and his enthusiasm had sounded quite genuine. "And I'll tell you now — of those in the know at party headquarters only O. V. Mere and myself believed you could pull it off."

"I haven't done yet," Saltana had replied rather gloomily. By this time he'd come to loathe the whole dreary business, together with the cut-off solitary (no Elfreda) life he'd been condemned to lead and all the damned idiotic secrecy. "Tenks and your fat smiler-with-the-knife and Leader of the House, Belworth, are to be there tonight, and of course Cumberland himself, and with the help of you and your boys, they're to sit in judgment on me and my handiwork, if you can call it that. I'm in a mood for getting quietly plastered."

All that was just after Saltana had put his two bags into the car boot. Now, miles away, they were rattling through Leicester, whose citizens, especially if they were only half-grown, were inclined to point, grin, and jeer at this ancient touring car, of a strange shape and a faded milk-chocolate hue.

It was just after seven. Leaving Melton Mowbray on the left, Oakham on the right, they groaned rather than rattled— the car seemed to be tired now — along a half-mile avenue towards Cumberland's mansion, very impressive — possibly Queen Anne, possibly not; and Saltana didn't want to know. Cumberland himself ought to have been big and fat, and Saltana was surprised, perhaps a trifle annoyed, to find that he was small-ish and thin, a fine-drawn type, who ought to have been selling old violins somewhere and not running hundreds of shops. He spoke with great care, and it was this rather than an obvious accent that suggested an alien. His wife was plump, looked older and more foreign than her husband, and was inclined to be apologetic about everything, like the genteel widows taking over *pensions,* whom Saltana had known as a student. It was a warm evening, and as Cumberland had begged him to help himself, he poured a fine old Scotch over two ice cubes, tried it, and began to feel a little better.

"I have heard and read about you, Professor Saltana," said Cumberland, smiling, "and especially from our friend Jimmy Kilburn. He sings your praises sometimes when we should be talking about financial matters. But tell me — are you happy about what you have been able to do for Ernest Itterby's image?"

"I ought to tell you I am — and it's all wonderful. But it's been a long job — I could only get to him in snatches of an hour or half an hour, so that I kept losing ground I'd already gained — and soon we didn't like each other much. I had to keep putting a lot of pressure on him — P.M.

or no P.M. — and it became wearing. You, Tenks, and Belworth will be able to decide for yourselves when we give you this little show after dinner — "

"Of course — but you are speaking very honestly and I would still like your own opinion, Professor Saltana."

"I think I've changed his image considerably," Saltana replied carefully. "Not a hundred percent of what I wanted, but perhaps about eighty-five percent. And I happen to think it's more than his whole Cabinet, together with every lobby correspondent in London, could have done."

A daughter, dark and shy, and a daughter-in-law, a vivacious redhead, joined them for dinner. So did Cliff, but not Ed and Pat, who were setting up the little Itterby show somewhere. It was a very good dinner and Saltana no longer felt gloomy or behaved grumpily, but as both Jimmy Tenks and Roger Belworth were tremendous talkers once they had an audience, Saltana hadn't to exert himself.

"Saltana, before we start," said Tenks, "I think you ought to say something. Unless of course you're feeling too weary — eh?"

"And any man might be excused," smiling Fatty Belworth chuckled away, "after he's spent two or three weeks trying to persuade our Ernest to change his image. Can't believe you've done it, Saltana."

"We'll see," said Saltana, addressing them all. "Very briefly then — and without any *Social Imagistics* jargon — this is what I found when I took on Itterby. He was still playing the country solicitor offering a little quiet advice. And the viewing voters don't want a solicitor. And still less do they want an obviously insincere or bogus solicitor, an actor who's played the part too long. And they no longer want quiet advice; they want leadership. Well, first I had to convince Itterby that I was right, then I had to insist upon his making various changes in his appearance, manner, speech — and this was really hard going because he was very much set in his ways and secretly, behind a dry modest persona, very vain — "

"A-ha — you've got him. Eh, Jimmy?" This was Knifer Belworth, of course. Saltana ignored the interruption.

"You're now going to see and hear Itterby making a speech yesterday — the first and very rough projection of his new image. If you're not impressed, I'm sorry. I've done my best with the man. Right, Cliff?"

There was only about a quarter of an hour of it. Saltana tried to think about other things; he was tired of Itterby. When the lights were on again and the screen blank and silent, he got up. "I don't think I should say anything now," he cried through the buzz of comment, "but as it was Cliff who first showed me the old Itterby image, who agreed at once with my criticism of it, I hope you'll allow him to tell you what he feels about the changes I've made. Cliff?"

Cliff went forward and stood by the screen. "Well, I've had to work with the P.M.'s image — not the man, the image — for several years now. And I was in despair before Professor Saltana came along. What he's done seems to me absolutely marvellous. Nobody else could have done it. Even if we'd known exactly what was wrong with Ernest Itterby's image, we could never have persuaded him to change it and then shown him what he must do. I told Itterby yesterday, after he'd made his speech, what a marvellous job had been done. He said, of course, it was mostly his own idea — "

The yelp of laughter came from Belworth. "What do you expect, young man? I'd have said the same myself." Chuckle, chuckle. "But I might have been more appreciative in private — "

"No, no, Roger," said Tenks. "And don't worry about Ernest. I can take care of him. Congratulations, Saltana! A very clever job indeed!"

"Of course, of course," said Belworth, "I entirely concur. Even though it's likely to land us with another five years of Ernest." Chuckle, chuckle. "Mr. Cumberland, Professor Saltana deserves a drink. And even if I don't, I'll be glad to keep him company. Ladies, after you."

Half an hour later, Cumberland took Saltana to one side. "I start for London early in the morning, Professor Saltana, so perhaps you and I might spend a few minutes in my little office here. You don't object? Then please allow me to lead the way." While they were on the way, he continued: "You have done more than I would have thought possible, Professor Saltana. Though I knew you were a clever man, when Sir James Tenks first approached me and I agreed to provide the fee if necessary — after all, he is President of the Board of Trade — my private reaction was negative. I knew something of Itterby. So I was pessimistic. And I was wrong."

He sat down at a small desk — it really was a little office — and quickly wrote a cheque, which, after scanning carefully, he passed to Saltana. "With my compliments. That is correct, I think."

It was for five thousand pounds. "It is — and thank you."

"You return to London tomorrow — to your Institute, Professor Saltana?"

"No, Mr. Cumberland, I have a better plan." He hesitated for a moment. "And to carry it out — I need a little help, please. First I want to find a really charming out-of-the-way country hotel or inn. You see, I've been away from England for nearly twenty years — and places change. And then when I've found the right place, I want to send some telegrams — and you must allow me to pay for them. But I must get them off tonight."

"But first you must know where you are going. Now I suggest you stay here — it will be best for the telegrams — and instead of offering you handbooks and guides I will send you an expert. Yes, you have already met her. My son's wife, Sonia. This surprises you. But just as you are in images and I am in shops, my son Paul is in hotels — not large city hotels but small country hotels of charm and character — and Sonia, who has excellent taste, works with him. Now wait here, please — perhaps think about your telegrams — and I will send Sonia to you."

Sonia was the vivacious redhead, and like a sensible woman in the hotel business she didn't come empty-handed but arrived with a little drink tray. She seemed delighted to advise him, but first made him explain as best he could what he had in mind. "And it hasn't to be in this part of the country?" she asked when he had done explaining.

"No — anywhere in reason — not Land's End or the Hebrides — "

"This would be nothing like that, though it may involve a rather awkward cross-country journey for you tomorrow, if you're not going by car. It's one of our last acquisitions and in many ways my favourite so far. We had to close it for some weeks, not to spoil it but just to instal a few more bathrooms, and it's only just re-opened. Which means it won't be full. How many rooms do you require?"

"Well — " and Saltana rather drew this out — "I suppose I'd better say — four single rooms — "

"And perhaps fairly close together too — um?" Her tone was demure, but her greenish eyes had a gleam in them. "But it's quite a small hotel. Really an inn. It's called The Rose and Heifer, and it's just outside Earlsfield, a tiny place in Herefordshire, near the Shropshire border. I'll give you the details after I've phoned them to make sure they have the rooms for you." As she waited for the call to be answered, she said, "It's getting late, but there must be somebody up. I do hope you're not married, Professor Saltana."

"I get your point, Mrs. Cumberland. And you'll be relieved to hear I hope to marry one of the single-room occupants — very soon indeed."

She had just time to flash him a grin, and then she was telling somebody at the Rose and Heifer that she was Mrs. Paul Cumberland and was ringing up specially for Professor Saltana.

## 12

That mad and lovely telegram came up with Elfreda's breakfast. She phoned down about trains and then went buzzing round her bedroom like a crazy woman, pulling out dress-hangers, trying to pack but not knowing what, for how long, for where. She took a fast train from Paddington and then, just after lunch, she had to change and take a slow train. It stopped at anything that looked like a platform and never hurried itself even between stations, but it showed her the great golden mid-September afternoon and a countryside she'd never seen before. This

Earlsfield place — and wasn't it just like Cosmo Saltana to *order* her to go there? — hadn't a station, cared nothing for railway services, so her next ride was in a creaky old taxi; but the driver, though a dreamy fellow, knew where Earlsfield and The Rose and Heifer Inn were.

At last the thatched cottages and their gardens vanished; there were ancient black-and-white timbered houses, a tall spire, a market square — sheep still wandering round it — and even a little market hall with weathered pillars and steps leading to deep shadow. The taxi went along one sleepy street, up another, even narrower, and then suddenly was out of the tiny town. And there where roads crossed — and one of them began climbing towards wooded hills — was the Rose and Heifer, as its sign proclaimed. It was black-and-white timbered too; and above its fat little bay windows it seemed to bulge a bit here and there, and it had tubs of scarlet geraniums round its doorways and baskets of pink geraniums hanging from the walls.

Though she'd never seen this part of England before — couldn't have found Earlsfield on any map, if it *was* on any map — Elfreda knew where she was now. She'd come at last to the place always somewhere behind the hill, the place there'd never been time nor opportunity to reach, the place at the end of that road on which you'd always had to turn back. And when she went inside — where it was cool, dim, modest, out of the huge brazen afternoon — she moved rather slowly, quietly and carefully, as if when she called out or sent one of those copper things clattering down, the whole scene might burst like a bubble.

Elfreda was against receptionists, in hotels or elsewhere, because the last thing they wanted to do was to receive, to welcome; you almost always arrived as a tiresome interruption to something mysterious they were doing, perhaps writing their memoirs. But this woman, about her own age, seemed quite glad to see Elfreda. She knew Professor Saltana was coming — though he hadn't arrived yet — and the rooms booked for him were ready. She offered to send tea up to Elfreda's room. This room had an uneven floor, rather a low ceiling, and small windows, and was all wrong — except that Elfreda loved it. After she'd unpacked, tidied up, had tea, she decided to pass waiting-for-Cosmo time by exploring the long garden, at the back of the inn, that she could see from her window. A lawn ran down between two borders in what looked to be a rather elaborate rose garden, into which a woman in a dark yellow dress was disappearing.

The sun was still well above the wooded hills as she inspected, like a president his troops, the border dahlias, delphiniums, bright yellow pansies, and below them the scarlet salvias and michaelmas daisies. Then she passed under a pergola and went winding among the roses. There was a curious kind of faintly hazy, gold-dusted light in this hollow of a rose garden, and for a moment or two she didn't recognise the woman in the dark yellow dress who'd found a seat and was reading there.

"Lois?"

"My God — Elfreda!"

"But what are *you* doing here, Lois?"

"Sit down, my dear, sit down. We'll never work this out, standing up. That's better."

"Well, I had this telegram from Cosmo — not asking me but *telling* me, *ordering* me — to come here. And it was sent from somewhere the other side of the country — Rutland."

"And here we are, darling, *obeying* them — looking like two dormice caught in a searchlight. And *loving* it." Lois's eyes seemed larger than ever: half the rose garden could be seen in them. "Well, of course, my story's just the same. Tuby — still in the Isle of Man with his mind gone — wired me this morning to meet him here, and I jumped into my car and never stopped, except to buy a bar of chocolate and an apple for lunch, until I saw the sign of the Rose and Heifer — "

"A delightful place, though — "

"Yes, but even if it wasn't, we'd think it was. I've been considering the appalling weakness of our sex, Elfreda. Here am I, into my thirties, a Master of Arts, a Doctor of Philosophy, no less, a career woman, as they say, who's just turned down an offer, bloated with dollars, from America and an enquiry from the Oxford University Press — and what happens? A little fat lunatic, seventeen years older than I am, after disappearing for weeks sends me a telegram not asking me but, as you said, *ordering* me to come to this inn. And do I tell him I won't stir until I've had an abject apology? Well, you know the answer to that, my dear."

"I didn't really know what I was packing, Lois."

"If the old drama is anything to go by, we're not stronger and more independent but even weaker and sillier, when we're in love, than our female ancestors were. Because we have to be more masculine, then as soon as the female element takes over — we're just *blancmanges*. Our great-great-grandmothers would despise us."

"I don't care about them. When will these men arrive?"

"Probably as soon as the bar's open. That's where we'll find them — boozing away, roaring with laughter — " And there she stopped, to stare at Elfreda in silence.

"I know, Lois. Now you're thinking just what I've been thinking. If we're to meet them here, then they're to meet each other. So where's this famous quarrel?"

"Nowhere. And that's where it always was, Elfreda. Oh — the artful stinkers!"

"You know, darling, I never really could quite believe in it. I was always having to go from one to the other of them, and instead of attacking each other they were always praising each other. That was what was so maddening. It didn't make sense to me, my dear. When I quarrel, I *quarrel*."

"So do I. And from then on, I'm spiteful as hell, a spitting cat. That row they had and then the separation were all a fake. And I believe it's something to do with this political nonsense Tuby's been so mysterious about. But even so — why, for God's sake, the Isle of Man? At least you haven't had that to contend with. Or have you?"

"No, that must be something different — "

"Don't suggest my Tuby's got a wife and four children there — perhaps running a boarding house — "

"No, of course not, Lois you idiot! But it's something political, which he couldn't tell me about, that's kept Saltana away. And I'm sure it explains the fake quarrel. They had to make people think they'd split up."

"Let's move, shall we? Now the sun's going down into Wales, I find it rather chilly here. And that's another curious thing," Lois went on as they walked out of the rose garden. "I know this part of the country, near the Welsh border, though it's years since I was here last. There's a kind of ancient magic haunting it, as if Merlin or some other great wizard put it under a spell that's only just wearing off. Perhaps you don't feel that — um?"

"Yes, I do," said Elfreda. "Though I didn't know how to describe it."

"So I thought how artful it was of Tuby to make me come here. It's just his kind of place, I thought, just where I'll have to forgive all his disappearances, and garden-fête and Isle of Man lunacies. But then, when I arrived, my dear, I had a shock." And Lois touched Elfreda's arm and stopped walking and they stood together on the lawn. "I asked for the room that Dr. Tuby had booked for me, and the rather nice woman at the reception desk said she didn't know anything about a Dr. Tuby, which of course made me feel a complete fool. I must have looked witless, because she asked me then if I knew a Professor Saltana, in whose name four rooms had been booked. So of course I said I did know him and was sure one of those rooms had been meant for me. She probably thinks we're holding a secret scholastic conference, which is a hell of a long way from anything I have in my besotted mind, my dear."

They moved on. "Cosmo must have met somebody who recommended this place, and he must have wired or phoned Tuby, who then wired you your marching orders — "

"Dam' cheek too, when you remember he's kept me for weeks hanging on in Tarbury, which I'd be delighted never to see again. Now either that man marries me or I try America and probably get sozzled night after night on bourbon."

"Perhaps Tuby thinks you're against marriage — "

"So I am — except to him. And if he still thinks by this time I don't want to marry *him*, then his insight into the feminine mind and heart is utterly bogus."

"What do we do now, Lois? I want to be around when Cosmo arrives — "

"And all the host of Heaven forbid I'm somewhere else when Tuby turns up! I want to discover at once if I remember what he looks like. Perhaps he's now a tall beaky man with a ginger moustache."

"What do we do, then? It's too early to have a drink. If we go up to our rooms or have a bath, we won't be around when they arrive. There must be some quiet place where we can talk while keeping an eye on the reception desk."

There was, and it called itself Writing Room, though nobody was writing in it. They settled down in two adjoining small armchairs, their heads fairly close together.

"You do realize, don't you, my dear," said Elfreda, "that Cosmo and Owen Tuby are now out of this image business?"

"Are you sure, Elfreda?"

"Positively. It's been sold to the Americans. And what with one thing and another, Cosmo comes out with fifty thousand pounds and Owen, as Deputy Director, with forty-two thousand — "

Lois gave a little scream. "Did you say forty-two thousand? Why — I was ready to marry this man even if I had to keep him, and now with forty-two thousand he hasn't a hope of getting away. Where is it and when can we start spending it? No, don't tell me. Tuby must do that. Remember, my dear, that sums like these may seem little or nothing to you, but to me they look like diamond mines. And what's all this money going to do to these men? I hope to God they won't want to sit about in Bermuda or somewhere, just drinking and boasting — "

"Don't be silly, Lois. You know very well they aren't that kind. I only hope it isn't politics."

Lois was serious now. "I don't know about Saltana. I can just imagine him a politician. But I know for certain Tuby hasn't any such thing in mind. He told me so, after I'd pestered him about his plans. My guess is — they're cooking up something between them — not any more images and nothing to do with politics."

"And they weren't going to say anything until they were sure of the money. That certainly applies to Cosmo, because he'd be afraid I'd offer to lend or give him the money he needed. And if he couldn't say what they wanted to do, then he'd ask Tuby to keep quiet about it."

"But how could the Isle of Man come into it? They couldn't be thinking of buying a holiday camp or running motorcycle races. They're daft — but not *that* daft. And of course Tuby's Isle-of-Manning may have nothing to do with Saltana — just some idiocy of his own, or not idiocy, being kind to an old aunt or six young nieces and nephews. He *is* kind and very generous, and he's earned quite a lot of money already with your *Social Imagistics* — as well as not sleeping with Meldy Glebe, which was very sweet of him." She stopped because they had left the door open and now caught sight of two people approaching the reception desk. But it was an elderly couple, not their men.

"If it were a little later," Lois said darkly, "I'd be inclined to think our two were boozing together somewhere along the way."

"Now, be fair. Cosmo has to come across country from Rutland, and Tuby from the Isle of Man. I'll bet they're just as eager to get here as we were. You ought to know by this time, Lois, that Tuby adores you."

"And I him. And from now on, I'll never be able to let him go far out of sight, the way women fall for this Casanova-disguised-as-Mr.-Pickwick. All kinds too — snobbish and snooty Isabel Lapford, all-for-a-cuddle Hazel Honeyfield, glamour-puss-deluxe Meldy Glebe — all kinds. He looks safe and then before we know where we are he's talked us into anything he fancies."

"Well, he hasn't fancied anything, except with you, for months. And you know it, Lois. Why, before he realized he was in love with you, the woman where he lodged — she's Eden Mere's cousin — soon began to dote on him, and her husband was neglecting her, and Owen was sorry for her, but he made up his mind nothing should happen — "

"Oh yes — I know, Elfreda. And it certainly won't be boring being married to a man who has such a dangerous effect on other females. Can you be jealous?"

"Me? My dear, before Cosmo did or said anything to me, and I knew he was off with all sorts of handsome unscrupulous creatures — it was murder. What about you?"

"Like a half-poisoned cat. I'm a horrible creature." She grinned — and in spite of her large-eyed, delicately sensitive face, Lois could produce a good grin. But then she looked serious. "I've come to know Tuby very well now. We've talked for hours and hours and hours. Part of what I'm going to say applies to Saltana too, so you must let me run on. But I'll begin with Tuby. And this isn't his girl friend talking now but a fellow academic, Dr. Terry of the English Department of Brockshire University. Tuby is an original and very perceptive critic of literature — and a *divine* teacher, making almost everybody I've known in the profession look like a dustbin. And he had to spend twenty years in the East. Nobody cared a damn. He wasn't one of the trendy boys. He was far away and out of the movement. So he'd had enough, like Saltana."

"And when they met me," said Elfreda, "they were almost broke. And no more sociologists than I am. Cosmo's admitted everything, though I'd already guessed some of it — and didn't mind. Good God! I've had more out of life in the last year than in all the forty years before it — but I'm sorry, dear, go on."

"I was furious with Saltana because I thought he was taking Tuby away from criticism and teaching, but now I know it wasn't as simple as that. In a way Tuby's more mischievous than Saltana. But there's a rather innocent kind of revenge in it too. Who wanted Tuby to do his proper work? Nobody, it seemed. But everybody was writing and talking about images. All right — images then. The same people who want images want experts. Then why not *Social Imagistics?* It was a great piece of luck, their meeting you."

"Yes, dear, I made it easier for them to make a start," Elfreda told her. Was she sounding a bit smug? She tried a different tone. "But Cosmo says they would have gone on with their *Social Imagistics* somehow or other, Lois."

"While knowing all the time it was just a lot of clever nonsense. They didn't *believe* in their image expertise. Tuby admits that, Elfreda dear."

Frowning, Elfreda hesitated a moment before replying. "I think you have to be careful here, Lois. Don't turn them into a pair of frauds or con men. Just remember you were outside it all while I was working with them the whole time. They didn't swindle anybody. They really earned the money they were paid. And even after they staged that mock quarrel — the wretches — and separated, more and more enquiries were coming in. We'd have made far more money these next six months than we did in the past six. Only of course they didn't want to go on — "

"Because they didn't *believe* in what they were doing — "

"I'm sorry to break in, dear. And I know you're much cleverer than I am." Then Elfreda stopped sounding apologetic. "But I can tell you what Cosmo said — and it was the last real long talk we had — after that we just gabbled on the phone. He said that what he and Tuby *didn't* believe in was the kind of world in which you have to bother about images and *Social Imagistics.* And when he and Tuby came back, after being so long away, it was at first a world quite strange to them, full of all this talking and writing about images — "

But Lois gave a little shriek, called out "Tuby darling!" and was gone, leaving Elfreda feeling rather envious. However, it was probably quicker and easier to fly from the Isle of Man to Liverpool or somewhere and then come down here than to cross the country, without a car, from Rutland. After a minute or two, Tuby appeared in the doorway.

"Elfreda, my dear, you're looking splendid. I'm just going up to my room to instal myself and wash, then we'll have a drink. Can't talk in here. And the bar's open."

"How do you know it is?"

"I always know when bars are open. Lois was already beginning to mutter something about blackmail, so I cut her short. I'll join you in five minutes."

"What's this about blackmail?" Elfreda asked Lois, who was standing, apparently entranced, near the stairs.

Lois closed one enormous bright eye. "You'll find out when Tuby does. And I need a witness. Shall we start drinking or wait for him? We might as well explore, don't you think? It may be already packed with farmers."

There were two bars, and the nearer and smaller one, perhaps kept for hotel guests, was empty and looked ready to encourage intimate talk. A middle-aged woman, a severe type who might have been a smaller version of Eden Mere, came behind the counter from the public bar and gave them a sternly enquiring look. She made them feel they ought to have a man with them. "We're meeting a friend here," said Elfreda. "He'll be down quite soon."

They sat down in a snug corner, just right for four, and Lois said, "It's a funny thing about barmaids. Whenever I read about them — in novels — they're always voluptuous if rather brassy creatures, inflaming the men. But whenever I actually see one, she's always more or less like that woman who popped in and out, a kind of prohibition fifth columnist. Elfreda dear, I hope you're not worrying about Saltana. He'll turn up any minute now. And Tuby, who knows about trains, says there could hardly be a worse journey."

"He's probably in a foul temper somewhere — poor Cosmo! What are you going to drink, Lois?"

"My dear, I haven't given it a thought. But now that I do, I realize I'm in the mood for saké or tequilla or Danziger Goldwasser, some exotic tipple that would inevitably make me feel sick. So I'll keep my Tuby company — which at the moment is all I want to do in this world — and drink whisky. But I daren't ask that woman for it."

"Then I'll do it. Saves times — and Tuby will be more than ready — "

"Of course — and that means I must do it, my dear. Whisky — or gin-and-tonic for you? Gin, eh? Good! I think I'll be even more severe than she is. I'll *top her,* as they say on the boards."

When Tuby, clean, rosy, and smiling, joined them, he said at once, "You've chosen well, ladies. We ought to reserve this corner until bedtime. Chin, chin, girls!"

"Cut that out, Tuby," Lois told him. "Unless of course you're regressing, turning back into one of those bronzed manly fellows — old China hands and whatnot. By the way, when I got your first telegram from the Isle of Man, I rang up Elfreda and told her we'd tied ourselves to madmen. And for a whole day I thought you must have a wife and four children there. And if not, why the Isle of Man?"

"Later, my love. Then all will be revealed — "

"There isn't going to be *more* mystery-mongering, is there?"

"We're waiting for Cosmo Saltana. Aren't we, Elfreda?"

"Of course we are," cried Lois penitently. "Sorry, darling! I mean you, Elfreda. I'm not apologizing to this man. I'm about to present him with an ultimatum. Now listen carefully, Dr. Tuby. I gather you're now one of the rich. So either you marry me at the very first opportunity or you're in for some appalling blackmail — I pester you at all hours on the telephone, I write horrible letters not only to you but to all your associates, and when you're entertaining influential people, also rich, of course, I burst in to stage the most distressing scenes — "

"And I wouldn't put it past you, my delicate sweet poppet," Tuby told her. "So we'll marry as soon as you like."

"Thank you, kind sir. But you won't insist on the Isle of Man, will you?"

"Quiet, girl!" He looked at Elfreda. "I'm certainly not one of the rich. But how much do I get?"

"Altogether — forty-two thousand pounds — "

"A tidy sum, souls!" cried Tuby. "And as I've just earned another five thousand and have my share of previous earnings tucked away, I'll be worth more than fifty thousand — and more than I was paid altogether for twenty years' hard slogging under hot suns."

"And I hope this doesn't mean, my darling," said Lois, "that now you'll want to loll about in Antibes or somewhere — um?"

"No, my love. As you know, I'm a self-indulgent man, but even so I shrink from a life of pleasure. Now and then I met people in the East, just passing through, who were entirely devoted to amusing themselves, and most of them would have been happier serving lorry-drivers with tea and sausages — "

"Listen!" And Elfreda jumped up. "I thought I heard Cosmo." They all listened for a moment, and then Elfreda, still uncertain, moved towards the door. It opened — and there he was, and then they were eagerly embracing.

"A detestable journey," said Saltana, "but well worth it. Lois — Owen — your servant! But let's waste no time on polite trivia." He strode to the bar counter and rapped on it. The severe woman looked in. "The same again in the corner, please, and if you happen to have an old malt whisky — I'll take a double of it."

The severity vanished, the woman was now all appreciative nods and smiles; evidently Saltana represented her idea of a generous if masterful customer. "I ought to clean up," he said as he joined the others, "but that can wait. I've been half over England — in trains, but, you might say, *tacking*. Any news?"

"Yes, Cosmo," said Elfreda. "Lois and Owen are getting married as soon as possible." And she gave him a look.

"They are, are they? Well, my dear, how did I come out finally? Money, I mean."

"You get fifty thousand."

"Good! Then *we'll* marry as soon as possible."

"Darling!"

"Congratulations! In the Isle of Man?" Lois enquired sweetly.

Saltana frowned at her, then looked at Tuby. "What does she know?"

"Nothing," replied Tuby. "I said firmly, *Later*. But the woman's half out of her mind with curiosity."

"And so am I," said Elfreda. "And surely, now you're here, we can be told?"

"No, my love," Saltana told her. "Not the right time or the right place. During and after dinner, I suggest. Which reminds me. Has anything been done about dinner? This is no ordinary occasion. The usual *table d'hôte* couldn't live up to it. One of us must go along to enquire, persuade, command."

"Then it ought to be one of you two men," Lois declared. "And I'd say — Tuby. He fancies himself a gourmet. He can certainly enquire and persuade — and if commands should be necessary, he can always send for you, Saltana." After Tuby had gone, Lois continued: "And now I think you ought to tell us — don't you, Elfreda? — what you've been up to with all this political hush-hush hanky-panky. At least tell me what Tuby's been doing."

"Certainly," said Saltana. Then he lowered his voice. "But you must keep it strictly to yourselves. There's to be a general election next month. So Tuby has been working on the image of the Leader of the Opposition, Sir Henry Flinch-Epworth. And I've been busy — indeed, a dam' sight busier than Tuby's been — attending to the image of Ernest Itterby, the Prime Minister. Each for a fee of five thousand pounds. Our last and noblest job. We're now out of the image business forever."

"And I'm sorry in a way," said Elfreda.

"I'm not, my dear," Lois told her. "Saltana, what did you do to those two? I've seen them both on the telly a good many times, and they're very different types. Will they still be very different — or rather more alike?"

His reply was quiet and careful. "I haven't had a chance yet to compare notes properly with Tuby. But there's a possibility — just a possibility — they may seem now quite astonishingly alike — "

Lois let out a little scream of laughter. "Why — you impudent villains!"

"But Cosmo — " and Elfreda stared at him wonderingly — "you don't mean you two did it *deliberately*, do you?"

"Well, my love — yes and no. We gave them the best possible advice, honestly earning our fees. But starting from opposite ends, so to speak, we had to move each of them towards the middle. And there in the middle, they might not seem very different — I mean as images, not men. But we'll see. Now what about another drink?"

Before they could reply, Tuby returned bringing with him a pretty girl in her twenties who was wearing a chef's hat. "A delightful surprise, you'll agree. Miss Jocelyn Farris — Mrs. Drake, Dr. Terry, Professor Saltana. Jocelyn, who's taken a *cordon bleu* course in London, is our chef. And settling dinner, we have a question for you. First course — trout with almonds. *D'accord?* Good! Next — a special partridge dish Jocelyn already had going for us. We agree? Of course! Now for the soufflé — and Jocelyn assures me she can make a good soufflé — "

"Then I wish she'd show me," said Lois.

"Which brings us to the question. A cheese soufflé or what Jocelyn calls a soufflé Marie Brizard — "

"It's sweet, of course," said Jocelyn, "but not too sweet — made with liqueurs. And I'm sorry, but it must be one or the other — so will you please decide?"

While Elfreda and Lois were exchanging glances, Saltana came in masterfully: "I am by temperament and habit a cheese man. But I know very well that these ladies are longing to try soufflé Marie Brizard, and I say, Dr. Tuby, that should be our choice."

"Well spoken, Professor Saltana!" cried Tuby, "It's what you want, isn't it? Elfreda? Lois? Then we're *chez* Madame Brizard, Jocelyn. Now — who looks after the wine here?" And out they went.

Elfreda and Lois refused another drink and talked about going up to have a bath. "The sooner I go the better, Cosmo," said Elfreda demurely, "because as it happens you and I seem to be sharing a bathroom between our rooms."

"And by a strange coincidence — so are Tuby and I," Lois added, closing her brilliant eyes and making her mouth very small. "By the way, who found this marvellous hotel?"

"I did — by chance, last night. But I'll explain later."

"They're great men for explaining later," said Elfreda as she got up.

"Yes, and they've hardly started yet," said Lois, following her. "Wait till we've turned them into husbands. In a few years they'll owe us hundreds of hours of later explanations."

Saltana ordered another drink for himself and for Tuby, who returned to say he'd ordered a bottle of Traminer for the trout and two bottles of Château Talbot. "That name always fascinates me," he added. "I'd like to make a public speech in Gascony — aimed at de Gaulle — pointing out that we English were there — and for two or three centuries — long before his French were. *Gascony libre,* I might cry."

They settled into the corner. "I've told our women what we were up to with our politicians," said Saltana. "No details, of course. What happened with Flinch-Epworth — and how's his new image?" And later they were laughing so much that the elderly couple of fellow-guests — they were tall and thin and had already arrived at that brother-and-sister look — who came in to ask for two small dry sherries, and were shocked to hear anything above a whisper in an English hotel, retreated almost at once.

In her bedroom, doing her face, Elfreda wasn't thinking about money or politicians or where the Isle of Man came in; she was wondering about having a baby. She wasn't too old yet, though quite soon she might be — a first baby too. She'd never said anything to Cosmo. It was hard to imagine him with a baby around; perhaps he'd glare and thunder at the mere mention of it, yet you never know with men, and several wives had told her how their husbands had hated the *idea* of a baby but then had proudly and joyfully welcomed the actual son or daughter. Perhaps it would be better to say nothing to Cosmo until she found herself pregnant, and that wasn't impossible, as that specialist in Portland had assured her.

Lois, in her bedroom, was staring fiercely at herself in the glass, which was charming but too old and made her look spotty, which she wasn't. Her eyes were ridiculously large, but, as she'd told Tuby, this had nothing to do with thyroid and they wouldn't start bulging; there'd been a mistake and she'd been given eyes that really belonged to some other and much bigger creature. But now she was being fierce with her reflection. "The truth is, you fool," she told it, "you're afraid of happiness. This is what this world's done to you — and it's the dirtiest trick of all. Even the nice people say you mustn't be happy until everybody else is happy — and by that time nobody will be happy, they'll all be too tired. You can see how far we've come, Dr. Terry. If a modern dramatist ended a play as Shakespeare did his comedies, he'd be howled down as a hack entertainer or a cowardly escapist. We can't — you can't, you idiot — risk feeling happy even for one day and night. There must be a catch in it. Life is now like those toys and boxes of chocolates the horrible Nazis left behind when they retreated — gloat over one of them and it blows up in your face. One part of you, Lois you fool, sulking in a dark corner because the rest of you is lit up, is just waiting for Tuby to drop dead just when he's undressing tonight or, if that's a bit much, for the whole four of us to have a flaming row at dinner so that you'll find yourself back here weeping. We're all nannies to ourselves, saying if we don't stop those grins and giggles and jumping about, we'll be crying before the day's out. Get rid of all that tonight, you fool — for God's sake. Yes, for God's sake. People didn't really believe God was dead when Nietzsche said He was. But they did start believing He *didn't want us to be happy*. Oh — shut up, idiot! And where's my bag?"

Lois and Elfreda agreed on their way down together that they didn't want another drink before dinner. "We ought to have booked a sitting room," said Elfreda, "if there's one to be had."

"I've never been a sitting-room booker — never had enough money — but I'm ready to begin splashing Tuby's dubious gains. You mean — so that we've somewhere to talk in, after dinner?"

"Yes, dear. Otherwise, we'll linger on and on in the dining room when the staff are dying to get rid of us. I'll ask at the desk."

Yes, there was one private sitting room, and Mrs. Drake could have it and was given the key. It had rather a forlorn parlour atmosphere and had been deliberately kept Victorian — two glass cases of stuffed birds, imposing photographs of Lord Beaconsfield and Mr. Gladstone and various be-whiskered athletic teams — but it offered them three armchairs and a sofa. They switched on the lights, though it was barely dusk, and closed the curtains, to see how the room would look later, and Elfreda changed a few things round.

"I've read for years about those little feminine touches that make all the difference," said Lois, "and I've never known what the hell they were — except for some dusting and bringing a few flowers in." She tried the sofa. "I heard Tuby making all those bathroom noises, as if he'd turned himself into a couple of sea lions, but I kept my door firmly locked against him. I'm all for what he has in mind, but I wasn't going to be all mussed up and then be droopy and yawny all through dinner — not when we have the whole night."

Elfreda looked at her watch and then sat down. "We can stay here for at least another ten minutes. And if we don't, we'll find ourselves back in the bar. Lois, do you think Cosmo and Owen drink too much?"

"I know one of them does. The first time I met Tuby — it was at a Lapford party, where they were always terribly stingy with food and drink — he was sitting in a darkish corner of the hall, with the largest whisky I've ever seen and an enormous plate of food — Isabel of course, spoiling him — and I was very cheeky and he was very sweet and we did some sharing. He seemed like a friendly elf or troll in a fairy tale," she went on dreamily. "Still does — in a way. Or a disguised enchanter — "

"Cosmo's like that," Elfreda declared proudly.

"I'm sure he is. They're mythopoeic beings, both of them. If they hadn't been, they couldn't have done what they have done — with their *Social Imagistics* — and laughing up their sleeves. Nobody else I've ever met could have done it."

"I feel that too, Lois. But ought they to drink so much?"

"Perhaps not. And perhaps they don't when they're really serious about something — and working hard at it. Anyhow I feel men ought to be *too much*. I seem to have spent years with *just-enough* men, who have one small sherry or cocktail, one slice of meat, and one weeny, weeny nightcap — mini-men."

"I know. Poor Judson was rather like that. And I always knew what he was going to do or say. But Cosmo might do or say *anything*. I never know what's next. One minute he'll be terrifying, and the next minute he'll melt my bones, he's so sweet. And I'm sure now he's mixed up in this Isle of Man thing with Tuby. What if they say we must live there?"

"My dear — don't give me away — but if Tuby said we must live in Greenland, I might argue against it — but I'd go."

"I'm just the same. But we'll insist upon being told what they're planning, not during dinner but afterwards, up here." Elfreda looked at her watch again and stood up. "We ought to go down. I think I'll ask them to light a fire, just for the look of it. And bring up some glasses and things."

Lois gave Tuby a quick kiss in the entrance to the dining room. "Are you happy, my darling?"

"A bad question — but I am. And I oughtn't to be."

"Now really — why?" They were moving in now behind the other two.

"Because almost as long as I can remember, whenever I've had good reason to be happy — and everybody has expected it — I haven't been happy. Then suddenly — walking down a dusty road, watching a leaf in the wind, towelling my back — happiness has come floating in, unaccountable joy has spouted like a fountain."

"Oh — I'm like that. And no, I shouldn't have asked."

"What I certainly am is hellishly hungry."

It was a long, low-ceilinged room, with off-white walls, dark wood, and clever lighting. There were only six other people dining: the elderly couple and a nondescript quartet, and they were at the other end of the room. "This corner's perfect," said Lois as she sat down. "And no head waiter — thank the Lord! I detest head waiters."

"That's because you've been compelled to patronise a low class of restaurant, my love," Tuby told her.

"The *ah-mais-oui* West End types — character actors really — are worse still," said Saltana.

"Robinson's has had three head waiters since I've been there," said Elfreda. "The middle one was the nicest, but he was offered a better job in Bournemouth. Oh — don't look — but our waitress has the oddest shape — as broad as she's high."

"She'll give us a square deal," said Tuby. And she was in fact an exceptionally good waitress. Over the trout, Saltana explained how he'd come to discover this hotel, at Ilbert Cumberland's, and this led inevitably to some exchange between the two men on their brief political careers and how the improved images of the two Leaders might make them look almost exactly alike.

"And we can only hope it won't confuse the floating viewer-voters," Saltana concluded with mock solemnity. "Elfreda and Lois, drink some more of this excellent claret before Marie Brizard raids your palate."

It was while they were waiting for the soufflé that Tuby suddenly exclaimed: "Cosmo — what a callous pair we are! Not a thought for the people who've been working with us! The Institute and the Society have been disposed of — so what about Primrose, Eden, young Beryl?"

"Owen, I share your shame," cried Saltana. "What indeed? Elfreda?"

"I was waiting to tell you," she replied, smiling. But first she described the dismal return of Primrose from Sardinia. "So then I got busy.

I suggested that she and Eden should run a boutique and that I would put up the money — about three thousand — to start it. Eden's back from Brittany, and now the pair of them are rushing round trying to find suitable premises. And young Beryl is about to take a job — better than ours was — in Dan Luckett's London office. So, you see, everything's fine."

"Elfreda," said Tuby, raising his glass, "I salute you."

"And I double that, my love," said Saltana, drinking to her. "Incidentally, what the devil *is* a boutique? I'm always seeing the term — and it baffles me."

"What would you say, Lois?" This was deliberate, because Elfreda felt Lois oughtn't to be left out any longer.

"It's where you spend ten pounds on something quaint but modish that they've knocked up for about thirty bob."

"Then Primrose and Eden ought to make a good team. Primrose can dream up the imbecilities while Eden challenges the customers to query the outrageous prices. By the way, Owen," Saltana continued, "while O. V. Mere will be busy at the headquarters of both parties — right up to the general election, I imagine — we ought to let him know what we're planning to do."

"And what *are* you planning to do?" Lois asked rather sharply. "Isn't it about time — "

"You eat this soufflé Marie Brizard first," said the extraordinarily square waitress. "It won't wait — and Jocelyn will be disappointed if you let it spoil."

"She was quite right," declared Lois a little later. "And it's heavenly. Elfreda, we must ask Jocelyn how she does it. And I won't ask these men to tell us their plans until we're up in our sitting room."

"Where I've asked them to bring our coffee," Elfreda announced comfortably.

"My dear, you think of everything." Saltana was genuinely admiring.

"I do too," said Lois rather mournfully, "but, unlike Elfreda, never in the right order or at the right time. Better keep that in mind, Dr. Tuby. It's chaos for you as soon as we're man and wife."

"That's home to me, girl. I've never lived anywhere else."

Saltana had now eaten a morsel of bread, drunk a little water, and was back with the claret. "Follow my excellent example, Owen, and prepare yourself to return to old Talbot. This wine will clear my mind and strengthen your oratory — before we talk seriously to these women upstairs. Because if we fail to convince them, my boy, we're dished — I don't know what the hell we'll do. Ladies, you go ahead — and sink into a receptive mood without going to sleep."

"Remembering," said Tuby, smiling at them both, "that the ancient

Chinese — who knew more about everything than Chairman Mao will ever discover — said that Woman should be *willing*."

"And have her feet bound, I suppose," said Lois as she and Elfreda prepared to leave them.

In the sitting room, the wood fire was giving them more and better light than the one standard lamp they kept on in the corner. Perched on the sofa in a pleasant flicker, Lois began to sip her coffee. "The trouble is," she began, though she didn't sound greatly troubled, "that what we're waiting for those men to reveal could equally well be original, brave, and glorious, or something in our opinion utterly daft."

"And here we are — just waiting — "

"Yes."

"And *my* trouble," said Elfreda, a smiling golden image in this light, "is that I don't mind, don't care. My dear, I *like it*."

"Elfreda, I'm now deeply devoted to you. No — I really am. The more I see of you, my dear, the greater my enjoyment, the higher my esteem. You're like a lovely loaf of special bread. Whereas I'm just a bit of stale cake."

Lois hardly heard what Elfreda replied to this. The thought of Tuby, the dinner and the wine, the firelight and this flickering mid-Victorian room, together floated her into one of those moments, which come and go as they please and may not return for years, when we seem to perceive — or in a flash may know — that life is a dream.

The men came in, Tuby with his pipe, Saltana with a cheroot; they accepted coffee and drank it rather quickly, still standing; then Saltana sat near Elfreda, and Tuby shared Lois's sofa and when she reached out he took her hand.

"You start, Cosmo," said Tuby.

"It's an idea we've been nursing for some time. We had it in our minds long before we thought about images. Indeed, the images were taken on to serve it." Saltana sounded as if he had rehearsed this speech. "With your help, Tuby and I want to create a university — or simply a college, we don't care which — entirely for people over forty. No degree factory here. We're not worried about youth, as so many solemn fellows seem to be. It can live on its rich blood and the hope and promise of the unknown. But many people past forty, already looking down the hill towards the cemetery, have a desperate need to learn, to understand, to enjoy, to enrich the spirit, to live before they die. They may have money, position, prestige, and authority, but they find themselves asking *So what, so what?* And we want to offer them an answer. Yes, Owen?"

"We want to wash the dust out of their mouths and then spread before them the treasures — " But Tuby checked himself. "No — no, I'm beginning to sound like one of those advertisements for mail-order art books — "

"Yes, you were, darling," said Lois. "Couldn't you come down from yonder lofty heights?"

"Minx!" Saltana growled.

"Cosmo!" came Elfreda's warning.

Lois stared at him. "Did you really mean that? I was talking to Tuby, not to you.'

"Of course he didn't, Lois," Tuby put in hastily. "And let's get on. What we have in mind isn't just another dose of adult education. Nobody passes an examination. Nobody gets — or doesn't get — a diploma, a certificate, a medal, or a gold watch. It won't be a cheap imitation of something going on more expensively somewhere else. It'll be education in the very broadest but best sense, something people can go on with themselves after they've left us, and something that intelligent and sensitive but stale and bewildered over-forties urgently need. Do you doubt that?"

"*I* don't," cried Elfreda. "But perhaps I'm not intelligent and sensitive enough — "

"Certainly you are, my dear," said Saltana sharply. "Though you're not stale — and so-whatting. But there's a great deal you'd like to know more about, isn't there? We don't like the word, but *culture* comes into it. As for you, Lois, you can teach — we hope you will — but you can learn too."

"I don't know about you, Saltana," said Lois, serious now. "And I'm not being catty. I just don't know about you. I don't know about me either. But Tuby would be wonderful with such people, bringing literature to life and not worrying it in some dusty corner, like a terrier with a rat. But you'd need a whole staff — "

"We know that, Lois," Tuby told her. "We'd try to give people a world picture — "

"No economists, though," cried Saltana. "And no technologists and the like. Our people will have had them. I'll attend to the history of philosophy. You and Tuby take over literature. Then we'll need a broadly based scientist or two, a first-class art historian, a musicologist, and a practising musician — sooner or later a resident string quartet — "

"That's so he can play the Mozart and Brahms clarinet quintets — "

"Shut up! No medicine, there's plenty of that outside, but a lively depth psychologist, preferably a Jungian, if only to provoke argument. And one good historian, two when we can afford them. Plus every sensible device for showing people what we mean — a specially built record player, films, slide projectors, closed-circuit television if necessary — "

"But Cosmo, my dear," said Elfreda apologetically, "isn't this going to cost a whole heap of money? And then you'll have to have your own buildings — "

"I know, I know, my love. And you and I will have to work it out. Tuby and Lois can be thinking about staff and courses. But we've enough money to make a start, Elfreda. If Tuby and I put up fifty thousand each, and you do the same, as I hope you will — "

"You know I will, darling — "

"And Jimmy Kilburn will match us, I know — "

"And so he ought — "

"Then we start with two hundred thousand pounds. Now that ought to pay for places for us, a few lecture rooms, a smallish auditorium-cum-cinema-cum-theatre-cum-concert-hall, and a kitchen and restaurant. Don't imagine we're hoping to build hostels, dormitories, junior common rooms, laboratories, and all the rest. This isn't another University of Brockshire, y'know, Lois."

"Thank God for that! But look, Saltana, I don't know how many students — or whatever you want to call them — you hope to have, but they'll have to be lodged somewhere — "

"In hotels and digs, my love," Tuby told her.

Lois shrieked "Isle of Man!" at him just a second before Elfreda did.

Tuby nodded and smiled. "Have you ever been there, either of you? I know Saltana hasn't. No? Then I'm the Manx expert here."

"You are," said Saltana. "Your report, please, Dr. Tuby."

"But what's the point?" Elfreda demanded. "It's all very well talking about hotels and digs, but won't they be bursting with holiday people?"

"Our college — and we must find a name for it soon — will be closed from the first week in July until the third week in September," Saltana announced gravely. "On the other hand, there will be no real vacations between September and July — only two or three days at Christmas and Easter."

"That could work," said Lois. "But isn't it a dreadful place?"

"We await Dr. Tuby's report, Dr. Terry — "

"Oh — do stop that, Cosmo," Elfreda protested. "Go on, Owen."

"In the morning," Tuby began, "when you're sober and perhaps feeling bilious, I'll let you examine some brochures, illustrating in colour everything there from casinos and dance halls to glens and high cliffs. It's as if bits of Galloway had floated down to join broken-off pieces of Ulster, with here and there a kind of fungus growth from Blackpool and Margate. But this last can be avoided, even though the island is only 33 miles long, pointed at both ends and with a maximum width of only 12½ miles. But with an area of 227 square miles, it has a total population of just over fifty thousand — "

"Darling, you sound like a talking guidebook," cried Lois. "Do be more human."

"Certainly," said Tuby. "As you probably know, the island governs itself. One disappointment here, Cosmo. I'd hoped for cheap tobacco and booze, but the duties and prices are the same as Britain's. However, if they still went up and up, perhaps we might go in for a little smuggling. And anyhow the saving in tax — you know about Manx taxation, Lois, Elfreda?"

No, they didn't.

"Then allow me, Owen," said Saltana. "Ladies, income tax in the Isle of Man stands at four-and-threepence in the pound, and there's no surtax — "

"No surtax?" It was a kind of squeal from Elfreda.

"No surtax," said Tuby. "And rents are very low."

"I'm going to put this to a tax accountant, Owen, as soon as I get back to London." Saltana was now giving his performance as a shrewd man of affairs. "I want to know if our students — though we won't call them that, of course — can't establish residence for tax purposes and possibly save a devil of a lot. I'm thinking now of successful professional men taking a sabbatical, industrialists, managerial types, perhaps senior civil servants — "

"But, Cosmo, have they all to be successful and important? Can't there be any unsuccessful hard-up people?"

"Of course, of course." For once Saltana sounded impatient with her. "We've been unsuccessful hard-up people ourselves — and only a year ago. As soon as we can afford it, Elfreda, we'll offer some scholarships, bursaries, fellowships — call 'em what you like."

Seeing that Elfreda looked hurt, Lois created a diversion. "Tuby darling, what were you doing all those days on the Isle of Man? Looking for possible places?"

"Yes, my dear, and it's not my kind of work. It's yours and Elfreda's — "

"Elfreda's certainly. But I'm ready to trot alongside her. Any possibilities?"

"Two. Both decently away from holiday fun and games. One in the north of the island, a few miles from Ramsay. The other at the southern end, no great distance from either Castletown or Port Erin. One a group of ex-naval buildings no longer in use. The other a hotel that was mismanaged to death. Neither right yet, of course. And there might possibly be something better that I missed. I ate a lot of kippers and then sprawled in hot glens, thinking about you, my love."

Lois was about to try a pretty speech of thanks but noticed that Saltana, bursting wtih leadership, wanted to address them. "We need a plan now. Otherwise, we'll waste a lot of time. So here it is. Elfreda and I go to London, to clear things up and to marry as soon as Caxton Hall — or wherever it ought to be — can look after us. Lois, you take Tuby back to Tarbury — I imagine you'll have some clearing up to do — "

"I will indeed, Marshal — "

"Then on an agreed convenient date, we fly to the Isle of Man — easier to reach these days than this place is — "

"Certainly," said Tuby.

"And Elfreda and I make the best of a kippery honeymoon," cried Lois. And both of them giggled a little.

"If they giggle, then we drink, Cosmo. After you with that bottle. And it's a good plan. A few more days in Tarbury won't hurt me. I can stay at The Bell — "

"You'll stay with me, my fine fellow," Lois told him severely. "And spend hours and hours packing books into tea chests — after you've found the tea chests. Is it *chests?* Sounds absurd somehow."

"A small one for the road, ladies?" Tuby had the bottle now. "Just a touch — eh? You keep this bottle, Cosmo. I've one in my bag."

"You always have one in your bag, you old boozer," cried Lois.

"Yes, woman," Tuby thundered, "and I propose to keep right on having one in my bag."

"That's the way to talk to her, my boy. But leave that bottle alone now. Well, here's to us — and to all the over-forty so-whats we'll bring out of the desert!"

They drank to that, and then Elfreda and Lois drifted out, chattering, and Saltana took the bottle and two glasses and Tuby opened the door and returned to switch out the standard lamp, gave what was left of the fire a fond glance, and followed his friend into the corridor.

Much later, in one darkened bedroom, Elfreda murmured sleepily, "Darling, I've been trying to think of a name for our university or college, but I can't — " And that, of course — as she ought to have known — was just as if she'd pressed the lid of a jack-in-the-box. Saltana was up, into his dressing gown, switching on a light, reaching for the bottle, finding a cheroot, talking all the time. Oh dear!

"The right name'll come, my love. Better not to press for it. Might be good if we could bring the Isle of Man into it — symbolic. I ought to have asked Tuby to give me one or two of his brochures tonight. We could be looking at them now." He paused to light his cheroot.

"You could, Cosmo. I couldn't. I'd never see a thing properly. But I can listen. You needn't stop talking — yet, darling."

"Brochures and pretty pictures in the morning then, my dear. Haven't a notion what the place looks like. And talking of brochures, we'll have to get something in print as soon as we know where we're going to be. But that's all. No advertising. No, no, no — we waste no money on advertising."

"But people will have to know about us," came sleepily from the bed.

"My dear girl, aren't you forgetting we never advertised the Institute? Which reminds me that we might use *Institute* again. *Isle of Man Institute?* No — not right. Something'll come. But whatever we call it, we're not going to waste good money advertising it. Not necessary at all. The mass media are far more effective when you don't pay them but they pay you. And of course this story of the politicians' images must leak out, probably has already. But Tuby and I kept our word not to tell anybody what we were doing. We'd discussed certain possibilities beforehand, of course, but once we'd given our word we never even told each other anything. And that's why I couldn't tell you what I was doing. Elfreda my love, you understand that now, don't you?" But she had fallen asleep.

Lois's room wasn't quite dark; she had opened the curtains, and though the window faced the hills it admitted a faint glimmer of starlight, and the space she and Tuby were sharing most intimately wasn't black but a mysterious darkish blue.

She gave the lobe (rather large) of his left ear a gentle tug. "Tuby darling — I've been thinking — and I've suddenly realized that all the time I'll be teaching people years and years older than I am."

"What of it, my sugarplum?"

"You must have been thinking about Hazel Honeyfield. I'm no sugarplum, man."

"As you please, girl. My helping of sweet-and-sour, then. But I'm years and years older than you — and you've been busy teaching me for some time — "

"*Me? You?* Why — you monster of Oriental eroticism — "

"What I had in mind then — about teaching — was Jacobean drama. And you'll have to enlarge your field now, my girl." Tuby was speaking slowly, rather dreamily. "The Bard, for instance. And there's a packet for you — "

"Hoy — steady, mate! *You* must do Shakespeare — "

"We might — split him." Tuby was close enough but sounded further away than ever. "I do — social background — characters . . . You do verse, imagery — symbolism . . . And it won't be — teaching — not exactly . . . Need another term — for what we're — trying to do — don't we. . . ?"

"Don't go to sleep. No, my darling, do if you want to. Anyhow if it isn't exactly teaching, it won't be *Social Imagistics* — thank God! But I ought to have told you — I don't like kippers. So will there be anything else to eat?"

"Almost . . ." — and it came from a great distance now — "everything . . . everything . . . every . . . thing . . ."

Though he'd obviously stopped attending to her, she told him he was her clever, brave, sweet love, and then for some minutes she listened to his regular breathing as if it might turn into the Eroica.